North Carolina grade 7

HOLT SCIENCE & TECHNOLOGY

HOLT, RINEHART AND WINSTON

A Harcourt Education Company

Orlando • Austin • New York • San Diego • Toronto • London

Acknowledgments

Contributing Authors

Katy Z. Allen
Science Writer
Wayland, Massachusetts

Linda Ruth Berg, Ph.D.
Adjunct Professor
Natural Sciences
St. Petersburg College
St. Petersburg, Florida

Barbara Christopher
Science Writer and Editor
Austin, Texas

Leila Dumas
Former Physics Teacher
Austin, Texas

Jennie Dusheck
Science Writer
Santa Cruz, California

Kathleen Kaska
Former Life and Earth Science Teacher and Science Department Chair

William G. Lamb, Ph.D.
Winningstad Chair in the Physical Sciences
Oregon Episcopal School
Portland, Oregon

Robert J. Sager, M.S., J.D., L.G.
Coordinator and Professor of Earth Science
Pierce College
Lakewood, Washington

Mark F. Taylor, Ph.D.
Associate Professor of Biology
Biology Department
Baylor University
Waco, Texas

North Carolina Teacher Consultants

Pamela B. Heath
Director of Middle Grades Education
Lenoir County Public Schools
Kinston, North Carolina

James Thomas Heldreth III
Science Teacher
Eastern Guilford Middle School
Gibsonville, North Carolina

Brian Herndon
Instructional Specialist
Gaston County Schools
Gastonia, North Carolina

Dorothea Holley
Teacher
Southwest Middle School
Charlotte, North Carolina

Larry Hollis
Earth and Environmental Science Teacher
Southwest Middle School
Charlotte, North Carolina

Beverly Lyons
Science Teacher and Department Chair
Hanes Middle School
Winston-Salem, North Carolina

Donna Roberts
Science Teacher
Concord Middle School
Concord, North Carolina

Patricia Sherron-Underwood
K–8 Math and Science Curriculum Specialist
Curriculum and Instruction Department
Randolph County School District
Asheboro, North Carolina

Carolyn Woolsey
Science Teacher
Southwest Middle School
Charlotte, North Carolina

Inclusion Specialists

Karen Clay
Inclusion Specialist Consultant
Boston, Massachusetts

Ellen McPeek Glisan
Special Needs Consultant
San Antonio, Texas

Safety Reviewer

Jack Gerlovich, Ph.D.
Associate Professor
School of Education
Drake University
Des Moines, Iowa

Academic Reviewers

David M. Armstrong, Ph.D.
Professor
Ecology and Evolutionary Biology
University of Colorado
Boulder, Colorado

John Brockhaus, Ph.D.
Professor of Geospatial Information Science and Director of Geospatial Information Science Program
Department of Geography and Environmental Engineering
United States Military Academy
West Point, New York

Howard L. Brooks, Ph.D.
Professor of Physics and Astronomy
Department of Physics and Astronomy
DePauw University
Greencastle, Indiana

Joe W. Crim, Ph.D.
Professor and Head of Cellular Biology
Department of Cellular Biology
University of Georgia
Athens, Georgia

William E. Dunscombe
Chairman
Biology Department
Union County College
Cranford, New Jersey

Acknowledgments
continued on page 691

Contents in Brief

Contents

Contents   **vii**

Contents **xv**

Chapter Labs and LabBook

The more labs, the better!
Take a minute to browse the variety of exciting **labs** in this textbook. Labs appear within the chapters and in a special LabBook in the back of the textbook. All labs are designed to help you experience science firsthand. But please don't forget to be safe. Read the Safety First! section before starting any of the labs.

Start your engines with an activity!

Get motivated to learn by doing the two activities at the beginning of each chapter. The **Pre-Reading Activity** helps you organize information as you read the chapter. The **Start-up Activity** helps you gain scientific understanding of the topic through hands-on experience.

PRE-READING ACTIVITY

START-UP ACTIVITY

READING STRATEGY

Remembering what you read doesn't have to be hard!

A **Reading Strategy** at the beginning of every section provides tips to help you remember and/or organize the information covered in the section.

Quick Lab

SCHOOL to HOME

Activity

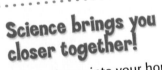

Science brings you closer together!

Bring science into your home by doing **School-to-Home Activities** with a parent or another adult in your household.

INTERNET ACTIVITY

Get caught in the Web!

Go to **go.hrw.com** for **Internet Activities** related to each chapter. To find the Internet Activity for a particular chapter, just type in the keyword listed below.

MATH PRACTICE

MATH FOCUS

Science and math go hand in hand.

The **Math Focus** and **Math Practice** items show you many ways that math applies directly to science and vice versa.

...ection to...

One subject leads to another.

You may not realize it at first, but different subjects are related to each other in many ways. Each **Connection** explores a topic from the viewpoint of another discipline. In this way, all of the subjects you learn about in school merge to improve your understanding of the world around you.

Science in Action

Science moves beyond the classroom!

Read **Science in Action** articles to learn more about science in the real world. These articles will give you an idea of how interesting, strange, helpful, and action-packed science is. At the end of each chapter, you will find three short articles. And if your thirst is still not quenched, go to **go.hrw.com** for in-depth coverage.

How to Use Your Textbook

Your Roadmap for Success with Holt Science and Technology

Reading Warm-Up

A Reading Warm-Up at the beginning of every section provides you with the section's objectives and key terms. The objectives tell you what you'll need to know after you finish reading the section.

Key terms are listed for each section. Learn the definitions of these terms because you will most likely be tested on them. Each key term is highlighted in the text and is defined at point of use and in the margin. You can also use the glossary to locate definitions quickly.

STUDY TIP Reread the objectives and the definitions to the key terms when studying for a test to be sure you know the material.

Get Organized

A Reading Strategy at the beginning of every section provides tips to help you organize and remember the information covered in the section. Keep a science notebook so that you are ready to take notes when your teacher reviews the material in class. Keep your assignments in this notebook so that you can review them when studying for the chapter test.

SECTION 1

Introduction to Body Systems

Imagine jumping into a lake. At first, your body feels very cold. You may even shiver. But eventually you get used to the cold water. How does this happen?

Your body gets used to cold water because of homeostasis (HOH mee OH STAY sis). **Homeostasis** is the maintenance of a stable internal environment in the body. When you jump into a cold lake, homeostasis helps your body stay warm.

READING WARM-UP

Objectives
- Describe homeostasis and what happens when it is disrupted.
- Describe how tissues, organs, and organ systems are related.
- List 12 organ systems.
- Identify how organ systems work together to maintain homeostasis.

Terms to Learn
homeostasis
tissue
organ

READING STRATEGY

Reading Organizer As you read this section, make a concept map by using the terms above.

homeostasis the maintenance of a constant internal state in a changing environment

Staying in Balance

The environment around you is always changing. Your body has to adjust to these conditions. For example, generally, on a hot day, your body is able to react to maintain your body temperature and avoid overheating. As shown in **Figure 1,** all living organisms have to maintain homeostasis.

Maintaining homeostasis is not easy. Your body needs nutrients and oxygen. Your body needs wastes removed. And your body needs to defend itself against disease. A single cell cannot do all of these jobs for the entire body. Fortunately, your body has many kinds of cells. Some cells remove wastes. Other cells carry oxygen or defend your body against disease. Together, these cells help your internal environment stay stable.

Figure 1 *These penguins have adaptations that help them maintain homeostasis in the cold environment in which they live.*

148   Chapter 5   Body Organization and Structure

Be Resourceful—Use the Web

SCiLINKS.

Internet Connect
boxes in your textbook take you to resources that you can use for science projects, reports, and research papers. Go to scilinks.org, and type in the SciLinks code to get information on a topic.

go.hrw.com

Visit go.hrw.com
Find worksheets, Current Science® magazine articles online, and other materials that go with your textbook at **go.hrw.com.** Click on the textbook icon and the table of contents to see all of the resources for each chapter.

Falling Out of Balance

Sometimes, your body cannot maintain homeostasis. For example, if you don't eat the right foods, your cells may not get the nutrients they need. Maybe your body systems can't fight off a disease caused by bacteria or viruses. So, homeostasis is disrupted. What happens when homeostasis is disrupted? Cells may be damaged or may die. When this happens, you can become sick, as shown in **Figure 2**. Sometimes, people die when homeostasis is disrupted.

Temperature Regulation

When you are hot, your body gives off heat. You also sweat. When sweat evaporates from your skin, your body is cooled. Sweating is a process that helps your body maintain homeostasis. Sometimes, the body cannot cool down. This happens when cells do not get what they need, such as water for sweat. If the body gets too hot, cells may be damaged.

The body also has ways to keep you warm on cold days. When you are cold, you shiver, which helps you stay warm. Sometimes, the body cannot stay warm. Body temperature falls below normal in a condition called *hypothermia*.

Figure 2 When homeostasis is disrupted, a person can become sick.

Moving Materials

Your cells need nutrients for life processes. If nutrients are not delivered, the cells cannot complete their life processes. So, the cells will die. These life processes often make wastes, which must be removed from cells. Many wastes are toxic. If a cell cannot get rid of them, the wastes will damage the cell.

Reading Check Explain the importance of moving materials into and out of cells. *(See the Appendix for answers to Reading Checks.)*

CONNECTION
Chemis
WRITING A
SKILL re
tors may rem
because of d
make adjustn
Examine how
disease or inj
tain a stable
a newspaper

Nervous System Your nervous system receives and sends electrical messages throughout your body.

Digestive System Your digestive system breaks down the food you eat into nutrients that your body can absorb.

Lymphatic System The lymphatic system returns leaked fluids to blood vessels and helps defend against disease.

Endocrine System Your glands send out chemical messages, which control body functions.

SECTION Review

Summary

- Homeostasis is the maintenance of a stable internal environment.
- A group of cells that work together is a tissue. Tissues form organs. Organs that work together form organ systems.
- There are 12 major organ systems in the human body.
- Organ systems work together to help the body maintain homeostasis.

Using Key Terms

1. In your own words, write a definition for the term *homeostasis*.

Understanding Key Ideas

2. Which of the following statements describes how tissues, organs, and organ systems are related?
   a. Organs form tissues, which form organ systems.
   b. Organ systems form organs, which form tissues.
   c. Tissues form organs, which form organ systems.
   d. None of the above

3. List the 12 organ systems.

Math Skills

4. The human skeleton has 206 bones. The human skull has 22 bones. What percentage of human bones are skull bones?

Critical Thinking

5. **Applying Concepts** The circulatory system delivers nutrients to cells in the body. What might happen to homeostasis if this system were disrupted? Explain your answer.

6. **Predicting Consequences** Predict what might happen if the human body did not have specialized cells, tissues, organs, and organ systems to maintain homeostasis.

SciLINKS. **NSTA**
Developed and maintained by the National Science Teachers Association

For a variety of links related to this chapter, go to www.scilinks.org

Topic: Tissues and Organs; Body Systems
SciLinks code: HSM1530; HSM0184

153

Use the Illustrations and Photos

Art shows complex ideas and processes. Learn to analyze the art so that you better understand the material you read in the text.

Tables and graphs display important information in an organized way to help you see relationships.

A picture is worth a thousand words. Look at the photographs to see relevant examples of science concepts that you are reading about.

Answer the Section Reviews

Section Reviews test your knowledge of the main points of the section. Critical Thinking items challenge you to think about the material in greater depth and to find connections that you infer from the text.

STUDY TIP When you can't answer a question, reread the section. The answer is usually there.

Do Your Homework

Your teacher may assign worksheets to help you understand and remember the material in the chapter.

STUDY TIP Don't try to answer the questions without reading the text and reviewing your class notes. A little preparation up front will make your homework assignments a lot easier. Answering the items in the Chapter Review will help prepare you for the chapter test.

Visit Holt Online Learning

If your teacher gives you a special password to log onto the Holt Online Learning site, you'll find your complete textbook on the Web. In addition, you'll find some great learning tools and practice quizzes. You'll be able to see how well you know the material from your textbook.

Visit CNN Student News

You'll find up-to-date events in science at cnnstudentnews.com.

SAFETY FIRST!

Exploring, inventing, and investigating are essential to the study of science. However, these activities can also be dangerous. To make sure that your experiments and explorations are safe, you must be aware of a variety of safety guidelines. You have probably heard of the saying, "It is better to be safe than sorry." This is particularly true in a science classroom where experiments and explorations are being performed. Being uninformed and careless can result in serious injuries. Don't take chances with your own safety or with anyone else's.

The following pages describe important guidelines for staying safe in the science classroom. Your teacher may also have safety guidelines and tips that are specific to your classroom and laboratory. Take the time to be safe.

Safety Rules!

Start Out Right

Always get your teacher's permission before attempting any laboratory exploration. Read the procedures carefully, and pay particular attention to safety information and caution statements. If you are unsure about what a safety symbol means, look it up or ask your teacher. You cannot be too careful when it comes to safety. If an accident does occur, inform your teacher immediately regardless of how minor you think the accident is.

If you are instructed to note the odor of a substance, wave the fumes toward your nose with your hand. Never put your nose close to the source.

Safety Symbols

All of the experiments and investigations in this book and their related worksheets include important safety symbols to alert you to particular safety concerns. Become familiar with these symbols so that when you see them, you will know what they mean and what to do. It is important that you read this entire safety section to learn about specific dangers in the laboratory.

Eye protection

Clothing protection

Hand safety

Heating safety

Electric safety

Chemical safety

Animal safety

Sharp object

Plant safety

Eye Safety

Wear safety goggles when working around chemicals, acids, bases, or any type of flame or heating device. Wear safety goggles any time there is even the slightest chance that harm could come to your eyes. If any substance gets into your eyes, notify your teacher immediately and flush your eyes with running water for at least 15 minutes. Treat any unknown chemical as if it were a dangerous chemical. Never look directly into the sun. Doing so could cause permanent blindness.

Avoid wearing contact lenses in a laboratory situation. Even if you are wearing safety goggles, chemicals can get between the contact lenses and your eyes. If your doctor requires that you wear contact lenses instead of glasses, wear eye-cup safety goggles in the lab.

Safety Equipment

Know the locations of the nearest fire alarms and any other safety equipment, such as fire blankets and eyewash fountains, as identified by your teacher, and know the procedures for using the equipment.

Neatness

Keep your work area free of all unnecessary books and papers. Tie back long hair, and secure loose sleeves or other loose articles of clothing, such as ties and bows. Remove dangling jewelry. Don't wear open-toed shoes or sandals in the laboratory. Never eat, drink, or apply cosmetics in a laboratory setting. Food, drink, and cosmetics can easily become contaminated with dangerous materials.

Certain hair products (such as aerosol hair spray) are flammable and should not be worn while working near an open flame. Avoid wearing hair spray or hair gel on lab days.

Sharp/Pointed Objects

Use knives and other sharp instruments with extreme care. Never cut objects while holding them in your hands. Place objects on a suitable work surface for cutting.

Be extra careful when using any glassware. When adding a heavy object to a graduated cylinder, tilt the cylinder so that the object slides slowly to the bottom.

Heat

Wear safety goggles when using a heating device or a flame. Whenever possible, use an electric hot plate as a heat source instead of using an open flame. When heating materials in a test tube, always angle the test tube away from yourself and others. To avoid burns, wear heat-resistant gloves whenever instructed to do so.

Electricity

Be careful with electrical cords. When using a microscope with a lamp, do not place the cord where it could trip someone. Do not let cords hang over a table edge in a way that could cause equipment to fall if the cord is accidentally pulled. Do not use equipment with damaged cords. Be sure that your hands are dry and that the electrical equipment is in the "off" position before plugging it in. Turn off and unplug electrical equipment when you are finished.

Chemicals

Wear safety goggles when handling any potentially dangerous chemicals, acids, or bases. If a chemical is unknown, handle it as you would a dangerous chemical. Wear an apron and protective gloves when you work with acids or bases or whenever you are told to do so. If a spill gets on your skin or clothing, rinse it off immediately with water for at least 5 minutes while calling to your teacher.

Never mix chemicals unless your teacher tells you to do so. Never taste, touch, or smell chemicals unless you are specifically directed to do so. Before working with a flammable liquid or gas, check for the presence of any source of flame, spark, or heat.

Animal Safety

Always obtain your teacher's permission before bringing any animal into the school building. Handle animals only as your teacher directs. Always treat animals carefully and respectfully. Wash your hands thoroughly after handling any animal.

Plant Safety

Do not eat any part of a plant or plant seed used in the laboratory. Wash your hands thoroughly after handling any part of a plant. When in nature, do not pick any wild plants unless your teacher instructs you to do so.

Glassware

Examine all glassware before use. Be sure that glassware is clean and free of chips and cracks. Report damaged glassware to your teacher. Glass containers used for heating should be made of heat-resistant glass.

1

Science in Our World

About the PHOTO

What happened to the legs of these frogs? Science can help answer this question. Deformed frogs, such as the ones in this photo, have been found in the northern United States and southern Canada. Scientists and students like you have been using science to find out how frogs may develop deformities.

PRE-READING ACTIVITY

FOLDNOTES **Layered Book** Before you read the chapter, create the FoldNote entitled "Layered Book" described in the **Study Skills** section of the Appendix. Label the tabs of the layered book with "Examples of life scientists," "Scientific methods," "Scientific models," and "Tools, measurement, and safety." As you read the chapter, write information you learn about each category under the appropriate tab.

START-UP ACTIVITY

A Little Bit of Science

In this activity, you'll find out that you can learn about the unknown without having to see it.

Procedure

1. Your teacher will give you a **coffee can** to which a **sock** has been attached. Do not look into the can.

2. Reach through the opening in the sock. You will feel **several objects** inside the can.

3. Record observations you make about the objects by feeling them, shaking the can, and so on.

4. What do you think is in the can? List your guesses. State some reasons for your guesses.

5. Pour the contents of the can onto your desk. Compare your list with what was in the can.

Analysis

1. Did you guess the contents of the can correctly? What might have caused you to guess wrongly?

2. What observations did you make about each of the objects while they were in the can? Which of your senses did you use?

Science and Scientists

You are enjoying a picnic on a summer day. Crumbs from your sandwich fall to the ground, and ants carry the crumbs away. You wonder, Why do ants show up at picnics?

Congratulations! You just took one of the first steps of being a scientist. How did you do it? You observed the world around you. Then, you asked a question about your observations. And asking a question is part of what science is all about.

Start with a Question

The world around you is full of amazing things. Single-celled algae float unseen in ponds. Volcanoes erupt with explosive force. Mars may have had water in the past. And 40-ton whales glide through the oceans. These things or others, such as those shown in **Figure 1,** may lead you to ask a question. A question is the beginning of science. **Science** is the knowledge obtained by observing the natural world in order to discover facts and to formulate laws and principles that can be verified or tested.

✓ **Reading Check** What is science? (*See the Appendix for answers to Reading Checks.*)

In Your Own Neighborhood

Take a look around your home, school, and neighborhood. Often, you take things that you use or see every day for granted. But one day you might look at something in a new way. That's when a question hits you! The student in **Figure 1** didn't have to look very far to realize that he had some questions to ask.

The World and Beyond

You don't have to stop at questions about things in your neighborhood. Ask questions about atoms or galaxies, pandas and bamboo, or earthquakes. A variety of plants and animals live in a variety of places. And each place has a unique combination of rocks, soil, and water.

You can even ask questions about places other than those on Earth. Look outward to the moon, the sun, and the planets in our solar system. Beyond that, you have the rest of the universe! There are enough questions to keep scientists busy for a long time.

READING WARM-UP

Objectives
- Describe three methods of investigation.
- Identify benefits of science in the world around you.
- Describe five jobs that use science.

Terms to Learn
science

READING STRATEGY

Prediction Guide Before reading this section, write the title of each heading in this section. Next, under each heading, write what you think you will learn.

science the knowledge obtained by observing natural events and conditions in order to discover facts and formulate laws or principles that can be verified or tested

Why do leaves change color in the fall?

Why did the dinosaurs die out?

How do birds know where to go when they migrate?

Figure 1 *Part of science is asking questions about the world around you.*

Investigation: The Search for Answers

After you ask a question, it's time to look for an answer. But how do you start your investigation? Several methods may be used.

Research

You can find answers to some of your questions by doing research, as **Figure 2** shows. You can ask someone who knows a lot about the subject of your question. You can find information in textbooks, encyclopedias, and magazines. You can search on the Internet. You might read a report of an experiment that someone did. But be sure to think about the sources of your information. Use information only from reliable sources.

Figure 2 *A library is a good place to begin your search for answers.*

Observation

You can also find answers to questions by making careful observations. For example, if you want to know how spiders spin their webs, look for a web. When you find one, return to observe the spider as it spins. But be careful in making observations. Sometimes, what people expect to observe affects what they do observe. For example, most plants need light to grow. Does that mean that all plants need bright sunlight? Do some plants prefer shade? Some people might "observe" that bright light is the only answer. To test an observation, you may have to do an experiment.

Ask a Question

The next time you're outside, look carefully around you. Think of a science-related question that you would like to answer. Write the question in your **science journal.** Discuss with a parent which methods of investigation would be most likely to help you answer your question.

Experimentation

You might answer the question about light and shade by doing a simple experiment, such as the one shown in **Figure 3.** Your research and your observations can help you plan your experiment. What should you do if your experiment needs something that is hard to get? For example, what do you do if you want to know whether a certain plant grows in space? Don't give up! Try to find results from someone else's experiment!

Figure 3 *This student is doing an experiment to find out whether this type of plant grows better in shade or in direct sunlight.*

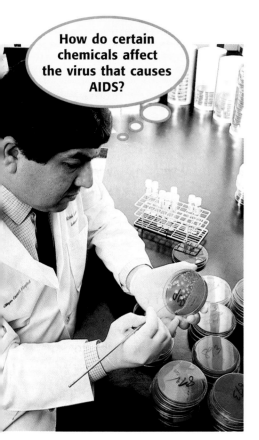

How do certain chemicals affect the virus that causes AIDS?

Figure 4 *Abdul Lakhani studies AIDS to find a cure for the disease.*

Why Ask Questions?

Although scientists cannot answer every question immediately, they do find some interesting answers. Do any of the answers really matter? Absolutely! As you study science, you will see how science affects you and society around you.

Fighting Diseases

Polio is a disease that can cause paralysis by affecting the brain and nerves. Do you know anyone who has had polio? You probably don't. But in 1952, polio infected 58,000 Americans. Fortunately, vaccines developed in 1955 and 1956 have eliminated polio in the United States. In fact, the virus that causes polio has been wiped out in most of the world.

Today, scientists are searching for cures for diseases such as mad cow disease, tuberculosis, and acquired immune deficiency syndrome (AIDS). The scientist in **Figure 4** is learning more about AIDS, which kills millions of people every year.

Saving Resources

Science also helps answer the question, How can we make resources last longer? Recycling is one answer. Think about the last time that you recycled an aluminum can. By recycling that can, you saved more than just the aluminum, as **Figure 5** shows. Using science, people have developed more-efficient methods and better equipment for recycling aluminum, paper, steel, glass, and even some plastics. In this way, science helps make resources last longer.

Figure 5 **Resources Saved Through Recycling**

Compared with producing aluminum from its ore, recycling 1 metric ton (1.1 tons) of aluminum:

 produces 95% less air pollution

 saves 4 metric tons (4.4 tons) of ore

 produces 4 metric tons (4.4 tons) fewer chemical products

 uses 14,000 kWh less energy

 produces 97% less water pollution

Answering Society's Questions

Sometimes, society faces a question that does not seem to have an immediate answer. For example, at one time, the question of how to reduce air pollution did not have any obvious, reasonable answers. The millions of people who depended on their cars could not just stop driving. As the problem of air pollution became more important to people, scientists developed different technologies to address it. For example, one source of air pollution is exhaust from cars. Through science, people have developed cleaner-burning gasoline. People have even developed new ways to clean up exhaust before it leaves the tailpipe of a car!

Reading Check How can society influence the types of technologies that are developed?

Scientists All Around You

Believe it or not, scientists work in many different places. If you think about it, any person who asks questions and looks for answers could be called a scientist! Keep reading to learn about just a few people who use science in their jobs.

Zoologist

A *zoologist* (zoh AHL uh jist) is a person who studies the lives of animals. Dale Miquelle, shown in **Figure 6,** is part of a team of Russian and American zoologists studying the Siberian tiger. The tigers have almost become extinct after being hunted and losing their homes. By learning about the tigers' living space and food needs, zoologists hope to make a plan that will help the tigers survive better in the wild.

Figure 6 *To learn how much land a Siberian tiger covers, Dale Miquelle tracks a tiger that is wearing a radio-transmitting collar.*

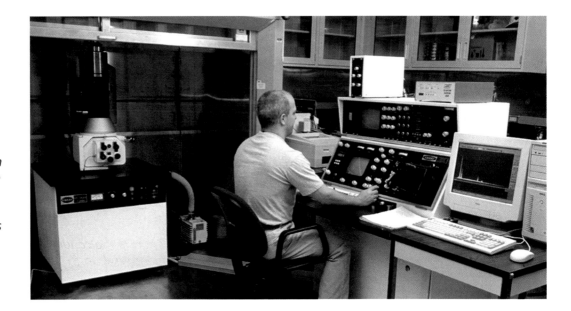

Figure 7 *This geochemist may work outdoors when collecting rock samples from the field. Then, he may work indoors as he analyzes the samples in his laboratory.*

Geochemist

Some scientists work outdoors most of the time. Other scientists spend much of their time in the laboratory. A geochemist (JEE oh KEM ist), such as the one shown in **Figure 7,** may work in both places. A *geochemist* is a person who specializes in the chemistry of rocks, minerals, and soil.

Geochemists determine the economic value of these materials. They also try to find out what the environment was like when these materials formed and what has happened to the materials since they first formed.

Mechanic

Do you have a machine that needs repairs? Call a mechanic, such as Gene Webb in **Figure 8.** Mechanics work on everything from cars to the space shuttle. Mechanics use science to solve problems. Mechanics must find answers to questions about why a machine is not working. Then, they must find a way to make it work. Mechanics also think of ways to improve the machine, to make it work faster or more efficiently.

Oceanographer

An *oceanographer* studies the ocean. Some oceanographers study waves and ocean currents. Others study plants and animals that live in the ocean. Still others study the ocean floor, including how it forms.

Figure 8 *A mechanic can help keep a car's engine running smoothly.*

While studying the ocean floor, oceanographers discovered black smokers. Black smokers are cracks where hot water (around 300°C!) from beneath Earth's surface comes up. These vents in the ocean floor are home to some strange animals, including red-tipped tube worms and blind white crabs.

Volcanologist

If black smokers aren't hot enough for you, perhaps you would like to become a volcanologist (VAHL kuh NAHL uh jist). A *volcanologist* studies one of Earth's most interesting processes—volcanoes. The volcanologist shown in **Figure 9** is photographing lava flowing from Mt. Etna, a volcano in Italy. Mt. Etna's lava may reach temperatures of 1,050°C. By learning more about volcanoes, volcanologists hope to get better at predicting when a volcano will erupt. Being able to predict eruptions would help save lives.

Reading Check What does a volcanologist do?

Figure 9 *Volcanologists gain a better understanding of the inside of the Earth by studying the makeup of lava.*

SECTION Review

Summary

- Science is a process of gathering knowledge about the natural world by making observations and asking questions.
- Science begins by asking a question.
- Even if science cannot answer the question right away, the answers that scientists find may be very important.
- A question may lead to a scientific investigation, including research, observations, and experimentation.
- Science can help save lives, fight diseases, save resources, and protect the environment.
- A variety of people may become scientists for a variety of reasons.

Using Key Terms

1. In your own words, write a definition for the term *science*.

Understanding Key Ideas

2. A zoologist might study any of the following EXCEPT
   a. shellfish living in ponds.
   b. the reason that mole rats live in large groups underground.
   c. environmental threats to sea turtles.
   d. rocks and minerals in the Painted Desert.

3. Describe five careers that use science.

4. How are observation and experimentation different?

5. How may what people expect to observe affect what they do observe? How can people avoid this problem?

Math Skills

6. Students in a science class collected 50 frogs from a pond. They found that 15 of the frogs had serious deformities. What percentage of the frogs had deformities?

Critical Thinking

7. **Making Inferences** An ad for deluxe garbage bags says that the bags are 30% stronger than regular garbage bags. Describe how science can help you find out if this claim is true.

8. **Identifying Relationships** Make a list of three things that you consider to be a problem in society. Give an example of how new technology might solve these problems.

9. **Applying Concepts** Look at **Figure 9**. Write five questions about what you see. Describe how science might help you answer your questions. Share your questions with your classmates.

SCILINKS

NSTA
Developed and maintained by the National Science Teachers Association

For a variety of links related to this chapter, go to www.scilinks.org

Topic: Careers in Science
SciLinks code: HSM0244

Scientific Methods

Imagine that your class is on a field trip to a wildlife refuge. You discover several deformed frogs. You wonder what could be causing the frogs' deformities.

A group of students from Le Sueur, Minnesota, actually made this discovery! By making observations and asking questions about the observations, the students used scientific methods.

What Are Scientific Methods?

When scientists observe the natural world, they often think of a question or problem. But scientists don't just guess at answers. They use scientific methods. **Scientific methods** are the ways in which scientists follow steps to answer questions and solve problems. The steps used for all investigations are the same. But the order in which the steps are followed may vary, as shown in **Figure 1.** Scientists may use all of the steps or just some of the steps during an investigation. They may even repeat some of the steps. The order depends on what works best to answer the question. No matter where scientists work or what questions they try to answer, all scientists have two things in common. They are curious about the natural world, and they use similar methods to investigate it.

✓ **Reading Check** What are scientific methods? (*See the Appendix for answers to Reading Checks.*)

scientific methods a series of steps followed to solve problems

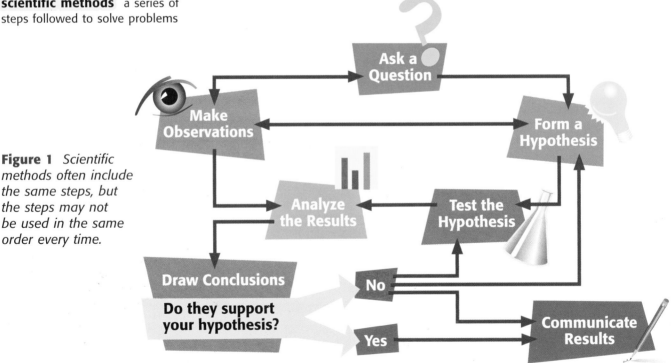

Figure 1 *Scientific methods often include the same steps, but the steps may not be used in the same order every time.*

Ask a Question

Have you ever observed something out of the ordinary or difficult to explain? Such an observation usually raises questions. For example, about the deformed frogs you might ask, "Could something in the water be causing the frog deformities?" Looking for answers may include making more observations.

Make Observations

After the students in Minnesota realized something was wrong with the frogs, they decided to make additional, careful observations, as shown in **Figure 2.** They counted the number of deformed frogs and the number of normal frogs they caught. They also photographed the frogs, took measurements, and wrote a thorough description of each frog.

In addition, the students collected data on other organisms living in the pond. They also conducted many tests on the pond water and measured things such as the level of acidity. The students carefully recorded their data and observations.

Figure 2 *Making careful observations is often the first step in an investigation.*

Accurate Observations

Any information that you gather through your senses is an observation. Observations can take many forms. They may be measurements of length, volume, time, speed, or loudness. They may describe the color or shape of an organism. Or they may record the behavior of organisms in an area. The range of observations that a scientist can make is endless. But no matter what observations reveal, they are useful only if they are accurately made and recorded. Scientists use many standard tools and methods to make and record observations. Examples of these tools are shown in **Figure 3.**

Figure 3 *Microscopes, rulers, and thermometers are some of the many tools scientists use to collect information.*

Form a Hypothesis

After asking questions and making observations, scientists may form a hypothesis. A **hypothesis** (hie PAHTH uh sis) is a possible explanation or answer to a question. A good hypothesis is based on observation and can be tested. When scientists form hypotheses, they think logically and creatively and consider what they already know.

To be useful, a hypothesis must be testable. A hypothesis is testable if an experiment can be designed to test the hypothesis. Yet if a hypothesis is not testable, it is not always wrong. An untestable hypothesis is simply one that cannot be supported or disproved. Sometimes, it may be impossible to gather enough observations to test a hypothesis.

Scientists may form different hypotheses for the same problem. In the case of the Minnesota frogs, scientists formed the hypotheses shown in **Figure 4.** Were any of these explanations correct? To find out, scientists had to test each hypothesis.

✓ Reading Check What makes a hypothesis testable?

hypothesis an explanation that is based on prior scientific research or observations and that can be tested

Figure 4
More than one hypothesis can be made for a single question.

Hypothesis 1:

The deformities were caused by one or more chemical pollutants in the water.

Hypothesis 2:

The deformities were caused by attacks from parasites or other frogs.

Hypothesis 3:

The deformities were caused by an increase in exposure to ultraviolet light from the sun.

Predictions

Before scientists can test a hypothesis, they must first make predictions. A prediction is a statement of cause and effect that can be used to set up a test for a hypothesis. Predictions are usually stated in an if-then format, as shown in **Figure 5.**

Figure 5 lists the predictions made for the hypotheses shown in **Figure 4.** More than one prediction may be made for each hypothesis. After predictions are made, scientists can conduct experiments to see which predictions, if any, prove to be true and support the hypotheses.

Figure 5 *More than one prediction may be made for a single hypothesis.*

Hypothesis 1:

Prediction: If *a substance in the pond water is causing the deformities,* then *the water from ponds that have deformed frogs will be different from the water from ponds in which no abnormal frogs have been found.*

Prediction: If *a substance in the pond water is causing the deformities,* then *some tadpoles will develop deformities when they are raised in pond water collected from ponds that have deformed frogs.*

Hypothesis 2:

Prediction: If *a parasite is causing the deformities,* then *this parasite will be found more often in frogs that have deformities.*

Hypothesis 3:

Prediction: If *an increase in exposure to ultraviolet light is causing the deformities,* then *some frog eggs exposed to ultraviolet light in a laboratory will develop into deformed frogs.*

CONNECTION TO
Language Arts

WRITING SKILL **"Leading doctors say . . ."** Suppose that you and a friend see an ad for a cold remedy on TV. According to the ad, "Leading doctors recommend this product for their patients." Then, a famous actor comes on and says that he or she uses the product, too. Write a dialogue of the debate you might have with your friend about whether these claims are believable.

Test the Hypothesis

After scientists make a prediction, they test the hypothesis. Scientists try to design experiments that will clearly show whether a particular factor caused an observed outcome. In an experiment, a *factor* is anything that can influence the experiment's outcome. Factors can be anything from temperature to the type of organism being studied.

Under Control

Scientists studying the frogs in Minnesota observed many factors that affect the development of frogs in the wild, as shown in **Figure 6.** But it was hard to tell which factor could be causing the deformities. To sort factors out, scientists perform controlled experiments. A **controlled experiment** tests only one factor at a time and consists of a control group and one or more experimental groups. All of the factors for the control group and the experimental groups are the same except for one. The one factor that differs is called the **variable.** Because only the variable differs between the control group and the experimental groups, any differences observed in the outcome of the experiment are probably caused by the variable.

✔ **Reading Check** How many factors should an experiment test?

Designing an Experiment

Designing a good experiment requires planning. Every factor should be considered. Examine the prediction for Hypothesis 3: *If an increase in exposure to ultraviolet light is causing the deformities, then some frog eggs exposed to ultraviolet light in a laboratory will develop into deformed frogs.* An experiment to test this hypothesis is summarized in **Table 1.** In this case, the variable is the length of time the eggs are exposed to ultraviolet (UV) light. All other factors, such as the temperature of the water, are the same in the control group and in the experimental groups.

Figure 6 *Many factors affect this tadpole in the wild. These factors include chemicals, light, temperature, and parasites.*

controlled experiment an experiment that tests only one factor at a time by using a comparison of a control group with an experimental group

variable a factor that changes in an experiment in order to test a hypothesis

Table 1 Experiment to Test Effect of UV Light on Frogs				
	Control factors			**Variable**
Group	**Kind of frog**	**Number of Eggs**	**Temperature of water**	**UV light exposure**
#1 (control)	leopard frog	100	25°C	0 days
#2 (experimental)	leopard frog	100	25°C	15 days
#3 (experimental)	leopard frog	100	25°C	24 days

Figure 7 UV Light Experiment

Control Group	Experimental Groups	
Group #1 No UV light exposure	**Group #2** UV light exposure for 15 days	**Group #3** UV light exposure for 24 days
Result: 0 deformed frogs	Result: 0 deformed frogs	Result: 47 deformed frogs

Collecting Data

Figure 7 shows the experimental setup to test Hypothesis 3. As **Table 1** shows, there are 100 eggs in each group. Scientists always try to test many individuals. They want to be sure that differences between control and experimental groups are caused by the variable and not by differences between individuals. The larger the groups are, the smaller the effect of a difference between individual frogs will be. The larger the groups are, the more likely it is that the variable is responsible for any changes and the more accurate the data collected are likely to be.

Scientists test a result by repeating the experiment. If an experiment gives the same results each time, scientists are more certain about the variable's effect on the outcome. Scientists keep clear, accurate, honest records of their data so that other scientists can repeat the experiment and verify the results.

Analyze the Results

After scientists finish their tests, they must organize their data and analyze the results. Scientists may organize data in a table or a graph. The data collected from the UV light experiment are shown in the bar graph in **Figure 8.** Analyzing the results helps scientists explain and focus on the effect of the variable. For example, the graph shows that the length of UV exposure has an effect on the development of frog deformities.

Figure 8 *This graph shows that 24 days of UV exposure had an effect on frog deformities, while less exposure had no effect.*

Averages

Finding the average, or mean, of a group of numbers is a common way to analyze data.

For example, three seeds were kept at 25°C and sprouted in 8, 8, and 5 days. To find the average number of days that it took the seeds to sprout, add 8, 8, and 5 and divide the sum by 3, the number of subjects (seeds). It took these seeds an average of 7 days to sprout.

Suppose three seeds were kept at 30°C and sprouted in 6, 5, and 4 days. What's the average number of days that it took these seeds to sprout?

Figure 9 *This student scientist is communicating the results of his investigation at a science fair.*

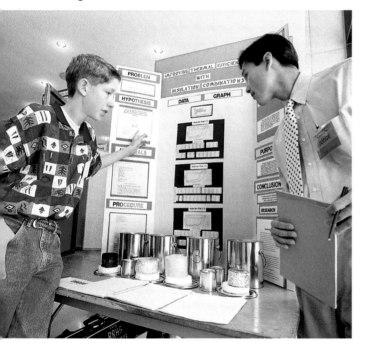

Draw Conclusions

After scientists have analyzed the data from several experiments, they can draw conclusions. They decide whether the results of the experiments support a hypothesis. When scientists find that a hypothesis is not supported by the tests, they must try to find another explanation for what they have observed. Proving that a hypothesis is wrong is just as helpful as supporting it. Why? Either way, the scientist has learned something, which is the purpose of using scientific methods.

✓ Reading Check How can a wrong hypothesis be helpful?

Is It the Answer?

The UV light experiment supports the hypothesis that frog deformities can be caused by exposure to UV light. Does this mean that UV light definitely caused frogs living in the Minnesota wetland to be deformed? No, the only thing this experiment shows is that UV light may be a cause of frog deformities. Results of tests done in a laboratory may differ from results of tests performed in the wild. In addition, the experiment did not investigate the effects of parasites or some other substance on the frogs. In fact, many scientists now think that more than one factor could be causing the deformities.

Sometimes, similar investigations or experiments give different results. For example, another research team may have had results that did not support the UV light hypothesis. In such a case, scientists must work together to decide if the differences in the results are scientifically significant. Often, making that decision takes more experiments and more evidence.

Communicate Results

Scientists form a global community. After scientists complete their investigations, they communicate their results to other scientists. The student in **Figure 9** is explaining the results of a science project.

Scientists regularly share their results for several reasons. First, other scientists may then repeat the experiments to see if they get the same results. Second, the information can be considered by other scientists with similar interests. The scientists can then compare hypotheses and form consistent explanations. New data may strengthen existing hypotheses or show that the hypotheses need to be altered. There are many paths from observations and questions to communicating results.

Summary

- Scientific methods are the ways in which scientists follow steps to answer questions and solve problems.

- Any information you gather through your senses is an observation. Observations often lead to the formation of questions and hypotheses.

- A hypothesis is a possible explanation or answer to a question. A well-formed hypothesis is testable by experiment.

- A controlled experiment tests only one factor at a time and consists of a control group and one or more experimental groups.

- After testing a hypothesis, scientists analyze the results and draw conclusions about whether the hypothesis is supported.

- Communicating results allows others to check the results, add to their knowledge, and design new experiments.

Using Key Terms

1. Use the following terms in the same sentence: *hypothesis, controlled experiment,* and *variable.*

Understanding Key Ideas

2. The steps of scientific methods
   a. are exactly the same in every investigation.
   b. must be used in the same order every time.
   c. are not used in the same order every time.
   d. always end with a conclusion.

3. What is the appropriate design of a controlled experiment?

4. What causes scientific knowledge to change?

Math Skills

5. Calculate the average of the following values: 4, 5, 6, 6, and 9.

Critical Thinking

6. **Analyzing Methods** Why was UV light chosen to be the variable in the frog experiment?

7. **Analyzing Processes** Why are there many ways to follow the steps of scientific methods?

8. **Making Inferences** Why might two scientists working on the same problem draw different conclusions?

9. **Making Inferences** Why do scientists use scientific methods?

Interpreting Graphics

10. The table below shows how long it takes for bacteria to double. Plot the information on a graph. Put temperature on the *x*-axis and the time to double on the *y*-axis. Do not graph values for which there is no growth. At what temperature do the bacteria multiply the fastest?

Temperature (°C)	Time to double (min)
10	130
20	60
25	40
30	29
37	17
40	19
45	32
50	no growth

11. What would happen if you changed the scale of the graph by using values of 0 to 300 minutes on the *y*-axis? How might that change affect your interpretation of the data?

SCILINKS

Developed and maintained by the National Science Teachers Association

For a variety of links related to this chapter, go to www.scilinks.org

Topic: Scientific Methods; Deformed Frogs
SciLinks code: HSM1359; HSM0383

Scientific Models

How can you see the parts of a cell? Unless you had superhuman eyesight, you couldn't see inside most cells without using a microscope.

What would you do if you didn't have a microscope? Looking at a model of a cell would help! A model of a cell can help you understand what the parts of a cell look like.

Types of Scientific Models

A **model** is a representation of an object or system. Scientific models are used to help explain how something works or to describe the structure of something. A model may be used to predict future events. However, models have limitations. A model is never exactly like the real thing. If it were, it would not be a model. Three major kinds of scientific models are physical, mathematical, and conceptual models.

Physical Models

A model volcano and a miniature steam engine are examples of physical models. Some physical models, such as a model of a cell, look like the thing that they model. But a limitation of the model of a cell is that the model is not alive and doesn't act exactly like a cell. Other physical models, such as the model of a skyscraper in **Figure 1,** look and act at least somewhat like the thing that they model. Scientists often use the model that is simplest to use but that still serves their purpose.

Figure 1 *The model of the skyscraper doesn't act like the real building in every way, which is both a benefit and a limitation of the model.*

Figure 2   **Mathematical Model: A Punnett Square**

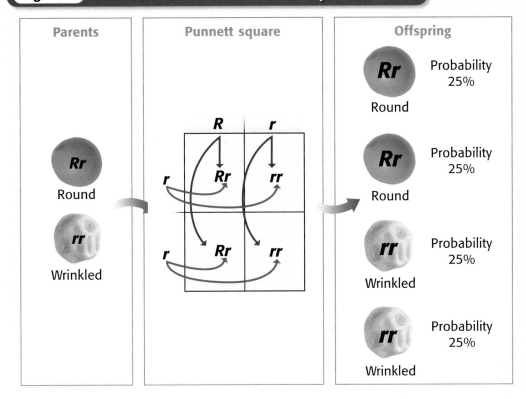

Mathematical Models

A mathematical model may be made up of numbers, equations, and other forms of data. Some mathematical models are simple and can be used easily. The Punnett square shown in **Figure 2** helps scientists study the passing of traits from parents to offspring. Using this model, scientists can predict how often certain traits will appear in the offspring of certain parents.

Computers are useful for creating and manipulating mathematical models. They make fewer mistakes and can keep track of more variables than a person can. But a computer model can also be incorrect in many ways. The more complex a model is, the more carefully scientists must build and test the model.

✓ **Reading Check** What type of model is a Punnett square? (*See the Appendix for answers to Reading Checks.*)

Conceptual Models

The third type of model is the conceptual model. Some conceptual models are systems of ideas. Others compare unfamiliar things with familiar things to help explain unfamiliar ideas. The idea that the solar system formed from a spinning disk of gas is a conceptual model. Scientists also use conceptual models to classify behaviors of animals. Scientists can then predict how an animal might respond to a certain action based on behaviors that have already been observed.

CONNECTION TO Environmental Science

Samples Scientists studying deformed frogs in Minnesota wanted to know at what stage in the frogs' development the deformities happened. So, the scientists collected a large sample of frogs in all stages of development.

The larger a sample is, the more accurately it represents the whole population. If, for example, a sample of frogs is too small, one unusual frog may make the results of the study inaccurate. If the sample has too many old frogs or too many tadpoles, the sample is unrepresentative of the whole population. Give an example of an unrepresentative sample. Make a poster describing how that sample might make the experimental results inaccurate.

ACTIVITY

Figure 3 *This computer-generated model doesn't just look like a dinosaur. It may also open and close its jaws in much the same way that a dinosaur does.*

Benefits of Models

Models often represent things that are small, large, or complicated. Models can also represent things that do not exist. For example, **Figure 3** is a model of one type of dinosaur. Dinosaurs died out millions of years ago. Some popular movies about dinosaurs have used computer models like this one because dinosaurs are extinct. But the movies would not be as realistic if they did not have the scientific models.

A model can be a kind of hypothesis, and scientists can test a model. To build a model of an organism, even an extinct one, scientists gather information from fossils and other observations. Then, scientists can test whether the model fits their ideas about how an organism moved or what it ate.

Limits of Models

Models are useful, but they are not perfect. For example, the model in **Figure 3** gives scientists an idea of how the dinosaur looked. But to find out how strong the dinosaur's jaws were, scientists might build a physical model that has pressure sensors in the jaw. That model would provide data about bite strength. Scientists may use different models to represent the same thing, such as the dinosaur's jaw. But the kind of model and the model's complexity depend on the model's purpose.

Even a model jaw that has pressure sensors is not perfect. Scientists can compare the dinosaur bite with the bite of a crocodile. Next, scientists use their model to conduct tests. Scientists might then estimate how hard the dinosaur could bite. But without a live dinosaur, the result is still a hypothesis.

Building Scientific Knowledge

Sometimes, scientists draw different conclusions from the same data. Other times, new results show that old conclusions are wrong. Scientists are always asking new questions or looking at old questions from a different angle. As scientists find new answers, scientific knowledge continues to grow and change.

Scientific Theories

For every hypothesis, more than one prediction can be made. Each time another prediction is proven true, the hypothesis gains more support. Over time, scientists tie together everything that they have learned. An explanation that ties together many related observations, facts, and tested hypotheses is called a **theory.** Theories are conceptual models that help organize scientific thinking. Theories are used to explain observations and to predict what might happen in the future.

theory an explanation that ties together many hypotheses and observations

law a summary of many experimental results and observations; a law tells how things work

✔ **Reading Check** How do scientists use theories?

Scientific Laws

What happens when a theory and its models correctly predict the results of many experiments? A scientific law may be formed. In science, a **law** is a summary of many experimental results and observations. A scientific law is a statement of what *will* happen in a specific situation. A law tells you how things work.

Scientific laws are at work around you every day. For example, the law of gravity states that objects will always fall toward the center of Earth. And inside your cells, many laws of chemistry are at work to keep you alive.

Scientific Change

New scientific ideas may take time to be accepted as facts, scientific theories, or scientific laws. Scientists should be open to new ideas but should always test new ideas by using scientific methods. If new evidence challenges an accepted idea, scientists must reexamine the old evidence and reevaluate the old idea. In this way, the process of building scientific knowledge never ends.

SECTION Review

Summary

- Models represent objects or systems. Often, they use familiar things to represent unfamiliar things. Three main types of models are physical, mathematical, and conceptual models. Models have limitations but are useful and can be changed based on new evidence.

- Scientific knowledge is built as scientists form and revise scientific hypotheses, models, theories, and laws.

Using Key Terms

In each of the following sentences, replace the incorrect term with the correct term from the word bank.

> theory   law   hypothesis

1. A conclusion is an explanation that matches many hypotheses but may still change.

2. A model tells you exactly what to expect in certain situations.

Understanding Key Ideas

3. A limitation of models is that
   a. they are large enough to see.
   b. they do not act exactly like the things that they model.
   c. they are smaller than the things that they model.
   d. they model unfamiliar things.

4. What type of model would you use to test the hypothesis that global warming is causing polar icecaps to melt? Explain.

Math Skills

5. If Jerry is 2.1 m tall, how tall is a scale model of Jerry that is 10% of his size?

Critical Thinking

6. **Applying Concepts** You want to make a model of an extinct plant. What are two kinds of models that you might use? Describe the advantages and disadvantages of each type of model.

Tools, Measurement, and Safety

Would you use a hammer to tighten a bolt on a bicycle? No, you wouldn't. You need the right tools to fix a bike.

Scientists use a variety of tools in their experiments. A tool is anything that helps you do a task.

Tools for Measuring

You might remember that one way to collect data is to take measurements. To get the best measurements, you need the proper tools. Stopwatches, metersticks, and balances are tools that you can use to make measurements. Thermometers, spring scales, and graduated cylinders are also helpful tools. Some of the uses of these tools are shown in **Figure 1.**

✓ **Reading Check** Name six tools used for taking measurements. (*See the Appendix for answers to Reading Checks.*)

Tools for Analyzing

After you collect data, you need to analyze them. Perhaps you need to find the average of your data. Calculators are handy tools to help you do calculations quickly. Or you might show your data in a graph or a figure. A computer that has the correct software can help you make neat, colorful figures. Of course, even a pencil and graph paper are tools that you can use to graph your data.

Figure 1 **Measurement Tools**

You can use a **graduated cylinder** to measure volume.

You can use a **stopwatch** to measure time.

You can use a **thermometer** to measure temperature.

You can use a **meterstick** to measure length.

You can use a **balance** to measure mass.

You can use a **spring scale** to measure force.

Units of Measurement

The ability to make accurate and reliable measurements is an important skill in science. Many systems of measurement are used throughout the world. At one time in England, the standard for an inch was three grains of barley placed end to end. Other modern standardized units were originally based on parts of the body, such as the foot. Such systems were not very reliable. Their units were based on objects that had different sizes.

The International System of Units

In the late 1700s, the French Academy of Sciences began to form a global measurement system now known as the *International System of Units,* or SI. Today, most scientists and almost all countries use this system. One advantage of using SI measurements is that doing so helps scientists share and compare their observations and results.

Another advantage of SI units is that all units are based on the number 10, which makes conversions from one unit to another easy. The table in **Table 1** contains commonly used SI units for length, volume, mass, and temperature.

No Rulers Allowed

1. Measure the width of your desk, but don't use a ruler.
2. Select another object to use as your unit of measurement.
3. Compare your measurement with those of your classmates.
4. Explain why it is important to use standard units of measurement.

Table 1 Common SI Units and Conversions		
Length	**meter (m)** kilometer (km) decimeter (dm) centimeter (cm) millimeter (mm) micrometer (μm) nanometer (nm)	1 km = 1,000 m 1 dm = 0.1 m 1 cm = 0.01 m 1 mm = 0.001 m 1 μm = 0.000001 m 1 nm = 0.000000001 m
Volume	**cubic meter (m³)** cubic centimeter (cm³) liter (L) milliliter (mL)	$1\ cm^3 = 0.000001\ m^3$ $1\ L = 1\ dm^3 = 0.001\ m^3$ $1\ mL = 0.001\ L = 1\ cm^3$
Mass	**kilogram (kg)** gram (g) milligram (mg)	1 g = 0.001 kg 1 mg = 0.000001 kg
Temperature	**Kelvin (K)** **Celsius (°C)**	0°C = 273 K 100°C = 373 K

Measurement

Scientists report measured quantities in a way that shows the precision of the measurement. To do so, they use significant figures. *Significant figures* are the digits in a measurement that are known with certainty. The MathFocus below will help you understand significant figures and will teach you how to use the correct number of digits. Now that you have a standardized system of units for measuring things, you can use the system to measure length, area, mass, volume, and temperature.

Length

How long is a lizard? Well, a **meter** (m) is the basic SI unit of length. However, a scientist, such as the one in **Figure 2,** would use centimeters (cm) to describe a small lizard's length. If you divide 1 m into 100 parts, each part equals 1 cm. So, 1 cm is one-hundredth of a meter. Even though 1 cm seems small, some things are even smaller. Scientists describe the length of very small objects in micrometers (μm) or nanometers (nm). To see these small objects, scientists use powerful microscopes.

Area

How much paper would you need to cover the top of your desk? To answer this question, you must find the area of the desk. **Area** is a measure of the size of the surface of an object. To calculate the area of a square or a rectangle, measure the length and width. Then, use the following equation:

$$area = length \times width$$

Units for area are square units, such as square meters (m^2), square centimeters (cm^2), and square kilometers (km^2).

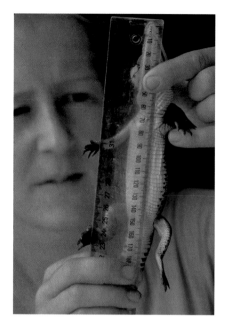

Figure 2 *This scientist is using a metric ruler to measure a lizard's length. The unit chosen to describe an object, such as this lizard, depends on the size of the object being measured.*

meter the basic unit of length in the SI (symbol, m)

area a measure of the size of a surface or a region

Significant Figures Calculate the area of a carpet that is 3.145 m long (four significant figures) and 5.75 m (three significant figures) wide. (Hint: In multiplication and division problems, the answer cannot have more significant figures than the measurement that has the smallest number of significant figures does.)

Step 1: Write the equation for area.

$$area = length \times width$$

Step 2: Replace *length* and *width* with the measurements given, and solve.

$$area = 3.125 \text{ m} \times 5.75 \text{ m} = 18.08375 \text{ m}^2$$

Step 3: Round the answer to get the correct number of significant figures. Here, the correct number of significant figures is three, because the value with the smallest number of significant figures has three significant figures.

$$area = 18.1 \text{ m}^2$$

Now Its Your Turn

1. Use a calculator to perform the following calculation: 125.5 km × 8.225 km. Write the answer with the correct number of significant figures.

Figure 3 *Adding the rock changes the water level from 70 mL to 80 mL. So, the rock displaces 10 mL of water. Because 1 mL = 1 cm³, the volume of the rock is 10 cm³.*

Mass

How large a rock can a rushing stream move? The answer depends on the energy of the stream and the mass of the rock. **Mass** is a measure of the amount of matter in an object. The kilogram (kg) is the basic unit for mass in the SI. Kilograms are used to describe the mass of a large rock. Grams are used to measure the mass of smaller objects. One thousand grams equals 1 kg. For example, a medium-sized apple has a mass of about 100 g. Masses of very large objects are given in metric tons. A metric ton equals 1,000 kg.

✓ **Reading Check** What is the basic SI unit for mass?

Volume

Think about moving some magnets to a laboratory. How many magnets will fit into a box? The answer depends on the volume of the box and the volume of each magnet. **Volume** is a measure of the size of a body in three-dimensional space. In this case, you need the volumes of the box and of the magnets.

The volume of a liquid is often given in liters (L). Liters are based on the meter. A cubic meter (1 m³) is equal to 1,000 L. So, 1,000 L will fit into a box measuring 1 m on each side. A milliliter (mL) will fit into a box measuring 1 cm on each side. So, 1 mL = 1 cm³. Graduated cylinders are used to measure the volume of liquids.

The volume of a large, solid object is given in cubic meters (m³). The volumes of smaller objects can be given in cubic centimeters (cm³) or cubic millimeters (mm³). The volume of a box can be calculated by multiplying the object's length, width, and height. The volume of an irregularly shaped object can be found by measuring the volume of liquid that the object displaces. You can see how this works in **Figure 3.**

mass a measure of the amount of matter in an object

volume a measure of the size of a body or region in three-dimensional space

Figure 4 *This thermometer shows the relationship between degrees Fahrenheit and degrees Celsius.*

°F	°C
212°F Water boils	100°C Water boils
98.6°F Normal body temperature	37°C Normal body temperature
32°F Water freezes	0°C Water freezes

temperature the measure of how hot (or cold) something is

density the ratio of the mass of a substance to the volume of the substance

Temperature

How hot is melted iron? To answer this question, a scientist would measure the temperature of the liquid metal. **Temperature** is a measure of how hot or cold something is. You probably use degrees Fahrenheit (°F) to describe temperature. Scientists commonly use degrees Celsius (°C), although the kelvin (K) is the official SI base unit for temperature. You will use degrees Celsius in this book. The thermometer in **Figure 4** compares the Fahrenheit and Celsius scales.

Density

If you measure the mass and volume of an object, you have the measurements that you need to find the density of the object. **Density** is the amount of matter in a given volume. You cannot measure density directly. But after you have measured the mass and the volume, you can use the following equation to calculate density:

$$density = \frac{mass}{volume}$$

Density is the ratio of mass to volume, so units often used for density are grams per milliliter (g/mL) and grams per cubic centimeter (g/cm^3). Density may be difficult to understand. Think of a table-tennis ball and a golf ball. They have similar volumes. But a golf ball has more mass than a table-tennis ball does. So the golf ball has a greater density.

Safety Rules!

Science is exciting and fun, but it can also be dangerous. Don't take any chances! Always follow your teacher's instructions. Don't take shortcuts—even when you think there is no danger. Before starting an experiment, get your teacher's permission. Read the lab procedures carefully. Pay special attention to safety information and caution statements. **Figure 5** shows the safety symbols used in this book. Get to know these symbols and their meanings. Do so by reading the safety information in the front of this book. **This is important!** If you are still unsure about what a safety symbol means, ask your teacher.

Reading Check Why are safety symbols important?

Figure 5 **Safety Symbols**

 Eye Protection
 Clothing Protection
 Hand Safety
 Heating Safety
 Electric Safety
 Sharp Object
 Chemical Safety
 Animal Safety
 Plant Safety

SECTION Review

Summary

- Scientists use a variety of tools to measure and analyze the world around them.

- The International System of Units (SI) is a simple, reliable, and uniform system of measurement that is used by most scientists.

- The basic units of measurement in the SI are the meter (for length), the kilogram (for mass), and the Kelvin (for temperature).

- Before starting any science activity or science lab, review the safety symbols and the safety rules for that activity or lab. Don't take chances with your health and safety.

Using Key Terms

Complete each of the following sentences by choosing the correct term from the word bank.

mass   area
volume   temperature

1. A measure of the size of a surface or a region is called ___.

2. Scientists use kilograms when measuring an object's ___.

3. The ___ of a liquid is usually described in liters.

Understanding Key Ideas

4. SI units are
   a. based on standardized measurements of body parts.
   b. almost always based on the number 10.
   c. used to measure only length.
   d. used only in France.

5. What is temperature?

6. If you wanted to measure the mass of a fly, which SI unit would be most appropriate?

Math Skills

7. What is the area of a soccer field that is 110 m long and 85 m wide?

8. What is the density of silver if a 6 cm³ piece of silver has a mass of 63 g?

Critical Thinking

9. **Applying Concepts** Some people are thinking about sending humans to the moon and then to the planet Mars. Why is it important for scientists around the world to use the International System of Units as they make these plans?

10. **Making Inferences** Give an example of something that can happen if you do not follow safety rules.

11. **Applying Concepts** What tool would you use to measure the mass of the air in a basketball?

SCLINKS®

Developed and maintained by the National Science Teachers Association

For a variety of links related to this chapter, go to www.scilinks.org

Topic: Tools of Science; SI Units
SciLinks code: HSM1535; HSM1390

Skills Practice Lab

OBJECTIVES

Apply scientific methods to predict, measure, and observe the mixing of two unknown liquids.

MATERIALS

- beakers, 100 mL (2)
- Celsius thermometer
- glass-labeling marker
- graduated cylinders, 50 mL (3)
- liquid A, 75 mL
- liquid B, 75 mL
- protective gloves

SAFETY

Does It All Add Up?

Your math teacher won't tell you this, but did you know that sometimes 2 + 2 does not appear to equal 4?! In this experiment, you will use scientific methods to predict, measure, and observe the mixing of two unknown liquids. You will learn that a scientist does not set out to prove a hypothesis but to test it and that sometimes the results just don't seem to add up!

Make Observations

1 Put on your safety goggles, gloves, and lab apron. Examine the beakers of liquids A and B provided by your teacher. Write down as many observations as you can about each liquid. **Caution:** Do not taste, touch, or smell the liquids.

2 Pour exactly 25 mL of liquid A from the beaker into each of two 50 mL graduated cylinders. Combine these samples in one of the graduated cylinders. Record the final volume. Pour the liquid back into the beaker of liquid A. Rinse the graduated cylinders. Repeat this step for liquid B.

Form a Hypothesis

3 Based on your observations and on prior experience, formulate a testable hypothesis that states what you expect the volume to be when you combine 25 mL of liquid A with 25 mL of liquid B.

4 Make a prediction based on your hypothesis. Use an if-then format. Explain the basis for your prediction.

Data Table				
	Contents of cylinder A	Contents of cylinder B	Mixing results: predictions	Mixing results: observations
Volume				
Appearance		*DO NOT WRITE IN BOOK*		
Temperature				

Test the Hypothesis

5 Make a data table like the one above.

6 Mark one graduated cylinder "A." Carefully pour exactly 25 mL of liquid A into this cylinder. In your data table, record its volume, appearance, and temperature.

7 Mark another graduated cylinder "B." Carefully pour exactly 25 mL of liquid B into this cylinder. Record its volume, appearance, and temperature in your data table.

8 Mark the empty third cylinder "A + B."

9 In the "Mixing results: predictions" column in your table, record the prediction you made earlier. Each classmate may have made a different prediction.

10 Carefully pour the contents of both cylinders into the third graduated cylinder.

11 Observe and record the total volume, appearance, and temperature in the "Mixing results: observations" column of your table.

Analyze the Results

1 **Analyzing Data** Discuss your predictions as a class. How many different predictions were there? Which predictions were supported by testing? Did any measurements surprise you?

Draw Conclusions

2 **Drawing Conclusions** Was your hypothesis supported or disproven? Either way, explain your thinking. Describe everything that you think you learned from this experiment.

3 **Analyzing Methods** Explain the value of incorrect predictions.

Chapter Review

USING KEY TERMS

1 Use the following terms in the same sentence: *science* and *scientific methods*.

2 Use the following terms in the same sentence: *controlled experiment* and *variable*.

For each pair of terms, explain how the meanings of the terms differ.

3 *theory* and *hypothesis*

4 *controlled experiment* and *variable*

5 *area* and *volume*

6 *physical model* and *conceptual model*

UNDERSTANDING KEY IDEAS

Multiple Choice

7 The steps of scientific methods
  a. must all be used in every scientific investigation.
  b. must always be used in the same order.
  c. often start with a question.
  d. always result in the development of a theory.

8 In a controlled experiment,
  a. a control group is compared with one or more experimental groups.
  b. there are at least two variables.
  c. all factors should be different.
  d. a variable is not needed.

9 Which of the following tools is best for measuring 100 mL of water?
  a. 10 mL graduated cylinder
  b. 150 mL graduated cylinder
  c. 250 mL beaker
  d. 500 mL beaker

10 Which of the following is NOT an SI unit?
  a. meter
  b. foot
  c. liter
  d. kilogram

11 A pencil is 14 cm long. How many millimeters long is it?
  a. 1.4 mm
  b. 140 mm
  c. 1,400 mm
  d. 1,400,000 mm

12 The directions for a lab include the safety icons shown below. These icons mean that

  a. you should be careful.
  b. you are going into the laboratory.
  c. you should wash your hands first.
  d. you should wear safety goggles, a lab apron, and gloves during the lab.

Short Answer

13 List three ways that science is beneficial to living things.

14 Why do hypotheses need to be testable?

15 Give an example of how a scientist might use computers and technology.

16 List three types of models, and give an example of each.

17 What are some advantages and limitations of models?

18 Which SI units can be used to describe the volume of an object? Which SI units can be used to describe the mass of an object?

19 In a controlled experiment, why should there be several individuals in the control group and in each of the experimental groups?

CRITICAL THINKING

20 **Concept Mapping** Use the following terms to create a concept map: *observations, predictions, questions, controlled experiments, variable,* and *hypothesis.*

21 **Making Inferences** Investigations often begin with observation. What limits the observations that scientists can make?

22 **Forming Hypotheses** A scientist who studies mice makes the following observation: on the day the mice are fed vitamins with their meals, they perform better in mazes. What hypothesis would you form to explain this phenomenon? Write a testable prediction based on your hypothesis.

INTERPRETING GRAPHICS

The pictures below show how an egg can be measured by using a beaker and water. Use the pictures below to answer the questions that follow.

Before: 125 mL   After: 200 mL

23 What kind of measurement is being taken?

a. area

b. length

c. mass

d. volume

24 Which of the following is an accurate measurement of the egg in the picture?

a. 75 cm^3

b. 125 cm^3

c. 125 mL

d. 200 mL

25 Make a double line graph using the data in the table below.

Number of Frogs		
Date	Normal	Deformed
1995	25	0
1996	21	0
1997	19	1
1998	20	2
1999	17	3
2000	20	5

READING

Read each of the passages below. Then, answer the questions that follow the passage.

Passage 1 Zoology is the study of animals. Zoology dates back more than 2,300 years, to ancient Greece. There, the philosopher Aristotle observed and theorized about animal behavior. About 200 years later, Galen, a Greek physician, began dissecting and experimenting with animals. However, there were few advances in zoology until the 1700s and 1800s. During this period, the Swedish <u>naturalist</u> Carolus Linnaeus developed a classification system for plants and animals, and British naturalist Charles Darwin published his theory of evolution by natural selection.

1. According to the passage, when did major advances in Zoology begin?
   A About 2,300 years ago
   B About 2,100 years ago
   C During the 1700s and 1800s
   D Only during recent history

2. Which of the following is a possible meaning of the word *naturalist,* as used in the passage?
   F a scientist who studies plants and animals
   G a scientist who studies animals
   H a scientist who studies theory
   I a scientist who studies animal behavior

3. Which of the following is the **best** title for this passage?
   A Greek Zoology
   B Modern Zoology
   C The Origins of Zoology
   D Zoology in the 1700s and 1800s

Passage 2 When looking for answers to a problem, scientists build on existing knowledge. For example, scientists have wondered if there is some relationship between Earth's core and Earth's magnetic field. To form a hypothesis, scientists started with what they knew: Earth has a dense, solid inner core and a molten outer core. Scientists then created a computer <u>model</u> to simulate how Earth's magnetic field might be generated.

They tried different things with their model until the model produced a magnetic field that matched that of the real Earth. The model predicted that Earth's inner core spins in the same direction as the rest of the Earth, but the inner core spins slightly faster than Earth's surface. If the hypothesis is correct, it might explain how Earth's magnetic field is produced. Although scientists cannot reach the Earth's core to examine it directly, they can test whether other observations match what is predicted by their hypothesis.

1. What does the word *model* refer to in this passage?
   A a giant plastic globe
   B a representation of the Earth created on a computer
   C a computer terminal
   D a technology used to drill into the Earth's core

2. Which of the following is the **best** summary of the passage?
   F Scientists can use models to help them answer difficult and complex questions.
   G Scientists have discovered the source of Earth's magnetic field.
   H The spinning of Earth's molten inner core causes Earth's magnetic field.
   I Scientists make a model of a problem and then ask questions about the problem.

The table below shows the plans for an experiment in which bees will be observed visiting flowers. Use the table to answer the questions that follow.

Bee Experiment				
Group	Type of bee	Time of day	Type of plant	Flower color
#1	Honey-bee	9:00 A.M.– 10:00 A.M.	Portland rose	red
#2	Honey-bee	9:00 A.M.– 10:00 A.M.	Portland rose	yellow
#3	Honey-bee	9:00 A.M.– 10:00 A.M.	Portland rose	white
#4	Honey-bee	9:00 A.M.– 10:00 A.M.	Portland rose	pink

1. Which factor is the variable in this experiment?
   A the type of bee
   B the time of day
   C the type of plant
   D the color of the flowers

2. Which of the following hypotheses could be tested by this experiment?
   F Honeybees prefer to visit rose plants.
   G Honeybees prefer to visit red flowers.
   H Honeybees prefer to visit flowers in the morning.
   I Honey bees prefer to visit Portland rose flowers between 9 and 10 A.M.

3. Which of the following is the **best** reason why the Portland rose plant is included in all of the groups to be studied?
   A The type of plant is a control factor; any type of flowering plant could be used as long as all plants were of the same type.
   B The experiment will test whether bees prefer the Portland rose over other flowers.
   C An experiment should always have more than one variable.
   D The Portland rose is a very common plant.

Read each question below, and choose the best answer.

1. A survey of students was conducted to find out how many people were in each student's family. The replies from five students were as follows: 3, 3, 4, 4, and 6. What was the average family size?
   A 3
   B 3.5
   C 4
   D 5

2. In the survey above, if one more student were surveyed, which reply would make the average lower?
   F 3
   G 4
   H 5
   I 6

3. If an object that is 5 μm long were magnified by 1,000, how long would that object then appear?
   A 5 μm
   B 5 mm
   C 1,000 μm
   D 5,000 mm

4. How many meters are in 50 km?
   F 50 m
   G 500 m
   H 5,000 m
   I 50,000 m

5. What is the area of a square whose sides measure 4 m each?
   A 16 m
   B 16 m^2
   C 32 m
   D 32 m^2

Standardized Test Preparation

Science in Action

Scientific Debate

Should We Stop All Forest Fires?

Since 1972, the policy of the National Park Service has been to manage the national parks as naturally as possible. Because fire is a natural event in forests, this policy includes allowing most fires caused by lightning to burn. The only lightning-caused fires that are put out are those that threaten lives, property, uniquely scenic areas, or endangered species. All human-caused fires are put out. However, this policy has caused some controversy. Some people want this policy followed in all public forests and even grasslands. Others think that all fires should be put out.

Science Fiction

"The Homesick Chicken" by Edward D. Hoch

Why did the chicken cross the road? You think you know the answer to this old riddle, don't you? But "The Homesick Chicken," by Edward D. Hoch, may surprise you. That old chicken may not be exactly what it seems.

You see, one of the chickens at the high-tech Tangaway Research Farms has escaped. Then, it was found in a vacant lot across the highway from Tangaway, pecking away contentedly. Why did it bother to escape? Barnabus Rex, a specialist in solving scientific riddles, is called in to work on this mystery. As he investigates, he finds clues and forms a hypothesis. Read the story, and see if you can explain the mystery before Mr. Rex does.

Social Studies ACTiViTY

WRITING SKILL Research a location where there is a debate about controlling forest fires. You might look into national forests or parks. Write a newspaper article about the issue. Be sure to present all sides of the debate.

Language Arts ACTiViTY

WRITING SKILL Write your own short story about a chicken crossing a road for a mysterious reason. Give clues (evidence) to the reader about the mysterious reason but do not reveal the truth until the end of the story. Be sure the story makes sense scientifically.

Matthew Henson

Arctic Explorer Matthew Henson was born in Maryland in 1866. His parents were freeborn sharecroppers. When Henson was a young boy, his parents died. He then went to look for work as a cabin boy on a ship. Several years later, Henson had traveled around the world and had become educated in the areas of geography, history, and mathematics. In 1898, Henson met U.S. Naval Lieutenant Robert E. Peary. Peary was the leader of Arctic expeditions between 1886 and 1909.

Peary asked Henson to accompany him as a navigator on several trips, including trips to Central America and Greenland. One of Peary's passions was to be the first person to reach the North Pole. It was Henson's vast knowledge of mathematics and carpentry that made Peary's trek to the North Pole possible. In 1909, Henson was the first person to reach the North Pole. Part of Henson's job as navigator was to drive ahead of the party and blaze the first trail. As a result, he often arrived ahead of everyone else. On April 6, 1909, Henson reached the approximate North Pole 45 minutes ahead of Peary. Upon his arrival, he exclaimed, "I think I'm the first man to sit on top of the world!"

Math ACTiViTY

On the last leg of their journey, Henson and Peary traveled 664.5 km in 16 days! On average, how far did Henson and Peary travel each day?

To learn more about these Science in Action topics, visit go.hrw.com and type in the keyword HZ5SW7F.

Current Science

Check out Current Science® articles related to this chapter by visiting go.hrw.com. Just type in the keyword HZ5CS01.

UNIT 1

TIMELINE

The Atmosphere, Weather, and Climate

In this unit, you will learn about Earth's atmosphere, including how it affects conditions on the Earth's surface. The constantly changing weather is always a good topic for conversation, but forecasting the weather is not an easy task. Climate, on the other hand, is much more predictable. This timeline shows some of the events that have occurred as scientists have tried to better understand Earth's atmosphere, weather, and climate.

1281

A sudden typhoon destroys a fleet of Mongolian ships about to reach Japan. This "divine wind," or *kamikaze* in Japanese, saves the country from invasion and conquest.

1778

Carl Scheele concludes that air is mostly made of nitrogen and oxygen.

1838

John James Audubon publishes *The Birds of America*.

1974

Chlorofluorocarbons (CFCs) are recognized as harmful to the ozone layer.

1982

Weather information becomes available 24 hours a day, 7 days a week, on commercial TV.

1655

Saturn's rings are recognized as such. Galileo Galilei had seen them in 1610, but his telescope was not strong enough to show that they were rings.

1718

Gabriel Fahrenheit builds the first mercury thermometer.

1749

Benjamin Franklin explains how updrafts of air are caused by the sun's heating of the local atmosphere.

1920

Serbian scientist Milutin Milankovitch determines that over tens of thousands of years, changes in the Earth's motion through space have profound effects on climate.

1945

The first atmospheric test of an atomic bomb takes place near Alamogordo, New Mexico.

1985

Scientists discover an ozone hole over Antarctica.

1986

The world's worst nuclear accident takes place at Chernobyl, Ukraine, and spreads radiation through the atmosphere as far as the western United States.

1999

The first nonstop balloon trip around the world is successfully completed when Brian Jones and Bertrand Piccard land in Egypt.

2003

A record 393 tornadoes are observed in the United States during one week in May.

The path of radioactive material released from Chernobyl

The Breitling Orbiter 3 lands in Egypt on March 21, 1999.

2

The Atmosphere

About the

Imagine climbing a mountain and taking only one out of three breaths! As altitude increases, the density of the atmosphere decreases. At the heights shown in this picture, the atmosphere is so thin that it contains only 30% of the amount of oxygen found in the atmosphere at sea level. So, most mountaineers carry part of their atmosphere with them—in the form of oxygen tanks.

PRE-READING ACTIVITY

FOLDNOTES **Booklet** Before you read the chapter, create the FoldNote entitled "Booklet" described in the **Study Skills** section of the Appendix. Label each page of the booklet with a main idea from the chapter. As you read the chapter, write what you learn about each main idea on the appropriate page of the booklet.

START-UP ACTIVITY

Does Air Have Mass?

In this activity, you will compare an inflated balloon with a deflated balloon to find out if air has mass.

Procedure

1. In a **notebook,** answer the following questions: Does air have mass? Will an inflated balloon weigh more than a deflated balloon?

2. Inflate **two large balloons,** and tie the balloons closed. Attach each balloon to opposite ends of a **meterstick** using identical **pushpins.** Balance the meterstick on a **pencil** held by a volunteer. Check that the meterstick is perfectly balanced.

3. Predict what will happen when you pop one balloon. Record your predictions.

4. Put on **safety goggles,** and carefully pop one of the balloons with a **pushpin.**

5. Record your observations.

Analysis

1. Explain your observations. Was your prediction correct?

2. Based on your results, does air have mass? If air has mass, is the atmosphere affected by Earth's gravity? Explain your answers.

Characteristics of the Atmosphere

If you were lost in the desert, you could survive for a few days without food and water. But you wouldn't last more than five minutes without the atmosphere.

READING WARM-UP

Objectives

● Describe the composition of Earth's atmosphere.

● Explain why air pressure changes with altitude.

● Explain how air temperature changes with atmospheric composition.

● Describe the layers of the atmosphere.

Terms to Learn

atmosphere   stratosphere
air pressure   mesosphere
troposphere   thermosphere

READING STRATEGY

Mnemonics As you read this section, create a mnemonic device to help you remember the layers of the Earth's atmosphere.

The **atmosphere** is a mixture of gases that surrounds Earth. In addition to containing the oxygen you need to breathe, the atmosphere protects you from the sun's damaging rays. The atmosphere is always changing. Every breath you take, every tree that is planted, and every vehicle you ride in affects the atmosphere's composition.

The Composition of the Atmosphere

As you can see in **Figure 1,** the atmosphere is made up mostly of nitrogen gas. The oxygen you breathe makes up a little more than 20% of the atmosphere. In addition to containing nitrogen and oxygen, the atmosphere contains small particles, such as dust, volcanic ash, sea salt, dirt, and smoke. The next time you turn off the lights at night, shine a flashlight, and you will see some of these tiny particles floating in the air.

Water is also found in the atmosphere. Liquid water (water droplets) and solid water (snow and ice crystals) are found in clouds. But most water in the atmosphere exists as an invisible gas called *water vapor.* When atmospheric conditions change, water vapor can change into solid or liquid water, and rain or snow might fall from the sky.

✓ **Reading Check** Describe the three physical states of water in the atmosphere. (*See the Appendix for answers to Reading Checks.*)

Figure 1   **Composition of the Atmosphere**

Nitrogen 78%

Oxygen 21%

1%

Nitrogen, the most common atmospheric gas, is released when dead plants and dead animals break down and when volcanoes erupt.

Oxygen, the second most common atmospheric gas, is made by phytoplankton and plants.

The remaining 1% of the atmosphere is made up of argon, carbon dioxide, water vapor, and other gases.

Atmospheric Pressure and Temperature

You may be surprised to learn that you carry a 700 km column of air every day. Although air is not heavy, at sea level, a square inch of surface area is under almost 15 lb of air.

As Altitude Increases, Air Pressure Decreases

The atmosphere is held around the Earth by gravity. Gravity acts to move gas molecules in the atmosphere toward Earth's center. The force of gravity is balanced by air pressure. **Air pressure** is the measure of the force with which air molecules push on a surface. Air pressure is strongest at the Earth's surface because more air is above you. As you move farther away from the Earth's surface, fewer gas molecules are above you. So, as altitude (distance from sea level) increases, air pressure decreases. Think of the forces of air pressure and gravity as a human pyramid, as shown in **Figure 2.** The people at the bottom of the pyramid can feel all the weight of the people on top. The people at the bottom push up to balance the weight of the people above them. In a similar way, air pressure and gravity exist near a state of balance or equilibrium.

Atmospheric Composition Affects Air Temperature

Air temperature also changes as altitude increases. The temperature differences result mainly from the way solar energy is absorbed as it moves through the atmosphere. Some parts of the atmosphere are warmer because they contain a high percentage of gases that absorb solar energy. Other parts of the atmosphere contain less of these gases and are cooler.

CONNECTION TO Physics

Air-Pressure Experiment
Does air pressure push only downward? Try this experiment to find out. Fill a plastic cup to the brim with water. Firmly hold a piece of cardboard over the mouth of the cup. Quickly invert the glass over a sink, and observe what happens. How do the effects of air pressure explain your observations?

ACTIVITY

atmosphere a mixture of gases that surrounds a planet or moon

air pressure the measure of the force with which air molecules push on a surface

Lower pressure

Higher pressure

Figure 2 *As in a human pyramid, air pressure increases closer to the Earth's surface.*

Modeling the Atmosphere
In teams, use a metric ruler to create an illustrated scale model of the atmosphere similar to the one shown on this page. Assume that the atmosphere is about 700 km high. If you reduced the height of the atmosphere by a factor of 100,000, your scale model would be 7 m long, and the troposphere would be 16 cm long. Think of a creative way to display your model. You could use sidewalk chalk, stakes and string, poster board, or other materials approved by your teacher. Do some research to add interesting information about each layer.

Figure 3 *The layers of the atmosphere are defined by changes in temperature.*

Layers of the Atmosphere

Based on temperature changes, the Earth's atmosphere is divided into four layers, as shown in **Figure 3.** These layers are the *troposphere, stratosphere, mesosphere,* and *thermosphere.* Although these words might sound complicated, the name of each layer gives you clues about its features.

For example, *-sphere* means "ball," which suggests that each layer of the atmosphere surrounds the Earth like a hollow ball. *Tropo-* means "turning" or "change," and the troposphere is the layer where gases turn and mix. *Strato-* means "layer," and the stratosphere is the sphere where gases are layered and do not mix very much. *Meso-* means "middle," and the mesosphere is the middle layer. Finally, *thermo-* means "heat," and the thermosphere is the sphere where temperatures are highest.

✓ **Reading Check** What does the name of each atmospheric layer mean?

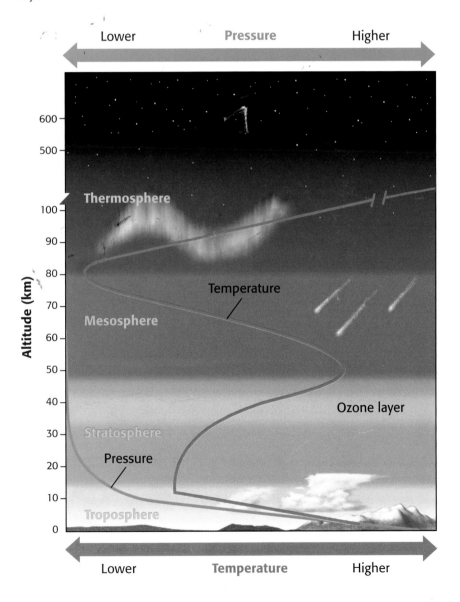

The Troposphere: The Layer in Which We Live

The lowest layer of the atmosphere, which lies next to the Earth's surface, is called the **troposphere.** The troposphere is also the densest atmospheric layer. It contains almost 90% of the atmosphere's total mass! Almost all of the Earth's carbon dioxide, water vapor, clouds, air pollution, weather, and life-forms are in the troposphere. As shown in **Figure 4,** temperatures vary greatly in the troposphere. Differences in air temperature and density cause gases in the troposphere to mix continuously.

The Stratosphere: Home of the Ozone Layer

The atmospheric layer above the troposphere is called the **stratosphere. Figure 5** shows the boundary between the stratosphere and the troposphere. Gases in the stratosphere are layered and do not mix as much as gases in the troposphere. The air is also very thin in the stratosphere and contains little moisture. The lower stratosphere is extremely cold. Its temperature averages –60°C. But temperature rises as altitude increases in the stratosphere. This rise happens because ozone in the stratosphere absorbs ultraviolet radiation from the sun, which warms the air. Almost all of the ozone in the stratosphere is contained in the ozone layer. The *ozone layer* protects life on Earth by absorbing harmful ultraviolet radiation.

The Mesosphere: The Middle Layer

Above the stratosphere is the mesosphere. The **mesosphere** is the middle layer of the atmosphere. It is also the coldest layer. As in the troposphere, the temperature decreases as altitude increases in the mesosphere. Temperatures can be as low as –93°C at the top of the mesosphere.

Figure 4 *As altitude increases in the troposphere, temperature decreases. Snow remains all year on this mountaintop.*

troposphere the lowest layer of the atmosphere, in which temperature decreases at a constant rate as altitude increases

stratosphere the layer of the atmosphere that is above the troposphere and in which temperature increases as altitude increases

mesosphere the layer of the atmosphere between the stratosphere and the thermosphere and in which temperature decreases as altitude increases

Figure 5 *This photograph of Earth's atmosphere was taken from space. The troposphere is the yellow layer; the stratosphere is the white layer.*

The Thermosphere: The Edge of the Atmosphere

thermosphere the uppermost layer of the atmosphere, in which temperature increases as altitude increases

The uppermost atmospheric layer is called the **thermosphere.** In the thermosphere, temperature again increases with altitude. Atoms of nitrogen and oxygen absorb high-energy solar radiation and release thermal energy, which causes temperatures in the thermosphere to be 1,000°C or higher.

When you think of an area that has high temperatures, you probably think of a place that is very hot. Although the thermosphere has very high temperatures, it does not feel hot. Temperature is different from heat. Temperature is a measure of the average energy of particles in motion. The high temperature of the thermosphere means that particles in that layer are moving very fast. Heat, however, is the transfer of thermal energy between objects of different temperatures. Particles must touch one another to transfer thermal energy. The space between particles in the thermosphere is so great that particles do not transfer much energy. In other words, the density of the thermosphere is so low that particles do not often collide and transfer energy. **Figure 6** shows how air density affects the heating of the troposphere and the thermosphere.

Reading Check Why doesn't the thermosphere feel hot?

Figure 6 Temperature in the Troposphere and the Thermosphere

The **thermosphere** is less dense than the troposphere. So, although particles are moving very fast, they do not transfer much thermal energy.

The **troposphere** is denser than the thermosphere. So, although particles in the troposphere are moving much slower than particles in the thermosphere, they can transfer much more thermal energy.

The Ionosphere: Home of the Auroras

In the upper mesosphere and the lower thermosphere, nitrogen and oxygen atoms absorb harmful solar energy. As a result, the thermosphere's temperature rises, and gas particles become electrically charged. Electrically charged particles are called *ions*. Therefore, this part of the thermosphere is called the *ionosphere*. As shown in **Figure 7,** in polar regions these ions radiate energy as shimmering lights called *auroras*. The ionosphere also reflects AM radio waves. When conditions are right, an AM radio wave can travel around the world by reflecting off the ionosphere. These radio signals bounce off the ionosphere and are sent back to Earth.

Figure 7 *Charged particles in the ionosphere cause auroras, or northern and southern lights.*

SECTION Review

Summary

- Nitrogen and oxygen make up most of Earth's atmosphere.
- Air pressure decreases as altitude increases.
- The composition of atmospheric layers affects their temperature.
- The troposphere is the lowest atmospheric layer. It is the layer in which we live.
- The stratosphere contains the ozone layer, which protects us from harmful UV radiation.
- The mesosphere is the coldest atmospheric layer.
- The thermosphere is the uppermost layer of the atmosphere.

Using Key Terms

1. Use each of the following terms in a separate sentence: *air pressure, atmosphere, troposphere, stratosphere, mesosphere,* and *thermosphere.*

Understanding Key Ideas

2. Why does the temperature of different layers of the atmosphere vary?
   a. because air temperature increases as altitude increases
   b. because the amount of energy radiated from the sun varies
   c. because of interference by humans
   d. because of the composition of gases in each layer

3. Why does air pressure decrease as altitude increases?

4. How can the thermosphere have high temperatures but not feel hot?

5. What determines the temperature of atmospheric layers?

6. What two gases make up most of the atmosphere?

Math Skills

7. If an average cloud has a density of 0.5 g/m^3 and has a volume of 1,000,000,000 m^3, what is the weight of an average cloud?

Critical Thinking

8. **Applying Concepts** Apply what you know about the relationship between altitude and air pressure to explain why rescue helicopters have a difficult time flying at altitudes above 6,000 m.

9. **Making Inferences** If the upper atmosphere is very thin, why do space vehicles heat up as they enter the atmosphere?

10. **Making Inferences** Explain why gases such as helium can escape Earth's atmosphere.

SCI*L*INKS®

NSTA
Developed and maintained by the
National Science Teachers Association

For a variety of links related to this chapter, go to www.scilinks.org

Topic: Composition of the Atmosphere
SciLinks code: HSM0328

Atmospheric Heating

You are lying in a park. Your eyes are closed, and you feel the warmth of the sun on your face. You may have done this before, but have you ever stopped to think that it takes a little more than eight minutes for the energy that warms your face to travel from a star that is 149,000,000 km away?

READING WARM-UP

Objectives

● Describe what happens to solar energy that reaches Earth.

● Summarize the processes of radiation, conduction, and convection.

● Explain the relationship between the greenhouse effect and global warming.

Terms to Learn

radiation
thermal conduction
convection
global warming
greenhouse effect

READING STRATEGY

Reading Organizer As you read this section, make a table comparing radiation, conduction, and convection.

Energy in the Atmosphere

In the scenario above, your face was warmed by energy from the sun. Earth and its atmosphere are also warmed by energy from the sun. In this section, you will find out what happens to solar energy as it enters the atmosphere.

Radiation: Energy Transfer by Waves

The Earth receives energy from the sun by radiation. **Radiation** is the transfer of energy as electromagnetic waves. Although the sun radiates a huge amount of energy, Earth receives only about two-billionths of this energy. But this small fraction of energy is enough to drive the weather cycle and make Earth habitable. **Figure 1** shows what happens to solar energy once it enters the atmosphere.

Figure 1 *Energy from the sun is absorbed by the atmosphere, land, and water and is changed into thermal energy.*

About **25%** is scattered and reflected by clouds and air.

About **20%** is absorbed by ozone, clouds, and atmospheric gases.

About **5%** is reflected by Earth's surface.

About **50%** is absorbed by Earth's surface.

Conduction: Energy Transfer by Contact

If you have ever touched something hot, you have experienced the process of conduction. **Thermal conduction** is the transfer of thermal energy through a material. Thermal energy is always transferred from warm to cold areas. When air molecules come into direct contact with the warm surface of Earth, thermal energy is transferred to the atmosphere.

Convection: Energy Transfer by Circulation

If you have ever watched a pot of water boil, you have observed convection. **Convection** is the transfer of thermal energy by the circulation or movement of a liquid or gas. Most thermal energy in the atmosphere is transferred by convection. For example, as air is heated, it becomes less dense and rises. Cool air is denser, so it sinks. As the cool air sinks, it pushes the warm air up. The cool air is eventually heated by the Earth's surface and begins to rise again. This cycle of warm air rising and cool air sinking causes a circular movement of air, called a *convection current,* as shown in **Figure 2.**

✓ Reading Check How do differences in air density cause convection currents? (*See the Appendix for answers to Reading Checks.*)

radiation the transfer of energy as electromagnetic waves

thermal conduction the transfer of energy as heat through a material

convection the transfer of thermal energy by the circulation or movement of a liquid or gas

Figure 2 *The processes of radiation, thermal conduction, and convection heat Earth and its atmosphere.*

Radiation is the transfer of energy by electromagnetic waves.

Convection currents are created as warm air rises and cool air sinks.

Near the Earth's surface, air is heated by **thermal conduction.**

Figure 3 The Greenhouse Effect

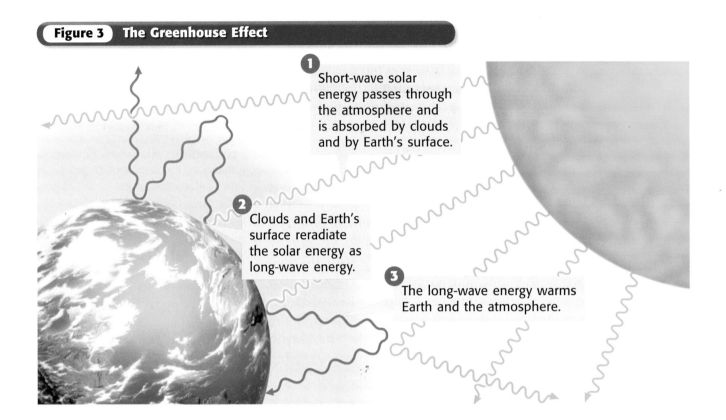

1 Short-wave solar energy passes through the atmosphere and is absorbed by clouds and by Earth's surface.

2 Clouds and Earth's surface reradiate the solar energy as long-wave energy.

3 The long-wave energy warms Earth and the atmosphere.

The Greenhouse Effect and Life on Earth

As you have learned, about 70% of the radiation that enters Earth's atmosphere is absorbed by clouds and by the Earth's surface. This energy is converted into thermal energy that warms the planet. In other words, short-wave visible light is absorbed and reradiated into the atmosphere as long-wave thermal energy. So, why doesn't this thermal energy escape back into space? Most of it does, but the atmosphere is like a warm blanket that traps enough energy to make Earth livable. This process, shown in **Figure 3,** is called the greenhouse effect. The **greenhouse effect** is the process by which gases in the atmosphere, such as water vapor and carbon dioxide, absorb thermal energy and radiate it back to Earth. This process is called the greenhouse effect because the gases function like the glass walls and roof of a greenhouse, which allow solar energy to enter but prevent thermal energy from escaping.

greenhouse effect the warming of the surface and lower atmosphere of Earth that occurs when water vapor, carbon dioxide, and other gases absorb and reradiate thermal energy

The Radiation Balance: Energy In, Energy Out

For Earth to remain livable, the amount of energy received from the sun and the amount of energy returned to space must be approximately equal. Solar energy that is absorbed by the Earth and its atmosphere is eventually reradiated into space as thermal energy. Every day, the Earth receives more energy from the sun. The balance between incoming energy and outgoing energy is known as the *radiation balance.*

Greenhouse Gases and Global Warming

Many scientists have become concerned about data that show that average global temperatures have increased in the past 100 years. Such an increase in average global temperatures is called **global warming.** Some scientists have hypothesized that an increase of greenhouse gases in the atmosphere may be the cause of this warming trend. Greenhouse gases are gases that absorb thermal energy in the atmosphere.

Human activity, such as the burning of fossil fuels and deforestation, may be increasing levels of greenhouse gases, such as carbon dioxide, in the atmosphere. If this hypothesis is correct, increasing levels of greenhouse gases may cause average global temperatures to continue to rise. If global warming continues, global climate patterns could be disrupted. Plants and animals that are adapted to live in specific climates would be affected. However, climate models are extremely complex, and scientists continue to debate whether the global warming trend is the result of an increase in greenhouse gases.

global warming a gradual increase in average global temperature

✓ **Reading Check** What is a greenhouse gas?

SECTION Review

Summary

- Energy from the sun is transferred through the atmosphere by radiation, thermal conduction, and convection.

- Radiation is energy transfer by electro-magnetic waves. Thermal conduction is energy transfer by direct contact. Convection is energy transfer by circulation.

- The greenhouse effect is Earth's natural heating process. Increasing levels of greenhouse gases could cause global warming.

Using Key Terms

1. Use each of the following terms in a separate sentence: *thermal conduction, radiation, convection, greenhouse effect,* and *global warming.*

Understanding Key Ideas

2. Which of the following is the best example of thermal conduction?
   a. a light bulb warming a lampshade
   b. an egg cooking in a frying pan
   c. water boiling in a pot
   d. gases circulating in the atmosphere

3. Describe three ways that energy is transferred in the atmosphere.

4. What is the difference between the greenhouse effect and global warming?

5. What is the radiation balance?

Math Skills

6. Find the average of the following temperatures: 73.2°F, 71.1°F, 54.6°F, 65.5°F, 78.2°F, 81.9°F, and 82.1°F.

Critical Thinking

7. **Identifying Relationships** How does the process of convection rely on radiation?

8. **Applying Concepts** Describe global warming in terms of the radiation balance.

SCI*L*INKS

NSTA
Developed and maintained by the National Science Teachers Association

For a variety of links related to this chapter, go to www.scilinks.org

Topic: Energy in the Atmosphere
SciLinks code: HSM0512

Global Winds and Local Winds

If you open the valve on a bicycle tube, the air rushes out. Why? The air inside the tube is at a higher pressure than the air is outside the tube. In effect, letting air out of the tube created a wind.

READING WARM-UP

Objectives

● Explain the relationship between air pressure and wind direction.

● Describe global wind patterns.

● Explain the causes of local wind patterns.

Terms to Learn

wind
Coriolis effect
polar easterlies
westerlies
trade winds
jet stream

READING STRATEGY

Prediction Guide Before reading this section, write the title of each heading in this section. Next, under each heading, write what you think you will learn.

wind the movement of air caused by differences in air pressure

Why Air Moves

The movement of air caused by differences in air pressure is called **wind.** The greater the pressure difference, the faster the wind moves. The devastation shown in **Figure 1** was caused by winds that resulted from extreme differences in air pressure.

Air Rises at the Equator and Sinks at the Poles

Differences in air pressure are generally caused by the unequal heating of the Earth. The equator receives more direct solar energy than other latitudes, so air at the equator is warmer and less dense than the surrounding air. Warm, less dense air rises and creates an area of low pressure. This warm, rising air flows toward the poles. At the poles, the air is colder and denser than the surrounding air, so it sinks. As the cold air sinks, it creates areas of high pressure around the poles. This cold polar air then flows toward the equator.

Figure 1 *In 1992, Hurricane Andrew became the most destructive hurricane in U.S. history. The winds from the hurricane reached 264 km/h.*

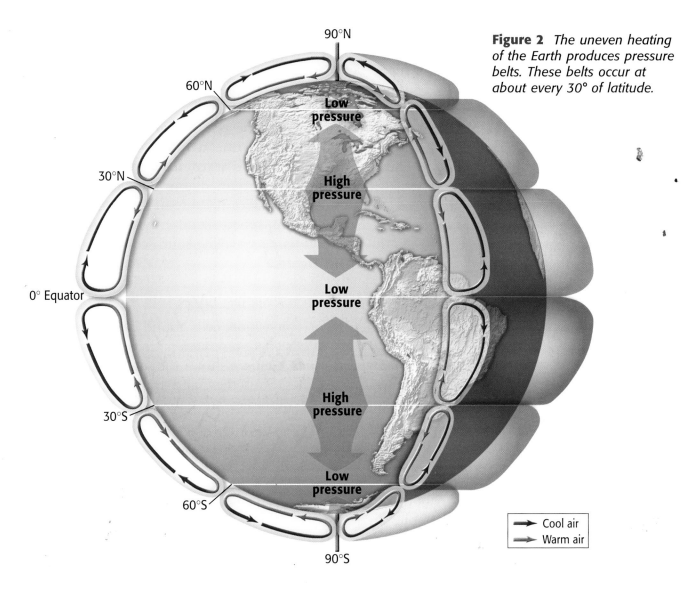

90°N

60°N

Low pressure

30°N

High pressure

0° Equator

Low pressure

30°S

High pressure

60°S

Low pressure

90°S

→ Cool air
→ Warm air

Pressure Belts Are Found Every 30°

You may imagine that wind moves in one huge, circular pattern from the poles to the equator. In fact, air travels in many large, circular patterns called *convection cells*. Convection cells are separated by *pressure belts,* bands of high pressure and low pressure found about every 30° of latitude, as shown in **Figure 2.** As warm air rises over the equator and moves toward the poles, the air begins to cool. At about 30° north and 30° south latitude, some of the cool air begins to sink. Cool, sinking air causes high pressure belts near 30° north and 30° south latitude. This cool air flows back to the equator, where it warms and rises again. At the poles, cold air sinks and moves toward the equator. Air warms as it moves away from the poles. Around 60° north and 60° south latitude, the warmer air rises, which creates a low pressure belt. This air flows back to the poles.

✔ Reading Check Why does sinking air cause areas of high pressure? (*See the Appendix for answers to Reading Checks.*)

Earth's rotation

→ Path of wind without Coriolis effect
→ Approximate path of wind

Figure 3 *The Coriolis effect in the Northern Hemisphere causes winds traveling north to appear to curve to the east and winds traveling south to appear to curve to the west.*

Coriolis effect the apparent curving of the path of a moving object from an otherwise straight path due to the Earth's rotation

polar easterlies prevailing winds that blow from east to west between 60° and 90° latitude in both hemispheres

westerlies prevailing winds that blow from west to east between 30° and 60° latitude in both hemispheres

trade winds prevailing winds that blow east to west from 30° latitude to the equator in both hemispheres

The Coriolis Effect

As you have learned, pressure differences cause air to move between the equator and the poles. But try spinning a globe and using a piece of chalk to trace a straight line from the equator to the North Pole. The chalk line curves because the globe was spinning. Like the chalk line, winds do not travel directly north or south, because the Earth is rotating. The apparent curving of the path of winds and ocean currents due to the Earth's rotation is called the **Coriolis effect.** Because of the Coriolis effect in the Northern Hemisphere, winds traveling north curve to the east, and winds traveling south curve to the west, as shown in **Figure 3.**

Global Winds

The combination of convection cells found at every 30° of latitude and the Coriolis effect produces patterns of air circulation called *global winds.* **Figure 4** shows the major global wind systems: polar easterlies, westerlies, and trade winds. Winds such as easterlies and westerlies are named for the direction from which they blow.

Polar Easterlies

The wind belts that extend from the poles to 60° latitude in both hemispheres are called the **polar easterlies.** The polar easterlies are formed as cold, sinking air moves from the poles toward 60° north and 60° south latitude. In the Northern Hemisphere, polar easterlies can carry cold arctic air over the United States, producing snow and freezing weather.

Westerlies

The wind belts found between 30° and 60° latitude in both hemispheres are called the **westerlies.** The westerlies flow toward the poles from west to east. The westerlies can carry moist air over the United States, producing rain and snow.

Trade Winds

In both hemispheres, the winds that blow from 30° latitude almost to the equator are called **trade winds.** The Coriolis effect causes the trade winds to curve to the west in both hemispheres. Early traders used the trade winds to sail from Europe to the Americas. As a result, the winds became known as "trade winds."

✓ Reading Check If the trade winds carried traders from Europe to the Americas, what wind system carried traders back to Europe?

The Doldrums

The trade winds of the Northern and Southern Hemispheres meet in an area around the equator called the *doldrums*. In the doldrums, there is very little wind because the warm, rising air creates an area of low pressure. The name *doldrums* means "dull" or "sluggish."

The Horse Latitudes

At about 30° north and 30° south latitude, sinking air creates an area of high pressure. The winds at these locations are weak. These areas are called the *horse latitudes*. According to legend, this name was given to these areas when sailing ships carried horses from Europe to the Americas. When the ships were stuck in this windless area, horses were sometimes thrown overboard to save drinking water for the sailors. Most of the world's deserts are located in the horse latitudes because the sinking air is very dry.

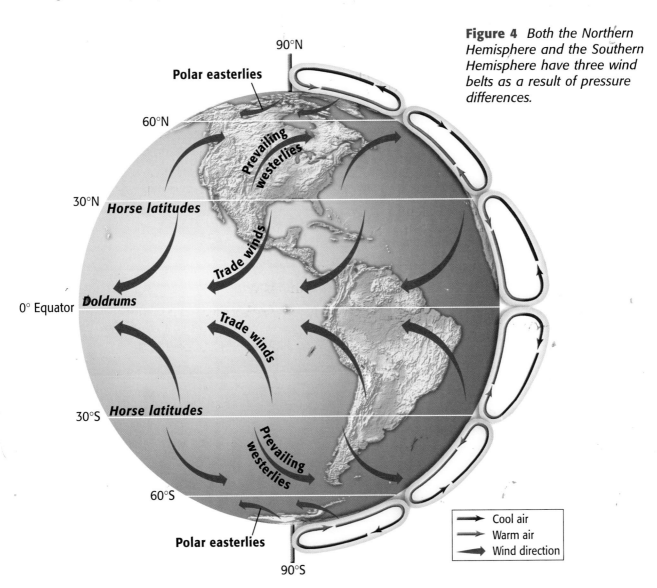

Figure 4 *Both the Northern Hemisphere and the Southern Hemisphere have three wind belts as a result of pressure differences.*

Figure 5 *The jet stream forms this band of clouds as it flows above the Earth.*

jet stream a narrow belt of strong winds that blow in the upper troposphere

Jet Streams: Atmospheric Conveyor Belts

The flight from Seattle to Boston can be 30 minutes faster than the flight from Boston to Seattle. Why? Pilots take advantage of a jet stream similar to the one shown in **Figure 5.** The **jet streams** are narrow belts of high-speed winds that blow in the upper troposphere and lower stratosphere. These winds can reach maximum speeds of 400 km/h. Unlike other global winds, the jet streams do not follow regular paths around the Earth. Knowing the path of a jet stream is important not only to pilots but also to meteorologists. Because jet streams affect the movement of storms, meteorologists can track a storm if they know the location of a jet stream.

Local Winds

Local winds generally move short distances and can blow from any direction. Local geographic features, such as a shoreline or a mountain, can produce temperature differences that cause local winds. For example, the formation of sea and land breezes is shown in **Figure 6.** During the day, the land heats up faster than the water, so the air above the land becomes warmer than the air above the ocean. The warm land air rises, and the cold ocean air flows in to replace it. At night, the land cools faster than water, so the wind blows toward the ocean.

Figure 6   Sea and Land Breezes

During the day, air over the ocean is cooler and forms an area of high pressure. The cool air flows to the land, producing a sea breeze.

Air over the land is warmer. As warm air rises, it creates an area of low pressure.

At night, air over the ocean is warmer. As the warm air rises, it forms an area of low pressure.

Air over land is cooler and forms an area of high pressure. The cool air moves toward the ocean, producing a land breeze.

Mountain Breezes and Valley Breezes

Mountain and valley breezes are other examples of local winds caused by an area's geography. Campers in mountainous areas may feel a warm afternoon quickly change into a cold night soon after the sun sets. During the day, the sun warms the air along the mountain slopes. This warm air rises up the mountain slopes, creating a valley breeze. At nightfall, the air along the mountain slopes cools. This cool air moves down the slopes into the valley, producing a mountain breeze.

✓ **Reading Check** Why does the wind tend to blow down from mountains at night?

CONNECTION TO Social Studies

Local Breezes The chinook, the shamal, the sirocco, and the Santa Ana are all local winds. Find out about an interesting local wind, and create a poster-board display that shows how the wind forms and how it affects human cultures.

ACTIVITY

SECTION Review

Summary

- Winds blow from areas of high pressure to areas of low pressure.
- Pressure belts are found approximately every 30° of latitude.
- The Coriolis effect causes wind to appear to curve as it moves across the Earth's surface.
- Global winds include the polar easterlies, the westerlies, and the trade winds.
- Local winds include sea and land breezes and mountain and valley breezes.

Using Key Terms

1. In your own words, write a definition for each of the following terms: *wind, Coriolis effect, jet stream, polar easterlies, westerlies,* and *trade winds.*

Understanding Key Ideas

2. Why does warm air rise and cold air sink?
   a. because warm air is less dense than cold air
   b. because warm air is denser than cold air
   c. because cold air is less dense than warm air
   d. because warm air has less pressure than cold air does

3. What are pressure belts?

4. What causes winds?

5. How does the Coriolis effect affect wind movement?

6. How are sea and land breezes similar to mountain and valley breezes?

7. Would there be winds if the Earth's surface were the same temperature everywhere? Explain your answer.

Math Skills

8. Flying an airplane at 500 km/h, a pilot plans to reach her destination in 5 h. But she finds a jet stream moving 250 km/h in the direction she is traveling. If she gets a boost from the jet stream for 2 h, how long will the flight last?

Critical Thinking

9. **Making Inferences** In the Northern Hemisphere, why do westerlies flow from the west but trade winds flow from the east?

10. **Applying Concepts** Imagine you are near an ocean in the daytime. You want to go to the ocean, but you don't know how to get there. How might a local wind help you find the ocean?

SCiLINKS

NSTA Developed and maintained by the National Science Teachers Association

For a variety of links related to this chapter, go to www.scilinks.org

Topic: Atmospheric Pressure and Winds
SciLinks code: HSM0115

Air Pollution

In December 1952, one of London's dreaded "pea souper" fogs settled on the city. But this was no ordinary fog—it was thick with coal smoke and air pollution. It burned people's lungs, and the sky grew so dark that people could not see their hands in front of their faces. When the fog lifted four days later, thousands of people were dead!

London's killer fog shocked the world and caused major changes in England's air-pollution laws. People began to think that air pollution was not simply a part of urban life that had to be endured. Air pollution had to be reduced. Although this event is an extreme example, air pollution is common in many parts of the world. However, nations are taking major steps to reduce air pollution. But what is air pollution? **Air pollution** is the contamination of the atmosphere by the introduction of pollutants from human and natural sources. Air pollutants are classified according to their source as either primary pollutants or secondary pollutants.

Primary Pollutants

Pollutants that are put directly into the air by human or natural activity are *primary pollutants*. Primary pollutants from natural sources include dust, sea salt, volcanic gases and ash, smoke from forest fires, and pollen. Primary pollutants from human sources include carbon monoxide, dust, smoke, and chemicals from paint and other substances. In urban areas, vehicle exhaust is a common source of primary pollutants. Examples of primary pollutants are shown in **Figure 1.**

✓ **Reading Check** List three primary pollutants from natural sources. (*See the Appendix for answers to Reading Checks.*)

air pollution the contamination of the atmosphere by the introduction of pollutants from human and natural sources

Figure 1 **Examples of Primary Pollutants**

Industrial emissions

Vehicle exhaust

Volcanic ash

Secondary Pollutants

Pollutants that form when primary pollutants react with other primary pollutants or with naturally occurring substances are *secondary pollutants*. Ozone and smog are examples of secondary pollutants. Ozone is formed when sunlight reacts with vehicle exhaust and air. You may have heard of "Ozone Action Day" warnings in your community. When such a warning is issued, people are discouraged from outdoor physical activity because ozone can damage their lungs. In the stratosphere, ozone forms a protective layer that absorbs harmful radiation from the sun. Near the Earth's surface, however, ozone is a dangerous pollutant that negatively affects the health of organisms. **Figure 2** shows how smog is formed.

Point and Nonpoint-Source Pollutants

All sources of pollutants can be classified as either point-source pollutants or non-point source pollutants. *Point-source pollutants* are pollutants that are released from a single source. Examples of point-source pollutants in North Carolina are smoke from burning brush, chemical wastes and gases from agricultural industries as shown in **Figure 3,** and particulate matter. Particulate matter is any small particle of dust, dirt, or soot in the air. *Nonpoint-source pollutants* are pollutants that come from many different sources and are often difficult to identify. Examples of nonpoint-source pollutants in North Carolina include ozone and haze. Ozone forms when emissions from industries and motor vehicles react with air and sunlight. Haze forms when emissions from power plants react with air.

② Ozone reacts with vehicle exhaust to form smog.

Smog

Ozone

① Vehicle exhaust reacts with air and sunlight to form ozone.

Automobile exhaust

Figure 2 *Smog forms when sunlight reacts with ozone and vehicle exhaust.*

Figure 3 *Chemicals such as methane from animal waste, are considered point-source pollutants.*

Sources of Human-Caused Air Pollution

Human-caused air pollution comes from a variety of sources. A major source of air pollution today is transportation. Cars contribute about 10% to 20% of the human-caused air pollution in the United States. Vehicle exhaust contains nitrogen oxide, which contributes to smog formation and acid precipitation. However, pollution controls and cleaner gasoline have greatly reduced air pollution from vehicles.

Industrial Air Pollution

Many industrial plants and electric power plants burn fossil fuels, such as coal, to produce energy. Burning some types of coal without pollution controls can release large amounts of air pollutants. Some industries also produce chemicals that can pollute the air. Oil refineries, chemical manufacturing plants, dry-cleaning businesses, furniture refinishers, and auto body shops are all potential sources of air pollution.

Indoor Air Pollution

Sometimes, the air inside a building can be more polluted than the air outside. Some sources of indoor air pollution are shown in **Figure 4.** *Ventilation,* or the mixing of indoor air with outdoor air, can reduce indoor air pollution. Another way to reduce indoor air pollution is to limit the use of chemical solvents and cleaners.

Figure 4 *There are many sources of indoor air pollution. Indoor air pollution can be difficult to detect because it is often invisible.*

Nitrogen oxides from unvented gas stove, wood stove, or kerosene heater

Fungi and bacteria from dirty heating and air conditioning ducts

Chlorine and ammonia from household cleaners

Carbon monoxide from faulty furnace and car left running

Solvents from paint strippers and thinners

Chemicals from dry cleaning

Formaldehyde from furniture, carpeting, particleboard, and foam insulation

Gasoline from car and lawn mower

Acid Precipitation

When fossil fuels are burned, they can release sulfur dioxide and nitrogen oxide into the atmosphere. When these pollutants combine with water in the atmosphere, they form sulfuric acid and nitric acid. Precipitation such as rain, sleet, or snow that contains these acids from air pollution is called **acid precipitation.** Precipitation is naturally acidic, but sulfuric acid and nitric acid can make it so acidic that it can negatively affect the environment. In most areas of the world, pollution controls have helped reduce acid precipitation.

Acid Precipitation and Plants

Plant communities have adapted over long periods of time to the natural acidity of the soil in which they grow. Acid precipitation can cause the acidity of soil to increase. This process, called *acidification*, changes the balance of a soil's chemistry in several ways. When the acidity of soil increases, some nutrients are broken down. Nutrients that plants need for growth get washed away by acidic rainwater. Increased acidity also releases aluminum and other toxic metals from the soil. Some of these toxic metals are absorbed by the roots of plants.

Reading Check How does acid precipitation affect plants?

The Effects of Acid Precipitation on Forests

Forest ecology is complex. Scientists are still trying to fully understand the long-term effects of acid precipitation on groups of plants and their habitats. In some areas of the world, however, acid precipitation has damaged large areas of forest. The effects of acid precipitation are most noticeable in Eastern Europe, as shown in **Figure 5.** Forests in the northeastern United States and in eastern Canada have also been affected by acid precipitation.

acid precipitation rain, sleet, or snow that contains a high concentration of acids

Testing for Particulates

1. Particulates are pollutants such as dust that are extremely small. In this lab, you will measure the amount of particulates in the air. Begin by covering **ten 5 in. × 7 in. index cards** with a thin coat of **petroleum jelly.**

2. Hang the cards in various locations inside and outside your school.

3. One day later, use a **magnifying lens** to count the number of particles on the cards. Which location had the fewest number of particulates? Which location had the highest number of particulates? Hypothesize why.

Figure 5 *This forest in Poland was damaged by acid precipitation.*

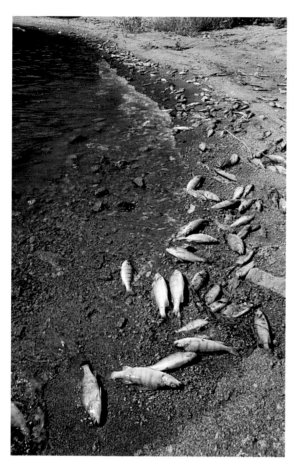

Figure 6 *Acid shock, which is a rapid change in a body of water's acidity, can prevent fish from absorbing oxygen and nutrients. Acid shock can cause populations of fish to die.*

Acid Precipitation and Aquatic Ecosystems

Aquatic organisms have adapted to live in water that has a particular range of acidity. If acid precipitation increases the acidity of a lake or stream, aquatic plants, fish, and other aquatic organisms living in the lake or stream may die.

The effects of acid precipitation are worst in the spring, when the acidic snow that built up in the winter melts and acidic water flows into lakes and rivers. A rapid change in a body of water's acidity is called *acid shock*. Acid shock can cause large numbers of fish in a population to die, as shown in **Figure 6.** Acid shock can affect how fish absorb oxygen and nutrients. To reduce the effects of acid precipitation on aquatic ecosystems, some communities add powdered limestone (calcium carbonate) to acidified lakes in the spring. Limestone neutralizes acids in the lakes. Unfortunately, limestone cannot prevent all acid damage to lakes.

Reading Check Why is powdered limestone added to lakes in the spring instead of the fall?

Acid Precipitation and Humans

Acid precipitation can also affect humans. An increase in soil acidity can cause toxic metals, such as aluminum and mercury, to be released from the soil. These toxic metals can find their way into crops, water, fish, and then eventually into the human body. Studies have also shown that acid precipitation may harm the respiratory health of children.

Neutralizing Acid Precipitation

1. Pour 1/2 tbsp of **vinegar** into one cup of **distilled water,** and stir the mixture well. Check the pH of the mixture by using pH paper. The pH should be about 4.

2. Crush one stick of **blackboard chalk** into powder. Pour the powder into the vinegar and water mixture. Check the pH of the mixture.

3. Did the vinegar and water mixture become more or less acidic after the powdered chalk was poured in?

International Cooperation

Controlling acid precipitation is complicated. Pollutants that are released in one area may later fall to the ground as acid precipitation in an area hundreds of kilometers away. Sometimes, pollution from one country results in acid precipitation in another country. For example, almost half of the acid precipitation that falls in southeastern Canada results from pollution produced in the United States. In the spirit of cooperation, the governments of Canada and the United States signed the Canada-U.S. Air Quality Agreement in 1991. Both countries agreed to reduce acidic emissions that flowed across the Canada-U.S. boundary. More of these international agreements may be necessary to control acid precipitation.

CONNECTION TO Chemistry

Acidity of Precipitation
Acidity is measured by using a pH scale, the units of which range from 1 to 14. Solutions that have a pH of less than 7 are acidic. Research recorded pH levels of acid rain in your area. Then, compare these pH levels with the pH levels of other common acids, such as lemon juice and acetic acid.

SECTION Review

Summary

- Primary pollutants are pollutants that are put directly into the air by human or natural activity. Secondary pollutants form when primary pollutants react with other primary pollutants or with naturally occurring substances.

- Point-source pollutants in North Carolina are smoke, outdoor odors, and particulate matter. Nonpoint-source pollutants in North Carolina are ozone and haze.

- Transportation, industry, and natural sources are the main sources of air pollution.

- Acid precipitation can have harmful effects on plants, animals, and humans.

Using Key Terms

The statements below are false. For each statement, replace the underlined term to make a true statement.

1. <u>Air pollution</u> is a sudden change in the acidity of a stream or lake.

2. <u>Smog</u> is rain, sleet, or snow that has a high concentration of acid.

Understanding Key Ideas

3. Which of the following is a primary pollutant?
   a. ozone
   b. smog
   c. vehicle exhaust
   d. rain

4. List the main point-source pollutants and nonpoint-source pollutants in North Carolina.

Critical Thinking

5. **Expressing Opinions** How do you think that nations should resolve air-pollution problems that cross national boundaries?

Interpreting Graphics

Use the map to answer the questions below.

6. Which areas have the most acidic precipitation?

7. Boston is a larger city than Buffalo is, but the precipitation measured in Buffalo is more acidic than the precipitation in Boston. Explain why.

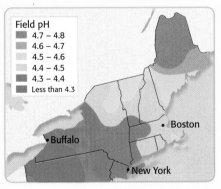

Field pH
- 4.7 – 4.8
- 4.6 – 4.7
- 4.5 – 4.6
- 4.4 – 4.5
- 4.3 – 4.4
- Less than 4.3

Boston
Buffalo
New York

Maintaining Air Quality

Have you ever seen or heard a weather forecaster report the day's air quality? Have you ever had to stay indoors because the air outside was unhealthy?

The air quality in your area affects your health and your everyday life. It's important to learn about the air quality in your area and to know the short-term and long-term effects of air pollution on your health.

Air Pollution and Human Health

Daily exposure to small amounts of air pollution can cause serious health problems. Children, elderly people, and people who have asthma, allergies, lung problems, and heart problems are especially vulnerable to the effects of air pollution.

Short-Term and Long-Term Effects

Many of the effects of air pollution on the human body are short-term effects and are immediately noticeable. Coughing, headaches, irritation to the eyes, nose, and throat, and an increase in asthma-related problems are only a few short-term effects. One good way to avoid experiencing any short-term effects of air pollution is staying indoors on days when the air quality is poor in your area. People who cannot stay indoors because of their jobs, such as the police officer in **Figure 1,** can wear masks and other gear to protect themselves from air pollution.

Long-term effects of air pollution, such as lung cancer and heart disease, may not be noticed until many years after an individual has been exposed to pollutants.

✓ **Reading Check** List three short-term effects of air pollution on human health. (*See the Appendix for answers to Reading Checks.*)

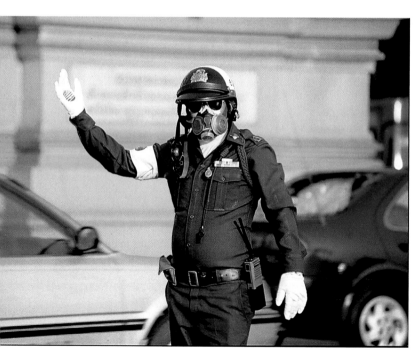

Figure 1 *This police officer wears a mask to protect him from harmful pollutants as he directs traffic in Bangkok, Thailand.*

Monitoring Air Quality

In 1970, the United States Congress passed the Clean Air Act. The Clean Air Act is a law that gives the Environmental Protection Agency (EPA) the authority to regulate the amount of air pollutants that can be released from any source, such as cars and factories.

Air Quality Standards

The EPA sets air quality standards for each state to follow. There are specific standards regarding levels of pollutants, such as carbon monoxide, lead, and ozone. These standards restrict how much of each pollutant can be released. The EPA works to improve air quality in areas where the air quality is poor and to prevent air pollution in areas where the air quality is healthy. There are two types of standards—primary and secondary. Primary standards protect against the effects of air pollution on human health and secondary standards protect against the effects of air pollution on crops, vegetation, and buildings. If air quality worsens, the EPA can set stricter standards. The Clean Air Act was strengthened in 1990.

Air Quality Index

The EPA and local governments are responsible for setting and enforcing air quality standards, as well as for reporting the air quality to the public. The Air Quality Index (AQI), shown in **Table 1,** is used to provide the public with daily air quality information. The AQI measures the air quality of an area with a value from 0 to 500. The AQI is determined after air pollution monitors record the concentrations of the major pollutants in an area. The higher the AQI, the higher the level of air pollution, and the higher the health risk. Once the AQI value is determined for a certain area, a level of health concern and color is also given.

CONNECTION TO Environmental Science

WRITING SKILL **The Ozone Hole**
In 1985, scientists reported an alarming discovery about the Earth's protective ozone layer. Over the Antarctic regions, the ozone layer was thinning. Chemicals called *CFCs* were causing ozone to break down into oxygen, which does not block the sun's harmful ultraviolet (UV) rays. The thinning of the ozone layer creates an ozone hole, which allows more UV radiation to reach the Earth's surface. UV radiation is dangerous to organisms because it damages genes and can cause skin cancer. Using the Internet or library resources research the current state of the ozone layer. Also, find out if *CFCs* are still being used today.

Table 1 Air Quality Index		
Air Quality Index (AQI) Values	**Levels of Health Concern**	**Colors**
0 to 50	Good	Green
51 to 100	Moderate	Yellow
101 to 150	Unhealthy for sensitive groups	Orange
151 to 200	Unhealthy	Red
201 to 300	Very Unhealthy	Purple
301 to 500	Hazardous	Maroon

Figure 2 *This power plant is leading the way in clean-coal technology. The plant turns coal into a gas before it is burned, so fewer pollutants are released.*

Figure 3 *Many states require cars to get emissions tests. Regulating the amount of emissions that vehicles release helps reduce air pollution.*

Reducing Air Pollution

Much progress has been made in reducing air pollution. The Clean Air Act, stricter air quality standards, advancements in technology, and lifestyle changes all help reduce air pollution.

Controlling Air Pollution from Industry

The Clean Air Act requires many industries to use pollution-control devices such as scrubbers. A *scrubber* is a device that is used to remove some pollutants before they are released by smokestacks. Scrubbers in coal-burning power plants remove particles such as ash from the smoke. Other industrial plants, such as the power plant shown in **Figure 2,** focus on burning fuel more efficiently so that fewer pollutants are released.

Reducing Motor Vehicle Emissions

A large percentage of air pollution in the United States comes from the vehicles we drive. To reduce air pollution from vehicles, the EPA requires car makers to meet a certain standard for vehicle exhaust. Devices such as catalytic converters remove many pollutants from exhaust and help cars meet this standard. To make sure that cars continue to meet this standard, some states require vehicles to pass an emissions inspection, as shown in **Figure 3.**

Cleaner fuels and more-efficient engines have also helped reduce air pollution from vehicles. Car makers are also designing cars that run on fuels other than gasoline. Some of these cars run on hydrogen or natural gas. Hybrid cars, which are becoming more common, use gasoline and electric power to reduce emissions.

Ways To Reduce Air Pollution

People can make choices that can help reduce air pollution. For example, you can reduce air pollution by carpooling, using public transportation, walking, or biking to your destination, as shown in **Figure 4.** Planning ahead to combine trips or errands instead of making multiple trips also helps reduce pollution. Keeping cars and other gas-powered machines in good condition helps reduce the amount of fuel the engine consumes, and therefore reduces the amount of emissions the engine releases.

Conserving electricity also helps reduce air pollution. Turning off lights and other electrical appliances when they are not in use can reduce the amount of air pollution that is created when electricity is generated. You can also learn more about reducing air pollution by talking to your state environmental agency or by joining a group that is working to reduce air pollution in your area.

✓ Reading Check Describe one way that you can help reduce air pollution.

Figure 4 *In Copenhagen, Denmark, companies loan free bicycles in exchange for publicity. The program helps reduce air pollution and auto traffic.*

SECTION Review

Summary

- Coughing, headaches, and an increase in asthma-related problems are three effects of air pollution on the human body.

- The EPA and local governments set and enforce air quality standards, and inform the public about air quality.

- Air pollution can be reduced by legislation, such as the Clean Air Act; by technology, such as scrubbers; and by changes in lifestyle.

Understanding Key Ideas

1. Which of the following is a long-term effect of air pollution on the human body?
   a. irritation to the eyes
   b. lung cancer
   c. headaches
   d. coughing

2. Describe the Clean Air Act. When was the Clean Air Act passed by Congress?

3. Explain how the EPA ensures that areas maintain healthy air quality.

4. What do the EPA's primary and secondary air quality standards protect?

5. Describe three effects of air pollution on human health.

6. How can industries help reduce the air pollution they release?

7. What is the Air Quality Index?

Critical Thinking

8. **Identifying Relationships** How can advancements in technology help reduce motor vehicle emissions?

9. **Applying Concepts** List three ways that your community can reduce air pollution. How can you raise awareness in your community about how to reduce air pollution?

SCI LINKS®

NSTA
Developed and maintained by the
National Science Teachers Association

For a variety of links related to this chapter, go to www.scilinks.org

Topic: Air Pollution
SciLinks code: HSM0033

Under Pressure!

Imagine that you are planning a picnic with your friends, so you look in the newspaper for the weather forecast. The temperature this afternoon should be in the low 80s. This temperature sounds quite comfortable! But you notice that the newspaper's forecast also includes the barometer reading. What's a barometer? And what does the reading tell you? In this activity, you will build your own barometer and will discover what this tool can tell you.

OBJECTIVES

Predict how changes in air pressure affect a barometer.

Build a barometer to test your hypothesis.

MATERIALS

- balloon
- can, coffee, large, empty, 10 cm in diameter
- card, index
- scissors
- straw, drinking
- tape, masking, or rubber band

SAFETY

Ask a Question

1 How can I use a barometer to detect changes in air pressure?

Form a Hypothesis

2 Write a few sentences that answer the question above.

Test the Hypothesis

3 Stretch the balloon a few times. Then, blow up the balloon, and let the air out. This step will make your barometer more sensitive to changes in atmospheric pressure.

4 Cut off the open end of the balloon. Next, stretch the balloon over the open end of the coffee can. Then, attach the balloon to the can with masking tape or a rubber band.

5 Cut one end of the straw at an angle to make a pointer.

6 Place the straw on the stretched balloon so that the pointer is directed away from the center of the balloon. Five centimeters of the end of the straw should hang over the edge of the can. Tape the straw to the balloon as shown in the illustration at right.

7 Tape the index card to the side of the can as shown in the illustration at right. Congratulations! You have just made a barometer!

8 Now, use your barometer to collect and record information about air pressure. Place the barometer outside for 3 or 4 days. On each day, mark on the index card where the tip of the straw points.

Analyze the Results

1 **Explaining Events** What atmospheric factors affect how your barometer works? Explain your answer.

2 **Recognizing Patterns** What does it mean when the straw moves up?

3 **Recognizing Patterns** What does it mean when the straw moves down?

Draw Conclusions

4 **Applying Conclusions** Compare your results with the barometric pressures listed in your local newspaper. What kind of weather is associated with high pressure? What kind of weather is associated with low pressure?

5 **Evaluating Results** Does the barometer you built support your hypothesis? Explain your answer.

Applying Your Data

Now, you can use your barometer to measure the actual air pressure! Get the weather section from your local newspaper for the same 3 or 4 days that you were testing your barometer. Find the barometer reading in the newspaper for each day, and record the reading beside that day's mark on your index card. Use these markings on your card to create a scale with marks at regular intervals. Transfer this scale to a new card and attach it to your barometer.

Chapter Review

USING KEY TERMS

For each pair of terms, explain how the meanings of the terms differ.

1 *air pressure* and *wind*

2 *troposphere* and *thermosphere*

3 *greenhouse effect* and *global warming*

4 *convection* and *thermal conduction*

5 *global wind* and *local wind*

6 *stratosphere* and *mesosphere*

UNDERSTANDING KEY IDEAS

Multiple Choice

7 What is the most abundant gas in the atmosphere?

a. oxygen

b. hydrogen

c. nitrogen

d. carbon dioxide

8 A major source of oxygen for the Earth's atmosphere is

a. sea water.

b. the sun.

c. plants.

d. animals.

9 The bottom layer of the atmosphere, where almost all weather occurs, is the

a. stratosphere.

b. troposphere.

c. thermosphere.

d. mesosphere.

10 What percentage of the solar energy that reaches the outer atmosphere is absorbed at the Earth's surface?

a. 20%   c. 50%

b. 30%   d. 70%

11 The ozone layer is located in the

a. stratosphere.

b. troposphere.

c. thermosphere.

d. mesosphere.

12 By which method does most thermal energy in the atmosphere circulate?

a. conduction   c. advection

b. convection   d. radiation

13 The balance between incoming energy and outgoing energy is called

a. the convection balance.

b. the conduction balance.

c. the greenhouse effect.

d. the radiation balance.

14 Which of the following pollutants is NOT a primary pollutant?

a. car exhaust

b. acid precipitation

c. smoke from a factory

d. fumes from burning plastic

15 The Clean Air Act

a. controls the amount of air pollutants that can be released from many sources.

b. requires cars to run on fuels other than gasoline.

c. requires many industries to use scrubbers.

d. Both (a) and (c)

Short Answer

16 Why does the atmosphere become less dense as altitude increases?

17 Explain why air rises when it is heated.

18 What is the main cause of temperature changes in the atmosphere?

19 What are secondary pollutants, and how do they form? Give an example of a secondary pollutant.

20 Give one example of a point-source pollutant and one example of a nonpoint-source pollutant in North Carolina.

21 Describe two sources of human-caused air pollution and describe what can be done to reduce the air pollution each creates.

22 What do the primary and secondary air quality standards protect?

23 How is air quality information communicated to the public? Why is this information important to the public?

CRITICAL THINKING

24 Concept Mapping Use the following terms to create a concept map: *mesosphere, stratosphere, layers, temperature, troposphere,* and *atmosphere.*

25 Identifying Relationships What is the relationship between the greenhouse effect and global warming?

26 Applying Concepts How does acid precipitation affect plants, animals, and humans? What can be done to reduce acid precipitation?

27 Making Inferences The atmosphere of Venus has a very high level of carbon dioxide. How might this fact influence the greenhouse effect on Venus?

INTERPRETING GRAPHICS

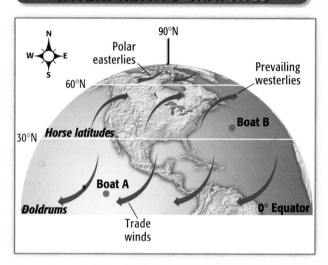

Use the diagram above to answer the questions that follow. When answering the questions that follow, assume that ocean currents do not affect the path of the boats.

28 If Boat A traveled to 50°N, from which direction would the prevailing winds blow?

29 If Boat B sailed with the prevailing westerlies in the Northern Hemisphere, in which direction would the boat be traveling?

Standardized Test Preparation

EOG Prep

Read each of the passages below. Then, answer the questions that follow each passage.

Passage 1 An important part of the EPA's Acid Rain Program is the allowance trading system, which is designed to reduce sulfur dioxide emissions. In this system, 1 ton of sulfur dioxide (SO_2) emission is equivalent to one <u>allowance</u>. A limited number of allowances are allocated for each year. Companies purchase the allowances from the EPA and are allowed to produce as many tons of SO_2 as they have allowances for the year. Companies can buy, sell, or trade allowances, but if they exceed their allowances, they must pay a fine. The system allows a company to determine the most cost-effective ways to comply with the Clean Air Act. A company can reduce emissions by using technology that conserves energy, using renewable energy sources, or updating its pollution-control devices and using low-sulfur fuels.

1. According to the passage, which of the following methods can a company use to reduce emissions?
   A preserving wildlife habitat
   B lobbying Congress
   C using high-sulfur fuels
   D using technology that conserves energy

2. In the passage, what does *allowance* mean?
   F an allotment for a pollutant
   G an allocation of money for reducing pollution
   H an alleviation of pollution
   I an allegation of pollution

Passage 2 The chinook, or "snow eater," is a dry wind that blows down the eastern side of the Rocky Mountains from New Mexico to Alaska. Arapaho Indians gave the chinook its name because of its ability to melt large amounts of snow very quickly. Chinooks form when moist air is forced over a mountain range. The air cools as it rises. As the air cools, it releases moisture by raining or snowing. As the dry air flows over the mountaintop, it compresses and heats the air below. The warm, dry wind that results is worthy of the name "snow eater" because it melts a half meter of snow in a few hours! The temperature change caused when a chinook rushes down a mountainside can also be dramatic. In 1943 in Spearfish, South Dakota, the temperature at 7:30 in the morning was −4°F. But two minutes later, a chinook caused the temperature to soar 49° to 45°F.

1. Which of the following descriptions best explains why the chinook is called "the snow eater"?
   A The chinook is so cold that it prevents the formation of snow in the atmosphere.
   B The chinook is so warm that it prevents the formation of snow in the atmosphere.
   C The chinook is a warm wind that has high humidity.
   D The chinook is a warm wind that has low humidity.

2. According to the passage, at what time did the temperature reach 45°F in Spearfish, South Dakota?
   F 7:30 P.M.
   G 7:32 P.M.
   H 7:30 A.M.
   I 7:32 A.M.

Use the illustration below to answer the questions that follow.

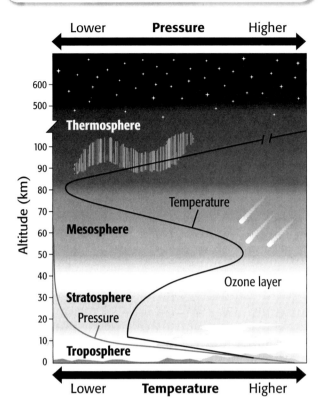

1. Which of the following statements describes how temperature changes in the mesosphere?

A Temperature increases as altitude increases.

B Temperature decreases as altitude increases.

C Temperature decreases as pressure increases.

D Temperature does not change as pressure increases.

2. In which layers does temperature decrease as pressure decreases?

F the troposphere and the mesosphere

G the troposphere and the stratosphere

H the ozone layer and the troposphere

I the ozone layer and the thermosphere

3. A research balloon took measurements at 23 km, 35 km, 52 km, 73 km, 86 km, 92 km, 101 km, and 110 km. Which measurements were taken in the mesosphere?

A measurements at 23 km and 35 km

B measurements at 52 km and 73 km

C measurements at 86 km and 92 km

D measurements at 101 km and 110 km

Read each question below, and choose the best answer.

1. An airplane is flying at a speed of 500 km/h when it encounters a jet stream moving in the same direction at 150 km/h. If the plane flies with the jet stream, how much farther will the plane travel in 1.5 h?

A 950 km

B 525 km

C 225 km

D 150 km

2. Today's wind speed was measured at 18 km/h. What was the wind speed in meters per hour?

F 1.8 m/h

G 180 m/h

H 1,800 m/h

I 18,000 m/h

3. Rockport received 24.1 cm of rain on Monday, 12.5 cm of rain on Tuesday, and 5.8 cm of rain on Thursday. The rest of the week, it did not rain. How much rain did Rockport receive during the week?

A 18.3 cm

B 36.6 cm

C 42.4 cm

D 45.7 cm

4. A weather station recorded the following temperatures during a 5 h period: 15°C, 18°C, 13°C, 15°C, and 20°C. What was the average temperature during this period?

F 14.2°C

G 15.2°C

H 16.2°C

I 20.2°C

5. The temperature in Waterford, Virginia, increased 1.3°C every hour for 5 h. If the temperature in the morning was –4°C, what was the temperature 4 h later?

A 2.5°C

B 2.3°C

C 1.3°C

D 1.2°C

Standardized Test Preparation

Science in Action

Science, Technology, and Society

The HyperSoar Jet

Imagine traveling from Chicago to Tokyo in 72 minutes. If the HyperSoar jet becomes a reality, you may be able to travel to the other side of the world in less time than it takes to watch a movie! To accomplish this amazing feat, the jet would "skip" across the upper stratosphere. To begin skipping, the jet would climb above the stratosphere, turn off its engines, and glide for about 60 km. Then, gravity would pull the jet down to where the air is denser. The denser air would cause the jet to soar upward. In this way, the jet would skip across a layer of dense air until it was ready to land. Each 2-minute skip would cover about 450 km, and the HyperSoar would be able to fly at Mach 10—a speed of 3 km/s!

Math ACTIVITY

A trip on the HyperSoar from Chicago to Tokyo would require about 18 "skips." Each skip is 450 km. If the trip is 10,123 km, how many kilometers will the jet travel when it is not skipping?

Weird Science

Radar Zoology

"For tonight's forecast, expect a light shower of mayflies. A wave of warblers will approach from the south. Tomorrow will be cloudy, and a band of free-tailed bats will move to the south in the early evening." Such a forecast may not make the evening news, but it is a familiar scenario for radar zoologists. Radar zoologists use a type of radar called *NEXRAD* to track migrating birds, bands of bats, and swarms of insects. NEXRAD tracks animals in the atmosphere in the same way that it tracks storms. The system sends out a microwave signal. If the signal hits an object, some of the energy reflects back to a receiver. NEXRAD has been especially useful to scientists who study bird migration. Birds tend to migrate at night, when the atmosphere is more stable, so until now, nighttime bird migration has been difficult to observe. NEXRAD has also helped identify important bird migration routes and critical stopovers. For example, scientists have discovered that many birds migrate over the Gulf of Mexico instead of around it.

Social Studies ACTIVITY

Geography plays an important role in bird migration. Many birds ride the "thermals" produced by mountain ranges. Find out what thermals are, and create a map of bird migration routes over North America.

Ellen Paneok

Bush Pilot For Ellen Paneok, understanding weather patterns is a matter of life and death. As a bush pilot, she flies mail, supplies, and people to remote villages in Alaska that can be reached only by plane. Bad weather is one of the most serious challenges Paneok faces. "It's beautiful up here," she says, "but it can also be harsh." One dangerous situation is landing a plane in mountainous regions. "On top of a mountain you can't tell which way the wind is blowing," Paneok says. In this case, she flies in a rectangular pattern to determine the wind direction. Landing a plane on the frozen Arctic Ocean is also dangerous. In white-out conditions, the horizon can't be seen because the sky and the ground are the same color. "It's like flying in a milk bottle full of milk," Paneok says. In these conditions, she fills black plastic garbage bags and drops them from the plane to help guide her landing.

Paneok had to overcome many challenges to become a pilot. As a child, she lived in seven foster homes before being placed in an all-girls' home at the age of 14. In the girls' home, she read a magazine about careers in aviation and decided then and there that she wanted to become a pilot. At first, she faced a lot of opposition from people telling her that she wouldn't be able to become a pilot. Now, she encourages young people to pursue their goals. "If you decide you want to go for it, go for it. There may be obstacles in your way, but you've just got to find a way to go over them, get around them, or dig under them," she says.

Ellen Paneok is shown at right with two of her Inupiat passengers.

Language Arts ACTIVITY

Beryl Markham lived an exciting life as a bush pilot delivering mail and supplies to remote areas of Africa. Read about her life or the life of Bessie Coleman, one of the most famous African American women in the history of flying.

To learn more about these Science in Action topics, visit go.hrw.com and type in the keyword HZ5ATMF.

Current Science

Check out Current Science® articles related to this chapter by visiting go.hrw.com. Just type in the keyword HZ5CS15.

3

Understanding Weather

About the PHOTO

Flamingos in the bathroom? This may look like someone's idea of a practical joke, but in fact, it's a practical idea! These flamingos reside at the Miami-Metro Zoo in Florida. They were put in the bathroom for protection against the incredibly dangerous winds of Hurricane Floyd in September of 1999.

PRE-READING ACTIVITY

FOLDNOTES **Four-Corner Fold**
Before you read the chapter, create the FoldNote entitled "Four-Corner Fold" described in the **Study Skills** section of the Appendix. Label the flaps of the four-corner fold with "Water in the air," "Air masses and fronts," "Severe weather," and "Forecasting the weather." Write what you know about each topic under the appropriate flap. As you read the chapter, add other information that you learn.

START-UP ACTIVITY

Meeting of the Masses

In this activity, you will model what happens when two air masses that have different temperature characteristics meet.

Procedure

1. Pour **500 mL of water** into a **beaker.** Pour **500 mL of cooking oil** into a **second beaker.** The water represents a dense cold air mass. The cooking oil represents a less dense warm air mass.

2. Predict what would happen to the two liquids if you tried to mix them.

3. Pour the contents of both beakers into a **clear, plastic, rectangular container** at the same time from opposite ends of the container.

4. Observe the interaction of the oil and water.

Analysis

1. What happens when the liquids meet?

2. Does the prediction that you made in step 2 of the Procedure match your results?

3. Using your results, hypothesize what would happen if a cold air mass met a warm air mass.

Water in the Air

What will the weather be this weekend? Depending on what you have planned, knowing the answer to this question could be important. A picnic in the rain can be a mess!

Have you ever wondered what weather is? **Weather** is the condition of the atmosphere at a certain time and place. The condition of the atmosphere is affected by the amount of water in the air. So, to understand weather, you need to understand how water cycles through Earth's atmosphere.

The Water Cycle

Water in liquid, solid, and gaseous states is constantly being recycled through the water cycle. The *water cycle* is the continuous movement of water from sources on Earth's surface—such as lakes, oceans, and plants—into the air, onto and over land, into the ground, and back to the surface. The movement of water through the water cycle is shown in **Figure 1.**

✓ **Reading Check** What is the water cycle? (*See the Appendix for answers to Reading Checks.*)

Figure 1 **The Water Cycle**

Condensation occurs when water vapor cools and changes from a gas to a liquid. Clouds form by this process.

Evaporation occurs when liquid water changes into water vapor, which is a gas.

Precipitation occurs when rain, snow, sleet, or hail falls from the clouds onto Earth's surface.

Runoff is water, usually from precipitation, that flows across land and collects in rivers, streams, and eventually the ocean.

Amount of Water Vapor Air Can Hold at Various Temperatures

Figure 2 *This graph shows that as air gets warmer, the amount of water vapor that the air can hold increases.*

Humidity

As water evaporates from lakes, oceans, and plants, it becomes *water vapor,* or moisture in the air. Water vapor is invisible. The amount of water vapor in the air is called **humidity.** As water evaporates and becomes water vapor, the humidity of the air increases. The air's ability to hold water vapor changes as the temperature of the air changes. **Figure 2** shows that as the temperature of the air increases, the air's ability to hold water vapor also increases.

Relative Humidity

One way to express humidity is through relative humidity. **Relative humidity** is the amount of water vapor in the air compared with the maximum amount of water vapor that the air can hold at a certain temperature. So, relative humidity is given as a percentage. When air holds all of the water that it can at a given temperature, it is said to be *saturated.* Saturated air has a relative humidity of 100%. But how do you find the relative humidity of air that is not saturated? If you know the maximum amount of water vapor that air can hold at a given temperature and the actual amount of water vapor in the air, you can calculate the relative humidity.

Suppose that 1 m³ of air at a certain temperature can hold 24 g of water vapor. However, you know that the air actually contains 18 g of water vapor. You can calculate the relative humidity by using the following formula:

$$\frac{actual\ water\ vapor\ content\ (g/m^3)}{saturation\ water\ vapor\ content\ (g/m^3)} \times 100 = relative\ humidity\ (\%)$$

$$\frac{18\ g/m^3}{24\ g/m^3} = 75\%$$

weather the short-term state of the atmosphere, including temperature, humidity, precipitation, wind, and visibility

humidity the amount of water vapor in the air

relative humidity the ratio of the amount of water vapor in the air to the maximum amount of water vapor the air can hold at a set temperature

Relative Humidity
Assume that 1 m³ of air at 25°C contains 11 g of water vapor. At this temperature, the air can hold 24 g/m³ of water vapor. Calculate the relative humidity of the air.

INTERNET ACTIVITY

For another activity related to this chapter, go to **go.hrw.com** and type in the keyword **HZ5WEAW**.

Factors Affecting Relative Humidity

Two factors that affect relative humidity are amount of water vapor and temperature. At constant temperature and pressure, as the amount of water vapor in air changes, the relative humidity changes. The more water vapor there is in the air, the higher the relative humidity is. If the amount of water vapor in the air stays the same but the temperature changes, the relative humidity changes. The relative humidity decreases as the temperature rises and increases as the temperature drops.

Measuring Relative Humidity

A *psychrometer* (sie KRAHM uht uhr) is an instrument that is used to measure relative humidity. A psychrometer consists of two thermometers, one of which is a wet-bulb thermometer. The bulb of a wet-bulb thermometer is covered with a damp cloth. The other thermometer is a dry-bulb thermometer.

The difference in temperature readings between the thermometers indicates the amount of water vapor in the air. The larger the difference between the two readings is, the less water vapor the air contains and thus the lower the humidity is. **Figure 3** shows how to use a table of differences between wet-bulb and dry-bulb readings to determine relative humidity.

✓ Reading Check What tool is used to measure relative humidity?

Figure 3 Determining Relative Humidity

Find the relative humidity by locating the column head that is equal to the difference between the wet-bulb and dry-bulb readings. Then, locate the row head that equals the temperature reading on the dry-bulb thermometer. The value that lies where the column and row intersect equals the relative humidity. You can see a psychrometer below.

	Relative Humidity (%)							
Dry-bulb reading (°C)	Difference between wet-bulb reading and dry-bulb reading (°C)							
	1	2	3	4	5	6	7	8
0	81	64	46	29	13			
2	84	68	52	37	22	7		
4	85	71	57	43	29	16		
6	86	73	60	48	35	24	11	
8	87	75	63	51	40	29	19	8
10	88	77	66	55	44	34	24	15
12	89	78	68	58	48	39	29	21
14	90	79	70	60	51	42	34	26
16	90	81	71	63	54	46	38	30
18	91	82	73	65	57	49	41	34
20	91	83	74	66	59	51	44	37

How a Wet-Bulb Thermometer Works

A wet-bulb thermometer works differently than a dry-bulb thermometer, which measures only air temperature. As air passes over the wet-bulb thermometer, the water in the cloth evaporates. As the water evaporates, the cloth cools. If the humidity is low, the water will evaporate more quickly and the temperature reading on the wet-bulb thermometer will drop. If the humidity is high, only a small amount of water will evaporate from the cloth of the wet-bulb thermometer and the change in temperature will be small.

Reading Check Explain how a wet-bulb thermometer works.

Condensation

You have probably seen water droplets form on the outside of a glass of ice water, as shown in **Figure 4.** Where did those water drops come from? The water came from the surrounding air, and droplets formed as a result of condensation. **Condensation** is the process by which a gas, such as water vapor, becomes a liquid. Before condensation can occur, the air must be saturated, which means that the air must have a relative humidity of 100%. Condensation occurs when saturated air cools.

Figure 4 *Condensation occurred when the air next to the glass cooled to its dew point.*

Dew Point

Air can become saturated when water vapor is added to the air through evaporation. Air can also become saturated when it cools to its dew point. The *dew point* is the temperature at which a gas condenses into a liquid. At its dew point, air is saturated. The ice in the glass of water causes the air surrounding the glass to cool to its dew point.

Before water vapor can condense, though, it must have a surface to condense on. In the case of the glass of ice water, water vapor condenses on the outside of the glass.

condensation the change of state from a gas to a liquid

Out of Thin Air

1. Pour **room-temperature water** into a **plastic container,** such as a drinking cup, until the water level is near the top of the cup.
2. Observe the outside of the container, and record your observations.
3. Add **one or two ice cubes** to the container of water.
4. Watch the outside of the container for any changes.
5. What happened to the outside of the container?
6. What is the liquid on the container?
7. Where did the liquid come from? Explain your answer.

Figure 5 Three Forms of Clouds

Cumulus clouds look like piles of cotton balls.

Stratus clouds are not as tall as cumulus clouds, but they cover more area.

Cirrus clouds are made of ice crystals.

cloud a collection of small water droplets or ice crystals suspended in the air, which forms when the air is cooled and condensation occurs

CONNECTION TO Language Arts

Cloud Clues Did you know that the name of a cloud actually describes the characteristics of the cloud? For example, the word *cumulus* comes from the Latin word meaning "heap." A cumulus cloud is a puffy, white cloud, which could be described as a "heap" of clouds. Use a dictionary or the Internet to find the word origins of the names of the other cloud types you learn about in this section.

Clouds

Have you ever wondered what clouds are and how they form? A **cloud** is a collection of millions of tiny water droplets or ice crystals. Clouds form as warm air rises and cools. As the rising air cools, it becomes saturated. When the air is saturated, the water vapor changes to a liquid or a solid, depending on the air temperature. At temperatures above freezing, water vapor condenses on small particles in the air and forms tiny water droplets. At temperatures below freezing, water vapor changes to a solid to form ice crystals. Clouds are classified by form, as shown in **Figure 5,** and by altitude.

Cumulus Clouds

Puffy, white clouds that tend to have flat bottoms are called *cumulus clouds* (KYOO myoo luhs KLOWDZ). Cumulus clouds form when warm air rises. These clouds generally indicate fair weather. However, when these clouds get larger, they produce thunderstorms. Thunderstorms come from a kind of cumulus cloud called a *cumulonimbus cloud* (KYOO myoo loh NIM buhs KLOWD). Clouds that have names that include *-nimbus* or *nimbo-* are likely to produce precipitation.

Stratus Clouds

Clouds called *stratus clouds* (STRAYT uhs KLOWDZ) are clouds that form in layers. Stratus clouds cover large areas of the sky and often block out the sun. These clouds can be caused by a gentle lifting of a large body of air into the atmosphere. *Nimbostratus clouds* (NIM boh STRAYT uhs KLOWDZ) are dark stratus clouds that usually produce light to heavy, continuous rain. *Fog* is a stratus cloud that has formed near the ground.

Cirrus Clouds

As you can see in **Figure 5,** *cirrus clouds* (SIR uhs KLOWDZ) are thin, feathery, white clouds found at high altitudes. Cirrus clouds form when the wind is strong. If they get thicker, cirrus clouds indicate that a change in the weather is coming.

Clouds and Altitude

Clouds are also classified by the altitude at which they form. **Figure 6** shows two altitude groups used to describe clouds and the altitudes at which they form in the middle latitudes. The prefix *cirro-* is used to describe clouds that form at high altitudes. For example, a cumulus cloud that forms high in the atmosphere is called a *cirrocumulus cloud.* The prefix *alto-* describes clouds that form at middle altitudes. Clouds that form at low altitudes do not have a specific prefix to describe them.

✓ **Reading Check** At what altitude does an altostratus cloud form?

Figure 6 **Cloud Types Based on Form and Altitude**

High Clouds Because of the cold temperatures at high altitude, high clouds are made up of ice crystals. The prefix *cirro-* is used to describe high clouds.

Middle Clouds Middle clouds can be made up of both water drops and ice crystals. The prefix *alto-* is used to describe middle clouds.

Low Clouds Low clouds are made up of water drops. There is no specific prefix used to describe low clouds.

8,000 m Cirrocumulus   Cirrus

Cirrostratus

6,000 m

Altostratus   Cumulonimbus

4,000 m
Altocumulus

Cumulus

2,000 m

Stratocumulus
Nimbostratus   Stratus

Figure 7 *Snowflakes are six-sided ice crystals that can be several millimeters to several centimeters in size.*

precipitation any form of water that falls to the Earth's surface from the clouds

Precipitation

When water from the air returns to Earth's surface, it returns as precipitation. **Precipitation** is water, in solid or liquid form, that falls from the air to Earth. There are four major forms of precipitation—rain, snow, sleet, and hail.

Rain

The most common form of precipitation is *rain*. A cloud produces rain when the water drops in the cloud become large enough to fall. A water drop in a cloud begins as a droplet that is smaller than the period at the end of this sentence. Before such a water drop falls as rain, it must become about 100 times its original size.

Sleet and Snow

Sleet forms when rain falls through a layer of freezing air. The rain freezes in the air, which produces falling ice. *Snow* forms when temperatures are so cold that water vapor changes directly to a solid. Snow can fall as single ice crystals or can join to form snowflakes, as shown in **Figure 7.**

Hail

Balls or lumps of ice that fall from clouds are called *hail*. Hail forms in cumulonimbus clouds. When updrafts of air in the clouds carry raindrops high in the clouds, the raindrops freeze and hail forms. As hail falls, water drops coat it. Another updraft of air can send the hail up again. Here, the water drops collected on the hail freeze to form another layer of ice on the hail. This process can happen many times. Eventually, the hail becomes too heavy to be carried by the updrafts and so falls to Earth's surface, as shown in **Figure 8.**

Figure 8 *The impact of large hailstones can damage property and crops. The inset photograph shows layers inside of a hailstone, which reveal how it formed.*

Summary

- Weather is the condition of the atmosphere at a certain time and place. Weather is affected by the amount of water vapor in the air.

- The water cycle describes the movement of water above, on, and below Earth's surface.

- Humidity describes the amount of water vapor in the air. Relative humidity is a way to express humidity.

- When the temperature of the air cools to its dew point, the air has reached saturation and condensation occurs.

- Clouds form as air cools to its dew point. Clouds are classified by form and by the altitude at which they form.

- Precipitation occurs when the water vapor that condenses in the atmosphere falls back to Earth in solid or liquid form.

Using Key Terms

1. In your own words, write a definition for each of the following terms: *relative humidity, condensation, cloud,* and *precipitation*.

Understanding Key Ideas

2. Which of the following clouds is most likely to produce light to heavy, continuous rain?
   a. cumulus cloud
   b. cumulonimbus cloud
   c. nimbostratus cloud
   d. cirrus cloud

3. How is relative humidity affected by the amount of water vapor in the air?

4. What does a relative humidity of 75% mean?

5. Describe the path of water through the water cycle.

6. What are four types of precipitation?

Critical Thinking

7. **Applying Concepts** Why are some clouds formed from water droplets, while others are made up of ice crystals?

8. **Applying Concepts** How can rain and hail fall from the same cumulonimbus cloud?

9. **Identifying Relationships** What happens to relative humidity as the air temperature drops below the dew point?

Interpreting Graphics

Use the image below to answer the questions that follow.

10. What type of cloud is shown in the image?

11. How is this type of cloud formed?

12. What type of weather can you expect when you see this type of cloud? Explain.

SCiLINKS®

NSTA
Developed and maintained by the
National Science Teachers Association

For a variety of links related to this chapter, go to www.scilinks.org

Topic: The Water Cycle
SciLinks code: HSM1626

Air Masses and Fronts

Have you ever wondered how the weather can change so quickly? For example, the weather may be warm and sunny in the morning and cold and rainy by afternoon.

Changes in weather are caused by the movement and interaction of air masses. An **air mass** is a large body of air where temperature and moisture content are similar throughout. In this section, you will learn about air masses and their effect on weather.

Air Masses

Air masses are characterized by their moisture content and temperature. The moisture content and temperature of an air mass are determined by the area over which the air mass forms. These areas are called *source regions*. An example of a source region is the Gulf of Mexico. An air mass that forms over the Gulf of Mexico is warm and wet because this area is warm and has a lot of water that evaporates. There are many types of air masses, each of which is associated with a particular source region. The characteristics of these air masses are represented on maps by a two-letter symbol, as shown in **Figure 1.** The first letter indicates the moisture content that is characteristic of the air mass. The second letter represents the temperature that is characteristic of the air mass.

Figure 1   Air Masses That Affect Weather in North America

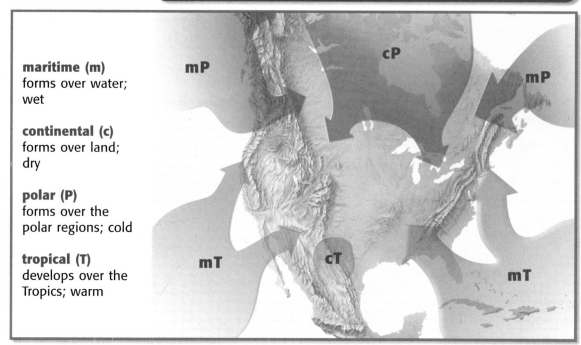

maritime (m) forms over water; wet

continental (c) forms over land; dry

polar (P) forms over the polar regions; cold

tropical (T) develops over the Tropics; warm

Figure 2 *Cold air masses that form over the North Atlantic Ocean can bring severe weather, such as blizzards, in the winter.*

Cold Air Masses

Most of the cold winter weather in the United States is influenced by three polar air masses. A continental polar (cP) air mass forms over northern Canada, which brings extremely cold winter weather to the United States. In the summer, a cP air mass generally brings cool, dry weather.

A maritime polar (mP) air mass that forms over the North Pacific Ocean is cool and very wet. This air mass brings rain and snow to the Pacific Coast in the winter and cool, foggy weather in the summer.

A maritime polar air mass that forms over the North Atlantic Ocean brings cool, cloudy weather and precipitation to New England in the winter, as shown in **Figure 2.** In the summer, the air mass brings cool weather and fog.

Warm Air Masses

Four warm air masses influence the weather in the United States. A maritime tropical (mT) air mass that develops over warm areas in the Pacific Ocean is milder than the maritime polar air mass that forms over the Pacific Ocean.

Other maritime tropical air masses develop over the warm waters of the Gulf of Mexico and the Atlantic Ocean. These air masses move north across the East Coast and into the Midwest. In the summer, they bring hot and humid weather, hurricanes, and thunderstorms, as shown in **Figure 3.** In the winter, they bring mild, often cloudy weather.

A continental tropical (cT) air mass forms over the deserts of northern Mexico and the southwestern United States. This air mass moves northward and brings clear, dry, and hot weather in the summer.

✓ Reading Check What type of air mass contributes to the hot and humid summer weather in the midwestern United States? (*See the Appendix for answers to Reading Checks.*)

air mass a large body of air where temperature and moisture content are constant throughout

Figure 3 *Warm air masses that develop over the Gulf of Mexico bring thunderstorms in the summer.*

Figure 4   **Fronts That Affect Weather in North America**

Cold Front

Warm Front

Fronts

Air masses that form from different areas often do not mix. The reason is that the air masses have different densities. For example, warm air is less dense than cold air. So, when two types of air masses meet, warm air generally rises. The area in which two types of air masses meet is called a **front.** The four kinds of fronts—cold fronts, warm fronts, occluded fronts, and stationary fronts—are shown in **Figure 4.** Fronts are associated with weather in the middle latitudes.

front the boundary between air masses of different densities and usually different temperatures

Cold Front

A cold front forms where cold air moves under warm air, which is less dense, and pushes the warm air up. Cold fronts can move quickly and bring thunderstorms, heavy rain, or snow. Cooler weather usually follows a cold front because the air mass behind the cold front is cooler and drier than the air mass that it is replacing.

Warm Front

A warm front forms where warm air moves over cold, denser air. In a warm front, the warm air gradually replaces the cold air. Warm fronts generally bring drizzly rain and are followed by clear and warm weather.

Occluded Front   **Stationary Front**

Occluded Front

An occluded front forms when a warm air mass is caught between two colder air masses. The coldest air mass moves under and pushes up the warm air mass. The coldest air mass then moves forward until it meets a cold air mass that is warmer and less dense. The colder of these two air masses moves under and pushes up the warmer air mass. Sometimes, though, the two colder air masses mix. An occluded front has cool temperatures and large amounts of rain and snow.

✓ **Reading Check** What type of weather would you expect an occluded front to produce?

Stationary Front

A stationary front forms when a cold air mass meets a warm air mass. In this case, however, both air masses do not have enough force to lift the warm air mass over the cold air mass. So, the two air masses remain separated. This may happen because there is not enough wind to keep the air masses pushing against each other. A stationary front often brings many days of cloudy, wet weather.

Figure 5 *This satellite image shows a cyclone system forming.*

Air Pressure and Weather

You may have heard a weather reporter on TV or radio talking about areas of low pressure and high pressure. These areas of different pressure affect the weather.

Cyclones

Areas that have lower pressure than the surrounding areas do are called **cyclones.** Cyclones are areas where air masses come together, or converge, and rise. **Figure 5** shows a satellite image of the formation of a cyclone system.

Anticyclones

Areas that have high pressure are called **anticyclones.** Anticyclones are areas where air moves apart, or diverges, and sinks. The sinking air is denser than the surrounding air, and the pressure is higher. Cooler, denser air moves out of the center of these high-pressure areas toward areas of lower pressure. **Figure 6** shows how wind can spiral out of an anticyclone and into a cyclone.

cyclone an area in the atmosphere that has lower pressure than the surrounding areas and has winds that spiral toward the center

anticyclone the rotation of air around a high-pressure center in the direction opposite to Earth's rotation

Figure 6 *As the colder, denser air spirals out of the anticyclone, it moves towards areas of low pressure, which sometimes forms a cyclone.*

High pressure

Low pressure

Anticyclone

Cyclone

Cyclones, Anticyclones, and Weather

You have learned what cyclones and anticyclones are. So, now you might be wondering how do cyclones and anticyclones affect the weather? As the air in the center of a cyclone rises, it cools and forms clouds and rain. The rising air in a cyclone causes stormy weather. In an anticyclone, the air sinks. As the air sinks, it gets warmer and absorbs moisture. The sinking air in an anticyclone brings dry, clear weather. By keeping track of cyclones and anticyclones, meteorologists can predict the weather.

✓ **Reading Check** Describe the different types of weather that a cyclone and an anticyclone can produce.

CONNECTION TO Astronomy

Storms on Jupiter Cyclones and anticyclones occur on Jupiter, too! Generally, cyclones on Jupiter appear as dark ovals, and anticyclones appear as bright ovals. Jupiter's Great Red Spot is an anticyclone that has existed for centuries. Research the existence of cyclones and anticyclones on other bodies in our solar system.

SECTION Review

Summary

- Air masses are characterized by moisture content and temperature.
- A front occurs where two air masses meet.
- Four major types of fronts are cold, warm, occluded, and stationary fronts.
- Differences in air pressure cause cyclones, which bring stormy weather, and anticyclones, which bring dry, clear weather.

Using Key Terms

For each pair of terms, explain how the meanings of the terms differ.

1. *front* and *air mass*

2. *cyclone* and *anticyclone*

Understanding Key Ideas

3. What kind of front forms when a cold air mass displaces a warm air mass?
    a. a cold front
    b. a warm front
    c. an occluded front
    d. a stationary front

4. What are the major air masses that influence the weather in the United States?

5. What is one source region of a maritime polar air mass?

6. What are the characteristics of an air mass whose two-letter symbol is cP?

7. What are the four major types of fronts?

8. How do fronts cause weather changes?

9. How do cyclones and anticyclones affect the weather?

Math Skills

10. A cold front is moving toward the town of La Porte at 35 km/h. The front is 200 km away from La Porte. How long will it take the front to get to La Porte?

Critical Thinking

11. **Applying Concepts** How do air masses that form over the land and ocean affect weather in the United States?

12. **Identifying Relationships** Why does the Pacific Coast have cool, wet winters and warm, dry summers? Explain.

13. **Applying Concepts** Which air masses influence the weather where you live? Explain.

SCiLINKS

NSTA
Developed and maintained by the National Science Teachers Association

For a variety of links related to this chapter, go to www.scilinks.org

Topic: Air Masses and Fronts
SciLinks code: HSM0032

Severe Weather

CRAAAACK! BOOM! What made that noise? You didn't expect it, and it sure made you jump.

A big boom of thunder has probably surprised you at one time or another. And the thunder was probably followed by a thunderstorm. A thunderstorm is an example of severe weather. *Severe weather* is weather that can cause property damage and sometimes death.

Thunderstorms

Thunderstorms can be very loud and powerful. **Thunderstorms,** such as the one shown in **Figure 1,** are small, intense weather systems that produce strong winds, heavy rain, lightning, and thunder. Thunderstorms can occur along cold fronts. But thunderstorms can develop in other places, too. There are only two atmospheric conditions required to produce thunderstorms: warm and moist air near Earth's surface and an unstable atmosphere. The atmosphere is unstable when the surrounding air is colder than the rising air mass. The air mass will continue to rise as long as the surrounding air is colder than the air mass.

When the rising warm air reaches its dew point, the water vapor in the air condenses and forms cumulus clouds. If the atmosphere is extremely unstable, the warm air will continue to rise, which causes the cloud to grow into a dark, cumulonimbus cloud. Cumulonimbus clouds can reach heights of more than 15 km.

READING WARM-UP

Objectives

● Describe how lightning forms.
● Describe the formation of thunderstorms, tornadoes, and hurricanes.
● Describe the characteristics of thunderstorms, tornadoes, and hurricanes.
● Explain how to stay safe during severe weather.

Terms to Learn

thunderstorm   tornado
lightning   hurricane
thunder

READING STRATEGY

Reading Organizer As you read this section, create an outline of the section. Use the headings from the section in your outline.

thunderstorm a usually brief, heavy storm that consists of rain, strong winds, lightning, and thunder

Figure 1 *A typical thunderstorm, such as this one over Dallas, Texas, generates an enormous amount of electrical energy.*

Figure 2 *The upper part of a cloud usually carries a positive electric charge, while the lower part of the cloud carries mainly negative charges.*

Lightning

Thunderstorms are very active electrically. **Lightning** is an electric discharge that occurs between a positively charged area and a negatively charged area, as shown in **Figure 2.** Lightning can happen between two clouds, between Earth and a cloud, or even between two parts of the same cloud. Have you ever touched someone after scuffing your feet on the carpet and received a mild shock? If so, you have experienced how lightning forms. While you walk around, friction between the floor and your shoes builds up an electric charge in your body. When you touch someone else, the charge is released.

When lightning strikes, energy is released. This energy is transferred to the air and causes the air to expand rapidly and send out sound waves. **Thunder** is the sound that results from the rapid expansion of air along the lightning strike.

Severe Thunderstorms

Severe thunderstorms can produce one or more of the following conditions: high winds, hail, flash floods, and tornadoes. Hailstorms damage crops, dent the metal on cars, and break windows. Flash flooding that results from heavy rains causes millions of dollars in property damage annually. And every year, flash flooding is a leading cause of weather-related deaths.

Lightning, as shown in **Figure 3,** happens during all thunderstorms and is very powerful. Lightning is responsible for starting thousands of forest fires each year and for killing or injuring hundreds of people a year in the United States.

Reading Check What is a severe thunderstorm? (*See the Appendix for answers to Reading Checks.*)

lightning an electric discharge that takes place between two oppositely charged surfaces, such as between a cloud and the ground, between two clouds, or between two parts of the same cloud

thunder the sound caused by the rapid expansion of air along an electrical strike

Figure 3 *Lightning often strikes the tallest object in an area, such as the Eiffel Tower in Paris, France.*

Tornadoes

tornado a destructive, rotating column of air that has very high wind speeds, is visible as a funnel-shaped cloud, and touches the ground

Tornadoes happen in only 1% of all thunderstorms. A **tornado** is a small, spinning column of air that has high wind speeds and low central pressure and that touches the ground. A tornado starts out as a funnel cloud that pokes through the bottom of a cumulonimbus cloud and hangs in the air. The funnel cloud becomes a tornado when it makes contact with Earth's surface. **Figure 4** shows how a tornado forms.

Figure 4 **How a Tornado Forms**

❶ Wind moving in two directions causes a layer of air in the middle to begin to spin like a roll of toilet paper.

❷ The spinning column of air is turned to a vertical position by strong updrafts of air in the cumulonimbus cloud. The updrafts of air also begin to spin.

❸ The spinning column of air moves to the bottom of the cumulonimbus cloud and forms a funnel cloud.

❹ The funnel cloud becomes a tornado when it touches the ground.

Figure 5 *The tornado that hit Kissimmee, Florida, in 1998 had wind speeds of up to 416 km/h.*

Twists of Terror

About 75% of the world's tornadoes occur in the United States. Most of these tornadoes happen in the spring and early summer when cold, dry air from Canada meets warm, moist air from the Tropics. The size of a tornado's path of destruction is usually about 8 km long and 10 to 60 m wide. Although most tornadoes last only a few minutes, they can cause a lot of damage. Their ability to cause damage is due to their strong spinning winds. The average tornado has wind speeds between 120 and 180 km/h, but rarer, more violent tornadoes can have spinning winds of up to 500 km/h. The winds of tornadoes have been known to uproot trees and destroy buildings, as shown in **Figure 5.** Tornadoes are capable of picking up heavy objects, such as mobile homes and cars, and hurling them through the air.

hurricane a severe storm that develops over tropical oceans and whose strong winds of more than 120 km/h spiral in toward the intensely low-pressure storm center

Hurricanes

A large, rotating tropical weather system that has wind speeds of at least 120 km/h is called a **hurricane,** shown in **Figure 6.** Hurricanes are the most powerful storms on Earth. Hurricanes have different names in different parts of the world. In the western Pacific Ocean, hurricanes are called *typhoons.* Hurricanes that form over the Indian Ocean are called *cyclones.*

Most hurricanes form in the areas between 5° and 20° north latitude and between 5° and 20° south latitude over warm, tropical oceans. At higher latitudes, the water is too cold for hurricanes to form. Hurricanes vary in size from 160 to 1,500 km in diameter and can travel for thousands of kilometers.

✓ Reading Check What are some other names for hurricanes?

Figure 6 *This photograph of Hurricane Fran was taken from space.*

How a Hurricane Forms

A hurricane begins as a group of thunderstorms moving over tropical ocean waters. Winds traveling in two different directions meet and cause the storm to spin. Because of the Coriolis effect, the storm turns counterclockwise in the Northern Hemisphere and clockwise in the Southern Hemisphere.

A hurricane gets its energy from the condensation of water vapor. Once formed, the hurricane is fueled through contact with the warm ocean water. Moisture is added to the warm air by evaporation from the ocean. As the warm, moist air rises, the water vapor condenses and releases large amounts of energy. The hurricane continues to grow as long as it is over its source of warm, moist air. When the hurricane moves into colder waters or over land, it begins to die because it has lost its source of energy. **Figure 7** and **Figure 8** show two views of a hurricane.

✓ Reading Check Where do hurricanes get their energy?

Figure 7 *The photo above gives you a bird's-eye view of a hurricane.*

Rain bands

Eye

Eye wall

Figure 8 **Cross Section of a Hurricane**

Surrounding the eye is the **eye wall**—a group of cumulonimbus clouds that produce heavy rains and strong winds. The winds can reach speeds of 300 km/h. The eye wall is the strongest part of the hurricane.

At the center of the hurricane is the **eye**—a core of warm, relatively calm air with low pressure and light winds.

Beyond the eye wall, spiraling bands of clouds called **rain bands** circle the center of the hurricane. The rain bands produce heavy rains and high winds. Within this area of the hurricane, wind speed decreases as the distance from the eye wall increases.

Updraft

Downdraft

Damage Caused by Hurricanes

Hurricanes can cause a lot of damage when they move near or onto land. Wind speeds of most hurricanes range from 120 to 150 km/h. Some can reach speeds as high as 300 km/h. Hurricane winds can knock down trees and telephone poles and can damage and destroy buildings and homes.

While high winds cause a great deal of damage, most hurricane damage is caused by flooding associated with heavy rains and storm surges. A *storm surge* is a wall of water that builds up over the ocean because of the strong winds and low atmospheric pressure. The wall of water gets bigger as it nears the shore, and it reaches its greatest height when it crashes onto the shore. Depending on the hurricane's strength, a storm surge can be 1 to 8 m high and 65 to 160 km long. Flooding causes tremendous damage to property and lives when a storm surge moves onto shore, as shown in **Figure 9.**

Severe Weather Safety

Severe weather can be very dangerous, so it is important to keep yourself safe. One way to stay safe is to turn on the radio or TV during a storm. Your local radio and TV stations will let you know if a storm has gotten worse.

Thunderstorm Safety

Lightning is one of the most dangerous parts of a thunderstorm. Lightning is attracted to tall objects. If you are outside, stay away from trees, which can get struck down. If you are in the open, crouch down. Otherwise, you will be the tallest object in the area! Stay away from bodies of water. If lightning hits water while you are in it, you could be hurt or could even die.

Figure 9 *A hurricane's storm surge can cause severe damage to homes near the shoreline.*

Natural Disaster Plan

WRITING SKILL Every family should have a plan to deal with weather emergencies. With a parent, discuss what your family should do in the event of severe weather. Together, write up a plan for your family to follow in case of a natural disaster. Also, make a disaster supply kit that includes enough food and water to last several days.

Figure 10 *During a tornado warning, it is best to protect yourself by crouching against a wall and covering the back of your head and neck with your hands or a book.*

Tornado Safety

Weather forecasters use watches and warnings to let people know about tornadoes. A *watch* is a weather alert that lets people know that a tornado may happen. A *warning* is a weather alert that lets people know that a tornado has been spotted.

If there is a tornado warning for your area, find shelter quickly. The best place to go is a basement or cellar. Or you can go to a windowless room in the center of the building, such as a bathroom, closet, or hallway, as **Figure 10** shows. If you are outside, lie down in a large, open field or a deep ditch.

Flood Safety

An area can get so much rain that it begins to flood. So, like tornadoes, floods have watches and warnings. However, little warning can usually be given. A flash flood is a flood that rises and falls very suddenly. The best thing to do during a flood is to find a high place to wait out the flood. You should always stay out of floodwaters. Even shallow water can be dangerous if it is moving fast.

Figure 11 *These store owners are boarding up their windows to protect the windows from strong winds during a hurricane.*

Hurricane Safety

If a hurricane is in your area, your local TV or radio station will keep you updated on its condition. People living on the shore may be asked to evacuate the area. If you live in an area where hurricanes strike, your family should have a disaster supply kit that includes enough water and food to last several days. To protect the windows in your home, you should cover them with plywood, as shown in **Figure 11.** Most important, you must stay indoors during the storm.

Summary

- Thunderstorms are intense weather systems that produce strong winds, heavy rain, lightning, and thunder.

- Lightning is a large electric discharge that occurs between two oppositely charged surfaces. Lightning releases a great deal of energy and can be very dangerous.

- Tornadoes are small, rotating columns of air that touch the ground and can cause severe damage.

- A hurricane is a large, rotating tropical weather system. Hurricanes cause strong winds and can cause severe property damage.

- In the event of severe weather, it is important to stay safe. Listening to your local TV or radio station for updates and remaining indoors and away from windows are good rules to follow.

Using Key Terms

Complete each of the following sentences by choosing the correct term from the word bank.

hurricane	storm surge
tornado	lightning

1. Thunderstorms are very active electrically and often cause ___.

2. A ___ forms when a funnel cloud pokes through the bottom of a cumulonimbus cloud and makes contact with the ground.

Understanding Key Ideas

3. The safest thing to do if you are caught outdoors during a tornado is to
   a. stay near buildings and roads.
   b. head for an open area.
   c. seek shelter near a large tree.
   d. None of the above

4. Describe how tornadoes form.

5. At what latitudes do hurricanes usually form?

6. What is lightning? What happens when lightning strikes?

Critical Thinking

7. **Applying Concepts** What items do you think you would need in a disaster kit? Explain.

8. **Identifying Relationships** What happens to a hurricane as it moves over land? Explain.

Interpreting Graphics

Use the diagram below to answer the questions that follow.

9. Describe what is happening at point C.

10. What is point B?

11. What kind of weather can you expect at point A?

SCI LINKS.

NSTA
Developed and maintained by the
National Science Teachers Association

For a variety of links related to this chapter, go to www.scilinks.org

Topic: Severe Weather
SciLinks code: HSM1383

Forecasting the Weather

You watch the weather forecast on the evening news. The news is good—there's no rain in sight. But how can the weather forecasters tell that it won't rain?

READING WARM-UP

Objectives

● Describe the different types of instruments used to take weather measurements.

● Explain how radar and weather satellites help meteorologists forecast the weather.

● Explain how to interpret a weather map.

Terms to Learn

thermometer
barometer
anemometer

READING STRATEGY

Reading Organizer As you read this section, make a table comparing the different instruments used to collect weather data.

Weather affects how you dress and how you plan your day, so it is important to get accurate weather forecasts. But where do weather reporters get their information? And how do they predict the weather? A *weather forecast* is a prediction of weather conditions over the next 3 to 5 days. A *meteorologist* is a person who observes and collects data on atmospheric conditions to make weather predictions. In this section, you will learn how weather data are collected and shown.

Weather-Forecasting Technology

To accurately forecast the weather, meteorologists need to measure various atmospheric conditions, such as air pressure, humidity, precipitation, temperature, wind speed, and wind direction. Meteorologists use special instruments to collect data on weather conditions both near and far above Earth's surface.

High in the Sky

Weather balloons carry electronic equipment that can measure weather conditions as high as 30 km above Earth's surface. Weather balloons, such as the one in **Figure 1,** carry equipment that measures temperature, air pressure, and relative humidity. By tracking the balloons, meteorologists can also measure wind speed and direction.

✔ **Reading Check** How do meteorologists gather data on atmospheric conditions above Earth's surface? (*See the Appendix for answers to Reading Check.*)

Figure 1 *Weather balloons carry radio transmitters that send measurements to stations on the ground.*

Windsock

Figure 2 *Meteorologists use these tools to collect atmospheric data.*

Thermometer

Anemometer

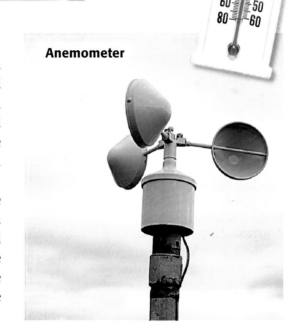

Measuring Air Temperature and Pressure

A tool used to measure air temperature is called a **thermometer.** Most thermometers use a liquid sealed in a narrow glass tube, as shown in **Figure 2.** When air temperature increases, the liquid expands and moves up the glass tube. As air temperature decreases, the liquid shrinks and moves down the tube.

A **barometer** is an instrument used to measure air pressure. A mercurial barometer consists of a glass tube that is sealed at one end and placed in a container full of mercury. As the air pressure pushes on the mercury inside the container, the mercury moves up the glass tube. The greater the air pressure is, the higher the mercury will rise.

Measuring Wind Direction

Wind direction can be measured by using a windsock or a wind vane. A windsock, shown in **Figure 2,** is a cone-shaped cloth bag open at both ends. The wind enters through the wide end and leaves through the narrow end. Therefore, the wide end points into the wind. A wind vane is shaped like an arrow with a large tail and is attached to a pole. As the wind pushes the tail of the wind vane, the wind vane spins on the pole until the arrow points into the wind.

Measuring Wind Speed

An instrument used to measure wind speed is called an **anemometer.** An anemometer, as shown in **Figure 2,** consists of three or four cups connected by spokes to a pole. The wind pushes on the hollow sides of the cups and causes the cups to rotate on the pole. The motion sends a weak electric current that is measured and displayed on a dial.

thermometer an instrument that measures and indicates temperature

barometer an instrument that measures atmospheric pressure

anemometer an instrument used to measure wind speed

Figure 3 *Using Doppler radar, meteorologists can predict a tornado up to 20 minutes before it touches the ground.*

Radar and Satellites

Radar is used to find the location, movement, and amount of precipitation. It can also detect what form of precipitation a weather system is carrying. You might have seen a kind of radar called *Doppler radar* used in a local TV weather report. **Figure 3** shows how Doppler radar is used to track precipitation. *Weather satellites* that orbit Earth provide the images of weather systems that you see on TV weather reports. Satellites can track storms and measure wind speeds, humidity, and temperatures at different altitudes.

Weather Maps

In the United States, the National Weather Service (NWS) and the National Oceanic and Atmospheric Administration (NOAA) collect and analyze weather data. The NWS produces weather maps based on information gathered from about 1,000 weather stations across the United States. On these maps, each station is represented by a station model. A *station model* is a small circle that shows the location of the weather station. As shown in **Figure 4,** surrounding the small circle is a set of symbols and numbers, which represent the weather data.

Figure 4 **A Station Model**

Temperature (°F) — 38
Type of precipitation — ●
Dew point temperature (°F) — 27
Wind speed
Wind direction
Amount of cloud cover
196 — Abbreviated version of barometric pressure in millibars

Reading a Weather Map

Weather maps that you see on TV include lines called *isobars*. Isobars are lines that connect points of equal air pressure. Isobars that form closed circles represent areas of high or low pressure. These areas are usually marked on a map with a capital *H* or *L*. Fronts are also labeled on weather maps, as you can see on the weather map in **Figure 5**.

Legend

Cold front		**H** High pressure	
Warm front		**L** Low pressure	
Low pressure trough		Rain	
Isobar		Fog	

Figure 5 *Can you identify the fronts shown on the weather map?*

SECTION Review

Summary

- Meteorologists use several instruments, such as weather balloons, thermometers, barometers, anemometers, windsocks, weather vanes, radar, and weather satellites, to forecast the weather.
- Station models show the weather conditions at various points across the United States.
- Weather maps show areas of high and low pressure as well as the location of fronts.

Using Key Terms

1. In your own words, write a definition for each of the following terms: *thermometer, barometer,* and *anemometer*.

Understanding Key Ideas

2. Which of the following instruments measures air pressure?
   a. thermometer
   b. barometer
   c. anemometer
   d. windsock

3. How does radar help meteorologists forecast the weather?

4. What does a station model represent?

Math Skills

5. If it is 75°F outside, what is the temperature in degrees Celsius? (Hint: °F = (°C × 9/5) + 32)

Critical Thinking

6. **Applying Concepts** Why would a meteorologist compare a new weather map with one that is 24 h old?

7. **Making Inferences** In the United States, why is weather data gathered from a large number of station models?

8. **Making Inferences** How might several station models from different regions plotted on a map help a meteorologist?

SCILINKS.

NSTA

Developed and maintained by the National Science Teachers Association

For a variety of links related to this chapter, go to www.scilinks.org

Topic: Forecasting the Weather
SciLinks code: HSM0606

OBJECTIVES

Construct a device that uses water to measure temperature.

Calibrate the new device by using a mercury thermometer.

MATERIALS

- bottle, plastic
- can, aluminum soda
- card, index, 3 in. × 5 in.
- clay, modeling (1 lb)
- container, yogurt, with lid
- cup, plastic-foam, large (2)
- film canister
- food coloring, red (1 bottle)
- funnel, plastic or paper cone
- gloves, heat-resistant
- hot plate
- ice, cube (5 or 6)
- pan, aluminum pie
- pitcher
- plastic tubing, 5 mm diameter, 30 cm long
- ruler, metric
- straw, plastic, inflexible, clear (1)
- tape, transparent (1 roll)
- thermometer, Celsius
- water, tap

SAFETY

Boiling Over!

Safety Industries, Inc., would like to produce and sell thermometers that are safer than mercury thermometers. The company would like your team of inventors to design a thermometer that uses water instead of mercury. The company will offer a contract to the team that creates the best design of a water thermometer. Good luck!

Ask a Question

1 What causes the liquid in a thermometer to rise? How can I use this information to make a thermometer?

Form a Hypothesis

2 Brainstorm with a classmate to design a thermometer that uses only water to measure temperature. Sketch your design. Write a one-sentence hypothesis that describes how your thermometer will work.

Test the Hypothesis

3 Following your design, build a thermometer by using only materials from the materials list. Like a mercury thermometer, your thermometer needs a bulb and a tube. However, the liquid in your thermometer will be water.

4 To test your design, place the aluminum pie pan on a hot plate. Use the pitcher to carefully pour water into the pan until the pan is half full. Turn on the hot plate, and heat the water.

5 Put on your safety goggles and heat-resistant gloves, and carefully place the "bulb" of your thermometer in the hot water. Observe the water level in the tube. Does the water level rise?

6 If the water level does not rise, change your design as necessary and repeat steps 3–5. When the water level in your thermometer does rise, sketch the design of this thermometer as your final design.

7 After you decide on your final design, you must calibrate your thermometer by using a laboratory thermometer. Tape an index card to your thermometer's tube so that the part of the tube that sticks out from the "bulb" of your thermometer touches the card.

8 Place the plastic funnel or the cone-shaped paper funnel into a plastic-foam cup. Carefully pour hot water from the pie pan into the funnel. Be sure that no water splashes or spills.

9 Place your thermometer and a laboratory thermometer in the hot water. As your thermometer's water level rises, mark the level on the index card. At the same time, observe and record the temperature of the laboratory thermometer, and write this value beside your mark on the card.

10 Repeat steps 8–9 using warm tap water.

11 Repeat steps 8–9 using ice water.

12 Draw evenly spaced scale markings between your temperature markings on the index card. Write the temperatures that correspond to the scale marks on the index card.

Analyze the Results

1 **Analyzing Results** How well does your thermometer measure temperature?

Draw Conclusions

2 **Drawing Conclusions** Compare your thermometer design with other students' designs. How would you change your design to make your thermometer measure temperature better?

3 **Applying Conclusions** Take a class vote to see which design should be used by Safety Industries. Why was this thermometer design chosen? How did it differ from other designs in the class?

Chapter Review

USING KEY TERMS

For each pair of terms, explain how the meanings of the terms differ.

1 *relative humidity* and *dew point*

2 *condensation* and *precipitation*

3 *air mass* and *front*

4 *lightning* and *thunder*

5 *tornado* and *hurricane*

6 *barometer* and *anemometer*

UNDERSTANDING KEY IDEAS

Multiple Choice

7 The process in which water changes from a liquid to gas is called

  a. precipitation.

  b. condensation.

  c. evaporation.

  d. water vapor.

8 What is the relative humidity of air at its dew point?

  a. 0%   **c.** 75%

  b. 50%   **d.** 100%

9 Which of the following is NOT a type of condensation?

  a. fog   **c.** snow

  b. cloud   **d.** dew

10 High clouds made of ice crystals are called ___ clouds.

  a. stratus   **c.** nimbostratus

  b. cumulus   **d.** cirrus

11 Large thunderhead clouds that produce precipitation are called ___ clouds.

  a. nimbostratus   **c.** cumulus

  b. cumulonimbus **d.** stratus

12 Strong updrafts within a thunderhead can produce

  a. snow.   **c.** sleet.

  b. rain.   **d.** hail.

13 A maritime tropical air mass contains

  a. warm, wet air. **c.** warm, dry air.

  b. cold, moist air. **d.** cold, dry air.

14 A front that forms when a warm air mass is trapped between cold air masses and is forced to rise is a(n)

  a. stationary front. **c.** occluded front.

  b. warm front.   **d.** cold front.

15 A severe storm that forms as a rapidly rotating funnel cloud is called a

  a. hurricane.   **c.** typhoon.

  b. tornado.   **d.** thunderstorm.

16 The lines connecting points of equal air pressure on a weather map are called

  a. contour lines. **c.** isobars.

  b. highs.   **d.** lows.

Short Answer

17 Explain the relationship between condensation and dew point.

18 Describe the conditions along a stationary front.

19 What are the characteristics of an air mass that forms over the Gulf of Mexico?

20 Explain how a hurricane develops.

21 Describe the water cycle, and explain how it affects weather.

22 List the major similarities and differences between hurricanes and tornadoes.

23 Explain how a tornado forms.

24 Describe an interaction between weather and ocean systems.

25 What is a station model? What types of information do station models provide?

26 What type of technology is used to locate and measure the amount of precipitation in an area?

27 List two ways to keep yourself informed during severe weather.

28 Explain why staying away from flood-water is important even when the water is shallow.

CRITICAL THINKING

29 Concept Mapping Use the following terms to create a concept map: *evaporation, relative humidity, water vapor, dew, psychrometer, clouds,* and *fog.*

30 Making Inferences If both the air temperature and the amount of water vapor in the air change, is it possible for the relative humidity to stay the same? Explain.

31 Applying Concepts What can you assume about the amount of water vapor in the air if there is no difference between the wet- and dry-bulb readings of a psychrometer?

32 Identifying Relationships Explain why the concept of relative humidity is important to understanding weather.

INTERPRETING GRAPHICS

Use the weather map below to answer the questions that follow.

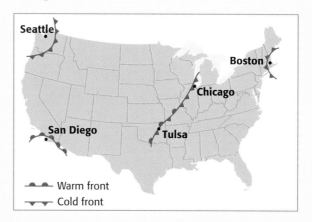

33 Where are thunderstorms most likely to occur? Explain your answer.

34 What are the weather conditions in Tulsa, Oklahoma? Explain your answer.

Standardized Test Preparation

READING

Read each of the passages below. Then, answer the questions that follow each passage.

Passage 1 In May 1997, a springtime tornado <u>wreaked</u> havoc on Jarrell, Texas. The Jarrell tornado was a powerful tornado, whose wind speeds were estimated at more than 410 km/h. The winds of the twister were so strong that they peeled the asphalt from paved roads, stripped fields of corn bare, and destroyed an entire neighborhood. Some tornadoes, such as the one that struck the town of Jarrell, are classified as violent tornadoes. Only 2% of the tornadoes that occur in the United States are categorized as violent tornadoes. Despite the fact that these types of tornadoes do not occur often, 70% of all tornado-related deaths are a result of violent tornadoes.

1. In the passage, what does the word *wreaked* mean?

　　A smelled

　　B caused

　　C prevented

　　D removed

2. Which of the following can be concluded from the passage?

　　F Tornadoes often hit Jarrell, Texas.

　　G Most tornadoes fall into the violent category.

　　H The tornado that hit Jarrell was a rare type of tornado.

　　I Tornadoes always happen during the spring.

3. Which of the following **best** describes a characteristic of violent tornadoes?

　　A Violent tornadoes destroy paved roads.

　　B Violent tornadoes damage crops.

　　C Violent tornadoes damage homes.

　　D Violent tornadoes have extremely strong winds.

Passage 2 Water evaporates into the air from Earth's surface. This water returns to Earth's surface as <u>precipitation</u>. Precipitation is water, in solid or liquid form, that falls from the air to Earth. The four major types of precipitation are rain, snow, sleet, and hail. The most common form of precipitation is rain.

A cloud produces rain when the cloud's water drops become large enough to fall. A raindrop begins as a water droplet that is smaller than the period at the end of this sentence. Before a water drop falls as rain, it must become about 100 times this beginning size. Water drops get larger by joining with other water drops. When the water drops become too heavy, they fall as precipitation.

1. In this passage, what does *precipitation* mean?

　　A acceleration

　　B haste

　　C water that falls from the atmosphere to Earth

　　D separating a substance from a solution as a solid

2. What is the main idea of the second paragraph?

　　F Rain occurs when the water droplets in clouds become large enough to fall.

　　G Raindrops are very small at first.

　　H Water droplets join with other water droplets to become larger.

　　I Rain is a form of precipitation.

3. According to the passage, which step happens last in the formation of precipitation?

　　A Water droplets join.

　　B Water droplets fall to the ground.

　　C Water droplets become heavy.

　　D Water evaporates into the air.

Use each diagram below to answer the question that follows each diagram.

A   B

1. During an experiment, the setup shown in the diagram above is maintained for 72 h. Which of the following is the most likely outcome?

   A Beaker A will hold less water than beaker B will.

   B The amount of water in beaker A and beaker B will stay the same.

   C The amount of water in beaker A and beaker B will change by about the same amount.

   D Beaker B will hold less water than beaker A will.

Amount of Water Vapor That Air Can Hold at Various Temperatures

2. Look at the line graph above. Which statement is consistent with the line graph?

   F The ability of air to hold moisture increases as temperature increases.

   G The ability of air to hold moisture decreases as temperature increases.

   H The ability of air to hold moisture decreases and then increases as temperature increases.

   I The ability of air to hold moisture stays the same regardless of temperature.

Read each question below, and choose the best answer.

1. The speed of light is 3.00×10^8 m/s. What is another way to express this measure?

   A 3,000,000,000 m/s

   B 300,000,000 m/s

   C 3,000,000 m/s

   D 300,000 m/s

2. A hurricane is moving 122 km/h. How long will it take to hit the coast, which is 549 km away?

   F 4.2 h

   G 4.5 h

   H 4.8 h

   I 5.2 h

3. A front is moving 15 km/h in an easterly direction. At that rate, how far will the front travel in 12 h?

   A 0.8 km

   B 1.25 km

   C 27 km

   D 180 km

4. On average, 2 out of every 100 tornadoes are classified as violent tornadoes. If there are 400 tornadoes in 1 year, which is the best prediction of the number of tornadoes that will be classified as violent tornadoes during that year?

   F 2

   G 4

   H 8

   I 16

5. The air temperature in the morning was 27°C. During the day, a front moved into the region and caused the temperature to drop to 18°C. By how many degrees did the temperature drop?

   A 1°C

   B 9°C

   C 11°C

   D 19°C

Standardized Test Preparation

Science in Action

Science Fiction

"All Summer in a Day" by Ray Bradbury

It is raining, just as it has been for seven long years. For the people who live on Venus, constant rain is a fact of life. But today is a special day—a day when the rain stops and the sun shines. This day comes once every seven years. At school, the students have been looking forward to this day for weeks. But Margot longs to see the sun even more than the others do. The reason for her longing makes the other kids jealous, and jealous kids can be cruel. What happens to Margot? Find out by reading Ray Bradbury's "All Summer in a Day" in the *Holt Anthology of Science Fiction*.

Language Arts ACTiViTY

WRITING SKILL What would living in a place where it rained all day and every day for seven years be like? Write a short story describing what your life would be like if you lived in such a place. In your story, describe what you and your friends would do for fun after school.

Weird Science

Can Animals Forecast the Weather?

Before ways of making sophisticated weather forecasts were developed, people observed animals and insects for evidence of changing weather. By observing the behavior of certain animals and insects, you, too, can detect changing weather! For example, did you know that birds fly higher when fair weather is coming? And a robin's song is high pitched in fair weather and low pitched as rain approaches. Ants travel in lines when rain is coming and scatter when the weather is clear. You can tell how hot the weather is by listening for the chirping of crickets—crickets chirp faster as the temperature rises!

Math ACTiViTY

To estimate the outdoor temperature in degrees Fahrenheit, count the number of times that a cricket chirps in 15 s and add 37. If you count 40 chirps in 15 s, what is the estimated temperature?

Cristy Mitchell

Meteorologist Predicting floods, observing a tornado develop inside a storm, watching the growth of a hurricane, and issuing flood warnings are all in a day's work for Cristy Mitchell. As a meteorologist for the National Weather Service, Mitchell spends each working day observing the powerful forces of nature. When asked what made her job interesting, Mitchell replied, "There's nothing like the adrenaline rush you get when you see a tornado coming!"

Perhaps the most familiar field of meteorology is weather forecasting. However, meteorology is also used in air-pollution control, weather control, agricultural planning, and even criminal and civil investigations. Meteorologists also study trends in Earth's climate.

Meteorologists such as Mitchell use high-tech tools—computers and satellites—to collect data. By analyzing such data, Mitchell is able to forecast the weather.

Social Studies ACTiViTY

An almanac is a type of calendar that contains various information, including weather forecasts and astronomical data, for every day of the year. Many people used almanacs before meteorologists started to forecast the weather on TV. Use an almanac from the library to find out what the weather was on the day that you were born.

go.hrw.com

To learn more about these Science in Action topics, visit go.hrw.com and type in the keyword HZ5WEAF.

Current Science

Check out Current Science® articles related to this chapter by visiting go.hrw.com. Just type in the keyword HZ5CS16.

Climate

About the

Would you like to hang out on this ice with the penguins? You probably would not. You would be shivering, and your teeth would be chattering. However, these penguins feel comfortable. They have thick feathers and lots of body fat to keep them warm. Like other animals, penguins have adapted to their climate, which allows them to live comfortably in that climate. So, you will never see one of these penguins living comfortably on a hot, sunny beach in Florida!

PRE-READING ACTIVITY

FOLDNOTES **Pyramid** Before you read the chapter, create the FoldNote entitled "Pyramid" described in the **Study Skills** section of the Appendix. Label the sides of the pyramid with "Tropical climate," "Temperate climate," and "Polar climate." As you read the chapter, define each climate zone, and write characteristics of each climate zone on the appropriate pyramid side.

START-UP ACTIVITY

What's Your Angle?

Try this activity to see how the angle of the sun's solar rays influences temperatures on Earth.

Procedure

1. Place a **lamp** 30 cm from a **globe.**

2. Point the lamp so that the light shines directly on the globe's equator.

3. Using **adhesive putty,** attach a **thermometer** to the globe's equator in a vertical position. Attach **another thermometer** to the globe's North Pole so that the tip points toward the lamp.

4. Record the temperature reading of each thermometer.

5. Turn on the lamp, and let the light shine on the globe for 3 minutes.

6. After 3 minutes, turn off the lamp and record the temperature reading of each thermometer again.

Analysis

1. Was there a difference between the final temperature at the globe's North Pole and the final temperature at the globe's equator? If so, what was it?

2. Explain why the temperature readings at the North Pole and the equator may be different.

What Is Climate?

Suppose you receive a call from a friend who is coming to visit you tomorrow. To decide what clothing to bring, he asks about the current weather in your area.

You step outside to see if rain clouds are in the sky and to check the temperature. But what would you do if your friend asked you about the climate in your area? What is the difference between weather and climate?

Climate Vs. Weather

The main difference between weather and climate is the length of time over which both are measured. **Weather** is the condition of the atmosphere at a particular time. Weather conditions vary from day to day and include temperature, humidity, precipitation, wind, and visibility. **Climate,** on the other hand, is the average weather condition in an area over a long period of time. Climate is mostly determined by two factors—temperature and precipitation. Different parts of the world can have different climates, as shown in **Figure 1.** But why are climates so different? The answer is complicated. It includes factors in addition to temperature and precipitation, such as latitude, wind patterns, mountains, large bodies of water, and ocean currents.

✓ Reading Check How is climate different from weather? (*See the Appendix for answers to Reading Checks.*)

READING WARM-UP

Objectives

● Explain the difference between weather and climate.

● Identify five factors that determine climates.

● Identify the three climate zones of the world.

Terms to Learn

weather	elevation
climate	surface current
latitude	biome
prevailing winds	

READING STRATEGY

Discussion Read this section silently. Write down questions that you have about this section. Discuss your questions in a small group.

Figure 1 *How does the climate in northern Africa differ from the climate where you live?*

North America

Africa

South America

Latitude

Think of the last time you looked at a globe. Do you recall the thin, horizontal lines that circle the globe? Those lines are called lines of latitude. **Latitude** is the distance north or south, measured in degrees, from the equator. In general, the temperature of an area depends on its latitude. The higher the latitude is, the colder the climate tends to be. One of the coldest places on Earth, the North Pole, is 90° north of the equator. However, the equator, at latitude 0°, is usually hot.

As shown in **Figure 2,** if you were to take a trip to different latitudes in the United States, you would experience different climates. For example, the climate in Washington, D.C., which is at a higher latitude, is different from the climate in Texas.

Solar Energy and Latitude

Solar energy, which is energy from the sun, heats the Earth. The amount of direct solar energy a particular area receives is determined by latitude. **Figure 3** shows how the curve of the Earth affects the amount of direct solar energy at different latitudes. Notice that the sun's rays hit the equator directly, at almost a 90° angle. At this angle, a small area of the Earth's surface receives more direct solar energy than at a lesser angle. As a result, that area has high temperatures. However, the sun's rays strike the poles at a lesser angle than they do the equator. At this angle, the same amount of direct solar energy that hits the area at the equator is spread over a larger area at the poles. The result is lower temperatures at the poles.

Figure 2 *Winter in south Texas (top) is different from winter in Washington D.C. (bottom).*

weather the short-term state of the atmosphere, including temperature, humidity, precipitation, wind, and visibility

climate the average weather condition in an area over a long period of time

latitude the distance north or south from the equator; expressed in degrees

Figure 3 The sun's rays strike the Earth's surface at different angles because the surface is curved.

Sun's rays

Equator

Seasons and Latitude

In most places in the United States, the year consists of four seasons. But there are places in the world that do not have such seasonal changes. For example, areas near the equator have approximately the same temperatures and same amount of daylight year-round. Seasons happen because the Earth is tilted on its axis at a 23.5° angle. This tilt affects how much solar energy an area receives as Earth moves around the sun. **Figure 4** shows how latitude and the tilt of the Earth determine the seasons and the length of the day in a particular area.

✓ **Reading Check** Why is there less seasonal change near the equator?

Figure 4 **The Seasons**

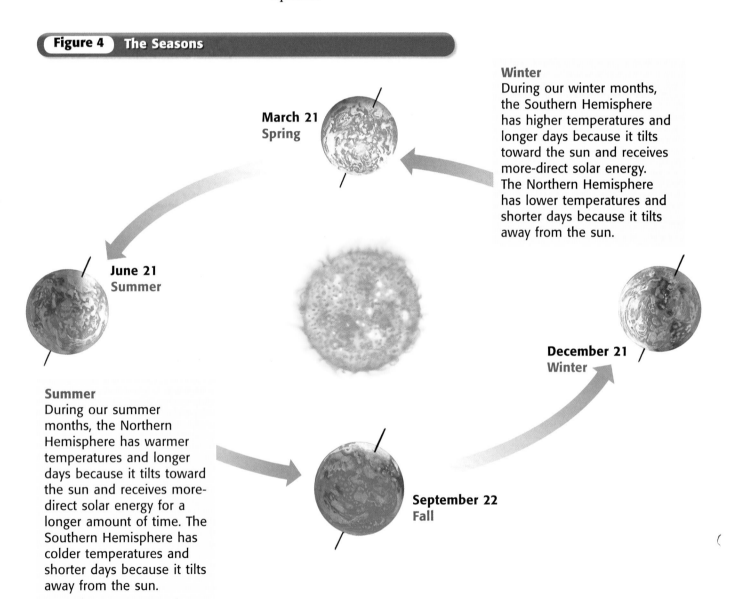

March 21
Spring

June 21
Summer

Winter
During our winter months, the Southern Hemisphere has higher temperatures and longer days because it tilts toward the sun and receives more-direct solar energy. The Northern Hemisphere has lower temperatures and shorter days because it tilts away from the sun.

December 21
Winter

Summer
During our summer months, the Northern Hemisphere has warmer temperatures and longer days because it tilts toward the sun and receives more-direct solar energy for a longer amount of time. The Southern Hemisphere has colder temperatures and shorter days because it tilts away from the sun.

September 22
Fall

Figure 5   The Circulation of Warm Air and Cold Air

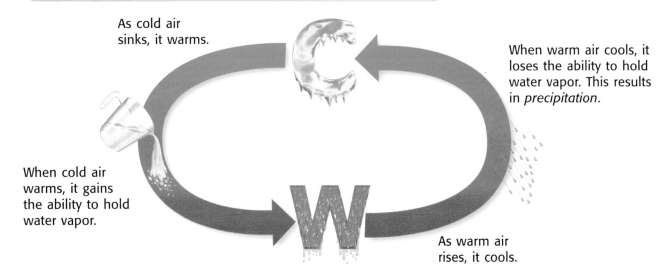

As cold air sinks, it warms.

When warm air cools, it loses the ability to hold water vapor. This results in *precipitation*.

When cold air warms, it gains the ability to hold water vapor.

As warm air rises, it cools.

Prevailing Winds

Winds that blow mainly from one direction are **prevailing winds**. Before you learn how the prevailing winds affect climate, take a look at **Figure 5** to learn about some of the basic properties of air.

Prevailing winds affect the amount of precipitation that a region receives. If the prevailing winds form from warm air, they may carry moisture. If the prevailing winds form from cold air, they will probably be dry.

The amount of moisture in prevailing winds is also affected by whether the winds blow across land or across a large body of water. Winds that travel across large bodies of water absorb moisture. Winds that travel across land tend to be dry. Even if a region borders the ocean, the area might be dry. **Figure 6** shows an example of how dry prevailing winds can cause the land to be dry though the land is near an ocean.

prevailing winds winds that blow mainly from one direction during a given period

A Cool Breeze

1. Hold a **thermometer** next to the top edge of a **cup** of **water** containing two **ice cubes**. Record the temperature next to the cup.

2. Have your lab partner fan the surface of the cup with a **paper fan**. Record the temperature again. Has the temperature changed? Why or why not?

Sahara

Prevailing winds

Africa

Figure 6 *The Sahara Desert, in northern Africa, is extremely dry because of the dry prevailing winds that blow across the continent.*

School to Home

Using a Map

With your parent, use a physical map to locate the mountain ranges in the United States. Does climate vary from one side of a mountain range to the other? If so, what does this tell you about the climatic conditions on either side of the mountain? From what direction are the prevailing winds blowing?

Mountains

Mountains can influence an area's climate by affecting both temperature and precipitation. Kilimanjaro is the tallest mountain in Africa. It has snow-covered peaks year-round, even though it is only about 3° (320 km) south of the equator. Temperatures on Kilimanjaro and in other mountainous areas are affected by elevation. **Elevation** is the height of surface landforms above sea level. As the elevation increases, the ability of air to transfer energy from the ground to the atmosphere decreases. Therefore, as elevation increases, temperature decreases.

Mountains also affect the climate of nearby areas by influencing the distribution of precipitation. **Figure 7** shows how the climates on two sides of a mountain can be very different.

Reading Check Why does the atmosphere become cooler at higher elevations?

Figure 7 *Mountains block the prevailing winds and affect the climate on the other side.*

The Wet Side
Mountains force air to rise. The air cools as it rises, releasing moisture as snow or rain. The land on the windward side of the mountain is usually green and lush because the wind releases its moisture.

The Dry Side
After dry air crosses the mountain, the air begins to sink. As the air sinks, it is warmed and absorbs moisture. The dry conditions created by the sinking, warm air usually produce a desert. This side of the mountain is in a *rain shadow*.

Large Bodies of Water

Large bodies of water can influence an area's climate. Water absorbs and releases heat slower than land does. Because of this quality, water helps to moderate the temperatures of the land around it. So, sudden or extreme temperature changes rarely take place on land near large bodies of water. For example, the state of Michigan, which is surrounded by the Great Lakes, has more-moderate temperatures than other places at the same latitude. The lakes also increase the moisture content of the air, which leads to heavy snowfall in the winter. This "lake effect" can cause 350 inches of snow to drop in one year!

Ocean Currents

The circulation of ocean surface currents has a large effect on an area's climate. **Surface currents** are streamlike movements of water that occur at or near the surface of the ocean. **Figure 8** shows the pattern of the major ocean surface currents.

As surface currents move, they carry warm or cool water to different locations. The surface temperature of the water affects the temperature of the air above it. Warm currents heat the surrounding air and cause warmer temperatures. Cool currents cool the surrounding air and cause cooler temperatures. The Gulf Stream current carries warm water northward off the east coast of North America and past Iceland. Iceland is an island country located just below the Arctic Circle. The warm water from the Gulf Stream heats the surrounding air and creates warmer temperatures in southern Iceland. Iceland experiences milder temperatures than Greenland, its neighboring island. Greenland's climate is cooler because Greenland is not influenced by the Gulf Stream.

elevation the height of an object above sea level

surface current a horizontal movement of ocean water that is caused by wind and that occurs at or near the ocean's surface

☑ **Reading Check** Why does Iceland experience milder temperatures than Greenland?

Figure 8 *The red arrows represent the movement of warm surface currents. The blue arrows represent the movement of cold surface currents.*

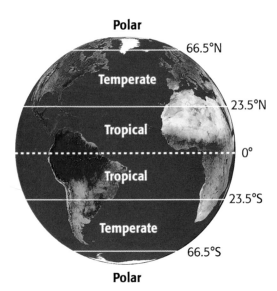

Polar

66.5°N

Temperate

23.5°N

Tropical

0°

Tropical

23.5°S

Temperate

66.5°S

Polar

Figure 9 *The three major climate zones are determined by latitude.*

biome a large region characterized by a specific type of climate and certain types of plant and animal communities

Climates of the World

Have you seen any polar bears in your neighborhood lately? You probably have not. That's because polar bears live only in very cold arctic regions. Why are the animals in one part of the world so different from the animals in other parts? One of the differences has to do with climate. Plants and animals that have adapted to one climate may not be able to live in another climate. For example, frogs would not be able to survive at the North Pole.

Climate Zones

The Earth's three major climate zones—tropical, temperate, and polar—are shown in **Figure 9.** Each zone has a temperature range that relates to its latitude. However, in each of these zones, there are several types of climates because of differences in the geography and the amount of precipitation. Because of the various climates in each zone, there are different biomes in each zone. A **biome** is a large region characterized by a specific type of climate and certain types of plant and animal communities. **Figure 10** shows the distribution of the Earth's land biomes. In which biome do you live?

✓ *Reading Check* What factors distinguish one biome from another biome?

Figure 10 The Earth's Land Biomes

Tundra
Taiga
Temperate forest
Tropical rain forest

Temperate grassland
Tropical savanna
Temperate desert
Tropical desert

Chaparral
Mountains

Equator

SECTION Review

Summary

- Weather is the condition of the atmosphere at a particular time. This condition includes temperature, humidity, precipitation, wind, and visibility.

- Climate is the average weather condition in an area over a long period of time.

- The higher the latitude, the cooler the climate.

- Prevailing winds affect the climate of an area by the amount of moisture they carry.

- Mountains influence an area's climate by affecting both temperature and precipitation.

- Large bodies of water and ocean currents influence the climate of an area by affecting the temperature of the air over the water.

- The three climate zones of the world are the tropical zone, the temperate zone, and the polar zone.

Using Key Terms

1. In your own words, write a definition for each of the following terms: *weather, climate, latitude, prevailing winds, elevation, surface currents,* and *biome.*

Understanding Key Ideas

2. Which of the following affects climate by causing the air to rise?
   a. mountains
   b. ocean currents
   c. large bodies of water
   d. latitude

3. What is the difference between weather and climate?

4. List five factors that determine climates.

5. Explain why there is a difference in climate between areas at 0° latitude and areas at 45° latitude.

6. List the three climate zones of the world.

Critical Thinking

7. **Analyzing Relationships** How would seasons be different if the Earth did not tilt on its axis?

8. **Applying Concepts** During what months does Australia have summer? Explain.

Interpreting Graphics

Use the map below to answer the questions that follow.

9. Would you expect the area that the arrow points to to be moist or dry? Explain your answer.

10. Describe how the climate of the same area would change if the prevailing winds traveled from the opposite direction. Explain how you came to this conclusion.

For a variety of links related to this chapter, go to www.scilinks.org

Topic: What Is Climate?
SciLinks code: HSM1659

119

The Tropics

Where in the world do you think you could find a flying dragon gliding above you from one treetop to the next?

Don't worry. This flying dragon, or tree lizard, is only about 20 cm long, and it eats only insects. With winglike skin flaps, the flying dragon can glide from one treetop to the next. But, you won't find this kind of animal in the United States. These flying dragons live in Southeast Asia, which is in the tropical zone.

The Tropical Zone

The region that surrounds the equator and that extends from about 23.5° north latitude to 23.5° south latitude is called the **tropical zone.** The tropical zone is also known as the Tropics. Latitudes in the tropical zone receive the most solar radiation. Temperatures are therefore usually hot, except at high elevations.

Within the tropical zone, there are three major types of biomes—tropical rain forest, tropical desert, and tropical savanna. These three biomes have high temperatures. But they differ in the amount of precipitation, soil characteristics, vegetation, and kinds of animals. **Figure 1** shows the distribution of these biomes.

✓ **Reading Check** At what latitudes would you find the tropical zone? (*See the Appendix for answers to Reading Checks.*)

Figure 1 Biomes of the Tropical Zone

23.5° N
0°
23.5° S

Tropical
Tropical

Equator

- Tropical rain forest
- Tropical savanna
- Tropical desert

Tropical Rain Forests

Tropical rain forests are always warm and wet. Because they are located near the equator, they receive strong sunlight year-round. So, there is little difference between seasons in tropical rain forests.

Tropical rain forests contain the greatest number of animal and plant species of any biome. Animals found in tropical rain forests include monkeys, parrots, tree frogs, tigers, and leopards. Plants found in tropical rain forests include mahogany, vines, ferns, and bamboo. But in spite of the lush vegetation, shown in **Figure 2,** the soil in rain forests is poor. The rapid decay of plants and animals returns nutrients to the soil. But these nutrients are quickly absorbed and used by the plants. The nutrients that are not immediately used by the plants are washed away by the heavy rains. The soil is left thin and nutrient poor.

Figure 2 *In tropical rain forests, many of the trees form above-ground roots that provide extra support for the trees in the thin, nutrient-poor soil.*

tropical zone the region that surrounds the equator and that extends from about 23.5° north latitude to 23.5° south latitude

CONNECTION TO Social Studies

WRITING SKILL **Living in the Tropics** The tropical climate is very hot and humid. People who live in the Tropics have had to adapt to feel comfortable in that climate. For example, in the country of Samoa, some people live in homes that have no walls, which are called *fales.* Fales have only a roof, which provides shade. The openness of the home allows cool breezes to flow through the home. Research other countries in the Tropics. See how the climate influences the way the people live in those countries. Then, in your **science journal,** describe how the people's lifestyle helps them adapt to the climate.

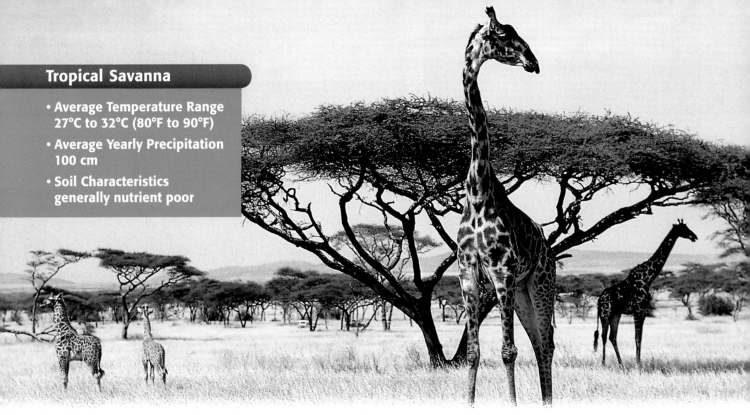

Tropical Savanna

- **Average Temperature Range 27°C to 32°C (80°F to 90°F)**
- **Average Yearly Precipitation 100 cm**
- **Soil Characteristics generally nutrient poor**

Figure 3 *The grass of a tropical savanna can be as tall as 5 m.*

Tropical Savannas

Tropical savannas, or grasslands, are composed of tall grasses and a few scattered trees. The climate is usually very warm. Tropical savannas have a dry season that lasts four to eight months and that is followed by short periods of rain. Savanna soils are generally nutrient poor. However, grass fires, which are common during the dry season, leave the soils nutrient enriched. An African savanna is shown in **Figure 3.**

Many plants have adapted to fire and use it to promote development. For example, some species need fire to break open their seeds' outer skin. Only after this skin is broken can each seed grow. For other species, heat from the fire triggers the plants to drop their seeds into the newly enriched soil.

Animals that live in tropical savannas include giraffes, lions, crocodiles, and elephants. Plants include tall grasses, trees, and thorny shrubs.

CONNECTION TO
Biology

WRITING SKILL **Animal and Plant Adaptations** Animals and plants adapt to the climate in which they live. These adaptations cause certain animals and plants to be unique to particular biomes. For example, the camel, which is unique to the desert, has adapted to going for long periods of time without water. Research other animals or plants that live in the Tropics. Then, in your **science journal,** describe the characteristics that help them survive in the Tropics.

Tropical Deserts

A desert is an area that receives less than 25 cm of rainfall per year. Because of this low yearly rainfall, deserts are the driest places on Earth. Desert plants, such as those shown in **Figure 4,** are adapted to survive in places that have little water. Animals such as rats, lizards, snakes, and scorpions have also adapted to survive in these deserts.

There are two kinds of deserts—hot deserts and cold deserts. Hot deserts are caused by cool, sinking air masses. Many hot deserts, such as the Sahara, in Africa, are tropical deserts. Daily temperatures in tropical deserts often vary from very hot daytime temperatures (50°C) to cool nighttime temperatures (20°C). Because of the dryness of deserts, the soil is poor in organic matter, which is needed for plants to grow.

Reading Check What animals would you find in a tropical desert?

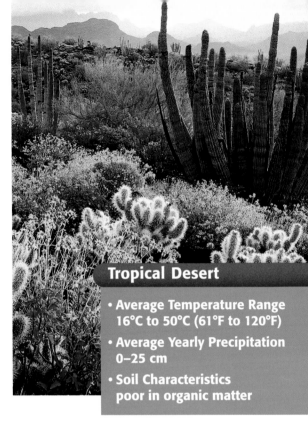

Tropical Desert

• **Average Temperature Range**
  16°C to 50°C (61°F to 120°F)

• **Average Yearly Precipitation**
  0–25 cm

• **Soil Characteristics**
  poor in organic matter

Figure 4 *Plants such as succulents have fleshy stems and leaves to store water.*

SECTION Review

Summary

● The tropical zone is located around the equator, between 23.5° north and 23.5° south latitude.

● Temperatures are usually hot in the tropical zone.

● Tropical rain forests are warm and wet. They have the greatest number of plant and animal species of any biome.

● Tropical savannas are grasslands that have a dry season.

● Tropical deserts are hot and receive little rain.

Using Key Terms

1. In your own words, write a definition for the term *tropical zone*.

Understanding Key Ideas

2. Which of the following tropical biomes has less than 50 cm of precipitation a year?
   a. rain forest   c. grassland
   b. desert   d. savanna

3. What are the soil characteristics of a tropical rain forest?

4. In what ways have savanna vegetation adapted to fire?

Math Skills

5. Suppose that in a tropical savanna, the temperature was recorded every hour for 4 h. The recorded temperatures were 27°C, 28°C, 29°C, and 29°C. Calculate the average temperature for this 4 h period.

Critical Thinking

6. **Analyzing Relationships** How do the tropical biomes differ?

7. **Making Inferences** How would you expect the adaptations of a plant in a tropical rain forest to differ from the adaptations of a tropical desert plant? Explain.

8. **Analyzing Data** An area has a temperature range of 30°C to 40°C and received 10 cm of rain this year. What biome is this area in?

SCILINKS.

NSTA
Developed and maintained by the
National Science Teachers Association

For a variety of links related to this chapter, go to www.scilinks.org

Topic: Climates of the World
SciLinks code: HSM0302

Temperate and Polar Zones

Which season is your favorite? Do you like the change of colors in the fall, the flowers in the spring, or do you prefer the hot days of summer?

READING WARM-UP

Objectives

- Locate and describe the temperate zone and the polar zone.
- Describe the different biomes found in the temperate zone and the polar zone.
- Explain what a microclimate is.

Terms to Learn

temperate zone
polar zone
microclimate

READING STRATEGY

Reading Organizer As you read this section, create an outline of the section. Use the headings from the section in your outline.

If you live in the continental United States, chances are you live in a biome that experiences seasonal change. Seasonal change is one characteristic of the temperate zone. Most of the continental United States is in the temperate zone, which is the climate zone between the Tropics and the polar zone.

The Temperate Zone

The climate zone between the Tropics and the polar zone is the **temperate zone.** Latitudes in the temperate zone receive less solar energy than latitudes in the Tropics do. Because of this, temperatures in the temperate zone tend to be lower than in the Tropics. Some biomes in the temperate zone have a mild change of seasons. Other biomes in the country can experience freezing temperatures in the winter and very hot temperatures in the summer. The temperate zone consists of the following four biomes—temperate forest, temperate grassland, chaparral, and temperate desert. Although these biomes have four distinct seasons, the biomes differ in temperature and precipitation and have different plants and animals. **Figure 1** shows the distribution of the biomes found in the temperate zone.

✓ **Reading Check** Where is the temperate zone? (*See the Appendix for answers to Reading Checks.*)

Figure 1 **Biomes of the Temperate Zone**

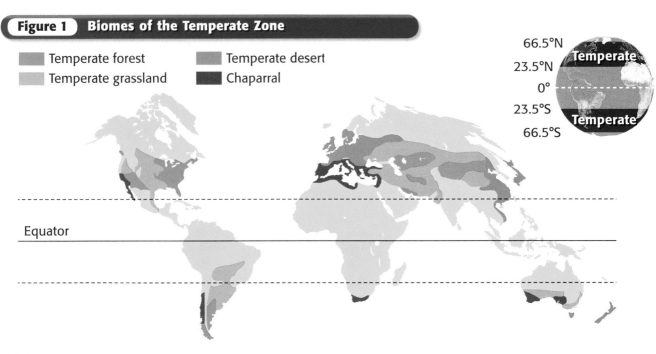

- Temperate forest
- Temperate grassland
- Temperate desert
- Chaparral

66.5°N
23.5°N
0°
23.5°S
66.5°S
Temperate
Temperate

Equator

Temperate Forest

- Average Temperature Range
  0°C to 28°C (32°F to 82°F)
- Average Yearly Precipitation
  76 to 250 cm
- Soil Characteristics
  very fertile, organically rich

Temperate Forests

The temperate forest biomes tend to have high amounts of rainfall and seasonal temperature differences. Summers are often warm, and winters are often cold. Animals such as deer, bears, and foxes live in temperate forests. **Figure 2** shows deciduous trees in a temperate forest. *Deciduous* describes trees that lose their leaves at the end of the growing season. The soils in deciduous forests are usually fertile because of the high organic content from decaying leaves that drop every winter. Another type of tree found in the temperate forest is the evergreen. *Evergreens* are trees that keep their leaves year-round.

Figure 2 *Deciduous trees have leaves that change color and drop when temperatures become cold.*

temperate zone the climate zone between the Tropics and the polar zone

Temperate Grasslands

Temperate grasslands, such as those shown in **Figure 3,** are regions that receive too little rainfall for trees to grow. This biome has warm summers and cold winters. Examples of animals that are found in temperate grasslands include bison in North America and kangaroo in Australia. Grasses are the most common kind of plant found in this biome. Because grasslands have the most-fertile soils of all biomes, much of the grassland has been plowed to make room for croplands.

Temperate Grassland

- Average Temperature Range
  −6°C to 26°C (21°F to 78°F)
- Average Yearly Precipitation
  38 to 76 cm
- Soil Characteristics
  most-fertile soils of all biomes

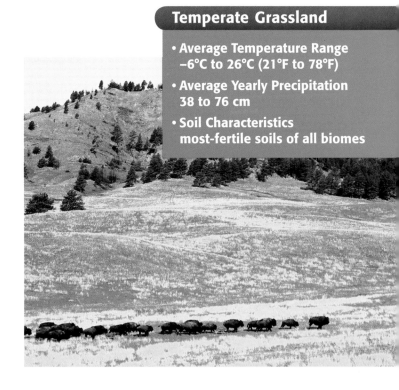

Figure 3 *At one time, the world's grasslands covered about 42% of Earth's total land surface. Today, they occupy only about 12% of the Earth's total land surface.*

Chaparral

- **Average Temperature Range**
  11°C to 26°C (51°F to 78°F)
- **Average Yearly Precipitation**
  48 to 56 cm
- **Soil Characteristics**
  rocky, nutrient-poor soils

Figure 4 *Some plant species found in chaparral require fire to reproduce.*

Figure 5 *The Great Basin Desert is in the rain shadow of the Sierra Nevada.*

Chaparrals

Chaparral regions, as shown in **Figure 4,** have cool, wet winters and hot, dry summers. Animals, such as coyotes and mountain lions live in chaparrals. The vegetation is mainly evergreen shrubs. These shrubs are short, woody plants with thick, waxy leaves. The waxy leaves are adaptations that help prevent water loss in dry conditions. These shrubs grow in rocky, nutrient-poor soil. Like tropical-savanna vegetation, chaparral vegetation has adapted to fire. In fact, some plants, such as chamise, can grow back from their roots after a fire.

Temperate Deserts

The temperate desert biomes, like the one shown in **Figure 5,** tend to be cold deserts. Like all deserts, cold deserts receive less than 25 cm of precipitation yearly. Examples of animals that live in temperate deserts are lizards, snakes, bats, and toads. And the types of plants found in temperate deserts include cacti, shrubs, and thorny trees.

Temperate deserts can be very hot in the daytime. But, unlike hot deserts, they are often very cold at night. This large change in temperature between day and night is caused by low humidity and cloudless skies. These conditions allow for a large amount of energy to heat the Earth's surface during the day. However, these same characteristics allow the energy to escape at night. This causes temperatures to drop. You probably rarely think of snow and deserts together. But temperate deserts often receive light snow during the winter.

✓ Reading Check Why are temperate deserts cold at night?

Temperate Desert

- **Average Temperature Range**
  1°C to 50°C (34°F to 120°F)
- **Average Yearly Precipitation**
  0 to 25 cm
- **Soil Characteristics**
  poor in organic matter

Figure 6 Biomes of the Polar Zone

Polar
66.5°N

0°

66.5°S
Polar

Equator

- Tundra
- Taiga

The Polar Zone

The climate zone located at the North or South Pole and its surrounding area is called the **polar zone.** Polar climates have the coldest average temperatures of all the climate zones. Temperatures in the winter stay below freezing. The temperatures during the summer remain cool. **Figure 6** shows the distribution of the biomes found in the polar zone.

polar zone the North or South Pole and its surrounding area

Tundra

The tundra biome, as shown in **Figure 7,** has long, cold winters with almost 24 hours of night. It also has short, cool summers with almost 24 hours of daylight. In the summer, only the top meter of soil thaws. Underneath the thawed soil lies a permanently frozen layer of soil, called *permafrost*. This frozen layer prevents the water in the thawed soil from draining. Because of the poor drainage, the upper soil layer is muddy. This muddy layer of soil makes a great breeding ground for insects, such as mosquitoes. Many birds migrate to the tundra during the summer to feed on the insects. Other animals that live in the tundra are caribou, reindeer, and polar bears. Plants in this biome include mosses and lichens.

Figure 7 *In the tundra, mosses and lichens cover rocks.*

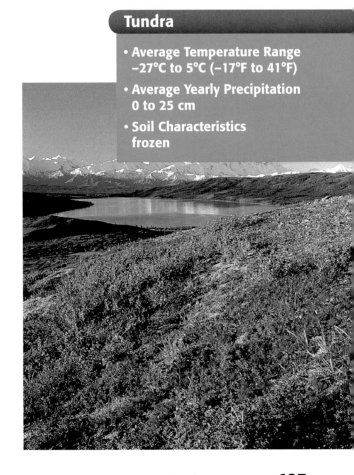

Tundra

- **Average Temperature Range** −27°C to 5°C (−17°F to 41°F)
- **Average Yearly Precipitation** 0 to 25 cm
- **Soil Characteristics** frozen

Taiga

- **Average Temperature Range**
  −10°C to 15°C (14°F to 59°F)
- **Average Yearly Precipitation**
  40 to 61 cm
- **Soil Characteristics**
  acidic

Figure 8 *The taiga, such as this one in Washington, have mostly evergreens for trees.*

microclimate the climate of a small area

Taiga (Northern Coniferous Forest)

Just south of the tundra lies the taiga biome. The taiga, as shown in **Figure 8,** has long, cold winters and short, warm summers. Animals commonly found here are moose, bears, and rabbits. The majority of the trees are evergreen needle-leaved trees called *conifers,* such as pine, spruce, and fir trees. The needles and flexible branches allow these trees to shed heavy snow before they can be damaged. Conifer needles are made of acidic substances. When the needles die and fall to the soil, they make the soil acidic. Most plants cannot grow in acidic soil. Because of the acidic soil, the forest floor is bare except for some mosses and lichens.

Microclimates

The climate and the biome of a particular place can also be influenced by local conditions. **Microclimate** is the climate of a small area. The alpine biome is a cold biome found on mountains all around the world. The alpine biome can even be found on mountains in the Tropics! How is this possible? The high elevation affects the area's climate and therefore its biome. As the elevation increases, the air's ability to transfer heat from the ground to the atmosphere by conduction decreases, which causes temperatures to decrease. In winter, the temperatures are below freezing. In summer, average temperatures range from 10°C to 15°C. Plants and animals have had to develop special adaptations to live in this severe climate.

Cities

Cities are also microclimates. In a city, temperatures can be 1°C to 2°C warmer than the surrounding rural areas. Have you ever walked barefoot on a black asphalt street on a hot summer day? Doing so burns your feet because buildings and pavement made of dark materials absorb solar radiation instead of reflecting it. There is also less vegetation in a city to take in the sun's rays. This absorption and re-radiation of heat by buildings and pavement heats the surrounding air. In turn, the temperatures rise.

✓ Reading Check Why do cities have higher temperatures than the surrounding rural areas?

CONNECTION TO Physics

Hot Roofs! Scientists studied roofs on a sunny day when the air temperature was 13°C. They recorded roof temperatures ranging from 18°C to 61°C depending on color and material of the roof. Place thermometers on outside objects that are made of different types of materials and that are different colors. Please stay off the roof! Is there a difference in temperatures?

ACTIVITY

SECTION Review

Summary

- The temperate zone is located between the Tropics and the polar zone. It has moderate temperatures.

- Temperate forests, temperate grasslands, and temperate deserts are biomes in the temperate zone.

- The polar zone includes the North or South Pole and its surrounding area. The polar zone has the coldest temperatures.

- The tundra and the taiga are biomes within the polar zone.

Using Key Terms

1. In your own words, write a definition for the term *microclimate*.

Complete each of the following sentences by choosing the correct term from the word bank.

> temperate zone   polar zone   microclimate

2. The coldest temperatures are found in the ___.

3. The ___ has moderate temperatures.

Understanding Key Ideas

4. Which of the following biomes has the driest climate?
   a. temperate forests
   b. temperate grasslands
   c. chaparrals
   d. temperate deserts

5. Explain why the temperate zone has lower temperatures than the Tropics.

6. Describe how the latitude of the polar zone affects the climate in that area.

7. Explain why the tundra can sometimes experience 24 hours of daylight or 24 hours of night.

8. How do conifers make the soil they grow in too acidic for other plants to grow?

Math Skills

9. Texas has an area of about 700,000 square kilometers. Grasslands compose about 20% of this area. About how many square kilometers of grassland are there in Texas?

Critical Thinking

10. **Identifying Relationships** Which biome would be more suitable for growing crops, temperate forest or taiga? Explain.

11. **Making Inferences** Describe the types of animals and vegetation you might find in the Alpine biome.

SCLINKS

NSTA
Developed and maintained by the National Science Teachers Association

For a variety of links related to this chapter, go to www.scilinks.org

Topic: Modeling Earth's Climate
SciLinks code: HSM0976

Changes in Climate

As you have probably noticed, the weather changes from day to day. Sometimes, the weather can change several times in one day! But have you ever noticed the climate change?

On Saturday, your morning baseball game was canceled because of rain, but by that afternoon the sun was shining. Now, think about the climate where you live. You probably haven't noticed a change in climate, because climates change slowly. What causes climatic change? Studies indicate that human activity may cause climatic change. However, natural factors also can influence changes in the climate.

Ice Ages

The geologic record indicates that the Earth's climate has been much colder than it is today. In fact, much of the Earth was covered by sheets of ice during certain periods. An **ice age** is a period during which ice collects in high latitudes and moves toward lower latitudes. Scientists have found evidence of many major ice ages throughout the Earth's geologic history. The most recent ice age began about 2 million years ago.

Glacial Periods

During an ice age, there are periods of cold and periods of warmth. These periods are called glacial and interglacial periods. During *glacial periods,* the enormous sheets of ice advance. As they advance, they get bigger and cover a larger area, as shown in **Figure 1.** Because a large amount of water is frozen during glacial periods, the sea level drops.

ice age a long period of climate cooling during which ice sheets cover large areas of Earth's surface; also known as a glacial period

Figure 1 *During glacial periods, ice sheets (as shown in light blue), cover a larger portion of the Earth.*

Interglacial Periods

Warmer times that happen between glacial periods are called *interglacial periods*. During an interglacial period, the ice begins to melt and the sea level rises again. The last interglacial period began 10,000 years ago and is still happening. Why do these periods occur? Will the Earth have another glacial period in the future? These questions have been debated by scientists for the past 200 years.

Motions of the Earth

There are many theories about the causes of ice ages. Each theory tries to explain the gradual cooling that begins an ice age. This cooling leads to the development of large ice sheets that periodically cover large areas of the Earth's surface.

The *Milankovitch theory* explains why an ice age isn't just one long cold spell. Instead, the ice age alternates between cold and warm periods. Milutin Milankovitch, a Yugoslavian scientist, proposed that changes in the Earth's orbit and in the tilt of the Earth's axis cause ice ages. His theory is shown in **Figure 2.** In a 100,000 year period, the Earth's orbit changes from elliptical to circular. This changes the Earth's distance from the sun. In turn, it changes the temperature on Earth. Changes in the tilt of the Earth also influence the climate. The more the Earth is tilted, the closer the poles are to the sun.

✓ Reading Check What are the two things Milankovitch says causes ice ages? (*See the Appendix for answers to Reading Checks.*)

INTERNET ACTIVITY

For another activity related to this chapter, go to **go.hrw.com** and type in the keyword **HZ5CLMW.**

Figure 2 **The Milankovitch Theory**

❶ Over a period of 100,000 years, the Earth's orbit slowly changes from a more circular shape to a more elliptical shape and back again. When Earth's orbit is elliptical, Earth receives more energy from the sun. When its orbit is more circular, Earth receives less energy from the sun.

❷ Over a period of 41,000 years, the tilt of the Earth's axis varies between 22.2° and 24.5°. When the tilt is at 24.5°, the poles receive more solar energy.

❸ The Earth's axis traces a complete circle every 26,000 years. The circular motion of the Earth's axis determines the time of year that the Earth is closest to the sun.

Figure 3 *Much of Pangaea—the part that is now Africa, South America, India, Antarctica, Australia, and Saudi Arabia— was covered by continental ice sheets.*

Plate Tectonics

The Earth's climate is further influenced by plate tectonics and continental drift. One theory proposes that ice ages happen when the continents are positioned closer to the polar regions. About 250 million years ago, all the continents were connected near the South Pole in one giant landmass called *Pangaea,* as shown in **Figure 3.** During this time, ice covered a large area of the Earth's surface. As Pangaea broke apart, the continents moved toward the equator, and the ice age ended. During the last ice age, many large landmasses were positioned in the polar zones. Antarctica, northern North America, Europe, and Asia were covered by large sheets of ice.

Volcanic Eruptions

Many natural factors can affect global climate. Catastrophic events, such as volcanic eruptions, can influence climate. Volcanic eruptions send large amounts of dust, ash, and smoke into the atmosphere. Once in the atmosphere, the dust, smoke, and ash particles act as a shield. This shield blocks the sun's rays, which causes the Earth to cool. **Figure 4** shows how dust particles from a volcanic eruption block the sun.

✓ Reading Check How can volcanoes change the climate?

Figure 4 **Volcanic Dust in the Atmosphere**

Volcanic eruptions, such as the 1980 eruption of Mount St. Helens, as shown at right, produce dust that reflects sunlight.

Sun's rays

Mount St. Helens

Dust layer

Atmosphere

Figure 5 *Some scientists believe that a 10 km chunk of rock smashed into the Earth 65 million years ago, which caused the climatic change that resulted in the extinction of dinosaurs.*

Asteroid Impact

Imagine a rock the size of a car flying in from outer space and crashing in your neighborhood. This rock, like the one shown in **Figure 5,** is called an asteroid. An *asteroid* is a small, rocky object that orbits the sun. Sometimes, asteroids enter our atmosphere and crash into the Earth. What would happen if an asteroid 1 km wide, which is more than half a mile long, hit the Earth? Scientists believe that if an asteroid this big hit the Earth, it could change the climate of the entire world.

When a large piece of rock slams into the Earth, it causes debris to shoot into the atmosphere. *Debris* is dust and smaller rocks. This debris can block some of the sunlight and thermal energy. This would lower average temperatures, which would change the climate. Plants wouldn't get the sunlight they needed to grow, and animals would find surviving difficult. Scientists believe such an event is what caused dinosaurs to become extinct 65 million years ago when a 10 km asteroid slammed into the Earth and changed the Earth's climate.

The Sun's Cycle

Some changes in the climate can be linked to changes in the sun. You might think that the sun always stays the same. However, the sun follows an 11-year cycle. During this cycle, the sun changes from a solar maximum to a solar minimum. During a solar minimum, the sun produces a low percentage of high-energy radiation. But when the sun is at its solar maximum, it produces a large percentage of high-energy radiation. This increase in high-energy radiation warms the winds in the atmosphere. This change in turn affects climate patterns around the world.

CONNECTION TO Astronomy

Sunspots Sunspots are dark areas on the sun's surface. The number of sunspots changes with the sun's cycle. When the cycle is at a solar maximum, there are many sunspots. When the cycle is at a solar minimum, there are fewer sunspots. If the number of sunspots was low in 1997, in what year will the next low point in the cycle happen?

1. The round-trip distance from your home to school is 20 km.

2. You traveled from home to school and from school to home 23 times in a month.

3. The vehicle in which you took your trips travels 30 km/gal.

4. If burning 1 gal of gasoline produces 9 kg of carbon dioxide, how much carbon dioxide did the vehicle release during the month?

global warming a gradual increase in the average global temperature

greenhouse effect the warming of the surface and lower atmosphere of Earth that occurs when carbon dioxide, water vapor, and other gases in the air absorb and trap thermal energy

Global Warming

A gradual increase in the average global temperature that is due to a higher concentration of gases, such as carbon dioxide in the atmosphere, is called **global warming.** To understand how global warming works, you must first learn about the greenhouse effect.

Greenhouse Effect

The Earth's natural heating process, in which gases in the atmosphere trap thermal energy, is called the **greenhouse effect.** The car in **Figure 6** shows how the greenhouse effect works. The car's windows stop most of the thermal energy from escaping, and the inside of the car gets hot. On Earth, instead of glass stopping the thermal energy, atmospheric gases absorb the thermal energy. When this happens, the thermal energy stays in the atmosphere and keeps the Earth warm. Many scientists believe that the rise in global temperatures is due to an increase of carbon dioxide, an atmospheric gas. Most evidence shows that the increase in carbon dioxide is caused by the burning of fossil fuels.

Another factor that may add to global warming is the clearing of forests. In many countries, forests are being burned to clear land for farming. Burning of the forests releases more carbon dioxide. Because plants use carbon dioxide to make food, destroying the trees decreases a natural way of removing carbon dioxide from the atmosphere.

Figure 6 *Sunlight streams into the car through the clear, glass windows. The seats absorb the radiant energy and change it into thermal energy. The energy is then trapped in the car.*

Consequences of Global Warming

Many scientists think that if the global temperature continues to rise, the ice caps will melt and cause flooding. Melted ice-caps would raise the sea level and flood low-lying areas, such as the coasts.

Areas that receive little rainfall, such as deserts, might receive even less because of increased evaporation. Desert animals and plants would find surviving harder. Warmer and drier climates could harm crops in the Midwest of the United States. But farther north, such as in Canada, weather conditions for farming could improve.

✓ Reading Check How would warmer temperatures affect deserts?

SCHOOL to HOME

Reducing Pollution
Your city just received a warning from the Environmental Protection Agency for exceeding the automobile fuel emissions standards. Discuss with your parent ways that the city can reduce the amount of automobile emissions.

SECTION Review

Summary

- The Earth's climate experiences glacial and interglacial periods.
- The Milankovitch theory states that the Earth's climate changes as its orbit and the tilt of its axis change.
- Climate changes can be caused by volcanic eruptions, asteroid impact, the sun's cycle, and by global warming.
- Excess carbon dioxide is believed to contribute to global warming.

Using Key Terms

1. Use the following term in a sentence: *ice age*.

2. In your own words, write a definition for each of the following terms: *global warming* and *greenhouse effect*.

Understanding Key Ideas

3. Describe the possible causes of an ice age.

4. Which of the following can cause a change in the climate due to dust particles?
   a. volcanic eruptions
   b. plate tectonics
   c. solar cycles
   d. ice ages

5. How has the Earth's climate changed over time?

6. What might have caused the Earth's climate to change?

7. Which period of an ice age are we in currently? Explain.

8. Explain how the greenhouse effect warms the Earth.

Math Skills

9. After a volcanic eruption, the average temperature in a region dropped from 30° to 18°C. By how many degrees Celsius did the temperature drop?

Critical Thinking

10. **Analyzing Relationships** How will the warming of the Earth affect agriculture in different parts of the world? Explain.

11. **Predicting Consequences** How would deforestation (the cutting of trees) affect global warming?

SCILINKS.

NSTA
Developed and maintained by the
National Science Teachers Association

For a variety of links related to this chapter, go to www.scilinks.org

Topic: Changes in Climate
SciLinks code: HSM0252

Skills Practice Lab

OBJECTIVES

Interpret data in a climatograph.

Identify the biome for each climatograph.

- Tundra
- Taiga
- Temperate forest
- Tropical rain forest
- Temperate grassland
- Tropical savanna
- Temperate desert
- Tropical desert
- Chaparral
- Mountains

Biome Business

You have just been hired as an assistant to a world-famous botanist. You have been provided with climatographs for three biomes. A *climatograph* is a graph that shows the monthly temperature and precipitation of an area in a year.

You can use the information provided in the three graphs to determine what type of climate each biome has. Next to the climatograph for each biome is an unlabeled map of the biome. Using the maps and the information provided in the graphs, you must figure out what the environment is like in each biome. You can find the exact location of each biome by tracing the map of the biome and matching it to the map at the bottom of the page.

Procedure

1. Look at each climatograph. The shaded areas show the average precipitation for the biome. The red line shows the average temperature.

2. Use the climatographs to determine the climate patterns for each biome. Compare the map of each biome with the map below to find the exact location of each biome.

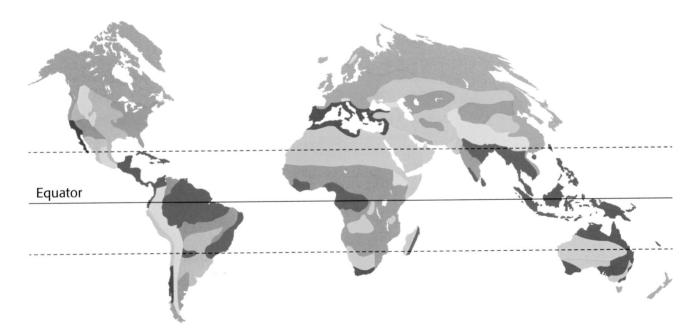

Equator

Analyze Results

1 **Analyzing Data** Describe the precipitation patterns of each biome by answering the following questions:

  a. In which month does the biome receive the most precipitation?

  b. Do you think that the biome is dry, or do you think that it is wet from frequent rains?

2 **Analyzing Data** Describe the temperature patterns of each biome by answering the following questions:

  a. In the biome, which months are warmest?

  b. Does the biome seem to have temperature cycles, like seasons, or is the temperature almost always the same?

  c. Do you think that the biome is warm or cold? Explain.

Draw Conclusions

3 **Drawing Conclusions** Name each biome.

4 **Applying Conclusions** Where is each biome located?

Biome B

Biome A

Biome C

Chapter Review

USING KEY TERMS

For each pair of terms, explain how the meanings of the terms differ.

1 *biome* and *tropical zone*

2 *weather* and *climate*

3 *temperate zone* and *polar zone*

Complete each of the following sentences by choosing the correct term from the word bank.

biome   microclimate
ice age   global warming

4 One factor that could add to ___ is an increase in pollution.

5 A city is an example of a(n) ___.

UNDERSTANDING KEY IDEAS

Multiple Choice

6 Which of the following is a factor that affects climate?

a. prevailing winds

b. latitude

c. ocean currents

d. All of the above

7 The biome that has a temperature range of 28°C to 32°C and an average yearly precipitation of 100 cm is the

a. tropical savanna.

b. tropical desert.

c. tropical rain forest.

d. None of the above

8 Which of the following biomes is NOT found in the temperate zone?

a. temperate forest

b. taiga

c. chaparral

d. temperate grassland

9 In which of the following is the tilt of the Earth's axis considered to have an effect on climate?

a. global warming

b. the sun's cycle

c. the Milankovitch theory

d. asteroid impact

10 Which of the following substances contributes to the greenhouse effect?

a. smoke

b. smog

c. carbon dioxide

d. All of the above

11 In which of the following climate zones is the soil most fertile?

a. the tropical climate zone

b. the temperate climate zone

c. the polar climate zone

d. None of the above

Short Answer

12 Why do higher latitudes receive less solar radiation than lower latitudes do?

13 How does wind influence precipitation patterns?

14 Give an example of a microclimate. What causes the unique temperature and precipitation characteristics of this area?

15 How are tundras and deserts similar?

16 How does deforestation influence global warming?

17 **Concept Mapping** Use the following terms to create a concept map: *global warming, deforestation, changes in climate, greenhouse effect, ice ages,* and *the Milankovitch theory.*

18 **Analyzing Processes** Explain how ocean surface currents cause milder climates.

19 **Identifying Relationships** Describe how the tilt of the Earth's axis affects seasonal changes in different latitudes.

20 **Evaluating Conclusions** Explain why the climate on the eastern side of the Rocky Mountains differs drastically from the climate on the western side.

21 **Applying Concepts** What are some steps you and your family can take to reduce the amount of carbon dioxide that is released into the atmosphere?

22 **Applying Concepts** If you wanted to live in a warm, dry area, which biome would you choose to live in?

23 **Evaluating Data** Explain why the vegetation in areas that have a tundra climate is sparse even though these areas receive precipitation that is adequate to support life.

INTERPRETING GRAPHICS

Use the diagram below to answer the questions that follow.

24 At what position—1, 2, 3, or 4—is it spring in the Southern Hemisphere?

25 At what position does the South Pole receive almost 24 hours of daylight?

26 Explain what is happening in each climate zone in both the Northern and Southern Hemispheres at position 4.

Standardized Test Preparation

EOG Prep

READING

Read each of the passages below. Then, answer the questions that follow each passage.

Passage 1 Earth's climate has gone through many changes. For example, 6,000 years ago today's desert in North Africa was grassland and shallow lakes. Hippopotamuses, crocodiles, and early Stone Age people shared the shallow lakes that covered the area. For many years, scientists have known that Earth's climate has changed. What they didn't know was why it changed. Today, scientists can use supercomputers and complex computer programs to help them find the answer. Now, scientists may be able to <u>decipher</u> why North Africa's lakes and grasslands became a desert. And that information may be useful for predicting future heat waves and ice ages.

1. In this passage, what does *decipher* mean?

   A to question

   B to cover up

   C to explain

   D to calculate

2. According to the passage, which of the following statements is true?

   F Scientists did not know that Earth's climate has changed.

   G Scientists have known that Earth's climate has changed.

   H Scientists have known why Earth's climate has changed.

   I Scientists know that North Africa was always desert.

3. Which of the following is a fact in the passage?

   A North African desert areas never had lakes.

   B North American desert areas never had lakes.

   C North African desert areas had shallow lakes.

   D North Africa is covered with shallow lakes.

Passage 2 El Niño, which is Spanish for "the child," is the name of a weather event that occurs in the Pacific Ocean. Every 2 to 12 years, the interaction between the ocean surface and atmospheric winds creates El Niño. This event influences weather patterns in many regions of the world. For example, in Indonesia and Malaysia, El Niño meant <u>drought</u> and forest fires in 1998. Thousands of people in these countries suffered respiratory ailments caused by breathing the smoke from these fires. Heavy rains in San Francisco created extremely high mold-spore counts. These spores caused problems for people who have allergies. In San Francisco, the spore count in February is usually between 0 and 100. In 1998, the count was often higher than 8,000.

1. In this passage, what does *drought* mean?

   A windy weather

   B stormy weather

   C long period of dry weather

   D rainy weather

2. What can you infer about mold spores from reading the passage?

   F Some people in San Francisco are allergic to mold spores.

   G Mold spores are only in San Francisco.

   H A higher mold-spore count helps people with allergies.

   I The mold-spore count was low in 1998.

3. According to the passage, which of the following statements is true?

   A El Niño causes droughts in Indonesia and Malaysia.

   B El Niño occurs every year.

   C El Niño causes fires in San Francisco.

   D El Niño last occurred in 1998.

The chart below shows types of organisms in an unknown biome. Use the chart below to answer the questions that follow.

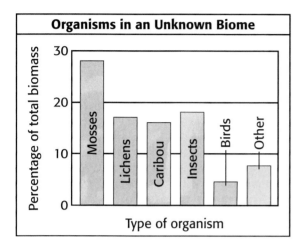

Organisms in an Unknown Biome

1. *Biomass* is a term that means "the total mass of all living things in a certain area." The graph above shows the relative percentages of the total biomass for different plants and animals in a given area. What type of biome does the graph represent?
   A rain forest
   B chaparral
   C tundra
   D taiga

2. Approximately what percentage of biomass is made up of caribou?
   F 28%
   G 25%
   H 16%
   I 5%

3. Approximately what percentage of biomass is made up of lichens and mosses?
   A 45%
   B 35%
   C 25%
   D 16%

Read each question below, and choose the best answer.

1. In a certain area of the savanna that is 12 km long and 5 km wide, there are 180 giraffes. How many giraffes are there per square kilometer in this area?
   A 12
   B 6
   C 4
   D 3

2. If the air temperature near the shore of a lake measures 24°C and the temperature increases by 0.055°C every 10 m traveled away from the lake, what would the air temperature 1 km from the lake be?
   F 5°C
   G 25°C
   H 29.5°C
   I 35°C

3. In a temperate desert, the temperature dropped from 50°C at noon to 37°C by nightfall. By how many degrees Celsius did the noon temperature drop?
   A 13°C
   B 20°C
   C 26°C
   D 50°C

4. Earth is tilted on its axis at a 23.5° angle. What is the measure of the angle that is complementary to a 23.5° angle?
   F 66.5°
   G 67.5°
   H 156.5°
   I 336.5°

5. After a volcanic eruption, the average temperature in a region dropped from 30°C to 18°C. By what percentage did the temperature drop?
   A 30%
   B 25%
   C 40%
   D 15%

Standardized Test Preparation

Science in Action

Scientific Debate

Global Warming

Many scientists believe that pollution from burning fossil fuels is causing temperatures on Earth to rise. Higher average temperatures can cause significant changes in climate. These changes may make survival difficult for animals and plants that have adapted to a biome.

However, other scientists believe that there isn't enough evidence to prove that global warming exists. They argue that any increase in temperatures around the world can be caused by a number of factors other than pollution, such as the sun's cycle.

Language Arts ACTiViTY

WRITING SKILL Read articles that present a variety of viewpoints on global warming. Then, write your own article supporting your viewpoint on global warming.

Science, Technology, and Society

Ice Cores

How do scientists know what Earth's climate was like thousands of years ago? Scientists learn about Earth's past climates by studying ice cores. An ice core is collected by drilling a tube of ice from glaciers and polar ice sheets. Layers in the ice core contain substances that landed in the snow during a particular year or season, such as dust from desert storms, ash from volcanic eruptions, and carbon dioxide from pollution. By studying the layers of the ice cores, scientists can learn what factors influenced the past climates.

Math ACTiViTY

An area has an average yearly rainfall of 20 cm. In 1,000 years, if the average yearly rainfall decreases by 6%, what would the new average yearly rainfall be?

Mercedes Pascual

Climate Change and Disease Mercedes Pascual is a theoretical ecologist at the University of Michigan. Pascual has been able to help the people of Bangladesh save lives by using information about climate changes to predict outbreaks of the disease cholera. Cholera can be a deadly disease that people usually contract by drinking contaminated water. Pascual knew that in Bangladesh, outbreaks of cholera peak every 3.7 years. She noticed that this period matches the frequency of the El Niño Southern Oscillations, which is a weather event that occurs in the Pacific Ocean. El Niño affects weather patterns in many regions of the world, including Bangladesh. El Niño increases the temperatures of the sea off the coast of Bangladesh. Pascual found that increased sea temperatures lead to higher numbers of the bacteria that cause cholera. In turn, more people contract cholera. But because of the research conducted by Pascual and other scientists, the people of Bangladesh can better predict and prepare for outbreaks of cholera.

Social Studies ACTIVITY

WRITING SKILL Research the effects of El Niño. Write a report describing El Niño and its affect on a country other than Bangladesh.

go.hrw.com
To learn more about these Science in Action topics, visit go.hrw.com and type in the keyword HZ5CLMF.

Current Science
Check out Current Science® articles related to this chapter by visiting go.hrw.com. Just type in the keyword HZ5CS17.

UNIT 2

TIMELINE

Human Body Systems

Like a finely tuned machine, your body is made up of many systems that work together. Your lungs take in oxygen. Your brain reacts to things you see, hear, and smell and sends signals through your nervous system that cause you to react to those things. Your digestive system converts the food you eat into energy that the cells of your body can use. And those are just a few things that your body can do!

In this unit, you will study the systems of your body. You'll discover how the parts of your body work together.

Around 3000 BCE

Ancient Egyptian doctors are the first to study the human body scientifically.

1824

Jean Louis Prevost and Jean Batiste Dumas prove that sperm is essential for fertilization.

1766

Albrecht von Haller determines that nerves control muscle movement and that all nerves are connected to the spinal cord or to the brain.

1940

During World War II in Italy, Rita Levi-Montalcini is forced to leave her work at a medical school laboratory because she is Jewish. She sets up a laboratory in her bedroom and studies the development of the nervous system.

Around 500 BCE

Indian surgeon Susrata performs operations to remove cataracts.

1492

Christopher Columbus lands in the West Indies.

1543

Andreas Vesalius publishes the first complete description of the structure of the human body.

1616

William Harvey discovers that blood circulates and that the heart acts as a pump.

1893

Daniel Hale Williams, an African American surgeon, becomes the first person to repair a tear in the pericardium, the sac around the heart.

1922

Frederick Banting, Charles Best, and John McLeod discover insulin.

1930

Karl Landsteiner receives a Nobel Prize for his discovery of the four human blood types.

1982

Dr. William DeVries implants an artificial heart in Barney Clark.

1998

The first sucessful hand transplant is performed in France.

2001

Drs. Laman A. Gray, Jr. and Robert D. Dowling at Jewish Hospital in Louisville, Kentucky, implant the first self-contained mechanical human heart.

Body Organization and Structure

About the

Lance Armstrong has won the Tour de France several times. These victories are especially remarkable because he was diagnosed with cancer in 1996. But with medicine and hard work, he grew strong enough to win one of the toughest events in all of sports.

PRE-READING ACTIVITY

 Four-Corner Fold
Before you read the chapter, create the FoldNote entitled "Four-Corner Fold" described in the **Study Skills** section of the Appendix. Label the flaps of the four-corner fold with "The skeletal system," "The muscular system," and "The integumentary system." Write what you know about each topic under the appropriate flap. As you read the chapter, add other information that you learn.

START-UP ACTIVITY

Too Cold for Comfort

Your nervous system sends you messages about your body. For example, if someone steps on your toe, your nervous system sends you a message. The pain you feel is a message that tells you to move your toe to safety. Try this exercise to watch your nervous system in action.

Procedure

1. Hold **a few pieces of ice** in one hand. Allow the melting water to drip into a **dish.** Hold the ice until the cold is uncomfortable. Then, release the ice into the dish.

2. Compare the hand that held the ice with your other hand. Describe the changes you see.

Analysis

1. What message did you receive from your nervous system while you held the ice?

2. How quickly did the cold hand return to normal?

3. What organ systems do you think helped restore your hand to normal?

4. Think of a time when your nervous system sent you a message, such as an uncomfortable feeling of heat, cold, or pain. How did your body react?

Introduction to Body Systems

Imagine jumping into a lake. At first, your body feels very cold. You may even shiver. But eventually you get used to the cold water. How does this happen?

Your body gets used to cold water because it returns to *homeostasis*. **Homeostasis** (HOH mee OH STAY sis) is the maintenance of a stable internal environment in the body. When you jump into a cold lake, homeostasis helps your body stay warm.

Staying in Balance

The environment around you is always changing. Your body has to adjust to these conditions. For example, generally, on a hot day, your body is able to react to maintain your body temperature and avoid overheating. As shown in **Figure 1,** all living organisms have to maintain homeostasis.

Maintaining homeostasis is not easy. Your body needs nutrients and oxygen. Your body needs wastes removed. And your body needs to defend itself against disease. A single cell cannot do all of these jobs for the entire body. Fortunately, your body has many kinds of cells. Some cells remove wastes. Other cells carry oxygen or defend your body against disease. Together, these cells help your internal environment stay stable.

READING WARM-UP

Objectives

- Describe homeostasis and what happens when it is disrupted.
- Describe how tissues, organs, and organ systems are related.
- List 12 organ systems.
- Identify how organ systems work together to maintain homeostasis.

Terms to Learn

homeostasis
tissue
organ

READING STRATEGY

Reading Organizer As you read this section, make a concept map by using the terms above.

homeostasis the maintenance of a constant internal state in a changing environment

Figure 1 *These penguins have adaptations that help them maintain homeostasis in the cold environment in which they live.*

Falling Out of Balance

Sometimes, your body cannot maintain homeostasis. For example, if you don't eat the right foods, your cells may not get the nutrients they need. Maybe your body systems can't fight off a disease caused by bacteria or viruses. So, homeostasis is disrupted. What happens when homeostasis is disrupted? Cells may be damaged or may die. When this happens, you can become sick, as shown in **Figure 2.** Sometimes, people die when homeostasis is disrupted.

Temperature Regulation

When you are hot, your body gives off heat. You also sweat. When sweat evaporates from your skin, your body is cooled. Sweating is a process that helps your body maintain homeostasis. Sometimes, the body cannot cool down. This happens when cells do not get what they need, such as water for sweat. If the body gets too hot, cells may be damaged.

The body also has ways to keep you warm on cold days. When you are cold, you shiver, which helps you stay warm. Sometimes, the body cannot stay warm. Body temperature falls below normal in a condition called *hypothermia.*

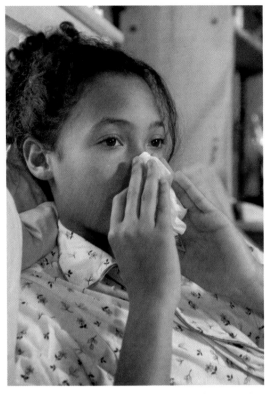

Figure 2 *When homeostasis is disrupted, a person can become sick.*

Moving Materials

Your cells need nutrients for life processes. If nutrients are not delivered, the cells cannot complete their life processes. So, the cells will die. These life processes often make wastes, which must be removed from cells. Many wastes are toxic. If a cell cannot get rid of them, the wastes will damage the cell.

✓ Reading Check Explain the importance of moving materials into and out of cells. (*See the Appendix for answers to Reading Checks.*)

CONNECTION TO
Chemistry

WRITING SKILL **Adapting After Surgery** People can survive the removal of some parts of the body. For example, doctors may remove a patient's gall bladder, spleen, or large intestine because of disease or injury. However, the patient's body must make adjustments to maintain a stable internal environment. Examine how the body adjusts to the loss of a body part due to disease or injury. Identify how the body changes in order to maintain a stable internal environment. In your **science journal,** write a newspaper article about your findings.

Body Organization

As you may know, your body is made up of billions of cells. A cell is the basic unit of all living things. You have many kinds of cells. For example, you have muscle cells and nerve cells.

Cells Form Tissues

Various kinds of cells make up the parts of the body. These cells work together in much the same way that players on a soccer team do. Just as each person on a soccer team has a role during a game, each cell in your body has a job in maintaining homeostasis. For example, muscle cells are cells that can contract, or become shorter. They allow movement. Nerve cells receive and transmit electrical impulses, or messages.

A group of similar cells working together forms a **tissue.** Your body has four main kinds of tissue. The four kinds of tissue are shown in **Figure 3.** Each kind of tissue is made up of its own kind of cells. For example, muscle cells make up muscle tissue, and nerve cells make up nervous tissue.

Each kind of tissue may have variations based on the specific function of the tissue. For example, both bone and blood are kinds of connective tissue. However, the tissues differ. The connective tissue of bones supports the body and protects organs, so it is a solid. The connective tissue of blood moves throughout the body, so it is a liquid.

tissue a group of similar cells that perform a common function

✓**Reading Check** How are cells and tissues related?

Figure 3 **Four Kinds of Tissue**

Epithelial tissue covers and protects underlying tissue. When you look at the surface of your skin, you see epithelial tissue. The cells form a continuous sheet.

Nervous tissue sends electrical signals through the body. It is found in the brain, nerves, and sense organs.

Figure 4 **Organization of the Stomach**

The stomach is an organ. The four kinds of tissue work together so that the stomach can carry out digestion.

Nervous tissue in the stomach partly controls the production of acids that aid in the digestion of food. Nervous tissue signals when the stomach is full.

Epithelial tissue lines the stomach.

Blood and another **connective tissue** called *collagen* are found in the wall of the stomach.

Layers of **muscle tissue** break up and mix stomach contents.

Tissues Form Organs

One kind of tissue alone cannot do all of the things that several kinds of tissue working together can do. Two or more tissues working together form an **organ.** Your stomach, shown in **Figure 4,** uses all four kinds of tissue to carry out digestion.

organ a collection of tissues that carry out a specialized function of the body

Organs Form Systems

Your stomach does a lot to help you digest your food. But the stomach doesn't do it all. Your stomach works with other organs, such as the small and large intestines, to digest your food. Organs that work together make up an *organ system.*

Reading Check How is the stomach part of an organ system?

Muscle tissue is made of cells that contract and relax to produce movement.

Connective tissue joins, supports, protects, insulates, nourishes, and cushions organs. It also keeps organs from falling apart.

Working Together

Organ systems work together to maintain homeostasis. Your body has 12 major organ systems, as shown in **Figure 5.** The circulatory and cardiovascular systems are shown together. The cardiovascular system includes your heart and blood vessels. Additionally, these organs are part of the circulatory system, which also includes blood. Together, these two systems deliver the materials your cells need to survive. This is just one example of how organ systems work together to keep you healthy.

✓ Reading Check Give an example of how organ systems work together in the body.

Figure 5   Organ Systems

Integumentary System Your skin protects you from disease and regulates body temperature.

Muscular System Your muscular system works with the skeletal system to help you move.

Skeletal System Your bones provide a frame to support and protect your body parts.

Cardiovascular and Circulatory Systems Your heart pumps blood through all of your blood vessels.

Respiratory System Your lungs absorb oxygen and release carbon dioxide.

Urinary System Your urinary system removes wastes from the blood and regulates your body's fluids.

Male Reproductive System The male reproductive system produces and delivers sperm.

Female Reproductive System The female reproductive system produces eggs and nourishes and protects the fetus.

Nervous System Your nervous system receives and sends electrical messages throughout your body.

Digestive System Your digestive system breaks down the food you eat into nutrients that your body can absorb.

Lymphatic System The lymphatic system returns leaked fluids to blood vessels and helps defend against disease.

Endocrine System Your glands send out chemical messages, which control body functions.

SECTION Review

Summary

- Homeostasis is the maintenance of a stable internal environment.
- A group of cells that work together is a tissue. Tissues form organs. Organs that work together form organ systems.
- There are 12 major organ systems in the human body.
- Organ systems work together to help the body maintain homeostasis.

Using Key Terms

1. In your own words, write a definition for the term *homeostasis*.

Understanding Key Ideas

2. Which of the following statements describes how tissues, organs, and organ systems are related?
   a. Organs form tissues, which form organ systems.
   b. Organ systems form organs, which form tissues.
   c. Tissues form organs, which form organ systems.
   d. None of the above

3. List the 12 organ systems.

Math Skills

4. The human skeleton has 206 bones. The human skull has 22 bones. What percentage of human bones are skull bones?

Critical Thinking

5. **Applying Concepts** The circulatory system delivers nutrients to cells in the body. What might happen to homeostasis if this system were disrupted? Explain your answer.

6. **Predicting Consequences** Predict what might happen if the human body did not have specialized cells, tissues, organs, and organ systems to maintain homeostasis.

The Skeletal System

When you hear the word skeleton, *you may think of the remains of something that has died. But your skeleton is not dead. It is very much alive.*

You may think your bones are dry and brittle. But they are alive and active. Bones, cartilage, and the connective tissue that holds bones together make up your **skeletal system.**

Bones

The average adult human skeleton has 206 bones. Bones help support and protect parts of your body. They work with your muscles so you can move. Bones also help your body maintain homeostasis by storing minerals and making blood cells. **Figure 1** shows the functions of your skeleton.

skeletal system the organ system whose primary function is to support and protect the body and to allow the body to move

Figure 1   The Skeleton

Skull
Ribs
Radius
Clavicle
Humerus
Patella
Femur
Ulna
Tibia
Fibula
Pelvic girdle
Vertebral column

Protection Your heart and lungs are protected by ribs, your spinal cord is protected by vertebrae, and your brain is protected by the skull.

Storage Bones store minerals that help your nerves and muscles function properly. Long bones store fat that can be used for energy.

Movement Skeletal muscles pull on bones to produce movement. Without bones, you would not be able to sit, stand, walk, or run.

Blood Cell Formation Some of your bones are filled with a special material that makes blood cells. This material is called *marrow.*

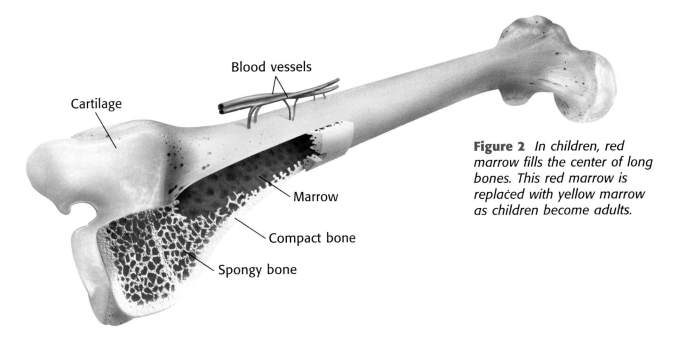

Blood vessels

Cartilage

Marrow

Compact bone

Spongy bone

Figure 2 *In children, red marrow fills the center of long bones. This red marrow is replaced with yellow marrow as children become adults.*

Bone Structure

A bone may seem lifeless. But a bone is a living organ made of several different tissues. Bone is made of connective tissue and minerals. These minerals are deposited by living cells called *osteoblasts* (AHS tee oh BLASTS).

If you look inside a bone, you will notice two kinds of bone tissue. If the bone tissue does not have any visible open spaces, it is called *compact bone*. Compact bone is rigid and dense. Tiny canals within compact bone contain small blood vessels. Bone tissue that has many open spaces is called *spongy bone*. Spongy bone provides most of the strength and support for a bone.

Bones contain a soft tissue called *marrow*. There are two types of marrow. Red marrow produces both red and white blood cells. Yellow marrow, found in the central cavity of long bones, stores fat. **Figure 2** shows a cross section of a long bone, the femur.

Bone Growth

Did you know that most of your skeleton used to be soft and rubbery? Most bones start out as a flexible tissue called *cartilage*. When you were born, you didn't have much true bone. But as you grew, most of the cartilage was replaced by bone. During childhood, most bones still have growth plates of cartilage. These growth plates provide a place for bones to continue to grow.

Feel the end of your nose. ●r bend the top of your ear. These areas are two places where cartilage is never replaced by bone. These areas stay flexible.

✓ Reading Check How do bones grow? (*See the Appendix for answers to Reading Checks.*)

Pickled Bones

1. Place a **clean chicken bone** in a **jar of vinegar.**
2. After 1 week, remove the bone and rinse it with **water.**
3. Describe the changes that you can see or feel.
4. How has the bone's strength changed?
5. What did the vinegar remove?

Figure 3 **Three Joints**

Gliding Joint

Gliding joints allow bones in the hand and wrist to glide over one another and give some flexibility to the area.

Ball-and-Socket Joint

As a video-game joystick lets you move your character all around, the shoulder lets your arm move freely in all directions.

Hinge Joint

As a hinge allows a door to open and close, the knee enables you to flex and extend your lower leg.

Joints

joint a place where two or more bones meet

A place where two or more bones meet is called a **joint.** Your joints allow your body to move when your muscles contract. Some joints, such as fixed joints, allow little or no movement. Many of the joints in the skull are fixed joints. Other joints, such as your shoulder, allow a lot of movement. Joints can be classified based on how the bones in a joint move. For example, your shoulder is a ball-and-socket joint. Three joints are shown in **Figure 3.**

Joints are held together by *ligaments* (LIG uh muhnts). Ligaments are strong elastic bands of connective tissue. They connect the bones in a joint. Also, cartilage covers the ends of many bones. Cartilage helps cushion the area in a joint where bones meet.

✓ *Reading Check* Describe the basic structure of joints.

CONNECTION TO
Environmental Science

WRITING SKILL **Bones from the Ocean** Sometimes, a bone or joint may become so damaged that it needs to be repaired or replaced with surgery. Often, replacement parts are made from a metal, such as titanium. However, some scientists have discovered that coral skeletons from coral reefs in the ocean can be used to replace human bone. Research bone surgery. Identify why doctors use metals such as titanium. Then, identify the advantages that coral may offer. Write a report discussing your findings.

Skeletal System Injuries and Diseases

Sometimes, parts of the skeletal system are injured. As shown in **Figure 4,** bones may be fractured, or broken. Joints can also be injured. A dislocated joint is a joint in which one or more bones have been moved out of place. Another joint injury, called a *sprain*, happens if a ligament is stretched too far or torn.

There are also diseases of the skeletal system. *Osteoporosis* (AHS tee OH puh ROH sis) is a disease that causes bones to become less dense. Bones become weak and break more easily. Age and poor eating habits can make it more likely for people to develop osteoporosis. Other bone diseases affect the marrow or make bones soft. A disease that affects the joints is called *arthritis* (ahr THRIET is). Arthritis is painful. Joints may swell or stiffen. As they get older, some people are more likely to have some types of arthritis.

Figure 4 *This X ray shows that the two bones of the forearm have been fractured, or broken.*

SECTION Review

Summary

- The skeletal system includes bones, cartilage, and the connective tissue that connects bones.

- Bones protect the body, store minerals, allow movement, and make blood cells.

- Joints are places where two or more bones meet.

- Skeletal system injuries include fractures, dislocations, and sprains. Skeletal system diseases include osteoporosis and arthritis.

Using Key Terms

1. In your own words, write a definition for the term *skeletal system*.

Understanding Key Ideas

2. Which of the following is NOT an organ of the skeletal system?
   a. bone
   b. cartilage
   c. muscle
   d. None of the above

3. Describe four functions of bones.

4. What are three joints?

5. Describe two diseases that affect the skeletal system.

Math Skills

6. A broken bone usually heals in about six weeks. A mild sprain takes one-third as long to heal. In days, about how long does it take a mild sprain to heal?

Critical Thinking

7. **Identifying Relationships** Red bone marrow produces blood cells. Children have red bone marrow in their long bones, while adults have yellow bone marrow, which stores fat. Why might adults and children have different kinds of marrow?

8. **Predicting Consequences** What might happen if children's bones didn't have growth plates of cartilage?

SCiLINKS.

NSTA
Developed and maintained by the
National Science Teachers Association

For a variety of links related to this chapter, go to www.scilinks.org

Topic: Skeletal System
SciLinks code: HSM1399

The Muscular System

Have you ever tried to sit still, without moving any muscles at all, for one minute? It's impossible! Somewhere in your body, muscles are always working.

You use muscles when you eat and breathe. Muscles, along with your skeleton, hold you upright and let you move. If all of your muscles rested at once, you would collapse. The **muscular system** is made up of the muscles that let you move.

Kinds of Muscle

Figure 1 shows the three kinds of muscle in your body. *Smooth muscle* is found in the digestive tract and in the walls of blood vessels. *Cardiac muscle* is found only in your heart. *Skeletal muscle* is attached to your bones for movement. Skeletal muscle also helps protect your inner organs.

Muscle action can be voluntary or involuntary. Muscle action that is under your control is *voluntary*. Muscle action that is not under your control is *involuntary*. Smooth muscle and cardiac muscle are involuntary muscles. Skeletal muscles can be both voluntary and involuntary muscles. For example, you can blink your eyes anytime you want to. But your eyes will also blink automatically.

READING WARM-UP

Objectives

● List three kinds of muscle tissue.

● Describe how skeletal muscles move bones.

● Compare aerobic exercise with resistance exercise.

● Describe two muscular system injuries.

Terms to Learn

muscular system

READING STRATEGY

Discussion Read this section silently. Write down questions that you have about this section. Discuss your questions in a small group.

Figure 1 Three Kinds of Muscle

Skeletal muscle enables bones to move.

Smooth muscle moves food through the digestive system.

Cardiac muscle pumps blood around the body.

Figure 2 **A Pair of Muscles in the Arm**

Skeletal muscles, such as the biceps and triceps muscles, work in pairs. When the biceps muscle contracts, the arm bends. When the triceps muscle contracts, the arm straightens.

Biceps muscle

Triceps muscle

Flexor   **Extensor**

Movement

Skeletal muscles can make hundreds of movements. You can see many of these movements by watching a dancer, a swimmer, or even someone smiling or frowning. When you want to move, signals travel from your brain to your skeletal muscle cells. The muscle cells then contract, or get shorter.

Muscles Attach to Bones

Strands of tough connective tissue connect your skeletal muscles to your bones. These strands are called *tendons*. When a muscle that connects two bones gets shorter, the bones are pulled closer to each other. For example, tendons attach the biceps muscle to a bone in your shoulder and to a bone in your forearm. When the biceps muscle contracts, your forearm bends toward your shoulder.

Muscles Work in Pairs

Your skeletal muscles often work in pairs. Usually, one muscle in the pair bends part of the body. The other muscle straightens part of the body. A muscle that bends part of your body is called a *flexor* (FLEKS uhr). A muscle that straightens part of your body is an *extensor* (ek STEN suhr). As shown in **Figure 2,** the biceps muscle of the arm is a flexor. The triceps muscle of the arm is an extensor.

✓ Reading Check Describe how muscles work in pairs. (*See the Appendix for answers to Reading Checks.*)

muscular system the organ system whose primary function is movement and flexibility

Power in Pairs

Ask a parent to sit in a chair and place a hand palm up under the edge of a table. Tell your parent to apply gentle upward pressure. Feel the front and back of your parent's upper arm. Next, ask your parent to push down on top of the table. Feel your parent's arm again. What did you notice about the muscles in your parent's arm when he or she was pressing up? pushing down?

Figure 3 *This girl is strengthening her heart and improving her endurance by doing aerobic exercise. This boy is doing resistance exercise to build strong muscles.*

Use It or Lose It

What happens when someone wears a cast for a broken arm? Skeletal muscles around the broken bone become smaller and weaker. The muscles weaken because they are not exercised. Exercised muscles are stronger and larger. Strong muscles can help other organs, too. For example, contracting muscles squeeze blood vessels. This action increases blood flow without needing more work from the heart.

Certain exercises can give muscles more strength and endurance. More endurance lets muscles work longer without getting tired. Two kinds of exercise can increase muscle strength and endurance. They are resistance exercise and aerobic exercise. You can see an example of each kind in **Figure 3.**

Resistance Exercise

Resistance exercise is a great way to strengthen skeletal muscles. During resistance exercise, people work against the resistance, or weight, of an object. Some resistance exercises, such as curl-ups, use your own weight for resistance.

Aerobic Exercise

Steady, moderately intense activity is called *aerobic exercise.* Jogging, cycling, skating, swimming, and walking are aerobic exercises. This kind of exercise can increase muscle strength. However, aerobic exercise mostly strengthens the heart and increases endurance.

CONNECTION TO Chemistry

Muscle Function Body chemistry is very important for healthy muscle function. Spasms or cramps happen if too much sweating, poor diet, or illness causes a chemical imbalance in muscles. Identify three chemicals that the body needs for muscles to work properly. Make a poster explaining how people can make sure that they have enough of each chemical.

ACTIVITY

Muscle Injury

Any exercise program should be started slowly. Starting slowly means you are less likely to get hurt. You should also warm up for exercise. A *strain* is an injury in which a muscle or tendon is overstretched or torn. Strains often happen because a muscle has not been warmed up. Strains also happen when muscles are worked too hard.

People who exercise too much can hurt their tendons. The body can't repair an injured tendon before the next exercise session. So, the tendon becomes inflamed. This condition is called *tendinitis*. Often, a long rest is needed for the injured tendon to heal.

Some people try to make their muscles stronger by taking drugs. These drugs are called *anabolic steroids* (A nuh BAH lik STER OIDZ). They can cause long-term health problems. Anabolic steroids can damage the heart, liver, and kidneys. They can also cause high blood pressure. If taken before the skeleton is mature, anabolic steroids can cause bones to stop growing.

Reading Check What are the risks of using anabolic steroids?

Runner's Time
Jan has decided to enter a 5 km road race. She now runs 5 km in 30 min. She would like to decrease her time by 15% before the race. What will her time be when she reaches her goal?

SECTION Review

Summary

- The three kinds of muscle tissue are smooth muscle, cardiac muscle, and skeletal muscle.

- Skeletal muscles work in pairs. Skeletal muscles contract to move bones.

- Resistance exercise improves muscle strength. Aerobic exercise improves heart strength and muscle endurance.

- Strains are injuries that affect muscles and tendons. Tendinitis affects tendons.

Using Key Terms

1. In your own words, write a definition for the term *muscular system*.

Understanding Key Ideas

2. Muscles
   a. work in pairs.
   b. move bones by relaxing.
   c. get smaller when exercised.
   d. All of the above

3. Describe three kinds of muscle.

4. List two kinds of exercise. Give an example of each.

5. Describe two muscular system injuries.

Math Skills

6. If Trey can do one curl-up every 2.5 s, about how long will it take him to do 35 curl-ups?

Critical Thinking

7. **Applying Concepts** Describe some of the muscle action needed to pick up a book. Include flexors and extensors in your description.

8. **Predicting Consequences** If aerobic exercise improves heart strength, what likely happens to heart rate as the heart gets stronger? Explain your answer.

For a variety of links related to this chapter, go to www.scilinks.org

Topic: Muscular System
SciLinks code: HSM1008

The Integumentary System

What part of your body has to be partly dead to keep you alive? Here are some clues: It comes in many colors, it is the largest organ in the body, and it is showing right now!

Did you guess your skin? If you did, you guessed correctly. Your skin, hair, and nails make up your **integumentary system** (in TEG yoo MEN tuhr ee SIS tuhm). The integumentary system covers your body and helps you maintain homeostasis.

Functions of Skin

Why do you need skin? Here are four good reasons:

- Skin protects you by keeping water in your body and foreign particles out of your body.

- Skin keeps you in touch with the outside world. Nerve endings in your skin let you feel things around you.

- Skin helps regulate your body temperature. Small organs in the skin called *sweat glands* make sweat. Sweat is a salty liquid that flows to the surface of the skin. As sweat evaporates, the skin cools.

- Skin helps get rid of wastes. Several kinds of waste chemicals can be removed in sweat.

As shown in **Figure 1,** skin comes in many colors. Skin color is determined by a chemical called *melanin*. If a lot of melanin is present, skin is very dark. If little melanin is present, skin is very light. Melanin absorbs ultraviolet light from the sun. So, melanin reduces damage that can lead to skin cancer. However, all skin, even dark skin, is vulnerable to cancer. Skin should be protected from sunlight whenever possible.

integumentary system the organ system that forms a protective covering on the outside of the body

Figure 1 *Variety in skin color is caused by the pigment melanin. The amount of melanin varies from person to person.*

Figure 2 **Structures of the Skin**

Beneath the surface, your skin is a complex organ made of blood vessels, nerves, glands, and muscles.

Blood vessels transport substances and help regulate body temperature.

Nerve fibers carry messages to and from the brain.

Hair follicles in the dermis make hair.

Muscle fibers attached to a hair follicle can contract and cause the hair to stand up.

Oil glands release oil that keeps hair flexible and waterproofs the epidermis.

Sweat glands release sweat to cool the body. Sweating is also a way to remove waste materials from the body.

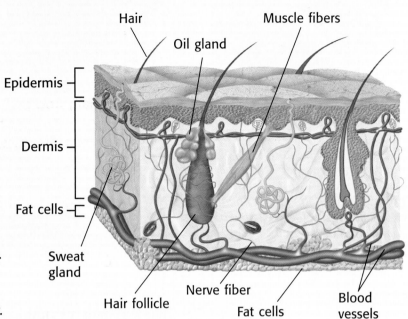

Layers of Skin

Skin is the largest organ of your body. In fact, the skin of an adult covers an area of about 2 m²! However, there is more to skin than meets the eye. Skin has two main layers: the epidermis (EP uh DUHR mis) and the dermis. The **epidermis** is the outermost layer of skin. You see the epidermis when you look at your skin. The thicker layer of skin that lies beneath the epidermis is the **dermis.**

epidermis the surface layer of cells on a plant or animal

dermis the layer of skin below the epidermis

Epidermis

The epidermis is made of epithelial tissue. Even though the epidermis has many layers of cells, it is as thick as only two sheets of paper over most of the body. It is thicker on the palms of your hands and on the soles of your feet. Most cells in the epidermis are dead. These cells are filled with a protein called *keratin*. Keratin helps make the skin tough.

Dermis

The dermis lies beneath the epidermis. The dermis has many fibers made of a protein called *collagen*. These fibers provide strength. They also let skin bend without tearing. The dermis contains many small structures, as shown in **Figure 2.**

Your epidermis is showing!

Reading Check Describe the dermis. How does it differ from the epidermis? (*See the Appendix for answers to Reading Checks.*)

Lunula

Nail body

Free edge

Hair

Figure 3 *A hair is made up of layers of dead, tightly packed, keratin-filled cells. In nails, new cells are produced in the nail root, just beneath the lunula. The new cells push older cells toward the outer edge of the nail.*

CONNECTION TO
Social Studies

WRITING SKILL **Using Hair** Many traditional cultures use animal hair to make products, such as rugs and blankets. Identify a culture that uses animal hair. In your **science journal,** write a report describing how the culture uses animal hair.

Hair and Nails

Hair and nails are important parts of the integumentary system. Like skin, hair and nails are made of living and dead cells. **Figure 3** shows hair and nails.

A hair forms at the bottom of a tiny sac called a *hair follicle.* The hair grows as new cells are added at the hair follicle. Older cells get pushed upward. The only living cells in a hair are in the hair follicle. Like skin, hair gets its color from melanin.

Hair helps protect skin from ultraviolet light. Hair also keeps particles, such as dust and insects, out of your eyes and nose. In most mammals, hair helps regulate body temperature. A tiny muscle attached to the hair follicle contracts. If the follicle contains a hair, the hair stands up. The lifted hairs work like a sweater. They trap warm air around the body.

A nail grows from living cells in the *nail root* at the base of the nail. As new cells form, the nail grows longer. Nails protect the tips of your fingers and toes. So, your fingers and toes can be soft and sensitive for a keen sense of touch.

✓ **Reading Check** Describe how nails grow.

Skin Injuries

Skin is often damaged. Fortunately, your skin can repair itself, as shown in **Figure 4.** Some damage to skin is very serious. Damage to the genetic material in skin cells can cause skin cancer. Skin may also be affected by hormones that cause oil glands in skin to make too much oil. This oil combines with dead skin cells and bacteria to clog hair follicles. The result is acne. Proper cleansing can help but often cannot prevent this problem.

Figure 4 **How Skin Heals**

1 A blood clot forms over a cut to stop bleeding and to keep bacteria from entering the wound. Bacteria-fighting cells then come to the area to kill bacteria.

2 Damaged cells are replaced through cell division. Eventually, all that is left on the surface is a scar.

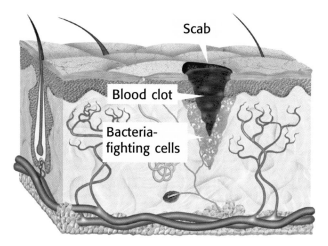

Scab

Blood clot

Bacteria-fighting cells

New cells

SECTION Review

Summary

- Skin keeps water in the body, keeps foreign particles out of the body, lets people feel things around them, regulates temperature, and removes wastes.

- The two layers of skin are the epidermis and the dermis.

- Hair grows from hair follicles. Nails grow from nail roots.

- Skin may develop skin cancer. Acne may develop if skin produces too much oil.

Using Key Terms

1. In your own words, write a definition for each of the following terms: *integumentary system*, *epidermis*, and *dermis*.

Understanding Key Ideas

2. Which of the following is NOT a function of skin?
   a. to regulate body temperature
   b. to keep water in the body
   c. to move your body
   d. to get rid of wastes

3. Describe the two layers of skin.

4. How do hair and nails develop?

5. Describe how a cut heals.

Math Skills

6. On average, hair grows 0.3 mm per day. How many millimeters does hair grow in 30 days? in a year?

Critical Thinking

7. **Making Inferences** Why do you feel pain when you pull on your hair or nails, but not when you cut them?

8. **Analyzing Ideas** The epidermis on the palms of your hands and on the soles of your feet is thicker than it is anywhere else on your body. Why might this skin need to be thicker?

SCiLINKS.

NSTA

Developed and maintained by the
National Science Teachers Association

For a variety of links related to this chapter, go to www.scilinks.org

Topic: Integumentary System
SciLinks code: HSM0803

Skills Practice Lab

Seeing Is Believing

OBJECTIVES

Measure nail growth over time.

Draw a graph of nail growth.

MATERIALS

- graph paper (optional)
- metric ruler
- permanent marker

SAFETY

Like your hair and skin, fingernails are part of your body's integumentary system. Nails, shown in the figure below, are a modification of the outer layer of the skin. Nails grow from the nail bed and will grow continuously throughout your life. In this activity, you will measure the rate at which fingernails grow.

Procedure

1. Use a permanent marker to mark the center of the nail bed on your right index finger, as shown in the figure below. **Caution:** Do not get ink on your clothing.

2. Measure from the mark to the base of your nail. Record the measurement, and label the measurement "Day 1."

3. Repeat steps 1 and 2 for your left index finger.

4. Let your fingernails grow for 2 days. Normal daily activity will not wash away the mark completely, but you may need to freshen the mark.

5. Measure the distance from the mark on your nail to the base of your nail. Record this distance, and label the measurement "Day 3."

6 Continue measuring and recording the growth of your nails every other day for 2 weeks. Refresh the mark as necessary. You may continue to file or trim your nails as usual throughout the course of the lab.

7 After you have completed your measurements, use them to create a graph similar to the graph below.

Fingernail Growth

Analyze the Results

1 **Describing Events** Did the nail on one hand grow faster than the nail on the other hand?

2 **Examining Data** Did your nails grow at a constant rate, or did your nails grow more quickly at certain times?

Draw Conclusions

3 **Making Predictions** If one nail grew more quickly than the other nail, what might explain the difference in growth?

4 **Analyzing Graphs** Compare your graph with the graphs of your classmates. Do you notice any differences in the graphs based on gender or physical characteristics, such as height? If so, describe the difference.

Applying Your Data

Do additional research to find out how nails are important to you. Also, identify how nails can be used to indicate a person's health or nutrition. Based on what you learn, describe how your nail growth indicates your health or nutrition.

Chapter Review

USING KEY TERMS

Complete each of the following sentences by choosing the correct term from the word bank.

homeostasis   organ
joint   skeletal system
tissue   muscular system
epidermis   dermis
integumentary system

1 A(n) ___ is a place where two or more bones meet.

2 ___ is the maintenance of a stable internal environment.

3 The outermost layer of skin is the ___.

4 The organ system that includes skin, hair, and nails is the ___.

5 A(n) ___ is made up of two or more tissues working together.

6 The ___ supports and protects the body, stores minerals, and allows movement.

UNDERSTANDING KEY IDEAS

Multiple Choice

7 Which of the following lists shows the way in which the body is organized?

a. cells, organs, organ systems, tissues
b. tissues, cells, organs, organ systems
c. cells, tissues, organs, organ systems
d. cells, tissues, organ systems, organs

8 Which muscle tissue can be both voluntary and involuntary?

a. smooth muscle
b. cardiac muscle
c. skeletal muscle
d. All of the above

9 The integumentary system

a. helps regulate body temperature.
b. helps the body move.
c. stores minerals.
d. None of the above

10 Muscles

a. work in pairs.
b. can be voluntary or involuntary.
c. become stronger if exercised.
d. All of the above

Short Answer

11 How do muscles move bones?

12 Describe the skeletal system, and list four functions of bones.

13 Give an example of how organ systems work together.

14 List three injuries and two diseases that affect the skeletal system.

15 Compare aerobic exercise and resistance exercise.

16 What are two kinds of damage that may affect skin?

17 **Concept Mapping** Use the following terms to create a concept map: *tissues, muscle tissue, connective tissue, cells, organ systems, organs, epithelial tissue,* and *nervous tissue*.

18 **Making Comparisons** Compare the shapes of the bones of the human skull with the shapes of the bones of the human leg. How do the shapes differ? Why are the shapes important?

19 **Making Inferences** Compare your elbows and fingertips in terms of the texture and sensitivity of the skin on these parts of your body. Why might the skin on these body parts differ?

20 **Making Inferences** Imagine that you are building a robot. Your robot will have a skeleton similar to a human skeleton. If the robot needs to be able to move a limb in all directions, what kind of joint would be needed? Explain your answer.

21 **Analyzing Ideas** Human bones are dense and are often filled with marrow. But many bones of birds are hollow. Why might birds have hollow bones?

22 **Identifying Relationships** Why might some muscles fail to work properly if a bone is broken?

Use the cross section of skin below to answer the questions that follow.

23 What is d called? What substance is most abundant in this layer?

24 What is the name and function of a?

25 What is the name and function of b?

26 Which letter corresponds to the part of the skin that is made up of epithelial tissue that contains dead cells?

27 Which letter corresponds to the part of the skin from which hair grows? What is this part called?

Standardized Test Preparation

EOG Prep

Read the passages below. Then, answer the questions that follow each passage.

Passage 1 Sometimes, doctors perform a <u>skin graft</u> to transfer some of a person's healthy skin to an area where skin has been damaged. Doctors perform skin grafts because skin is often the best "bandage" for a wound. Like cloth or plastic bandages, skin protects the wound. Skin allows the wound to breathe. Unlike cloth or plastic bandages, skin can regenerate itself as it covers a wound. But sometimes a person's skin is so severely damaged (by burns, for example) that the person doesn't have enough skin to spare.

1. Based on the passage, what can skin do that manufactured bandages can't do?
   - **A** Skin can protect a wound.
   - **B** Skin can stop more skin from being damaged.
   - **C** Skin can regenerate itself.
   - **D** Skin can prevent burns.

2. In the passage, what does the term *skin graft* most likely mean?
   - **F** a piece of skin transplanted from one part of the body to another
   - **G** a piece of skin made of plastic
   - **H** a piece of damaged skin that has been removed from the body
   - **I** burned skin

3. Based on the passage, why might a severe burn victim not receive a skin graft?
   - **A** Manufactured bandages are better.
   - **B** He or she doesn't have enough healthy skin.
   - **C** There isn't enough damaged skin to repair.
   - **D** Skin is the best bandage for a wound.

Passage 2 Making sure that your body maintains homeostasis is not an easy task. The task is difficult because your internal environment is always changing. Your body must do many different jobs to maintain homeostasis. Each cell in your body has a specific job in maintaining homeostasis. Your cells are organized into groups. A group of similar cells working together forms a tissue. Your body has four main kinds of tissue—epithelial tissue, connective tissue, muscle tissue, and nervous tissue. These tissues work together to form organs, which help maintain homeostasis.

1. Based on the passage, which of the following statements about tissues is true?
   - **A** Tissues do not help maintain homeostasis.
   - **B** Tissues form organ systems.
   - **C** Tissues are changing because the body's internal environment is always changing.
   - **D** There are four kinds of tissue.

2. According to the passage, which of the following statements about homeostasis is true?
   - **F** It is easy for the body to maintain homeostasis.
   - **G** The body must do different jobs to maintain homeostasis.
   - **H** Your internal environment rarely changes.
   - **I** Organs and organ systems do not help maintain homeostasis.

3. Which of the following statements about cells is false?
   - **A** Cells are organized into different groups.
   - **B** Cells form tissues.
   - **C** Cells work together.
   - **D** Cells don't maintain homeostasis.

The line graph below shows hair growth over time. Use the graph to answer the questions that follow.

Hair Length over Time

1. How long was the hair on day 60?
   - **A** 20.0 cm
   - **B** 21.0 cm
   - **C** 22.5 cm
   - **D** 23.0 cm

2. On which day was hair length 23 cm?
   - **F** day 60
   - **G** day 90
   - **H** day 120
   - **I** day 150

3. From day 0 to day 150, what is the average amount that hair grows every 30 days?
   - **A** 0.5 cm
   - **B** 1.2 cm
   - **C** 1.5 cm
   - **D** 2.0 cm

4. Based on the average amount of hair growth per 30-day period, how long would it take the hair to grow another 3.6 cm?
   - **F** 30 days
   - **G** 60 days
   - **H** 90 days
   - **I** 120 days

Read each question below, and choose the best answer.

1. About 40% of a person's mass is muscle tissue. If Max has a mass of 40 kg, about how much muscle tissue does he have?
   - **A** 16 kg
   - **B** 20 kg
   - **C** 24 kg
   - **D** 30 kg

2. When running, an adult inhales about 72 L of air per minute. That amount is 12 times the amount that an adult needs while resting. How much air does an adult inhale while resting?
   - **F** 6 L/min
   - **G** 12 L/min
   - **H** 60 L/min
   - **I** 64 L/min

3. Maggie likes to do bench presses, a resistance exercise. She bench presses 10 kg. If Maggie added 2 kg every 2 weeks, how long would it take her to reach 20 kg?
   - **A** 4 weeks
   - **B** 5 weeks
   - **C** 10 weeks
   - **D** 12 weeks

4. A box of 25 bandages costs $4.00. A roll of tape costs $1.50. Troy needs 125 bandages and 3 rolls of tape for a first-aid kit. Which of the following equations shows the cost of first-aid supplies, x?
   - **F** $x = (125 \times 4.00) + (3 \times 1.50)$
   - **G** $x = (25 \times 4.00) + (3 \times 1.50)$
   - **H** $x = [(25 \times 4.00) \div 125] + (3 \times 1.50)$
   - **I** $x = [(125 \div 25) \times 4.00] + (3 \times 1.50)$

5. Stephen wants to run a 10 K race. Right now, he can run 5 K. What is the percentage increase from 5 K to 10 K?
   - **A** 50%
   - **B** 100%
   - **C** 200%
   - **D** 500%

Science in Action

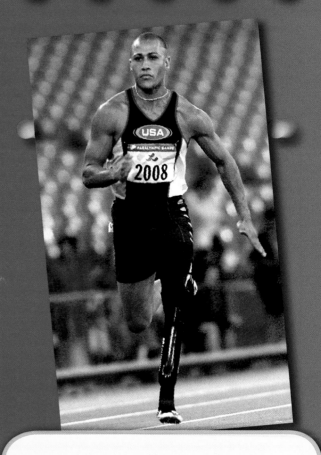

Weird Science

Engineered Skin

Your skin is your first line of defense against the outside world. Your skin keeps you safe from dehydration and infection, helps regulate body temperature, and helps remove some wastes. But what happens if a large portion of skin is damaged? Skin may not be able to function properly. For someone who has a serious burn, a doctor often uses skin from an undamaged part of the person's body to repair the damaged skin. But some burn victims don't have enough undamaged skin to spare. Doctors have discovered ways to engineer skin that can be used in place of human skin.

Math ACTIVITY

A doctor repaired 0.35 m^2 of an adult patient's skin with engineered skin. If an adult has about 2 m^2 of skin, what percentage of the patient's skin was repaired?

Science, Technology, and Society

Beating the Odds

Sometimes, people are born without limbs or lose limbs in accidents. Many of these people have prostheses (prahs THEE seez), or human-made replacements for the body parts. Until recently, many of these prostheses made it more difficult for many people to participate in physical activities, such as sports. But new designs have led to lighter, more comfortable prostheses that move the way that a human limb does. These new designs have allowed athletes with physical disabilities to compete at higher levels.

Social Studies ACTIVITY

Research the use of prostheses throughout history. Create a timeline showing major advances in prosthesis use and design.

Careers

Zahra Beheshti

Physical Therapist A physical therapist is a licensed professional who helps people recover from injuries by using hands-on treatment instead of medicines. Dr. Zahra Beheshti is a physical therapist at the Princeton Physical Therapy Center in New Jersey. She often helps athletes who suffer from sports injuries.

After an injury, a person may go through a process called *rehabilitation* to regain the use of the injured body part. The most common mistake made by athletes is that they play sports before completely recovering from injuries. Dr. Beheshti explains, "Going back to their usual pre-injury routine could result in another injury."

Dr. Beheshti also teaches patients about preventing future sports injuries. "Most injuries happen when an individual engages in strenuous activities without a proper warm-up or cool-down period." Being a physical therapist is rewarding work. Dr. Beheshti says, "I get a lot of satisfaction when treating patients and see them regain their function and independence and return to their normal life."

Language Arts ACTiViTY

WRITING SKILL Interview a physical therapist who works in or near your community. Write a newspaper article about your interview.

To learn more about these Science in Action topics, visit go.hrw.com and type in the keyword **HL5BD1F.**

Current Science

Check out Current Science® articles related to this chapter by visiting go.hrw.com. Just type in the keyword **HL5CS22.**

Circulation and Respiration

About the

Your circulatory system is made up of the heart, blood vessels, and blood. This picture is a colored scanning electron micrograph of red and white blood cells and cell fragments called *platelets*. Red blood cells are disk shaped, white blood cells are rounded, and platelets are the small green fragments. There are millions of blood cells in a drop of blood. Blood cells are so important that your body makes about 200 billion red blood cells every day.

PRE-READING ACTIVITY

FOLDNOTES **Four-Corner Fold**
Before you read the chapter, create the FoldNote entitled "Four-Corner Fold" described in the **Study Skills** section of the Appendix. Label the flaps of the four-corner fold with the section titles "Cardiovascular system," "Blood," "Lymphatic system," and "Respiratory system." Write what you know about each topic under the appropriate flap. As you read the chapter, add other information that you learn.

STARTUP ACTIVITY

Exercise Your Heart

How does your heart respond to exercise? You can see this reaction by measuring your pulse.

Procedure

1. Take your pulse while remaining still. (Take your pulse by placing your fingers on the inside of your wrist just below your thumb.)

2. Using a **watch with a second hand,** count the number of heart beats in 15 s. Then, multiply this number by 4 to calculate the number of beats in 1 minute.

3. Do some moderate physical activity, such as jumping jacks or jogging in place, for 30 s.

4. Stop and calculate your heart rate again.
   Caution: Do not perform this exercise if you have difficulty breathing, if you have high blood pressure or asthma, or if you get dizzy easily.

5. Rest for 5 min.

6. Take your pulse again.

Analysis

1. How did exercise affect your heart rate? Why do you think this happened?

2. How does your heart rate affect the rate at which red blood cells travel throughout your body?

3. Did your heart rate return to normal (or almost normal) after you rested? Why or why not?

The Cardiovascular System

When you hear the word heart, *what do you think of first? Many people think of romance. Some people think of courage. But the heart is much more than a symbol of love or bravery. Your heart is an amazing pump.*

The heart is an organ that is part of your circulatory system. The *circulatory system* includes your heart; your blood; your veins, capillaries, and arteries; and your lymphatic system.

Your Cardiovascular System

Your heart creates pressure every time it beats. This pressure moves blood to every cell in your body through your cardiovascular system (KAR dee OH VAS kyoo luhr SIS tuhm). The **cardiovascular system** consists of the heart and the three types of blood vessels that carry blood throughout your body. The word *cardio* means "heart," and *vascular* means "blood vessel." The blood vessels—arteries, capillaries, and veins—carry blood pumped by the heart. **Figure 1** shows the major arteries and veins.

Vein — Artery

Heart

✔️ **Reading Check** What are the four main parts of the cardiovascular system? (*See the Appendix for answers to Reading Checks.*)

Figure 1 *The cardiovascular system carries blood to every cell in your body.*

cardiovascular system a collection of organs that transport blood throughout the body

The Heart

Your *heart* is an organ made mostly of cardiac muscle tissue. It is about the size of your fist and is almost in the center of your chest cavity. Like hearts of all mammals, your heart has a left side and a right side that are separated by a thick wall. The right side of the heart pumps oxygen-poor blood to the lungs. The left side pumps oxygen-rich blood to the body. As you can see in **Figure 2,** each side has an upper chamber and a lower chamber. Each upper chamber is called an *atrium* (plural, *atria*). Each lower chamber is called a *ventricle*.

Flaplike structures called *valves* are located between the atria and ventricles and in places where large arteries are attached to the heart. As blood moves through the heart, these valves close to prevent blood from going backward. The "lub-dub, lub-dub" sound of a beating heart is caused by the valves closing. **Figure 3** shows the flow of blood through the heart.

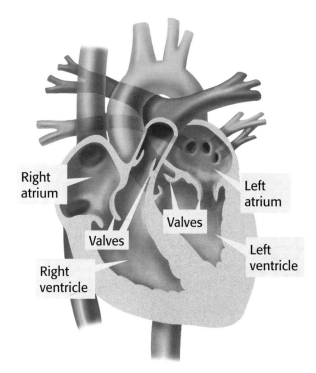

Figure 2 *The heart pumps blood through blood vessels. The vessels carrying oxygen-rich blood are shown in red. The vessels carrying oxygen-poor blood are shown in blue.*

Figure 3   The Flow of Blood Through the Heart

❶ Blood enters the atria first. The left atrium receives oxygen-rich blood from the lungs. The right atrium receives oxygen-poor blood from the body.

❷ When the atria contract, blood is squeezed into the ventricles.

❸ While the atria relax, the ventricles contract and push blood out of the heart. Blood from the right ventricle goes to the lungs. Blood from the left ventricle goes to the rest of the body.

Figure 4 *Large arteries branch into smaller arteries, which branch into capillaries. Capillaries join small veins, which join to form large veins.*

From heart

To heart

Vein

Capillaries

Wall of vein

Artery

Wall of artery

artery a blood vessel that carries blood away from the heart to the body's organs

capillary a tiny blood vessel that allows an exchange between blood and cells in other tissue

vein in biology, a vessel that carries blood to the heart

Blood Vessels

Blood travels throughout your body in hollow tubes called *blood vessels*. The three types of blood vessels—arteries, capillaries, and veins—are shown in **Figure 4.**

Arteries

A blood vessel that carries blood away from the heart is an **artery.** Arteries have thick walls, which contain a layer of smooth muscle. Each heartbeat pumps blood into your arteries at high pressure. This pressure is your *blood pressure.* Artery walls stretch and are usually strong enough to stand the pressure. Your *pulse* is caused by the rhythmic change in your blood pressure.

Capillaries

Nutrients, oxygen, and other substances must leave blood and get to your body's cells. Carbon dioxide and other wastes leave body cells and are carried away by blood. A **capillary** is a tiny blood vessel that allows these exchanges between body cells and blood. These exchanges can take place because capillary walls are only one cell thick. Capillaries are so narrow that blood cells must pass through them in single file. No cell in the body is more than three or four cells away from a capillary.

Veins

After leaving capillaries, blood enters veins. A **vein** is a blood vessel that carries blood back to the heart. As blood travels through veins, valves in the veins keep the blood from flowing backward. When skeletal muscles contract, they squeeze nearby veins and help push blood toward the heart.

Reading Check Describe the three types of blood vessels.

Two Types of Circulation

Where does blood get the oxygen to deliver to your body? From your lungs! Your heart pumps blood to the lungs. In the lungs, carbon dioxide leaves the blood and oxygen enters the blood. The oxygen-rich blood then flows back to the heart. This circulation of blood between your heart and lungs is called **pulmonary circulation** (PUL muh NER ee SUHR kyoo LAY shuhn).

The oxygen-rich blood returning to the heart from the lungs is then pumped to the rest of the body. The circulation of blood between the heart and the rest of the body is called **systemic circulation** (sis TEM ik SUHR kyoo LAY shuhn). Both types of circulation are shown in **Figure 5.**

pulmonary circulation the flow of blood from the heart to the lungs and back to the heart through the pulmonary arteries, capillaries, and veins

systemic circulation the flow of blood from the heart to all parts of the body and back to the heart

Figure 5 The Flow of Blood Through the Body

Pulmonary circulation

Systemic circulation

a The right ventricle pumps oxygen-poor blood into arteries that lead to the lungs. These are the only arteries in the body that carry oxygen-poor blood.

b In the capillaries of the lungs, blood takes up oxygen and releases carbon dioxide. Oxygen-rich blood travels through veins to the left atrium. These are the only veins in the body that carry oxygen-rich blood.

c The heart pumps oxygen-rich blood from the left ventricle into arteries and then into capillaries.

d As blood travels through capillaries, it transports oxygen, nutrients, and water to the cells of the body. At the same time, waste materials and carbon dioxide are carried away.

e Oxygen-poor blood travels back to the heart and is delivered into the right atrium by two large veins.

Cardiovascular Problems

More than just your heart and blood vessels are at risk if you have cardiovascular problems. Your whole body may be harmed. Cardiovascular problems can be caused by smoking, high levels of cholesterol in the blood, stress, physical inactivity, or heredity. Eating a healthy diet and getting plenty of exercise can reduce the risk of having cardiovascular problems.

Atherosclerosis

Heart diseases are the leading cause of death in the United States. A major cause of heart diseases is a cardiovascular disease called *atherosclerosis* (ATH uhr OH skluh ROH sis). Athero-sclerosis happens when cholesterol (kuh LES tuhr AWL) builds up inside of blood vessels. This cholesterol buildup causes the blood vessels to become narrower and less elastic. **Figure 6** shows how clogged the pathway through a blood vessel can become. When an artery that supplies blood to the heart becomes blocked, the person may have a heart attack.

✓ Reading Check Why is atherosclerosis dangerous?

High Blood Pressure

Atherosclerosis may be caused by hypertension. *Hypertension* is abnormally high blood pressure. The higher the blood pressure, the greater the risk of a heart attack, heart failure, kidney disease, and stroke. A *stroke* is when a blood vessel in the brain becomes clogged or ruptures. As a result, that part of the brain receives no oxygen. Without oxygen, brain cells die.

Figure 6 *This illustration shows the narrowing of an artery as the result of high levels of cholesterol in the blood. Lipid deposits (yellow) build up inside the blood vessel walls and block the flow of blood. Red blood cells and lipid particles (yellow balls) are shown escaping.*

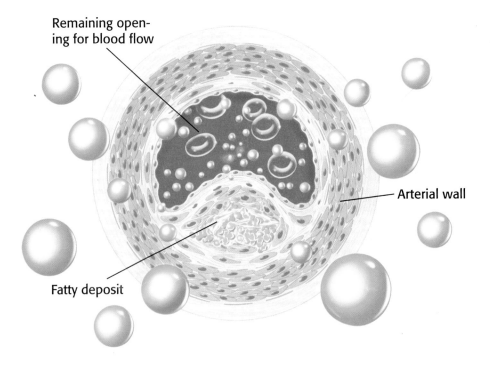

Remaining opening for blood flow

Arterial wall

Fatty deposit

Heart Attacks and Heart Failure

Two cardiovascular problems are heart attacks and heart failure. A *heart attack* happens when heart muscle cells die and part of the heart muscle is damaged. As shown in **Figure 7,** arteries that deliver oxygen to the heart may be blocked. Without oxygen, heart muscle cells die quickly. When enough heart muscle cells die, the heart may stop.

Heart failure is different. *Heart failure* happens when the heart cannot pump enough blood to meet the body's needs. Organs, such as the brain, lungs, and kidneys, may be damaged by lack of oxygen or nutrients, or by the buildup of fluids or wastes.

Figure 7   Heart Attack

Artery delivering blood to heart muscle

Location of blocked artery

Area of heart damaged by lack of oxygen to heart muscle

SECTION Review

Summary

- The cardiovascular system is made up of the heart and three types of blood vessels.
- The three types of blood vessels are arteries, veins, and capillaries.
- Oxygen-poor blood flows from the heart through the lungs, where it picks up oxygen.
- Oxygen-rich blood flows from the heart to the rest of the body.
- Cardiovascular problems include atherosclerosis, hypertension, heart attacks, and strokes.

Using Key Terms

For each pair of terms, explain how the meanings of the terms differ.

1. *artery* and *vein*

2. *systemic circulation* and *pulmonary circulation*

Understanding Key Ideas

3. Which of the following is true of blood in the pulmonary veins?
   a. The blood is going to the body.
   b. The blood is oxygen poor.
   c. The blood is going to the lungs.
   d. The blood is oxygen rich.

4. What are the four parts of the cardiovascular system? Describe the functions of each part.

5. What is the difference between a heart attack and heart failure?

Math Skills

6. An adult male's heart pumps about 2.8 million liters of blood a year. If his heart beats 70 times a minute, how much blood does his heart pump with each beat?

Critical Thinking

7. **Identifying Relationships** How is the heart's structure related to its function?

8. **Making Inferences** One of aspirin's effects is that it prevents platelets from being too "sticky." Why might doctors prescribe aspirin for patients who have had a heart attack?

9. **Analyzing Ideas** Veins and arteries are everywhere in your body. When a pulse is taken, it is usually taken at an artery in the neck or wrist. Explain why.

10. **Making Comparisons** Why is the structure of arteries different from the structure of capillaries?

SCiLINKS®

NSTA
Developed and maintained by the National Science Teachers Association

For a variety of links related to this chapter, go to www.scilinks.org
Topic: The Cardiovascular System; Cardiovascular Problems
SciLinks code: HSM0221; HSM0220

181

Blood

Blood is part of the circulatory system. It travels through miles and miles of blood vessels to reach every cell in your body. So, you must have a lot of blood, right?

Well, actually, an adult human body has about 5 L of blood. Your body probably has a little less than that. All the blood in your body would not fill two 3 L soda bottles.

What Is Blood?

Your *circulatory system* is made up of your heart, your blood vessels, and blood. **Blood** is a connective tissue made up of plasma, red blood cells, platelets, and white blood cells. Blood carries oxygen and nutrients to all parts of your body.

✓ **Reading Check** What are the four main components of blood? (*See the Appendix for answers to Reading Checks.*)

Plasma

The fluid part of the blood is called plasma (PLAZ muh). *Plasma* is a mixture of water, minerals, nutrients, sugars, proteins, and other substances. Red blood cells, white blood cells, and platelets are found in plasma.

Red Blood Cells

Most blood cells are *red blood cells,* or RBCs. RBCs, such as the ones shown in **Figure 1,** take oxygen to every cell in your body. Cells need oxygen to carry out their functions. Each RBC has hemoglobin (HEE moh GLOH bin). *Hemoglobin* is an oxygen-carrying protein. Hemoglobin clings to the oxygen you inhale. RBCs can then transport oxygen throughout the body. Hemoglobin also gives RBCs their red color.

blood the fluid that carries gases, nutrients, and wastes through the body and that is made up of plasma, red blood cells, platelets, and white blood cells

Figure 1 *Red blood cells are made in the bone marrow of certain bones. As red blood cells mature, they lose their nucleus and their DNA.*

Red blood cell

Platelet

Fibers

Figure 2 *Platelets release chemicals in damaged vessels and cause fibers to form. The fibers make a "net" that traps blood cells and stops bleeding.*

Platelets

Drifting among the blood cells are tiny particles called platelets. *Platelets* are pieces of larger cells found in bone marrow. These larger cells remain in the bone marrow, but fragments are pinched off and enter the bloodstream as platelets. Platelets last for only 5 to 10 days, but they are an important part of blood. When you cut or scrape your skin, you bleed because blood vessels have been opened. As soon as bleeding starts, platelets begin to clump together in the damaged area. They form a plug that helps reduce blood loss, as shown in **Figure 2.** Platelets also release chemicals that react with proteins in plasma. The reaction causes tiny fibers to form. The fibers help create a blood clot.

White Blood Cells

Sometimes *pathogens* (PATH uh juhnz)—bacteria, viruses, and other microscopic particles that can make you sick— enter your body. When they do, they often meet *white blood cells,* or WBCs. WBCs, shown in **Figure 3,** help keep you healthy by destroying pathogens. WBCs also help clean wounds.

WBCs fight pathogens in several ways. Some WBCs squeeze out of blood vessels and move around in tissues, searching for pathogens. When they find a pathogen, they destroy it. Other WBCs release antibodies. *Antibodies* are chemicals that identify or destroy pathogens. WBCs also keep you healthy by destroying body cells that have died or been damaged. Most WBCs are made in bone marrow. Some WBCs mature in the lymphatic system.

✓ **Reading Check** Why are WBCs important to your health?

Figure 3 *White blood cells defend the body against pathogens. These white blood cells have been colored yellow to make their shape easier to see.*

Body Temperature Regulation

Your blood does more than supply your cells with oxygen and nutrients. It also helps regulate your body temperature. When your brain senses that your body temperature is rising, it signals blood vessels in your skin to enlarge. As the vessels enlarge, heat from your blood is transferred to your skin. This transfer helps lower your temperature. When your brain senses that your temperature is normal, it instructs your blood vessels to return to their normal size.

Blood Pressure

Every time your heart beats, it pushes blood out of the heart and into your arteries. The force exerted by blood on the inside walls of arteries is called **blood pressure.**

Blood pressure is expressed in millimeters of mercury (mm Hg). For example, a blood pressure of 110 mm Hg means the pressure on the artery walls can push a narrow column of mercury to a height of 110 mm.

Blood pressure is usually given as two numbers, such as 110/70 mm Hg. Systolic (sis TAHL ik) pressure is the first number. *Systolic pressure* is the pressure inside large arteries when the ventricles contract. The surge of blood causes the arteries to bulge and produce a pulse. The second number, *diastolic* (DIE uh STAHL ik) *pressure,* is the pressure inside arteries when the ventricles relax. For adults, a blood pressure of 120/80 mm Hg or below is considered healthy. High blood pressure can cause heart or kidney damage.

Reading Check What is the difference between systolic pressure and diastolic pressure?

Blood Types

Every person has one of four blood types: A, B, AB, or O. Your blood type refers to the type of chemicals you have on the surface of your RBCs. These surface chemicals are called *antigens* (AN tuh juhnz). Type A blood has A antigens; type B has B antigens; and type AB has both A and B antigens. Type O blood has neither the A nor the B antigen.

The different blood types have different antigens on their RBCs. They may also have different antibodies in the plasma. These antibodies react to antigens of other blood types as if the antigens were pathogens. As shown in **Figure 4,** type A blood has antibodies that react to type B blood. If a person with type A blood receives type B blood, the type B antibodies attach themselves to the type B RBCs. These RBCs begin to clump together, and the clumps may block blood vessels. A reaction to the wrong blood type may be fatal.

blood pressure the force that blood exerts on the walls of the arteries

Figure 4 *This figure shows which antigens and antibodies may be present in each blood type.*

Blood Types and Transfusions

Sometimes, a person must be given a blood transfusion. A *transfusion* is the injection of blood or blood components into a person to replace blood that has been lost because of surgery or an injury. **Figure 5** shows bags of blood that may be given in a transfusion. The blood type is clearly marked. Because the ABO blood types have different antigen-antibody reactions, a person receiving blood cannot receive blood from just anyone. **Table 1** shows blood transfusion possibilities.

Figure 5 *The blood type must be clearly labeled on blood stored for transfusions.*

Table 1 Blood Transfusion Possibilities

Type	Can receive	Can donate to
A	A, O	A, AB
B	B, O	B, AB
AB	all	AB only
O	O	all

Reading Check People with type O blood are sometimes called universal donors. Why might this be true?

SECTION Review

Summary

- Blood's four main components are plasma, red blood cells, platelets, and white blood cells.

- Blood carries oxygen and nutrients to cells, helps protect against disease, and helps regulate body temperature.

- Blood pressure is the force blood exerts on the inside walls of arteries.

- Every person has one of four ABO blood types.

- Mixing blood types may be fatal.

Using Key Terms

1. Use each of the following terms in a separate sentence: *blood* and *blood pressure.*

Understanding Key Ideas

2. A person with type B blood can donate blood to people with which type(s) of blood?
   a. B, AB
   b. A, AB
   c. AB only
   d. All types

3. List the four main components of blood and tell what each component does.

4. Why is it important for a doctor to know a patient's blood type?

Math Skills

5. A person has a systolic pressure of 174 mm Hg. What percentage of normal (120 mm Hg) is this?

Critical Thinking

6. **Identifying Relationships** How does the body use blood and blood vessels to help maintain proper body temperature?

7. **Predicting Consequences** Some blood conditions and diseases affect the ability of red blood cells to deliver oxygen to cells of the body. Predict what might happen to a person with a disease of that type.

SCiLINKS

NSTA

Developed and maintained by the National Science Teachers Association

For a variety of links related to this chapter, go to www.scilinks.org

Topic: Blood; Blood Donations
SciLinks code: HSM0175; HSM0178

The Lymphatic System

Every time your heart pumps, a little fluid is forced out of the thin walls of the capillaries. Some of this fluid collects in the spaces around your cells. What happens to this fluid?

Most of the fluid is reabsorbed through the capillaries into your blood. But some is not. Your body has a second circulatory system called the lymphatic (lim FAT ik) system.

The **lymphatic system** is the group of organs and tissues that collect the excess fluid and return it to your blood. The lymphatic system also helps your body fight pathogens.

Vessels of the Lymphatic System

The fluid collected by the lymphatic system is carried through vessels. The smallest vessels of the lymphatic system are *lymph capillaries*. Lymph capillaries absorb some of the fluid and particles from between the cells. These particles are too large to enter blood capillaries. Some of these particles are dead cells or pathogens. The fluid and particles absorbed into lymph capillaries are called **lymph.**

As shown in **Figure 1,** lymph capillaries carry lymph into larger vessels called *lymphatic vessels*. Skeletal muscles squeeze these vessels to force lymph through the lymphatic system. Valves inside lymphatic vessels stop backflow. Lymph drains into the large neck veins of the cardiovascular system.

✓ **Reading Check** How is the lymphatic system related to the cardiovascular system? (*See the Appendix for answers to Reading Checks.*)

lymphatic system a collection of organs whose primary function is to collect extracellular fluid and return it to the blood

lymph the fluid that is collected by the lymphatic vessels and nodes

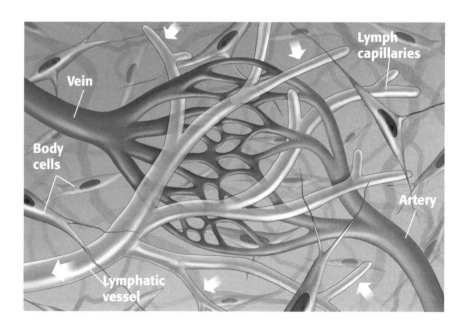

Figure 1 *The white arrows show the movement of lymph into lymph capillaries and through lymphatic vessels.*

Lymph capillaries

Vein

Body cells

Artery

Lymphatic vessel

Other Parts of the Lymphatic System

In addition to vessels and capillaries, several organs and tissues are part of the lymphatic system. These organs and tissues are shown in **Figure 2.** Bone marrow plays an important role in your lymphatic system. The other parts of the lymphatic system are the lymph nodes, the thymus gland, the spleen, and the tonsils.

Bone Marrow

Bones—part of your skeletal system—are very important to your lymphatic system. *Bone marrow* is the soft tissue inside of bones. Bone marrow is where most red and white blood cells, including lymphocytes (LIM foh SIETS), are produced. *Lymphocytes* are a type of white blood cell that helps your body fight pathogens.

Lymph Nodes

As lymph travels through lymphatic vessels, it passes through lymph nodes. **Lymph nodes** are small, bean-shaped masses of tissue that remove pathogens and dead cells from the lymph. Lymph nodes are concentrated in the armpits, neck, and groin.

Lymph nodes contain lymphocytes. Some lymphocytes—called *killer T cells*—surround and destroy pathogens. Other lymphocytes—called *B cells*—produce antibodies that attach to pathogens. These marked pathogens clump together and are then destroyed by other cells.

When bacteria or other pathogens cause an infection, WBCs may multiply greatly. The lymph nodes fill with WBCs that are fighting the infection. As a result, some lymph nodes may become swollen and painful. Your doctor may feel these swollen lymph nodes to see if you have an infection. In fact, if your lymph nodes are swollen and sore, you or your parent can feel them, too. Swollen lymph nodes are sometimes an early clue that you have an infection.

Thymus

T cells develop from immature lymphocytes produced in the bone marrow. Before these cells are ready to fight infections, they develop further in the thymus. The **thymus** is the gland that produces T cells that are ready to fight infection. The thymus is located behind the breastbone, just above the heart. Mature lymphocytes from the thymus travel through the lymphatic system to other areas of your body.

lymph node an organ that filters lymph and that is found along the lymphatic vessels

thymus the main gland of the lymphatic system; it produces mature T lymphocytes

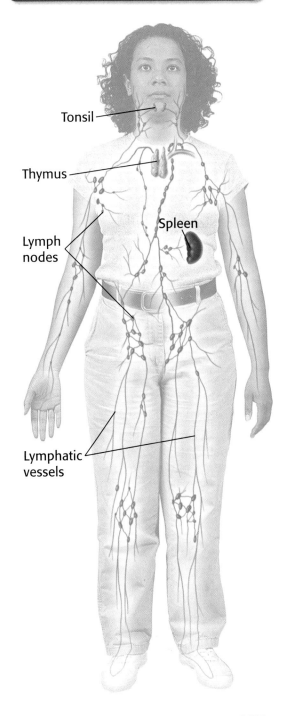

Figure 2 **The Lymphatic System**

Tonsil

Thymus

Spleen

Lymph nodes

Lymphatic vessels

Spleen

Your spleen is the largest lymphatic organ. The **spleen** stores and produces lymphocytes. It is a purplish organ about the size of your fist. Your spleen is soft and spongy. It is located in the upper left side of your abdomen. As blood flows through the spleen, lymphocytes attack or mark pathogens in the blood. If pathogens cause an infection, the spleen may also release lymphocytes into the bloodstream.

In addition to being part of the lymphatic system, the spleen produces, monitors, stores, and destroys blood cells. When red blood cells (RBCs) are squeezed through the spleen's capillaries, the older and more fragile cells burst. These damaged RBCs are then taken apart by some of the cells in the spleen. Some parts of these RBCs may be reused. For this reason, you can think of the spleen as the red-blood-cell recycling center.

The spleen has two important functions. The *white pulp,* shown in **Figure 3,** is part of the lymphatic system. It helps to fight infections. The *red pulp,* also shown in **Figure 3,** removes unwanted material, such as defective red blood cells, from the blood. However, it is possible to lead a healthy life without your spleen. If the spleen is damaged or removed, other organs in the body take over many of its functions.

Reading Check What are two important functions of the spleen?

spleen the largest lymphatic organ in the body

CONNECTION TO Social Studies

WRITING SKILL **Vent Your Spleen** Why do we say that someone is "venting his spleen"? What does it mean? Conduct library or Internet research about this phrase. Write a report on what you have learned.

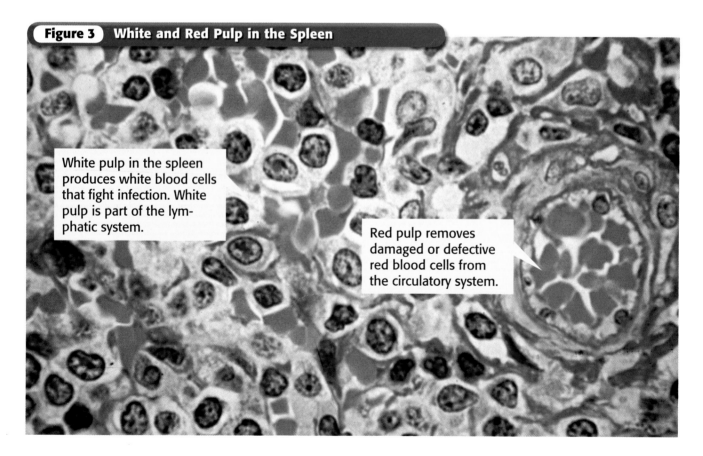

Figure 3 White and Red Pulp in the Spleen

White pulp in the spleen produces white blood cells that fight infection. White pulp is part of the lymphatic system.

Red pulp removes damaged or defective red blood cells from the circulatory system.

Tonsils

The lymphatic system includes your tonsils. **Tonsils** are lymphatic tissue in the nasal cavity and at the back of the mouth on either side of the tongue. Each tonsil is about the size of a large olive.

Tonsils help defend the body against infection. Lymphocytes in the tonsils trap pathogens that enter the throat. Sometimes, tonsils become infected and are red, swollen, and very sore. Severely infected tonsils may be covered with patches of white, infected tissue. Sore, swollen tonsils, such as those in **Figure 4,** make swallowing difficult.

Sometimes, a doctor will suggest surgery to remove the tonsils. In the past, this surgery was frequently done in childhood. It is less common today. Surgery is now done only if a child has frequent, severe tonsil infections or if a child's tonsils are so enlarged that breathing is difficult.

tonsils small, rounded masses of lymphatic tissue located in the pharynx and in the passage from the mouth to the pharynx

Figure 4 *Tonsils help protect your throat and lungs from infection by trapping pathogens.*

Inflamed tonsils

SECTION
Review

Summary

- The lymphatic system collects fluid from between the cells and returns it to the blood.
- The lymphatic system contains cells that help the body fight disease.
- The lymphatic system consists of lymphatic vessels, lymph, and tissues and organs throughout the body.
- The thymus, spleen, and tonsils contain lymphocytes that help fight pathogens.

Using Key Terms

1. Use each of the following terms in a separate sentence: *lymph nodes, spleen,* and *tonsils.*

Understanding Key Ideas

2. Lymph
   a. is the same as blood.
   b. is fluid in the cells.
   c. drains into your muscles.
   d. is fluid collected by lymphatic vessels.

3. Name six parts of the lymphatic system. Tell what each part does.

4. How are your cardiovascular and lymphatic systems related?

Math Skills

5. One cubic millimeter of blood contains 5 million RBCs and 10,000 WBCs. How many times more RBCs are there than WBCs?

Critical Thinking

6. **Expressing Opinions** Some people have frequent, severe tonsil infections. These infections can be treated with medicine, and the infections usually go away after a few days. Do you think removing tonsils in such a case is a good idea? Explain.

7. **Analyzing Ideas** Why is it important that lymphatic tissue is spread throughout the body?

SCILINKS®

NSTA
Developed and maintained by the
National Science Teachers Association

For a variety of links related to this chapter, go to www.scilinks.org

Topic: The Lymphatic System
SciLinks code: HSM0891

The Respiratory System

Breathing—you do it all the time. You're doing it right now. You hardly ever think about it, though, unless you suddenly can't breathe.

Then, it becomes very clear that you have to breathe in order to live. But why is breathing important? Your body needs oxygen in order to get energy from the foods you eat. Breathing makes this process possible.

Respiration and the Respiratory System

The words *breathing* and *respiration* are often used to mean the same thing. However, breathing is only one part of respiration. **Respiration** is the process by which a body gets and uses oxygen and releases carbon dioxide and water. Respiration is divided into two parts. The first part is breathing, which involves inhaling and exhaling. The second part is cellular respiration, which involves chemical reactions that release energy from food.

Breathing is made possible by your respiratory system. The **respiratory system** is the group of organs that take in oxygen and get rid of carbon dioxide. The nose, throat, lungs, and passageways that lead to the lungs make up the respiratory system. **Figure 1** shows the parts of the respiratory system.

respiration the exchange of oxygen and carbon dioxide between living cells and their environment; includes breathing and cellular respiration

respiratory system a collection of organs whose primary function is to take in oxygen and expel carbon dioxide

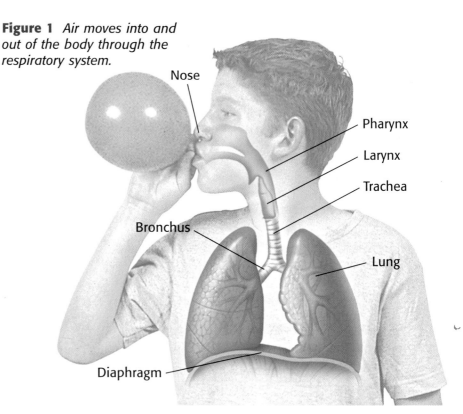

Figure 1 *Air moves into and out of the body through the respiratory system.*

Nose

Pharynx

Larynx

Trachea

Bronchus

Lung

Diaphragm

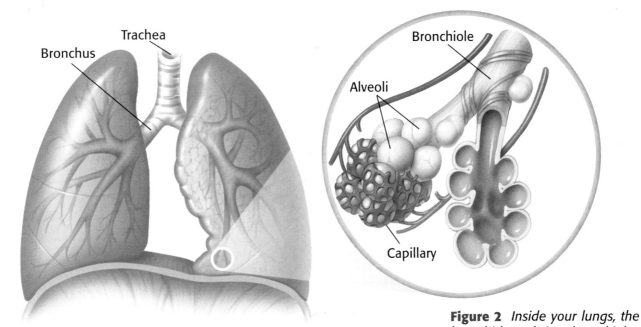

Trachea

Bronchus

Bronchiole

Alveoli

Capillary

Figure 2 *Inside your lungs, the bronchi branch into bronchioles. The bronchioles lead to tiny sacs called alveoli.*

Nose, Pharynx, and Larynx

Your *nose* is the main passageway into and out of the respiratory system. Air can be breathed in through and out of the nose. Air can also enter and leave through the mouth.

From the nose, air flows into the **pharynx** (FAR ingks), or throat. Food and drink also travel through the pharynx on the way to the stomach. The pharynx branches into two tubes. One tube, the *esophagus,* leads to the stomach. The other tube is the larynx (LAR ingks). The larynx leads to the lungs.

The **larynx** is the part of the throat that contains the vocal cords. The *vocal cords* are a pair of elastic bands that stretch across the larynx. Muscles connected to the larynx control how much the vocal cords are stretched. When air flows between the vocal cords, the cords vibrate. These vibrations make sound.

Trachea

The larynx guards the entrance to a large tube called the **trachea** (TRAY kee uh), or windpipe. Your body has two large, spongelike lungs. The trachea, shown in **Figure 2,** is the passageway for air traveling from the larynx to the lungs.

Bronchi and Alveoli

The trachea splits into two branches called **bronchi** (BRAHNG KIE) (singular, *bronchus*). One bronchus connects to each lung. Each bronchus branches into smaller tubes that are called *bronchioles* (BRAHNG kee OHLZ). In the lungs, each bronchiole branches to form tiny sacs that are called **alveoli** (al VEE uh LIE) (singular, *alveolus*). The alveoli provide a large amount of surface area.

✔ Reading Check Describe how the lung's structure relates to its function. (*See the Appendix for answers to Reading Checks.*)

pharynx the passage from the mouth to the larynx and esophagus

larynx the area of the throat that contains the vocal cords and produces vocal sounds

trachea the tube that connects the larynx to the lungs

bronchus one of the two tubes that connect the lungs with the trachea

alveoli any of the tiny air sacs of the lungs where oxygen and carbon dioxide are exchanged

Figure 3 The Role of Blood in Respiration

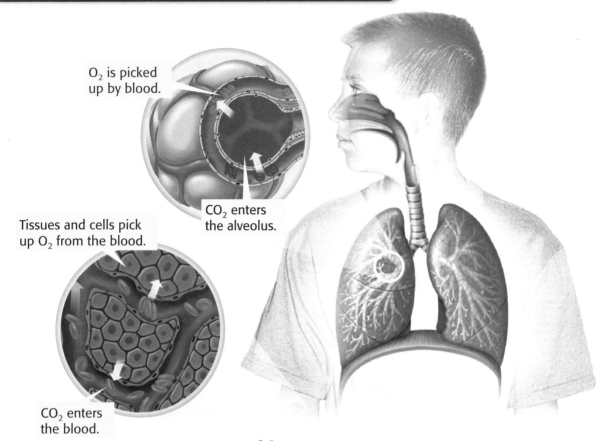

O₂ is picked up by blood.

CO₂ enters the alveolus.

Tissues and cells pick up O₂ from the blood.

CO₂ enters the blood.

Breathing

When you breathe, air is sucked into or forced out of your lungs. However, your lungs have no muscles of their own. Instead, breathing is done by the diaphragm (DIE uh FRAM) and rib muscles. The *diaphragm* is a dome-shaped muscle beneath the lungs. When you inhale, the diaphragm contracts and moves down. The chest cavity's volume increases. At the same time, some of your rib muscles contract and lift your rib cage. As a result, your chest cavity gets bigger and a vacuum is created. Air is sucked in. Exhaling is this process in reverse.

Breathing and Cellular Respiration

In *cellular respiration,* oxygen is used by cells to release energy stored in molecules of glucose. Where does the oxygen come from? When you inhale, you take in oxygen. This oxygen diffuses into red blood cells and is carried to tissue cells. The oxygen then diffuses out of the red blood cells and into each cell. Cells use the oxygen to release chemical energy. During the process, carbon dioxide (CO_2) and water are produced. Carbon dioxide is exhaled from the lungs. **Figure 3** shows how breathing and blood circulation are related.

Reading Check What is cellular respiration?

CONNECTION TO Chemistry

Oxygen and Blood When people who live at low elevations travel up into the mountains, they may find themselves breathing heavily even when they are not exerting themselves. Why might this happen?

Respiratory Disorders

Millions of people suffer from respiratory disorders. Respiratory disorders include asthma, emphysema, and severe acute respiratory syndrome (SARS). Asthma causes the bronchioles to narrow. A person who has asthma has difficulty breathing. An asthma attack may be triggered by irritants such as dust or pollen. SARS is caused by a virus. A person who has SARS may have a fever and difficulty breathing. Emphysema happens when the alveoli have been damaged. People who have emphysema have trouble getting the oxygen they need. **Figure 4** shows a lung damaged by emphysema.

Figure 4 *The photo on the left shows a healthy lung. The photo on the right shows the lung of a person who had emphysema.*

Quick Lab

Why Do People Snore?

1. Get a **15 cm² sheet of wax paper.**
2. Hum your favorite song.
3. Then, take the wax paper and press it against your lips. Hum the song again.
4. How was your humming different when wax paper was pressed to your mouth?
5. Use your observations to guess what might cause snoring.

SECTION Review

Summary

- Air travels to the lungs through the nose or mouth, pharynx, larynx, trachea, and bronchi.
- In the lungs, the bronchi branch into bronchioles, which branch into alveoli.
- Breathing involves lungs, muscles in the rib cage, and the diaphragm.
- Oxygen enters the blood through the alveoli in the lungs. Carbon dioxide leaves the blood and is exhaled.
- Respiratory disorders include asthma, SARS, and emphysema.

Using Key Terms

For each pair of terms, explain how the meanings of the terms differ.

1. *pharynx* and *larynx*

Understanding Key Ideas

2. Which of the following are respiratory disorders?
   a. SARS, alveoli, and asthma
   b. alveoli, emphysema, and SARS
   c. larynx, asthma, and SARS
   d. SARS, emphysema, and asthma

3. Explain how breathing happens.

4. Describe how your cardiovascular and respiratory systems work together.

Math Skills

5. Total lung capacity (TLC) is about 6 L. A person can exhale about 3.6 L. What percentage of TLC cannot be exhaled?

Critical Thinking

6. **Interpreting Statistics** About 6.3 million children in the United States have asthma. About 4 million of them had an asthma attack last year. What do these statistics tell you about the relationship between asthma and asthma attacks?

7. **Identifying Relationships** If a respiratory disorder causes lungs to fill with fluid, how might this affect a person's health?

SCi LINKS.

NSTA

Developed and maintained by the National Science Teachers Association

For a variety of links related to this chapter, go to www.scilinks.org

Topic: The Respiratory System; Respiratory Disorders

SciLinks code: HSM1307; HSM1306

Skills Practice Lab

Carbon Dioxide Breath

Carbon dioxide is important to both plants and animals. Plants take in carbon dioxide during photosynthesis and give off oxygen as a byproduct of the process. Animals—including you—take in oxygen during respiration and give off carbon dioxide as a byproduct of the process.

OBJECTIVES

Detect the presence of carbon dioxide in your breath.

Compare the data for carbon dioxide in your breath with the data from your classmates.

MATERIALS

- calculator (optional)
- clock with a second hand, or a stopwatch
- Erlenmeyer flask, 150 mL
- eyedropper
- gloves, protective
- graduated cylinder, 150 mL
- paper towels
- phenol red indicator solution
- plastic drinking straw
- water, 100 mL

SAFETY

Procedure

1. Put on your gloves, safety goggles, and apron.

2. Use the graduated cylinder to pour 100 mL of water into a 150 mL flask.

3. Using an eyedropper, carefully place four drops of phenol red indicator solution into the water. The water should turn orange.

4. Place a plastic drinking straw into the solution of phenol red and water. Drape a paper towel over the flask to prevent splashing.

5. Carefully blow through the straw into the solution.
   Caution: Do not inhale through the straw. Do not drink the solution, and do not share a straw with anyone.

6 Your lab partner should begin keeping time as soon as you start to blow through the straw. Have your lab partner time how long the solution takes to change color. Record the time.

Analyze the Results

1 **Describing Events** Describe what happens to the indicator solution.

2 **Examining Data** Compare your data with those of your classmates. What was the longest length of time it took to see a color change? What was the shortest? How do you account for the difference?

3 **Constructing Graphs** Make a bar graph that compares your data with the data of your classmates.

Draw Conclusions

4 **Interpreting Information** Do you think that there is a relationship between the length of time the solution takes to change color and the person's physical characteristics, such as which gender the tester is or whether the tester has an athletic build? Explain your answer.

5 **Making Predictions** Predict how exercise might affect the results of your experiment. For example, would you predict that the level of carbon dioxide in the breath of someone who was exercising would be higher or lower than the carbon dioxide level in the breath of someone who was sitting quietly? Would you predict that the level of carbon dioxide in the breath would affect the timing of any color change in the phenol solution?

Applying Your Data

Do jumping jacks or sit-ups for 3 minutes, and then repeat the experiment. Did the phenol solution still change color? Did your exercising change the timing? Describe and explain any change.

Chapter Review

USING KEY TERMS

Complete each of the following sentences by choosing the correct term from the word bank.

red blood cells   veins
white blood cells   arteries
lymphatic system   larynx
alveoli   bronchi
respiratory system   trachea

1 ___ deliver oxygen to the cells of the body.

2 ___ carry blood away from the heart.

3 The ___ helps the body fight pathogens.

4 The ___ contains the vocal cords.

5 The pathway of air through the respiratory system ends at the tiny sacs called ___.

UNDERSTANDING KEY IDEAS

Multiple Choice

6 Blood from the lungs enters the heart at the

a. left ventricle.
b. left atrium.
c. right atrium.
d. right ventricle.

7 Blood cells are made

a. in the heart.
b. from plasma.
c. from lymph.
d. in the bones.

8 Which of the following activities is a function of the lymphatic system?

a. returning excess fluid to the circulatory system
b. delivering nutrients to the cells
c. bringing oxygen to the blood
d. pumping blood to all parts of the body

9 Alveoli are surrounded by

a. veins.
b. muscles.
c. capillaries.
d. lymph nodes.

10 What prevents blood from flowing backward in veins?

a. platelets
b. valves
c. muscles
d. cartilage

11 Air moves into the lungs when the diaphragm muscle

a. contracts and moves down.
b. contracts and moves up.
c. relaxes and moves down.
d. relaxes and moves up.

Short Answer

12 What is the difference between pulmonary circulation and systemic circulation in the cardiovascular system?

13 Walton's blood pressure is 110/65. What do the two numbers mean?

14 What body process produces the carbon dioxide you exhale?

15 Describe how the circulatory system and the lymphatic system work together to keep your body healthy.

16 How is the spleen important to both the lymphatic system and the circulatory system?

17 Briefly describe the path that oxygen follows in your respiratory system and your circulatory system.

CRITICAL THINKING

18 **Concept Mapping** Use the following terms to create a concept map: *blood, oxygen, alveoli, capillaries,* and *carbon dioxide.*

19 **Making Comparisons** Compare and contrast the functions of the circulatory system and the lymphatic system.

20 **Identifying Relationships** Why do you think there are hairs in your nose?

21 **Applying Concepts** After a person donates blood, the blood is stored in one-pint bags until it is needed for a transfusion. A healthy person has about 5 million RBCs in each cubic millimeter (1 mm^3) of blood.

   a. How many RBCs are in 1 mL of blood? (One milliliter is equal to 1 cm^3 and to 1,000 mm^3.)

   b. How many RBCs are there in 1 pt? (One pint is equal to 473 mL.)

22 **Predicting Consequences** What would happen if all of the red blood cells in your blood disappeared?

23 **Identifying Relationships** When a person is not feeling well, a doctor may examine samples of the person's blood to see how many white blood cells are present. Why would this information be useful?

INTERPRETING GRAPHICS

The diagram below shows how the human heart would look in cross section. Use the diagram to answer the questions that follow.

24 Which letter identifies the chamber that receives blood from systemic circulation? What is this chamber's name?

25 Which letter identifies the chamber that receives blood from the lungs? What is this chamber's name?

26 Which letter identifies the chamber that pumps blood to the lungs? What is this chamber's name?

Standardized Test Preparation

EOG Prep

Read each of the passages below. Then, answer the questions that follow each passage.

Passage 1 For some reason, about one in five people sneeze when they step from a dimly lit area into a brightly lit area. In fact, some may sneeze a dozen times or more! Fortunately, the sneezing usually stops relatively quickly. This sneeze reaction is called a <u>photic</u> sneeze reflex (FOHT ik SNEEZ REE fleks). No one knows for certain why it happens. A few years ago, some geneticists studied the photic sneeze reflex. They named it the *ACHOO syndrome*. Scientists know that the ACHOO syndrome runs in families. So, the photic sneeze may be hereditary and can be passed from parent to child. Sometimes, even the number of times in a row that each person sneezes is the same throughout a family.

1. According to the passage, the ACHOO syndrome is most likely to be which of the following?
   A contagious
   B photosynthetic
   C hereditary
   D allergic

2. In the passage, what does *photic* mean?
   F having to do with sneezing
   G having to do with plants
   H having to do with genetics
   I having to do with light

3. Which of the following statements is one clue that the photic sneeze reflex can be passed from parent to child?
   A The reflex is triggered by bright light.
   B Sneezing usually stops after a few sneezes.
   C Family members even sneeze the same number of times.
   D Scientists do not know what causes the ACHOO syndrome.

Passage 2 The two main functions of blood are transporting nutrients and oxygen from the lungs to cells and carrying carbon dioxide and other waste materials away from cells to the lungs or other organs. Blood also transfers body heat to the body surface and plays a role in defending the body against disease. The respiratory system transports gases to and from blood. The respiratory system and blood work together to carry out external respiration and internal respiration. <u>External respiration</u> is the exchange of gases between the atmosphere and blood. Internal respiration is the exchange of gases between blood and the cells of the body.

1. In the passage, what does *external respiration* mean?
   A the exchange of gases outdoors
   B the inhalation of gases as you breathe in
   C the exchange of gases between blood and the atmosphere
   D the exhalation of gases as you breathe out

2. Which of the following statements is a fact in the passage?
   F The respiratory system transports oxygen to all the cells of the body.
   G The respiratory system is part of the circulatory system.
   H Blood is a kind of cardiac tissue.
   I Blood transports oxygen to cells.

3. According to the passage, what are two of the roles blood plays in the human body?
   A transferring body heat and defending against disease
   B defending against disease and transporting gases to the circulatory system
   C transporting carbon dioxide to body cells and transferring body heat
   D external respiration and atmosphere

Use the graph below to answer the questions that follow.

Change in Heart Rate over Time

1. What is the most likely explanation for the change seen after the two-minute mark?
   A The person started exercising.
   B The person fell asleep.
   C The person inhaled.
   D The person sat down.

2. How much faster is the heart beating during minute 5 than during minute 2?
   F 10 beats per minute more
   G 12 beats per minute more
   H 15 beats per minute more
   I 17 beats per minute more

3. About how many minutes did it take for this person's heart rate to go from 65 beats per minute to 75 beats per minute?
   A 0.7 minute
   B 1.0 minute
   C 1.7 minutes
   D 4.0 minutes

4. After how many minutes does this person's heart rate return to its resting rate?
   F 1.0 minute
   G 2.0 minutes
   H 5.0 minutes
   I There is not enough information to determine the answer.

Read each question below, and choose the best answer.

1. If Jim's heart beats 73 times every minute, Jen's heart beats 68 times every minute, and Leigh's heart beats 81 times every minute, what is the average heart rate for these 3 people?
   A 73 beats per minute
   B 74 beats per minute
   C 141 beats per minute
   D 222 beats per minute

2. The Griffith family has 4 dogs. Each of the dogs eats between 0.9 kg and 1.3 kg of food every day. Which is a reasonable estimate of the total amount of food all 4 dogs eat every day?
   F 1 kg of food
   G 3 kg of food
   H 4 kg of food
   I 8 kg of food

3. Assume that the average person's resting heart rate is 70 beats per minute. The resting heart rate of a particular person is 10 beats per minute more than the average person's. If a person with the higher heart rate lives 75 years, about how many more times will his or her heart beat than the average person's heart in that time?
   A 3,942
   B 394,200
   C 3,942,000
   D 394,200,000

4. At rest, the cells of the human body use about 250 mL of oxygen per minute. At that rate, how much oxygen would the cells of the human body use every 24 hours?
   F about 36 L
   G about 360 L
   H about 36,000 L
   I about 360,000 L

Standardized Test Preparation

Science in Action

Science, Technology, and Society

Artificial Blood

What happens when someone loses blood rapidly? Loss of blood can be fatal in a very short time, so lost blood must be replaced as quickly as possible. But what if enough blood, or blood of the right type, is not immediately available? Scientists are developing different types of artificial blood—including one based on cow hemoglobin—that may soon be used to save lives that would otherwise be lost.

Weird Science

Circular Breathing and the Didgeridoo

Do you play a musical instrument such as a clarinet, flute, or tuba? How long can you blow into it before you have to take a breath? Can you blow into it for one minute? two minutes? And what happens when you stop to breathe? The Aboriginal people of Australia have a musical instrument called the *didgeridoo* (DIJ uh ree DOO). Didgeridoo players can play for hours without stopping to take a breath. They use a technique called *circular breathing* that lets them inhale and exhale at the same time. Circular breathing lets a musician play music without having to take breaths as often. With a little practice, maybe you can do it, too.

Language Arts ACTiViTY

WRITING SKILL Imagine that you are a doctor and one of your patients needs surgery. Create a pamphlet or brochure that explains what artificial blood is and how it may be used in surgical procedures.

Social Studies ACTiViTY

WRITING SKILL Select a country from Africa or Asia. Research that country's traditional musical instruments or singing style. Write a description of how the instruments or singing style of that country differs from those of the United States. Illustrate your report.

Anthony Roberts, Jr.

Leader in Training Anthony Roberts, Jr., has asthma. When he was in the 5th grade, his school counselor told him about a summer camp—The Boggy Creek Gang Camp—that was just being built. His counselor said that the camp was designed to serve kids who have asthma or other disabilities and diseases, such as AIDS, cancer, diabetes, epilepsy, hemophilia, heart disease, kidney disease, rheumatic diseases, and sickle cell anemia. Kids, in other words, who might otherwise never go to summer camp. Anthony jumped at the chance to go. Now, Anthony is too old to be a camper, and he is too young to be a regular counselor. But he can be a *Leader in Training* (LIT). Some camps have LIT programs that help young people make the transition from camper to counselor.

For Anthony, the chance to be an LIT fit perfectly with his love of camping and with his desire to work with kids with disabilities. Anthony remembers the fun he had and wants to help other kids have the same summer fun he did.

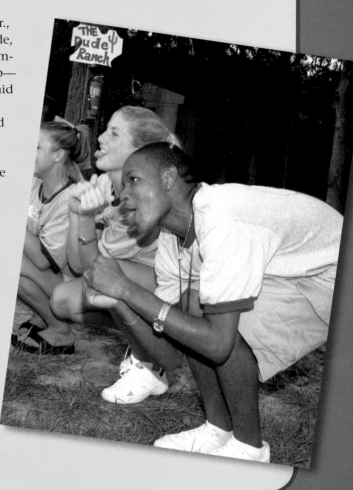

Math ACTiViTY

Research how many children under 17 years of age in the United States have asthma. Make a bar graph that shows how the number of children who have asthma has changed since 1981. What does this graph tell you about rates of asthma among children in the United States?

To learn more about these Science in Action topics, visit go.hrw.com and type in the keyword **HL5BD2F.**

Current Science

Check out Current Science® articles related to this chapter by visiting go.hrw.com. Just type in the keyword **HL5CS23.**

The Digestive and Urinary Systems

About the PHOTO

Is this a giant worm? No, it's an X ray of a healthy large intestine! Your large intestine helps your body preserve water. As mostly digested food passes through your large intestine, water is drawn out of the food. This water is returned to the bloodstream. The gray shadow behind the intestine is the spinal column. The areas that look empty are actually filled with organs. A special liquid helps this large intestine show up on the X ray.

PRE-READING ACTIVITY

Graphic Organizer

Chain-of-Events Chart Before you read the chapter, create the graphic organizer entitled "Chain-of-Events Chart" described in the **Study Skills** section of the Appendix. As you read the chapter, fill in the chart with details about each step of the processes that your body uses to digest food.

START-UP ACTIVITY

Changing Foods

The stomach breaks down food by, in part, squeezing the food. You can model the action of the stomach in the following activity.

Procedure

1. Add **200 mL of flour** and **100 mL of water** to a **resealable plastic bag.**
2. Mix **100 mL of vegetable oil** with the flour and water.
3. Seal the plastic bag.
4. Shake the bag until the flour, water, and oil are well mixed.
5. Remove as much air from the bag as you can, and reseal the bag carefully.
6. Knead the bag carefully with your hands for 5 min. Be careful to keep the bag sealed.

Analysis

1. Describe the mixture before and after you kneaded the bag.
2. How might the changes you saw in the mixture relate to how your stomach digests food?
3. Do you think this activity is a good model of how your stomach works? Explain your answer.

The Digestive System

It's your last class before lunch, and you're starving! Finally, the bell rings, and you get to eat!

You feel hungry because your brain receives signals that your cells need energy to maintain homeostasis. Eating is just the beginning. Your body must change food into substances that your cells can use. Your **digestive system,** shown in **Figure 1,** is a group of organs that work together to break down food so that it can be used by the body.

Digestive System at a Glance

The most obvious part of your digestive system is a series of tubelike organs called the *digestive tract*. Food passes through the digestive tract. The digestive tract includes your mouth, pharynx, esophagus, stomach, small intestine, large intestine, rectum, and anus. The liver, gallbladder, pancreas, and salivary glands are also part of the digestive system. But food does not pass through these organs.

digestive system the organs that break down food so that it can be used by the body

Figure 1 The Digestive System

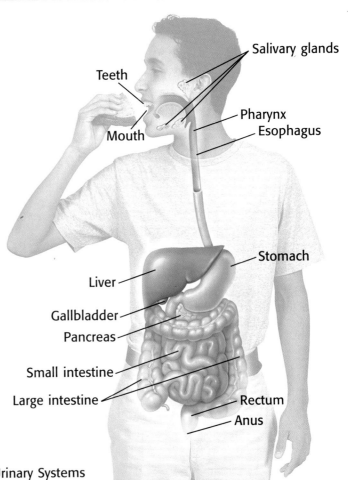

Teeth
Salivary glands
Mouth
Pharynx
Esophagus
Liver
Stomach
Gallbladder
Pancreas
Small intestine
Large intestine
Rectum
Anus

Breaking Down Food

The digestive system works with the circulatory system, which includes the heart, blood vessels, and blood, to deliver the materials cells need to function. Digestion is the process of breaking down food into a form that can pass from the digestive tract into the bloodstream. There are two types of digestion. The breaking, crushing, and mashing of food is called *mechanical digestion.* In *chemical digestion,* large molecules are broken down into nutrients. Nutrients are substances that the body needs for energy and for growth, maintenance, and repair.

Three major types of nutrients—carbohydrates, proteins, and fats—make up most of the food you eat. Substances called *enzymes* break some nutrients into smaller particles that the body can use. For example, proteins are chains of smaller molecules called *amino acids.* Proteins are too large to be absorbed into the bloodstream. So, enzymes cut up the chain of amino acids. The amino acids are small enough to pass into the bloodstream. This process is shown in **Figure 2.**

✓ Reading Check How do the digestive and circulatory systems work together? (*See the Appendix for answers to Reading Checks.*)

Break It Up!

1. Drop **one piece of hard candy** into a **clear plastic cup of water.**

2. Wrap an **identical candy** in a **towel,** and crush the candy with a **hammer.** Drop the candy into a **second clear cup of water.**

3. The next day, examine both cups. What is different about the two candies?

4. What type of digestion is represented by breaking the hard candy?

5. How does chewing your food help the process of digestion?

Figure 2 **The Role of Enzymes in Protein Digestion**

❶ Enzymes act as chemical scissors to cut the long chains of amino acids into small chains.

Enzymes

❷ The small chains are split by other enzymes.

❸ Individual amino acids are small enough to enter the bloodstream, where they can be used to make new proteins.

Digestion Begins in the Mouth

Chewing is important for two reasons. First, chewing creates small, slippery pieces of food that are easier to swallow than big, dry pieces are. Second, small pieces of food are easier to digest.

Teeth

Teeth are very important organs for mechanical digestion. With the help of strong jaw muscles, teeth break and grind food. The outermost layer of a tooth, the *enamel,* is the hardest material in the body. Enamel protects nerves and softer material inside the tooth. **Figure 3** shows a cross section of a tooth.

Have you ever noticed that your teeth have different shapes? Look at **Figure 4** to locate the different kinds of teeth. The molars are well suited for grinding food. The *premolars* are perfect for mashing food. The sharp teeth at the front of your mouth, the *incisors* and *canines,* are for shredding food.

Saliva

As you chew, the food mixes with a liquid called *saliva.* Saliva is made in salivary glands located in the mouth. Saliva contains an enzyme that begins the chemical digestion of carbohydrates. Saliva changes complex carbohydrates into simple sugars.

Leaving the Mouth

Once the food has been reduced to a soft mush, the tongue pushes it into the throat, which leads to a long, straight tube called the **esophagus** (i SAHF uh guhs). The esophagus squeezes the mass of food with rhythmic muscle contractions called *peristalsis* (PER uh STAL sis). Peristalsis forces the food into the stomach.

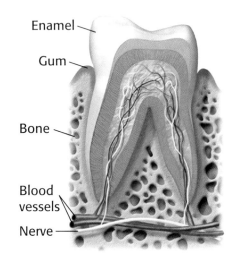

Figure 3 *A tooth, such as this molar, is made of many kinds of tissue.*

Enamel
Gum
Bone
Blood vessels
Nerve

esophagus a long, straight tube that connects the pharynx to the stomach

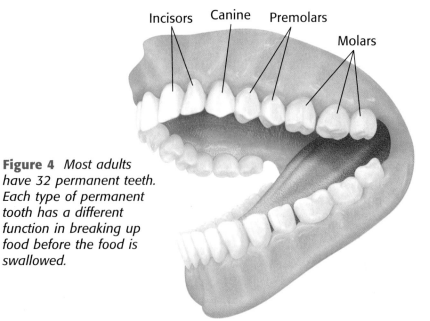

Incisors Canine Premolars Molars

Figure 4 *Most adults have 32 permanent teeth. Each type of permanent tooth has a different function in breaking up food before the food is swallowed.*

Figure 5 The Stomach

The stomach squeezes and mixes food for hours before it releases the mixture into the small intestine.

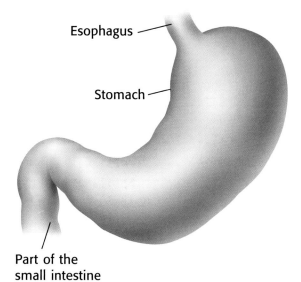

Esophagus

Stomach

Part of the small intestine

The Harsh Environment of the Stomach

The **stomach** is a muscular, saclike, digestive organ attached to the lower end of the esophagus. The stomach is shown in **Figure 5.** The stomach continues the mechanical digestion of your meal by squeezing the food with muscular contractions. While this squeezing is taking place, tiny glands in the stomach produce enzymes and acid. The enzymes and acid work together to break food into nutrients. Stomach acid also kills most bacteria that you might swallow with your food. After a few hours of combined mechanical and chemical digestion, your peanut butter and jelly sandwich has been reduced to a soupy mixture called *chyme* (KIEM).

stomach the saclike, digestive organ between the esophagus and the small intestine that breaks down food into a liquid by the action of muscles, enzymes, and acids .

✔ **Reading Check** How is the structure of the stomach related to its function?

Leaving the Stomach

The stomach slowly releases the chyme into the small intestine through a small ring of muscle that works like a valve. This valve keeps food in the stomach until the food has been thoroughly mixed with digestive fluids. Each time the valve opens and closes, it lets a small amount of chyme into the small intestine. Because the stomach releases chyme slowly, the intestine has more time to mix the chyme with fluids from the liver and pancreas. These fluids help digest food and stop the harsh acids in chyme from hurting the small intestine.

Tooth Truth

Young children get a first set of 20 teeth called *baby teeth*. These teeth usually fall out and are replaced by 32 permanent teeth. How many more permanent teeth than baby teeth does a person have? What is the ratio of baby teeth to permanent teeth? Be sure to express the ratio in its most reduced form.

The Pancreas and Small Intestine

Most chemical digestion takes place after food leaves the stomach. Proteins, carbohydrates, and fats in the chyme are digested by the small intestine and fluids from the pancreas.

The Pancreas

When the chyme leaves the stomach, the chyme is very acidic. The pancreas makes fluids that protect the small intestine from the acid. The **pancreas** is an oval organ located between the stomach and small intestine. The chyme never enters the pancreas. Instead, the pancreatic fluid flows into the small intestine. This fluid contains enzymes that chemically digest chyme and contains bicarbonate, which neutralizes the acid in chyme. The pancreas also functions as a part of the endocrine system by making hormones that regulate blood sugar.

The Small Intestine

The **small intestine** is a muscular tube that is about 2.5 cm in diameter. Other than having a small diameter, it is really not that small. In fact, if you stretched the small intestine out, it would be longer than you are tall—about 6 m! If you flattened out the surface of the small intestine, it would be larger than a tennis court! How is this possible? The inside wall of the small intestine is covered with fingerlike projections called *villi,* shown in **Figure 6.** The surface area of the small intestine is very large because of the villi. The villi are covered with tiny, nutrient-absorbing cells. Once the nutrients are absorbed, they enter the bloodstream.

pancreas the organ that lies behind the stomach and that makes digestive enzymes and hormones that regulate sugar levels

small intestine the organ between the stomach and the large intestine where most of the breakdown of food happens and most of the nutrients from food are absorbed

CONNECTION TO Social Studies

WRITING SKILL **Parasites** Intestinal parasites are organisms, such as roundworms and hookworms, that infect people and live in their digestive tract. Worldwide, intestinal parasites infect more than 1 billion people. Some parasites can be deadly. Research intestinal parasites in a library or on the Internet. Then, write a report on a parasite, including how it spreads, what problems it causes, how many people have it, and what can be done to stop it.

Figure 6 **The Small Intestine and Villi**

The highly folded lining of the small intestine has many fingerlike projections called *villi.*

Villi are covered with nutrient-absorbing cells that pass nutrients to the bloodstream.

Figure 7 The Liver and the Gallbladder

Food does not move through the liver, gallbladder, and pancreas even though these organs are linked to the small intestine.

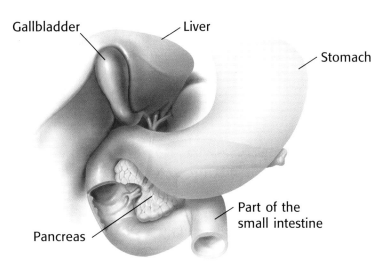

Gallbladder — Liver — Stomach — Part of the small intestine — Pancreas

The Liver and Gallbladder

The **liver** is a large, reddish brown organ that helps with digestion. A human liver can be as large as a football. Your liver is located toward your right side, slightly higher than your stomach, as shown in **Figure 7.** The liver helps with digestion in the following ways:

- It makes bile to break up fat.
- It stores nutrients.
- It breaks down toxins.

Breaking Up Fat

Although bile is made by the liver, bile is temporarily stored in a small, saclike organ called the **gallbladder,** shown in **Figure 7.** Bile is squeezed from the gallbladder into the small intestine, where the bile breaks large fat droplets into very small droplets. This mechanical process allows more fat molecules to be exposed to digestive enzymes.

Reading Check How does bile help digest fat?

Storing Nutrients and Protecting the Body

After nutrients are broken down, they are absorbed into the bloodstream and carried through the body. Nutrients that are not needed right away are stored in the liver. The liver then releases the stored nutrients into the bloodstream as needed. The liver also captures and detoxifies many chemicals in the body. For instance, the liver produces enzymes that break down alcohol and many other drugs.

liver the largest organ in the body; it makes bile, stores and filters blood, and stores excess sugars as glycogen

gallbladder a sac-shaped organ that stores bile produced by the liver

SCHOOL to HOME

Bile Model

You can model the way bile breaks down fat and oil. With a parent, put a small amount of water in a small jar. Then, add a few drops of vegetable oil to the water. Notice that the two liquids separate. Next, add a few drops of liquid dishwashing soap to the water, tighten the lid securely onto the jar, and shake the jar. What happened to the three liquids in the jar? Finally, make a model of the liver and investigate how its structure and functions are related.

large intestine the wider and shorter portion of the intestine that removes water from mostly digested food and that turns the waste into semisolid feces, or stool

The End of the Line

Material that can't be absorbed into the blood is pushed into the large intestine. The **large intestine** is the organ of the digestive system that stores, compacts, and then eliminates indigestible material from the body. The large intestine, shown in **Figure 8,** has a larger diameter than the small intestine. The large intestine is about 1.5 m long, and has a diameter of about 7.5 cm.

In the Large Intestine

Undigested material enters the large intestine as a soupy mixture. The large intestine absorbs most of the water in the mixture and changes the liquid into semisolid waste materials called *feces,* or *stool.*

Whole grains, fruits, and vegetables contain a carbohydrate, called *cellulose,* that humans cannot digest. We commonly refer to this material as *fiber.* Fiber keeps the stool soft and keeps material moving through the large intestine.

✓ *Reading Check* How does eating fiber help digestion?

Leaving the Body

The *rectum* is the last part of the large intestine. The rectum stores feces until they can be expelled. Feces pass to the outside of the body through an opening called the *anus.* It has taken each of your meals about 24 hours to make this journey through your digestive system.

CONNECTION TO Environmental Science

Waste Away Feces and other human wastes contain microorganisms and other substances that can contaminate drinking water. Every time you flush a toilet, the water and wastes go through the sewer to a wastewater treatment plant. At the wastewater treatment plant, the disease-causing microorganisms are removed, and the clean water is released back to rivers, lakes, and streams. Find out where the wastewater treatment plants are in your area. Report to your class where their wastewater goes.

ACTIVITY

Figure 8 *The large intestine is the final organ of digestion.*

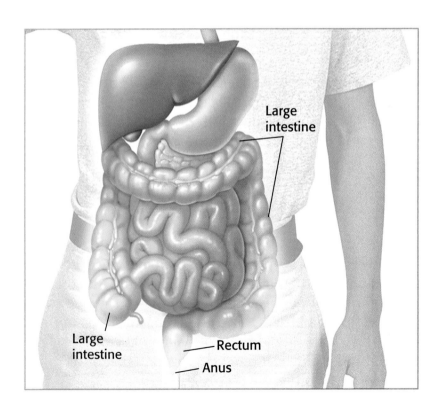

Large intestine

Large intestine

Rectum

Anus

SECTION
Review

Summary

- Your digestive system is a group of organs that work together to digest food so that the nutrients from food can be used by the body.

- The breaking and mashing of food is called *mechanical digestion*. Chemical digestion is the process that breaks large food molecules into simpler molecules.

- The stomach mixes food with acid and enzymes that break down nutrients. The mixture is called *chyme.*

- In the small intestine, pancreatic fluid and bile are mixed with chyme.

- From the small intestine, nutrients enter the bloodstream and are circulated to the body's cells.

- The liver makes bile, stores nutrients, and breaks down toxins.

- The large intestine absorbs water, changing liquid waste into semisolid stool, or feces.

Using Key Terms

1. Use each of the following terms in a separate sentence: *digestive system, large intestine,* and *small intestine.*

Understanding Key Ideas

2. Which of the following is NOT a function of the liver?

   a. to secrete bile   **c.** to detoxify chemicals

   b. to store nutrients   **d.** to compact wastes

3. What is the difference between mechanical digestion and chemical digestion?

4. What happens to the food that you eat when it gets to your stomach?

5. Describe the role of the liver, gallbladder, and pancreas in digestion.

6. Put the following steps of digestion in order.

   a. Food is chewed by the teeth in the mouth.

   b. Water is absorbed by the large intestine.

   c. Food is reduced to chyme in the stomach.

   d. Food moves down the esophagus.

   e. Nutrients are absorbed by the small intestine.

   f. The pancreas releases enzymes.

Critical Thinking

7. **Evaluating Conclusions** Explain the following statement: "Digestion begins in the mouth."

8. **Identifying Relationships** How would the inability to make saliva affect digestion?

Interpreting Graphics

9. Label and describe the function of each of the organs in the diagram below.

For a variety of links related to this chapter, go to www.scilinks.org

Topic: The Digestive System
SciLinks code: HSM0409

211

The Urinary System

As blood travels through the tissues, it picks up waste produced by the body's cells. Your blood is like a train that comes to town to drop off supplies and take away garbage. If the waste is not removed, your body can actually be poisoned.

Excretion is the process of removing waste products from the body. Three of your body systems have a role in excretion. Your integumentary system releases waste products and water when you sweat. Your respiratory system releases carbon dioxide and water when you exhale. Finally, the **urinary system** contains the organs that remove waste products from your blood.

Cleaning the Blood

As your body performs the chemical activities that keep you alive, waste products, such as carbon dioxide and ammonia, are made. Your body has to get rid of these waste products to stay healthy. The urinary system, shown in **Figure 1,** removes these waste products from the blood.

urinary system the organs that produce, store, and eliminate urine

Figure 1   Urinary System

- Kidney
- Ureter
- Urinary bladder
- Urethra

The Kidneys as Filters

The **kidneys** are a pair of organs that constantly clean the blood. Your kidneys filter about 2,000 L of blood each day. Your body holds only 5.6 L of blood, so your blood cycles through your kidneys about 350 times per day!

Inside each kidney, shown in **Figure 2,** are more than 1 million nephrons. **Nephrons** are microscopic filters in the kidney that remove wastes from the blood. Nephrons remove many harmful substances. One of the most important substances removed by nephrons is urea (yoo REE uh), which contains nitrogen and is formed when cells use protein for energy.

Reading Check How are nephrons related to the function of kidneys? (*See the Appendix for answers to Reading Checks.*)

kidney one of the pair of organs that filter water and wastes from the blood and that excrete products as urine

nephron the unit in the kidney that filters blood

Figure 2 **How the Kidneys Filter Blood**

❶ A large artery brings blood into each kidney.

❷ Tiny blood vessels branch off the main artery and pass through part of each nephron.

❸ Water and other small substances, such as glucose, salts, amino acids, and urea, are forced out of the blood vessels and into the nephrons.

❹ As these substances flow through the nephrons, most of the water and some nutrients are moved back into blood vessels that wrap around the nephrons. A concentrated mixture of waste materials is left behind in the nephrons.

❺ The cleaned blood, which has slightly less water and much less waste material, leaves each kidney in a large vein to recirculate in the body.

❻ The yellow fluid that remains in the nephrons is called *urine.* Urine leaves each kidney through a slender tube called the *ureter* and flows into the *urinary bladder,* where urine is stored.

❼ Urine leaves the body through another tube called the *urethra. Urination* is the process of expelling urine from the body.

Nephron

Artery

Unfiltered blood

Filtered blood

Vein

Ureter

Urine

Figure 3 *Drinking water when you exercise helps replace the water you lose when you sweat.*

Water In, Water Out

You drink water every day. You lose water every day in sweat and urine. You need to get rid of as much water as you drink. If you don't, your body will swell up. So, how does your body keep the water levels in balance? The balance of fluids is controlled by chemical messengers in the body called *hormones*.

Sweat and Thirst

When you are too warm, as the boy in **Figure 3** is, you lose a lot of water in the form of sweat. The evaporation of water from your skin cools you down. As the water content of the blood drops, the salivary glands produce less saliva. This is one of the reasons you feel thirsty.

Antidiuretic Hormone

When you get thirsty, other parts of your body react to the water shortage, too. A hormone called *antidiuretic hormone* (AN tee DIE yoo RET ik HAWR MOHN), or ADH, is released. ADH signals the kidneys to take water from the nephrons. The nephrons return the water to the bloodstream. Thus, the kidneys make less urine. When your blood has too much water, small amounts of ADH are released. The kidneys react by allowing more water to stay in the nephrons and leave the body as urine.

Diuretics

Some beverages contain caffeine, which is a *diuretic* (DIE yoo RET ik). Diuretics cause the kidneys to make more urine, which decreases the amount of water in the blood. When you drink a beverage that contains water and caffeine, the caffeine increases fluid loss. So, your body gets to use less of the water from the caffeinated beverage than from a glass of water.

 Reading Check What are diuretics?

Urinary System Problems

The urinary system regulates body fluids and removes wastes from the blood. Any problems with water regulation can become dangerous for your body and disrupt homeostasis. Some common urinary system problems are described below.

- **Bacterial Infections** Bacteria can get into the bladder and ureters through the urethra and cause painful infections. Infections should be treated early, before they spread to the kidneys. Infections in the kidneys can permanently damage the nephrons.

- **Kidney Stones** Sometimes, salts and other wastes collect inside the kidneys and form kidney stones like the one in **Figure 4.** Some kidney stones interfere with urine flow and cause pain. Most kidney stones pass naturally from the body, but sometimes they must be removed by a doctor.

- **Kidney Disease** Damage to nephrons can prevent normal kidney functioning and can lead to kidney disease. If a person's kidneys do not function properly, a kidney machine can be used to filter waste from the blood.

Figure 4 *This kidney stone had to be removed from a patient's urinary system.*

SECTION Review

Summary

- The urinary system removes liquid waste as urine. The filtering structures in the kidney are called *nephrons.*

- Most of the water in the blood is returned to the bloodstream. Urine passes through the ureter, into the bladder, and out of the body through the urethra.

- Disorders of the urinary system include infections, kidney stones, and kidney disease.

Using Key Terms

1. In your own words, write a definition for the term *urinary system.*

Understanding Key Ideas

2. Which event happens first?
   a. Water is absorbed into blood.
   b. A large artery brings blood into the kidney.
   c. Water enters the nephrons.
   d. The nephron separates water from wastes.

3. How do kidneys filter blood?

4. Describe three disorders of the urinary system.

Math Skills

5. A study has shown that 75% of teenage boys drink 34 oz of soda per day. How many 12 oz cans of soda would a boy drink in a week if he drank 34 oz per day?

Critical Thinking

6. **Applying Concepts** Which of the following contains more water: the blood going into the kidney or the blood leaving it?

7. **Predicting Consequences** When people have one kidney removed, their other kidney can often keep their blood clean. But the remaining kidney often changes. Predict how the remaining kidney may change to do the work of two kidneys.

SCI**LINKS**®

NSTA
Developed and maintained by the
National Science Teachers Association

For a variety of links related to this chapter, go to www.scilinks.org
Topic: The Urinary System; Urinary System Ailments
SciLinks code: HSM1583; HSM1584

Skills Practice Lab

As the Stomach Churns

The stomach, as you know, performs not only mechanical digestion but also chemical digestion. As the stomach churns, which moves the food particles around, the digestive fluids—acid and enzymes—are added to begin protein digestion.

Commercially prepared meat tenderizers contain enzymes from plants that break down, or digest, proteins. Two types of meat tenderizer are commonly available at grocery stores. One type of tenderizer contains an enzyme called *papain,* from papaya. Another type of tenderizer contains an enzyme called *bromelain,* from pineapple. In this lab, you will test the effects of these two types of meat tenderizers on beef stew meat.

Ask a Question

1 Determine which question you will answer through your experiment. That question may be one of the following: Which meat tenderizer will work faster? Which one will make the meat more tender? Will the meat tenderizers change the color of the meat or water? What might these color changes, if any, indicate?

Form a Hypothesis

2 Form a hypothesis from the question you formed in step 1. **Caution:** Do not taste any of the materials in this activity.

Test the Hypothesis

3 Identify all variables and controls present in your experiment. In your notebook, make a data table that includes these variables and controls. Use this data table to record your observations and results.

4 Label one test tube with the name of one tenderizer, and label the other test tube with the name of the other tenderizer. Label the third test tube "Control." What will the test tube labeled "Control" contain?

OBJECTIVES

Demonstrate chemical digestion in the stomach.

Investigate three forms of chemical digestion.

MATERIALS

- beef stew meat, 1 cm cubes (3)
- eyedropper
- gloves, protective
- graduated cylinder, 25 mL
- hydrochloric acid, very dilute, 0.1 M
- measuring spoon, 1/4 tsp
- meat tenderizer, commercially prepared, containing bromelain
- meat tenderizer, commercially prepared, containing papain
- tape, masking
- test tubes (4)
- test-tube marker
- test-tube rack
- water

SAFETY

5 Pour 20 mL of water into each test tube.

6 Use the eyedropper to add four drops of very dilute hydrochloric acid to each test tube. **Caution:** Hydrochloric acid can burn your skin. If any acid touches your skin, rinse the area with running water and tell your teacher immediately.

7 Use the measuring spoon to add 1/4 tsp of each meat tenderizer to its corresponding test tube.

8 Add one cube of beef to each test tube.

9 Record your observations for each test tube immediately, after 5 min, after 15 min, after 30 min, and after 24 h.

Analyze the Results

1 **Describing Events** Did you immediately notice any differences in the beef in the three test tubes? At what time interval did you notice a significant difference in the appearance of the beef in the test tubes? Explain the differences.

2 **Examining Data** Did one meat tenderizer perform better than the other? Explain how you determined which performed better.

Draw Conclusions

3 **Evaluating Results** Was your hypothesis supported? Explain your answer.

4 **Applying Conclusions** Many animals that sting have venom composed of proteins. Explain how applying meat tenderizer to the wound helps relieve the pain of such a sting.

Chapter Review

USING KEY TERMS

Complete each of the following sentences by choosing the correct term from the word bank.

pancreas	digestive system
large intestine	stomach
kidney	small intestine
nephron	urinary system

1 The ____ secretes juices into the small intestine.

2 The saclike organ at the end of the esophagus is called the ____.

3 The ____ is an organ that contains millions of nephrons.

4 A group of organs that removes waste from the blood and excretes it from the body is called the ____.

5 The ____ is a group of organs that work together to break down food.

6 Indigestible material is formed into feces in the ____.

UNDERSTANDING KEY IDEAS

Multiple Choice

7 The hormone that signals the kidneys to make less urine is

a. urea.　　　c. ADH.

b. caffeine.　　d. ATP.

8 Which of the following organs aids digestion by producing bile?

a. stomach　　c. small intestine

b. pancreas　　d. liver

9 The part of the kidney that filters the blood is the

a. artery.　　　c. nephron.

b. ureter.　　　d. urethra.

10 The fingerlike projections that line the small intestine are called

a. emulsifiers.

b. fats.

c. amino acids.

d. villi.

11 Which of the following is NOT part of the digestive tract?

a. mouth　　　c. stomach

b. kidney　　　d. rectum

12 The soupy mixture of food, enzymes, and acids in the stomach is called

a. chyme.　　　c. urea.

b. villi.　　　　d. vitamins.

13 The stomach helps with

a. storing food.

b. chemical digestion.

c. physical digestion.

d. All of the above

14 The gall bladder stores

a. food.　　　c. bile.

b. urine.　　　d. villi.

15 The esophagus connects the

a. pharynx to the stomach.

b. stomach to the small intestine.

c. kidneys to the nephrons.

d. stomach to the large intestine.

Short Answer

16 Why is it important for the pancreas to release bicarbonate into the small intestine?

17 How does the structure of the small intestine help the small intestine absorb nutrients?

18 What is a kidney stone?

CRITICAL THINKING

19 **Concept Mapping** Use the following terms to create a concept map: *teeth, stomach, digestion, bile, saliva, mechanical digestion, gallbladder,* and *chemical digestion.*

20 **Predicting Consequences** How would digestion be affected if the liver were damaged?

21 **Analyzing Processes** When you put a piece of carbohydrate-rich food, such as bread, a potato, or a cracker, into your mouth, the food tastes bland. But if this food sits on your tongue for a while, the food will begin to taste sweet. What digestive process causes this change in taste?

22 **Making Comparisons** The recycling process for one kind of plastic begins with breaking the plastic into small pieces. Next, chemicals are used to break the small pieces of plastic down to its building blocks. Then, those building blocks are used to make new plastic. How is this process both like and unlike human digestion?

INTERPRETING GRAPHICS

The bar graph below shows how long the average meal spends in each portion of your digestive tract. Use the graph below to answer the questions that follow.

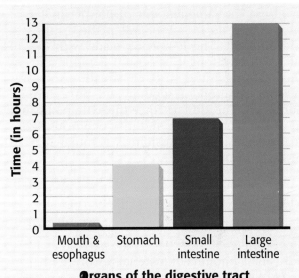

Length of Time in Digestive Organs

23 In which part of your digestive tract does the food spend the longest amount of time?

24 On average, how much longer does food stay in the small intestine than in the stomach?

25 Which organ mixes food with special substances to make chyme? Approximately how long does food remain in this organ?

26 Bile breaks large fat droplets into very small droplets. How long is the food in your body before it comes into contact with bile?

Standardized Test Preparation

READING

Read the passage below. Then, read each question that follows the passage. Decide which is the best answer to each question.

Passage 1 When you lose water, your blood becomes <u>more concentrated</u>. Think about how you make a powdered drink, such as lemonade. If you use the same amount of powder in 1 L of water as you do in 2 L of water, the drinks will taste different. The lemonade made with 1 L of water will be stronger because it is more concentrated. Losing water through sweating increases the concentration of sodium and potassium in your blood. The kidneys force the extra potassium out of the blood stream and into nephrons. From the nephrons, the potassium is eliminated from the body in urine.

1. The words *more concentrated* in this passage refer to
   A the same amount of water with different amounts of material dissolved in it.
   B small amounts of material dissolved in small amounts of water.
   C large amounts of material dissolved in large amounts of water.
   D a given amount of material dissolved in a smaller amount of water.

2. Which of the following statements is a fact from the passage?
   F Blood contains both potassium and sodium.
   G Losing too much sodium is dangerous.
   H Potassium and sodium can be replaced by drinking an exercise drink.
   I Tears contain sodium.

Passage 2 Three major types of nutrients—<u>carbohydrates</u>, proteins, and fats—make up most of the food you eat. Chemical substances called *enzymes* break these nutrients into smaller particles for the body to use. For example, proteins, which are chains of smaller molecules called *amino acids,* are too large to be absorbed into the bloodstream. So, enzymes cut the chain of amino acids. These amino acids are small enough to pass into the bloodstream to be used by the body.

1. According to the passage, what is a carbohydrate?
   A an enzyme
   B a substance made of amino acids
   C a nutrient
   D the only substance in a healthy diet

2. Which of the following statements is a fact from the passage?
   F Carbohydrates, fats, and proteins are three major types of nutrients.
   G Proteins are made of fats and carbohydrates.
   H Some enzymes create chains of proteins.
   I Fats are difficult to digest.

3. Which of the following can be inferred from the passage?
   A To be useful to the body, nutrients must be small enough to enter the bloodstream.
   B Carbohydrates are made of amino acids.
   C Amino acids are made of proteins.
   D Without enough protein, the body cannot grow.

Use the figure below to answer the questions that follow.

1. The container is divided by a membrane. What can you conclude from the diagram?

A Water molecules can pass through the membrane.

B Food-coloring molecules can pass through the membrane.

C Both water molecules and food-coloring molecules can pass through the membrane.

D Neither water molecules nor food-coloring molecules can pass through the membrane.

2. If the membrane has holes that separate molecules by size,

F food-coloring molecules are larger than water molecules.

G water molecules are larger than food-coloring molecules.

H water molecules and food-coloring molecules are the same size.

I the holes are smaller than both water molecules and food-coloring molecules.

3. The concentration of food-coloring molecules in the columns labeled "Water and food coloring"

A is greater in 2 than in 1.

B is greater in 1 than in 2.

C is the same in 1 and 2.

D cannot change.

Read each question below, and choose the best answer.

1. Cora is 1.5 m tall. Cora's small intestine is 6 m long. How many times longer is Cora's small intestine than her height?

A 3 times longer

B 4 times longer

C 5 times longer

D 6 times longer

2. During a water-balance study that was performed for one day, a woman drank 1,500 mL of water. The food she ate contained 750 mL of water, and her body produced 250 mL of water internally during normal body processes. She lost 900 mL of water in sweat, 1,500 mL in urine, and 100 mL in feces. Overall, how much water did she gain or lose during the day?

F She gained 1,500 mL of water.

G She lost 900 mL of water.

H She gained as much water as she lost.

I She lost twice as much water as she gained.

3. There are 6 blue marbles, 2 red marbles, and 4 green marbles in a bag. If someone selects 1 marble at random from the bag, what is the probability that the marble will be blue?

A 1/5

B 1/4

C 1/3

D 1/2

Standardized Test Preparation

Science in Action

Weird Science

Tapeworms

What if you found out that you had a constant mealtime companion who didn't want just a bite but wanted it all? And what if that companion never asked for your permission? This mealtime companion might be a tapeworm. Tapeworms are invertebrate flatworms. These flatworms are parasites. A parasite is an organism that obtains its food by living in or on another organism. A tapeworm doesn't have a digestive tract of its own. Instead, a tapeworm absorbs the nutrients digested by the host. Some tape worms can grow to be over 10 m long. Cooking beef, pork, and fish properly can help prevent people from getting tapeworms. People or animals who get tapeworms can be treated with medicines.

Science, Technology, and Society

Pill Cameras

Open wide and say "Ahhhh." When you have a problem with your mouth or teeth, doctors can examine you pretty easily. But when people have problems that are further down their digestive tract, examination becomes more difficult. So, some doctors have recently created a tiny, disposable camera that patients can swallow. As the camera travels down the digestive tract, the camera takes pictures and sends them to a tiny recorder that patients wear on their belt. The camera takes about 57,000 images during its trip. Later, doctors can review the pictures and see the pictures of the patient's entire digestive tract.

Social Studies

WRITING SKILL The World Health Organization and the Pan American Health Organization have made fighting intestinal parasites in children a high priority. Conduct library or Internet research on Worm Busters, which is a program for fighting parasites. Write a brief report of your findings.

Math ACTIVITY

If a pill camera takes 57,000 images while it travels through the digestive system and takes about two pictures per second, how many hours is the camera in the body?

Christy Krames

Medical Illustrator Christy Krames is a medical illustrator. For 19 years, she has created detailed illustrations of the inner workings of the human body. Medical illustrations allow doctors and surgeons to share concepts, theories, and techniques with colleagues and allow students to learn about the human body.

Medical illustrators often draw tiny structures or body processes that would be difficult or impossible to photograph. For example, a photograph of a small intestine can show the entire organ. But a medical illustrator can add to the photograph an enlarged drawing of the tiny villi inside the intestine. Adding details helps to better explain how small parts of organs work together so that the organs can function.

Medical illustration requires knowledge of both art and science. So, Christy Krames studied both art and medicine in college. Often, Krames must do research before she draws a subject. Her research may include reading books, observing surgical procedures, or even dissecting a pig's heart. This research results in accurate and educational drawings of the inner body.

Language Arts ACTIVITY

WRITING SKILL Pretend you are going to publish an atlas of the human body. Write a classified advertisement to hire medical illustrators. Describe the job, and describe the qualities that the best candidates will have. As you write the ad, remember you are trying to persuade the best illustrators to contact you.

To learn more about these Science in Action topics, visit go.hrw.com and type in the keyword HL5BD3F.

Current Science

Check out Current Science® articles related to this chapter by visiting go.hrw.com. Just type in the keyword HL5CS24.

Communication and Control

About the PHOTO

This picture may look like it shows a flower garden or a coral reef. But it really shows something much closer to home. It shows the human tongue (magnified thousands of times, of course). Those round bumps are taste buds. You use taste and other senses to gather information about your surroundings.

PRE-READING ACTIVITY

Graphic Organizer

Concept Map Before you read the chapter, create the graphic organizer entitled "Concept Map" described in the **Study Skills** section of the Appendix. As you read the chapter, fill in the concept map with details about each part or division of the nervous system. Include details about what each part or division does.

START-UP ACTIVITY

Act Fast!

If you want to catch an object, your brain sends a message to the muscles in your arm. In this exercise, you will see how long sending that message takes.

Procedure

1. Sit in a **chair** with one arm in a "handshake" position. Your partner should stand facing you, holding a **meterstick** vertically. The stick should be positioned so that it will fall between your thumb and fingers.

2. Tell your partner to let go of the meterstick without warning you. Catch the stick between your thumb and fingers. Your partner should catch the meterstick if it tips over.

3. Record the number of centimeters that the stick dropped before you caught it. That distance represents your reaction time.

4. Repeat steps 1–3 three times. Calculate the average distance.

5. Repeat steps 1–4 with your other hand.

6. Trade places with your partner, and repeat steps 1–5.

Analysis

1. Compare the reaction times of your own hands. Why might one hand react more quickly than the other?

2. Compare your results with your partner's. Why might one person react more quickly than another?

The Nervous System

Which of the following activities do NOT involve your nervous system: eating, playing a musical instrument, reading a book, running, or sleeping?

This is a trick question. All of these activities involve your nervous system. In fact, your nervous system controls almost everything you do.

Two Systems Within a System

The nervous system acts as the body's central command post. Its has two basic functions. First, it gathers and interprets information. This information comes from inside your body and from the world outside your body. Then, the nervous system responds to that information as needed.

The nervous system has two parts: the central nervous system and the peripheral (puh RIF uhr uhl) nervous system. The **central nervous system** (CNS) is your brain and spinal cord. The CNS processes and responds to all messages coming from the peripheral nervous system. The **peripheral nervous system** (PNS) is all of the parts of the nervous system except for the brain and the spinal cord. The PNS connects all parts of the body to the CNS. The PNS uses specialized structures, called *nerves,* to carry information between your body and your CNS. **Figure 1** shows the major divisions of the nervous system.

✓ **Reading Check** Explain the difference between the CNS and the PNS. (*See the Appendix for answers to Reading Checks.*)

central nervous system (CNS) the brain and the spinal cord

peripheral nervous system (PNS) all of the parts of the nervous system except for the brain and the spinal cord

Figure 1 *The CNS (in orange) acts as the control center for your body. The PNS (in purple) carries information to and from the CNS.*

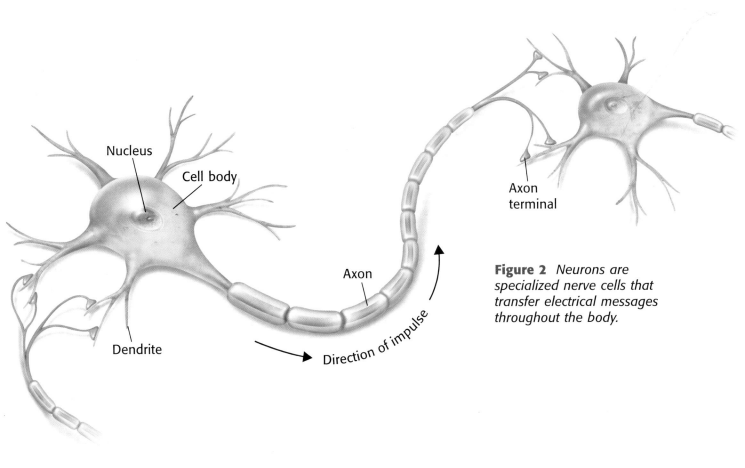

Figure 2 *Neurons are specialized nerve cells that transfer electrical messages throughout the body.*

Nucleus

Cell body

Axon terminal

Axon

Direction of impulse

Dendrite

The Peripheral Nervous System

Messages about your environment travel through the nervous system along neurons. A **neuron** (NOO RAHN) is a nerve cell that is specialized to transfer messages in the form of fast-moving electrical energy. These electrical messages are called *impulses*. Impulses may travel as fast as 150 m/s or as slow as 0.2 m/s. **Figure 2** shows a typical neuron transferring an impulse.

Neuron Structure

In many ways, a neuron is similar to other cells. A neuron has a large region in its center called the *cell body.* The cell body has a nucleus and cell organelles. But neurons also have special structures called dendrites and axons. *Dendrites* are usually short, branched extensions of the cell. Neurons receive information from other cells through their dendrites. A neuron may have many dendrites, which allows it to receive impulses from thousands of other cells.

Impulses are carried away from the cell body by axons. *Axons* are elongated extensions of a neuron. They can be very short or quite long. Some long axons extend almost 1 m from your lower back to your toes. The end of an axon often has branches that allow information to pass to other cells. The tip of each branch is called an *axon terminal.*

Reading Check In your own words, describe a neuron.

neuron a nerve cell that is specialized to receive and conduct electrical impulses

Time to Travel

To calculate how long an impulse takes to travel a certain distance, you can use the following equation:

$$time = \frac{distance}{speed}$$

If an impulse travels 100 m/s, about how long would it take an impulse to travel 10 m?

Information Collection

Remember that neurons are a type of nerve cell that carries impulses. Some neurons are *sensory neurons*. These neurons gather information about what is happening in and around your body. They have specialized nerve endings called *receptors*. Receptors detect changes inside and outside the body. For example, receptors in your eyes detect light. Sensory neurons then send this information to the CNS for processing.

Delivering Orders

Neurons that send impulses from the brain and spinal cord to other systems are called *motor neurons*. When muscles get impulses from motor neurons, they respond by contracting. For example, motor neurons cause muscles around your eyes to contract when you are in bright light. These muscles make you squint. Squinting lets less light enter the eyes. Motor neurons also send messages to your glands, such as sweat glands. These messages tell sweat glands to start or stop making sweat.

Nerves

The central nervous system is connected to the rest of your body by nerves. A **nerve** is a collection of axons bundled together with blood vessels and connective tissue. Nerves are everywhere in your body. Most nerves have axons of both sensory neurons and motor neurons. Axons are parts of nerves, but nerves are more than just axons. **Figure 3** shows the structure of a nerve. The axon in this nerve transmits information from the spinal cord to muscle fibers.

Reading Check What is a nerve?

nerve a collection of nerve fibers (axons) through which impulses travel between the central nervous system and other parts of the body

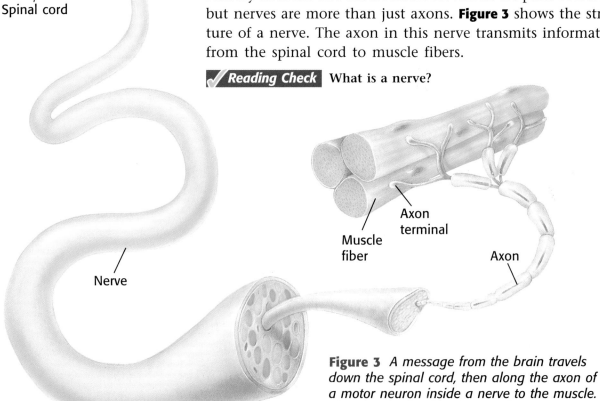

Spinal cord

Nerve

Muscle fiber

Axon terminal

Axon

Figure 3 *A message from the brain travels down the spinal cord, then along the axon of a motor neuron inside a nerve to the muscle. The message makes the muscle contract.*

Somatic and Autonomic Nervous Systems

Remember, the PNS connects your CNS to the rest of your body. And the PNS has two main parts—the sensory part (sensory neurons) and the motor part (motor neurons). You know that sensory nerves collect information from your senses and send that information to the CNS. You also know that motor nerves carry out the CNS's responses to that sensory information. To carry those responses, the motor part of the PNS has two kinds of nerves: somatic nerves and autonomic nerves.

Somatic Nervous System

Most of the neurons that are part of the *somatic nervous system* are under your conscious control. These are the neurons that stimulate skeletal muscles. They control voluntary movements, such as writing, talking, smiling, or jumping.

Autonomic Nervous System

Autonomic nerves do not need your conscious control. These neurons are part of the autonomic nervous system. The *autonomic nervous system* controls body functions that you don't think about, such as digestion and heart rate (the number of times your heart beats per minute).

The main job of the autonomic nervous system is to keep all the body's functions in balance. Depending on the situation, the autonomic nervous system can speed up or slow down these functions. The autonomic nervous system has two divisions: the *sympathetic division* and the *parasympathetic division*. These two divisions work together to keep your internal environment stable. This is called *homeostasis*. Some of these functions are shown in **Table 1.**

Reading Check Describe three functions of the PNS.

CONNECTION TO Chemistry

Keeping Your Balance The autonomic nervous system has two parts—the sympathetic division and the parasympathetic division. These parts of your nervous system help keep all of your body systems in balance. Research these two parts of the nervous system, and make a poster showing how they keep your body healthy.

ACTIVITY

Table 1 Effects of the Autonomic Nervous System on the Body

Organ	Effect of sympathetic division	Effect of parasympathetic division
Eyes	pupils dilate (grow larger; makes it easier to see objects)	pupils constrict (vision normal)
Heart	heart rate increases (increases blood flow)	heart rate slows (blood flow slows)
Lungs	bronchioles dilate (grow larger; increases oxygen in blood)	bronchioles constrict
Blood vessels	blood vessels dilate (increases blood flow except to digestion)	little or no effect
Intestines	digestion slows (reduces blood flow to stomach and intestines)	digestion returns to normal

The Central Nervous System

The central nervous system receives information from the sensory neurons. Then it responds by sending messages to the body through motor neurons in the PNS.

The Control Center

brain the mass of nerve tissue that is the main control center of the nervous system

The largest organ in the nervous system is the brain. The **brain** is the main control center of the nervous system. Many processes that the brain controls happen automatically. These processes are called *involuntary*. For example, you couldn't stop digesting food even if you tried. On the other hand, some actions controlled by your brain are *voluntary*. When you want to move your arm, your brain sends signals along motor neurons to muscles in your arm. Then, the muscles contract, and your arm moves. The brain has three main parts—the cerebrum (suh REE bruhm), the cerebellum (SER uh BEL uhm), and the medulla (mi DUHL uh). Each part has its own job.

✔ **Reading Check** What is the difference between a voluntary action and an involuntary action?

The Cerebrum

The largest part of your brain is called the *cerebrum*. It looks like a mushroom cap. This dome-shaped area is where you think and where most memories are stored. It controls voluntary movements and allows you to sense touch, light, sound, odors, taste, pain, heat, and cold.

The cerebrum has two halves, called *hemispheres*. The left hemisphere directs the right side of the body, and the right hemisphere directs the left side of the body. **Figure 4** shows some of the activities that each hemisphere controls. However, most brain activities use both hemispheres.

Figure 4 **The Cerebral Hemispheres**

The **left hemisphere** primarily controls activities such as speaking, reading, writing, and solving problems.

$$x = \frac{-b \pm \sqrt{b^2 - 4ac}}{2a}$$

$e = mc^2$

$\pi = 3.14159625$

Top of Brain

The **right hemisphere** primarily controls activities such as spatial thinking, processing music, and interpreting emotions.

The Cerebellum

The second-largest part of your brain is the *cerebellum*. It lies beneath the back of the cerebrum. The cerebellum processes sensory information from your body, such as from skeletal muscles and joints. This allows the brain to keep track of your body's position. If you begin to lose your balance, the cerebellum sends impulses telling different skeletal muscles to contract. Those muscles shift a person's weight and keep a person, such as the girl in **Figure 5,** from losing her balance.

The Medulla

The *medulla* is the part of the brain that connects to your spinal cord. The medulla is about 3 cm long, and you can't live without it. It controls involuntary processes in other body systems, such as the circulatory system (blood pressure and heart rate) and the respiratory system (involuntary breathing).

Your medulla constantly receives sensory impulses from receptors in your blood vessels. It uses this information to regulate your blood pressure. If your blood pressure gets too low, the medulla sends out impulses that tell blood vessels to tighten up. As a result, blood pressure rises. The medulla also sends impulses to the heart to make the heart beat faster or slower. **Figure 6** shows the location of the parts of the brain and some of the functions of each part.

Figure 5 *Your cerebellum causes skeletal muscles to make adjustments so that you will stay upright.*

✔ **Reading Check** Explain why the medulla is important.

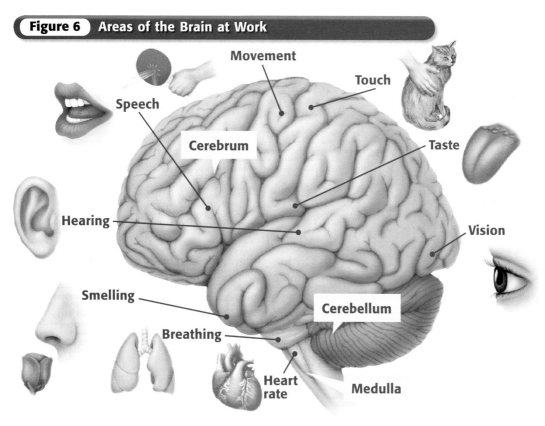

Figure 6 **Areas of the Brain at Work**

Movement

Touch

Speech

Cerebrum

Taste

Hearing

Vision

Smelling

Cerebellum

Breathing

Heart rate

Medulla

Spinal cord

Vertebra

Motor
information

Sensory
information

Figure 7 *The spinal cord carries information to and from the brain. Vertebrae protect the spinal cord.*

The Spinal Cord

Your spinal cord, which is part of your central nervous system, is about as big around as your thumb. The spinal cord is made of neurons and bundles of axons that pass impulses to and from the brain. As shown in **Figure 7,** the spinal cord is surrounded by protective bones called *vertebrae* (VUHR tuh BRAY).

The nerve fibers in your spinal cord allow your brain to communicate with your peripheral nervous system. Sensory neurons in your skin and muscles send impulses along their axons to your spinal cord. The spinal cord carries impulses to your brain. The brain interprets these impulses as pain, temperature, or other sensations. The brain then responds to the situation. Impulses moving from the brain down the spinal cord are relayed to motor neurons. Motor neurons carry the impulses along their axons to muscles and glands all over your body.

Reading Check Describe the path of an impulse from the skin to the brain and the path of the response.

Spinal Cord Injury

A spinal cord injury may block all information to and from the brain. Sensory information coming from below the injury may not get to the brain. For example, a spinal cord injury may block all sensory impulses from the feet and legs. People with such an injury would not be able to sense pain, touch, or temperature with their feet. And motor commands from the brain to the injured area may not reach the peripheral nerves. So, the person would not be able to move his or her legs.

Each year, thousands of people are paralyzed by spinal cord injuries. Many of these injuries happen in car accidents and could be avoided by wearing a seat belt. Among young people, spinal cord injuries are sometimes related to sports or other activities. These injuries might be prevented by wearing proper safety equipment.

Building a Neuron

1. Your teacher will provide at least four different colors of **modeling clay.** Build a model of a neuron by using different-colored clay for the various parts of the neuron.

2. Use **tape** to attach your model neuron to a **piece of plain white paper.**

3. On the paper, label each part of the neuron. Draw an arrow from the label to the part.

4. Using a **colored pencil, marker,** or **crayon,** draw arrows showing the path of an impulse traveling in your neuron. Tell whether the impulse is a sensory impulse or a motor impulse. Then, describe what will happen when the impulse reaches its destination.

Summary

- The central nervous system (CNS) includes the brain and the spinal cord.

- The peripheral nervous system (PNS) is all the parts of the nervous system except the brain and spinal cord.

- The peripheral nervous system has nerves made up of axons of neurons.

- Sensory neurons have receptors that detect information about the body and its environment. Motor neurons carry messages from the brain and spinal cord to other parts of the body.

- The PNS has two types of motor nerves—somatic nerves and autonomic nerves.

- The cerebrum is the largest part of the brain and controls thinking, sensing, and voluntary movement.

- The cerebellum is the part of the brain that keeps track of the body's position and helps maintain balance.

- The medulla controls involuntary processes, such as heart rate, blood pressure, body temperature, and breathing.

Using Key Terms

1. In your own words, write a definition for each of the following terms: *neuron* and *nerve*.

2. Use the following terms in the same sentence: *brain* and *peripheral nervous system*.

Understanding Key Ideas

3. Someone touches your shoulder and you turn around. Which sequence do your impulses follow?

   a. motor neuron, sensory neuron, CNS response

   b. motor neuron, CNS response, sensory neuron

   c. sensory neuron, motor neuron, CNS response

   d. sensory neuron, CNS response, motor neuron

4. Describe one function of each part of the brain.

5. Compare the somatic nervous system with the autonomic nervous system.

6. Explain how a severe injury to the spinal cord can affect other parts of the body.

Critical Thinking

7. **Applying Concepts** Some medications slow a person's nervous system. These drugs are often labeled "May cause drowsiness." Explain why a person needs to know about this side effect.

8. **Making Inferences** Explain how the structure of your brain is adapted to perform specific functions within one or more systems.

Interpreting Graphics

Use the figure below to answer the questions that follow.

9. Which hemisphere of the brain recognizes and processes words, numbers, and letters? faces, places, and objects?

10. For a person whose left hemisphere is primarily in control, would it be easier to learn to play a new computer game by reading the rules and following instructions or by watching a friend play and imitating his actions?

SCI LINKS®

NSTA
Developed and maintained by the
National Science Teachers Association

For a variety of links related to this chapter, go to www.scilinks.org

Topic: Nervous System
SciLinks code: HSM1023

Responding to the Environment

You feel a tap on your shoulder. Who tapped you? You turn to look, hoping to see a friend. Your senses are on the job!

The tap produces impulses in sensory receptors on your shoulder. These impulses travel to your brain. Once the impulses reach your brain, they create an awareness called a *sensation*. In this case, the sensation is of your shoulder being touched. But you still do not know who tapped you. So, you turn around. The sensory receptors in your eyes send impulses to your brain. Now, your brain recognizes your best friend.

Sense of Touch

Touch is what you feel when sensory receptors in the skin are stimulated. It is the sensation you feel when you shake hands or feel a breeze. As shown in **Figure 1,** skin has different kinds of receptors. Each kind of receptor responds mainly to one kind of stimulus. For example, *thermoreceptors* respond to temperature change. Each kind of receptor produces a specific sensation of touch, such as pressure, temperature, pain, or vibration. Skin is part of the integumentary (in TEG yoo MEN tuhr ee) system. The **integumentary system** protects the body from damage. It includes hair, skin, and nails.

✓ **Reading Check** List four sensations that your skin can detect. *(See the Appendix for answers to Reading Checks.)*

integumentary system the organ system that forms a protective covering on the outside of the body

Figure 1 *Each type of receptor in your skin has its own structure and function.*

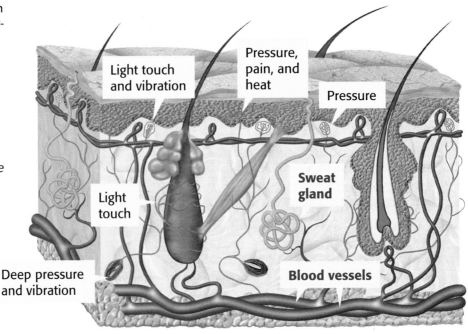

Light touch and vibration

Pressure, pain, and heat

Pressure

Light touch

Sweat gland

Blood vessels

Deep pressure and vibration

Responding to Sensory Messages

Think about how all your body systems interact to provide for everything that you need. For example, when you step on something sharp, as the man in **Figure 2** did, pain receptors in the skin on your foot or toe send impulses to your spinal cord. Almost immediately, a message to move your foot travels back to the muscles in your leg and foot. Without thinking, you quickly lift your foot. This immediate, involuntary action is called a **reflex.** Your brain isn't telling your leg to move. In fact, by the time the message reaches your brain, your leg and foot have already moved. If you had to wait for your brain to act, you toes might be seriously hurt!

reflex an involuntary and almost immediate movement in response to a stimulus

feedback mechanism a cycle of events in which information from one step controls or affects a previous step

✓ **Reading Check** Why are reflexes important?

Feedback Mechanisms

Most of the time, the brain processes information from skin receptors. For example, on a hot day, heat receptors in your skin detect an increase in your temperature. The receptors send impulses to the brain. Your brain responds by sending messages to sweat glands to make sweat. As sweat evaporates, it cools your body. Your brain also signals blood vessels in your skin to dilate (open wider). Blood flow increases. Thermal energy from blood in your skin moves to the air around you. This also cools your body. As your body cools, it sends messages to your brain. The brain responds by signalling sweat glands and blood vessels to reduce their activity.

This cooling process is one of your body's feedback mechanisms. A **feedback mechanism** is a cycle of events in which information from one step controls or affects a previous step. The temperature-regulating feedback mechanism helps keep your body temperature within safe limits. This cooling mechanism works like a thermostat on an air conditioner. Once a room reaches the right temperature, the thermostat sends a message to the air conditioner to stop blowing cold air.

Figure 2 *A reflex, such as lifting your foot when you step on something sharp, is one way your nervous system responds to your environment.*

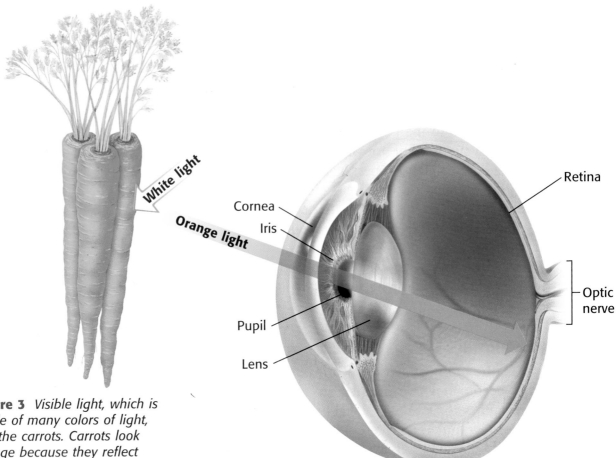

Figure 3 *Visible light, which is made of many colors of light, hits the carrots. Carrots look orange because they reflect orange light to your eyes.*

White light

Orange light

Cornea

Iris

Pupil

Lens

Retina

Optic nerve

retina the light-sensitive inner layer of the eye; it receives images formed by the lens and transmits them through the optic nerve to the brain

For another activity related to this chapter, go to **go.hrw.com** and type in the keyword **HL5BD4W.**

Sense of Sight

Sight is the sense that allows you to see the size, shape, motion, and color of objects around you. You see an object when it sends or reflects visible light toward your eyes. Your eyes detect this light, which enables your brain to form visual images.

Your eyes are complex sensory organs, as you can see in **Figure 3.** The front of the eye is covered by a clear membrane called the *cornea*. The cornea protects the eye but allows light to enter. Light from an object enters the front of your eye through an opening called the *pupil*. The light then travels through the lens to the back of the eye. There, the light strikes the **retina,** a layer of light-sensitive cells.

The retina is packed with photoreceptors. A *photoreceptor* is a special neuron that changes light into electrical impulses. The retina has two kinds of photoreceptors: rods and cones. Rods are very sensitive to dim light. They are important for night vision. Impulses from rods are interpreted as black-and-white images. Cones are very sensitive to bright light. Impulses from cones allow you to see fine details and colors.

Impulses from the rods and cones travel along axons. The impulses leave the back of each eye through an optic nerve. The optic nerve carries the impulses to your brain, where the impulses are interpreted as the images that you see.

✓ Reading Check Describe how light and sight are related.

Reacting to Light

Your pupil looks like a black dot in the center of your eye. In fact, it is an opening that lets light enter the eye. The pupil is surrounded by the *iris*, a ring of muscle. The iris controls the amount of light that enters the eye and gives the eye its color. In bright light, the iris contracts, which makes the pupil smaller. A smaller pupil reduces the amount of light entering the eye and passing onto the retina. In dim light, the iris opens the pupil and lets in more light.

✓ Reading Check How does your iris react to bright light?

Focusing the Light

Light travels in straight lines until it passes through the cornea and the lens. The *lens* is an oval-shaped piece of clear, curved material behind the iris. Muscles in the eye change the shape of the lens in order to focus light onto the retina. When you look at objects close to the eye, the lens becomes more curved. When you look at objects far away, the lens gets flatter.

Figure 4 shows some common vision problems. In some eyes, the lens focuses the light in front of the retina, which results in nearsightedness. If the lens focuses the light just behind the retina, the result is farsightedness. Glasses, contact lenses, or surgery can usually correct these vision problems.

Where's the Dot?

1. Hold your **book** at arm's length, and close your right eye. Focus your left eye on the black dot below.

2. Slowly move the book toward your face until the white dot disappears. You may need to try a few times to get this result. The white dot doesn't always disappear for every person.

3. Describe your observations.

4. Use the library or the Internet to research the optic nerve and to find out why the white dot disappears.

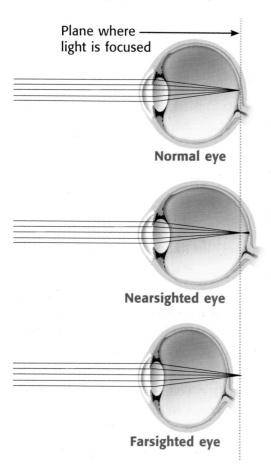

Plane where light is focused

Normal eye

Nearsighted eye

Farsighted eye

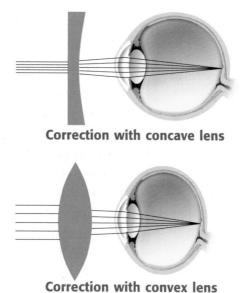

Figure 4 *A concave lens bends light rays outward to correct nearsightedness. A convex lens bends light rays inward to correct farsightedness.*

Correction with concave lens

Correction with convex lens

Auditory nerve

Ear canal

Cochlea

Ear bones

Eardrum

Sound waves

Figure 5 *A sound wave travels into the outer ear. It is converted into bone vibrations in the middle ear, then into liquid vibrations in the inner ear, and finally, into nerve impulses that travel to the brain.*

cochlea a coiled tube that is found in the inner ear and that is essential to hearing

CONNECTION TO Physics

WRITING SKILL **Elephant Talk** Sound is produced by vibrating objects. Some sounds, called *infrasonic sounds*, are too low for human ears to detect. Research how elephants use infrasonic sounds to communicate with each other, and write a report about what you learn.

Sense of Hearing

Sound is produced when something, such as a drum, vibrates. Vibrations push on nearby air particles, which push on other air particles. The vibrations create waves of sound energy. Hearing is the sense that allows you to experience sound energy.

Ears are organs specialized for hearing. Each ear has an outer, middle, and inner portion, as shown in **Figure 5.** Sound waves reaching the outer ear are funneled into the middle ear. There, the waves make the eardrum vibrate. The eardrum is a thin membrane separating the outer ear from the middle ear. The vibrating eardrum makes tiny bones in the middle ear vibrate. One of these bones vibrates against the **cochlea** (KAHK lee uh), a fluid-filled organ of the inner ear. Inside the cochlea, vibrations make waves just like the waves you make by tapping on a glass of water. Neurons in the cochlea change the waves into electrical impulses. These impulses travel along the auditory nerve to the area of the brain that interprets sound.

Reading Check Why is the cochlea important to hearing?

Sense of Taste

Taste is the sense that allows you to detect chemicals and distinguish flavors. Your tongue is covered with tiny bumps called *papillae* (puh PIL ee). Most papillae contain taste buds. Taste buds contain clusters of *taste cells,* the receptors for taste. Taste cells respond to dissolved food molecules. Taste cells react to four basic tastes: sweetness, sourness, saltiness, and bitterness. When the brain combines information from all of the taste buds, you taste a "combination" flavor.

Sense of Smell

As you can see in **Figure 6,** receptors for smell are located on *olfactory cells* in the upper part of your nasal cavity. An olfactory cell is a nerve cell that responds to chemical molecules in the air. You smell something when the receptors react to molecules that have been inhaled. The molecules dissolve in the moist lining of the nasal cavity and trigger an impulse. Olfactory cells send those impulses to the brain, which interprets the impulses as odors.

Taste buds and olfactory cells both detect dissolved molecules. Your brain combines information from both senses to give you sensations of flavor.

Figure 6 *Olfactory cells line the nasal cavity. These cells are sensory receptors that react to chemicals in the air.*

SECTION Review

Summary

- Touch allows you to respond to temperature, pressure, pain, and vibration on the skin.
- Reflexes and feedback mechanisms help you respond to your environment.
- Sight allows you to respond to light energy.
- Hearing allows you to respond to sound energy.
- Taste allows you to distinguish flavors.
- Smell allows you to perceive different odors.

Using Key Terms

1. In your own words, write a definition for each of the following terms: *reflex* and *feedback mechanism.*

2. Use each of the following terms in a separate sentence: *retina* and *cochlea.*

Understanding Key Ideas

3. Three sensations that receptors in the skin detect are
   a. light, smell, and sound.
   b. touch, pain, and odors.
   c. temperature, pressure, and pain.
   d. pressure, sound, and touch.

4. Explain how light and sight are related.

5. Describe how your senses of hearing, taste, and smell work.

6. Explain why you might have trouble seeing bright colors at a candlelit dinner.

7. How is your sense of taste similar to your sense of smell, and how do these senses work together?

8. Describe how the feedback mechanism that regulates body temperature works.

Math Skills

9. Suppose a nerve impulse must travel 0.90 m from your toe to your central nervous system. If the impulse travels at 150 m/s, calculate how long it will take the impulse to arrive. If the impulse travels at 0.2 m/s, how long will it take the impulse to arrive?

Critical Thinking

10. **Making Inferences** Why is it important for the human body to have reflexes?

11. **Applying Concepts** Rods help you detect objects and shapes in dim light. Explain why it is important for human eyes to have both rods and cones.

SCILINKS®

NSTA
Developed and maintained by the
National Science Teachers Association

For a variety of links related to this chapter, go to www.scilinks.org

Topic: The Senses; The Eye
SciLinks code: HSM1378; HSM0560

The Endocrine System

Have you ever heard of an epinephrine (EP uh NEPH rin) rush? You might have had one without realizing it. Exciting situations, such as riding a roller coaster or watching a scary movie, can cause your body to release epinephrine.

Epinephrine is a chemical messenger produced by the adrenal glands. Adrenal glands are part of a second body-control system, the endocrine system.

Glands and Hormones

The **endocrine system** is a collection of glands and groups of cells that secrete hormones. A **gland** is a group of cells that make special chemical messengers for your body. These chemical messengers are called hormones. A **hormone** is a chemical messenger made in one cell or tissue that causes a change in another cell or tissue in another part of the body. Endocrine system hormones regulate growth, development, and homeostasis. Hormones flow through the bloodstream to all parts of the body. Thus, an endocrine gland near your brain can control an organ—or many organs—somewhere else in your body.

In the situation shown in **Figure 1,** the adrenal glands release the hormone *epinephrine*. Epinephrine increases your heartbeat and breathing rate. This response is called the "fight-or-flight" response. When you are frightened, angry, or excited, the "fight-or-flight" response prepares you to fight the danger or to run from it.

endocrine system a collection of glands and groups of cells that secrete hormones that regulate growth, development, and homeostasis

gland a group of cells that make special chemicals for the body

Figure 1 *When you have to move quickly to avoid danger, your adrenal glands make more blood-glucose available for energy.*

More Endocrine Glands

Your body has several other endocrine glands. Some of these glands have many functions. For example, your pituitary gland stimulates skeletal growth and helps the thyroid gland work properly. It also regulates the amount of water in the blood. And the pituitary gland stimulates the birth process in women.

Your thyroid gland is very important during infancy and childhood. Thyroid hormones control the secretion of growth hormones for normal body growth. Thyroid hormones also control the development of the central nervous system. And they control your metabolism. *Metabolism* is the sum of all the chemical processes that take place in an organism.

Your thymus gland is important to your immune system. Cells called *killer T cells* grow and mature in the thymus gland. These T cells help destroy or neutralize cells or substances that invade your body. The names and some of the functions of endocrine glands are shown in **Figure 2.**

Reading Check Name two endocrine glands, and explain why they are important to your body. *(See the Appendix for answers to Reading Checks.)*

hormone a substance that is made in one cell or tissue and that causes a change in another cell or tissue in a different part of the body

CONNECTION TO Language Arts

WRITING SKILL **Working Together** Write a report analyzing how your nervous system and your endocrine system work together to provide for your needs. Especially, evaluate how these two systems work together to help regulate your internal environment. Illustrate your report.

Figure 2 Endocrine Glands and Their Functions

The **pituitary gland** secretes hormones that affect other glands and organs.

The **parathyroid glands** (behind the thyroid) regulate calcium levels in the blood.

The **adrenal glands** help the body respond to danger.

The **pancreas** regulates blood-glucose levels.

The **ovaries** (in females) produce hormones needed for reproduction.

Your **thyroid gland** increases the rate at which you use energy.

The **thymus gland** regulates the immune system, which helps your body fight disease.

The **testes** (in males) produce hormones needed for reproduction.

Controlling the Endocrine Glands

Do you remember the feedback mechanisms at work in the nervous system? Endocrine glands control similar feedback mechanisms. For example, the pancreas has specialized cells that make two different hormones, *insulin* and *glucagon.* As shown in **Figure 3,** these two hormones control the level of glucose in the blood. Insulin lowers blood-glucose levels by telling the liver to convert glucose into glycogen and to store glycogen for future use. Glucagon has the opposite effect. It tells the liver to convert glycogen into glucose and to release the glucose into the blood.

✓ *Reading Check* What does insulin do?

Figure 3 **Blood-Glucose Feedback Control**

5b Sometimes, to raise your blood-glucose level, you must eat something.

1 Glucose is fuel for your body. Glucose is absorbed into the bloodstream from the small intestine.

2 When the glucose level in the blood is high, such as after a meal, the pancreas releases the hormone insulin into the blood.

5a If your blood-glucose falls too far, glucagon tells the liver to break down glycogen and release the glucose into your blood.

Pancreas

Pancreas

4 When the pancreas detects that your blood-glucose level has returned to normal, it stops releasing insulin.

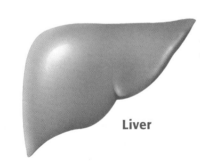

3 Insulin signals the liver to take in glucose from the blood, convert the glucose into glycogen, and to store glycogen for future energy needs.

Liver

Hormone Imbalances

Occasionally, an endocrine gland makes too much or not enough of a hormone. For example, when a person's blood-glucose level rises, the pancreas secretes insulin. Insulin sends a message to the liver to convert glucose into glycogen. The liver stores glycogen for future use. But a person whose body does not use insulin properly or whose pancreas does not make enough insulin has a condition called *diabetes mellitus* (DIE uh BEET EEZ muh LIET uhs). A person who has diabetes may need daily injections of insulin to keep his or her blood-glucose levels within safe limits. Some patients, such as the woman in **Figure 4,** receive their insulin automatically from a small machine worn next to the body.

Another hormone imbalance is when a child's pituitary gland doesn't make enough growth hormone. As a result, the child's growth is stunted. Fortunately, if the problem is detected early, a doctor can prescribe growth hormone and monitor the child's growth. If the pituitary makes too much growth hormone, a child may grow taller than expected.

Figure 4 *This woman has diabetes and receives insulin from a device that monitors her blood-glucose level.*

SECTION Review

Summary

- Glands in the endocrine system use chemical messengers called *hormones.*
- Hormones regulate body functions by causing changes in cells or tissues.
- Feedback mechanisms tell endocrine glands when to turn hormones on and off.
- A hormone imbalance is when a gland releases too much or too little of a hormone.

Using Key Terms

1. Use the following terms in the same sentence: *endocrine system, glands,* and *hormone.*

Understanding Key Ideas

2. Identify five endocrine glands, and explain why their hormones are important to your body.

3. Hormone imbalances may cause
   a. feedback and insulin.
   b. diabetes and stunted growth.
   c. thyroid and pituitary.
   d. glucose and glycogen.

4. How do feedback mechanisms control hormone production?

Math Skills

5. One's bedtime blood-glucose level is normally 140 mg/dL. Ty's blood-glucose level is 189 mg/dL at bedtime. What percentage above 140 mg/dL is Ty's level?

Critical Thinking

6. **Making Inferences** Glucose is a source of energy. Epinephrine quickly increases the blood-glucose level. Why is epinephrine important in times of stress?

7. **Applying Concepts** The hormone glucagon is released when glucose levels fall below normal. Explain how the hormones glucagon and insulin work together to control blood-glucose levels.

SCILINKS®

NSTA
Developed and maintained by the National Science Teachers Association

For a variety of links related to this chapter, go to www.scilinks.org

Topic: Hormones
SciLinks code: HSM0758

Skills Practice Lab

You've Gotta Lotta Nerve

Your skin has thousands of nerve receptors that detect sensations, such as temperature, pain, and pressure. Your brain is designed to filter out or ignore most of the input it receives from these skin receptors. If the brain did not filter input, simply wearing clothes would trigger so many responses that you couldn't function.

Some areas of the skin, such as the back of your hand, are more sensitive than others. In this activity, you will map the skin receptors for heat, cold, and pressure on the back of your hand.

OBJECTIVES

Locate areas on the skin that respond to certain stimuli.

Determine which areas on the skin are more sensitive to certain kinds of stimuli.

MATERIALS

- dissecting pin with a small piece of cork or a small rubber stopper covering the sharp end
- eyedropper, plastic
- paper, graphing
- pens or markers, washable, fine point
- ruler, metric
- tap water, hot
- water, very cold

SAFETY

Procedure

1. Form a group of three. One of you will volunteer the back of your hand for testing, one will do the testing, and the third will record the results.

2. Use a fine-point, washable marker or pen and a metric ruler to mark a 3 cm × 3 cm square on the back of one person's hand. Draw a grid within the area. Space the lines approximately 0.5 cm apart. You will have 36 squares in the grid when you are finished, as shown in the photograph below.

3. Mark off three 3 cm × 3 cm areas on a piece of graph paper. Make a grid in each area exactly as you did on the back of your partner's hand. Label one grid "Cold," another grid "Hot," and the third grid "Pressure."

4 Use the eyedropper to apply one small droplet of cold water on each square in the grid on your partner's hand. Your partner should turn away while being tested. On your graph paper, mark an X on the "Cold" grid to show where your partner felt the cold droplet. Carefully blot the water off your partner's hand after several drops.

5 Repeat the test using hot-water droplets. The hot water should not be hot enough to hurt your partner. Mark an X on the "Hot" grid to indicate where your partner felt the hot droplet.

6 Repeat the test by using the head (not the point!) of the pin. Touch the skin to detect pressure receptors. Use a very light touch. On the graph paper, mark an X on the "Pressure" grid to indicate where your partner felt the pressure.

Analyze the Results

1 **Organizing Data** Count the number of Xs in each grid. How many heat receptor responses are there per 3 cm²? How many cold receptor responses are there? How many pressure receptor responses are there?

2 **Explaining Events** Do you have areas on the back of your hand where the receptors overlap? Explain your answer.

3 **Recognizing Patterns** How do you think the results of this experiment would be similar or different if you mapped an area of your forearm? of the back of your neck? of the palm of your hand?

Draw Conclusions

4 **Interpreting Information** Prepare a written report that includes a description of your investigation and a discussion of your answers to items 1–3. What conclusions can you draw from your results?

Applying Your Data

Use the library or the Internet to research what happens if a receptor is continuously stimulated. Does the kind of receptor make a difference? Does the intensity or strength of the stimulus make a difference? Explain your answers.

Chapter Review

USING KEY TERMS

Complete each of the following sentences by choosing the correct term from the word bank.

insulin

hormone

retina

neuron

reflex

axon

nerve

central nervous
    system

1 The two parts of your _____ are your brain and spinal cord.

2 Sensory receptors in the _____ detect light.

3 Epinephrine is a(n) _____ that triggers the fight-or-flight response.

4 A(n) _____ is an involuntary and almost immediate movement in response to a stimulus.

5 One hormone that helps to regulate blood-glucose levels is _____ .

6 A(n) _____ is a specialized cell that receives and conducts electrical impulses.

UNDERSTANDING KEY IDEAS

Multiple Choice

7 Which of the following has receptors for smelling?

a. cochlea cells

b. thermoreceptors

c. olfactory cells

d. optic nerve

8 Which of the following allow you to see the world in color?

a. cones

b. rods

c. lenses

d. retinas

9 Which of the following glands makes insulin?

a. adrenal gland

b. pituitary gland

c. thyroid gland

d. pancreas

10 The peripheral nervous system does NOT include

a. the spinal cord.

b. axons.

c. sensory receptors.

d. motor neurons.

11 Which part of the brain regulates blood pressure?

a. right cerebral hemisphere

b. left cerebral hemisphere

c. cerebellum

d. medulla

12 The process in which the endocrine system, the digestive system, and the circulatory system control the level of blood glucose is an example of

a. a reflex.

b. an endocrine gland.

c. the fight-or-flight response.

d. a feedback mechanism.

Short Answer

13 What is the difference between the somatic nervous system and the autonomic nervous system? Why are both systems important to the body?

14 Why is the endocrine system important to your body?

15 What is the relationship between the CNS and the PNS?

16 What is the function of the bones in the middle ear?

17 Describe two interactions between the endocrine system and the body that happen when a person is frightened.

CRITICAL THINKING

18 **Concept Mapping** Use the following terms to create a concept map: *nervous system, spinal cord, medulla, peripheral nervous system, brain, cerebrum, central nervous system,* and *cerebellum.*

19 **Making Comparisons** Compare a feedback mechanism with a reflex.

20 **Analyzing Ideas** Why is it important to have a lens that can change shape inside the eye?

21 **Applying Concepts** Why is it important that reflexes happen without thinking about them?

22 **Predicting Consequences** What would happen if your autonomic nervous system stopped working?

23 **Making Comparisons** How are the nervous system and the endocrine system similar? How are they different?

INTERPRETING GRAPHICS

Use the diagram below to answer the questions that follow.

24 Which letter identifies the gland that regulates blood-glucose level?

25 Which letter identifies the gland that releases a hormone that stimulates the birth process?

26 Which letter identifies the gland that helps the body fight disease?

READING

Read each of the passages below. Then, answer the questions that follow each passage.

Passage 1 The axon terminals of neurons usually do not touch the other cells. There is a small gap between an axon terminal and another cell. This space where a neuron meets another cell is called a *synapse*. When a nerve impulse arrives at an axon terminal, the impulse cannot cross the gap. Instead, the impulse triggers the release of chemicals called *neurotransmitters*. These neurotransmitters cross the synapse between the axon terminal and the cell. When neurotransmitters reach the next cell, they signal the cell to react in a certain way. There are many kinds of neurotransmitters. Some neurotransmitters tell cells to start an action. Other neurotransmitters tell cells to stop an action.

1. What is the space between a neuron terminal and a receiving cell called?
   A a neurotransmitter
   B a synapse
   C an axon
   D a nerve

2. Why are neurotransmitters necessary?
   F They tell muscle cells to contract or relax.
   G They create a gap that axons must cross.
   H They carry messages across the synapse.
   I They release chemical signals called *impulses*.

3. Which of the following statements is a fact in the passage?
   A A synapse is an extension of a nerve cell.
   B The space between an axon terminal and another cell is filled with neurons.
   C Nerve impulses jump from an axon to another cell.
   D There are many kinds of neurotransmitters.

Passage 2 Hormones are chemical messengers released by cells that <u>regulate</u> other cells in the body. Hormones regulate many body processes. Hormones control growth, direct the production and use of energy, keep body temperature within normal limits, and direct responses to stimuli outside the body. Hormones carry chemical messages that tell cells to change their activities. For example, one hormone tells the heart to beat faster. Another hormone tells certain cells to make proteins and stimulates bone and muscle growth. Each hormone communicates with specific cells. Each hormone is like a key that opens only one kind of lock. A hormone's message can be received only by cells that have the right kind of lock. Hormones control many important body functions, so their messages must be delivered properly.

1. According to the passage, which of the following statements about hormones is true?
   A Hormones tell cells to change their activities.
   B Hormones are electrical messengers.
   C Hormones are like locks.
   D Hormones are not important to your body.

2. What does the word *regulate* mean?
   F to control or direct
   G to beat faster
   H to raise your temperature
   I to reverse

3. According to the passage, what are two ways that one particular hormone affects the body?
   A controls your temperature and heart rate
   B responds to stimuli and makes proteins
   C stimulates bone growth and makes proteins
   D coordinates energy production and use and decreases temperature

The diagram below shows a typical neuron. Use the diagram below to answer the questions that follow.

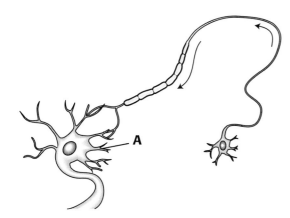

1. What does A represent?
   A a cell body   C a dendrite
   B an axon   D an axon terminal

2. Which of the following represents the path that an impulse in a neuron travels?
   F dendrite, cell body, axon, axon terminal
   G axon, axon terminal, cell body, dendrite
   H dendrite, nucleus, cell body, axon
   I nucleus, cell body, nucleus, axon

3. To where is an impulse that reaches an axon terminal transmitted?
   A another axon terminal
   B the brain
   C a reflex
   D dendrites of another neuron

4. What does having many dendrites allow a neuron to do?
   F to be locked into place in the body
   G to receive impulses from many other cells
   H to send impulses to surrounding cells
   I to get necessary nutrition

5. Which of the following statements about an axon is true?
   A An axon is part of a gland.
   B An axon connects the cell body to the axon terminal.
   C An axon detects sights and sounds.
   D An axon carries chemical messages.

Read each question below, and choose the best answer.

1. Sound travels about 335 m/s. How many kilometers would a sound travel in 1 min? (One kilometer is equal to 1,000 meters.)
   A 335,000 km
   B 20,100 km
   C 20.1 km
   D 0.335 km

2. Some axons send one impulse every 2.5 milliseconds. How many impulses could one of these axons send every second? (One second is equal to 1,000 milliseconds.)
   F 4 impulses
   G 40 impulses
   H 400 impulses
   I 4,000 impulses

3. The table below shows the results of Miguel's blood-glucose tests. Miguel ate lunch at 12:00 noon. His blood glucose was measured every hour after that time. What was the average hourly decrease in blood-glucose level?

Blood Glucose	
Time tested	Blood-glucose level (mg/1,000 mL)
1:00 P.M.	178
2:00 P.M.	112
3:00 P.M.	100
4:00 P.M.	89

   A approximately 160 mg/1,000 mL
   B approximately 120 mg/1,000 mL
   C approximately 30 mg/1,000 mL
   D approximately 22 mg/1,000 mL

4. Your brain has about 1 billion neurons. How is 1 billion expressed in scientific notation?
   F 1×10^3
   G 1×10^6
   H 1×10^9
   I 1×10^{12}

Standardized Test Preparation

Science in Action

Scientific Discoveries

The Placebo Effect

A placebo (pluh SEE boh) is an inactive substance, such as a sugar pill, used in experimental drug trials. Some of the people who are test subjects are given a placebo as if it were the drug being tested. Usually, neither the doctor conducting the trial nor the test subjects know whether a person is taking a placebo or the test drug. In theory, any change in a subject's condition should be the result of the test drug. But for many years, scientists have known about the *placebo effect,* the effect of feeling better after taking the placebo pill. What makes someone who takes the placebo feel better? By studying brain activity, scientists are beginning to understand the placebo effect.

Science, Technology, and Society

Robotic Limbs

Cyborgs, or people that are part human and part robot, have been part of science fiction for many years and usually have super-human strength and X-ray vision. Meanwhile there are ordinary people on Earth who have lost the use of their arms and legs and could use some robot power. However, until recently, they have had to settle for clumsy mechanical limbs that were not a very good substitute for a real arm or hand. Today, thanks to advances in technology, scientists are developing artificial limbs—and eyes and ears—that can be wired directly into the nervous system and can be controlled by the brain. In the near future, artificial limbs and some artificial organs will be much more like the real thing.

Social Studies ACTiViTY

Research the differences and similarities between ancient Chinese medical practices and traditional Western medical treatment. Both types of treatment rely in part on a patient's mental and emotional response to treatment. How might the placebo effect be part of both medical traditions? Create a poster showing the results of your research.

Language Arts ACTiViTY

WRITING SKILL At the library or on the Internet, find examples of optical or visual illusions. Research how the brain processes visual information and how the brain "sees" and interprets these illusions. Write a report about why the brain seems to be fooled by visual tricks. How can understanding the brain's response to illusions help scientists create artificial vision?

Bertha Madras

Studying Brain Activity The brain is an amazing organ. Sometimes, though, drugs or disease keep the brain from working properly. Bertha Madras is a biochemist who studies drug addiction. Dr. Madras studies brain activity to see how substances, such as cocaine, target cells or areas in the brain. Using a variety of brain scanning techniques, Dr. Madras can observe a brain on drugs. She can see how a drug affects the normal activity of the brain. During her research, Dr. Madras realized that some of her results could be applied to Parkinson's disease and to attention deficit hyperactivity disorder (ADHD) in adults. Her research has led to new treatments for both problems.

Math ACTIVITY

Using a search engine on a computer connected to the Internet, search the Internet for "reaction time experiment." Go to one of the Web sites and take the response-time experiment. Record the time that it took you to respond. Repeat the test nine more times, and record your response time for each trial. Then, make a line graph or a bar graph of your response times. Did your response times change? In what way did they change?

NORMAL

COCAINE ABUSER (10 DA)

COCAINE ABUSER (100 DA)

To learn more about these Science in Action topics, visit go.hrw.com and type in the keyword **HL5BD4F.**

Current Science

Check out Current Science® articles related to this chapter by visiting go.hrw.com. **Just type in the keyword HL5CS25.**

9

Reproduction and Development

About the PHOTO

If someone had taken your picture when your mother was about 13 weeks pregnant with you, that picture would have looked much like this photograph. You have changed a lot since then, haven't you? You started out as a single cell, and you became a complete person. And you haven't stopped growing and changing yet. In fact, you will continue to change for the rest of your life.

PRE-READING ACTIVITY

Graphic Organizer

Spider Map Before you read the chapter, create the graphic organizer entitled "Spider Map" described in the **Study Skills** section of the Appendix. Label the circle "Reproduction and Development." Create a leg for each section title. As you read the chapter, fill in the map with details about reproduction and development from each section.

START-UP ACTIVITY

How Grows It?

As you read this paragraph, you are slowly aging. Your body is growing into the body of an adult. But does your body have the same proportions that an adult's body has? Complete this activity to find out.

Procedure

1. Have a classmate use a **tape measure** and **meterstick** to measure your total height, head height, and leg length. Your teacher will tell you how to take these measurements.

2. Use the following equations to calculate your head height–to–total body height proportion and your leg length–to–total body height proportion.

$$\text{head proportion} = \frac{\text{head height}}{\text{body height}} \times 100$$

$$\text{leg proportion} = \frac{\text{leg length}}{\text{body height}} \times 100$$

3. Your teacher will give you the head, body, and leg measurements of three adults. Calculate the head-body and leg-body proportions of each of the three adults. Record all of the measurements and calculations.

Analysis

1. Compare your proportions with the proportions of the three adults.

Animal Reproduction

The life span of some living things is short compared with ours. For example, a fruit fly lives only about 40 days. Other organisms live much longer than we do. Some bristlecone pine trees, for example, are nearly 5,000 years old.

But all living things eventually die. If a species is to survive, its members must reproduce.

Asexual Reproduction

Some animals, particularly simpler ones, reproduce asexually. In **asexual reproduction,** a single parent has offspring that are genetically identical to the parent.

One kind of asexual reproduction is called budding. *Budding* happens when a part of the parent organism pinches off and forms a new organism. The new organism separates from the parent and lives independently. The hydra, shown in **Figure 1,** reproduces by budding. The new hydra is genetically identical to its parent.

Fragmentation is a second kind of asexual reproduction. In *fragmentation,* parts of an organism break off and then develop into a new individual that is identical to the original one. Certain organisms, such as flatworms called *planaria,* reproduce by fragmentation. A third type of asexual reproduction, similar to fragmentation, is *regeneration.* When an organism capable of regeneration, such as the sea star in **Figure 2,** loses a body part, that part may develop into an entirely new organism.

asexual reproduction reproduction that does not involve the union of sex cells and in which a single parent produces offspring that are genetically identical to the parent

Figure 1 *The hydra bud will separate from its parent. Buds from other organisms, such as certain corals, remain attached to the parent.*

Figure 2 *The largest arm on this sea star was a fragment, from which a new sea star will regenerate. In time, all of the sea star's arms will grow to the same size.*

Sexual Reproduction

Most animals reproduce sexually. In **sexual reproduction,** off-spring are formed when genetic information from more than one parent combines. Sexual reproduction in animals usually requires two parents—a male and a female. The female parent produces sex cells called **eggs.** The male parent produces sex cells called **sperm.** When an egg's nucleus and a sperm's nucleus join, a fertilized egg, called a *zygote* (ZIE GOHT), is created. This joining of an egg and sperm is known as *fertilization.*

Human cells—except eggs and sperm and mature red blood cells—contain 46 chromosomes. Eggs and sperm are formed by a process called *meiosis*. In humans, meiosis is the division of one cell that has 46 chromosomes into four cells that have 23 chromosomes each. When an egg and a sperm join to form a zygote, the original number of 46 chromosomes is restored.

Genetic information is found in *genes*. Genes are located on *chromosomes* (KROH muh SOHMZ) made of the cell's DNA. During fertilization, the egg and sperm each contribute chromosomes to the zygote. The combination of genes from the two parents results in a zygote that grows into a unique individual. **Figure 3** shows how genes mix through three generations.

✔ Reading Check What is sexual reproduction? (*See the Appendix for answers to Reading Checks.*)

sexual reproduction reproduction in which sex cells from two parents unite to produce offspring that share traits from both parents

egg a sex cell produced by a female

sperm the male sex cell

Figure 3   Inheriting Genes

Eggs and sperm contain chromosomes. You inherit chromosomes—and the genes on them—from both of your parents. Your parents each inherited chromosomes from their parents.

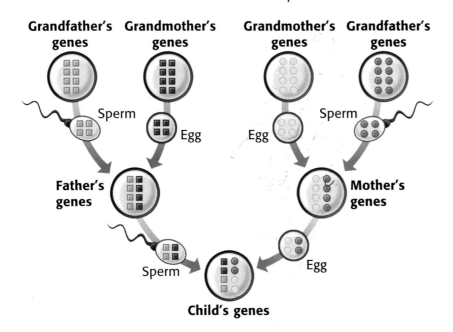

Grandfather's genes   Grandmother's genes   Grandmother's genes   Grandfather's genes

Sperm   Egg   Egg   Sperm

Father's genes   Mother's genes

Sperm   Egg

Child's genes

CONNECTION TO Language Arts

WRITING SKILL   Nature or Nurture? Scientists debate whether genetics or upbringing is more important in shaping people. Use the Internet or library to research the issue of "nature versus nurture." Find information about identical twins who were raised apart. When you finish your research, write a persuasive essay supporting one side of the debate. Include evidence to support your argument.

Figure 4 *Some fish, such as these clownfish, fertilize their eggs externally. The eggs are the orange mass on the rock.*

external fertilization the union of sex cells outside the bodies of the parents

internal fertilization fertilization of an egg by sperm that occurs inside the body of a female

Internal and External Fertilization

Fertilization can happen either outside or inside the female's body. When the sperm fertilizes the eggs outside the female's body, the process is called **external fertilization.** External fertilization must take place in a moist environment so that the delicate zygotes won't dry out. Some fishes, such as those in **Figure 4,** reproduce by external fertilization.

Many amphibians, such as frogs, use external fertilization. For example, the female frog releases her eggs. At the same time, the male frog releases his sperm over the eggs to fertilize them. Frogs usually leave the zygotes to develop on their own. In about two weeks, the fertilized eggs hatch into tadpoles.

Internal Fertilization

When the egg and sperm join inside the female's body, the process is called **internal fertilization**. Internal fertilization allows the female animal to protect the developing egg inside her body. Reptiles, birds, mammals, and some fishes reproduce by internal fertilization. Many animals that use internal fertilization can lay fertilized eggs. Female chickens, for example, usually lay one or two eggs after internal fertilization has taken place.

In most mammals, one or more fertilized eggs develop inside the mother's body. Many mammals give birth to young that are well developed. Young zebras, such as the one in **Figure 5,** can stand up and nurse almost immediately after birth.

Reading Check What is the difference between external and internal fertilization?

Figure 5 *This zebra has just been born, but he is already able to stand. Within an hour, he will be able to run.*

Mammals

All mammals reproduce sexually. All mammals nurture their young with milk. And all mammals reproduce in one of the following three ways:

- **Monotreme** *Monotremes* (MAHN oh TREEMZ) are mammals that lay eggs. After the eggs are incubated and hatch, the young are nourished by milk that oozes from pores on the mother's belly. Echidnas and platypuses are monotremes.

- **Marsupial** Mammals that give birth to partially developed live young, such as the kangaroo in **Figure 6,** are *marsupials* (mahr SOO pee uhlz). Most marsupials have pouches where their young continue to develop after birth. Opossums, koalas, wombats, and Tasmanian devils are marsupials.

- **Placental Mammal** There are more than 4,000 species of placental mammals, including armadillos, humans, and bats. Placental mammals are nourished inside their mother's body before birth. Newborn placental mammals are more developed than newborn monotremes or marsupials are.

Figure 6 *The red kangaroo is a marsupial. A young kangaroo, such as this one in its mother's pouch, is called a* joey.

 Reading Check Name two ways that all mammals are alike.

SECTION Review

Summary

- In asexual reproduction, a single parent produces offspring that are genetically identical to the parent.

- In sexual reproduction, an egg from one parent combines with a sperm from the other parent.

- Fertilization can be external or internal.

- All mammals reproduce sexually and nurture their young with milk.

Using Key Terms

For each pair of terms, explain how the meanings of the terms differ.

1. *internal fertilization* and *external fertilization*

2. *asexual reproduction* and *sexual reproduction*

Understanding Key Ideas

3. In humans, each egg and each sperm contain
   a. 23 chromosomes.
   b. 46 chromosomes.
   c. 69 chromosomes.
   d. 529 chromosomes.

4. List three types of asexual reproduction.

5. How do monotremes differ from marsupials?

6. Describe the process of meiosis.

7. Are humans placental mammals, monotremes, or marsupials? Explain.

Math Skills

8. Some bristlecone pine needles last 40 years. If a tree lives for 3,920 years, how many sets of needles might it grow?

Critical Thinking

9. **Making Inferences** Why is reproduction as important to a bristlecone pine as it is to a fruit fly?

10. **Applying Concepts** Describe one advantage of internal fertilization over external fertilization.

SCLINKS.

NSTA

Developed and maintained by the National Science Teachers Association

For a variety of links related to this chapter, go to www.scilinks.org

Topic: Reproduction

SciLinks code: HSM1293

257

Human Reproduction

About nine months after a human sperm and egg combine, a mother gives birth to her baby. But how do humans make eggs and sperm?

The Male Reproductive System

The male reproductive system, shown in **Figure 1,** produces sperm and delivers it to the female reproductive system. The **testes** (singular, *testis*) are a pair of organs that make sperm and testosterone (tes TAHS tuhr OHN). Testosterone is the main male sex hormone. It helps regulate the production of sperm and the development of male characteristics.

As sperm leave a testis, they are stored in a tube called an *epididymis* (EP uh DID i mis). Sperm mature in the epididymis. Another tube, called a *vas deferens* (vas DEF uh RENZ), passes from the epididymis into the body and through the *prostate gland*. The prostate gland surrounds the neck of the bladder. As sperm move through the vas deferens, they mix with fluids from several glands, including the prostate gland. This mixture of sperm and fluids is called *semen.*

To leave the body, semen passes through the vas deferens into the *urethra* (yoo REE thruh). The urethra is the tube that runs through the penis. The **penis** is the external organ that transfers semen into the female's body.

✓ **Reading Check** Describe the path that sperm take from the testes to the penis. (*See the Appendix for answers to Reading Checks.*)

testes the primary male reproductive organs, which produce sperm and testosterone (singular, *testis*)

penis the male organ that transfers sperm to a female and that carries urine out of the body

Figure 1   **The Male Reproductive System**

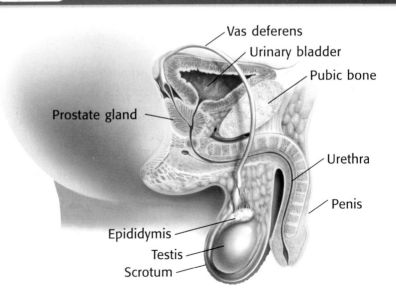

Vas deferens
Urinary bladder
Pubic bone
Prostate gland
Urethra
Penis
Epididymis
Testis
Scrotum

Figure 2 The Female Reproductive System

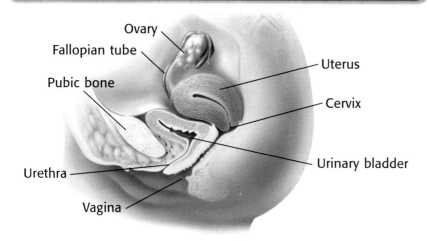

The Female Reproductive System

The female reproductive system, shown in **Figure 2,** produces eggs, nurtures fertilized eggs (zygotes), and gives birth. The two **ovaries** are the organs that make eggs. Ovaries also release estrogen (ES truh juhn) and progesterone (proh JES tuhr OHN), the main female sex hormones. These hormones regulate the release of eggs and development of female characteristics.

The Egg's Journey

During *ovulation* (AHV yoo LAY shuhn), an egg is released from an ovary and passes into a *fallopian* (fuh LOH pee uhn) *tube.* A fallopian tube leads from each ovary to the uterus. The egg passes through the fallopian tube into the uterus. Fertilization usually happens in the fallopian tube. If the egg is fertilized, the resulting zygote enters the uterus. The zygote may become embedded in the thickened lining of the uterus. The **uterus** is the organ in which a zygote develops into a baby.

When a baby is born, he or she passes from the uterus through the vagina and emerges outside the body. The **vagina** is the canal between the outside of the body and the uterus.

Menstrual Cycle

From puberty through her late 40s or early 50s, a woman's reproductive system goes through monthly changes. These changes prepare the body for pregnancy and are called the *menstrual cycle* (MEN struhl SIE kuhl). The first day of *menstruation* (MEN STRAY shuhn), the monthly discharge of blood and tissue from the uterus, is counted as the first day of the cycle. Menstruation lasts about 5 days. When menstruation ends, the lining of the uterus thickens. Ovulation occurs on about the 14th day of the cycle. If the egg is not fertilized within a few days, menstruation begins and flushes the egg away. The cycle—which usually takes about 28 days—starts again.

ovary in the female reproductive system of animals, an organ that produces eggs

uterus in female mammals, the hollow, muscular organ in which a fertilized egg is embedded and in which the embryo and fetus develop

vagina the female reproductive organ that connects the outside of the body to the uterus

Counting Eggs

1. The average woman ovulates each month from about age 12 to about age 50. How many mature eggs could she produce from age 18 to age 50?

2. A female's ovaries typically contain 2 million immature eggs. If she ovulates regularly from age 12 to age 50, what percentage of her eggs will mature?

Multiple Births

Have you ever seen identical twins? Sometimes, they are so similar that even their parents have trouble telling them apart. The boys in **Figure 3** are identical twins. Fraternal twins, the other type of twins, are more common than identical twins are. Fraternal twins can look very different from each other. In every 1,000 births, there are about 30 sets of twins. About one-third of all twin births are identical twins.

Twins are the most common multiple births. But humans sometimes have triplets (3 babies). In the United States, there are about two sets of triplets in every 1,000 births. Humans also have quadruplets (4 babies), quintuplets (5 babies), and more. These types of multiple births are rare. Births of quintuplets or more happen only once in about 53,000 births.

✔ **Reading Check** What is the frequency of twin births?

Reproductive System Problems

In most cases, the reproductive system functions flawlessly. But like any body system, the reproductive system sometimes has problems. These problems include disease and infertility.

STDs

Chlamydia, herpes, and hepatitis B are common sexually transmitted diseases. A *sexually transmitted disease,* or STD, is a disease that can pass from a person who is infected with the STD to an uninfected person during sexual contact. STDs are also called *sexually transmitted infections,* or STIs. These diseases affect many people each year, as shown in **Table 1.**

An STD you may have heard of is *acquired immune deficiency syndrome* (AIDS). AIDS is caused by *human immunodeficiency virus* (HIV). But you may not have heard of the STD *hepatitis B,* a liver disease also caused by a virus. This virus is spread in several ways, including sexual contact. In the United States, about 140,000 new cases of hepatitis B happen each year.

Figure 3 *Identical twins have genes that are exactly the same. Many identical twins who are raised apart have similar personalities and interests.*

Twins and More

With a parent, discuss some challenges that are created by the birth of twins, triplets, quadruplets, or other multiples. Include financial, mental, emotional, and physical challenges.

Create a poster that shows these challenges and ways to meet them.

If twins or other multiples are in your family, discuss how the individuals differ and how they are alike.

Table 1 The Spread of STDs in the United States	
STD	**Approximate number of new cases each year**
Chlamydia	3 to 10 million
Genital HPV (human papillomavirus)	5.5 million
Genital herpes	1 million
Gonorrhea	650,000
Syphilis	70,000
HIV/AIDS	40,000 to 50,000

Cancer

Sometimes, cancer happens in reproductive organs. *Cancer* is a disease in which cells grow at an uncontrolled rate. Cancer cells start out as normal cells. Then, something triggers uncontrolled cell growth. Different kinds of cancer have different triggers.

In men, the two most common reproductive system cancers are cancer of the testes and cancer of the prostate gland. In women, the two most common reproductive system cancers are breast cancer and cancer of the cervix. The *cervix* is the lower part, or neck, of the uterus. The cervix opens to the vagina.

Infertility

In the United States, about 15% of married couples have difficulty producing offspring. Many of these couples are *infertile,* or unable to have children. Men may be infertile if they do not produce enough healthy sperm. Women may be infertile if they do not ovulate normally.

Sexually transmitted diseases, such as gonorrhea and chlamydia, can lead to infertility in women. STD-related infertility occurs in men, but not as commonly as it does in women.

CONNECTION TO Social Studies

Understanding STDs Select one of the STDs in **Table 1.** Make a poster or brochure that identifies the cause of the disease, describes its symptoms, explains how it affects the body, and tells how it can be treated. Include a bar graph that shows the number of cases in different age groups.

ACTIVITY

SECTION Review

Summary

- The male reproductive system produces sperm and delivers it to the female reproductive system.
- The female reproductive system produces eggs, nurtures zygotes, and gives birth.
- Humans usually have one child per birth, but multiple births, such as those of twins or triplets, are possible.
- Human reproduction can be affected by cancer, infertility, and disease.

Using Key Terms

1. Use the following terms in the same sentence: *uterus* and *vagina.*

Understanding Key Ideas

2. Describe two problems of the reproductive system.

3. Identify the structures and functions of the male and female reproductive systems.

4. Identical twins happen once in 250 births. How many pairs of these twins might be at a school with 2,750 students?
   a. 1
   b. 11
   c. 22
   d. 250

Math Skills

5. In one country, 7 out of 1,000 infants die before their first birthday. Convert this figure to a percentage. Is your answer greater than or less than 1%?

Critical Thinking

6. **Making Inferences** What is the purpose of the menstrual cycle?

7. **Applying Concepts** Twins can happen when a zygote splits in two or when two eggs are fertilized. How can these two ways of twin formation explain how identical twins differ from fraternal twins?

8. **Predicting Consequences** How might cancer of the testes affect a man's ability to make sperm?

SCI LINKS

NSTA
Developed and maintained by the National Science Teachers Association

For a variety of links related to this chapter, go to www.scilinks.org
Topic: Reproduction System Irregularities or Disorders
SciLinks code: HSM1298

Growth and Development

Every one of us started out as a single cell. How did that cell become a person made of trillions of cells?

A single cell divides many times and develops into a baby. But the development of a baby from a single cell is only the first stage of human development. Think about how you will change between now and when you become a grandparent!

From Fertilization to Embryo

Ordinarily, the process of human development starts when a man deposits millions of sperm into a woman's vagina. A few hundred sperm make it through the uterus into a fallopian tube. There, a few sperm cover the egg. Usually, only one sperm gets through the outer coating of the egg. When this happens, it triggers a response—a membrane forms around the egg to keep other sperm from entering. When the sperm's nucleus joins with the nucleus of the egg, the egg becomes fertilized.

The fertilized egg (zygote) travels down the fallopian tube toward the uterus. This journey takes 5 to 6 days. During the trip, the zygote undergoes cell division many times. Eleven to 12 days after fertilization, the zygote has become a tiny ball of cells called an **embryo.** The embryo implants itself in the uterus. *Implantation* happens when the zygote embeds itself in the thick, nutrient-rich lining of the uterus. Fertilization and implantation are outlined in **Figure 1.**

✔ **Reading Check** Describe the process of fertilization and implantation. (*See the Appendix for answers to Reading Checks.*)

embryo a developing human, from fertilization through the first 8 weeks of development (the 10th week of pregnancy)

placenta the partly fetal and partly maternal organ by which materials are exchanged between fetus and mother

Figure 1 Fertilization and Implantation

ⓑ The egg is fertilized in the fallopian tube by a sperm.

ⓒ The embryo implants itself in the uterus's wall.

ⓐ The egg is released from the ovary.

From Embryo to Fetus

After implantation, the placenta (pluh SEN tuh) begins to grow. The **placenta** is a special two-way exchange organ. It has a network of blood vessels that provides the embryo with oxygen and nutrients from the mother's blood. Wastes produced by the embryo are removed in the placenta. They are carried by the mother's blood so that her body can excrete them. The embryo's blood and the mother's blood flow very near each other in the placenta, but they normally do not mix.

Reading Check Why is the placenta important?

Weeks 1 and 2

Doctors commonly count the time of a woman's pregnancy as starting from the first day of her last menstrual period. Even though fertilization has not yet taken place, that day is a convenient date from which to start counting. A normal pregnancy lasts about 280 days, or 40 weeks, from that day.

Weeks 3 and 4

Fertilization takes place at about the end of week 2. In week 3, after fertilization, the zygote moves to the uterus. As the zygote travels, it divides many times. It becomes a ball of cells that implants itself in the wall of the uterus. The zygote is now called an *embryo*. At the end of week 4, implantation is complete and the woman is pregnant. The embryo's blood cells begin to form. At this point, the embryo is about 0.2 mm long.

Weeks 5 to 8

Weeks 5 to 8 of pregnancy are weeks 3 to 6 of embryonic development. In this stage, the embryo becomes surrounded by a thin membrane called the *amnion* (AM nee AHN). The amnion is filled with amniotic fluid and protects the growing embryo from bumps and injury. During week 5, the umbilical cord forms. The **umbilical cord** (uhm BIL i kuhl KAWRD) is a cord that connects the embryo to the placenta. **Figure 2** shows the umbilical cord, amnion, and placenta.

In this stage, the heart, brain, other organs, and blood vessels start to form. They grow quickly. In weeks 5 and 6, eyes and ears take shape. The spinal cord begins to develop. In week 6, tiny limb buds appear. These buds will become arms and legs. In week 8, muscles start developing. Nerves grow into the shoulders and upper arms. Fingers and toes start to form. The embryo, now about 16 mm long, can swallow and blink.

Placenta

Umbilical cord

Amnion

Uterus

Cervix

Figure 2 *The placenta, amnion, and umbilical cord are the life support system for the fetus. This fetus is about 20 to 22 weeks old.*

umbilical cord the structure that connects the fetus to the placenta

Growing Up

With a parent, discuss the physical and mental changes that you went through between your birth and your first day of school. Make a poster illustrating those changes.

ACTIVITY

Weeks 9 to 16

At week 9, the fetus may begin to make tiny movements. After week 10, the embryo is called a **fetus** (FEET uhs). In about week 13, the fetus's face begins to look more human. During this stage, fetal muscles grow stronger. As a result, the fetus can make a fist and begins to move. The fetus grows rapidly during this stage. It doubles, and then triples, its size within a month. For example, in week 10, the fetus is about 36 mm long. A little later, at week 16, the fetus is about 108 mm to 116 mm long. Use **Figure 3** to follow some of the changes that take place in the fetus as it develops.

Reading Check Describe three changes the fetus undergoes during weeks 9 to 16.

Weeks 17 to 24

By week 17, the fetus can make faces. Usually, in week 18, the fetus starts to make movements that the mother can feel. By week 18, the fetus can hear sounds through the mother's uterus. It may even jump at loud noises. By week 23, the fetus's movements may be quite vigorous! If the fetus were born after week 24, it might survive. But babies born at 24 weeks require a lot of help. In weeks 17 to 24, the fetus grows to between 25 cm and 30 cm in length.

Weeks 25 to 36

At about 25 or 26 weeks, the fetus's lungs are well developed but not fully mature. The fetus still gets oxygen from its mother through the placenta. The fetus will not take its first breath of air until it is born. By the 32nd week, the fetus's eyes can open and close. Studies of fetal heart rate and brain activity show that fetuses respond to light. Some scientists have observed brain activity and eye movements in sleeping fetuses that resemble those activities in sleeping children or adults. These scientists think that a sleeping fetus may dream. After 36 weeks, the fetus is almost ready to be born.

Birth

At 37 to 38 weeks, the fetus is fully developed. A full-term pregnancy usually lasts about 40 weeks. Typically, as birth begins, the mother's uterus begins a series of muscular contractions called *labor*. Usually, these contractions push the fetus through the mother's vagina, and the baby is born. The newborn is still connected to the placenta by its umbilical cord, which is tied and cut. All that will remain of the point where the umbilical cord was attached is the baby's navel. Soon, the mother expels the placenta, and labor is complete.

CONNECTION TO Social Studies

WRITING SKILL **Nourishing the Fetus** The fetus gets its only nutrition from the food that its mother eats. To ensure the health of the fetus, the mother needs to eat healthy foods and take special vitamins. A mother can hurt her fetus's health by taking drugs, drinking alcohol, or smoking. Research the potential consequences of taking drugs, drinking alcohol, or smoking while pregnant. In your **science journal,** write a report about what you learn.

Figure 3 **Pregnancy Timeline**

Week

2 — Fertilization takes place.

4 — The fertilized egg becomes hundreds of cells.

Implantation is complete.

6 — The spinal cord and brain begin to form.

8 — Tiny fingers and toes begin to look like tiny fingers and toes.

10 — The embryo may make tiny movements that may be detected by ultrasound.

12 — The embryo is now called a fetus.

14 —

16 — Bones and bone marrow continue to form.

18 — A layer of fat begins to form under the skin.

20 —

22 —

24 —

26 — The fetus's lungs are almost ready to breathe air.

28 — The fetus practice breathes and has brain wave activity.

30 — The fetus's eyes are open and it may turn toward a bright light.

The fetus is developing taste buds and its brain is growing rapidly.

32 —

34 — The fetus's skin turns from red to pink.

36 — The fetus's skull has hardened.

38 —

The baby is born.

40 —

Figure 4 Stages of Human Development

Infant   4 years   7 years   11 years   Adult

Life Grows On

Use **Figure 4** to complete this activity.

1. Use a **ruler** to measure the infant's head height. Then, measure the infant's entire height, including the head.

2. Calculate the ratio of the infant's head height to the infant's total height.

3. Repeat these measurements and calculations for the other stages.

4. Does a baby's head grow faster or slower than the rest of the body? Why do you think this is so?

From Birth to Death

After birth, the human body goes through several stages of development. Some of those stages are shown in **Figure 4.**

Infancy and Childhood

Generally, infancy is the stage from birth to age 2. During infancy, you grew quickly and your baby teeth appeared. As your nervous system developed, you became more coordinated and started to walk.

Childhood—another period of fast growth—lasts from age 2 to puberty. Your baby teeth were replaced by permanent teeth. And your muscles became more coordinated, which allowed you to ride a bicycle, jump rope, and do other activities.

Adolescence

The stage from puberty to adulthood is adolescence. During puberty, a person's reproductive system becomes mature. In most boys, puberty takes place between the ages of 11 and 16. During this time, the young male's body becomes more muscular, his voice becomes deeper, and body and facial hair appear. In most girls, puberty takes place between the ages of 9 and 14. During puberty in females, the amount of fat in the hips and thighs increases, the breasts enlarge, body hair appears, and menstruation begins.

Reading Check Name an important change that takes place during adolescence.

Adulthood

From about age 20 to age 40, you will be a young adult. You will be at the peak of your physical development. Beginning around age 30, changes associated with aging begin. These changes are gradual and different for everyone. Some early signs of aging include loss of flexibility in muscles, deterioration of eyesight, increase in body fat, and some loss of hair.

The aging process continues in middle age (between 40 and 65 years old). During this time, hair may turn gray, athletic abilities will decline, and skin may wrinkle. A person who is more than 65 years old is considered an older adult. Although the aging process continues, many older adults lead very active lives, as is shown in **Figure 5.**

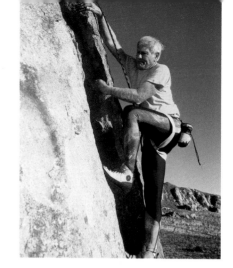

Figure 5 *Older adults can still enjoy activities that they enjoyed when they were younger.*

SECTION Review

Summary

- Fertilization occurs when a sperm from the male joins with an egg from the female.

- The embryo and fetus undergo many changes between implantation and birth.

- The first stage of human development lasts from fertilization to birth.

- After birth, a human goes through four more stages of growth and development.

Using Key Terms

1. In your own words, write a definition for the term *umbilical cord.*

2. Use the following terms in the same sentence: *embryo* and *fetus.*

Understanding Key Ideas

3. After birth, the two periods of most rapid growth are
   a. infancy and adolescence.
   b. childhood and adulthood.
   c. infancy and childhood.
   d. adolescence and adulthood.

4. After birth, which stage of human development is the longest?
   a. infancy
   b. childhood
   c. adolescence
   d. adulthood

5. Describe the development of the embryo and the fetus.

6. What is the function of the placenta?

7. Summarize the processes of fertilization and implantation.

8. What are five stages of human development?

Math Skills

9. Suppose a person is 80 years old and that puberty took place when he or she was 12 years old.
   a. Calculate the percentage of the person's life that he or she spent in each of the four stages of development that follow birth.
   b. Make a bar graph showing the percentage for each stage.

Critical Thinking

10. **Applying Concepts** Why does the egg's covering change after a sperm has entered the egg?

11. **Analyzing Ideas** Do you think any one stage of development is more important than other stages? Explain your answer.

SCILINKS®

NSTA
Developed and maintained by the National Science Teachers Association

For a variety of links related to this chapter, go to www.scilinks.org
Topic: Before Birth; Growth and Development
SciLinks code: HSM0140; HSM0700

Skills Practice Lab

It's a Comfy, Safe World!

OBJECTIVES

Construct a model of a human uterus protecting a fetus.

Compare the protection that a bird's egg gives a developing baby bird with the protection that a human uterus gives a fetus.

MATERIALS

- computer (optional)
- cotton, soft fabric, or other soft materials
- eggs, soft-boiled and in the shell (2 to 4)
- eggs, soft-boiled and peeled (3 or 4)
- gloves, protective
- mineral oil, cooking oil, syrup, or other thick liquid
- plastic bags, sealable
- water

SAFETY

Before birth, baby birds live inside a hard, protective shell until the baby has used up all the food supply. Most mammal babies develop within their mother's uterus, in which they are surrounded by fluid and connected to a placenta, before they are born. Before human babies are born, they lead a comfy life. By the seventh month, they lie around sucking their thumb, blinking their eyes, and perhaps even dreaming.

Ask a Question

1. Inside which structure is a developing organism better protected from bumps and blows: the uterus of a placental mammal or the egg of a bird?

Form a Hypothesis

2. A placental mammal's uterus protects a developing organism from bumps and blows better than a bird's egg does.

Test the Hypothesis

3. Brainstorm several ideas about how you will construct and test your model of a mammalian uterus. Then, use the materials provided by your teacher to build your model. A peeled, soft-boiled egg will represent the fetus inside your model uterus.

4. Make a data table similar to **Table 1** below. Test your model, examine the egg for damage, and record your results.

Table 1 First Model Test	
Original model	**Modified model**
DO NOT WRITE	
IN BOOK	

5. Modify your model as necessary; test this modified model using another peeled, soft-boiled egg; and record your results.

⑥ When you are satisfied with the design of your model, obtain another peeled, soft-boiled egg and an egg in the shell. The egg in the shell represents the baby bird inside the egg.

⑦ Make a data table similar to **Table 2** below. Test your new eggs, examine them for damage, and record your results in your data table.

Table 2 Final Model Test	
	Test Results
Model	DO NOT WRITE
Egg in shell	IN BOOK

Analyze the Results

① **Explaining Events** Explain any differences in the test results for the model and the egg in a shell.

② **Analyzing Results** What modification to your model was the most effective in protecting the fetus?

Draw Conclusions

③ **Evaluating Data** Review your hypothesis. Did your data support your hypothesis? Why or why not?

④ **Evaluating Models** What modifications to your model might make it more like a uterus?

Applying Your Data

Use the Internet or the library to find information about the development of monotremes, such as the echidna or the platypus, and marsupials, such as the koala or the kangaroo. Then, using what you have learned in this lab, compare the development of placental mammals with that of marsupials and monotremes.

Chapter Review

USING KEY TERMS

For each pair of terms, explain how the meanings of the terms differ.

1 *internal fertilization* and *external fertilization*

2 *testes* and *ovaries*

3 *asexual reproduction* and *sexual reproduction*

4 *fertilization* and *implantation*

5 *umbilical cord* and *placenta*

UNDERSTANDING KEY IDEAS

Multiple Choice

6 The sea star reproduces asexually by

a. fragmentation.

b. budding.

c. external fertilization.

d. internal fertilization.

7 Which list shows in order sperm's path through the male reproductive system?

a. testes, epididymis, urethra, vas deferens

b. epididymis, urethra, testes, vas deferens

c. testes, vas deferens, epididymis, urethra

d. testes, epididymis, vas deferens, urethra

8 Identical twins are the result of

a. a fertilized egg splitting in two.

b. two separate eggs being fertilized.

c. budding in the uterus.

d. external fertilization.

9 If the onset of menstruation is counted as the first day of the menstrual cycle, on what day of the cycle does ovulation typically occur?

a. 2nd day

b. 5th day

c. 14th day

d. 28th day

10 How do monotremes differ from placental mammals?

a. Monotremes are not mammals.

b. Monotremes have hair.

c. Monotremes nurture their young with milk.

d. Monotremes lay eggs.

11 All of the following are sexually transmitted diseases EXCEPT

a. chlamydia.

b. AIDS.

c. infertility.

d. genital herpes.

12 Where do fertilization and implantation, respectively, take place?

a. uterus, fallopian tube

b. fallopian tube, vagina

c. uterus, vagina

d. fallopian tube, uterus

Short Answer

13 Which human reproductive organs produce sperm? produce eggs?

14 Explain how the fetus gets oxygen and nutrients and how it gets rid of waste.

15 What are four stages of human life following birth?

16 Name three problems that can affect the human reproductive system, and explain why each is a problem.

17 Draw a diagram showing the structures of the male and female reproductive systems. Label each structure, and explain how each structure contributes to fertilization and implantation.

CRITICAL THINKING

18 **Concept Mapping** Use the following terms to create a concept map: *asexual reproduction, budding, external fertilization, fragmentation, reproduction, internal fertilization,* and *sexual reproduction.*

19 **Identifying Relationships** The environment in which organisms live may change over time. For example, a wet, swampy area may gradually become a grassy area with a small pond. Explain how sexual reproduction may give species that live in a changing environment a survival advantage.

20 **Applying Concepts** What is the function of the uterus? How is this function related to the menstrual cycle?

21 **Making Inferences** In most human body cells, the 46 chromosomes are duplicated during cell division so that each new cell receives 46 chromosomes. Cells that make eggs and sperm also split and duplicate their 46 chromosomes. But then, in the process of meiosis, the two cells split again to form four cells (egg or sperm) that each have 23 chromosomes. Why is meiosis important to human reproduction and to the human species?

INTERPRETING GRAPHICS

The following graph illustrates the cycles of the female hormone estrogen and the male hormone testosterone. The blue line shows the estrogen level in a female over 28 days. The red line shows the testosterone level in a male over the same amount of time. Use the graph below to answer the questions that follow.

Hormone Cycles

Testosterone

Estrogen

Amount of hormone

Days of cycle

0   7   14   21   28

22 What is the major difference between the levels of the two hormones over the 28 days?

23 What cycle do you think estrogen affects?

24 Why might the level of testosterone stay the same?

25 Do you think that the above estrogen cycle would change in a pregnant woman? Explain your answer.

Standardized Test Preparation

EOG Prep

READING

Read each of the passages below. Then, answer the questions that follow each passage.

Passage 1 The male reproductive system is made up of internal and external organs. The <u>external</u> organs of this system are the penis and the scrotum. The scrotum is a skin-covered sac that hangs outside the body. Normal human body temperature is about 37°C. Normal sperm production and development cannot take place at that temperature. Normal sperm production and development takes place at lower temperatures. That is why the testes rest in the scrotum, outside the body. The scrotum is about 2°C cooler than the body. Inside each testis are masses of tightly coiled tubes, called *seminiferous tubules,* in which sperm are produced when conditions are right.

1. In this passage, what does the word *external* mean?

  A not part of the body

  B outside the body

  C inside the body

  D lasting a long time

2. Which of the following statements is a fact according to the passage?

  F The temperature in the scrotum is higher than body temperature.

  G Testes are internal organs of the male reproductive system.

  H Normal sperm production cannot take place at normal body temperature.

  I Normal human body temperature is about 37°F.

3. What are the tubes in which sperm are made called?

  A testes

  B scrotum

  C seminiferous tubules

  D external organs

Passage 2 In a normal pregnancy, the fertilized egg travels to the uterus and implants itself in the uterus's wall. But, in about 7 out of 1,000 pregnancies in the United States, a woman has an <u>ectopic pregnancy</u>. The term *ectopic* is from two Greek words meaning "out of place." In an ectopic pregnancy, the fertilized egg implants itself in an ovary, a fallopian tube, or another area of the female reproductive system that is not the lining of the uterus. Because the zygote cannot develop properly outside of the uterus, an ectopic pregnancy can be very dangerous for both the mother and zygote. As the zygote grows, it causes the mother pain and bleeding. For example, an ectopic pregnancy in a fallopian tube can rupture the tube and cause abdominal bleeding. If an ectopic pregnancy is not treated quickly enough, the mother may die.

1. In the passage, what does the term *ectopic pregnancy* probably mean?

  A a pregnancy that takes place at the wrong time

  B a type of pregnancy that happens about 7 out of 100 times in the United States

  C a type of pregnancy caused by a problem with a fallopian tube

  D a pregnancy in which the zygote implants itself in the wrong place

2. Which of the following statements is a fact according to the passage?

  F Ectopic pregnancies take place in about 7% of all pregnancies.

  G The ectopic pregnancy rate in the United States is less than 1%.

  H Ectopic pregnancies take place in the uterus.

  I An ectopic pregnancy is harmless.

Use the diagrams below to answer the questions that follow.

Read each question below, and choose the best answer.

A.

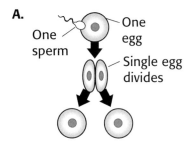

One sperm — One egg — Single egg divides

B. Two sperm

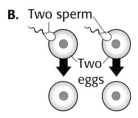

Two eggs

1. Which diagram of cell division would produce identical twins: A or B?

A diagram B, because each egg is fertilized by a separate sperm cell

B both diagram A and diagram B, because twins result in both cases

C diagram A, because a single fertilized egg separates into two halves

D diagram B, because two eggs are released by an ovary

2. Which of the following could describe fraternal twins?

F both boys

G both girls

H one girl and one boy

I any of these combinations

3. Which diagram of cell division could explain triplets, two of whom are identical and one of whom is fraternal?

A diagram A

B diagram B

C either diagram A or diagram B

D neither diagram A or diagram B

1. Identify the group that contains equivalent fractions, decimals, and percents.

A 7/10, 0.7, 7%

B 1/2, 0.5, 50%

C 3/8, 0.38, 38%

D 3/100, 0.3, 33%

2. A geologist was exploring a cave. She spent 2.7 h exploring on Saturday and twice as many hours exploring on Sunday. Which equation could be used to find n, the total number of hours the geologist spent exploring the cave on those 2 days?

F $n = 2 \div 2.7$

G $n = 2.7 + (2 \times 2.7)$

H $n = 2.7 + 2.7 + 2$

I $n = 2 \times 2.7$

3. Which of the following story problems can be solved by the equation below?

$$(60 + 70 + 68 + 80 + x) \div 5 = 70$$

A The heights of four buildings in South Braintree are 60 ft, 70 ft, 68 ft, and 80 ft. Find x, the average height of the buildings.

B The weights of four dogs Jason is raising are 60 lb, 70 lb, 68 lb, and 80 lb. Find x, the sum of the weights of the four dogs.

C Kayla's first four handmade bracelets sold for $60, $70, $68, and $80. Find x, the amount for which Kayla needs to sell her fifth bracelet to have an average selling price of $70.

D The times it took Taylor to complete each of four 100 m practice swims were 60 s, 70 s, 68 s, and 80 s. Find x, the average time it took Taylor to complete his practice swims.

Science in Action

Doctors operated on a fetus, whose hand is visible in this photo, to correct spina bifida.

Science, Technology, and Society

Fetal Surgery

Sometimes, a developing fetus has a serious medical problem. In many cases, surgery after birth can correct the problem. But some problems can be treated while the fetus is still in the uterus. For example, fetal surgery may be used to correct spina bifida (part of the spinal cord is exposed because the backbone doesn't form properly). Doctors now can fix several types of problems before a baby is born.

Social Studies ACTiViTy

WRITING SKILL Research the causes of spina bifida. Write a brochure telling expectant mothers what precautions they can take to prevent spina bifida.

Scientific Discoveries

Lasers and Acne

Many people think that acne affects only teenagers, but acne can strike at any age. Some acne is mild, but some is severe. Now, for some severe cases of acne, lasers may provide relief. That's right—lasers can be used to treat acne! Surgeons who specialize in the health and diseases of the skin use laser light to treat the skin disease known as *acne*.

In addition, laser treatments may stimulate the skin cells that produce collagen. Collagen is a protein found in connective tissue. Increased production of collagen in the skin improves the skin's texture and helps smooth out acne scars.

Language Arts ACTiViTy

WRITING SKILL Write a story about how severe acne affects a teen's life. Tell what happens when a doctor refers the teen to a specialist for laser treatment and how the successful treatment changes the teen's life.

Reva Curry

Diagnostic Medical Sonographer Sounds are everywhere in our world. But only some of those sounds—such as your favorite music playing on the stereo or the dog barking next door—are sounds that we can hear. There are sound waves whose frequency is too high for us to hear. These high-pitched sounds are called *ultrasound*. Some animals, such as bats, use ultrasound to hunt and to avoid midair collisions.

Humans use ultrasound, too. Ultrasound machines can peer inside the human body to look at hearts, blood vessels, and fetuses. Diagnostic medical sonographers are people who use sonography equipment to diagnose medical problems and to follow the growth and development of a fetus before it is born. One of the leading professionals in the field of diagnostic medical sonography is Dr. Reva Curry. Dr. Curry spent many years as a sonographer. Her primary job was to use high-tech instruments to create ultrasound images of parts of the body and interpret the results for other medical professionals. Today, Dr. Curry works with students as the dean of a community college.

Math

At 20°C, the speed of sound in water is 1,482 m/s and in steel is 5,200 m/s. How long would it take a sound to travel 815.1 m in water? In that same length of time, how far would a sound travel in a steel beam?

To learn more about these Science in Action topics, visit go.hrw.com and type in the keyword HL5BD5F.

Current Science

Check out Current Science® articles related to this chapter by visiting go.hrw.com. Just type in the keyword HL5CS26.

UNIT 3

TIMELINE

Human Health

In many ways, living in the 21st century is good for your health. Many deadly diseases that plagued our ancestors now have cures. Some diseases, such as smallpox, have been wiped out entirely. And others can be prevented by vaccines and other methods. Many researchers, including the people on this timeline, have worked to understand diseases and to find cures.

But people still get sick, and many diseases have no cure. In this unit, you will learn how your body protects itself and fights illness. You will also learn about ways to keep yourself healthy so that your body can operate in top form.

1403
The first quarantine is imposed in Venice, Italy, to stop the spread of the plague, or Black Death.

1717
Lady Mary Wortley Montague introduces a smallpox vaccine in England.

1854
Nurse Florence Nightingale introduces hygienic standards into military hospitals during the Crimean War.

1895
X rays are discovered by Wilhelm Roentgen.

1953
Cigarette smoking is linked to lung cancer.

1816
R. T. Laënnec invents the stethoscope.

1853
Charles Gerhardt synthesizes aspirin for the first time.

1900
Walter Reed discovers that yellow fever is carried by mosquitoes.

1906
Upton Sinclair writes *The Jungle*, which describes unsanitary conditions in the Chicago stockyards and leads to the creation of the Pure Food and Drug Act.

1921
A tuberculosis vaccine is produced.

1979
Smallpox is eradicated.

1997
Researchers discover that high doses of alcohol in early pregnancy switch off a gene that controls brain, heart, limb, and skull development in the fetus.

2003
More than 8,000 people are infected with severe acute respiratory syndrome (SARS), which is caused by a newly discovered virus.

Body Defenses and Disease

About the PHOTO

No, this photo is not from a sci-fi movie. It is not an alien insect soldier. This is, in fact, a greatly enlarged image of a house dust mite that is tinier than the dot of an *i*. Huge numbers of these creatures live in carpets, beds, and sofas in every home. Dust mites often cause problems for people who have asthma or allergies. The body's immune system fights diseases and alien factors, such as dust mites, that cause allergies.

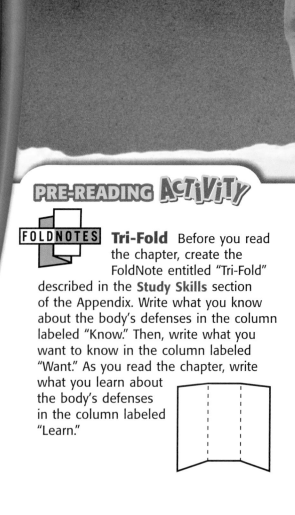

PRE-READING ACTIVITY

FOLDNOTES **Tri-Fold** Before you read the chapter, create the FoldNote entitled "Tri-Fold" described in the **Study Skills** section of the Appendix. Write what you know about the body's defenses in the column labeled "Know." Then, write what you want to know in the column labeled "Want." As you read the chapter, write what you learn about the body's defenses in the column labeled "Learn."

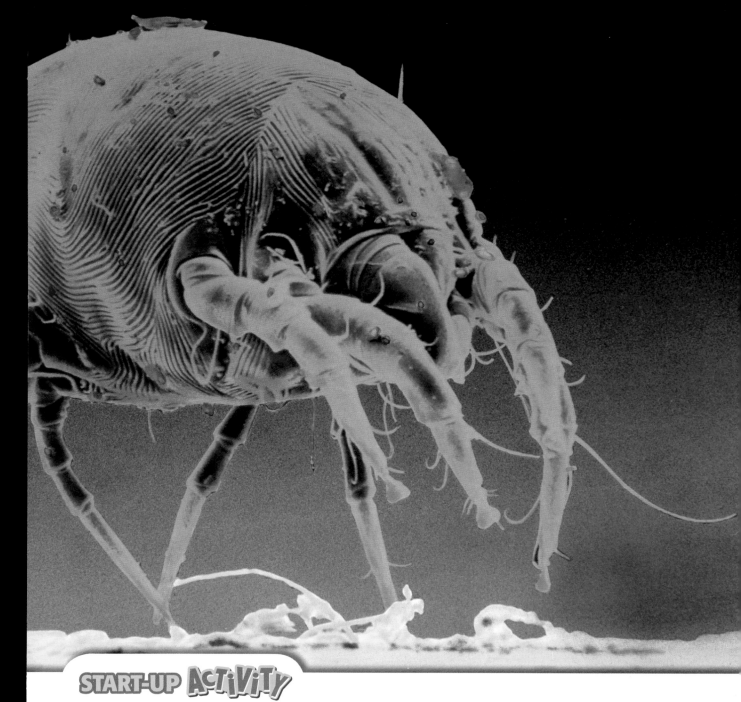

Invisible Invaders

In this activity, you will see tiny organisms grow.

Procedure

1. Obtain **two Petri dishes containing nutrient agar.** Label them "Washed" and "Unwashed."

2. Rub **two marbles** between the palms of your hands. Observe the appearance of the marbles.

3. Roll one marble in the Petri dish labeled "Unwashed."

4. Put on a pair of **disposable gloves.** Wash the other marble with **soap** and **warm water** for 4 min.

5. Roll the washed marble in the Petri dish labeled "Washed."

6. Secure the lids of the Petri dishes with **transparent tape.** Place the dishes in a warm, dark place. Do not open the Petri dishes after they are sealed.

7. Record changes in the Petri dishes for 1 week.

Analysis

1. How did the washed and unwashed marbles compare? How did the Petri dishes differ after several days?

2. Why is it important to wash your hands before eating?

Disease

You've probably heard it before: "Cover your mouth when you sneeze!" "Wash your hands!" "Don't put that in your mouth!"

What is all the fuss about? When people say these things to you, they are concerned about the spread of disease.

Causes of Disease

When you have a *disease,* your normal body functions are disrupted. Some diseases, such as most cancers and heart disease, are not spread from one person to another. They are called **noninfectious diseases.**

Noninfectious diseases can be caused by a variety of factors. For example, a genetic disorder causes the disease hemophilia (HEE moh FIL ee uh), in which a person's blood does not clot properly. Smoking, lack of physical activity, and a high-fat diet can greatly increase a person's chances of getting certain noninfectious diseases. Avoiding harmful habits may help you avoid noninfectious diseases.

A disease that can be passed from one living thing to another is an **infectious disease.** Infectious diseases are caused by agents called **pathogens.** Viruses and some bacteria, fungi, protists, and worms may all cause diseases. **Figure 1** shows some enlarged images of common pathogens.

noninfectious disease a disease that cannot spread from one individual to another

infectious disease a disease that is caused by a pathogen and that can be spread from one individual to another

pathogen a virus, microorganism, or other organism that causes disease

Figure 1   Pathogens

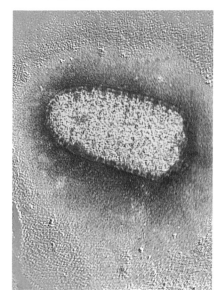

▲ This virus causes rabies.

▲ *Streptococcus* bacteria can cause strep throat.

Pathways to Pathogens

There are many ways pathogens can be passed from one person to another. Being aware of them can help you stay healthy.

Air

Some pathogens travel through the air. For example, a single sneeze, such as the one shown in **Figure 2,** releases thousands of tiny droplets of moisture that can carry pathogens.

Contaminated Objects

You may already know that if you drink from a glass that an infected person has just used, you could become infected with a pathogen. A person who is sick may leave bacteria or viruses on many other objects, too. For example, contaminated doorknobs, keyboards, combs, and towels can pass pathogens.

Person to Person

Some pathogens are spread by direct person-to-person contact. You can become infected with some illnesses by kissing, shaking hands, or touching the sores of an infected person.

Animals

Some pathogens are carried by animals. For example, humans can get a fungus called *ringworm* from handling an infected dog or cat. Also, ticks may carry bacteria that cause Lyme disease or Rocky Mountain spotted fever.

Food and Water

Drinking water in the United States is generally safe. But water lines can break, or treatment plants can become flooded. These problems may allow microorganisms to enter the public water supply. Bacteria growing in foods and beverages can cause illness, too. For example, meat, fish, and eggs that are not cooked enough can still contain dangerous bacteria or parasites. Even leaving food out at room temperature can give bacteria such as salmonella the chance to grow and produce toxins in the food. Refrigerating foods can slow the growth of many of these pathogens. Because bacteria grow in food, washing all used cooking surfaces and tools is also important.

Reading Check Why must you cook meat and eggs thoroughly? (*See the Appendix for answers to Reading Checks.*)

Figure 2 *A sneeze can force thousands of pathogen-carrying droplets out of your body at up to 160 km/h.*

CONNECTION TO Social Studies

Disease and History Many diseases have shaped history. For example, yellow fever, which is caused by a virus that is spread by mosquitoes, was one of the obstacles in building the Panama Canal. Only after people learned how to prevent the spread of the yellow fever virus could the canal be completed.

Use information from Internet and library research to create a poster describing how one infectious disease affected history.

ACTIVITY

immunity the ability to resist or to recover from an infectious disease

Putting Pathogens in Their Place

Until the twentieth century, surgery patients often died of bacterial infections. But doctors learned that simple cleanliness could help prevent the spread of some diseases. Today, hospitals and clinics use a variety of technologies to prevent the spread of pathogens. For example, ultraviolet radiation, boiling water, and chemicals are used to kill pathogens in health facilities.

Pasteurization

During the mid-1800s, Louis Pasteur, a French scientist, discovered that microorganisms caused wine to spoil. The uninvited microorganisms were bacteria. Pasteur devised a method of using heat to kill most of the bacteria in the wine. This method is called *pasteurization* (PAS tuhr i ZAY shuhn), and it is still used today. The milk that the girl in **Figure 3** is drinking has been pasteurized.

Vaccines and Immunity

In the late 1700s, no one knew what a pathogen was. During this time, Edward Jenner studied a disease called *smallpox*. He observed that people who had been infected with cowpox seemed to have protection against smallpox. These people had a resistance to the disease. The ability to resist or recover from an infectious disease is called **immunity.** Jenner's work led to the first modern vaccine. A *vaccine* is a substance that helps your body develop immunity to a disease.

Today, vaccines are used all over the world to prevent many serious diseases. Modern vaccines contain pathogens that are killed or specially treated so that they can't make you very sick. The vaccine is enough like the pathogen to allow your body to develop a defense against the disease.

Figure 3 *Today, pasteurization is used to kill pathogens in many different types of food, including dairy products, shellfish, and juices.*

Antibiotics

Have you ever had strep throat? If so, you have had a bacterial infection. Bacterial infections can be a serious threat to your health. Fortunately, doctors can usually treat these kinds of infections with antibiotics. An *antibiotic* is a substance that can kill bacteria or slow the growth of bacteria. Antibiotics may also be used to treat infections caused by other microorganisms, such as fungi. You may take an antibiotic when you are sick. Always take antibiotics according to your doctor's instructions to ensure that all the pathogens are killed.

Viruses, such as those that cause colds, are not affected by antibiotics. Antibiotics can kill only living things, and viruses are not alive. The only way to destroy viruses in your body is to locate and kill the cells they have invaded.

Reading Check Frank caught a bad cold just before the opening night of a school play. He visited his doctor and asked her to prescribe antibiotics for his cold. The doctor politely refused and advised Frank to stay home and get plenty of rest. Why do you think the doctor refused to give Frank antibiotics?

Epidemic!
You catch a cold and return to your school while sick. Your friends don't have immunity to your cold. On the first day, you expose five friends to your cold. The next day, each of those friends passes the virus to five more people. If this pattern continues for 5 more days, how many people will be exposed to the virus?

SECTION Review

Summary

- Noninfectious diseases cannot be spread from one person to another.
- Infectious diseases are caused by pathogens that are passed from one living thing to another.
- Pathogens can travel through the air or can be spread by contact with other people, contaminated objects, animals, food, or water.
- Cleanliness, pasteurization, vaccines, and antibiotics help control the spread of pathogens.

Using Key Terms

1. In your own words, write a definition for each of the following terms: *infectious disease, noninfectious disease,* and *immunity.*

Understanding Key Ideas

2. Vaccines contain
   a. treated pathogens.
   b. heat.
   c. antibiotics.
   d. pasteurization.

3. List five ways that you might come into contact with a pathogen.

4. Name four ways to help keep safe from pathogens.

Math Skills

5. If 10 people with the virus each expose 25 more people to the virus, how many people will be exposed to the virus?

Critical Thinking

6. **Identifying Relationships** Why might the risk of infectious disease be high in a community that has no water treatment facility?

7. **Analyzing Methods** Explain what might happen if a doctor did not wear gloves when treating patients.

8. **Applying Concepts** Why do vaccines for diseases in animals help prevent some illnesses in people?

Developed and maintained by the National Science Teachers Association

For a variety of links related to this chapter, go to www.scilinks.org

Topic: Pathogens; What Causes Diseases?
SciLinks code: HSM1118; HSM1653

Your Body's Defenses

Bacteria and viruses can be in the air, in the water, and on all the surfaces around you.

Your body must constantly protect itself against pathogens that are trying to invade it. But how does your body do that? Luckily, your body has its own built-in defense system.

First Lines of Defense

For a pathogen to harm you, it must attack a part of your body. Usually, though, very few of the pathogens around you make it past your first lines of defense.

Many organisms that try to enter your eyes or mouth are destroyed by special enzymes. Pathogens that enter your nose are washed down the back of your throat by mucus. The mucus carries the pathogens to your stomach, where most are quickly digested.

Your skin is made of many layers of flat cells. The outer-most layers are dead. As a result, many pathogens that land on your skin have difficulty finding a live cell to infect. As **Figure 1** shows, the dead skin cells are constantly dropping off your body as new skin cells grow from beneath. As the dead skin cells flake off, they carry away viruses, bacteria, and other microorganisms. In addition, glands secrete oil onto your skin's surface. The oil contains chemicals that kill many pathogens.

READING WARM-UP

Objectives

- Describe how your body keeps out pathogens.
- Explain how the immune system fights infections.
- Describe four challenges to the immune system.

Terms to Learn

immune system
macrophage
T cell
B cell
antibody

memory B cell
allergy
autoimmune
   disease
cancer

READING STRATEGY

Reading Organizer As you read this section, make a flowchart of the steps of how your body responds to a virus.

Figure 1 *Your body loses and replaces approximately 1 million skin cells every 40 min. In the process, countless pathogens are sloughed off.*

Failure of First Lines

Sometimes, skin is cut or punctured and pathogens can enter the body. The body acts quickly to keep out as many pathogens as possible. Blood flow to the injured area increases. Cell parts in the blood called *platelets* help seal the open wound so that no more pathogens can enter.

The increased blood flow also brings cells that belong to the **immune system,** the body system that fights pathogens. The immune system is not localized in any one place in your body. It is not controlled by any one organ, such as the brain. Instead, it is a team of individual cells, tissues, and organs that work together to keep you safe from invading pathogens.

Cells of the Immune System

The immune system consists mainly of three kinds of cells. One kind is the macrophage (MAK roh FAYJ). **Macrophages** engulf and digest many microorganisms or viruses that enter your body. If only a few microorganisms or viruses have entered a wound, the macrophages can easily stop them.

The other two main kinds of immune-system cells are T cells and B cells. **T cells** coordinate the immune system and attack many infected cells. **B cells** are immune-system cells that make antibodies. **Antibodies** are proteins that attach to specific antigens. *Antigens* are substances that stimulate an immune response. Your body is capable of making billions of different antibodies. Each antibody usually attaches to only one kind of antigen, as illustrated in **Figure 2.**

Reading Check How do macrophages help fight disease? (*See the Appendix for answers to Reading Checks.*)

Only Skin Deep

1. Cut an **apple** in half.
2. Place **plastic wrap** over each half. The plastic wrap will act as skin.
3. Use **scissors** to cut the plastic wrap on one of the apple halves, and then use an **eyedropper** to drip **food coloring** on each apple half. The food coloring represents pathogens coming into contact with your body.
4. What happened to each apple half?
5. How is the plastic wrap similar to skin?
6. How is the plastic wrap different from skin?

immune system the cells and tissues that recognize and attack foreign substances in the body

macrophage an immune system cell that engulfs pathogens and other materials

T cell an immune system cell that coordinates the immune system and attacks many infected cells

B cell a white blood cell that makes antibodies

antibody a protein made by B cells that binds to a specific antigen

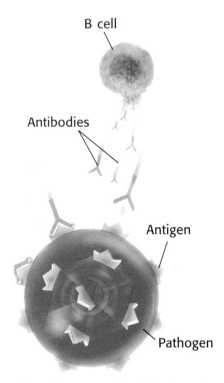

Figure 2 *An antibody's shape is very specialized. It matches an antigen like a key fits a lock.*

Responding to a Virus

If virus particles enter your body, some of the particles may pass into body cells and begin to replicate. Other virus particles will be engulfed and broken up by macrophages. This is just the beginning of the immune response. The process your immune system uses to fight an invading virus is summarized in the figure below.

Reading Check What are two things that can happen to virus particles when they enter the body?

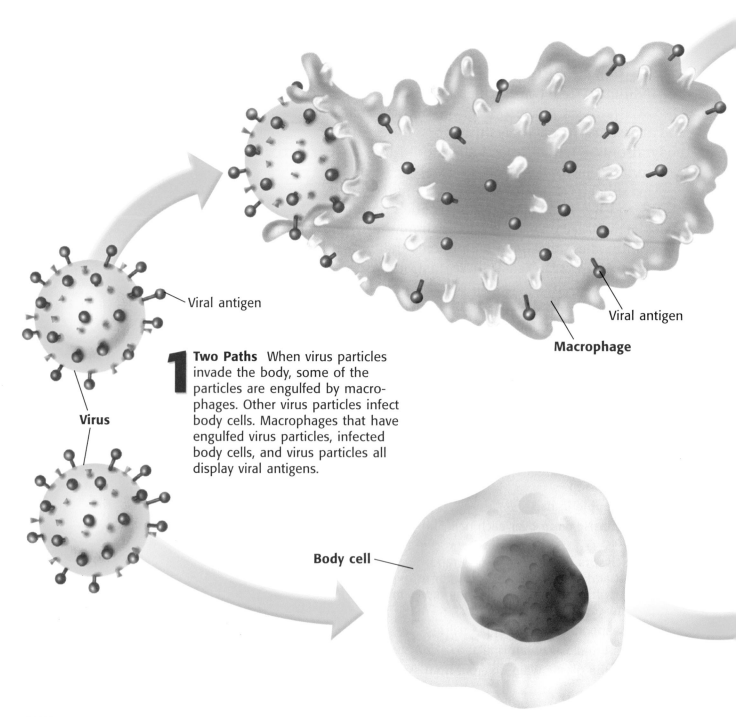

Viral antigen

Viral antigen

Macrophage

Virus

1 Two Paths When virus particles invade the body, some of the particles are engulfed by macrophages. Other virus particles infect body cells. Macrophages that have engulfed virus particles, infected body cells, and virus particles all display viral antigens.

Body cell

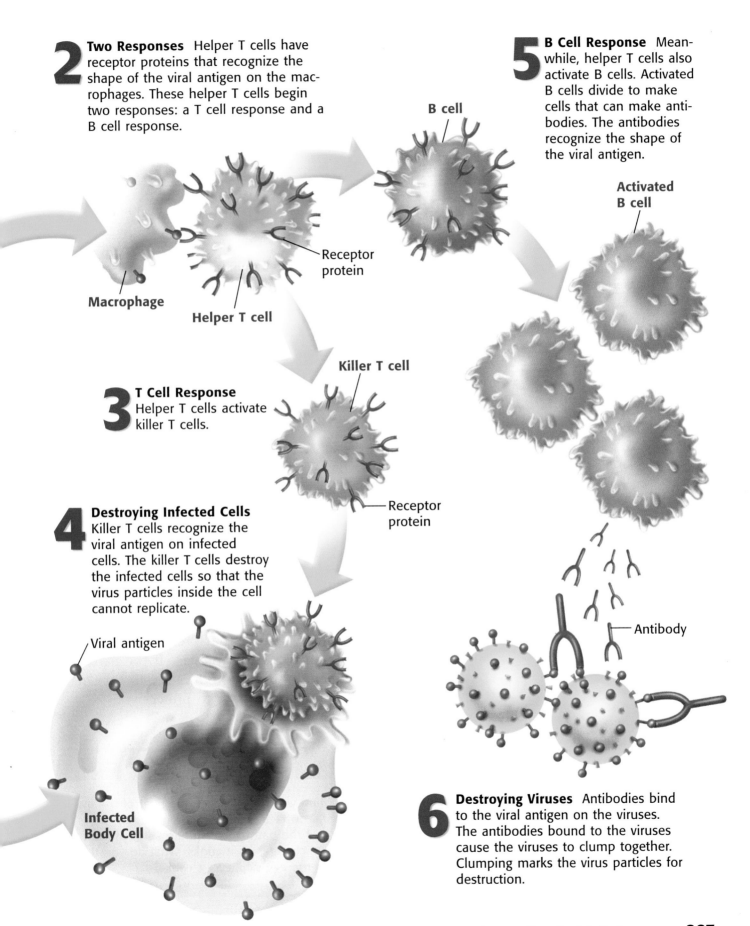

2 **Two Responses** Helper T cells have receptor proteins that recognize the shape of the viral antigen on the macrophages. These helper T cells begin two responses: a T cell response and a B cell response.

Macrophage

Helper T cell

Receptor protein

B cell

5 **B Cell Response** Meanwhile, helper T cells also activate B cells. Activated B cells divide to make cells that can make antibodies. The antibodies recognize the shape of the viral antigen.

Activated B cell

3 **T Cell Response** Helper T cells activate killer T cells.

Killer T cell

Receptor protein

4 **Destroying Infected Cells** Killer T cells recognize the viral antigen on infected cells. The killer T cells destroy the infected cells so that the virus particles inside the cell cannot replicate.

Viral antigen

Infected Body Cell

Antibody

6 **Destroying Viruses** Antibodies bind to the viral antigen on the viruses. The antibodies bound to the viruses cause the viruses to clump together. Clumping marks the virus particles for destruction.

Figure 3 *You may not feel well when you have a fever. But a fever is one way that your body fights infections.*

41°C
Dangerously high temperature

39°C
Best temperature for B cells and T cells to reproduce

37°C
Normal body temperature

Figure 4 *A slight fever helps immune cells reproduce. But a fever of more than a few degrees can become dangerous.*

memory B cell a B cell that responds to an antigen more strongly when the body is reinfected with an antigen than it does during its first encounter with the antigen

Fevers

The man in **Figure 3** is sick and has a fever. What is a fever? When macrophages activate the helper T cells, they send a chemical signal that tells your brain to turn up the thermostat. In a few minutes, your body's temperature can rise several degrees. A moderate fever of one or two degrees actually helps you get well faster because it slows the growth of some pathogens. As shown in **Figure 4,** a fever also helps B cells and T cells multiply faster.

Memory Cells

Your immune system can respond to a second encounter faster than it can respond the first time. B cells must have had previous contact with a pathogen before they can make the correct antibodies. During the first encounter with a new pathogen, specialized B cells make antibodies that are effective against that particular invader. This process takes about 2 weeks, which is far too long to prevent an infection. Therefore, the first time you are infected, you usually get sick.

A few of the B cells become memory B cells. **Memory B cells** are cells in your immune system that "remember" how to make an antibody for a particular pathogen. If the pathogen shows up again, the memory B cells produce B cells that make enough antibodies in just 3 or 4 days to protect you.

**CONNECTION TO
Chemistry**

Bent out of Shape When you have a fever, the heat of the fever changes the shape of viral or bacterial proteins, slowing or preventing the reproduction of the pathogen. With an adult present, observe how an egg white changes as it cooks. What do you think happens to the protein in the egg white as it cooks?

ACTIVITY

Challenges to the Immune System

The immune system is a very effective body-defense system, but it is not perfect. The immune system is unable to deal with some diseases. There are also conditions in which the immune system does not work properly.

Allergies

Sometimes, the immune system overreacts to antigens that are not dangerous to the body. This inappropriate reaction is called an **allergy.** Allergies may be caused by many things, including certain foods and medicines. Many people have allergic reactions to pollen, shown in **Figure 5.** Symptoms of allergic reactions range from a runny nose and itchy eyes to more serious conditions, such as asthma.

Doctors are not sure why the immune system overreacts in some people. Scientists think allergies might be useful because the mucus draining from your nose carries away pollen, dust, and microorganisms.

Autoimmune Diseases

A disease in which the immune system attacks the body's own cells is called an **autoimmune disease.** In an autoimmune disease, immune-system cells mistake body cells for pathogens. One autoimmune disease is rheumatoid arthritis (ROO muh TOYD ahr THRIET is), in which the immune system attacks the joints. A common location for rheumatoid arthritis is the joints of the hands, as shown in **Figure 6.** Other autoimmune diseases include type 1 diabetes, multiple sclerosis, and lupus.

✔ Reading Check Name four autoimmune diseases.

allergy a reaction to a harmless or common substance by the body's immune system

autoimmune disease a disease in which the immune system attacks the organism's own cells

Figure 5 *Pollen is one substance that can cause allergic reactions.*

Figure 6 *In rheumatoid arthritis, immune-system cells cause joint-tissue swelling, which can lead to joint deformities.*

Figure 7 Immune Cells Fighting Cancer

1 A killer T cell attacks an unregulated cell.

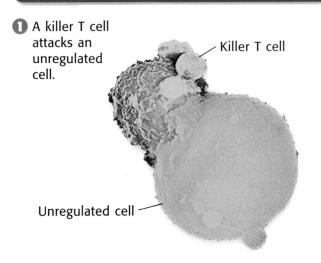

Killer T cell

Unregulated cell

2 The cell's membrane ruptures as the cell dies.

cancer a disease in which the cells begin dividing at an uncontrolled rate and become invasive

Cancer

Healthy cells divide at a carefully regulated rate. Occasionally, a cell doesn't respond to the body's regulation and begins dividing at an uncontrolled rate. As can be seen in **Figure 7,** killer T cells destroy this type of cell. Sometimes, the immune system cannot control the division of these cells. **Cancer** is the condition in which cells divide at an uncontrolled rate.

Many cancers will invade nearby tissues. They can also enter the cardiovascular system or lymphatic system. Cancers can then be transported to other places in the body. Cancers disrupt the normal activities of the organs they have invaded, sometimes leading to death. Today, though, there are many treatments for cancer. Surgery, radiation, and certain drugs can be used to remove or kill cancer cells or slow their division.

AIDS

The human immunodeficiency virus (HIV) causes acquired immune deficiency syndrome (AIDS). Most viruses infect cells in the nose, mouth, lungs, or intestines, but HIV is different. HIV infects the immune system itself, using helper T cells as factories to produce more viruses. You can see HIV particles in **Figure 8.** The helper T cells are destroyed in the process. Remember that the helper T cells put the B cells and killer T cells to work.

People with AIDS have very few helper T cells, so nothing activates the B cells and killer T cells. Therefore, the immune system cannot attack HIV or any other pathogen. People with AIDS don't usually die of AIDS itself. They die of other diseases that they are unable to fight off.

Figure 8 *The blue particles on this helper T cell are human immunodeficiency viruses. They replicated inside the T cell.*

Reading Check What virus causes AIDS?

Summary

- Macrophages engulf pathogens, display antigens on their surface, and activate helper T cells. The helper T cells put the killer T cells and B cells to work.
- Killer T cells kill infected cells. B cells make antibodies.
- Fever helps speed immune-cell growth and slow pathogen growth.
- Memory B cells remember how to make an antibody for a pathogen that the body has previously fought.

- An allergy is the overreaction of the immune system to a harmless antigen.
- Autoimmune diseases are responses in which the immune system attacks healthy tissue.
- Cancer cells are cells that undergo uncontrolled division.
- AIDS is a disease that results when the human immunodeficiency virus kills helper T cells.

Using Key Terms

For each pair of terms, explain how the meanings of the terms differ.

1. *B cell* and *T cell*

2. *autoimmune disease* and *allergy*

Understanding Key Ideas

3. Your body's first line of defense against pathogens includes
   a. skin.
   b. macrophages.
   c. T cells.
   d. B cells.

4. List three ways your body defends itself against pathogens.

5. Name three different cells in the immune system, and describe how they respond to pathogens.

6. Describe four challenges to the immune system.

7. What characterizes a cancer cell?

Critical Thinking

8. **Identifying Relationships** Can your body make antibodies for pathogens that you have never been in contact with? Why or why not?

9. **Applying Concepts** If you had chickenpox at age 7, what might prevent you from getting chickenpox again at age 8?

Interpreting Graphics

10. Look at the graph below. Over time, people with AIDS become very sick and are unable to fight off infection. Use the information in the graph below to explain why this occurs.

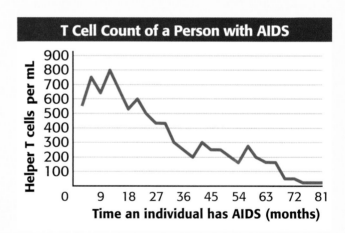

T Cell Count of a Person with AIDS

(Helper T cells per mL vs. Time an individual has AIDS (months))

For a variety of links related to this chapter, go to www.scilinks.org

Topic: Body Defenses; Allergies
SciLinks code: HSM0181; HSM0048

Skills Practice Lab

OBJECTIVES

Investigate how diseases spread.

Analyze data about how diseases spread.

MATERIALS

- beaker or a cup, 200 mL
- eyedropper
- gloves, protective
- solution, unknown, 50 mL

SAFETY

Passing the Cold

There are more than 100 viruses that cause the symptoms of the common cold. Any of the viruses can be passed from person to person—through the air or through direct contact. In this activity, you will track the progress of an outbreak in your class.

Ask a Question

1 With other members of your group, form a question about the spread of disease. For example "How are cold viruses passed from person to person?" or "How can the progress of an outbreak be modeled?"

Form a Hypothesis

2 Form a hypothesis based on the question you asked.

Test the Hypothesis

3 Obtain an empty cup or beaker, an eyedropper, and 50 mL of one of the solutions from your teacher. Only one student will have the "cold virus" solution. You will see a change in your solution when you have become "infected."

4 Your teacher will divide the class into two equal groups. If there is an extra student, that person will record data on the board. Otherwise, the teacher will act as the recorder.

5 The two groups should form straight lines, facing each other.

6 Each time your teacher says the word *mix,* fill your eyedropper with your solution, and place 10 drops of your solution in the beaker of the person in the line opposite you without touching your eyedropper to the other liquid.

7 Gently stir the liquid in your cup with your eyedropper. Do not put your eyedropper in anyone else's solution.

8 If your solution changes color, raise your hand so that the recorder can record the number of students who have been "infected."

9 Your teacher will instruct one line to move one person to the right. Then, the person at the end of the line without a partner should go to the other end of the line.

Results of Experiment			
Trial	Number of infected people	Total number of people	Percentage of infected people
1			
2			
3			
4			
5			
6			
7			
8			
9			
10			

DO NOT WRITE IN BOOK

10 Repeat steps 5–9 nine more times for a total of 10 trials.

11 Return to your desk, and create a data table in your notebook similar to the table above. The column with the title "Total number of people" will remain the same in every row. Enter the data from the board into your data table.

12 Find the percentage of infected people for the last column by dividing the number of infected people by the total number of people and multiplying by 100 in each line.

Analyze the Results

1 **Describing Events** Did you become infected? If so, during which trial did you become infected?

2 **Examining Data** Did everyone eventually become infected? If so, how many trials were necessary to infect everyone?

Draw Conclusions

3 **Interpreting Information** Explain at least one reason why this simulation may underestimate the number of people who might have been infected in real life.

4 **Applying Conclusions** Use your results to make a line graph showing the change in the infection percentage per trial.

Applying Your Data

Do research in the library or on the Internet to find out some of the factors that contribute to the spread of a cold virus. What is the best and easiest way to reduce your chances of catching a cold? Explain your answer.

Chapter Review

USING KEY TERMS

Complete each of the following sentences by choosing the correct term from the word bank.

antibody	cancer
infectious disease	B cell
noninfectious disease	T cell
pathogen	allergy

1 A(n) _____ is caused by a pathogen.

2 Antibiotics can be used to kill a(n) _____.

3 Macrophages attract helper _____.

4 A(n) _____ binds to an antigen.

5 An immune-system overreaction to a harmless substance is a(n) _____.

6 _____ is the unregulated growth of cells.

UNDERSTANDING KEY IDEAS

Multiple Choice

7 Pathogens are
  a. all viruses and microorganisms.
  b. viruses and microorganisms that cause disease.
  c. noninfectious organisms.
  d. all bacteria that live in water.

8 Which of the following is an infectious disease?
  a. allergies
  b. rheumatoid arthritis
  c. asthma
  d. a common cold

9 The skin keeps pathogens out by
  a. staying warm enough to kill pathogens.
  b. releasing killer T cells onto the surface.
  c. shedding dead cells and secreting oils.
  d. All of the above

10 Memory B cells
  a. kill pathogens.
  b. activate killer T cells.
  c. activate killer B cells.
  d. produce B cells that make antibodies.

11 A fever
  a. slows pathogen growth.
  b. helps B cells multiply faster.
  c. helps T cells multiply faster.
  d. All of the above

12 Macrophages
  a. make antibodies.
  b. release helper T cells.
  c. live in the gut.
  d. engulf pathogens.

Short Answer

13 Explain how macrophages start an immune response.

14 Describe the role of helper T cells in responding to an infection.

15 Name two ways that you come into contact with pathogens.

The graph below compares the concentration of antibodies in the blood the first time you are exposed to a pathogen with the concentration of antibodies the next time you are exposed to the pathogen. Use the graph below to answer the questions that follow.

Immune Response

Second exposure to pathogen

First exposure to pathogen

Concentration of antibodies

Days

CRITICAL THINKING

16 Concept Mapping Use the following terms to create a concept map: *macrophages, helper T cells, B cells, antibodies, antigens, killer T cells,* and *memory B cells.*

17 Identifying Relationships Why does the disappearance of helper T cells in AIDS patients damage the immune system?

18 Predicting Consequences Many people take fever-reducing drugs as soon as their temperature exceeds 37°C. Why might it not be a good idea to reduce a fever immediately with drugs?

19 Evaluating Data The risk of dying from a whooping cough vaccine is about one in 1 million. In contrast, the risk of dying from whooping cough is about one in 500. Discuss the pros and cons of this vaccination.

20 Are there more antibodies present during the first week of the first exposure or the first week of the second exposure? Why do you think this is so?

21 What is the difference in recovery time between the first exposure and second exposure? Why?

Standardized Test Preparation

EOG Prep

Read each of the passages below. Then, answer the questions that follow each passage.

Passage 1 Bacteria are becoming resistant to many human-made antibiotics, which means that the drugs no longer affect the bacteria. Scientists now face the challenge of developing new antibiotics that can overcome the resistant strains of bacteria.

Antibiotics from animals are different from some human-made antibiotics. These antibiotics bore holes through the membranes that surround bacterial cells, causing the cells to disintegrate and die. Bacterial membranes don't <u>mutate</u> often, so they are less likely to become resistant to the animal antibiotics.

1. In this passage, what does *mutate* mean?

  A to change

  B to grow

  C to form

  D to degrade

2. Based on the passage, which of the following statements is a fact?

  F Bacterial membranes are on the inside of the bacterial cell.

  G Bacterial membranes are on the outside of the bacterial cell.

  H All strains of bacteria mutate.

  I Bacterial membranes never change.

3. Based on the passage, which of the following sentences is false?

  A Antibiotics from animals are different from human-made antibiotics.

  B Antibiotics from animals bore holes in bacterial membranes.

  C Bacterial membranes don't change very often.

  D Bacteria rarely develop resistance to human-made antibiotics.

Passage 2 Drinking water in the United States is generally safe, but water lines can break, or treatment plants can become flooded, allowing microorganisms to enter the public water supply. Bacteria growing in foods and beverages can cause illness, too. Refrigerating foods can slow the growth of many of these <u>pathogens</u>, but meat, fish, and eggs that are not cooked enough can still contain dangerous bacteria or parasites. Leaving food out at room temperature can give bacteria such as *salmonella* time to grow and produce toxins in the food. For these reasons, it is important to wash all used cooking tools.

1. Which of the following statements can you infer from this passage?

  A Treatment plants help keep drinking water safe.

  B Treatment plants never become flooded.

  C Eliminating treatment plants would help keep water safe.

  D New treatment plants are better than old ones.

2. Which of the following statements can you infer from the passage?

  F Bacteria that live in food produce more toxins than molds produce.

  G Cooking food thoroughly kills bacteria living in the food.

  H Some bacteria are helpful to humans.

  I Illnesses caused by bacteria living in food are seldom serious.

3. According to this passage, what do pathogens cause?

  A disease

  B flooding

  C water-line breaks

  D water supplies

The graph below shows the reported number of people living with HIV/AIDS. Use the graph to answer the questions that follow.

Reported Number of People Living with HIV/AIDS

HIV cases worldwide (in millions)

Year

Source: Joint United Nations Program on HIV/AIDS

1. When did the number of people living with HIV/AIDS reach 5 million?

A 1985

B 1986

C 1987

D 1988

2. When did the number of people living with HIV/AIDS reach 30 million?

F 1996

G 1997

H 1998

I 1999

3. When was the rate of increase of people with HIV/AIDS the **greatest**?

A from 1980 to 1982

B from 1984 to 1986

C from 1988 to 1990

D from 1998 to 2000

4. What percentage of the people who are infected with HIV do not yet have AIDS?

F 10%

G 24%

H 75%

I There is not enough information to determine the answer.

5. If the virus continued to spread as the graph indicates, in the year 2002, about how many people would be infected with HIV?

A 30 million

B 35 million

C 39 million

D 60 million

6. Which part of the graph indicates the rate of infection?

F *x*-axis

G *y*-axis

H slope of the line being graphed

I number of years in the sample

MATH

Read each question below, and choose the best answer.

1. Suppose you have 50,000 flu viruses on your fingers and you rub your eyes. Only 20,000 viruses enter your eyes, 10,000 dissolve in chemicals, and 10,000 are washed down into your nose. Of those, you sneeze out 2,000. How many viruses are left to wash down the back of your throat and possibly start an infection?

A 50,000

B 10,000

C 8,000

D 5,000

2. In which of the following lists are the numbers in order from smallest to greatest?

F 0.027, 0.072, 0.270, 0.720

G 0.270, 0.072, 0.720, 0.270

H 0.072, 0.027, 0.270, 0.720

I 0.720, 0.270, 0.072, 0.027

Science in Action

Weird Science

Frogs in the Medicine Cabinet?

Frog skin, mouse intestines, cow lungs, and shark stomachs are all being tested to make more effective medicines to combat harmful bacteria. In 1896, a biologist named Michael Zasloff was studying African clawed frogs. He noticed that cuts in the frogs' skin healed quickly and never became infected. Zasloff decided to investigate further. He found that when a frog was cut, its skin released a liquid antibiotic that killed invading bacteria. Furthermore, sand sharks, moths, pigs, mice, and cows also contain chemicals that kill bacteria and other microorganisms. These useful antibiotics are even found in the small intestines of humans!

Scientific Discoveries

Medicine for Peanut Allergies

Scientists estimate that 1.5 million people in the United States suffer from peanut allergies. Every year 50 to 100 people in the United States die from an allergic reaction to peanuts. Peanuts and peanut oil are used to make many foods. People who have a peanut allergy sometimes mistakenly eat these foods and suffer severe reactions. A new drug has been discovered to help people control severe reactions. The drug is called TNX-901. The drug is actually an antibody that binds to the antibodies that the body makes during the allergic reaction to the peanuts. By binding these antibodies, the drug controls the allergic response.

Math Activity

During the testing of the new drug, 84 people were given four injections over the course of 4 months. One-fourth of the people participating received injections of a control that had no medicine in it. The rest of the people participating received different doses of the drug. How many people received the control? How many people received medicine? How many shots containing medicine were administered during the 4-month test?

Social Studies Activity

Many medicines were discovered in plants or animals by people living near those plants or animals. Research the origin of one or two common medicines discovered this way. Make a poster showing a world map and the location of the medicines that you researched.

Terrel Shepherd III

Nurse Terrel Shepherd III is a registered nurse (RN) at Texas Children's Hospital in Houston, Texas. RNs have many responsibilities. These responsibilities include giving patients their medications, assessing patients' health, and establishing intravenous access. Nurses also serve as a go-between for the patient and the doctor. Although most nurses work in hospitals or clinics, some nurses work for corporations. Pediatric nurses such as Shepherd work specifically with infants, children, and adolescents. The field of nursing offers a wide variety of job opportunities including home-care nurses, traveling nurses, and flight nurses. The hospital alone has many areas of expertise for nurses, including geriatrics (working with the elderly), intensive care, administration, and surgery. Traditionally, nursing has been considered to be a woman's career. However, since nursing began as a profession, men and women have practiced nursing. A career in nursing is possible for anyone who does well in science, enjoys people, and wants to make a difference in people's lives.

Language Arts ACTiViTY

WRITING SKILL Create a brochure that persuades people to consider a career in nursing. Describe nursing as a career, the benefits of becoming a nurse, and the education needed to be a nurse. Illustrate the brochure with pictures of nurses from the Internet or from magazines.

To learn more about these Science in Action topics, visit go.hrw.com and type in the keyword **HL5BD6F.**

Current Science

Check out Current Science® articles related to this chapter by visiting go.hrw.com. Just type in the keyword **HL5CS27.**

11

Staying Healthy

About the PHOTO

What do you see in this photo? Sure, you can see five students facing the camera, but what else does the picture tell you? The bright eyes, happy smiles, and shiny hair show radiant health. Having a clear mind and a long, active life depend on having a healthy body. Keeping your body healthy depends on eating well; avoiding drugs, cigarettes, and alcohol; and staying safe.

PRE-READING ACTIVITY

FOLDNOTES **Booklet** Before you read the chapter, create the FoldNote entitled "Booklet" described in the **Study Skills** section of the Appendix. Label each page of the booklet with a main idea from the chapter. As you read the chapter, write what you learn about each main idea on the appropriate page of the booklet.

START-UP ACTIVITY

Conduct a Survey

How healthy are the habits of your classmates? Find out for yourself.

Procedure

1. Copy and answer yes or no to each of the five questions at right. Do not put your name on the survey.

Analysis

1. As a class, record the data from the completed surveys in a chart. For each question, calculate the percentage of your class that answered yes.

2. What good and bad habits do your classmates have?

1. Do you exercise at least three times a week?

2. Do you wear a seat belt every time you ride in a car?

3. Do you eat five or more servings of fruits and vegetables every day?

4. Do you use sunscreen to protect your skin when you are outdoors?

5. Do you eat a lot of high-fat foods?

Good Nutrition

Does the saying "You are what you eat" mean that you are pizza? No, but substances in pizza help build your body.

Protein in the cheese may become part of your hair. Carbohydrates in the crust can give you energy for your next race.

READING WARM-UP

Objectives

● Identify the six groups of nutrients, and explain their importance to good health.

● Describe the Food Guide Pyramid.

● Understand how to read Nutrition Facts labels.

● Explain the dangers of various nutritional disorders.

Terms to Learn

nutrient   mineral
carbohydrate   vitamin
protein   malnutrition
fat

READING STRATEGY

Reading Organizer As you read this section, create an outline of the section. Use the headings from the section in your outline.

nutrient a substance in food that provides energy or helps form body tissues and that is necessary for life and growth

carbohydrate a class of energy-giving nutrients that includes sugars, starches, and fiber

Nutrients

Are you more likely to have potato chips or broccoli for a snack? If you eat many foods that are high in fat, such as potato chips, your food choices probably are not as healthy as they could be. Broccoli is a healthier food than potato chips. But eating only broccoli, as the person in **Figure 1** is doing, does not give you a balanced diet.

To stay healthy, you need to take in **nutrients,** or substances that provide the materials needed for life processes. Nutrients are grouped into six classes: *carbohydrates, proteins, fats, water, vitamins,* and *minerals.* Carbohydrates, proteins, and fats provide energy for the body in units called *Calories* (Cal).

Carbohydrates

Carbohydrates are your body's main source of energy. A **carbohydrate** is a chemical composed of simple sugars. There are two types of carbohydrates: simple and complex. *Simple carbohydrates* are sugars. They are easily digested and give you quick energy. *Complex carbohydrates* are made up of many sugar molecules linked together. They are digested slowly and give you long-lasting energy. Some complex carbohydrates are good sources of fiber. Fiber is a part of a healthy diet and is found in whole-grain foods, such as brown rice and whole-wheat bread. Many fruits and vegetables also contain fiber.

Figure 1 *Eating only one food, even a healthy food, will not give you all the substances your body needs.*

Protein

Proteins are found in body fluids, muscle, bone, and skin. **Proteins** are nutrients used to build and repair your body. Your body makes the proteins it needs, but it must have the necessary building blocks, called *amino acids*. Your digestive system breaks down protein into individual amino acids that are then used to make new proteins. Some foods, such as poultry, fish, milk, and eggs, provide all of the amino acids your body needs. Foods that contain all of these essential amino acids are called *complete proteins*. *Incomplete proteins* contain only some of the essential amino acids. Most plant foods contain incomplete protein, but eating a variety of plant foods will provide all of the amino acids your body needs.

✓ **Reading Check** What is an incomplete protein?
(*See the Appendix for answers to Reading Checks.*)

Figure 2 *This sample meal provides many of the nutrients a growing teenager needs.*

Fats

Another class of nutrients that is important to a healthy meal, such as the meal shown in **Figure 2,** is fat. **Fats** are energy-storage nutrients. Fats are needed to store and transport vitamins, produce hormones, keep skin healthy, and provide insulation. Fats also provide more energy than either proteins or carbohydrates. There are two types of fats: saturated and unsaturated. *Saturated fats* are found in meat, dairy products, coconut oil, and palm oil. Saturated fats raise blood cholesterol levels. Although *cholesterol* is a fat-like substance found naturally in the body, high levels can increase the risk of heart disease. *Unsaturated fats* and foods high in fiber may help reduce blood cholesterol levels. Your body cannot make unsaturated fats. They must come from vegetable oils and fish in your diet. The body needs both kinds of fats.

protein a molecule that is made up of amino acids and that is needed to build and repair body structures and to regulate processes in the body

fat an energy-storage nutrient that helps the body store some vitamins

Water

You cannot survive for more than a few days without water. Your body is about 70% water. Water is in every cell of your body. The main functions of water are to transport substances, regulate body temperature, and provide lubrication. Some scientists think you should drink at least eight glasses of water a day. When you exercise you need more water, as shown in **Figure 3.** You also get water from other liquids you drink and the foods you eat. Fresh fruits and vegetables, juices, soups, and milk are good sources of water.

Figure 3 *When you exercise, you need to drink more water.*

Table 1 Some Essential Vitamins

Vitamin	What it does	Where you get it
A	keeps skin and eyes healthy; builds strong bones and teeth	yellow and orange fruits and vegetables, leafy greens, meats, and milk
B (various forms)	helps body use carbohydrates; helps blood, nerves, and heart function	meats, whole grains, beans, peas, nuts, and seafood
C	strengthens tissues; helps the body absorb iron, fight disease	citrus fruits, leafy greens, broccoli, peppers, and cabbage
D	builds strong bones and teeth; helps the body use calcium and phosphorus	sunlight, enriched milk, eggs, and fish
E	protects red blood cells from destruction; keeps skin healthy	oils, fats, eggs, whole grains, wheat germ, liver, and leafy greens
K	assists with blood clotting	leafy greens, tomatoes, and potatoes

Minerals

If you eat a balanced diet, you should get all of the vitamins and minerals you need. **Minerals** are elements that are essential for good health. You need six minerals in large amounts: calcium, chloride, magnesium, phosphorus, potassium, and sodium. There are at least 12 minerals that are required in very small amounts. These include fluorine, iodine, iron, and zinc. Calcium is necessary for strong bones and teeth. Magnesium and sodium help the body use proteins. Potassium is needed to regulate your heartbeat and produce muscle movement, and iron is necessary for red blood cell production.

Vitamins

Vitamins are another class of nutrients. **Vitamins** are compounds that control many body functions. Only vitamin D can be made by the body, so you have to get most vitamins from food. **Table 1** provides information about six essential vitamins.

mineral a class of nutrients that are chemical elements that are needed for certain body processes

vitamin a class of nutrients that contain carbon and that are needed in small amounts to maintain health and allow growth

CONNECTION TO Oceanography

Nutritious Seaweed Kelp, a type of seaweed, is a good source of iodine. This nutritious food is grown on special farms off the coasts of China and Japan. What other nutritious foods come from the sea?

Eating for Good Health

Now you have learned which nutrients you need for good health. But how can you be sure to get all the important nutrients in the right amounts? To begin, keep in mind that most teenage girls need about 2,200 Cal per day, and most boys need about 2,800 Cal. Because different foods contain different nutrients, *where* you get your Calories is as important as *how many* you get. The Food Guide Pyramid, shown in **Figure 4,** can help you make good food choices.

✓ Reading Check Using the Food Guide Pyramid below, design a healthy lunch that includes one food from each food group.

Brown Bag Test

1. Cut a **brown paper bag** into squares.
2. Gather a variety of **foods.** Place a piece of each food on a different square and leave overnight.
3. What do you see when you remove the food?
4. Which food had the most oil? Which food had the least?

Figure 4 | **The Food Guide Pyramid**

The U.S. Department of Agriculture and the Department of Health and Human Services developed the Food Guide Pyramid to help Americans make healthy food choices. The Food Guide Pyramid divides foods into six groups. It shows how many servings you need daily from each group and gives examples of foods for each. This pyramid also provides sample serving sizes for each group. Within each group, the food choices are up to you.

Fats, oils, and sweets
Use sparingly.

Milk, yogurt, and cheese
2 to 3 servings
- 1 cup of milk or yogurt
- 1 1/2 oz of natural cheese
- 2 oz of processed cheese

Meat, poultry, fish, beans, eggs, and nuts 2 to 3 servings
- 2 to 3 oz of cooked poultry, fish, or lean meat
- 1/2 cup of cooked dried beans
- 1 egg

Vegetables 3 to 5 servings
- 1/2 cup of chopped vegetables
- 1 cup of raw, leafy vegetables
- 3/4 cup of cooked vegetables

Fruits 2 to 4 servings
- 1 medium apple, banana, or orange
- 1/2 cup of chopped, cooked, or canned fruit
- 3/4 cup of fruit juice

Bread, cereal, rice, and pasta 6 to 11 servings
- 1 slice of bread
- 1 oz of ready-to-eat cereal
- 1/2 cup of rice or pasta
- 1/2 cup of cooked cereal

Nutrition Facts	
Serving Size 1/2 cup (120 ml) — **Serving information**	
Servings per Container 2.5	

Amount per Serving	Prepared
Calories	70 — **Number of Calories per serving**
Calories from Fat	25

	% Daily Value
Total Fat 2.5 g	4%
Saturated Fat 1 g	5%
Cholesterol 15 mg	5%
Sodium 960 mg	40%
Total Carbohydrate 8 g	3%
Dietary Fiber less than 1 g	4%
Sugars 1 g	
Protein 3 g	
Vitamin A	15%
Vitamin C	0%
Calcium **Percentage of daily values**	0%
Iron	4%

*Percent Daily Values are based on a 2,000 Calorie diet. Your daily values may be higher or lower depending on your Calorie needs:

		Calories	2,000	2,500
Total Fat	Less than		65g	80g
Sat Fat	Less than		20g	25g
Cholesterol	Less than		300mg	300mg
Sodium	Less than		2,400mg	2,400mg
Total Carbohydrate			300g	375g
Dietary Fiber			25g	30g
Protein			50g	60g

Figure 5 *Nutrition Facts labels provide a lot of information.*

malnutrition a disorder of nutrition that results when a person does not consume enough of each of the nutrients that are needed by the human body

What Percentage?

Use the Nutrition Facts label above to answer the following question. The recommended daily value of fat is 72 g for teenage girls and 90 g for teenage boys. What percentage of the daily recommended fat value is provided in one cup of soup?

Reading Food Labels

Packaged foods must have Nutrition Facts labels. **Figure 5** shows a Nutrition Facts label for chicken noodle soup. Nutrition Facts labels show what amount of each nutrient is in one serving of the food. You can tell whether a food is high or low in a nutrient by looking at its daily value. Reading food labels can help you make healthy eating choices. The percentage of daily values shown is based on a diet that consists of 2,000 Cal per day. Most teenagers need more than 2,000 Cal per day. The number of Calories needed depends on factors such as height, weight, age, and level of activity. Playing sports and exercising use up Calories that need to be replaced for you to grow.

Reading Check For what nutrients does chicken noodle soup provide more than 10% of the daily value?

Nutritional Disorders

Unhealthy eating habits can cause nutritional disorders. **Malnutrition** occurs when someone does not eat enough of the nutrients needed by the body. Malnutrition can result from eating too few or too many Calories or not taking in enough of the right nutrients. Malnutrition affects how one looks and how quickly one's body can repair damage and fight illness.

Anorexia Nervosa and Bulimia Nervosa

Anorexia nervosa (AN uh REKS ee uh nuhr VOH suh) is an eating disorder characterized by self-starvation and an intense fear of gaining weight. Anorexia nervosa can lead to severe malnutrition.

Bulimia nervosa (boo LEE mee uh nuhr VOH suh) is a disorder characterized by binge eating followed by induced vomiting. Sometimes, people suffering from bulimia nervosa use laxatives or diuretics to rid their bodies of food and water. Bulimia nervosa can damage teeth and the digestive system and can lead to kidney and heart failure.

Both anorexia and bulimia can cause weak bones, low blood pressure, and heart problems. These eating disorders can be fatal if not treated. If you are worried that you or someone you know may have an eating disorder, talk to an adult.

Obesity

Eating too much food that is high in fat and low in other nutrients, such as junk food and fast food, can lead to malnutrition. *Obesity* (oh BEE suh tee) is having an extremely high percentage of body fat. People suffering from obesity may not be eating a variety of foods that provide them with the correct balance of essential nutrients. Having an inactive lifestyle can also contribute to obesity.

Obesity increases the risk of high blood pressure, heart disease, and diabetes. Eating a more balanced diet and exercising regularly can help reduce obesity. Obesity may also be caused by other factors. Scientists are studying the links between obesity and heredity.

SECTION Review

Summary

- A healthy diet has a balance of carbohydrates, proteins, fats, water, vitamins, and minerals.
- The Food Guide Pyramid is a good guide for healthy eating.
- Nutrition Facts labels provide information needed to plan a healthy diet.
- Anorexia nervosa and bulimia nervosa cause malnutrition and damage to many body systems.
- Obesity can lead to heart disease and diabetes.

Using Key Terms

1. In your own words, write a definition for each of the following terms: *nutrient, mineral,* and *vitamin.*

Understanding Key Ideas

2. Malnutrition can be caused by
   a. obesity.
   b. bulimia nervosa.
   c. anorexia nervosa.
   d. All of the above

3. What information is found on a Nutrition Facts label?

4. Give an example of a carbohydrate, a protein, and a fat.

5. If vitamins and minerals do not supply energy, why are they important to a healthy diet?

6. How do anorexia nervosa and bulimia nervosa differ?

7. How can someone who is obese suffer from malnutrition?

Math Skills

8. If you eat 2,500 Cal per day and 20% are from fat, 30% are from protein, and 50% are from carbohydrates, how many Calories of each nutrient do you eat?

Critical Thinking

9. **Applying Concepts** Name some of the nutrients that can be found in a glass of milk.

10. **Identifying Relationships** Explain how eating a variety of foods can help ensure good nutrition.

11. **Predicting Consequences** How would your growth be affected if your diet consistently lacked important nutrients?

12. **Applying Concepts** Explain how you can use the Nutrition Facts label to choose food that is high in calcium.

SCiLINKS®

NSTA
Developed and maintained by the
National Science Teachers Association

For a variety of links related to this chapter, go to www.scilinks.org

Topic: Food Pyramids; Nutritional Disorders
SciLinks code: HSM0598; HSM1057

Risks of Alcohol and Other Drugs

You see them in movies and on television and read about them in magazines. But what are drugs?

You are exposed to information, and misinformation, about drugs every day. So, how can you make the best decisions?

READING WARM-UP

Objectives

● Describe the difference between psychological and physical dependence.

● Explain the hazards of tobacco, alcohol, and illegal drugs.

● Distinguish between the positive and negative uses of drugs.

Terms to Learn

drug	alcoholism
addiction	narcotic
nicotine	

READING STRATEGY

Reading Organizer As you read this section, make a table comparing the positive and negative uses of drugs.

What Is a Drug?

Any chemical substance that causes a physical or psychological change is called a **drug.** Drugs come in many forms, as shown in **Figure 1.** Some drugs enter the body through the skin. Other drugs are swallowed, inhaled, or injected. Drugs are classified by their effects. *Analgesics* (AN'l JEE ziks) relieve pain. *Antibiotics* (AN tie bie AHT iks) fight bacterial infections, and *antihistamines* (AN tie HIS tuh MEENZ) control cold and allergy symptoms. *Stimulants* speed up the central nervous system, and *depressants* slow it down. When used correctly, legal drugs can help your body heal. When used illegally or improperly, however, drugs can do great harm.

Dependence and Addiction

The body can develop *tolerance* to a drug. Tolerance means that larger and larger doses of the drug are needed to get the same effect. The body can also form a *physical dependence* or need for a drug. If the body doesn't receive a drug that it is physically dependent on, withdrawal symptoms occur. Withdrawal symptoms include nausea, vomiting, pain, and tremors.

Addiction is the loss of control of drug-taking behavior. Once addicted, a person finds it very hard to stop taking a drug. Sometimes, the need for a drug is not due only to physical dependence. Some people also form *psychological dependence* on a drug, which means that they feel powerful cravings for the drug.

Figure 1 *All of these products contain drugs.*

Types of Drugs

There are many kinds of drugs. Some drugs are made from plants, and some are made in a lab. You can buy some drugs at the grocery store, while others can be prescribed only by a doctor. Some drugs are illegal to buy, sell, or possess.

Herbal Medicines

Information about herbal medicines has been handed down for centuries, and some herbs contain chemicals with important healing properties. The tea in **Figure 2** contains chamomile and is made from a plant. Chamomile has chemicals in it that can help you sleep. However, herbs are drugs and should be used carefully. The Federal Drug Administration does not regulate herbal medicines or teas and cannot guarantee their safety.

Over-the-Counter and Prescription Drugs

Over-the-counter drugs can be bought without a prescription. A prescription is written by a doctor and describes the drug, directions for use, and the amount of the drug to be taken.

Many over-the-counter and prescription drugs are powerful healing agents. However, some drugs also produce unwanted side effects. *Side effects* are uncomfortable symptoms, such as nausea, headaches, drowsiness, or more serious problems.

Whether purchased with or without a prescription, all drugs must be used with care. Information on proper use can be found on the label. **Figure 3** shows some general drug safety tips.

✓ Reading Check What is the difference between an over-the-counter drug and a prescription drug? (*See the Appendix for answers to Reading Checks.*)

drug any substance that causes a change in a person's physical or psychological state

addiction a dependence on a substance, such as alcohol or another drug

Figure 2 *Some herbs can be purchased in health-food stores. Medicinal herbs should always be used with care.*

Figure 3 **Drug Safety Tips**

- *Never take another person's prescription medicine.*
- *Read the label before each use. Always follow the instructions on the label and those provided by your doctor or pharmacist.*
- *Do not take more or less medication than prescribed.*
- *Consult a doctor if you have any side effects.*
- *Throw away leftover and out-of-date medicines.*

Figure 4 Effects of Smoking

▼ Healthy lung tissue of a nonsmoker

▼ Damaged lung tissue of a smoker

nicotine a toxic, addictive chemical that is found in tobacco and that is one of the major contributors to the harmful effects of smoking

alcoholism a disorder in which a person repeatedly drinks alcoholic beverages in an amount that interferes with the person's health and activities

Tobacco

Cigarettes are addictive, and smoking has serious health effects. **Nicotine** (NIK uh TEEN) is a chemical in tobacco that increases heart rate and blood pressure and is extremely addictive. Smokers experience a decrease in physical endurance. **Figure 4** shows the effects of smoking on the cilia of your lungs. Cilia clean the air you breathe and prevent debris from entering your lungs. Smoking increases the chances of lung cancer, and it has been linked to other cancers, emphysema, chronic bronchitis, and heart disease. Experts estimate that there are more than 430,000 deaths related to smoking each year in the United States. Secondhand smoke also poses significant health risks.

Like cigarettes, smokeless, or chewing, tobacco is addictive and can cause health problems. Nicotine is absorbed through the lining of the mouth. Smokeless tobacco increases the risk of several cancers, including mouth and throat cancer. It also causes gum disease and yellowing of the teeth.

Alcohol

It is illegal in most of the United States for people under the age of 21 to use alcohol. Alcohol slows down the central nervous system and can cause memory loss. Excessive use of alcohol can damage the liver, pancreas, brain, nerves, and cardiovascular system. In very large quantities, alcohol can cause death. Alcohol is a factor in more than half of all suicides, murders, and accidental deaths. **Figure 5** shows the results of one alcohol-related accident. Alcohol also affects decision making and can lead you to take unhealthy risks.

People can suffer from **alcoholism,** which means that they are physically and psychologically dependent on alcohol. Alcoholism is considered a disease, and genetic factors are thought to influence the development of alcoholism in some people.

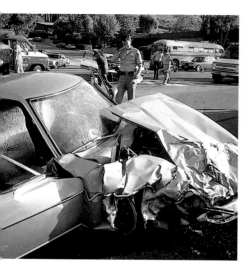

Figure 5 *This car was in an accident involving a drunk driver.*

310   Chapter 11   Staying Healthy

Figure 6 *Smoking marijuana can make your health and dreams go up in smoke.*

Marijuana

Marijuana is an illegal drug that comes from the Indian hemp plant. Marijuana affects different people in different ways. It may increase anxiety or cause feelings of paranoia. Marijuana slows reaction time, impairs thinking, and causes a loss of coordination. Regular use of marijuana can affect many areas of your life, as described in **Figure 6.**

narcotic a drug that is derived from opium and that relieves pain and induces sleep

Cocaine

Cocaine and its more purified form, crack, are made from the coca plant. Both drugs are illegal and highly addictive. Users can become addicted to them in a very short time. Cocaine can produce feelings of intense excitement followed by anxiety and depression. Both drugs increase heart rate and blood pressure and can cause heart attacks, even among first-time users.

✓ **Reading Check** What are two dangers to users of cocaine?

Narcotics and Designer Drugs

Drugs made from the opium plant are called **narcotics.** Some narcotics are used to treat severe pain. Narcotics are illegal unless prescribed by a doctor. Some narcotics are never legal. For example, heroin is one of the most addictive narcotics and is always illegal. Heroin is usually injected, and users often share needles. Therefore, heroin users have a high risk of becoming infected with diseases such as hepatitis and AIDS. Heroin users can also die of an overdose of the drug.

Other illegal drugs include inhalants, barbiturates (bahr BICH uhr itz), amphetamines (am FET uh MEENZ), and *designer drugs*. Designer drugs are made by making small changes to existing drugs. Ecstasy, or "X," is a designer drug that causes feelings of well-being. Over time, the drug causes lesions (LEE zhuhnz), or holes, in a user's brain, as shown in **Figure 7.** Ecstasy users are also more likely to develop depression.

Figure 7 *The brain scan on the left shows a healthy brain. The scan on the right is from a teenager who has regularly used Ecstasy.*

Figure 8 *Drug abuse can leave you depressed and feeling alone.*

Figure 9 **Drug Myths**

Myth **"It's only alcohol, not drugs."**

Reality Alcohol is a mood-altering and mind-altering drug. It affects the central nervous system and is addictive.

Myth **"I won't get hooked on one or two cigarettes a day."**

Reality Addiction is not related to the amount of a drug used. Some people become addicted after using a drug once or twice.

Myth **"I can quit any time I want."**

Reality Addicts may quit and return to drug usage many times. Their inability to stay drug-free shows how powerful the addiction is.

Good Reasons

WRITING SKILL Discuss with your parent the possible effects of drug abuse on your family. Then, write yourself a letter giving reasons why you should stay drug-free. Put your letter in a safe place. If you ever find yourself thinking about using drugs, take out your letter and read it. **ACTIVITY**

Hallucinogens

Hallucinogens (huh LOO si nuh juhnz) distort the senses and cause mood changes. Users have hallucinations, which means that they see and hear things that are not real. LSD and PCP are powerful, illegal hallucinogens. Sniffing glue or solvents can also cause hallucinations and serious brain damage.

Drug Abuse

A drug user takes a drug to prevent or improve a medical condition. The drug user obtains the drug legally and uses the drug properly. A drug abuser does not take a drug to relieve a medical condition. An abuser may take drugs for the temporary good feelings they produce, to escape from problems, or to belong to a group. The drug is often obtained illegally, and it is often taken without knowledge of the drug's dangers.

✓ **Reading Check** What is the difference between drug use and drug abuse?

How Drug Abuse Starts

Nicotine, alcohol, and marijuana are sometimes called *gateway drugs* because they are often the first drugs a person abuses. The abuse of other, more dangerous drugs may follow the abuse of gateway drugs. Peer pressure is often the reason that young people begin to use drugs. Teenagers may drink, smoke, or try marijuana to make friends or avoid being teased. Because drug abusers often stand out, it can sometimes be hard to see that many teenagers do not abuse drugs.

Many teenagers begin using illegal drugs to feel part of a group, but drug abuse has many serious consequences. Drug abuse can lead to problems with friends, family, school, and handling money. These problems often lead to depression and social isolation, as shown in **Figure 8.**

Many people who start using drugs do not recognize the dangers. Misinformation about drugs is everywhere. Several common drug myths are discussed in **Figure 9.**

Getting Off Drugs

People who abuse drugs undergo emotional and physical changes. Teenagers who had few problems often begin to have problems with school, family, and money when they start to use drugs.

The first step to quitting drugs is to admit to abusing drugs and to decide to stop. It is important for the addicted person to get the proper medical treatment. There are drug treatment centers, like the one shown in **Figure 10,** available to help. Getting off drugs can be extremely difficult. Withdrawal symptoms are often painful, and powerful cravings for a drug can continue long after a person quits. But people who stop abusing drugs lead happier and healthier lives.

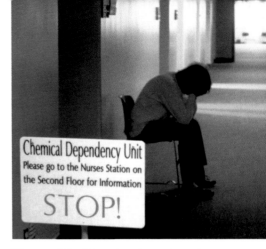

Figure 10 *Drug treatment centers help people get off drugs and back on track to healthier, happier lives.*

SECTION Review

Summary

- Physical dependence causes withdrawal symptoms when a person stops using a drug. Psychological dependence causes powerful cravings.

- There are many types of drugs, including over-the-counter, prescription, and herbal medicines.

- Tobacco contains the highly addictive chemical nicotine.

- Abuse of alcohol can lead to alcoholism.

- Illegal drugs include marijuana, cocaine, hallucinogens, designer drugs, and many narcotics.

- Getting off drugs requires proper medical treatment.

Using Key Terms

1. In your own words, write a definition for the terms *drug, addiction,* and *narcotic.*

Understanding Key Ideas

2. Which of the following products does NOT contain a drug?
   - **a.** cola
   - **b.** fruit juice
   - **c.** herbal tea
   - **d.** cough syrup

3. Describe the difference between physical and psychological dependence.

4. What is the difference between drug use and drug abuse?

5. How does addiction occur, and what are two consequences of drug addiction?

6. Name two different kinds of illegal drugs, and give examples of each.

Math Skills

7. If 2,200 people between the ages of 16 and 20 die every year in alcohol-related car crashes, how many die every day?

Critical Thinking

8. **Analyzing Relationships** How are nicotine, alcohol, heroin, and cocaine similar? How are they different?

9. **Analyzing Ideas** What are two ways that a person who abuses drugs can get in trouble with the law?

10. **Predicting Consequences** How can drug abuse damage family relationships?

11. **Making Inferences** Driving a car while under the influence of drugs can put others in danger. Describe another situation in which one person's drug abuse could put other people in danger.

SCLINKS

NSTA

Developed and maintained by the National Science Teachers Association

For a variety of links related to this chapter, go to www.scilinks.org

Topic: Drug and Alcohol Abuse
SciLinks code: HSM0428

Healthy Habits

Do you like playing sports or acting in plays? How does your health affect your favorite activities?

Whatever you do, the better your health is, the better you can perform. Keeping yourself healthy is a daily responsibility.

Taking Care of Your Body

The science of preserving and protecting your health is known as **hygiene.** It sounds simple, but washing your hands is the best way to prevent the spread of disease and infection. You should always wash your hands after using the bathroom and before and after handling food. Taking care of your skin, hair, and teeth is important for good hygiene. Good hygiene includes regularly using sunscreen, shampooing your hair, and brushing and flossing your teeth daily.

Good Posture

Posture is also important to health. Good posture helps you look and feel your best. Bad posture strains your muscles and ligaments and makes breathing difficult. To have good posture, imagine a vertical line passing through your ear, shoulder, hip, knee, and ankle when you stand, as shown in **Figure 1.** When working at a desk, you should maintain good posture by pulling your chair forward and planting your feet firmly on the floor.

READING WARM-UP

Objectives

● Describe three important aspects of good hygiene.

● Explain why exercise and sleep are important to good health.

● Describe methods of handling stress.

● List three ways to stay safe at home, on the road, and outdoors.

● Plan what you would do in the case of an accident.

Terms to Learn

hygiene
aerobic exercise
stress

READING STRATEGY

Prediction Guide Before reading this section, write the title of each heading in this section. Next, under each heading, write what you think you will learn.

hygiene the science of health and ways to preserve health

Figure 1 *A slumped posture strains your lower back.*

When you have good posture, your ear, shoulder, hip, knee, and ankle are in a straight line.

Bad posture strains your muscles and ligaments and can make breathing difficult.

Exercise

Aerobic exercise at least three times a week is essential to good health. **Aerobic exercise** is vigorous, constant exercise of the whole body for 20 minutes or more. Walking, running, swimming, and biking are all examples of aerobic exercise. **Figure 2** shows another popular aerobic exercise—basketball.

Aerobic exercise increases the heart rate. As a result, more oxygen is taken in and distributed throughout the body. Over time, aerobic exercise strengthens the heart, lungs, and bones. It burns Calories, helps your body conserve some nutrients, and aids digestion. It also gives you more energy and stamina. Aerobic exercise protects your physical and mental health.

Figure 2 *Aerobic exercise can be fun if you choose an activity you enjoy.*

Reading Check What are two benefits of regular exercise? (*See the Appendix for answers to Reading Checks.*)

Sleep

Believe it or not, teenagers actually need more sleep than younger children. Do you ever fall asleep in class, like the girl in **Figure 3,** or feel tired in the middle of the afternoon? If so, you may not be getting enough sleep. Scientists say that teenagers need about 9.5 hours of sleep each night.

At night, the body goes through several cycles of progressively deeper sleep, with periods of lighter sleep in between. If you do not sleep long enough, you will not enter the deepest, most restful period of sleep.

aerobic exercise physical exercise intended to increase the activity of the heart and lungs to promote the body's use of oxygen

Figure 3 *If you fall asleep easily during the day, you are probably not getting enough sleep.*

CONNECTION TO Language Arts

Dreamy Poetry

You are not wrong, who deem
That my days have been a dream;
Yet if hope has flown away
In a night, or in a day,
In a vision, or in none,
Is it therefore the less gone?
All that we see or seem
Is but a dream within a dream.

(Edgar Allan Poe,
"A Dream Within a Dream")

What do you think Poe means by "a dream within a dream?" Why do you think there are many poems written about dreams or sleep?

Coping with Stress

You have a big soccer game tomorrow. Are you excited and ready for action? You got a low grade on your English paper. Are you upset or angry? The game and the test are causing you stress. **Stress** is the physical and mental response to pressure.

Some stress is a normal part of life. Stress stimulates your body to prepare for difficult or dangerous situations. However, sometimes you may have no outlet for the stress, and it builds up. Many things are causing stress for the girl shown in **Figure 4.** Excess stress is harmful to your health and can decrease your ability to carry out your daily activities.

You may not even realize you are stressed until your body reacts. Perhaps you get a headache, have an upset stomach, or lie awake at night. You might feel tired all the time or begin an old nervous habit, such as nail-biting. You may become irritable or resentful. All of these things can be signs of too much stress.

Figure 4 *Can you identify all of the things in this picture that could cause stress?*

stress a physical or mental response to pressure

Dealing with Stress

Different people are stressed by different things. Once you identify the source of the stress, you can find ways to deal with it. If you cannot remove the cause of stress, here are some ideas for handling stress.

- Share your problems. Talk things over with someone you trust, such as a parent, friend, teacher, or school counselor.
- Make a list of all the things you would like to get done, and rank the things in order of importance. Do the most important things first.
- Exercise regularly, and get enough sleep.
- Pet a friendly animal.
- Spend some quiet time alone, or practice deep breathing or other relaxation techniques.

For another activity related to this chapter, go to **go.hrw.com** and type in the keyword **HL5BD7W.**

Injury Prevention

Have you ever fallen off your bike or sprained your ankle? Accidents happen, and they can cause injury and even death. It is impossible to prevent all accidents, but you can decrease your risk by using your common sense and following basic safety rules.

Safety Outdoors

Always dress appropriately for the weather and for the activity. Never hike or camp alone. Tell someone where you are going and when you expect to return. If you do not bring water from home, be sure to purify any water you drink in the wilderness.

Learn how to swim. It could save your life! Never swim alone, and do not dive into shallow water or water of unknown depth. When in a boat, wear a life jacket. If a storm threatens, get out of the water and seek shelter.

✓ **Reading Check** Name three safety tips for the outdoors.

Safety at Home

Many accidents can be avoided. **Figure 5** shows tips for safety around the house.

Figure 5 Home Safety Tips

Bathroom
- Never touch electrical switches or appliances while touching water.
- Use nonslip mats in the shower and tub.
- Use a night light.

- Have a parent install smoke detectors on every floor.

Kitchen
- Clean up spills quickly.
- Do not allow pot handles to extend over the edge of the stove.
- Use a stool to reach high shelves.
- Keep grease and drippings away from open flames.

Entrance and Stairs
- Use a railing.
- Never leave objects on stairs.

Living Room
- Keep electrical cords out of walkways.
- Do not plug too many electrical devices into one outlet.

Figure 6 *It is always important to use the appropriate safety equipment.*

Safety on the Road

In the car, always wear a seat belt, even if you are traveling only a short distance. Never ride in a car with someone who has been drinking. Safety equipment and common sense are your best defense against injury. When riding a bicycle, always wear a helmet like those shown in **Figure 6.** Ride with traffic, and obey all traffic rules. Be sure to signal when stopping or turning.

Safety in Class

Accidents can happen in school, especially in a lab class or during woodworking class. To avoid hurting yourself and others, always follow your teacher's instructions, and wear the proper safety equipment at all times.

When Accidents Happen

No matter how well you practice safety measures, accidents can still happen. What should you do if a friend chokes on food and cannot breathe? What if a friend is stung by a bee and has a violent allergic reaction?

Call for Help

Figure 7 *When calling 911, stay calm and listen carefully to what the dispatcher tells you.*

Once you've checked for other dangers, call for medical help immediately, as the person shown in **Figure 7** is doing. In most communities, you can dial 911. Speak slowly and clearly. Give the complete address and a description of the location. Describe the accident, the number of people injured, and the types of injuries. Ask what to do, and listen carefully to the instructions. Let the other person hang up first to be sure there are no more questions or instructions for you.

Learn First Aid

If you want to learn more about what to do in an emergency, you can take a first-aid or CPR course, such as the one shown in **Figure 8.** *CPR* can revive a person who is not breathing and has no heartbeat. If you are over 12 years old, you can become certified in both CPR and first aid. Some baby-sitting classes also provide information on first aid. The American Red Cross, community organizations, and local hospitals offer these classes. However, you should not attempt any lifesaving procedure unless you have been trained.

✓ Reading Check What is CPR, and how can you learn it?

Figure 8 *These teenagers are taking a CPR course to prepare themselves for emergency situations.*

SECTION Review

Summary

- Good hygiene includes taking care of your skin, hair, and teeth.
- Good posture is important to health.
- Exercise keeps your heart, lungs, and bones healthy.
- Teenagers need more than 9 hours of sleep to stay rested and healthy.
- Coping with stress is an important part of staying physically and emotionally healthy.
- It is important to be aware of the possible hazards around your home, outdoors, and at school. Using the appropriate safety equipment can also help keep you safe.

Using Key Terms

Complete each of the following sentences by choosing the correct term from the word bank.

hygiene   aerobic exercise
sleep   stress

1. The science of protecting your health is called ___.

2. ___ strengthens your heart, lungs, and bones.

3. ___ is the physical and mental response to pressure.

Understanding Key Ideas

4. Which of the following is important for good health?
    a. irregular exercise
    b. getting your hair cut
    c. taking care of your teeth
    d. getting plenty of sun

5. List two things you should do when calling for help in a medical emergency.

6. List three ways to stay safe when you are outside, and three ways to stay safe at home.

7. How do seat belts and safety equipment protect you?

Math Skills

8. It is estimated that only 65% of adults wear their seat belts. If there are 10,000 people driving in your area right now, how many of them are wearing their seat belts?

Critical Thinking

9. **Applying Concepts** What situations cause you stress? What can you do to help relieve the stress you are feeling?

10. **Making Inferences** According to the newspaper, the temperature outside is 61°F right now. Later, it will be 90°F outside. If you and your friends want to play soccer in the park, what should you wear? What should you bring with you?

SCiLINKS®

NSTA
Developed and maintained by the
National Science Teachers Association

For a variety of links related to this chapter, go to www.scilinks.org

Topic: Safety
SciLinks code: HSM1339

Skills Practice Lab

Keep It Clean

One of the best ways to prevent the spread of bacterial and viral infections is to frequently wash your hands with soap and water. Many companies advertise that their soap ingredients can destroy bacteria normally found on the body. In this activity, you will investigate how effective antibacterial soaps are at killing bacteria.

Procedure

1. Keeping the agar plates closed at all times, use the wax pencil to label the bottoms of three agar plates. Label one plate "Control," one plate "No soap," and one plate "Soap."

2. Without washing your hands, carefully press several surfaces of your hands on the agar plate marked "Control." Have your partner immediately put the cover back on the plate. After you touch the agar, do not touch anything with either hand.

3. Hold your right hand under running water for 2 min. Ask your partner to scrub all surfaces of your right hand with the scrub brush throughout these 2 min. Be sure that he or she scrubs under your fingernails. After scrubbing, your partner should turn off the water and open the plate marked "No soap." Touching only the agar, carefully press on the "No soap" plate with the same surfaces of your right hand that you used to press on the "Control" plate.

4 Repeat step 3, but use your left hand instead of your right. This time, ask your partner to scrub your left hand with liquid antibacterial soap and the scrub brush. Use the plate marked "Soap" instead of the plate marked "No soap."

5 Secure the lid of each plate to its bottom half with transparent tape. Place the plates upside down in the incubator. Incubate all three plates overnight at 37°C.

6 Remove the plates from the incubator, and turn them right side up. Check each plate for the presence of bacterial colonies, and count the number of colonies present on each plate. Record this information. **Caution:** Do not remove the lids on any of the plates.

Analyze the Results

1 **Examining Data** Compare the bacterial growth on the plates. Which plate contained the most growth? Which contained the least?

Draw Conclusions

2 **Drawing Conclusions** Does water alone effectively kill bacteria? Explain.

Applying Your Data

Repeat this experiment, but scrub with regular, not antibacterial, liquid soap. Describe how the results of the two experiments differ.

Chapter Review

USING KEY TERMS

Complete each of the following sentences by choosing the correct term from the word bank.

nutrients   Food Guide
addiction   Pyramid
malnutrition   drug

1 Carbohydrates, proteins, fats, vitamins, minerals, and water are the six categories of ___.

2 The ___ divides foods into six groups and gives a recommended number of servings for each group.

3 Both bulimia nervosa and anorexia nervosa cause ___.

4 A physical or psychological dependence on a drug can lead to ___.

5 A(n) ___ is any substance that causes a change in a person's physical or psychological state.

UNDERSTANDING KEY IDEAS

Multiple Choice

6 Which of the following statements about drugs is true?

a. A child cannot become addicted to drugs.

b. Smoking just one or two cigarettes is safe for anyone.

c. Alcohol is not a drug.

d. Withdrawal symptoms may be painful.

7 What does alcohol do to the central nervous system (CNS)?

a. It speeds the CNS up.

b. It slows the CNS down.

c. It keeps the CNS regulated.

d. It has no effect on the CNS.

8 To keep your teeth healthy,

a. brush your teeth as hard as you can.

b. use a toothbrush until it is worn out.

c. brush at least twice a day.

d. floss at least once a week.

9 According to the Food Guide Pyramid, what foods should you eat most?

a. meats

b. milk, yogurt, and cheese

c. fruits and vegetables

d. bread, cereal, rice, and pasta

10 Which of the following can help you deal with stress?

a. ignoring your homework

b. drinking a caffeinated drink

c. talking to a friend

d. watching television

11 Tobacco use increases the risk of

a. lung cancer.

b. car accidents.

c. liver damage.

d. depression.

Short Answer

12 Are all narcotics illegal? Explain.

13 What are three dangers of tobacco and alcohol use?

14 What are the three types of nutrients that provide energy in Calories, and what is the main function of each type in the body?

15 Name two conditions that can lead to malnutrition.

16 Explain why you should always wear safety equipment when you ride your bicycle.

CRITICAL THINKING

17 **Concept Mapping** Use the following terms to create a concept map: *carbohydrates, water, proteins, nutrients, fats, vitamins, minerals, saturated fats,* and *unsaturated fats.*

18 **Applying Concepts** You have recently become a vegetarian, and you worry that you are not getting enough protein. Name two foods that you could eat to get more protein.

19 **Analyzing Ideas** Your two-year-old cousin will be staying with your family. Name three things that you can do to make sure that the house is safe for a young child.

INTERPRETING GRAPHICS

Look at the photos below. The people in the photos are not practicing safe habits. List the unsafe habits shown in these photos. For each unsafe habit, tell what the corresponding safe habit is.

20

21

Standardized Test Preparation

EOG Prep

Read each of the passages below. Then, answer the questions that follow each passage.

Passage 1 A <u>chronic</u> disease is a disease that, once developed, is always present and will not go away. Chronic bronchitis is a disease that causes the airways in the lungs to become swollen. This irritation causes a lot of mucus to form in the lungs. As a result, a person who has chronic bronchitis coughs a lot. Another chronic condition is emphysema. Emphysema destroys the tiny air sacs and the walls in the lungs. The holes in the air sacs cannot heal. Eventually, the lung tissue dies, and the lungs can no longer work. Cigarette smoking causes more than 80% of all cases of chronic bronchitis and emphysema.

1. In the passage, what does the word *chronic* mean?
   A disappearing
   B temporary
   C always present
   D mucus filled

2. According to the passage, what disease destroys the tiny air sacs and walls of the lungs?
   F chronic bronchitis
   G emphysema
   H chronic cough
   I cigarette smoking

3. Which of the following is a true statement according to the passage?
   A Holes in the air sacs of lungs heal very quickly.
   B Cigarette smoking causes more than 80% of all cases of chronic bronchitis and emphysema.
   C Cigarette smoking does not cause chronic bronchitis or emphysema.
   D Chronic bronchitis will go away after a person stops smoking cigarettes.

Passage 2 Each body reacts differently to alcohol. Several factors affect how a body reacts to alcohol. A person who has several drinks in a short time is likely to be affected more than a person who has a single drink in the same amount of time. Food in a drinker's stomach can also slow alcohol absorption into the blood. Finally, the way that women absorb and process alcohol differs from the way that men do. If a man and a woman drink the same amount of alcohol, the woman's blood alcohol content (BAC) will be higher than the man's. As BAC increases, mental and physical abilities decline. Muscle coordination, which is especially important for walking and driving, decreases. Vision becomes blurred. Speech and memory are impaired. A high BAC can cause a person to pass out or even die.

1. According to the passage, what does *BAC* stand for?
   A blood alcohol content
   B blood alcohol contaminant
   C blurred alcohol capacity
   D blood alcoholic coordination

2. According to the passage, which of the following factors can affect BAC?
   F time of day
   G food in the stomach
   H age
   I physical activity

3. Which of the following is a fact according to the passage?
   A Alcohol does not affect mood or mental abilities.
   B Men absorb alcohol in the same way that women do.
   C Alcohol decreases muscle coordination.
   D Everybody reacts to alcohol in the same way.

INTERPRETING GRAPHICS

The figure below shows a sample prescription drug label. Use this figure to answer the questions that follow.

The People's Pharmacy
252 FIRST STREET   (713) 242-2299
HOUSTON, TX 77077   DEA# AS 3455

Rx 00674312C02/01/04   02/01/04

BAKER, RICHARD   CC

TAKE 1 TABLET BY MOUTH DAILY

TEQUIN   400MG TABS   (BMS)
DR. SANCHEZ, DAVID QTY: 10   NO REFILL

CAUTION: FEDERAL LAW PROHIBITS THE TRANSFER OF THIS DRUG TO ANY PERSON OTHER THAN THE PATIENT TO WHOM IT WAS PRESCRIBED.

Keep out of reach of children.

Patient's name
Directions for taking the medicine
Name of drug
Doctor's name

1. According to the label, what is the patient's name?

A Richard Baker

B Baker Richard

C David Sanchez

D James Beard

2. According to the label, how often should the medication be taken?

F once a day

G twice a day

H three times a day

I once a week

3. According to the label, how many refills remain on the prescription?

A 0

B 1

C 2

D 3

4. If this patient follows the directions exactly, how long will he need to take this medicine?

F 1 day

G 5 days

H 10 days

I There is not enough data to determine the answer.

MATH

Read each question below, and choose the best answer.

1. Which of the following ratios is equal to 2/4?

A 1/2

B 17/18

C 5/2

D 7/2

2. If 1 gal = 3.79 L, how many liters are in 3 gal?

F 3.79 L

G 7.58 L

H 11.37 L

I 15.16 L

3. Approximately how many liters are in 5 gal?

A 5 L

B 10 L

C 20 L

D 30 L

4. Ada has just built a car for a Pinewood Derby. She wants to find the average speed of her new car. During her first test run, she goes 5 mi/h. During her second run, she goes 4 mi/h, and in her third run, she goes 6 mi/h. What is her average speed?

F 4 mi/h

G 5 mi/h

H 6 mi/h

I 7 mi/h

5. Which of the following numbers is largest?

A 1×10^2

B 1×10^5

C 3×10^5

D 5×10^4

6. On Saturday, Mae won a goldfish at the school carnival. On the way home, Mae and her mother bought a fishbowl for $10.25, a container of fish food for $3.75, and a plastic coral for $8.15. How much money did Mae and her mother spend?

F $11.90

G $18.40

H $22.15

I $30.30

Science in Action

Bones can become severely weakened by the female athlete triad.

Science, Technology, and Society

Meatless Munching

Recent studies suggest that a vegetarian diet may reduce the risk of heart disease, adult-onset diabetes, and some forms of cancer. However, a vegetarian diet takes careful planning. Vegetarians must ensure that they get the proper balance of protein and vitamins in their diet. New foods that can help vegetarians remain healthy are being developed constantly. Meat substitutes are now made from soybeans, textured vegetable protein, and tofu. One new food, which is shown above, is made of a fungus that is a relative of mushrooms and truffles.

Scientific Discoveries

Female Athlete Triad

Getting enough exercise is an important part of staying healthy. But in 1992, doctors learned that too much exercise can be harmful for women. When a girl or woman exercises too much, three things can happen. She may lose too much weight. She may stop having her period. And her bones may become very weak. These three symptoms form the female athlete triad. To prevent this condition, female athletes need to take in enough Calories. Women who exercise heavily and try to lose weight may have a reduction in estrogen. Estrogen is the hormone that helps regulate the menstrual cycle. Low levels of estrogen and inadequate nutrition can cause bones to become weak and brittle. The photo above shows bone that has been weakened greatly.

Social Studies ACTiViTY

WRITING SKILL Research a culture that has a mostly vegetarian diet, such as Hindu or Buddhist. What kinds of food do the people eat? Why don't they eat animals? Write a short report on your findings.

Math ACTiViTY

Some scientists recommend that teenagers get 1,200 to 1,500 mg of calcium every day. A cup of milk has 300 mg of calcium, and a serving of yogurt has 400 mg of calcium. Calculate two combinations of milk and yogurt that would give you the recommended 1,500 mg of calcium.

Russell Selger

Guidance Counselor Guidance counselors help students think about their future by helping them discover their interests. After focusing their interests, a guidance counselor helps students plan a good academic schedule. A guidance counselor might talk to you about taking an art or computer science class that may help you discover a hidden talent. Many skills are vital to being a good guidance counselor. The job requires empathy, which is the ability to understand and sympathize with another person's feelings. Counselors also need patience, good listening skills, and a love of helping young people. Russell Selger, a guidance counselor at Timberlane Middle School, has a great respect for middle school students. "The kids are just alive. They want to learn. There's something about the spark that they have, and it's so much fun to guide them through all of this stuff," he explains.

Language Arts ACTiViTY

WRITING SKILL Visit the guidance counselor's office at your school. What services does your guidance counselor offer? Conduct an interview with a guidance counselor. Ask why he or she became a counselor. Write an article for the school paper about your findings.

To learn more about these Science in Action topics, visit **go.hrw.com** and type in the keyword **HL5BD7F.**

Current Science

Check out Current Science® articles related to this chapter by visiting go.hrw.com. Just type in the keyword HL5CS28.

UNIT

4

TIMELINE

Heredity and Genes

The differences and similarities between living things are the subject of this unit. You will learn how characteristics are passed from one generation to another, how living things are classified based on their characteristics, and how these characteristics help living things survive.

Scientists have not always understood these topics, and there is still much to be learned. This timeline will give you an idea of some things that have been learned so far.

1753

Carolus Linnaeus publishes the first of two volumes containing the classification of all known species.

1905

Nettie Stevens describes how human gender is determined by the X and Y chromosomes.

1930

The planet Pluto is discovered.

1969

Apollo 11 lands on the moon. Neil Armstrong becomes the first person to walk on the lunar surface.

1859
Charles Darwin suggests that natural selection is a mechanism of evolution.

1860
Abraham Lincoln is elected the 16th president of the United States.

1865
Gregor Mendel publishes the results of his studies of genetic inheritance in pea plants.

1951
Rosalind Franklin photographs DNA.

1953
James Watson and Francis Crick figure out the structure of DNA.

1960
Mary and Jonathan Leakey discover fossil bones of the human ancestor *Homo habilis* in Olduvai Gorge, Tanzania.

1974
Donald Johanson discovers a fossilized skeleton of one of the first hominids, *Australopithecus afarensis,* also called "Lucy."

1990
Ashanti DeSilva's white blood cells are genetically engineered to treat her immune deficiency disease.

2003
The Human Genome Project is completed. Scientists spent 13 years mapping out the 3 billion DNA subunits of chromosomes.

It's Alive!! Or Is It?

About the PHOTO

What does it mean to say something is *alive*? Machines have some of the characteristics of living things, but machines do not have all of these characteristics. This amazing robot insect can respond to changes in its environment. It can walk over obstacles. It can perform some tasks. But it is still not alive. How is it like and unlike a living insect?

PRE-READING ACTIVITY

Graphic Organizer

Concept Map Before you read the chapter, create the graphic organizer entitled "Concept Map" described in the **Study Skills** section of the Appendix. As you read the chapter, fill in the concept map with details about the characteristics of living things.

STARTUP ACTIVITY

Lights On!

In this activity, you will work with a partner to see how eyes react to changes in light.

Procedure

1. Observe a classmate's eyes in a lighted room. Note the size of your partner's pupils.

2. Have your partner keep both eyes open. Ask him or her to cover each one with a cupped hand. Wait about one minute.

3. Instruct your partner to pull away both hands quickly. Immediately, look at your partner's pupils. Record what happens.

4. Now, briefly shine a **flashlight** into your partner's eyes. Record how this affects your partner's pupils. **Caution:** Do not use the sun as the source of the light.

5. Change places with your partner, and repeat steps 1–4 so that your partner can observe your eyes.

Analysis

1. How did your partner's eyes respond to changes in the level of light?

2. How did changes in the size of your pupils affect your vision? What does this tell you about why pupils change size?

Characteristics of Living Things

While outside one day, you notice something strange in the grass. It's slimy, bright yellow, and about the size of a dime. You have no idea what it is. Is it a plant part that fell from a tree? Is it alive? How can you tell?

An amazing variety of living things exists on Earth. But living things are all alike in several ways. What does a dog have in common with a bacterium? What does a fish have in common with a mushroom? And what do *you* have in common with a slimy, yellow blob, known as a *slime mold*? Read on to find out about the six characteristics that all organisms share.

Living Things Have Cells

All living things, such as those in **Figure 1,** are composed of one or more cells. A **cell** is a membrane-covered structure that contains all of the materials necessary for life. The membrane that surrounds a cell separates the contents of the cell from the cell's environment. Most cells are too small to be seen with the naked eye.

Some organisms are made up of trillions of cells. In an organism with many cells, different kinds of cells perform specialized functions. For example, your nerve cells transport signals, and your muscle cells are specialized for movement.

In an organism made up of only one cell, different parts of the cell perform different functions. For example, a one-celled paramecium needs to eat. So, some parts of the cell take in food. Other parts of the cell break down the food. Still other parts of the cell excrete wastes.

cell the smallest unit that can perform all life processes; cells are covered by a membrane and have DNA and cytoplasm

Figure 1 *Some organisms, such as the protists on the right, are made of one cell or a few cells. The monkeys on the left are made up of trillions of cells.*

Figure 2 *The touch of an insect triggers the Venus' flytrap to close its leaves quickly.*

Living Things Sense and Respond to Change

All organisms have the ability to sense change in their environment and to respond to that change. When your pupils are exposed to light, they respond by becoming smaller. A change that affects the activity of the organism is called a **stimulus** (plural, *stimuli*).

Stimuli can be chemicals, gravity, light, sounds, hunger, or anything that causes organisms to respond in some way. A gentle touch causes a response in the plant shown in **Figure 2.**

Homeostasis

Even though an organism's outside environment may change, conditions inside an organism's body must stay the same. Many chemical reactions keep an organism alive. These reactions can take place only when conditions are exactly right, so an organism must maintain stable internal conditions to survive. The maintenance of a stable internal environment is called **homeostasis** (HOH mee OH STAY sis).

Responding to External Changes

Your body maintains a temperature of about 37°C. When you get hot, your body responds by sweating. When you get cold, your muscles twitch in an attempt to warm you up. This twitching is called *shivering.* Whether you are sweating or shivering, your body is trying to return itself to normal.

Other animals also need to have stable internal conditions. But many cannot respond the way you do. They have to control their body temperature by moving from one environment to another. If they get too warm, they move to the shade. If they get too cool, they move out into the sunlight.

✓ Reading Check How do some animals maintain homeostasis? (*See the Appendix for answers to Reading Checks.*)

stimulus anything that causes a reaction or change in an organism or any part of an organism

homeostasis the maintenance of a constant internal state in a changing environment

CONNECTION TO Physics

Temperature Regulation
Your body temperature does not change very much throughout the day. When you exercise, you sweat. Sweating helps keep your body temperature stable. As your sweat evaporates, your skin cools. Given this information, why do you think you feel cooler faster when you stand in front of a fan?

Figure 3 *Like most animals, bears produce offspring by sexual reproduction.*

Figure 4 *The hydra can reproduce asexually by forming buds that break off and grow into new individuals.*

sexual reproduction reproduction in which the sex cells from two parents unite, producing offspring that share traits from both parents

asexual reproduction reproduction that does not involve the union of sex cells and in which one parent produces offspring identical to itself

heredity the passing of genetic traits from parent to offspring

metabolism the sum of all chemical processes that occur in an organism

Living Things Reproduce

Organisms make other organisms similar to themselves. They do so in one of two ways: by sexual reproduction or by asexual reproduction. In **sexual reproduction,** two parents produce offspring that will share characteristics of both parents. Most animals and plants reproduce in this way. The bear cubs in **Figure 3** were produced sexually by their parents.

In **asexual reproduction,** a single parent produces offspring that are identical to the parent. **Figure 4** shows an organism that reproduces asexually. Most single-celled organisms reproduce in this way.

Living Things Have DNA

The cells of all living things contain the molecule **d**eoxyribo-**n**ucleic (dee AHKS uh RIE boh noo KLEE ik) **a**cid, or DNA. *DNA* controls the structure and function of cells. When organisms reproduce, they pass copies of their DNA to their offspring. Passing DNA ensures that offspring resemble parents. The passing of traits from one generation to the next is called **heredity.**

Living Things Use Energy

Organisms use energy to carry out the activities of life. These activities include such things as making food, breaking down food, moving materials into and out of cells, and building cells. An organism's **metabolism** (muh TAB uh LIZ uhm) is the total of all of the chemical activities that the organism performs.

✓ Reading Check Name four chemical activities in living things that require energy.

Living Things Grow and Develop

All living things, whether they are made of one cell or many cells, grow during periods of their lives. In a single-celled organism, the cell gets larger and divides, making other organisms. In organisms made of many cells, the number of cells gets larger, and the organism gets bigger.

In addition to getting larger, living things may develop and change as they grow. Just like the organisms in **Figure 5,** you will pass through different stages in your life as you develop into an adult.

Figure 5 *Over time, acorns develop into oak seedlings, which become oak trees.*

SECTION Review

Summary

- Organisms are made of one or more cells.
- Organisms detect and respond to stimuli.
- Organisms make more organisms like themselves by reproducing either asexually or sexually.
- Organisms have DNA.
- Organisms use energy to carry out the chemical activities of life.
- Organisms grow and develop.

Using Key Terms

Complete each of the following sentences by choosing the correct term from the word bank.

cells   stimulus
homeostasis   metabolism

1. Sunlight can be a ___.

2. Living things are made of ___.

Understanding Key Ideas

3. Homeostasis means maintaining
   a. stable internal conditions.
   b. varied internal conditions.
   c. similar offspring.
   d. varied offspring.

4. Explain the difference between asexual and sexual reproduction.

5. Describe the six characteristics of living things.

Math Skills

6. Bacteria double every generation. One bacterium is in the first generation. How many are in the sixth generation?

Critical Thinking

7. **Applying Concepts** How do you respond to some stimuli in your environment?

8. **Identifying Relationships** What does the fur coat of a bear have to do with homeostasis?

SCI LINKS®

NSTA
Developed and maintained by the
National Science Teachers Association

For a variety of links related to this chapter, go to www.scilinks.org

Topic: Characteristics of Living Things
SciLinks code: HSM0258

The Necessities of Life

Would it surprise you to learn that you have the same basic needs as a tree, a frog, and a fly?

In fact, almost every organism has the same basic needs: water, air, a place to live, and food.

READING WARM-UP

Objectives

● Explain why organisms need food, water, air, and living space.

● Describe the chemical building blocks of cells.

Terms to Learn

producer   lipid
consumer   phospholipid
decomposer   ATP
protein   nucleic acid
carbohydrate

READING STRATEGY

Discussion   Read this section silently. Write down questions that you have about this section. Discuss your questions in a small group.

Water

You may know that your body is made mostly of water. In fact, your cells and the cells of almost all living organisms are approximately 70% water. Most of the chemical reactions involved in metabolism require water.

Organisms differ greatly in terms of how much water they need and how they get it. You could survive for only about three days without water. You get water from the fluids you drink and the food you eat. The desert-dwelling kangaroo rat never drinks. It gets all of its water from its food.

Air

Air is a mixture of several different gases, including oxygen and carbon dioxide. Most living things use oxygen in the chemical process that releases energy from food. Organisms living on land get oxygen from the air. Organisms living in water either take in dissolved oxygen from the water or come to the water's surface to get oxygen from the air. The European diving spider in **Figure 1** goes to great lengths to get oxygen.

Green plants, algae, and some bacteria need carbon dioxide gas in addition to oxygen. These organisms produce food and oxygen by using photosynthesis (FOHT oh SIN thuh sis). In *photosynthesis*, green organisms convert the energy in sunlight to energy stored in food.

Reading Check What process do plants use to make food? (*See the Appendix for answers to Reading Checks.*)

Figure 1 *This spider surrounds itself with an air bubble that provides the spider with a source of oxygen underwater.*

A Place to Live

All organisms need a place to live that contains all of the things they need to survive. Some organisms, such as elephants, require a large amount of space. Other organisms may live their entire life in one place.

Space on Earth is limited. So, organisms often compete with each other for food, water, and other necessities. Many animals, including the warbler in **Figure 2,** will claim a particular space. After claiming a space, they try to keep other animals away.

Figure 2 *A warbler's song is more than just a pretty tune. The warbler is protecting its home by telling other warblers to stay out of its territory.*

Food

All living things need food. Food gives organisms energy and the raw materials needed to carry on life processes. Organisms use nutrients from food to replace cells and build body parts. But not all organisms get food in the same way. In fact, organisms can be grouped into three different groups based on how they get their food.

Making Food

Some organisms, such as plants, are called producers. **Producers** can make their own food. Like most producers, plants use energy from the sun to make food from water and carbon dioxide. Some producers get energy and food from the chemicals in their environment.

producer an organism that can make its own food by using energy from its surroundings

consumer an organism that eats other organisms or organic matter

decomposer an organism that gets energy by breaking down the remains of dead organisms or animal wastes and consuming or absorbing the nutrients

Taking Food

Other organisms are called **consumers** because they must eat (consume) other organisms to get food. The frog in **Figure 3** is an example of a consumer. It gets the energy it needs by eating insects and other organisms.

Some consumers are decomposers. **Decomposers** are organisms that get their food by breaking down the nutrients in dead organisms or animal wastes. The mushroom in **Figure 3** is a decomposer.

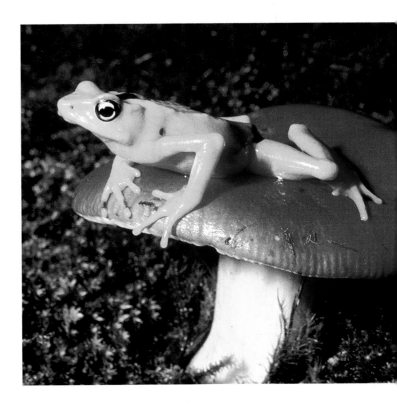

Figure 3 *The frog is a consumer. The mushroom is a decomposer. The green plants are producers.*

protein a molecule that is made up of amino acids and that is needed to build and repair body structures and to regulate processes in the body

Putting It All Together

Some organisms make their own food. Some organisms get food from eating other organisms. But all organisms need to break down that food in order to use the nutrients in it.

Nutrients are made up of molecules. A *molecule* is a substance made when two or more atoms combine. Molecules made of different kinds of atoms are *compounds*. Molecules found in living things are usually made of different combinations of six elements: carbon, hydrogen, nitrogen, oxygen, phosphorus, and sulfur. These elements combine to form proteins, carbohydrates, lipids, ATP, and nucleic acids.

Proteins

Almost all of the life processes of a cell involve proteins. **Proteins** are large molecules that are made up of smaller molecules called *amino acids*.

Making Proteins

Organisms break down the proteins in food to supply their cells with amino acids. These amino acids are then linked together to form new proteins. Some proteins are made up of only a few amino acids, but others contain more than 10,000 amino acids.

Proteins in Action

Proteins have many different functions. Some proteins form structures that are easy to see, such as those in **Figure 4.** Other proteins are very small and help cells do their jobs. Inside red blood cells, the protein hemoglobin (HEE moh GLOH bin) binds to oxygen to deliver and release oxygen throughout the body. Some proteins protect cells. Other proteins, called *enzymes* (EN ZIEMZ), start or speed up chemical reactions in cells.

Figure 4 *Spider webs, hair, horns, and feathers are all made from proteins.*

Figure 5 *The extra sugar in a potato plant is stored in the potato as starch, a complex carbohydrate.*

Carbohydrates

Molecules made of sugars are called **carbohydrates.** Cells use carbohydrates as a source of energy and for energy storage. An organism's cells break down carbohydrates to release the energy stored in them. There are two kinds of carbohydrates—simple carbohydrates and complex carbohydrates.

carbohydrate a class of energy-giving nutrients that includes sugars, starches, and fiber; contains carbon, hydrogen, and oxygen

Simple Carbohydrates

Simple carbohydrates are made up of one sugar molecule or a few sugar molecules linked together. Table sugar and the sugar in fruits are examples of simple carbohydrates.

Complex Carbohydrates

When an organism has more sugar than it needs, its extra sugar may be stored as complex carbohydrates. *Complex carbohydrates* are made of hundreds of sugar molecules linked together. Plants, such as the potato plant in **Figure 5,** store extra sugar as starch. When you eat mashed potatoes, you are eating a potato plant's stored starch. Your body then breaks down this complex carbohydrate to release the energy stored in the potato.

✓ Reading Check What is the difference between simple carbohydrates and complex carbohydrates?

How Much Oxygen?

Each red blood cell carries about 250 million molecules of hemoglobin. How many molecules of oxygen could a single red blood cell deliver throughout the body if every hemoglobin molecule attached to four oxygen molecules?

Starch Search

1. Obtain several **food samples** from your teacher.
2. Put **a few drops of iodine** on each sample. Record your observations. **Caution:** Iodine can stain clothing.
3. When iodine comes into contact with starch, a black substance appears. Which samples contain starch?

Figure 6   **Phospholipid Membranes**

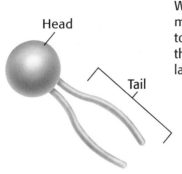

The head of a phospholipid molecule is attracted to water, but the tail is not. ▶

Head

Tail

Phospholipid molecule

When phospholipid molecules come together in water, they form two layers. ▶

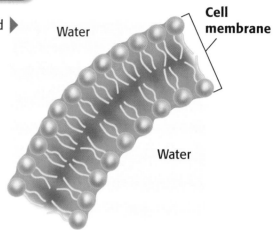

Water

Cell membrane

Water

Lipids

Lipids are compounds that cannot mix with water. Lipids have many important jobs in the cell. Like carbohydrates, some lipids store energy. Other lipids form the membranes of cells.

Phospholipids

All cells are surrounded by a cell membrane. The cell membrane helps protect the cell and keep the internal conditions of the cell stable. **Phospholipids** (FAHS foh LIP idz) are the molecules that form much of the cell membrane. The head of a phospholipid molecule is attracted to water. The tail is not. Cells are mostly water. When phospholipids are in water, the tails come together, and the heads face out into the water. **Figure 6** shows how phospholipid molecules form two layers in water.

Fats and Oils

Fats and oils are lipids that store energy. When an organism has used up most of its carbohydrates, it can get energy from these lipids. The structures of fats and oils are almost the same, but at room temperature, most fats are solid, and most oils are liquid. Most of the lipids stored in plants are oils. Most of the lipids stored in animals are fats.

✓ **Reading Check**   What is one difference between oils and fats?

ATP

Adenosine **tri**phosphate (uh DEN uh SEEN trie FAHS FAYT), also called ATP, is another important molecule. **ATP** is the major energy-carrying molecule in the cell. The energy in carbohydrates and lipids must be transferred to ATP, which then provides fuel for cellular activities.

lipid a type of biochemical that does not dissolve in water; fats and steroids are lipids

phospholipid a lipid that contains phosphorus and that is a structural component in cell membranes

ATP **a**denosine **tri**phosphate, a molecule that acts as the main energy source for cell processes

CONNECTION TO
Social Studies

Whaling In the 1900s, whales were hunted and killed for their oil. Whale oil was often used as fuel for oil lamps. Most of the oil taken from whales was taken from their fat, or *blubber*. Some whales had blubber over 18 in. thick, producing over 40 barrels of oil per whale. Research whether anyone still hunts whales or uses whale oil. Make a presentation to the class on your findings.

Nucleic Acids

Nucleic acids are sometimes called the blueprints of life because they have all the information needed for a cell to make proteins. **Nucleic acids** are large molecules made up of molecules called *nucleotides* (NOO klee oh TIEDZ). A nucleic acid may have thousands of nucleotides. The order of those nucleotides stores information. DNA is a nucleic acid. A DNA molecule is like a recipe book entitled *How to Make Proteins.* When a cell needs to make a certain protein, the cell gets information from the order of the nucleotides in DNA. This order of nucleotides tells the cell the order of the amino acids that are linked together to make that protein.

nucleic acid a molecule made up of subunits called *nucleotides*

SECTION Review

Summary

- Organisms need water for cellular processes.
- Organisms need oxygen to release the energy contained in their food.
- Organisms must have a place to live.
- Cells store energy in carbohydrates, which are made of sugars.
- Proteins are made up of amino acids. Some proteins are enzymes.
- Fats and oils store energy and make up cell membranes.
- Cells use molecules of ATP to fuel their activities.
- Nucleic acids, such as DNA, are made up of nucleotides.

Using Key Terms

For each pair of terms, explain how the meanings of the terms differ.

1. *producer* and *consumer*

2. *lipid* and *phospholipid*

Understanding Key Ideas

3. Plants store extra sugar as
    a. proteins.
    b. starch.
    c. nucleic acids.
    d. phospholipids.

4. Explain why organisms need food, water, air, and living space.

5. Describe the chemical building blocks of cells.

6. Why are decomposers categorized as consumers? How do they differ from producers?

7. What are the subunits of proteins?

Math Skills

8. Protein A is a chain of 660 amino acids. Protein B is a chain of 11 amino acids. How many times more amino acids does protein A have than protein B?

Critical Thinking

9. **Making Inferences** Could life as we know it exist on Earth if air contained only oxygen? Explain.

10. **Identifying Relationships** How might a cave, an ant, and a lake each meet the needs of an organism?

11. **Predicting Consequences** What would happen to the supply of ATP in your cells if you did not eat enough carbohydrates? How would this affect your cells?

12. **Applying Concepts** Which resource do you think is most important to your survival: water, air, a place to live, or food? Explain your answer.

Developed and maintained by the National Science Teachers Association

For a variety of links related to this chapter, go to www.scilinks.org

Topic: The Necessities of Life
SciLinks code: HSM1018

Inquiry Lab

Roly-Poly Races

OBJECTIVES

Observe responses to stimuli.

Analyze responses to stimuli.

MATERIALS

- chalk (1 stick)
- container, plastic, small, with lid
- gloves, protective
- isopod (4)
- potato, raw (1 small slice)
- ruler, metric
- soil (8 oz)
- stopwatch

SAFETY

Have you ever watched a bug run? Did you wonder why it was running? The bug you saw running was probably reacting to a stimulus. In other words, something happened to make the bug run! One characteristic of living things is that they respond to stimuli. In this activity, you will study the movement of roly-polies. Roly-polies are also called *pill bugs*. But they are not really bugs; they are land-dwelling animals called *isopods*. Isopods live in dark, moist areas under rocks or wood. You will provide stimuli to determine how fast your isopod can move and what affects its speed and direction. Remember that isopods are living things and must be treated gently and respectfully.

Ask a Question

① Ask a question such as, "Which stimuli cause pill bugs to run?"

Form a Hypothesis

② Using your question as a guide, form a hypothesis. For example, you could form the following hypothesis: "Light, sound, and touch stimulate pill bugs to run."

Test the Hypothesis

③ Choose a partner, and decide together how you will run your roly-poly race. Discuss some gentle ways to stimulate your isopods to move. Choose five or six things that might cause movement, such as a gentle nudge or a change in temperature, sound, or light. Check your choices with your teacher.

④ Make a data table similar to the table below. Label the columns with the stimuli that you've chosen. Label the rows "Isopod 1," "Isopod 2," "Isopod 3," and "Isopod 4."

Isopod Responses			
	Stimulus 1	Stimulus 2	Stimulus 3
Isopod 1			
Isopod 2			
Isopod 3			
Isopod 4			

DO NOT WRITE IN BOOK

5 Place a layer of soil that is 1 cm or 2 cm deep in a small plastic container. Add a small slice of potato and a piece of chalk. Your isopods will eat these items.

6 Place four isopods in your container. Observe them for a minute or two before you perform your tests. Record your observations.

7 Decide which stimulus you want to test first. Carefully arrange the isopods at the "starting line." The starting line can be an imaginary line at one end of the container.

8 Gently stimulate each isopod at the same time and in the same way. In your data table, record the isopods' responses to the stimulus. Be sure to record the distance that each isopod travels. Don't forget to time the race.

9 Repeat steps 7–8 for each stimulus. Be sure to wait at least 2 min between trials.

Analyze the Results

1 **Describing Events** Describe the way that isopods move. Do their legs move together?

2 **Analyzing Results** Did your isopods move before or between the trials? Did the movement seem to have a purpose, or were the isopods responding to a stimulus? Explain.

Draw Conclusions

3 **Interpreting Information** Did any of the stimuli make the isopods move faster or go farther? Explain.

Applying Your Data

Like isopods and all other living things, humans react to stimuli. Describe three stimuli that might cause humans to run.

Chapter Review

USING KEY TERMS

Complete each of the following sentences by choosing the correct term from the word bank.

lipid   carbohydrate
consumer   heredity
homeostasis   producer

1 The process of maintaining a stable internal environment is known as ___.

2 Offspring resemble their parents because of ___.

3 A ___ obtains food by eating other organisms.

4 Starch is a ___ and is made up of sugars.

5 Fat is a ___ that stores energy for an organism.

UNDERSTANDING KEY IDEAS

Multiple Choice

6 Which of the following statements about cells is true?

   a. Cells are the structures that contain all of the materials necessary for life.

   b. Cells are found in all organisms.

   c. Cells are sometimes specialized for particular functions.

   d. All of the above

7 Which of the following statements about all living things is true?

   a. All living things reproduce sexually.

   b. All living things have one or more cells.

   c. All living things must make their own food.

   d. All living things reproduce asexually.

8 Organisms must have food because

   a. food is a source of energy.

   b. food supplies cells with oxygen.

   c. organisms never make their own food.

   d. All of the above

9 A change in an organism's environment that affects the organism's activities is a

   a. response.   **c.** metabolism.

   b. stimulus.   **d.** producer.

10 Organisms store energy in

   a. nucleic acids.   **c.** lipids.

   b. phospholipids.   **d.** water.

11 The molecule that contains the information about how to make proteins is

   a. ATP.

   b. a carbohydrate.

   c. DNA.

   d. a phospholipid.

12 The subunits of nucleic acids are

   a. nucleotides.

   b. oils.

   c. sugars.

   d. amino acids.

Short Answer

13 What is the difference between asexual reproduction and sexual reproduction?

14 In one or two sentences, explain why living things must have air.

15 What is ATP, and why is it important to a cell?

CRITICAL THINKING

16 **Concept Mapping** Use the following terms to create a concept map: *cell, carbohydrates, protein, enzymes, DNA, sugars, lipids, nucleotides, amino acids,* and *nucleic acid.*

17 **Analyzing Ideas** A flame can move, grow larger, and give off heat. Is a flame alive? Explain.

18 **Applying Concepts** Based on what you know about carbohydrates, lipids, and proteins, why is it important for you to eat a balanced diet?

19 **Evaluating Hypotheses** Your friend tells you that the stimulus of music makes his goldfish swim faster. How would you design a controlled experiment to test your friend's claim?

INTERPRETING GRAPHICS

The pictures below show the same plant over a period of 3 days. Use the pictures below to answer the questions that follow.

Day 1

Day 2

Day 3

20 What is the plant doing?

21 What characteristic(s) of living things is the plant exhibiting?

Standardized Test Preparation

READING

Read each of the passages below. Then, answer the questions that follow each passage.

Passage 1 Organisms make other organisms similar to themselves. They do so in one of two ways: by sexual reproduction or by <u>asexual reproduction</u>. In sexual reproduction, two parents produce offspring that will share characteristics of both parents. Most animals and plants reproduce in this way. In asexual reproduction, a single parent produces offspring that are identical to the parent. Most single-celled organisms reproduce in this way.

1. In the passage, what does the term *asexual reproduction* mean?
   - **A** A single parent produces offspring.
   - **B** Two parents make identical offspring.
   - **C** Plants make offspring.
   - **D** Animals make offspring.

2. What is characteristic of offspring produced by sexual reproduction?
   - **F** They are identical to both parents.
   - **G** They share the traits of both parents.
   - **H** They are identical to one parent.
   - **I** They are identical to each other.

3. What is characteristic of offspring produced by asexual reproduction?
   - **A** They are identical to both parents.
   - **B** They share the traits of both parents.
   - **C** They are identical to one parent.
   - **D** They are usually plants.

4. What is the difference between sexual and asexual reproduction?
   - **F** the number of offspring produced
   - **G** the number of parents needed to produce offspring
   - **H** the number of traits produced
   - **I** the number of offspring that survive

Passage 2 In 1996, a group of researchers led by NASA scientists studied a 3.8-billion-year-old meteorite named ALH84001. These scientists agree that ALH84001 is a potato-sized piece of the planet Mars. They also agree that it fell to Earth about 13,000 years ago. It was discovered in Antarctica in 1984. According to the NASA team, ALH84001 brought with it evidence that life once existed on Mars.

Scientists found certain kinds of organic molecules (molecules containing carbon) on the surface of ALH84001. These molecules are similar to those left behind when living things break down substances for food. When these scientists examined the interior of the meteorite, they found the same organic molecules throughout. Because these molecules were spread throughout the meteorite, scientists concluded that the molecules were not contamination from Earth. The NASA team believes that these organic compounds are strong evidence that tiny organisms similar to bacteria lived, ate, and died on Mars millions of years ago.

1. How old is the meteorite named ALH84001?
   - **A** 13,000 years old
   - **B** millions of years old
   - **C** 3.8 billion years old
   - **D** 3.8 trillion years old

2. Which of the following would best support a claim that life might have existed on Mars?
   - **F** remains of organisms
   - **G** water
   - **H** meteorite temperatures similar to Earth temperatures
   - **I** oxygen

The graph below shows an ill person's body temperature. Use the graph below to answer the questions that follow.

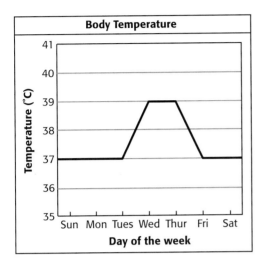

Body Temperature

1. A fever is a spike in temperature. On which day does this person have a fever?
   A Sunday
   B Monday
   C Wednesday
   D Saturday

2. A body with a fever is often fighting an infection. Fevers help eliminate the pathogens that cause the infection. According to the chart, when does this person probably have the highest fever?
   F Sunday
   G Monday
   H Wednesday
   I Saturday

3. What is the highest temperature that this fever reaches?
   A 37°C
   B 38°C
   C 39°C
   D 40°C

4. What is probably this person's normal body temperature?
   F 37°C
   G 38°C
   H 39°C
   I 40°C

Read each question below, and choose the best answer.

1. An aquarium is a place where fish can live. What is the volume of the aquarium shown below?

0.5 m
1 m
0.5 m

   A 0.25 m
   B 0.25 m²
   C 0.25 m³
   D 0.52 m³

2. The cost of admission to a natural history museum is $7 per adult. What is the total cost of admission for a group of five adults?
   F $25
   G $35
   H $45
   I $55

3. Lee biked 25.3 km on Monday, 20.7 km on Tuesday, and 15.6 km on Wednesday. How many kilometers did Lee bike during those three days?
   A 66.1 km
   B 61.6 km
   C 51.6 km
   D 16.6 km

4. Laura collected 24 leaves. One-third of the leaves were oak leaves. How many oak leaves did Laura collect?
   F 6
   G 8
   H 12
   I 24

Science in Action

HOLT ANTHOLOGY OF
Science Fiction

HOLT, RINEHART AND WINSTON

Science, Technology, and Society

Chess-Playing Computers

Computers can help us explore how humans think. One way to explore how humans think is to study how people and computers play chess against each other.

A computer's approach to chess is straightforward. By calculating each piece's possible board position for the next few moves, a computer creates what is called a *position tree*. A position tree shows how each move can lead to other moves. This way of playing requires millions of calculations.

Human chess champions play differently. Humans calculate only three or four moves every minute. Even so, human champions are still a match for computer opponents. By studying the ways that people and computers play chess, scientists are learning how people think and make choices.

Science Fiction

"They're Made Out of Meat" by Terry Bisson

Two space explorers millions of light-years from home are visiting an uncharted sector of the universe to find signs of life. Their mission is to contact, welcome, and log any and all beings in this part of the universe.

During their mission, they encounter a life-form quite unlike anything they have ever seen before. It looked too strange and, well, disgusting. The explorers have very strong doubts about adding this new organism to the list. But the explorers' official duty is to contact and welcome all life-forms no matter how ugly they are. Can the explorers bring themselves to perform their duty?

You'll find out by reading "They're Made Out of Meat," a short story by Terry Bisson. This story is in the *Holt Anthology of Science Fiction*.

Math ACTiViTY

A chess-playing computer needs to evaluate 3 million positions before a move. If you could evaluate two positions in 1 min, how long would it take you to evaluate 3 million possible positions?

Language Arts ACTiViTY

WRITING SKILL Write a story about what happens when the explorers next meet the creatures on the star in G445 zone.

People in Science

Janis Davis-Street

NASA Nutritionist Do astronauts eat shrimp cocktail in space? Yes, they do! Shrimp cocktail is nutritious and tastes so good that it is one of the most popular foods in the space program. And eating a proper diet helps astronauts stay healthy while they are in space.

But who figures out what astronauts need to eat? Janis Davis-Street is a nutritionist and laboratory supervisor for the Nutritional Biochemistry Laboratory at the Johnson Space Center in Houston, Texas. She was born in Georgetown, Guyana, on the north-eastern coast of South America. She was educated in Canada.

Davis-Street is part of a team that uses their knowledge of nutrition, biology, and chemistry to figure out the nutritional requirements for spaceflight. For example, they determine how many calories and other nutrients each astronaut needs per day during spaceflight.

The Nutritional Biochemistry Laboratory's work on the space shuttle missions and *Mir* space station developed into tests that allow NASA to help ensure astronaut health before, during, and after flight. These tests are important for understanding how the human body adapts to long space missions, and for determining whether treatments for preventing bone and muscle loss during spaceflight are working.

Social Studies ACTIVITY

Scientists from more than 30 countries have been on space missions. Research which countries have provided astronauts or cosmonauts for space missions. Using a map, place self-stick notes on countries that have provided scientists for space missions. Write the names of the appropriate scientists on the self-stick notes.

go.hrw.com

To learn more about these Science in Action topics, visit go.hrw.com and type in the keyword **HL5ALVF.**

Current Science

Check out Current Science® articles related to this chapter by visiting go.hrw.com. Just type in the keyword **HL5CS02.**

Cells: The Basic Units of Life

About the

Harmful bacteria may invade your body and make you sick. But wait—your white blood cells come to the rescue! In this image, a white blood cell (the large, yellowish cell) reaches out its pseudopod to destroy bacteria (the purple cells). The red discs are red blood cells.

PRE-READING ACTIVITY

FOLDNOTES **Key-Term Fold** Before you read the chapter, create the FoldNote entitled "Key-Term Fold" described in the **Study Skills** section of the Appendix. Write a key term from the chapter on each tab of the key-term fold. Under each tab, write the definition of the key term.

What Are Plants Made Of?

All living things, including plants, are made of cells. What do plant cells look like? Do this activity to find out.

Procedure

1. Tear off a **small leaf** from near the tip of an **Elodea sprig.**

2. Using **forceps,** place the whole leaf in a **drop of water** on a **microscope slide.**

3. Place a **coverslip** on top of the water drop by putting one edge of the coverslip on the slide near the water drop. Next, lower the coverslip slowly so that the coverslip does not trap air bubbles.

4. Place the slide on your **microscope.**

5. Using the lowest-powered lens first, find the plant cells. When you can see the cells under the lower-powered lens, switch to a higher-powered lens.

6. Draw a picture of what you see.

Analysis

1. Describe the shape of the *Elodea* cells. Are all of the cells in the *Elodea* the same?

2. Do you think human cells look like *Elodea* cells? How do you think they are different? How might they be similar?

The Diversity of Cells

Most cells are so small they can't be seen by the naked eye. So how did scientists find cells? By accident, that's how! The first person to see cells wasn't even looking for them.

All living things are made of tiny structures called cells. A **cell** is the smallest unit that can perform all the processes necessary for life. Because of their size, cells weren't discovered until microscopes were invented in the mid-1600s.

READING WARM-UP

Objectives

● State the parts of the cell theory.

● Explain why cells are so small.

● Describe the parts of a cell.

● Describe how eubacteria are different from archaebacteria.

● Explain the difference between prokaryotic cells and eukaryotic cells.

Terms to Learn

cell	nucleus
cell membrane	prokaryote
organelle	eukaryote

READING STRATEGY

Reading Organizer As you read this section, create an outline of the section. Use the headings from the section in your outline.

Cells and the Cell Theory

Robert Hooke was the first person to describe cells. In 1665, he built a microscope to look at tiny objects. One day, he looked at a thin slice of cork. Cork is found in the bark of cork trees. The cork looked like it was made of little boxes. Hooke named these boxes *cells*, which means "little rooms" in Latin. Hooke's cells were really the outer layers of dead cork cells. Hooke's microscope and his drawing of the cork cells are shown in **Figure 1.**

Hooke also looked at thin slices of living plants. He saw that they too were made of cells. Some cells were even filled with "juice." The "juicy" cells were living cells.

Hooke also looked at feathers, fish scales, and the eyes of houseflies. But he spent most of his time looking at plants and fungi. The cells of plants and fungi have cell walls. This makes them easy to see. Animal cells do not have cell walls. This absence of cell walls makes it harder to see the outline of animal cells. Because Hooke couldn't see their cells, he thought that animals weren't made of cells.

Figure 1 *Hooke discovered cells using this microscope. Hooke's drawing of cork cells is shown to the right of his microscope.*

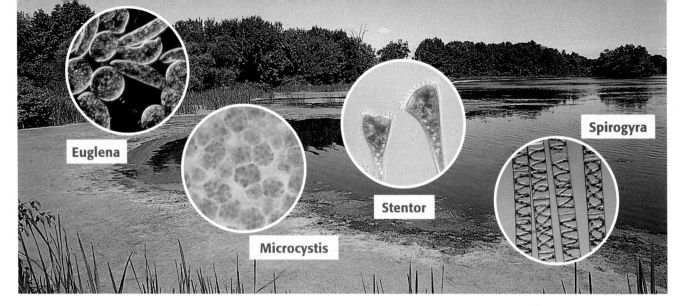

Euglena

Microcystis

Stentor

Spirogyra

Finding Cells in Other Organisms

In 1673, Anton van Leeuwenhoek (LAY vuhn HOOK), a Dutch merchant, made his own microscopes. Leeuwenhoek used one of his microscopes to look at pond scum. Leeuwenhoek saw small organisms in the water. He named these organisms *animalcules,* which means "little animals." Today, we call these single-celled organisms protists (PROH tists). Pond scum and some of the protists it contains are shown in **Figure 2.**

Leeuwenhoek also looked at animal blood. He saw differences in blood cells from different kinds of animals. For example, blood cells in fish, birds, and frogs are oval. Blood cells in humans and dogs are round and flat. Leeuwenhoek was also the first person to see bacteria. And he discovered that yeasts that make bread dough rise are single-celled organisms.

The Cell Theory

Almost 200 years passed before scientists concluded that cells are present in all living things. Scientist Matthias Schleiden (mah THEE uhs SHLIE duhn) studied plants. In 1838, he concluded that all plant parts were made of cells. Theodor Schwann (TAY oh dohr SHVAHN) studied animals. In 1839, Schwann concluded that all animal tissues were made of cells. Soon after that, Schwann wrote the first two parts of what is now known as the *cell theory.*

- All organisms are made of one or more cells.
- The cell is the basic unit of all living things.

Later, in 1858, Rudolf Virchow (ROO dawlf FIR koh), a doctor, stated that all cells could form only from other cells. Virchow then added the third part of the cell theory.

- All cells come from existing cells.

✓ Reading Check What are the three parts of the cell theory? (*See the Appendix for answers to Reading Checks.*)

Figure 2 *The green area at the edge of the pond is a layer of pond scum. This pond scum contains organisms called* protists, *such as those shown above.*

cell in biology, the smallest unit that can perform all life processes; cells are covered by a membrane and have DNA and cytoplasm

CONNECTION TO Physics

Microscopes The microscope Hooke used to study cells was much different from microscopes today. Research different kinds of microscopes, such as light microscopes, scanning electron microscopes (SEMs), and transmission electron microscopes (TEMs). Select one type of microscope. Make a poster or other presentation to show to the class. Describe how the microscope works and how it is used. Be sure to include images.

ACTIVITY

Cell Size

Most cells are too small to be seen without a microscope. It would take 50 human cells to cover the dot on this letter *i*.

A Few Large Cells

Most cells are small. A few, however, are big. The yolk of a chicken egg, shown in **Figure 3,** is one big cell. The egg can be this large because it does not have to take in more nutrients.

Many Small Cells

There is a physical reason why most cells are so small. Cells take in food and get rid of wastes through their outer surface. As a cell gets larger, it needs more food and produces more waste. Therefore, more materials pass through its outer surface.

As the cell's volume increases, its surface area grows too. But the cell's volume grows faster than its surface area. If a cell gets too large, the cell's surface area will not be large enough to take in enough nutrients or pump out enough wastes. So, the area of a cell's surface—compared with the cell's volume—limits the cell's size. The ratio of the cell's outer surface area to the cell's volume is called the *surface area–to-volume ratio,* which can be calculated by using the following equation:

$$surface\ area\text{–}to\text{-}volume\ ratio = \frac{surface\ area}{volume}$$

Figure 3 *The white and yolk of this chicken egg provide nutrients for the development of a chick.*

✓ Reading Check Why are most cells small?

MATH FOCUS

Surface Area–to-Volume Ratio Calculate the surface area–to-volume ratio of a cube whose sides measure 2 cm.

Step 1: Calculate the surface area.

*surface area of cube = number of sides ×
area of side*

surface area of cube = 6 × (2 cm × 2 cm)

surface area of cube = 24 cm²

Step 2: Calculate the volume.

volume of cube = side × side × side

volume of cube = 2 cm × 2 cm × 2 cm

volume of cube = 8 cm³

Step 3: Calculate the surface area–to-volume ratio.

$$surface\ area\text{–}to\text{-}volume\ ratio = \frac{surface\ area}{volume} = \frac{24}{8} = \frac{3}{1}$$

Now It's Your Turn

1. Calculate the surface area–to-volume ratio of a cube whose sides are 3 cm long.
2. Calculate the surface area–to-volume ratio of a cube whose sides are 4 cm long.
3. Of the cubes from questions 1 and 2, which has the greater surface area–to-volume ratio?
4. What is the relationship between the length of a side and the surface area–to-volume ratio of a cell?

Parts of a Cell

Cells come in many shapes and sizes. Cells have many different functions. But all cells have the following parts in common.

The Cell Membrane and Cytoplasm

All cells are surrounded by a cell membrane. The **cell membrane** is a protective layer that covers the cell's surface and acts as a barrier. It separates the cell's contents from its environment. The cell membrane also controls materials going into and out of the cell. Inside the cell is a fluid. This fluid and almost all of its contents are called the *cytoplasm* (SIET oh PLAZ uhm).

Organelles

Cells have organelles that carry out various life processes. **Organelles** are structures that perform specific functions within the cell. Different types of cells have different organelles. Most organelles are surrounded by membranes. For example, the algal cell in **Figure 4** has membrane-bound organelles. Some organelles float in the cytoplasm. Other organelles are attached to membranes or other organelles.

✓ *Reading Check* What are organelles?

Genetic Material

All cells contain DNA (**d**eoxyribo**n**ucleic **a**cid) at some point in their life. *DNA* is the genetic material that carries information needed to make new cells and new organisms. DNA is passed on from parent cells to new cells and controls the activities of a cell. **Figure 5** shows the DNA of a bacterium.

In some cells, the DNA is enclosed inside an organelle called the **nucleus.** For example, your cells have a nucleus. In contrast, bacterial cells do not have a nucleus.

In humans, mature red blood cells lose their DNA. Red blood cells are made inside bones. When red blood cells are first made, they have a nucleus with DNA. But before they enter the bloodstream, red blood cells lose their nucleus and DNA. They survive with no new instructions from their DNA.

Cell membrane
Organelles
DNA

Figure 4 *This green alga has organelles. The organelles and the fluid surrounding them make up the cytoplasm.*

cell membrane a phospholipid layer that covers a cell's surface; acts as a barrier between the inside of a cell and the cell's environment

organelle one of the small bodies in a cell's cytoplasm that are specialized to perform a specific function

nucleus in a eukaryotic cell, a membrane-bound organelle that contains the cell's DNA and that has a role in processes such as growth, metabolism, and reproduction

DNA
E. coli bacterium

Figure 5 *This photo shows an* Escherichia coli *bacterium. The bacterium's cell membrane has been treated so that the cell's DNA is released.*

Bacteria in Your Lunch?

Most of the time, you don't want bacteria in your food. Many bacteria make toxins that will make you sick. However, some foods—such as yogurt—are supposed to have bacteria in them! The bacteria in these foods are not dangerous.

In yogurt, masses of rod-shaped bacteria feed on the sugar (lactose) in milk. The bacteria convert the sugar into lactic acid. Lactic acid causes milk to thicken. This thickened milk makes yogurt.

1. Using a **cotton swab,** put a **small dot of yogurt** on a **microscope slide.**

2. Add a **drop of water.** Use the cotton swab to stir.

3. Add a **coverslip**.

4. Use a **microscope** to examine the slide. Draw what you observe.

prokaryote an organism that consists of a single cell that does not have a nucleus

Two Kinds of Cells

All cells have cell membranes, organelles, cytoplasm, and DNA in common. But there are two basic types of cells—cells without a nucleus and cells with a nucleus. Cells with no nucleus are *prokaryotic* (proh KAR ee AHT ik) *cells.* Cells that have a nucleus are *eukaryotic* (yoo KAR ee AHT ik) *cells.* Prokaryotic cells are further classified into two groups: *eubacteria* (yoo bak TIR ee uh) and *archaebacteria* (AHR kee bak TIR ee uh).

Prokaryotes: Eubacteria and Archaebacteria

Eubacteria and archaebacteria are prokaryotes (pro KAR ee OHTS). **Prokaryotes** are single-celled organisms that do not have a nucleus or membrane-bound organelles.

Eubacteria

The most common prokaryotes are eubacteria (or just *bacteria*). Bacteria are the world's smallest cells. These tiny organisms live almost everywhere. Bacteria do not have a nucleus, but they do have DNA. A bacteria's DNA is a long, circular molecule, shaped sort of like a rubber band. Bacteria have no membrane-covered organelles. But they do have ribosomes. *Ribosomes* are tiny, round organelles made of protein and other material.

Bacteria also have a strong, weblike exterior cell wall. This wall helps the cell retain its shape. A bacterium's cell membrane is just inside the cell wall. Together, the cell wall and cell membrane allow materials into and out of the cell.

Some bacteria live in the soil and water. Others live in, or on, other organisms. For example, you have bacteria living on your skin and teeth. You also have bacteria living in your digestive system. These bacteria help the process of digestion. A typical bacterial cell is shown in **Figure 6.**

Figure 6 *This diagram shows the DNA, cell membrane, and cell wall of a eubacterial cell. The flagellum helps the bacterium move.*

Figure 7 *This photograph, taken with an electron microscope, is of an archaebacterium that lives in the very high temperatures of deep-sea volcanic vents. The photograph has been colored so that the cell wall is green and the cell contents are pink.*

Archaebacteria

The second kind of prokaryote are the archaebacteria. These organisms are also called *archaea* (ahr KEE uh). Archaebacteria are similar to bacteria in some ways. For example, both are single-celled organisms. Both have ribosomes, a cell membrane, and circular DNA. And both lack a nucleus and membrane-bound organelles. But archaebacteria are different from bacteria. For example, archaebacterial ribosomes are different from eubacterial ribosomes.

Archaebacteria are similar to eukaryotic cells in some ways, too. For example, archaebacterial ribosomes are more like the ribosomes of eukaryotic cells. But archaebacteria also have some features that no other cells have. For example, the cell wall and cell membranes of archaebacteria are different from the cell walls of other organisms. And some archaebacteria live in places where no other organisms could live.

Three types of archaebacteria are *heat-loving, salt-loving,* and *methane-making.* Methane is a kind of gas frequently found in swamps. Heat-loving and salt-lovng archaebacteria are sometimes called extremophiles. *Extremophiles* live in places where conditions are extreme. They live in very hot water, such as in hot springs, or where the water is extremely salty. **Figure 7** shows one kind of methane-making archaebacteria that lives deep in the ocean near volcanic vents. The temperature of the water from those vents is extreme: it is above the boiling point of water at sea level.

✔ **Reading Check** What is one difference between eubacteria and archaebacteria?

CONNECTION TO Social Studies

Where Do They Live?
While most archaebacteria live in extreme environments, scientists have found that archaebacteria live almost everywhere. Do research about archaebacteria. Select one kind of archaebacteria. Create a poster showing the geographical location where the organism lives, describing its physical environment, and explaining how it survives in its environment.

ACTIVITY

Eukaryotic Cells and Eukaryotes

Eukaryotic cells are the largest cells. Most eukaryotic cells are still microscopic, but they are about 10 times larger than most bacterial cells. A typical eukaryotic cell is shown in **Figure 8.**

Unlike bacteria and archaebacteria, eukaryotic cells have a nucleus. The nucleus is one kind of membrane-bound organelle. A cell's nucleus holds the cell's DNA. Eukaryotic cells have other membrane-bound organelles as well. Organelles are like the different organs in your body. Each kind of organelle has a specific job in the cell. Together, organelles, such as the ones shown in **Figure 8,** perform all the processes necessary for life.

All living things that are not bacteria or archaebacteria are made of one or more eukaryotic cells. Organisms made of eukaryotic cells are called **eukaryotes.** Many eukaryotes are multicellular. *Multicellular* means "many cells." Multicellular organisms are usually larger than single-cell organisms. So, most organisms you see with your naked eye are eukaryotes. There are many types of eukaryotes. Animals, including humans, are eukaryotes. So are plants. Some protists, such as amoebas, are single-celled eukaryotes. Other protists, including some types of green algae, are multicellular eukaryotes. Fungi are organisms such as mushrooms or yeasts. Mushrooms are multicellular eukaryotes. Yeasts are single-celled eukaryotes.

Reading Check How are eukaryotes different from prokaryotes?

eukaryote an organism made up of cells that have a nucleus enclosed by a membrane; eukaryotes include animals, plants, and fungi, but not archaebacteria or eubacteria

For another activity related to this chapter, go to **go.hrw.com** and type in the keyword **HL5CELW.**

Figure 8 **Organelles in a Typical Eukaryotic Cell**

Organelles

Nucleus

Golgi complex

Nucleus

Mitochondrion

Lysosome

Endoplasmic reticulum

Ribosome

Cell membrane

Summary

● Cells were not discovered until microscopes were invented in the 1600s.

● Cell theory states that all organisms are made of cells, the cell is the basic unit of all living things, and all cells come from other cells.

● All cells have a cell membrane, cytoplasm, and DNA.

● Most cells are too small to be seen with the naked eye. A cell's surface area–to-volume ratio limits the size of a cell.

● The two basic kinds of cells are prokaryotic cells and eukaryotic cells. Eukaryotic cells have a nucleus and membrane-bound organelles. Prokaryotic cells do not.

● Prokaryotes are classified as archaebacteria and eubacteria.

● Archaebacterial cell walls and ribosomes are different from the cell walls and ribosomes of other organisms.

● Eukaryotes can be single-celled or multicellular.

Using Key Terms

1. In your own words, write a definition for the term *organelle*.

2. Use the following terms in the same sentence: *prokaryotic, nucleus,* and *eukaryotic*.

Understanding Key Ideas

3. Cell size is limited by the
   a. thickness of the cell wall.
   b. size of the cell's nucleus.
   c. cell's surface area–to-volume ratio.
   d. amount of cytoplasm in the cell.

4. What are the three parts of the cell theory?

5. Name three structures that every cell has.

6. Give two ways in which archaebacteria are different from bacteria.

Critical Thinking

7. **Applying Concepts** You have discovered a new single-celled organism. It has a cell wall, ribosomes, and long, circular DNA. Is it a eukaryote or a prokaryote cell? Explain.

8. **Identifying Relationships** One of your students brings you a cell about the size of the period at the end of this sentence. It is a single cell, but it also forms chains. What characteristics would this cell have if the organism is a eukaryote? If it is a prokaryote? What would you look for first?

Interpreting Graphics

The picture below shows a particular organism. Use the picture to answer the questions that follow.

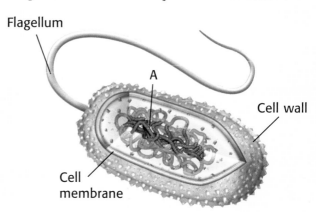

Flagellum

A

Cell wall

Cell membrane

9. What type of organism does the picture represent? How do you know?

10. Which structure helps the organism move?

11. What part of the organism does the letter *A* represent?

For a variety of links related to this chapter, go to www.scilinks.org

Topic: Prokaryotic Cells
SciLinks code: HSM1225

cell wall a rigid structure that surrounds the cell membrane and provides support to the cell

Eukaryotic Cells

Most eukaryotic cells are small. For a long time after cells were discovered, scientists could not see what was going on inside cells. They did not know how complex cells are.

Now, scientists know a lot about eukaryotic cells. These cells have many parts that work together and keep the cell alive.

Cell Wall

Some eukaryotic cells have cell walls. A **cell wall** is a rigid structure that gives support to a cell. The cell wall is the outermost structure of a cell. Plants and algae have cell walls made of cellulose (SEL yoo LOHS) and other materials. *Cellulose* is a complex sugar that most animals can't digest.

The cell walls of plant cells allow plants to stand upright. In some plants, the cells must take in water for the cell walls to keep their shape. When such plants lack water, the cell walls collapse and the plant droops. **Figure 1** shows a cross section of a plant cell and a close-up of the cell wall.

Fungi, including yeasts and mushrooms, also have cell walls. Some fungi have cell walls made of *chitin* (KIE tin). Other fungi have cell walls made from a chemical similar to chitin. Eubacteria and archaebacteria also have cell walls, but those walls are different from plant or fungal cell walls.

✓ **Reading Check** What types of cells have cell walls? (*See the Appendix for answers to Reading Checks.*)

Figure 1 *The cell walls of plant cells help plants retain their shape. Plant cell walls are made of cellulose.*

Cell wall

Cellulose fibers

Cell membrane

Cell Membrane

All cells have a cell membrane. The *cell membrane* is a protective barrier that encloses a cell. It separates the cell's contents from the cell's environment. The cell membrane is the outermost structure in cells that lack a cell wall. In cells that have a cell wall, the cell membrane lies just inside the cell wall.

The cell membrane contains proteins, lipids, and phospholipids. *Lipids,* which include fats and cholesterol, are a group of compounds that do not dissolve in water. The cell membrane has two layers of phospholipids (FAHS foh LIP idz), shown in **Figure 2.** A *phospholipid* is a lipid that contains phosphorus. Lipids are "water fearing," or *hydrophobic*. Lipid ends of phospholipids form the inner part of the membrane. Phosphorus-containing ends of the phospholipids are "water loving," or *hydrophilic*. These ends form the outer part of the membrane.

Some of the proteins and lipids control the movement of materials into and out of the cell. Some of the proteins form passageways. Nutrients and water move into the cell, and wastes move out of the cell, through these protein passageways.

Reading Check What are two functions of a cell membrane?

CONNECTION TO Language Arts

WRITING SKILL **The Great Barrier** In your **science journal,** write a science fiction story about tiny travelers inside a person's body. These little explorers need to find a way into or out of a cell to solve a problem. You may need to do research to find out more about how the cell membrane works. Illustrate your story.

Figure 2 *The cell membrane is made of two layers of phospholipids. It allows nutrients to enter and wastes to exit the cell.*

Hydrophilic heads

Phospholipids

Hydrophobic tails

Cell membrane

Figure 3 *The cytoskeleton, made of protein fibers, helps a cell retain its shape, move in its environment, and move its organelles.*

Figure 4 *The nucleus contains the cell's DNA. Pores allow materials to move between the nucleus and the cytoplasm.*

Cytoskeleton

The *cytoskeleton* (SIET oh SKEL uh tuhn) is a web of proteins in the cytoplasm. The cytoskeleton, shown in **Figure 3,** acts as both a muscle and a skeleton. It keeps the cell's membranes from collapsing. The cytoskeleton also helps some cells move.

The cytoskeleton is made of three types of protein. One protein is a hollow tube. The other two are long, stringy fibers. One of the stringy proteins is also found in muscle cells.

✔ **Reading Check** What is the cytoskeleton?

Nucleus

All eukaryotic cells have the same basic membrane-bound organelles, starting with the nucleus. The *nucleus* is a large organelle in a eukaryotic cell. It contains the cell's DNA, or genetic material. DNA contains the information on how to make a cell's proteins. Proteins control the chemical reactions in a cell. They also provide structural support for cells and tissues. But proteins are not made in the nucleus. Messages for how to make proteins are copied from the DNA. These messages are then sent out of the nucleus through the membranes.

The nucleus is covered by two membranes. Materials cross this double membrane by passing through pores. **Figure 4** shows a nucleus and nuclear pores. The nucleus of many cells has a dark area called the nucleolus (noo KLEE uh luhs). The *nucleolus* is where a cell begins to make its ribosomes.

Double membrane

Ribosomes

Organelles that make proteins are called **ribosomes.** Ribosomes are the smallest of all organelles. And there are more ribosomes in a cell than there are any other organelles. Some ribosomes float freely in the cytoplasm. Others are attached to membranes or the cytoskeleton. Unlike most organelles, ribosomes are not covered by a membrane.

Proteins are made within the ribosomes. Proteins are made of amino acids. An *amino acid* is any one of about 20 different organic molecules that are used to make proteins. All cells need proteins to live. All cells have ribosomes.

Endoplasmic Reticulum

Many chemical reactions take place in a cell. Many of these reactions happen on or in the endoplasmic reticulum (EN doh PLAZ mik ri TIK yuh luhm). The **endoplasmic reticulum,** or ER, is a system of folded membranes in which proteins, lipids, and other materials are made. The ER is shown in **Figure 5.**

The ER is part of the internal delivery system of the cell. Its folded membrane contains many tubes and passageways. Substances move through the ER to different places in the cell.

Endoplasmic reticulum is either rough ER or smooth ER. The part of the ER covered in ribosomes is rough ER. Rough ER is usually found near the nucleus. Ribosomes on rough ER make many of the cell's proteins. The ER delivers these proteins throughout the cell. ER that lacks ribosomes is smooth ER. The functions of smooth ER include making lipids and breaking down toxic materials that could damage the cell.

ribosome cell organelle composed of RNA and protein; the site of protein synthesis

endoplasmic reticulum a system of membranes that is found in a cell's cytoplasm and that assists in the production, processing, and transport of proteins and in the production of lipids

Figure 5 *The endoplasmic reticulum (ER) is a system of membranes. Rough ER is covered with ribosomes. Smooth ER does not have ribosomes.*

Smooth ER

Rough ER

Endoplasmic reticulum

Ribosomes

Smooth ER

Rough ER

Figure 6 *Mitochondria break down sugar and make ATP. ATP is produced on the inner membrane.*

mitochondrion in eukaryotic cells, the cell organelle that is surrounded by two membranes and that is the site of cellular respiration

Mitochondria

A mitochondrion (MIET oh KAHN dree uhn) is the main power source of a cell. A **mitochondrion** is the organelle in which sugar is broken down to produce energy. Mitochondria are covered by two membranes, as shown in **Figure 6.** Energy released by mitochondria is stored in a substance called *ATP* (**a**denosine **trip**hosphate). The cell then uses ATP to do work. ATP can be made at several places in a cell. But most of a cell's ATP is made in the inner membrane of the cell's mitochondria.

Most eukaryotic cells have mitochondria. Mitochondria are the size of some bacteria. Like bacteria, mitochondria have their own DNA, and mitochondria can divide within a cell.

Reading Check Where is most of a cell's ATP made?

Chloroplasts

Animal cells cannot make their own food. Plants and algae are different. They have chloroplasts (KLAWR uh PLASTS) in some of their cells. *Chloroplasts* are organelles in plant and algae cells in which photosynthesis takes place. Like mitochondria, chloroplasts have two membranes and their own DNA. A chloroplast is shown in **Figure 7.** *Photosynthesis* is the process by which plants and algae use sunlight, carbon dioxide, and water to make sugar and oxygen.

Chloroplasts are green because they contain *chlorophyll,* a green pigment. Chlorophyll is found inside the inner membrane of a chloroplast. Chlorophyll traps the energy of sunlight, which is used to make sugar. The sugar produced by photosynthesis is then used by mitochondria to make ATP.

Figure 7 *Chloroplasts harness and use the energy of the sun to make sugar. A green pigment—chlorophyll—traps the sun's energy.*

Golgi Complex

The organelle that packages and distributes proteins is called the **Golgi complex** (GOHL jee KAHM PLEKS). It is named after Camillo Golgi, the Italian scientist who first identified the organelle.

The Golgi complex looks like smooth ER, as shown in **Figure 8.** Lipids and proteins from the ER are delivered to the Golgi complex. There, the lipids and proteins may be modified to do different jobs. The final products are enclosed in a piece of the Golgi complex's membrane. This membrane pinches off to form a small bubble. The bubble transports its contents to other parts of the cell or out of the cell.

Cell Compartments

The bubble that forms from the Golgi complex's membrane is a vesicle. A **vesicle** (VES i kuhl) is a small sac that surrounds material to be moved into or out of a cell. All eukaryotic cells have vesicles. Vesicles also move material within a cell. For example, vesicles carry new protein from the ER to the Golgi complex. Other vesicles distribute material from the Golgi complex to other parts of the cell. Some vesicles form when part of the cell membrane surrounds an object outside the cell.

Golgi complex cell organelle that helps make and package materials to be transported out of the cell

vesicle a small cavity or sac that contains materials in a eukaryotic cell

Figure 8 *The Golgi complex processes proteins. It moves proteins to where they are needed, including out of the cell.*

Golgi complex

Golgi complex

Figure 9
Lysosomes digest materials inside a cell. In plant and fungal cells, vacuoles often perform the same function.

lysosome a cell organelle that contains digestive enzymes

Cellular Digestion

Lysosomes (LIE suh SOHMZ) are vesicles that are responsible for digestion inside a cell. **Lysosomes** are organelles that contain digestive enzymes. They destroy worn-out or damaged organelles, get rid of waste materials, and protect the cell from foreign invaders. Lysosomes, which come in a wide variety of sizes and shapes, are shown in **Figure 9.**

Lysosomes are found mainly in animal cells. When eukaryotic cells engulf particles, they enclose the particles in vesicles. Lysosomes bump into these vesicles and pour enzymes into them. These enzymes digest the particles in the vesicles.

✓ Reading Check Why are lysosomes important?

Vacuoles

A *vacuole* (VAK yoo OHL) is a large vesicle. In plant and fungal cells, some vacuoles act like large lysosomes. They store digestive enzymes and aid in digestion within the cell. Other vacuoles in plant cells store water and other liquids. Vacuoles that are full of water, such as the one in **Figure 9,** help support the cell. Some plants wilt when their vacuoles lose water. **Table 1** shows some organelles and their functions.

Table 1 **Organelles and Their Functions**	
Nucleus the organelle that contains the cell's DNA and is the control center of the cell	**Chloroplast** the organelle that uses the energy of sunlight to make food
Ribosome the organelle in which amino acids are hooked together to make proteins	**Golgi complex** the organelle that processes and transports proteins and other materials out of cell
Endoplasmic reticulum the organelle that makes lipids, breaks down drugs and other substances, and packages proteins for Golgi complex	**Vacuole** the organelle that stores water and other materials
Mitochondria the organelle that breaks down food molecules to make ATP	**Lysosome** the organelle that digests food particles, wastes, cell parts, and foreign invaders

Summary

- Eukaryotic cells have organelles that perform functions that help cells remain alive.
- All cells have a cell membrane. Some cells have a cell wall. Some cells have a cytoskeleton.
- The nucleus of a eukaryotic cell contains the cell's genetic material, DNA.
- Ribosomes are the organelles that make proteins. Ribosomes are not covered by a membrane.

- The endoplasmic reticulum (ER) and the Golgi complex make and process proteins before the proteins are transported to other parts of the cell or out of the cell.
- Mitochondria and chloroplasts are energy-producing organelles.
- Lysosomes are organelles responsible for digestion within a cell. In plant cells, organelles called *vacuoles* store cell materials and sometimes act like large lysosomes.

Using Key Terms

1. In your own words, write a definition for each of the following terms: *ribosome, lysosome,* and *cell wall.*

Understanding Key Ideas

2. Which of the following are found mainly in animal cells?
   a. mitochondria
   b. lysosomes
   c. ribosomes
   d. Golgi complexes

3. What is the function of a Golgi complex? What is the function of the endoplasmic reticulum?

Critical Thinking

4. **Making Comparisons** Describe three ways in which plant cells differ from animal cells.

5. **Applying Concepts** Every cell needs ribosomes. Explain why.

6. **Predicting Consequences** A certain virus attacks the mitochondria in cells. What would happen to a cell if all of its mitochondria were destroyed?

7. **Expressing Opinions** Do you think that having chloroplasts gives plant cells an advantage over animal cells? Support your opinion.

Interpreting Graphics

Use the diagram below to answer the questions that follow.

8. Is this a diagram of a plant cell or an animal cell? Explain how you know.

9. What organelle does the letter *b* refer to?

For a variety of links related to this chapter, go to www.scilinks.org

Topic: Eukaryotic Cells
SciLinks code: HSM0541

The Organization of Living Things

In some ways, organisms are like machines. Some machines have just one part. But most machines have many parts. Some organisms exist as a single cell. Other organisms have many—even trillions—of cells.

Most cells are smaller than the period that ends this sentence. Yet, every cell in every organism performs all the processes of life. So, are there any advantages to having many cells?

The Benefits of Being Multicellular

You are a *multicellular organism*. This means that you are made of many cells. Multicellular organisms grow by making more small cells, not by making their cells larger. For example, an elephant is bigger than you are, but its cells are about the same size as yours. An elephant just has more cells than you do. Some benefits of being multicellular are the following:

- **Larger Size** Many multicellular organisms are small. But they are usually larger than single-celled organisms. Larger organisms are prey for fewer predators. Larger predators can eat a wider variety of prey.

- **Longer Life** The life span of a multicellular organism is not limited to the life span of any single cell.

- **Specialization** Each type of cell has a particular job. Specialization makes the organism more efficient. For example, the cardiac muscle cell in **Figure 1** is a specialized muscle cell. Heart muscle cells contract and make the heart pump blood.

 Reading Check List three advantages of being multicellular. *(See the Appendix for answers to Reading Checks.)*

READING WARM-UP

Objectives

● List three advantages of being multicellular.

● Describe the four levels of organization in living things.

● Explain the relationship between the structure and function of a part of an organism.

Terms to Learn

tissue   organism
organ   structure
organ system   function

READING STRATEGY

Paired Summarizing Read this section silently. In pairs, take turns summarizing the material. Stop to discuss ideas that seem confusing.

Figure 1 *This photomicrograph shows a small part of one heart muscle cell. The green line surrounds one of many mitochondria, the powerhouses of the cell. The pink areas are muscle filaments.*

Figure 2 *This photomicrograph shows cardiac muscle tissue. Cardiac muscle tissue is made up of many cardiac cells.*

Cells Working Together

A **tissue** is a group of cells that work together to perform a specific job. The material around and between the cells is also part of the tissue. The cardiac muscle tissue, shown in **Figure 2,** is made of many cardiac muscle cells. Cardiac muscle tissue is just one type of tissue in a heart.

Animals have four basic types of tissues: nerve tissue, muscle tissue, connective tissue, and protective tissue. In contrast, plants have three types of tissues: transport tissue, protective tissue, and ground tissue. Transport tissue moves water and nutrients through a plant. Protective tissue covers the plant. It helps the plant retain water and protects the plant against damage. Photosynthesis takes place in ground tissue.

Tissues Working Together

A structure that is made up of two or more tissues working together to perform a specific function is called an **organ.** For example, your heart is an organ. It is made mostly of cardiac muscle tissue. But your heart also has nerve tissue and tissues of the blood vessels that all work together to make your heart the powerful pump that it is.

Another organ is your stomach. It also has several kinds of tissue. In the stomach, muscle tissue makes food move in and through the stomach. Special tissues make chemicals that help digest your food. Connective tissue holds the stomach together, and nervous tissue carries messages back and forth between the stomach and the brain. Other organs include the intestines, brain, and lungs.

Plants also have different kinds of tissues that work together as organs. A leaf is a plant organ that contains tissue that traps light energy to make food. Other examples of plant organs are stems and roots.

✓ Reading Check What is an organ?

tissue a group of similar cells that perform a common function

organ a collection of tissues that carry out a specialized function of the body

A Pet Protist
Imagine that you have a tiny box-shaped protist for a pet. To care for your pet protist properly, you have to figure out how much to feed it. The dimensions of your protist are roughly 25 μm × 20 μm × 2 μm. If seven food particles per second can enter through each square micrometer of surface area, how many particles can your protist eat in 1 min?

Organs Working Together

A group of organs working together to perform a particular function is called an **organ system.** Each organ system has a specific job to do in the body.

For example, the digestive system is made up of several organs, including the stomach and intestines. The digestive system's job is to break down food into small particles. Other parts of the body then use these small particles as fuel. In turn, the digestive system depends on the respiratory and cardiovascular systems for oxygen. The cardiovascular system, shown in **Figure 3,** includes organs and tissues such as the heart and blood vessels. Plants also have organ systems. They include leaf systems, root systems, and stem systems.

Reading Check List the levels of organization in living things.

Organisms

Anything that can perform life processes by itself is an **organism.** An organism made of a single cell is called a *unicellular organism.* Bacteria, most protists, and some kinds of fungi are unicellular. Although some of these organisms live in colonies, they are still unicellular. They are unicellular organisms living together, and all of the cells in the colony are the same. Each cell must carry out all life processes in order for that cell to survive. In contrast, even the simplest multicellular organism has specialized cells that depend on each other for the organism to survive.

organ system a group of organs that work together to perform body functions

organism a living thing; anything that can carry out life processes independently

structure the arrangement of parts in an organism

function the special, normal, or proper activity of an organ or part

Figure 3 Levels of Organization in the Cardiovascular System

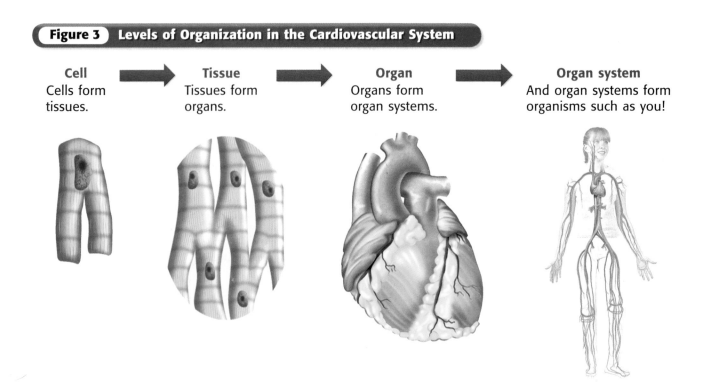

Cell
Cells form tissues.

Tissue
Tissues form organs.

Organ
Organs form organ systems.

Organ system
And organ systems form organisms such as you!

Structure and Function

In organisms, structure and function are related. **Structure** is the arrangement of parts in an organism. It includes the shape of a part and the material of which the part is made. **Function** is the job the part does. For example, the structure of the lungs is a large, spongy sac. In the lungs, there are millions of tiny air sacs called *alveoli*. Blood vessels wrap around the alveoli, as shown in **Figure 4.** Oxygen from air in the alveoli enters the blood. Blood then brings oxygen to body tissues. Also, in the alveoli, carbon dioxide leaves the blood and is exhaled.

The structures of alveoli and blood vessels enable them to perform a function. Together, they bring oxygen to the body and get rid of its carbon dioxide.

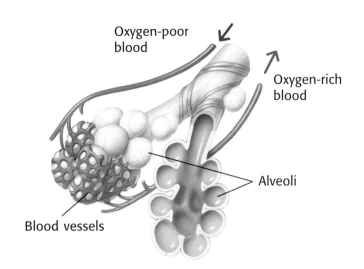

Figure 4 The Structure and Function of Alveoli

Oxygen-poor blood

Oxygen-rich blood

Alveoli

Blood vessels

SECTION Review

Summary

- Advantages of being multicellular are larger size, longer life, and cell specialization.

- Four levels of organization are cell, tissue, organ, and organ system.

- A *tissue* is a group of cells working together. An *organ* is two or more tissues working together. An *organ system* is two or more organs working together.

- In organisms, a part's structure and function are related.

Using Key Terms

1. Use each of the following terms in a separate sentence: *tissue, organ,* and *function.*

Understanding Key Ideas

2. What are the four levels of organization in living things?
   a. cell, multicellular, organ, organ system
   b. single cell, multicellular, tissue, organ
   c. larger size, longer life, specialized cells, organs
   d. cell, tissue, organ, organ system

Math Skills

3. One multicellular organism is a cube. Each of its sides is 3 cm long. Each of its cells is 1 cm^3. How many cells does it have? If each side doubles in length, how many cells will it then have?

Critical Thinking

4. **Applying Concepts** Explain the relationship between structure and function. Use alveoli as an example. Be sure to include more than one level of organization.

5. **Making Inferences** Why can multicellular organisms be more complex than unicellular organisms? Use the three advantages of being multicellular to help explain your answer.

SCi LINKS.

NSTA

Developed and maintained by the National Science Teachers Association

For a variety of links related to this chapter, go to www.scilinks.org

Topic: Organization of Life
SciLinks code: HSM1080

Model-Making Lab

OBJECTIVES

Explore why a single-celled organism cannot grow to the size of an elephant.

Create a model of a cell to illustrate the concept of surface area–to-volume ratio.

MATERIALS

- calculator (optional)
- cubic cell patterns
- heavy paper or poster board
- sand, fine
- scale or balance
- scissors
- tape, transparent

SAFETY

Elephant-Sized Amoebas?

An amoeba is a single-celled organism. Like most cells, amoebas are microscopic. Why can't amoebas grow as large as elephants? If an amoeba grew to the size of a quarter, the amoeba would starve to death. To understand how this can be true, build a model of a cell and see for yourself.

Procedure

1 Use heavy paper or poster board to make four cube-shaped cell models from the patterns supplied by your teacher. Cut out each cell model, fold the sides to make a cube, and tape the tabs on the sides. The smallest cell model has sides that are each one unit long. The next larger cell has sides of two units. The next cell has sides of three units, and the largest cell has sides of four units. These paper models represent the cell membrane, the part of a cell's exterior through which food and wastes pass.

Data Table for Measurements					
Length of side	Area of one side (A = S × S)	Total surface area of cube cell (TA = S × S × 6)	Volume of cube cell (V = S × S × S)	Mass of filled cube cell
1 unit	1 unit^2	6 unit^2	1 unit^3	
2 unit				
3 unit	*DO NOT WRITE IN BOOK*			
4 unit				

Key to Formula Symbols

S = the length of one side

A = area

6 = number of sides

V = volume

TA = total area

2 Copy the data table shown above. Use each formula to calculate the data about your cell models. Record your calculations in the table. Calculations for the smallest cell have been done for you.

3 Carefully fill each model with fine sand until the sand is level with the top edge of the model. Find the mass of the filled models by using a scale or a balance. What does the sand in your model represent?

4 Record the mass of each filled cell model in your Data Table for Measurements. (Always remember to use the appropriate mass unit.)

Analyze the Results

1 **Constructing Tables** Make a data table like the one shown at right.

2 **Organizing Data** Use the data from your Data Table for Measurements to find the ratios for each of your cell models. For each of the cell models, fill in the Data Table for Ratios .

Draw Conclusions

3 **Interpreting Information** As a cell grows larger, does the ratio of total surface area to volume increase, decrease, or stay the same?

4 **Interpreting Information** As a cell grows larger, does the total surface area–to-mass ratio increase, decrease, or stay the same?

5 **Drawing Conclusions** Which is better able to supply food to all the cytoplasm of the cell: the cell membrane of a small cell or the cell membrane of a large cell? Explain your answer.

6 **Evaluating Data** In the experiment, which is better able to feed all of the cytoplasm of the cell: the cell membrane of a cell that has high mass or the cell membrane of a cell that has low mass? You may explain your answer in a verbal presentation to the class, or you may choose to write a report and illustrate it with drawings of your models.

Data Table for Ratios		
Length of side	Ratio of total surface area to volume	Ratio of total surface area to mass
1 unit		
2 unit		
3 unit	*DO NOT WRITE IN BOOK*	
4 unit		

Chapter Review

USING KEY TERMS

Complete each of the following sentences by choosing the correct term from the word bank.

cell
cell membrane
organelles
cell wall
structure

organ
prokaryote
eukaryote
tissue
function

1 A(n) ___ is the most basic unit of all living things.

2 The job that an organ does is the ___ of that organ.

3 Ribosomes and mitochondria are types of ___.

4 A(n) ___ is an organism whose cells have a nucleus.

5 A group of cells working together to perform a specific function is a(n) ___.

6 Only plant cells have a(n) ___.

UNDERSTANDING KEY IDEAS

Multiple Choice

7 Which of the following best describes an organ?

a. a group of cells that work together to perform a specific job

b. a group of tissues that belong to different systems

c. a group of tissues that work together to perform a specific job

d. a body structure, such as muscles or lungs

8 The benefits of being multicellular include

a. small size, long life, and cell specialization.

b. generalized cells, longer life, and ability to prey on small animals.

c. larger size, more enemies, and specialized cells.

d. longer life, larger size, and specialized cells.

9 In eukaryotic cells, which organelle contains the DNA?

a. nucleus   c. smooth ER

b. Golgi complex   d. vacuole

10 Which of the following statements is part of the cell theory?

a. All cells suddenly appear by themselves.

b. All cells come from other cells.

c. All organisms are multicellular.

d. All cells have identical parts.

11 The surface area–to-volume ratio of a cell limits

a. the number of organelles that the cell has.

b. the size of the cell.

c. where the cell lives.

d. the types of nutrients that a cell needs.

12 Two types of organisms whose cells do not have a nucleus are

a. prokaryotes and eukaryotes.

b. plants and animals.

c. eubacteria and archaebacteria.

d. single-celled and multicellular organisms.

Short Answer

13 Explain why most cells are small.

14 Describe the four levels of organization in living things.

15 What is the difference between the structure of an organ and the function of the organ?

16 Name two functions of a cell membrane.

17 What are the structure and function of the cytoskeleton in a cell?

CRITICAL THINKING

18 **Concept Mapping** Use the following terms to create a concept map: *cells, organisms, Golgi complex, organ systems, organs, nucleus, organelle,* and *tissues.*

19 **Making Comparisons** Compare and contrast the functions of the endoplasmic reticulum and the Golgi complex.

20 **Identifying Relationships** Explain how the structure and function of an organism's parts are related. Give an example.

21 **Evaluating Hypotheses** One of your classmates states a hypothesis that all organisms must have organ systems. Is your classmate's hypothesis valid? Explain your answer.

22 **Predicting Consequences** What would happen if all of the ribosomes in your cells disappeared?

23 **Expressing Opinions** Scientists think that millions of years ago the surface of the Earth was very hot and that the atmosphere contained a lot of methane. In your opinion, which type of organism, a eubacterium or an archaebacterium, is the older form of life? Explain your reasoning.

INTERPRETING GRAPHICS

Use the diagram below to answer the questions that follow.

24 What is the name of the structure identified by the letter *a*?

25 Which letter identifies the structure that digests food particles and foreign invaders?

26 Which letter identifies the structure that makes proteins, lipids, and other materials and that contains tubes and passageways that enable substances to move to different places in the cell?

Standardized Test Preparation

READING

Read each of the passages below. Then, answer the questions that follow each passage.

Passage 1 Exploring caves can be dangerous but can also lead to interesting discoveries. For example, deep in the darkness of Cueva de Villa Luz, a cave in Mexico, are slippery formations called *snottites*. They were named snottites because they look just like a two-year-old's runny nose. If you use an electron microscope to look at them, you see that snottites are bacteria; thick, sticky fluids; and small amounts of minerals produced by the bacteria. As tiny as they are, these bacteria can build up snottite structures that may eventually turn into rock. Formations in other caves look like hardened snottites. The bacteria in snottites are acidophiles. Acidophiles live in environments that are highly acidic. Snottite bacteria produce sulfuric acid and live in an environment that is similar to the inside of a car battery.

1. Which statement best describes snottites?
   A Snottites are bacteria that live in car batteries.
   B Snottites are rock formations found in caves.
   C Snottites were named for a cave in Mexico.
   D Snottites are made of bacteria, sticky fluids, and minerals.

2. Based on this passage, which conclusion about snottites is most likely to be correct?
   F Snottites are found in caves everywhere.
   G Snottite bacteria do not need sunlight.
   H You could grow snottites in a greenhouse.
   I Snottites create other bacteria in caves.

3. What is the main idea of this passage?
   A Acidophiles are unusual organisms.
   B Snottites are strange formations.
   C Exploring caves is dangerous.
   D Snottites are large, slippery bacteria.

Passage 2 The world's smallest mammal may be a bat about the size of a jelly bean. The scientific name for this tiny animal, which was unknown until 1974, is *Craseonycteris thonglongyai*. It is so small that it is sometimes called the *bumblebee bat*. Another name for this animal is the *hog-nosed bat*. Hog-nosed bats were given their name because one of their distinctive features is a piglike muzzle. Hog-nosed bats differ from other bats in another way: they do not have a tail. But, like other bats, hog-nosed bats do eat insects that they catch in mid-air. Scientists think that the bats eat small insects that live on the leaves at the tops of trees. Hog-nosed bats live deep in limestone caves and have been found in only one country, Thailand.

1. According to the passage, which statement about hog-nosed bats is most accurate?
   A They are the world's smallest animal.
   B They are about the size of a bumblebee.
   C They eat leaves at the tops of trees.
   D They live in hives near caves in Thailand.

2. Which of the following statements describes distinctive features of hog-nosed bats?
   F The bats are very small and eat leaves.
   G The bats live in caves and have a tail.
   H The bats live in Thailand and are birds.
   I The bats have a piglike muzzle and no tail.

3. From the information in this passage, which conclusion is most likely to be correct?
   A Hog-nosed bats are similar to other bats.
   B Hog-nosed bats are probably rare.
   C Hog-nosed bats can sting like a bumblebee.
   D Hog-nosed bats probably eat fruit.

The diagrams below show two kinds of cells. Use these cell diagrams to answer the questions that follow.

Cell 1

Cell 2

1. What is the name of the organelle labeled *A* in Cell 1?

   A endoplasmic reticulum

   B mitochondrion

   C vacuole

   D nucleus

2. What type of cell is Cell 1?

   F a bacterial cell

   G a plant cell

   H an animal cell

   I a prokaryotic cell

3. What is the name and function of the organelle labeled *B* in Cell 2?

   A The organelle is a vacuole, and it stores water and other materials.

   B The organelle is the nucleus, and it contains the DNA.

   C The organelle is the cell wall, and it gives shape to the cell.

   D The organelle is a ribosome, where proteins are put together.

4. What type of cell is Cell 2? How do you know?

   F prokaryotic; because it does not have a nucleus

   G eukaryotic; because it does not have a nucleus

   H prokaryotic; because it has a nucleus

   I eukaryotic; because it has a nucleus

Read each question below, and choose the best answer.

1. What is the surface area–to-volume ratio of the rectangular solid shown in the diagram below?

6 cm

3 cm   2 cm

   A 0.5:1

   B 2:1

   C 36:1

   D 72:1

2. Look at the diagram of the cell below. Three molecules of food per cubic unit of volume per minute are required for the cell to survive. One molecule of food can enter through each square unit of surface area per minute. What will happen to this cell?

3

3   3

   F The cell is too small, and it will starve.

   G The cell is too large, and it will starve.

   H The cell is at a size that will allow it to survive.

   I There is not enough information to determine the answer.

Standardized Test Preparation

Science in Action

Scientific Discoveries

Discovery of the Stem Cell

What do Parkinson's disease, diabetes, aplastic anemia, and Alzheimer's disease have in common? All of these diseases are diseases for which stem cells may provide treatment or a cure. Stem cells are unspecialized cells from which all other kinds of cells can grow. And research on stem cells has been going on almost since microscopes were invented. But scientists have been able to culture, or grow, stem cells in laboratories for only about the last 20 years. Research during these 20 years has shown scientists that stem cells can be useful in treating—and possibly curing—a variety of diseases.

Weird Science

Extremophiles

Are there organisms on Earth that can give scientists clues about possible life elsewhere? Yes, there are! These organisms are called *extremophiles,* and they live where the environment is extreme. For example, some extremophiles live in the hot volcanic thermal vents deep in the ocean. Other extremophiles live in the extreme cold of Antarctica. But these organisms do not live only in extreme environments. Research shows that extremophiles may be abundant in plankton in the ocean. And not all extremophiles are archaebacteria; some extremophiles are eubacteria.

Language Arts ACTiViTy

WRITING SKILL Imagine that you are a doctor who treats diseases such as Parkinson's disease. Design and create a pamphlet or brochure that you could use to explain what stem cells are. Include in your pamphlet a description of how stem cells might be used to treat one of your patients who has Parkinson's disease. Be sure to include information about Parkinson's disease.

Social Studies ACTiViTy

Choose one of the four types of extremophiles. Do some research about the organism you have chosen and make a poster showing what you learned about it, including where it can be found, under what conditions it lives, how it survives, and how it is used.

People in Science

Caroline Schooley

Microscopist Imagine that your assignment is the following: Go outside. Look at 1 ft² of the ground for 30 min. Make notes about what you observe. Be prepared to describe what you see. If you look at the ground with just your naked eyes, you may quickly run out of things to see. But what would happen if you used a microscope to look? How much more would you be able to see? And how much more would you have to talk about? Caroline Schooley could tell you.

Caroline Schooley joined a science club in middle school. That's when her interest in looking at things through a microscope began. Since then, Schooley has spent many years studying life through a microscope. She is a microscopist. A *microscopist* is someone who uses a microscope to look at small things. Microscopists use their tools to explore the world of small things that cannot be seen by the naked eye. And with today's powerful electron microscopes, microscopists can study things we could never see before, things as small as atoms.

Math ACTIVITY

An average bacterium is about 0.000002 m long. A pencil point is about 0.001 m wide. Approximately how many bacteria would fit on a pencil point?

To learn more about these Science in Action topics, visit **go.hrw.com** and type in the keyword **HL5CELF.**

Current Science

Check out Current Science® articles related to this chapter by visiting go.hrw.com. Just type in the keyword **HL5CS03.**

The Cell in Action

About the

This adult katydid is emerging from its last immature, or nymph, stage. As the katydid changed from a nymph to an adult, every structure of its body changed. To grow and change, an organism must produce new cells. When a cell divides, it makes a copy of its genetic material.

PRE-READING ACTIVITY

FOLDNOTES **Tri-Fold** Before you read the chapter, create the FoldNote entitled "Tri-Fold" described in the **Study Skills** section of the Appendix. Write what you know about the actions of cells in the column labeled "Know." Then, write what you want to know in the column labeled "Want." As you read the chapter, write what you learn about the actions of cells in the column labeled "Learn."

Cells in Action

Yeast are single-celled fungi that are an important ingredient in bread. Yeast cells break down sugar molecules to release energy. In the process, carbon dioxide gas is produced, which causes bread dough to rise.

Procedure

1. Add **4 mL of a sugar solution** to **10 mL of a yeast-and-water mixture**. Use a **stirring rod** to thoroughly mix the two liquids.

2. Pour the stirred mixture into a small test tube.

3. Place a slightly **larger test tube** over the **small test tube.** The top of the small test tube should touch the bottom of the larger test tube.

4. Hold the test tubes together, and quickly turn both test tubes over. Place the test tubes in a test-tube rack.

5. Use a **ruler** to measure the height of the fluid in the large test tube. Wait 20 min, and then measure the height of the liquid again.

Analysis

1. What is the difference between the first height measurement and the second height measurement?

2. What do you think caused the change in the fluid's height?

The Cell in Action   **381**

Exchange with the Environment

What would happen to a factory if its power were shut off or its supply of raw materials never arrived? What would happen if the factory couldn't get rid of its garbage?

Like a factory, an organism must be able to obtain energy and raw materials and get rid of wastes. An organism's cells perform all of these functions. These functions keep cells healthy so that they can divide. Cell division allows organisms to grow and repair injuries.

The exchange of materials between a cell and its environment takes place at the cell's membrane. To understand how materials move into and out of the cell, you need to know about diffusion.

What Is Diffusion?

What happens if you pour dye on top of a layer of gelatin? At first, it is easy to see where the dye ends and the gelatin begins. But over time, the line between the two layers will blur, as shown in **Figure 1.** Why? Everything, including the gelatin and the dye, is made up of tiny moving particles. Particles travel from where they are crowded to where they are less crowded. This movement from areas of high concentration (crowded) to areas of low concentration (less crowded) is called **diffusion** (di FYOO zhuhn). Dye particles diffuse from where they are crowded (near the top of the glass) to where they are less crowded (in the gelatin). Diffusion also happens within and between living cells. Cells do not need to use energy for diffusion.

diffusion the movement of particles from regions of higher density to regions of lower density

Figure 1 *The particles of the dye and the gelatin slowly mix by diffusion.*

Figure 2 **Osmosis**

1 The side that holds only pure water has the higher concentration of water particles.

Pure water | Pure water and food coloring

2 During osmosis, water particles move to where they are less concentrated.

Pure water | Pure water and food coloring

Diffusion of Water

The cells of organisms are surrounded by and filled with fluids that are made mostly of water. The diffusion of water through cell membranes is so important to life processes that it has been given a special name—**osmosis** (ahs MOH sis).

Water is made up of particles, called *molecules*. Pure water has the highest concentration of water molecules. When you mix something, such as food coloring, sugar, or salt, with water, you lower the concentration of water molecules. **Figure 2** shows how water molecules move through a membrane that is semipermeable (SEM i PUHR mee uh buhl). *Semipermeable* means that only certain substances can pass through. The picture on the left in **Figure 2** shows liquids that have different concentrations of water. Over time, the water molecules move from the liquid with the high concentration of water molecules to the liquid with the lower concentration of water molecules.

The Cell and Osmosis

Osmosis is important to cell functions. For example, red blood cells are surrounded by plasma. Plasma is made up of water, salts, sugars, and other particles. The concentration of these particles is kept in balance by osmosis. If red blood cells were in pure water, water molecules would flood into the cells and cause them to burst. When red blood cells are put into a salty solution, the concentration of water molecules inside the cell is higher than the concentration of water outside. This difference makes water move out of the cells, and the cells shrivel up. Osmosis also occurs in plant cells. When a wilted plant is watered, osmosis makes the plant firm again.

✔ *Reading Check* Why would red blood cells burst if you placed them in pure water? (*See the Appendix for answers to Reading Checks.*)

osmosis the diffusion of water through a semipermeable membrane

Bead Diffusion

1. Put three groups of **colored beads** on the bottom of a **plastic bowl.** Each group should be made up of five beads of the same color.

2. Stretch some **clear plastic wrap** tightly over the top of the bowl. Gently shake the bowl for 10 seconds while watching the beads.

3. How is the scattering of the beads like the diffusion of particles? How is it different from the diffusion of particles?

Figure 3 *In passive transport, particles travel through proteins to areas of lower concentration. In active transport, cells use energy to move particles, usually to areas of higher concentration.*

Cell membrane

Passive transport

ATP Energy

Active transport

Moving Small Particles

Small particles, such as sugars, cross the cell membrane through passageways called *channels*. These channels are made up of proteins in the cell membrane. Particles travel through these channels by either passive or active transport. The movement of particles across a cell membrane without the use of energy by the cell is called **passive transport**, and is shown in **Figure 3.** During passive transport, particles move from an area of high concentration to an area of low concentration. Diffusion and osmosis are examples of passive transport.

A process of transporting particles that requires the cell to use energy is called **active transport.** Active transport usually involves the movement of particles from an area of low concentration to an area of high concentration.

Moving Large Particles

Small particles cross the cell membrane by diffusion, passive transport, and active transport. Large particles move into and out of the cell by processes called *endocytosis* and *exocytosis*.

Endocytosis

The active-transport process by which a cell surrounds a large particle, such as a large protein, and encloses the particle in a vesicle to bring the particle into the cell is called **endocytosis** (EN doh sie TOH sis). *Vesicles* are sacs formed from pieces of cell membrane. **Figure 4** shows endocytosis.

passive transport the movement of substances across a cell membrane without the use of energy by the cell

active transport the movement of substances across the cell membrane that requires the cell to use energy

endocytosis the process by which a cell membrane surrounds a particle and encloses the particle in a vesicle to bring the particle into the cell

Figure 4   Endocytosis

1. The cell comes into contact with a particle.

2. The cell membrane begins to wrap around the particle.

3. Once the particle is completely surrounded, a vesicle pinches off.

This photo shows the end of *endocytosis,* which means "within the cell."

Figure 5   Exocytosis

1 Large particles that must leave the cell are packaged in vesicles.

2 The vesicle travels to the cell membrane and fuses with it.

3 The cell releases the particle to the outside of the cell.

Exocytosis means "outside the cell."

Exocytosis

When large particles, such as wastes, leave the cell, the cell uses an active-transport process called **exocytosis** (EK soh sie TOH sis). During exocytosis, a vesicle forms around a large particle within the cell. The vesicle carries the particle to the cell membrane. The vesicle fuses with the cell membrane and releases the particle to the outside of the cell. **Figure 5** shows exocytosis.

exocytosis the process in which a cell releases a particle by enclosing the particle in a vesicle that then moves to the cell surface and fuses with the cell membrane

✓ **Reading Check**   What is exocytosis?

SECTION Review

Summary

● Diffusion is the movement of particles from an area of high concentration to an area of low concentration.

● Osmosis is the diffusion of water through a semipermeable membrane.

● Cells move small particles by diffusion, which is an example of passive transport, and by active transport.

● Large particles enter the cell by endocytosis, and exit the cell by exocytosis.

Using Key Terms

For each pair of terms, explain how the meanings of the terms differ.

1. *diffusion* and *osmosis*

2. *active transport* and *passive transport*

3. *endocytosis* and *exocytosis*

Understanding Key Ideas

4. The movement of particles from a less crowded area to a more crowded area requires
   a. sunlight.   c. a membrane.
   b. energy.   d. osmosis.

5. What structures allow small particles to cross cell membranes?

Math Skills

6. The area of particle 1 is 2.5 mm². The area of particle 2 is 0.5 mm². The area of particle 1 is how many times as big as the area of particle 2?

Critical Thinking

7. **Predicting Consequences** What would happen to a cell if its channel proteins were damaged and unable to transport particles? What would happen to the organism if many of its cells were damaged in this way? Explain your answer.

8. **Analyzing Ideas** Why does active transport require energy?

For a variety of links related to this chapter, go to www.scilinks.org

Topics: Diffusion; Osmosis
SciLinks code: HSM0406; HSM1090

Developed and maintained by the National Science Teachers Association

385

Cell Energy

Why do you get hungry? Feeling hungry is your body's way of telling you that your cells need energy.

All cells need energy to live, grow, and reproduce. Plant cells get their energy from the sun. Many animal cells get the energy they need from food.

From Sun to Cell

Nearly all of the energy that fuels life comes from the sun. Plants capture energy from the sun and change it into food through a process called **photosynthesis.** The food that plants make supplies them with energy. This food also becomes a source of energy for the organisms that eat the plants.

Photosynthesis

Plant cells have molecules that absorb light energy. These molecules are called *pigments.* Chlorophyll (KLAWR uh FIL), the main pigment used in photosynthesis, gives plants their green color. Chlorophyll is found in chloroplasts.

Plants use the energy captured by chlorophyll to change carbon dioxide and water into food. The food is in the form of the simple sugar glucose. Glucose is a carbohydrate. When plants make glucose, they convert the sun's energy into a form of energy that can be stored. The energy in glucose is used by the plant's cells. Photosynthesis also produces oxygen. Photosynthesis is summarized in **Figure 1.**

photosynthesis the process by which plants, algae, and some bacteria use sunlight, carbon dioxide, and water to make food

Photosynthesis

$$6CO_2 + 6H_2O + \text{Light energy} \longrightarrow C_6H_{12}O_6 + 6O_2$$

Carbon dioxide   Water   Glucose   Oxygen

Plant cell

Chloroplast

Figure 1 *Photosynthesis takes place in chloroplasts. Chloroplasts are found inside plant cells.*

Getting Energy from Food

Animal cells have different ways of getting energy from food. One way, called **cellular respiration,** uses oxygen to break down food. Many cells can get energy without using oxygen through a process called **fermentation.** Cellular respiration will release more energy from a given food than fermentation will.

Cellular Respiration

The word *respiration* means "breathing," but cellular respiration is different from breathing. Breathing supplies the oxygen needed for cellular respiration. Breathing also removes carbon dioxide, which is a waste product of cellular respiration. But cellular respiration is a chemical process that occurs in cells.

Most complex organisms, such as the cow in **Figure 2,** obtain energy through cellular respiration. During cellular respiration, food (such as glucose) is broken down into CO_2 and H_2O, and energy is released. Most of the energy released maintains body temperature. Some of the energy is used to form adenosine triphosphate (ATP). ATP supplies energy that fuels cell activities.

Most of the process of cellular respiration takes place in the cell membrane of prokaryotic cells. But in the cells of eukaryotes, cellular respiration takes place mostly in the mitochondria. The process of cellular respiration is summarized in **Figure 2.** Does the equation in the figure remind you of the equation for photosynthesis? **Figure 3** on the next page shows how photosynthesis and respiration are related.

✓ Reading Check What is the difference between cellular respiration and breathing? (*See the Appendix for answers to Reading Checks.*)

cellular respiration the process by which cells use oxygen to produce energy from food

fermentation the breakdown of food without the use of oxygen

Figure 2 *The mitochondria in the cells of this cow will use cellular respiration to release the energy stored in the grass.*

Cellular Respiration

$$C_6H_{12}O_6 + 6O_2 \rightarrow 6CO_2 + 6H_2O + \text{energy (ATP)}$$

Glucose   Oxygen   Carbon dioxide   Water

Mitochondria

Animal cell

Figure 3 The Connection Between Photosynthesis and Respiration

Light energy

Cellular Respiration

Cellular respiration releases carbon dioxide and water, which are used by plant cells to make glucose. During photosynthesis, oxygen is released.

ATP

$CO_2 + H_2O$

Mitochondrion

Chloroplast

$C_6H_{12}O_6 + O_2$

Photosynthesis

Photosynthesis makes glucose and oxygen, which are used by animal cells to make ATP. Cellular respiration releases carbon dioxide and water.

Plant Cell

Animal Cell

Connection Between Photosynthesis and Respiration

As shown in **Figure 3,** photosynthesis transforms energy from the sun into glucose. During photosynthesis, cells use CO_2 to make glucose, and the cells release O_2. During cellular respiration, cells use O_2 to break down glucose and release energy and CO_2. Each process makes the materials that are needed for the other process to occur elsewhere.

Fermentation

Have you ever felt a burning sensation in your leg muscles while you were running? When muscle cells can't get the oxygen needed for cellular respiration, they use the process of fermentation to get energy. One kind of fermentation happens in your muscles and produces lactic acid. The buildup of lactic acid contributes to muscle fatigue and causes a burning sensation. This kind of fermentation also happens in the muscle cells of other animals and in some fungi and bacteria. Another type of fermentation occurs in some types of bacteria and in yeast as described in **Figure 4.**

Figure 4 *Yeast forms carbon dioxide during fermentation. The bubbles of CO_2 gas cause the dough to rise and leave small holes in bread after it is baked.*

✓ **Reading Check** What are two kinds of fermentation?

SECTION Review

Summary

● Most of the energy that fuels life processes comes from the sun.

● The sun's energy is converted into food by the process of photosynthesis.

● Cellular respiration breaks down glucose into water, carbon dioxide, and energy.

● Fermentation is a way that cells get energy from their food without using oxygen.

Using Key Terms

1. In your own words, write a definition for the term *fermentation*.

Understanding Key Ideas

2. O_2 is released during
   a. cellular respiration.
   b. photosynthesis.
   c. breathing.
   d. fermentation.

3. How are photosynthesis and cellular respiration related?

4. How are respiration and fermentation similar? How are they different?

Math Skills

5. Cells of plant A make 120 molecules of glucose an hour. Cells of plant B make half as much glucose as plant A does. How much glucose does plant B make every minute?

Critical Thinking

6. **Analyzing Relationships** Why are plants important to the survival of all other organisms?

7. **Applying Concepts** You have been given the job of restoring life to a barren island. What types of organisms would you put on the island? If you want to have animals on the island, what other organisms must you bring? Explain your answer.

The Cell Cycle

In the time that it takes you to read this sentence, your body will have made millions of new cells! Making new cells allows you to grow and replace cells that have died.

The environment in your stomach is so acidic that the cells lining your stomach must be replaced every few days. Other cells are replaced less often, but your body is constantly making new cells.

The Life of a Cell

As you grow, you pass through different stages in life. Your cells also pass through different stages in their life cycle. The life cycle of a cell is called the **cell cycle.**

The cell cycle begins when the cell is formed and ends when the cell divides and forms new cells. Before a cell divides, it must make a copy of its deoxyribonucleic acid (DNA). DNA is the hereditary material that controls all cell activities, including the making of new cells. The DNA of a cell is organized into structures called **chromosomes.** Copying chromosomes ensures that each new cell will be an exact copy of its parent cell. How does a cell make more cells? It depends on whether the cell is prokaryotic (with no nucleus) or eukaryotic (with a nucleus).

Making More Prokaryotic Cells

Prokaryotic cells are less complex than eukaryotic cells are. Bacteria, which are prokaryotes, have ribosomes and a single, circular DNA molecule but don't have membrane-enclosed organelles. Cell division in bacteria is called *binary fission,* which means "splitting into two parts." Binary fission results in two cells that each contain one copy of the circle of DNA. A few of the bacteria in **Figure 1** are undergoing binary fission.

cell cycle the life cycle of a cell

chromosome in a eukaryotic cell, one of the structures in the nucleus that are made up of DNA and protein; in a prokaryotic cell, the main ring of DNA

Figure 1 *Bacteria reproduce by binary fission.*

Eukaryotic Cells and Their DNA

Eukaryotic cells are more complex than prokaryotic cells are. The chromosomes of eukaryotic cells contain more DNA than those of prokaryotic cells do. Different kinds of eukaryotes have different numbers of chromosomes. More-complex eukaryotes do not necessarily have more chromosomes than simpler eukaryotes do. For example, fruit flies have 8 chromosomes, potatoes have 48, and humans have 46. **Figure 2** shows the 46 chromosomes of a human body cell lined up in pairs. These pairs are made up of similar chromosomes known as **homologous chromosomes** (hoh MAHL uh guhs KROH muh SOHMZ).

✓ **Reading Check** Do more-complex organisms always have more chromosomes than simpler organisms do? (*See the Appendix for answers to Reading Checks.*)

Figure 2 *Human body cells have 46 chromosomes, or 23 pairs of chromosomes.*

Making More Eukaryotic Cells

The eukaryotic cell cycle includes three stages. In the first stage, called *interphase,* the cell grows and copies its organelles and chromosomes. After each chromosome is duplicated, the two copies are called *chromatids.* Chromatids are held together at a region called the *centromere.* The joined chromatids twist and coil and condense into an X shape, as shown in **Figure 3.** After this step, the cell enters the second stage of the cell cycle.

In the second stage, the chromatids separate. The complicated process of chromosome separation is called **mitosis.** Mitosis ensures that each new cell receives a copy of each chromosome. Mitosis is divided into four phases, as shown on the following pages.

In the third stage, the cell splits into two cells. These cells are identical to each other and to the original cell.

homologous chromosomes chromosomes that have the same sequence of genes and the same structure

mitosis in eukaryotic cells, a process of cell division that forms two new nuclei, each of which has the same number of chromosomes

Figure 3 *This duplicated chromosome consists of two chromatids. The chromatids are joined at the centromere.*

Chromatids

Centromere

CONNECTION TO Language Arts

Picking Apart Vocabulary

Brainstorm what words are similar to the parts of the term *homologous chromosome.* What can you guess about the meaning of the term's root words? Look up the roots of the words, and explain how they help describe the concept.

ACTIVITY

Figure 4 The Cell Cycle

Copying DNA (Interphase)

Before mitosis begins, chromosomes are copied. Each chromosome is then two chromatids.

Mitosis Phase 1 (Prophase)

Mitosis begins. The nuclear membrane dissolves. Chromosomes condense into rodlike structures.

Mitosis Phase 2 (Metaphase)

The chromosomes line up along the equator of the cell. Homologous chromosomes pair up.

Mitosis and the Cell Cycle

Figure 4 shows the cell cycle and the phases of mitosis in an animal cell. Mitosis has four phases that are shown and described above. This diagram shows only four chromosomes to make it easy to see what's happening inside the cell.

cytokinesis the division of the cytoplasm of a cell

Cytokinesis

In animal cells and other eukaryotes that do not have cell walls, division of the cytoplasm begins at the cell membrane. The cell membrane begins to pinch inward to form a groove, which eventually pinches all the way through the cell, and two daughter cells form. The division of cytoplasm is called **cytokinesis** and is shown at the last step of **Figure 4.**

Eukaryotic cells that have a cell wall, such as the cells of plants, algae, and fungi, reproduce differently. In these cells, a *cell plate* forms in the middle of the cell. The cell plate contains the materials for the new cell membranes and the new cell walls that will separate the new cells. After the cell splits into two, a new cell wall forms where the cell plate was. The cell plate and a late stage of cytokinesis in a plant cell are shown in **Figure 5.**

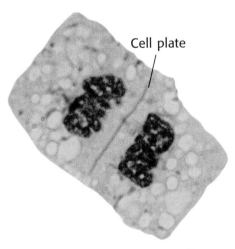

Cell plate

Figure 5 *When a plant cell divides, a cell plate forms and the cell splits into two cells.*

✓ **Reading Check** What is the difference between cytokinesis in an animal cell and cytokinesis in a plant cell?

Mitosis Phase 3 (Anaphase)

The chromatids separate and move to opposite sides of the cell.

Mitosis Phase 4 (Telophase)

A nuclear membrane forms around each set of chromosomes, and the chromosomes unwind. Mitosis is complete.

Cytokinesis

In cells that lack a cell wall, the cell pinches in two. In cells that have a cell wall, a cell plate forms between the two new cells.

SECTION Review

Summary

● A cell produces more cells by first copying its DNA.

● Eukaryotic cells produce more cells through the four phases of mitosis.

● Mitosis produces two cells that have the same number of chromosomes as the parent cell.

● At the end of mitosis, a cell divides the cytoplasm by cytokinesis.

● In plant cells, a cell plate forms between the two new cells during cytokinesis.

Using Key Terms

1. In your own words, write a definition for each of the following terms: *cell cycle* and *cytokinesis*.

Understanding Key Ideas

2. Eukaryotic cells
   a. do not divide.
   b. undergo binary fission.
   c. undergo mitosis.
   d. have cell walls.

3. Why is it important for chromosomes to be copied before cell division?

4. Describe mitosis.

Math Skills

5. Cell A takes 6 h to complete division. Cell B takes 8 h to complete division. After 24 h, how many more copies of cell A would there be than cell B?

Critical Thinking

6. **Predicting Consequences** What would happen if cytokinesis occurred without mitosis?

7. **Applying Concepts** How does mitosis ensure that a new cell is just like its parent cell?

8. **Making Comparisons** Compare the processes that animal cells and plant cells use to make new cells. How are the processes different?

SCI LINKS®

NSTA
Developed and maintained by the National Science Teachers Association

For a variety of links related to this chapter, go to www.scilinks.org

Topic: Cell Cycle
SciLinks code: HSM0235

The Perfect Taters Mystery

You are the chief food detective at Perfect Taters Food Company. The boss, Mr. Fries, wants you to find a way to keep his potatoes fresh and crisp before they are cooked. His workers have tried several methods, but these methods have not worked. Workers in Group A put the potatoes in very salty water, and something unexpected happened to the potatoes. Workers in Group B put the potatoes in water that did not contain any salt, and something else happened! Workers in Group C didn't put the potatoes in any water, and that didn't work either. Now, you must design an experiment to find out what can be done to make the potatoes stay crisp and fresh.

OBJECTIVES

Examine osmosis in potato cells.

Design a procedure that will give the best results.

MATERIALS

- cups, clear plastic, small
- potato pieces, freshly cut
- potato samples (A, B, and C)
- salt
- water, distilled

SAFETY

- Before you plan your experiment, review what you know. You know that potatoes are made of cells. Plant cells contain a large amount of water. Cells have membranes that hold water and other materials inside and keep some things out. Water and other materials must travel across cell membranes to get into and out of the cell.

- Mr. Fries has told you that you can obtain as many samples as you need from the workers in Groups A, B, and C. Your teacher will have these samples ready for you to observe.

- Make a data table like the one below. List your observations in the data table. Make as many observations as you can about the potatoes tested by workers in Groups A, B, and C.

Observations	
Group A	
Group B	
Group C	

Ask a Question

1 Now that you have made your observations, state Mr. Fries's problem in the form of a question that can be answered by your experiment.

Form a Hypothesis

2 Form a hypothesis based on your observations and your questions. The hypothesis should be a statement about what causes the potatoes not to be crisp and fresh. Based on your hypothesis, make a prediction about the outcome of your experiment. State your prediction in an if-then format.

Test the Hypothesis

3 Once you have made a prediction, design your investigation. Check your experimental design with your teacher before you begin. Mr. Fries will give you potato pieces, water, salt, and no more than six containers.

4 Keep very accurate records. Write your plan and procedure. Make data tables. To be sure your data is accurate, measure all materials carefully and make drawings of the potato pieces before and after the experiment.

Analyze the Results

1 **Explaining Events** Explain what happened to the potato cells in Groups A, B, and C in your experiment. Include a discussion of the cell membrane and the process of osmosis.

Draw Conclusions

2 **Analyzing Results** Write a letter to Mr. Fries that explains your experimental method, results, and conclusion. Then, make a recommendation about how he should handle the potatoes so that they will stay fresh and crisp.

Chapter Review

15 **Concept Mapping** Use the following terms to create a concept map: *chromosome duplication, cytokinesis, prokaryote, mitosis, cell cycle, binary fission,* and *eukaryote.*

16 **Making Inferences** Which one of the plants pictured below was given water mixed with salt, and which one was given pure water? Explain how you know, and be sure to use the word *osmosis* in your answer.

17 **Identifying Relationships** Why would your muscle cells need to be supplied with more food when there is a lack of oxygen than when there is plenty of oxygen present?

18 **Applying Concepts** A parent cell has 10 chromosomes.

  a. Will the cell go through binary fission or mitosis and cytokinesis to produce new cells?

  b. How many chromosomes will each new cell have after the parent cell divides?

The picture below shows a cell. Use the picture below to answer the questions that follow.

19 Is the cell prokaryotic or eukaryotic?

20 Which stage of the cell cycle is this cell in?

21 How many chromatids are present? How many pairs of homologous chromosomes are present?

22 How many chromosomes will be present in each of the new cells after the cell divides?

Standardized Test Preparation

EOG Prep

READING

Read each of the passages below. Then, answer the questions that follow each passage.

Passage 1 Perhaps you have heard that jogging or some other kind of exercise "burns" a lot of Calories. The word *burn* is often used to describe what happens when your cells release stored energy from food. The burning of food in living cells is not the same as the burning of logs in a campfire. When logs burn, the energy stored in wood is released as thermal energy and light in a single reaction. But this kind of reaction is not the kind that happens in cells. Instead, the energy that cells get from food molecules is released at each step of a series of chemical reactions.

1. According to the passage, how do cells release energy from food?

  A in a single reaction

  B as thermal energy and light

  C in a series of reactions

  D by burning

2. Which of the following statements is a fact in the passage?

  F Wood burns better than food does.

  G Both food and wood have stored energy.

  H Food has more stored energy than wood does.

  I When it is burned, wood releases only thermal energy.

3. According to the passage, why might people be confused between what happens in a living cell and what happens in a campfire?

  A The word *burn* may describe both processes.

  B Thermal energy is released during both processes.

  C Wood can be burned and broken down by living cells.

  D Jogging and other exercises use energy.

Passage 2 The word *respiration* means "breathing," but cellular respiration is different from breathing. Breathing supplies your cells with the oxygen that they need for cellular respiration. Breathing also rids your body of carbon dioxide, which is a waste product of cellular respiration. Cellular respiration is the chemical process that releases energy from food. Most organisms obtain energy from food through cellular respiration. During cellular respiration, oxygen is used to break down food (glucose) into CO_2 and H_2O, and energy is released. In humans, most of the energy released is used to maintain body temperature.

1. According to the passage, what is glucose?

  A a type of chemical process

  B a type of waste product

  C a type of organism

  D a type of food

2. According to the passage, how does cellular respiration differ from breathing?

  F Breathing releases carbon dioxide, but cellular respiration releases oxygen.

  G Cellular respiration is a chemical process that uses oxygen to release energy from food, but breathing supplies cells with oxygen.

  H Cellular respiration requires oxygen, but breathing does not.

  I Breathing rids your body of waste products, but cellular respiration stores wastes.

3. According to the passage, how do humans use most of the energy released?

  A to break down food

  B to obtain oxygen

  C to maintain body temperature

  D to get rid of carbon dioxide

The graph below shows the cell cycle. Use this graph to answer the questions that follow.

The Cell Cycle

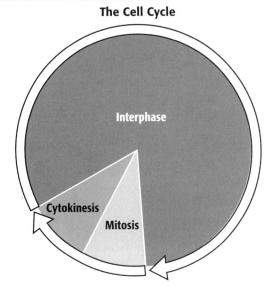

1. Which part of the cell cycle lasts longest?

   A interphase

   B mitosis

   C cytokinesis

   D There is not enough information to determine the answer.

2. Which of the following lists the parts of the cell cycle in the proper order?

   F mitosis, cytokinesis, mitosis

   G interphase, cytokinesis, mitosis

   H interphase, mitosis, interphase

   I mitosis, cytokinesis, interphase

3. Which part of the cell cycle is the briefest?

   A interphase

   B cell division

   C cytokinesis

   D There is not enough information to determine the answer.

4. Why is the cell cycle represented by a circle?

   F The cell cycle is a continuous process that begins again after it finishes.

   G The cell cycle happens only in cells that are round.

   H The cell cycle is a linear process.

   I The cell is in interphase for more than half of the cell cycle.

Read each question below, and choose the best answer.

1. A normal cell spends 90% of its time in interphase. How is 90% expressed as a fraction?

   A 3/4

   B 4/5

   C 85/100

   D 9/10

2. If a cell lived for 3 weeks and 4 days, how many days did it live?

   F 7

   G 11

   H 21

   I 25

3. How is $2 \times 3 \times 3 \times 3 \times 3$ expressed in exponential notation?

   A 3×2^4

   B 2×3^3

   C 3^4

   D 2×3^4

4. Cell A has 3 times as many chromosomes as cell B has. After cell B's chromosomes double during mitosis, cell B has 6 chromosomes. How many chromosomes does cell A have?

   F 3

   G 6

   H 9

   I 18

5. If $x + 2 = 3$, what does $x + 1$ equal?

   A 4

   B 3

   C 2

   D 1

6. If $3x + 2 = 26$, what does $x + 1$ equal?

   F 7

   G 8

   H 9

   I 10

Science in Action

Scientific Discoveries

Electrifying News About Microbes

Your car is out of fuel, and there isn't a service station in sight. This is not a problem! Your car's motor runs on electricity supplied by trillions of microorganisms. Some chemists think that "living" batteries will someday operate everything from watches to entire cities. A group of scientists at King's College in London have demonstrated that microorganisms can convert food into usable electrical energy. The microorganisms convert foods such as table sugar and molasses most efficiently. An efficient microorganism can convert more than 90% of its food into compounds that will fuel an electric reaction. A less efficient microbe will only convert 50% of its food into these types of compounds.

Math ACTIVITY

An efficient microorganism converts 90% of its food into fuel compounds, and an inefficient microorganism converts only 50%. If the inefficient microorganism makes 60 g of fuel out of a possible 120 g of food, how much fuel would an efficient microorganism make out of the same amount of food?

Science Fiction

"Contagion" by Katherine MacLean

A quarter mile from their spaceship, the *Explorer*, a team of doctors walk carefully along a narrow forest trail. Around them, the forest looks like a forest on Earth in the fall—the leaves are green, copper, purple, and fiery red. But it isn't fall. And the team is not on Earth.

Minos is enough like Earth to be the home of another colony of humans. But Minos might also be home to unknown organisms that could cause severe illness or death among the crew of *Explorer*. These diseases might be enough like diseases on Earth to be contagious, but they might be different enough to be very difficult to treat.

Something large moves among the shadows—it looks like a man. What happens next? Read Katherine's MacLean's "Contagion" in the *Holt Anthology of Science Fiction* to find out.

Language Arts ACTIVITY

WRITING SKILL Write two to three paragraphs that describe what you think might happen next in the story.

Jerry Yakel

Neuroscientist Jerry Yakel credits a sea slug for making him a neuroscientist. In a college class studying neurons, or nerve cells, Yakel got to see firsthand how ions move across the cell membrane of *Aplysia californica,* also known as a sea hare. He says, "I was totally hooked. I knew that I wanted to be a neurophysiologist then and there. I haven't wavered since."

Today, Yakel is a senior investigator for the National Institutes of Environmental Health Sciences, which is part of the U.S. government's National Institutes of Health. "We try to understand how the normal brain works," says Yakel of his team. "Then, when we look at a diseased brain, we train to understand where the deficits are. Eventually, someone will have an idea about a drug that will tweak the system in this or that way."

Yakel studies the ways in which nicotine affects the human brain. "It is one of the most prevalent and potent neurotoxins in the environment," says Yakel. "I'm amazed that it isn't higher on the list of worries for the general public."

Social Studies ACTiViTY

WRITING SKILL Research a famous or historical figure in science. Write a short report that outlines how he or she became interested in science.

go.hrw.com
To learn more about these Science in Action topics, visit go.hrw.com and type in the keyword **HL5ACTF.**

Current Science
Check out Current Science® articles related to this chapter by visiting go.hrw.com. Just type in the keyword **HL5CS04.**

15

Heredity

About the PHOTO

The guinea pig in the middle has dark fur, and the other two have light orange fur. The guinea pig on the right has longer hair than the other two. Why do these guinea pigs look different from one another? The length and color of their fur was determined before they were born. These are just two of the many traits determined by genetic information. Genetic information is passed on from parents to their offspring.

PRE-READING ACTIVITY

FOLDNOTES **Key-Term Fold** Before you read the chapter, create the FoldNote entitled "Key-Term Fold" described in the **Study Skills** section of the Appendix. Write a key term from the chapter on each tab of the key-term fold. Under each tab, write the definition of the key term.

STARTUP ACTIVITY

Clothing Combos

How do the same parents have children with many different traits?

Procedure

1. Gather **three boxes**. Put **five hats** in the first box, **five gloves** in the second, and **five scarves** in the third.

2. Without looking in the boxes, select one item from each box. Repeat this process, five students at a time, until the entire class has picked "an outfit." Record what outfit each student chooses.

Analysis

1. Were any two outfits exactly alike? Did you see all possible combinations? Explain your answer.

2. Choose a partner. Using your outfits, how many different combinations could you make by giving a third person one hat, one glove, and one scarf? How is this process like parents passing traits to their children?

3. After completing this activity, why do you think parents often have children who look very different from each other?

Mendel and His Peas

Why don't you look like a rhinoceros? The answer to this question seems simple: Neither of your parents is a rhinoceros. But there is more to this answer than meets the eye.

As it turns out, **heredity,** or the passing of traits from parents to offspring, is more complicated than you might think. For example, you might have curly hair, while both of your parents have straight hair. You might have blue eyes even though both of your parents have brown eyes. How does this happen? People have investigated this question for a long time. About 150 years ago, Gregor Mendel performed important experiments. His discoveries helped scientists begin to find some answers to these questions.

✓ **Reading Check** What is heredity? (*See the Appendix for answers to Reading Checks.*)

READING WARM-UP

Objectives

● Explain the relationship between traits and heredity.

● Describe the experiments of Gregor Mendel.

● Explain the difference between dominant and recessive traits.

Terms to Learn

heredity
dominant trait
recessive trait

READING STRATEGY

Brainstorming The key idea of this section is heredity. Brainstorm words and phrases related to heredity.

heredity the passing of genetic traits from parent to offspring

Who Was Gregor Mendel?

Gregor Mendel, shown in **Figure 1,** was born in 1822 in Heinzendorf, Austria. Mendel grew up on a farm and learned a lot about flowers and fruit trees.

When he was 21 years old, Mendel entered a monastery. The monks taught science and performed many scientific experiments. From there, Mendel was sent to Vienna where he could receive training in teaching. However, Mendel had trouble taking tests. Although he did well in school, he was unable to pass the final exam. He returned to the monastery and put most of his energy into research. Mendel discovered the principles of heredity in the monastery garden.

Unraveling the Mystery

From working with plants, Mendel knew that the patterns of inheritance were not always clear. For example, sometimes a trait that appeared in one generation (parents) was not present in the next generation (offspring). In the generation after that, though, the trait showed up again. Mendel noticed these kinds of patterns in several other living things, too. Mendel wanted to learn more about what caused these patterns.

To keep his investigation simple, Mendel decided to study only one kind of organism. Because he had studied garden pea plants before, they seemed like a good choice.

Figure 1 *Gregor Mendel discovered the principles of heredity while studying pea plants.*

Self-Pollinating Peas

In fact, garden peas were a good choice for several reasons. Pea plants grow quickly, and there are many different kinds available. They are also able to self-pollinate. A *self-pollinating plant* has both male and female reproductive structures. So, pollen from one flower can fertilize the ovule of the same flower or the ovule of another flower on the same plant. The flower on the right side of **Figure 2** is self-pollinating.

Why is it important that pea plants can self-pollinate? Because eggs (in an ovule) and sperm (in pollen) from the same plant combine to make a new plant, Mendel was able to grow true-breeding plants. When a *true-breeding plant* self-pollinates, all of its offspring will have the same trait as the parent. For example, a true-breeding plant with purple flowers will always have offspring with purple flowers.

Pea plants can also cross-pollinate. In *cross-pollination,* pollen from one plant fertilizes the ovule of a flower on a different plant. There are several ways that this can happen. Pollen may be carried by insects to a flower on a different plant. Pollen can also be carried by the wind from one flower to another. The left side of **Figure 2** shows these kinds of cross-pollination.

Self-pollination

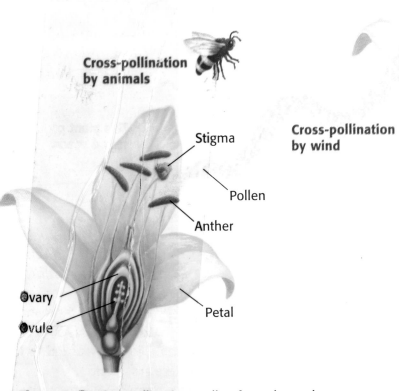

Cross-pollination by animals

Stigma

Cross-pollination by wind

Pollen

Anther

Ovary

Ovule

Petal

Figure 2 *During pollination, pollen from the anthers (male) is transferred to the stigma (female). Fertilization occurs when a sperm from the pollen travels through the stigma and enters the egg in an ovule.*

Seed Shape

Round   Wrinkled

Plant Height

Tall   Short

Flower Color

Purple   White

Figure 3 *These are some of the plant characteristics that Mendel studied.*

Characteristics

Mendel studied only one characteristic at a time. A *characteristic* is a feature that has different forms in a population. For example, hair color is a characteristic in humans. The different forms, such as brown or red hair, are called *traits*. Mendel used plants that had different traits for each of the characteristics he studied. For instance, for the characteristic of flower color, he chose plants that had purple flowers and plants that had white flowers. Three of the characteristics Mendel studied are shown in **Figure 3.**

Mix and Match

Mendel was careful to use plants that were true breeding for each of the traits he was studying. By doing so, he would know what to expect if his plants were to self-pollinate. He decided to find out what would happen if he bred, or crossed, two plants that had different traits of a single characteristic. To be sure the plants cross-pollinated, he removed the anthers of one plant so that the plant could not self-pollinate. Then, he used pollen from another plant to fertilize the plant, as shown in **Figure 4.** This step allowed Mendel to select which plants would be crossed to produce offspring.

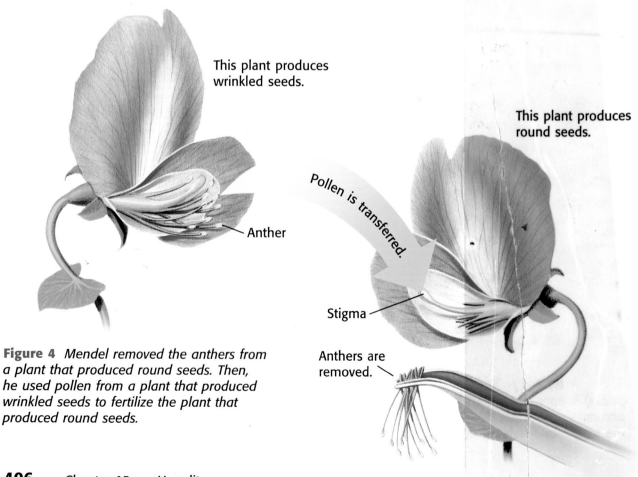

This plant produces wrinkled seeds.

This plant produces round seeds.

Pollen is transferred.

Anther

Stigma

Anthers are removed.

Figure 4 *Mendel removed the anthers from a plant that produced round seeds. Then, he used pollen from a plant that produced wrinkled seeds to fertilize the plant that produced round seeds.*

Mendel's First Experiments

In his first experiments, Mendel crossed pea plants to study seven different characteristics. In each cross, Mendel used plants that were true breeding for different traits for each characteristic. For example, he crossed plants that had purple flowers with plants that had white flowers. This cross is shown in the first part of **Figure 5.** The offspring from such a cross are called *first-generation plants.* All of the first-generation plants in this cross had purple flowers. Are you surprised by the results? What happened to the trait for white flowers?

Mendel got similar results for each cross. One trait was always present in the first generation, and the other trait seemed to disappear. Mendel chose to call the trait that appeared the **dominant trait.** Because the other trait seemed to fade into the background, Mendel called it the **recessive trait.** (To *recede* means "to go away or back off.") Dominant and recessive traits appear in all organisms, including humans. For example, dark hair is a dominant trait and light hair is a recessive trait.

Mendel's Second Experiments

To find out what happens to recessive traits, Mendel did more experiments. He allowed the first-generation plants to self-pollinate. **Figure 5** shows what happened when a first-generation plant with purple flowers could self-pollinate. The recessive trait for white flowers reappeared in the second generation. Mendel did this same experiment on each of the seven characteristics. In each case, some of the second-generation plants had the recessive trait.

✓ Reading Check Describe Mendel's second set of experiments.

dominant trait the trait observed in the first generation when parents that have different traits are bred

recessive trait a trait that reappears in the second generation after disappearing in the first generation when parents with different traits are bred

Parent Generation

Pollen transfer

First Generation
All flowers are purple.

A mature plant is allowed to self-pollinate.

Second Generation
For every three plants with purple flowers, there is one plant with white flowers.

Figure 5 *Mendel used the pollen from a plant with purple flowers to fertilize a plant with white flowers. Then, he allowed the offspring to self-pollinate.*

Ratios in Mendel's Experiments

Mendel then decided to count the number of plants with each trait that turned up in the second generation. He hoped that this might help him explain his results. Take a look at Mendel's results, shown in **Table 1.**

As you can see, the recessive trait did not show up as often as the dominant trait. Mendel decided to figure out the ratio of dominant traits to recessive traits. A *ratio* is a relationship between two different numbers that is often expressed as a fraction. Calculate the dominant-to-recessive ratio for each characteristic. (If you need help, look at the Math Practice at left.) Do you notice anything interesting about the ratios? Round to the nearest whole number. Are the ratios all the same, or are they different?

✓ **Reading Check** What is a ratio?

Table 1 Mendel's Results

Characteristic	Dominant traits		Recessive traits		Ratio
Flower color	705 purple		224 white		3.15:1
Seed color	6,002 yellow		2,001 green		?
Seed shape	5,474 round		1,850 wrinkled		?
Pod color	428 green		152 yellow		?
Pod shape	882 smooth		299 bumpy		?
Flower position	651 along stem		207 at tip		?
Plant height	787 tall		277 short		?

Gregor Mendel—Gone but Not Forgotten

Mendel realized that his results could be explained only if each plant had two sets of instructions for each characteristic. Each parent would then donate one set of instructions. In 1865, Mendel published his findings. But good ideas are sometimes overlooked or misunderstood at first. It wasn't until after his death, more than 30 years later, that Mendel's work was widely recognized. Once Mendel's ideas were rediscovered and understood, the door was opened to modern genetics. Genetic research, as shown in **Figure 6,** is one of the fastest changing fields in science today.

Figure 6 *This researcher is continuing the work started by Gregor Mendel more than 100 years ago.*

SECTION Review

Summary

- Heredity is the passing of traits from parents to offspring.

- Gregor Mendel made carefully planned experiments using pea plants that could self-pollinate.

- When parents with different traits are bred, dominant traits are always present in the first generation. Recessive traits are not visible in the first generation but reappear in the second generation.

- Mendel found a 3:1 ratio of dominant-to-recessive traits in the second generation.

Using Key Terms

1. Use each of the following terms in a separate sentence: *heredity, dominant trait,* and *recessive trait.*

Understanding Key Ideas

2. A plant that has both male and female reproductive structures is able to
   a. self-replicate.
   b. self-pollinate.
   c. change colors.
   d. None of the above

3. Explain the difference between self-pollination and cross-pollination.

4. What is the difference between a trait and a characteristic? Give one example of each.

5. Describe Mendel's first set of experiments.

6. Describe Mendel's second set of experiments.

Math Skills

7. In a bag of chocolate candies, there are 21 brown candies and 6 green candies. What is the ratio of brown to green? What is the ratio of green to brown?

Critical Thinking

8. **Predicting Consequences** Gregor Mendel used only true-breeding plants. If he had used plants that were not true breeding, do you think he would have discovered dominant and recessive traits? Explain.

9. **Applying Concepts** In cats, there are two types of ears: normal and curly. A curly-eared cat mated with a normal-eared cat, and all of the kittens had curly ears. Are curly ears a dominant or recessive trait? Explain.

10. **Identifying Relationships** List three other fields of study that use ratios.

Developed and maintained by the National Science Teachers Association

For a variety of links related to this chapter, go to www.scilinks.org

Topic: Heredity; Dominant and Recessive Traits

SciLinks code: HSM0738; HSM0423

Traits and Inheritance

Mendel calculated the ratio of dominant traits to recessive traits. He found a ratio of 3:1. What did this tell him about how traits are passed from parents to offspring?

Objectives

- Explain how genes and alleles are related to genotype and phenotype.
- Use the information in a Punnett square.
- Explain how probability can be used to predict possible genotypes in offspring.
- Describe three exceptions to Mendel's observations.

Terms to Learn

gene   genotype
allele   probability
phenotype

READING STRATEGY

Paired Summarizing Read this section silently. In pairs, take turns summarizing the material. Stop to discuss ideas that seem confusing.

gene one set of instructions for an inherited trait

allele one of the alternative forms of a gene that governs a characteristic, such as hair color

phenotype an organism's appearance or other detectable characteristic

Figure 1 *Albinism is an inherited disorder that affects a person's phenotype in many ways.*

A Great Idea

Mendel knew from his experiments with pea plants that there must be two sets of instructions for each characteristic. The first-generation plants carried the instructions for both the dominant trait and the recessive trait. Scientists now call these instructions for an inherited trait **genes.** Each parent gives one set of genes to the offspring. The offspring then has two forms of the same gene for every characteristic—one from each parent. The different forms (often dominant and recessive) of a gene are known as **alleles** (uh LEELZ). Dominant alleles are shown with a capital letter. Recessive alleles are shown with a lowercase letter.

✓ **Reading Check** What is the difference between a gene and an allele? (*See the Appendix for answers to Reading Checks.*)

Phenotype

Genes affect the traits of offspring. An organism's appearance is known as its **phenotype** (FEE noh TIEP). In pea plants, possible phenotypes for the characteristic of flower color would be purple flowers or white flowers. For seed color, yellow and green seeds are the different phenotypes.

Phenotypes of humans are much more complicated than those of peas. Look at **Figure 1** below. The man has an inherited condition called *albinism* (AL buh NIZ uhm). Albinism prevents hair, skin, and eyes from having normal coloring.

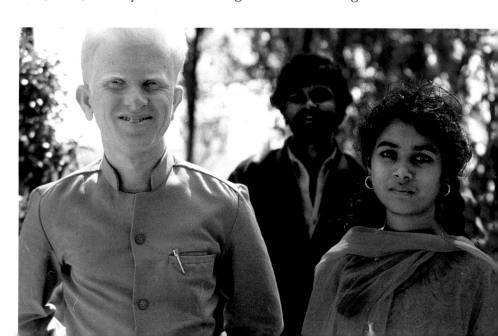

Genotype

Both inherited alleles together form an organism's **genotype.** Because the allele for purple flowers (*P*) is dominant, only one *P* allele is needed for the plant to have purple flowers. A plant with two dominant or two recessive alleles is said to be *homozygous* (HOH moh ZIE guhs). A plant that has the genotype *Pp* is said to be *heterozygous* (HET uhr OH ZIE guhs).

Punnett Squares

A Punnett square is used to organize all the possible combinations of offspring from particular parents. The alleles for a true-breeding, purple-flowered plant are written as *PP*. The alleles for a true-breeding, white-flowered plant are written as *pp*. The Punnett square for this cross is shown in **Figure 2.** All of the offspring have the same genotype: *Pp*. The dominant allele, *P*, in each genotype ensures that all of the offspring will be purple-flowered plants. The recessive allele, *p*, may be passed on to the next generation. This Punnett square shows the results of Mendel's first experiments.

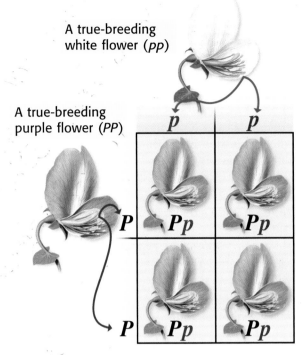

Figure 2 *All of the offspring for this cross have the same genotype—Pp.*

genotype the entire genetic makeup of an organism; also the combination of genes for one or more specific traits

Making a Punnett Square

1. Draw a square, and divide it into four sections.
2. Write the letters that represent alleles from one parent along the top of the box.
3. Write the letters that represent alleles from the other parent along the side of the box.
4. The cross shown at right is between two plants that produce round seeds. The genotype for each is *Rr*. Round seeds are dominant, and wrinkled seeds are recessive. Follow the arrows to see how the inside of the box was filled. The resulting alleles inside the box show all the possible genotypes for the offspring from this cross. What would the phenotypes for these offspring be?

Taking Your Chances

You have two guinea pigs. Each has brown fur and the genotype *Bb*. You want to predict what their offspring might look like. Try this to find out.

1. Stick a **piece of masking tape** on each side of **two quarters.**

2. Label one side with a capital *B* and the other side with a lowercase *b*.

3. Toss both coins 10 times, making note of your results each time.

4. How many times did you get the *bb* combination?

5. What is the probability that the next toss will result in *bb*?

6. What are the chances that the guinea pigs' offspring will have white fur (with the genotype *bb*)?

Figure 3 *This Punnett square shows the possible results from the cross* Pp × Pp.

More Evidence for Inheritance

In Mendel's second experiments, he allowed the first generation plants to self-pollinate. **Figure 3** shows a self-pollination cross of a plant with the genotype *Pp*. What are the possible genotypes of the offspring?

Notice that one square shows the genotype *Pp*, while another shows *pP*. These are exactly the same genotype. The other possible genotypes of the offspring are *PP* and *pp*. The combinations *PP*, *Pp*, and *pP* have the same phenotype—purple flowers. This is because each contains at least one dominant allele (*P*).

Only one combination, *pp*, produces plants that have white flowers. The ratio of dominant to recessive is 3:1, just as Mendel calculated from his data.

What Are the Chances?

Each parent has two alleles for each gene. When these alleles are different, as in *Pp*, offspring are equally likely to receive either allele. Think of a coin toss. There is a 50% chance you'll get heads and a 50% chance you'll get tails. The chance of receiving one allele or another is as random as a coin toss.

Probability

The mathematical chance that something will happen is known as **probability.** Probability is most often written as a fraction or percentage. If you toss a coin, the probability of tossing tails is 1/2—you will get tails half the time.

Reading Check What is probability?

probability the likelihood that a possible future event will occur in any given instance of the event

Probability If you roll a pair of dice, what is the probability that you will roll 2 threes?

Step 1: Count the number of faces on a single die. Put this number in the denominator: 6.

Step 2: Count how many ways you can roll a three with one die. Put this number in the numerator: 1/6.

Step 3: To find the probability that you will throw 2 threes, multiply the probability of throwing the first three by the probability of throwing the second three: 1/6 × 1/6 = 1/36.

Now It's Your Turn

If you roll a single die, what is the probability that you will roll an even number?

Calculating Probabilities

To find the probability that you will toss two heads in a row, multiply the probability of tossing the first head (1/2) by the probability of tossing the second head (1/2). The probability of tossing two heads in a row is 1/4.

Genotype Probability

To have white flowers, a pea plant must receive a *p* allele from each parent. Each offspring of a *Pp* × *Pp* cross has a 50% chance of receiving either allele from either parent. So, the probability of inheriting two *p* alleles is 1/2 × 1/2, which equals 1/4, or 25%. Traits in pea plants are easy to predict because there are only two choices for each trait, such as purple or white flowers and round or wrinkled seeds. Look at **Figure 4.** Do you see only two distinct choices for fur color?

Figure 4 *These kittens inherited one allele from their mother for each trait.*

CONNECTION TO Chemistry

Round and Wrinkled Round seeds may look better, but wrinkled seeds taste sweeter. The dominant allele for seed shape, *R*, causes sugar to be changed into starch (which is a storage molecule for sugar). This change makes the seed round. Seeds with the genotype *rr* do not make or store this starch. Because the sugar has not been changed into starch, the seed tastes sweeter. If you had a pea plant with round seeds (*Rr*), what would you cross it with to get some offspring with wrinkled seeds? Draw a Punnett square showing your cross.

ACTIVITY

More About Traits

Things are often more complicated than they first appear to be. Gregor Mendel uncovered the basic principles of how genes are passed from one generation to the next. But scientists have found exceptions to Mendel's principles.

Incomplete Dominance

Since Mendel's discoveries, researchers have found that sometimes one trait is not completely dominant over another. These traits do not blend together, but each allele has its own degree of influence. This is known as *incomplete dominance*. A curly-haired parent and a straight-haired parent have wavy-haired children because of incomplete dominance.

A classic example of incomplete dominance is found in the snapdragon flower. **Figure 5** shows a cross between a true-breeding red snapdragon (R^1R^1) and a true-breeding white snapdragon (R^2R^2). As you can see, all of the possible phenotypes for their offspring are pink because both alleles of the gene have some degree of influence.

Figure 5 *Cross-breeding two true-breeding snapdragons provides a good example of incomplete dominance.*

Reading Check What is incomplete dominance?

One Gene, Many Traits

Sometimes one gene influences more than one trait. An example of this phenomenon is shown by the white tiger in **Figure 6.** The white fur is caused by a single gene, but this gene influences more than just fur color. If you look closely, you'll see that the tiger has blue eyes. Here, the gene that controls fur color also influences eye color.

Many Genes, One Trait

Some traits, such as the color of your skin, hair, and eyes, are the result of several genes acting together. Therefore, it's difficult to tell if some traits are the result of a dominant or a recessive gene. Different combinations of alleles result in different eye-color shades.

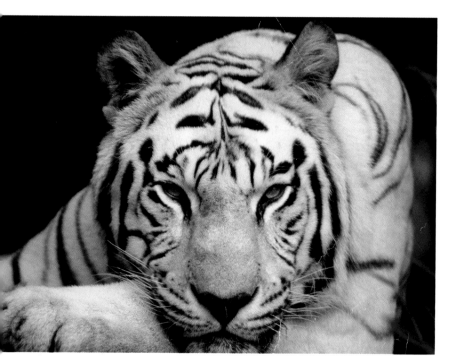

Figure 6 *The gene that gave this tiger white fur also influenced its eye color.*

The Importance of Environment

Genes aren't the only influences on traits. A guinea pig could have the genes for long fur, but its fur could be cut. In the same way, your environment influences how you grow. Your genes may make it possible that you will grow to be tall, but you need a healthy diet to reach your full potential height. Lifestyle choices can also affect a person's traits. The foods a person chooses to eat and the activities a person chooses to take part in affect how that person grows and develops. Choosing healthy foods and healthy activities can help you develop healthy traits. Together, the combination of genes, environmental factors, and lifestyle choices determine an individual's characteristics.

SECTION Review

Summary

- Instructions for an inherited trait are called *genes*. For each gene, there are two alleles, one inherited from each parent. Both alleles make up an organism's genotype. Phenotype is an organism's appearance.

- Punnett squares show all possible offspring genotypes.

- Probability can be used to describe possible outcomes in offspring and the likelihood of each outcome.

- Incomplete dominance occurs when one allele is not completely dominant over the other allele.

- Some genes influence more than one trait.

Using Key Terms

1. Use the following terms in the same sentence: *gene* and *allele*.

2. In your own words, write a definition for each of the following terms: *genotype* and *phenotype*.

Understanding Key Ideas

3. Use a Punnett square to determine the possible genotypes of the offspring of a *BB* × *Bb* cross.
   a. all *BB*   c. *BB, Bb, bb*
   b. *BB, Bb*   d. all *bb*

4. How are genes and alleles related to genotype and phenotype?

5. Describe three exceptions to Mendel's observations.

Math Skills

6. What is the probability that the offspring of a homozygous dominant parent and a heterozygous parent will show a recessive phenotype?

Critical Thinking

7. **Applying Concepts** The allele for a cleft chin, *C*, is dominant among humans. What are the results of a cross between parents with genotypes *Cc* and *cc*?

Interpreting Graphics

The Punnett square below shows the alleles for fur color in rabbits. Black fur, *B*, is dominant over white fur, *b*.

8. Given the combinations shown, what are the genotypes of the parents?

9. If black fur had incomplete dominance over white fur, what color would the offspring be?

Meiosis

Where are genes located? How do genes pass information? Understanding reproduction can provide some answers.

There are two kinds of reproduction: asexual and sexual. Asexual reproduction results in offspring with genotypes that are exact copies of their parent's genotype. Sexual reproduction produces offspring that share traits with their parents but are not exactly like either parent. In fact, offspring that share the same two parents vary a lot from each other, as well.

Asexual Reproduction

In *asexual reproduction,* only one parent cell is needed. The structures inside the cell are copied, and then the parent cell divides, making two exact copies. This type of cell reproduction is known as *mitosis.* Most of the cells in your body and most single-celled organisms reproduce in this way.

Sexual Reproduction

In sexual reproduction, two parent cells join together to form offspring that are different from both parents. The parent cells are called *sex cells.* Sex cells are different from ordinary body cells. Human body cells have 46, or 23 pairs of, chromosomes. One set of human chromosomes is shown in **Figure 1.** Chromosomes that carry the same sets of genes are called **homologous** (hoh MAHL uh guhs) **chromosomes.** Imagine a pair of shoes. Each shoe is like a homologous chromosome. The pair represents a homologous pair of chromosomes. But human sex cells are different. They have 23 chromosomes—half the usual number. Each sex cell has only one of the chromosomes from each homologous pair. Sex cells have only one "shoe."

Figure 1 *Human body cells have 23 pairs of chromosomes. One member of a pair of homologous chromosomes is shown below.*

Meiosis

Sex cells are made during meiosis (mie OH sis). **Meiosis** is a copying process that produces cells with half the usual number of chromosomes. Each sex cell receives one-half of each homologous pair. For example, a human egg cell has 23 chromosomes, and a sperm cell has 23 chromosomes. The new cell that forms when an egg cell and a sperm cell join has 46 chromosomes.

Because the genes of the parents are sorted and recombined randomly in the offspring, the offspring is different from the parents. If the same parents have more offspring, the genes will be sorted again, and these offspring will be different from each other as well as from the parents.

✓ Reading Check How many chromosomes does a human egg cell have? (*See the Appendix for answers to Reading Checks.*)

Genes and Chromosomes

What does all of this have to do with the location of genes? Not long after Mendel's work was rediscovered, a graduate student named Walter Sutton made an important observation. Sutton was studying sperm cells in grasshoppers. Sutton knew of Mendel's studies, which showed that the egg and sperm must each contribute the same amount of information to the offspring. That was the only way the 3:1 ratio found in the second generation could be explained. Sutton also knew from his own studies that although eggs and sperm were different, they did have something in common: Their chromosomes were located inside a nucleus. Using his observations of meiosis, his understanding of Mendel's work, and some creative thinking, Sutton proposed something very important:

Genes are located on chromosomes!

Understanding meiosis was critical to finding the location of genes. Before you learn about meiosis, review mitosis, shown in **Figure 2.** Meiosis is outlined in **Figure 3** on the next two pages.

Figure 2   Mitosis Revisited

❶ Each chromosome is copied.

❷ The chromosomes thicken and shorten. Each chromosome consists of two identical copies, called *chromatids.*

❸ The nuclear membrane dissolves. The chromatids line up along the equator (center) of the cell.

❹ The chromatids pull apart.

❺ The nuclear membrane forms around the separated chromatids. The chromosomes unwind, and the cell divides.

❻ The result is two identical copies of the original cell.

The Steps of Meiosis

During mitosis, chromosomes are copied once, and then the nucleus divides once. During meiosis, chromosomes are copied once, and then the nucleus divides twice. The resulting sperm and eggs have half the number of chromosomes of a normal body cell. **Figure 3** shows all eight steps of meiosis. Read about each step as you look at the figure. Different types of living things have different numbers of chromosomes. In this illustration, only four chromosomes are shown.

✓ **Reading Check** How many cells are made from one parent cell during meiosis?

Figure 3 Steps of Meiosis

Read about each step as you look at the diagram. Different types of living things have different numbers of chromosomes. In this diagram, only four chromosomes are shown.

One pair of homologous chromosomes

Two chromatids

1 Before meiosis begins, the chromosomes are in a threadlike form. Each chromosome makes an exact copy of itself, forming two halves called *chromatids*. The chromosomes then thicken and shorten into a form that is visible under a microscope. The nuclear membrane disappears.

2 Each chromosome is now made up of two identical chromatids. Similar chromosomes pair with one another, and the paired homologous chromosomes line up at the equator of the cell.

3 The chromosomes separate from their homologous partners and then move to opposite ends of the cell.

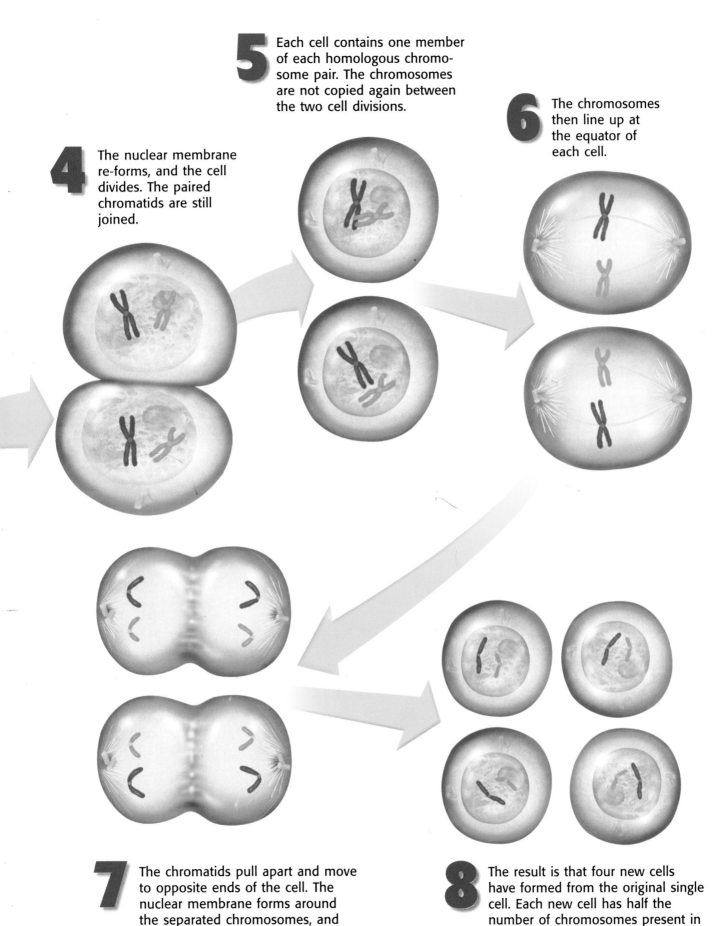

5 Each cell contains one member of each homologous chromosome pair. The chromosomes are not copied again between the two cell divisions.

6 The chromosomes then line up at the equator of each cell.

4 The nuclear membrane re-forms, and the cell divides. The paired chromatids are still joined.

7 The chromatids pull apart and move to opposite ends of the cell. The nuclear membrane forms around the separated chromosomes, and the cells divide.

8 The result is that four new cells have formed from the original single cell. Each new cell has half the number of chromosomes present in the original cell.

For another activity related
to this chapter, go to
go.hrw.com and type in the
keyword **HL5HERW**.

Meiosis and Mendel

As Walter Sutton figured out, the steps in meiosis explained Mendel's results. **Figure 4** shows what happens to a pair of homologous chromosomes during meiosis and fertilization. The cross shown is between a plant that is true breeding for round seeds and a plant that is true breeding for wrinkled seeds.

Each fertilized egg in the first generation had one dominant allele and one recessive allele for seed shape. Only one genotype was possible because all sperm formed by the male parent during meiosis had the wrinkled-seed allele, and all of the female parent's eggs had the round-seed allele. Meiosis also helped explain other inherited characteristics.

Figure 4 **Meiosis and Dominance**

Male Parent In the plant-cell nucleus below, each homologous chromosome has an allele for seed shape, and each allele carries the same instructions: to make wrinkled seeds.

Female Parent In the plant-cell nucleus below, each homologous chromosome has an allele for seed shape, and each allele carries the same instructions: to make round seeds.

Wrinkled-seed alleles (*rr*)

Round-seed alleles (*RR*)

Meiosis

Meiosis

Sperm cell nucleus

Egg cell nucleus

ⓐ Following **meiosis,** each sperm cell has a recessive allele for wrinkled seeds, and each egg cell has a dominant allele for round seeds.

Wrinkled-seed allele (*r*)

Round-seed allele (*R*)

Fertilization

ⓑ Fertilization of any egg by any sperm results in the same genotype (*Rr*) and the same phenotype (round). This result is exactly what Mendel found in his studies.

Wrinkled-seed allele (*r*)

Round-seed allele (*R*)

First generation (*Rr*)

Sex Chromosomes

Information contained on chromosomes determines many of our traits. **Sex chromosomes** carry genes that determine sex. In humans, females have two X chromosomes. But human males have one X chromosome and one Y chromosome.

During meiosis, one of each of the chromosome pairs ends up in a sex cell. Females have two X chromosomes in each body cell. When meiosis produces the egg cells, each egg gets one X chromosome. Males have both an X chromosome and a Y chromosome in each body cell. Meiosis produces sperm with either an X or a Y chromosome. An egg fertilized by a sperm with an X chromosome will produce a female. If the sperm contains a Y chromosome, the offspring will be male, as shown in **Figure 5.**

Figure 5 *Egg and sperm combine to form either the XX or XY combination.*

Sex-Linked Disorders

The Y chromosome does not carry all of the genes of an X chromosome. Females have two X chromosomes, so they carry two copies of each gene found on the X chromosome. This makes a backup gene available if one becomes damaged. Males have only one copy of each gene on their one X chromosome. The genes for certain disorders, such as colorblindness, are carried on the X chromosome. These disorders are called *sex-linked disorders*. Because the gene for such disorders is recessive, men are more likely to have sex-linked disorders.

People who are colorblind can have trouble distinguishing between shades of red and green. To help the colorblind, some cities have added shapes to their street lights, as shown in **Figure 6.** Hemophilia (HEE moh FIL ee uh) is another sex-linked disorder. Hemophilia prevents blood from clotting, and people with hemophilia bleed for a long time after small cuts. Hemophilia can be fatal.

sex chromosome one of the pair of chromosomes that determine the sex of an individual

Figure 6 *This stoplight in Canada is designed to help the colorblind see signals easily. This photograph was taken over a few minutes to show all three shapes.*

Figure 7 Pedigree for a Recessive Disease

☐ Males   ◯ Females

●┬☐ Vertical lines connect
◗ children to their parents.

■ or ● A solid square or circle
indicates that the person
has a certain trait.

◤ or ◑ A half-filled square or
circle indicates that the
person is a carrier of
the trait.

Generation

I

II

III

IV

pedigree a diagram that shows the occurrence of a genetic trait in several generations of a family

Genetic Counseling

Hemophilia and other genetic disorders can be traced through a family tree. If people are worried that they might pass a disease to their children, they may consult a genetic counselor. These counselors often make use of a diagram known as a **pedigree,** which is a tool for tracing a trait through generations of a family. By making a pedigree, a counselor can often predict whether a person is a carrier of a hereditary disease. The pedigree shown in **Figure 7** traces a disease called *cystic fibrosis* (SIS tik FIE broh sis). Cystic fibrosis causes serious lung problems. People with this disease have inherited two recessive alleles. Both parents need to be carriers of the gene for the disease to show up in their children.

Pedigrees can be drawn up to trace any trait through a family tree. You could even draw a pedigree that would show how you inherited your hair color. Many different pedigrees could be drawn for a typical family.

Selective Breeding

For thousands of years, humans have seen the benefits of the careful breeding of plants and animals. In *selective breeding*, organisms with desirable characteristics are mated. You have probably enjoyed the benefits of selective breeding, although you may not have realized it. For example, you have probably eaten an egg from a chicken that was bred to produce more eggs. Your pet dog may be a result of selective breeding. Roses, like the one shown in **Figure 8,** have been selectively bred to produce large flowers. Wild roses are much smaller and have fewer petals than roses that you could buy at a nursery.

Figure 8 *Roses have been selectively bred to create large, bright flowers.*

Summary

- In mitosis, chromosomes are copied once, and then the nucleus divides once. In meiosis, chromosomes are copied once, and then the nucleus divides twice.

- The process of meiosis produces sex cells, which have half the number of chromosomes. These two halves combine during reproduction.

- In humans, females have two X chromosomes. So, each egg contains one X chromosome. Males have both an X and a Y chromosome. So, each sperm cell contains either an X or a Y chromosome.

- Sex-linked disorders occur in males more often than in females. Colorblindness and hemophilia are examples of sex-linked disorders.

- A pedigree is a diagram used to trace a trait through many generations of a family.

Using Key Terms

In each of the following sentences, replace the incorrect term with the correct term from the word bank.

> pedigree   homologous chromosomes
>
> meiosis   mitosis

1. During fertilization, chromosomes are copied, and then the nucleus divides twice.

2. A Punnett square is used to show how inherited traits move through a family.

3. During meiosis, sex cells line up in the middle of the cell.

Understanding Key Ideas

4. Genes are found on
   a. chromosomes.
   b. proteins.
   c. alleles.
   d. sex cells.

5. If there are 14 chromosomes in pea plant cells, how many chromosomes are present in a sex cell of a pea plant?

6. Draw the eight steps of meiosis. Label one chromosome, and show its position in each step.

7. What alleles must be present in the parents of a child that is born with cystic fibrosis?

Interpreting Graphics

Use this pedigree to answer the question below.

8. Is this disorder sex linked? Explain your reasoning.

Critical Thinking

9. **Identifying Relationships** Put the following in order of smallest to largest: chromosome, gene, and cell.

10. **Applying Concepts** A pea plant has purple flowers. What alleles for flower color could the sex cells carry?

SCi LINKS®

NSTA

Developed and maintained by the
National Science Teachers Association

For a variety of links related to this chapter, go to www.scilinks.org

Topic: Meiosis; Genetic Diseases, Screening, Counseling
SciLinks code: HSM0935; HSM0651

OBJECTIVES

Build models to further your understanding of inheritance.

Examine the traits of a population of offspring.

MATERIALS

- allele sacks (14) (supplied by your teacher)
- gumdrops, green and black (feet)
- map pins (eyes)
- marshmallows, large (head and body segments)
- pipe cleaners (tails)
- pushpins, green and blue (noses)
- scissors
- toothpicks, red and green (antennae)

SAFETY

Bug Builders, Inc.

Imagine that you are a designer for a toy company that makes toy alien bugs. The president of Bug Builders, Inc., wants new versions of the wildly popular Space Bugs, but he wants to use the bug parts that are already in the warehouse. It's your job to come up with a new bug design. You have studied how traits are passed from one generation to another. You will use this knowledge to come up with new combinations of traits and assemble the bug parts in new ways. Model A and Model B, shown below, will act as the "parent" bugs.

Ask a Question

1. If there are two forms of each of the seven traits, then how many possible combinations are there?

Form a Hypothesis

2. Write a hypothesis that is a possible answer to the question above. Explain your reasoning.

Test the Hypothesis

3. Your teacher will display 14 allele sacks. The sacks will contain slips of paper with capital or lowercase letters on them. Take one piece of paper from each sack. (Remember: Capital letters represent dominant alleles, and lowercase letters represent recessive alleles.) One allele is from "Mom," and one allele is from "Dad." After you have recorded the alleles you have drawn, place the slips of paper back into the sack.

Model A ("Mom")
- red antennae
- 3 body segments
- curly tail
- 2 pairs of legs
- green nose
- black feet
- 3 eyes

Model B ("Dad")
- green antennae
- 2 body segments
- straight tail
- 3 pairs of legs
- blue nose
- green feet
- 2 eyes

Bug Family Traits				
Trait	Model A "Mom" allele	Model B "Dad" allele	New model "Baby" genotype	New model "Baby" phenotype
Antennae color				
Number of body segments				
Tail shape				
Number of leg pairs				
Nose color				
Foot color				
Number of eyes				

DO NOT WRITE IN BOOK

④ Create a table like the one above. Fill in the first two columns with the alleles that you selected from the sacks. Next, fill in the third column with the genotype of the new model ("Baby").

⑤ Use the information below to fill in the last column of the table.

Genotypes and Phenotypes	
RR or *Rr*—red antennae	*rr*—green antennae
SS or *Ss*—3 body segments	*ss*—2 body segments
CC or *Cc*—curly tail	*cc*—straight tail
LL or *Ll*—3 pairs of legs	*ll*—2 pairs of legs
BB or *Bb*—blue nose	*bb*—green nose
GG or *Gg*—green feet	*gg*—black feet
EE or *Ee*—2 eyes	*ee*—3 eyes

⑥ Now that you have filled out your table, you are ready to pick the parts you need to assemble your bug. (Toothpicks can be used to hold the head and body segments together and as legs to attach the feet to the body.)

Analyze the Results

① **Organizing Data** Take a poll of the traits of the offspring. What are the ratios for each trait?

② **Examining Data** Do any of the new models look exactly like the parents? Explain.

Draw Conclusions

③ **Interpreting Information** What are the possible genotypes of the parent bugs?

④ **Making Predictions** How many different genotypes are possible in the offspring?

Applying Your Data

Find a mate for your "Baby" bug. What are the possible genotypes and phenotypes of the offspring from this match?

Chapter Review

USING KEY TERMS

Complete each of the following sentences by choosing the correct term from the word bank.

sex cells   genotype
sex chromosomes   alleles
phenotype   meiosis

1 Sperm and eggs are known as _____.

2 The _____ is the expression of a trait and is determined by the combination of alleles called the _____.

3 _____ produces cells with half the normal number of chromosomes.

4 Different versions of the same genes are called _____.

UNDERSTANDING KEY IDEAS

Multiple Choice

5 Genes carry information that determines

a. alleles.

b. ribosomes.

c. chromosomes.

d. traits.

6 The process that produces sex cells is

a. mitosis.

b. photosynthesis.

c. meiosis.

d. probability.

7 The passing of traits from parents to offspring is called

a. probability.

b. heredity.

c. recessive.

d. meiosis.

8 If you cross a white flower with the genotype *pp* with a purple flower with the genotype *PP*, the possible genotypes in the offspring are

a. *PP* and *pp*.

b. all *Pp*.

c. all *PP*.

d. all *pp*.

9 For the cross in item 8, what would the phenotypes be?

a. all white

b. 3 purple and 1 white

c. all purple

d. half white, half purple

10 In meiosis,

a. chromosomes are copied twice.

b. the nucleus divides once.

c. four cells are produced from a single cell.

d. two cells are produced from a single cell.

11 When one trait is not completely dominant over another, it is called

a. recessive.

b. incomplete dominance.

c. environmental factors.

d. uncertain dominance.

Short Answer

12 Which sex chromosomes do females have? Which do males have?

13 In one or two sentences, define the term *recessive trait* in your own words.

14 How are sex cells different from other body cells?

15 What is a sex-linked disorder? Give one example of a sex-linked disorder that is found in humans.

CRITICAL THINKING

16 **Concept Mapping** Use the following terms to create a concept map: *meiosis, eggs, cell division, X chromosome, mitosis, Y chromosome, sperm,* and *sex cells.*

17 **Identifying Relationships** If you were a carrier of one allele for a certain recessive disorder, how could genetic counseling help you prepare for the future?

18 **Applying Concepts** If a child has blond hair and both of her parents have brown hair, what does that tell you about the allele for blond hair? Explain.

19 **Applying Concepts** What is the genotype of a pea plant that is true-breeding for purple flowers?

INTERPRETING GRAPHICS

Use the Punnett square below to answer the questions that follow.

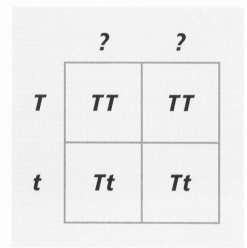

20 What is the unknown genotype?

21 If *T* represents the allele for tall pea plants and *t* represents the allele for short pea plants, what is the phenotype of each parent and of the offspring?

22 If each of the offspring were allowed to self-fertilize, what are the possible genotypes in the next generation?

23 What is the probability of each genotype in item 22?

Standardized Test Preparation

READING

Read the passages below. Then, answer the questions that follow each passage.

Passage 1 The different versions of a gene are called *alleles*. When two different alleles occur together, one is often expressed while the other has no obvious effect on the organism's appearance. The expressed form of the trait is dominant. The trait that was not expressed when the dominant form of the trait was present is called *recessive*. Imagine a plant that has both purple and white alleles for flower color. If the plant blooms purple, then purple is the dominant form of the trait. Therefore, white is the recessive form.

1. According to the passage, which of the following statements is true?

    A All alleles are expressed all of the time.

    B All traits for flower color are dominant.

    C When two alleles are present, the expressed form of the trait is dominant.

    D A recessive form of a trait is always expressed.

2. According to the passage, a trait that is not expressed when the dominant form is present is called

    F recessive.

    G an allele.

    H heredity.

    I a gene.

3. According to the passage, which allele for flower color is dominant?

    A white

    B pink

    C purple

    D yellow

Passage 2 Sickle cell anemia is a recessive genetic disorder. People inherit this disorder only when they inherit the disease-causing recessive allele from both parents. The disease causes the body to make red blood cells that bend into a sickle (or crescent moon) shape. The sickle-shaped red blood cells break apart easily. Therefore, the blood of a person with sickle cell anemia carries less oxygen. Sickle-shaped blood cells also tend to get stuck in blood vessels. When a blood vessel is blocked, the blood supply to organs can be cut off. But the sickle-shaped blood cells can also protect a person from malaria. Malaria is a disease caused by an organism that invades red blood cells.

1. According to the passage, sickle cell anemia is a

    A recessive genetic disorder.

    B dominant genetic disorder.

    C disease caused by an organism that invades red blood cells.

    D disease also called *malaria*.

2. According to the passage, sickle cell anemia can help protect a person from

    F blocked blood vessels.

    G genetic disorders.

    H malaria.

    I low oxygen levels.

3. Which of the following is a fact in the passage?

    A When blood vessels are blocked, vital organs lose their blood supply.

    B When blood vessels are blocked, it causes the red blood cells to bend into sickle shapes.

    C The blood of a person with sickle cell anemia carries more oxygen.

    D Healthy red blood cells never get stuck in blood vessels.

The Punnett square below shows a cross between two flowering plants. Use this Punnett square to answer the questions that follow.

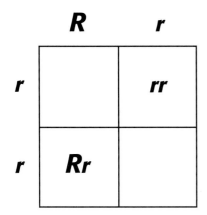

1. What is the genotype of the offspring represented in the upper left-hand box of the Punnett square?
   A *RR*
   B *Rr*
   C *rr*
   D *rrr*

2. What is the genotype of the offspring represented in the lower right-hand box of the Punnett square?
   F *RR*
   G *Rr*
   H *rr*
   I *rrr*

3. What is the ratio of *Rr* (purple-flowered plants) to *rr* (white-flowered plants) in the offspring?
   A 1:3
   B 2:2
   C 3:1
   D 4:0

Read each question below, and choose the best answer.

1. What is another way to write $4 \times 4 \times 4$?
   A 4^2
   B 4^3
   C 3^3
   D 3^4

2. Jane was making a design on top of her desk with pennies. She put 4 pennies in the first row, 7 pennies in the second row, and 13 pennies in the third row. If Jane continues this pattern, how many pennies will she put in the sixth row?
   F 25
   G 49
   H 97
   I 193

3. In which of the following lists are the numbers in order from smallest to greatest?
   A 0.012, 0.120, 0.123, 1.012
   B 1.012, 0.123, 0.120, 0.012
   C 0.123, 0.120, 0.012, 1.012
   D 0.123, 1.012, 0.120, 0.012

4. In which of the following lists are the numbers in order from smallest to greatest?
   F $-12.0, -15.5, 2.2, 4.0$
   G $-15.5, -12.0, 2.2, 4.0$
   H $-12.0, -15.5, 4.0, 2.2$
   I $2.2, 4.0, -12.0, -15.5$

5. Which of the following is equal to -11?
   A $7 + 4$
   B $-4 + 7$
   C $-7 + 4$
   D $-7 + -4$

6. Catherine earned $75 for working 8.5 h. How much did she earn per hour?
   F $10.12
   G $9.75
   H $8.82
   I $8.01

Standardized Test Preparation

Science in Action

This is a normal fruit fly under a scanning electron microscope.

This fruit fly has legs growing where its antennae should be.

Science, Technology, and Society

Mapping the Human Genome

In 2003, scientists finished one of the most ambitious research projects ever. Researchers with the Human Genome Project (HGP) mapped the human body's complete set of genetic instructions, which is called the *genome*. You might be wondering whose genome the scientists are decoding. Actually, it doesn't matter—only 0.1% of each person's genetic material is unique. The researchers' goals are to identify how tiny differences in that 0.1% make each of us who we are and to begin to understand how some differences can cause disease. Scientists are already using the map to think of new ways to treat genetic diseases, such as asthma, diabetes, and kidney disease.

Social Studies ACTiViTY

WRITING SKILL Research DNA fingerprinting. Write a short report describing how DNA fingerprinting has affected the way criminals are caught.

Weird Science

Lab Rats with Wings

Drosophila melanogaster (droh SAHF i luh muh LAN uh GAS tuhr) is the scientific name for the fruit fly. This tiny insect has played a big role in helping scientists understand many illnesses. Because fruit flies reproduce every 2 weeks, scientists can alter a fruit fly gene and see the results of the experiment very quickly. Another important reason for using these "lab rats with wings" is that their genetic code is simple and well understood. Fruit flies have 12,000 genes, but humans have more than 25,000. Scientists use fruit flies to find out about diseases like cancer, Alzheimer's, and muscular dystrophy.

Language Arts ACTiViTY

WRITING SKILL The mythical creature called the *Chimera* (kie MIR uh) was said to be part lion, part goat, and part serpent. According to legend, the Chimera terrorized people for years until it was killed by a brave hero. The word *chimera* now refers to any organism that has parts from many organisms. Write a short story about the Chimera that describes what it looks like and how it came to be.

Stacey Wong

Genetic Counselor If your family had a history of a particular disease, what would you do? Would you eat healthier foods, get more exercise, or visit your doctor regularly? All of those are good ideas, but Stacey Wong went a step farther. Her family's history of cancer helped her decide to become a genetic counselor. "Genetic counselors are usually part of a team of health professionals," she says, which can include physicians, nurses, dieticians, social workers, laboratory personnel, and others. "If a diagnosis is made by the geneticist," says Wong, "then I provide genetic counseling." When a patient visits a genetic counselor, the counselor asks many questions and builds a family medical history. Although counseling involves discussing what it means to have a genetic condition, Wong says "the most important part is to get to know the patient or family we are working with, listen to their concerns, gain an understanding of their values, help them to make decisions, and be their advocate."

Math ACTIVITY

The probability of inheriting genetic disease *A* is 1/10,000. The probability of inheriting genetic disease *B* is also 1/10,000. What is the probability that one person would inherit both genetic diseases *A* and *B*?

To learn more about these Science in Action topics, visit go.hrw.com and type in the keyword **HL5HERF.**

Current Science

Check out Current Science® articles related to this chapter by visiting go.hrw.com. Just type in the keyword HL5CS05.

16

Genes and DNA

About the PHOTO

These adult mice have no hair—not because their hair was shaved off but because these mice do not grow hair. In cells of these mice, the genes that normally cause hair to grow are not working. The genes were "turned off" by scientists who have learned to control the function of some genes. Scientists changed the genes of these mice to research medical problems such as cancer.

PRE-READING ACTIVITY

Graphic Organizer

Concept Map Before you read the chapter, create the graphic organizer entitled "Concept Map" described in the **Study Skills** section of the Appendix. As you read the chapter, fill in the concept map with details about DNA.

Fingerprint Your Friends

One way to identify people is by taking their finger-prints. Does it really work? Are everyone's fingerprints unique? Try this activity to find out.

Procedure

1. Rub the tip of a **pencil** back and forth across a **piece of tracing paper.** Make a large, dark mark.

2. Rub the tip of one of your fingers on the pencil mark. Then place a small **piece of transparent tape** over the darkened area on your finger.

3. Remove the tape, and stick it on **a piece of white paper.** Repeat steps 1–3 for the rest of your fingers.

4. Look at the fingerprints with a **magnifying lens.** What patterns do you see? Is the pattern the same on every finger?

Analysis

1. Compare your fingerprints with those of your classmates. Do any two people in your class have the same prints? Try to explain your findings.

What Does DNA Look Like?

For many years, the structure of a DNA molecule was a puzzle to scientists. In the 1950s, two scientists deduced the structure while experimenting with chemical models. They later won a Nobel Prize for helping solve this puzzle!

Inherited characteristics are determined by genes, and genes are passed from one generation to the next. Genes are parts of chromosomes, which are structures in the nucleus of most cells. Chromosomes are made of protein and DNA. **DNA** stands for *deoxyribonucleic acid* (dee AHKS ee RIE boh noo KLEE ik AS id). DNA is the genetic material—the material that determines inherited characteristics. But what does DNA look like?

The Pieces of the Puzzle

Scientists knew that the material that makes up genes must be able to do two things. First, it must be able to give instructions for building and maintaining cells. Second, it must be able to be copied each time a cell divides, so that each cell contains identical genes. Scientists thought that these things could be done only by complex molecules, such as proteins. They were surprised to learn how much the DNA molecule could do.

Nucleotides: The Subunits of DNA

DNA is made of subunits called nucleotides. A **nucleotide** consists of a sugar, a phosphate, and a base. The nucleotides are identical except for the base. The four bases are *adenine, thymine, guanine,* and *cytosine.* Each base has a different shape. Scientists often refer to a base by the first letter of the base, *A, T, G,* and *C.* **Figure 1** shows models of the four nucleotides.

DNA **d**eoxyribo**n**ucleic **a**cid, a molecule that is present in all living cells and that contains the information that determines the traits that a living thing inherits and needs to live

nucleotide in a nucleic-acid chain, a subunit that consists of a sugar, a phosphate, and a nitrogenous base

Figure 1 **The Four Nucleotides of DNA**

Adenine (A)

Thymine (T)

Guanine (G)

Cytosine (C)

Chargaff's Rules

In the 1950s, a biochemist named Erwin Chargaff found that the amount of adenine in DNA always equals the amount of thymine. And he found that the amount of guanine always equals the amount of cytosine. His findings are known as *Chargaff's rules*. At the time of his discovery, no one knew the importance of these findings. But Chargaff's rules later helped scientists understand the structure of DNA.

☑ Reading Check Summarize Chargaff's rules. (*See the Appendix for answers to Reading Checks*.)

Franklin's Discovery

More clues about the structure of DNA came from scientists in Britain. There, chemist Rosalind Franklin, shown in **Figure 2,** was able to make images of DNA molecules. She used a process known as *X-ray diffraction* to make these images. In this process, X rays are aimed at the DNA molecule. When an X ray hits a part of the molecule, the ray bounces off. The pattern made by the bouncing rays is captured on film. Franklin's images suggested that DNA has a spiral shape.

Watson and Crick's Model

At about the same time, two other scientists were also trying to solve the mystery of DNA's structure. They were James Watson and Francis Crick, shown in **Figure 3.** After seeing Franklin's X-ray images, Watson and Crick concluded that DNA must look like a long, twisted ladder. They were then able to build a model of DNA by using simple materials from their laboratory. Their model perfectly fit with both Chargaff's and Franklin's findings. The model eventually helped explain how DNA is copied and how it functions in the cell.

Figure 2 *Rosalind Franklin used X-ray diffraction to make images of DNA that helped reveal the structure of DNA.*

CONNECTION TO Chemistry

WRITING SKILL **Linus Pauling** Many scientists contributed to the discovery of DNA's structure. In fact, some scientists competed to be the first to make the discovery. One of these competitors was a chemist named Linus Pauling. Research and write a paragraph about how Pauling's work helped Watson and Crick.

Figure 3 *This photo shows James Watson (left) and Francis Crick (right) with their model of DNA.*

DNA's Double Structure

The shape of DNA is shown in **Figure 4.** As you can see, a strand of DNA looks like a twisted ladder. This shape is known as a *double helix* (DUB uhl HEE LIKS). The two sides of the ladder are made of alternating sugar parts and phosphate parts. The rungs of the ladder are made of a pair of bases. Adenine on one side of a rung always pairs with thymine on the other side. Guanine always pairs with cytosine.

Notice how the double helix structure matches Chargaff's observations. When Chargaff separated the parts of a sample of DNA, he found that the matching bases were always present in equal amounts. To model how the bases pair, Watson and Crick tried to match Chargaff's observations. They also used information from chemists about the size and shape of each of the nucleotides. As it turned out, the width of the DNA ladder matches the combined width of the matching bases. Only the correct pairs of bases fit within the ladder's width.

Making Copies of DNA

The pairing of bases allows the cell to *replicate*, or make copies of, DNA. Each base always bonds with only one other base. Thus, pairs of bases are *complementary* to each other, and both sides of a DNA molecule are complementary. For example, the sequence CGAC will bond to the sequence GCTG.

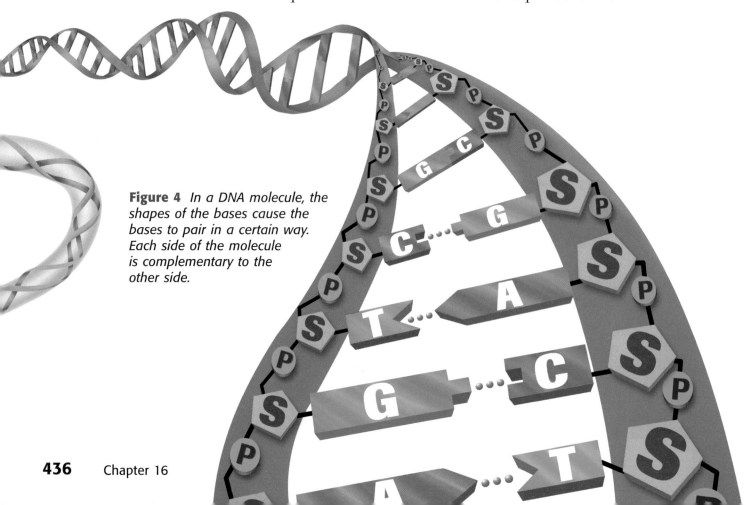

Figure 4 *In a DNA molecule, the shapes of the bases cause the bases to pair in a certain way. Each side of the molecule is complementary to the other side.*

How Copies Are Made

During replication, as shown in **Figure 5,** a DNA molecule is split down the middle, where the bases meet. The bases on each side of the molecule are used as a pattern for a new strand. As the bases on the original molecule are exposed, complementary nucleotides are added to each side of the ladder. Two DNA molecules are formed. Half of each of the molecules is old DNA, and half is new DNA.

When Copies Are Made

DNA is copied every time a cell divides. Each new cell gets a complete copy of all the DNA. The job of unwinding, copying, and re-winding the DNA is done by proteins within the cell. So, DNA is usually found with several kinds of proteins. Other proteins help with the process of carrying out the instructions written in the code of the DNA.

✔ **Reading Check** How often is DNA copied?

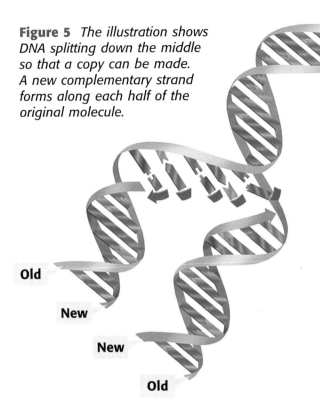

Figure 5 *The illustration shows DNA splitting down the middle so that a copy can be made. A new complementary strand forms along each half of the original molecule.*

Old

New

New

Old

SECTION Review

Summary

● DNA is the material that makes up genes. It carries coded information that is copied in each new cell.

● The DNA molecule looks like a twisted ladder. The two halves are long strings of nucleotides. The rungs are complementary pairs of bases.

● Because each base has a complementary base, DNA can be replicated accurately.

Using Key Terms

1. Use the term *DNA* in a sentence.

2. In your own words, write a definition for the term *nucleotide*.

Understanding Key Ideas

3. List three important events that led to understanding the structure of DNA.

4. Which of the following is NOT part of a nucleotide?
   a. base
   b. sugar
   c. fat
   d. phosphate

Math Skills

5. If a sample of DNA contained 20% cytosine, what percentage of guanine would be in this sample? What percentage of adenine would be in the sample? Explain.

Critical Thinking

6. **Making Inferences** Explain what is meant by the statement "DNA unites all organisms."

7. **Applying Concepts** What would the complementary strand of DNA be for the sequence of bases below?

   C T T A G G C T T A C C A

8. **Analyzing Processes** How are copies of DNA made? Draw a picture as part of your answer.

SCİLINKS®

NSTA

Developed and maintained by the
National Science Teachers Association

For a variety of links related to this chapter, go to www.scilinks.org

Topic: DNA; Genes and Traits
SciLinks code: HSM0418; HSM0647

How DNA Works

Almost every cell in your body contains about 2 m of DNA. How does all of the DNA fit in a cell? And how does the DNA hold a code that affects your traits?

DNA is found in the cells of all organisms, including bacteria, mosquitoes, and humans. Each organism has a unique set of DNA. But DNA functions the same way in all organisms.

Unraveling DNA

DNA is often wound around proteins, coiled into strands, and then bundled up even more. In a cell that lacks a nucleus, each strand of DNA forms a loose loop within the cell. In a cell that has a nucleus, the strands of DNA and proteins are bundled into chromosomes, as shown in **Figure 1.**

The structure of DNA allows DNA to hold information. The order of the bases on one side of the molecule is a code that carries information. A *gene* consists of a string of nucleotides that give the cell information about how to make a specific trait. There is an enormous amount of DNA, so there can be a large variety of genes.

✓ **Reading Check** What makes up a gene? (*See the Appendix for answers to Reading Checks.*)

Figure 1 Unraveling DNA

ⓐ A typical skin cell has a diameter of about 0.0025 cm. The DNA in the nucleus of each cell codes for proteins that determine traits such as skin color.

ⓑ The DNA in the nucleus is part of a material called *chromatin*. Long strands of chromatin are usually bundled loosely within the nucleus.

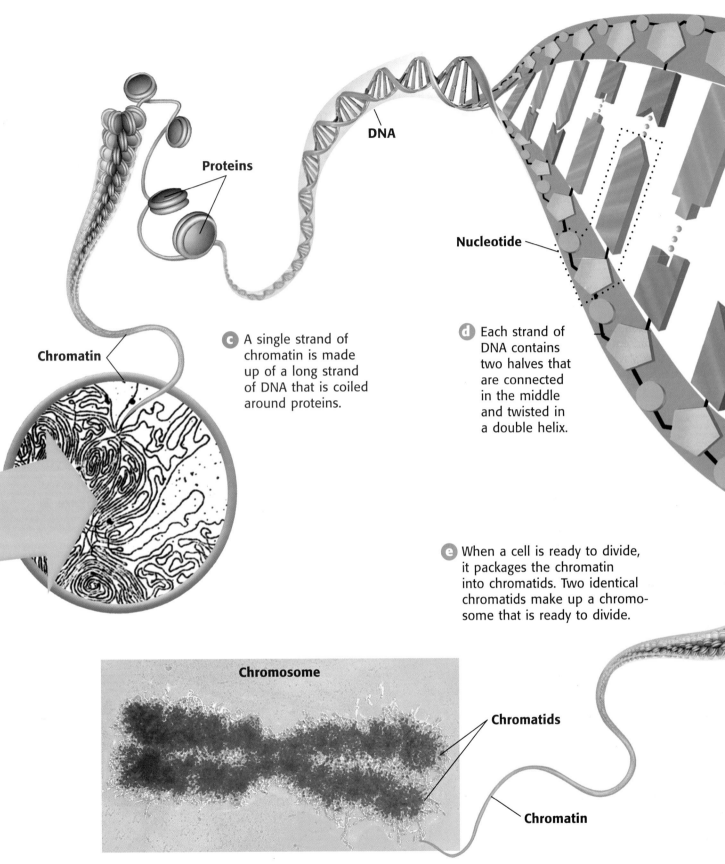

DNA

Proteins

Nucleotide

Chromatin

c A single strand of chromatin is made up of a long strand of DNA that is coiled around proteins.

d Each strand of DNA contains two halves that are connected in the middle and twisted in a double helix.

e When a cell is ready to divide, it packages the chromatin into chromatids. Two identical chromatids make up a chromosome that is ready to divide.

Chromosome

Chromatids

Chromatin

f Just before division, each human cell contains 46 chromosomes. These chromosomes contain two identical copies of all of the cell's genetic material.

Genes and Proteins

The DNA code is read like a book—from one end to the other and in one direction. The bases form the alphabet of the code. Groups of three bases are the codes for specific amino acids. For example, the three bases CCA form the code for the amino acid proline. The bases AGC form the code for the amino acid serine. A long string of amino acids forms a protein. Thus, each gene is usually a set of instructions for making a protein.

Proteins and Traits

How are proteins related to traits? Proteins are found throughout cells and cause most of the differences that you can see among organisms. Proteins act as chemical triggers and messengers for many of the processes within cells. Proteins help determine how tall you grow, what colors you can see, and whether your hair is curly or straight. Proteins exist in an almost limitless variety. A single organism may have thousands of genes that code for thousands of proteins.

Help from RNA

RNA ribonucleic acid, a molecule that is present in all living cells and that plays a role in protein production

Another type of molecule that helps make proteins is called **RNA,** or *ribonucleic acid* (RIE boh noo KLEE ik AS id). RNA is so similar to DNA that RNA can serve as a temporary copy of a DNA sequence. Several forms of RNA help in the process of changing the DNA code into proteins, as shown in **Figure 2.**

Figure 2 *Proteins are built in the cytoplasm by using RNA copies of a segment of DNA. The order of the bases on the RNA determines the order of amino acids that are assembled at the ribosome.*

Cytoplasm

1 A copy is made of one side of the DNA segment where a particular gene is located. This copy is transferred to the cytoplasm.

Nucleus

2 This mirrorlike copy of a DNA segment is called *messenger RNA* (mRNA).

mRNA

Base

3 Each group of three bases on the mRNA segment codes for one amino acid.

The Making of a Protein

The first step in making a protein is to copy one side of the segment of DNA containing a gene. A mirrorlike copy of the DNA segment is made out of RNA. This copy of the DNA segment is called *messenger RNA* (mRNA). It moves out of the nucleus and into the cytoplasm of the cell.

In the cytoplasm, the messenger RNA is fed through a protein assembly line. The "factory" that runs this assembly line is known as a ribosome. A **ribosome** is a cell organelle composed of RNA and protein. The messenger RNA is fed through the ribosome three bases at a time. Then, molecules of *transfer RNA* (tRNA) translate the RNA message. Each transfer RNA molecule picks up a specific amino acid from the cytoplasm. Inside the ribosome, bases on the transfer RNA match up with bases on the messenger RNA like pieces of a puzzle. The transfer RNA molecules then release their amino acids. The amino acids become linked in a growing chain. As the entire segment of messenger RNA passes through the ribosome, the growing chain of amino acids folds up into a new protein molecule.

✓ Reading Check What do the transfer RNA molecules transfer?

Code Combinations

A given sequence of three bases codes for one amino acid. For example, AGT is one possible sequence. How many different sequences of the four DNA base types are possible? (Hint: Make a list.)

ribosome a cell organelle composed of RNA and protein; the site of protein synthesis

Ribosome

4 The mRNA segment is fed through the ribosome.

Cytoplasm

mRNA

5 Molecules of transfer RNA (tRNA) deliver amino acids from the cytoplasm to the ribosome.

1st amino acid

2nd amino acid

3rd amino acid

4th amino acid

5th amino acid

7 The amino acids are joined to make a protein. Usually, one protein is produced for each gene.

6 The amino acids are dropped off at the ribosome.

tRNA

amino acid

Original sequence

a Base pair replaced

b Base pair added

c Base pair removed

Figure 3 *The original base sequence on the top has been changed to illustrate (a) a substitution, (b) an insertion, and (c) a deletion.*

mutation a change in the nucleotide-base sequence of a gene or DNA molecule

Changes in Genes

Imagine that you have been invited to ride on a new roller coaster at the state fair. Before you climb into the front car, you are told that some of the metal parts on the coaster have been replaced by parts made of a different substance. Would you still want to ride this roller coaster? Perhaps a strong metal was used as a substitute. Or perhaps a material that is not strong enough was used. Imagine what would happen if cardboard were used instead of metal!

Mutations

Substitutions like the ones in the roller coaster can accidentally happen in DNA. Changes in the number, type, or order of bases on a piece of DNA are known as **mutations.** Sometimes, a base is left out. This kind of change is known as a *deletion.* Or an extra base might be added. This kind of change is known as an *insertion.* The most common change happens when the wrong base is used. This kind of change is known as a *substitution.* **Figure 3** illustrates these three types of mutations.

Do Mutations Matter?

There are three possible consequences to changes in DNA: an improved trait, no change, or a harmful trait. Fortunately, cells make some proteins that can detect errors in DNA. When an error is found, it is usually fixed. But occasionally the repairs are not accurate, and the mistakes become part of the genetic message. If the mutation occurs in the sex cells, the changed gene can be passed from one generation to the next.

How Do Mutations Happen?

Mutations happen regularly because of random errors when DNA is copied. In addition, damage to DNA can be caused by abnormal things that happen to cells. Any physical or chemical agent that can cause a mutation in DNA is called a *mutagen.* Examples of mutagens include high-energy radiation from X rays and ultraviolet radiation. Ultraviolet radiation is one type of energy in sunlight. It is responsible for suntans and sunburns. Other mutagens include asbestos and the chemicals in cigarette smoke.

✓ Reading Check What is a mutagen?

An Example of a Substitution

A mutation, such as a substitution, can be harmful because it may cause a gene to produce the wrong protein. Consider the DNA sequence GAA. When copied as mRNA, this sequence gives the instructions to place the amino acid glutamic acid into the growing protein. If a mistake happens and the original DNA sequence is changed to GTA, the sequence will code for the amino acid valine instead.

This simple change in an amino acid can cause the disease *sickle cell disease*. Sickle cell disease affects red blood cells. When valine is substituted for glutamic acid in a blood protein, as shown in **Figure 4,** the red blood cells are changed into a sickle shape.

The sickle cells are not as good at carrying oxygen as normal red blood cells are. Sickle cells are also likely to get stuck in blood vessels and cause painful and dangerous clots.

✓ **Reading Check** What causes sickle cell disease?

An Error in the Message

The sentence below is the result of an error similar to a DNA mutation. The original sentence was made up of three-letter words, but an error was made in this copy. Explain the idea of mutations to your parent. Then, work together to find the mutation, and write the sentence correctly.

THE IGB ADC ATA TET HEB IGR EDR AT.

Figure 4 How Sickle Cell Disease Results from a Mutation

Original DNA
A C T C C T G A A G A A A A
T G A G G A C T T C T T T T

mRNA

Resulting amino acid chain
Threonine — Proline — Glutamic acid — Glutamic acid — Lysine → Normal red blood cell

Substitution

Mutated DNA
A C T C C T G T A G A A A A
T G A G G A C A T C T T T T

mRNA

Resulting amino acid chain
Threonine — Proline — Valine — Glutamic acid — Lysine → Sickle-shaped red blood cell

Uses of Genetic Knowledge

In the years since Watson and Crick made their model, scientists have learned a lot about genetics. This knowledge is often used in ways that benefit humans. But some uses of genetic knowledge also cause ethical and scientific debates.

Genetic Engineering

Scientists can manipulate individual genes within organisms. This kind of manipulation is called *genetic engineering*. In some cases, genes may be transferred from one type of organism to another. An example of a genetically engineered plant is shown in **Figure 5.** Scientists added a gene from fireflies to this plant. The gene produces a protein that causes the plant to glow.

Scientists may use genetic engineering to create new products, such as drugs, foods, or fabrics. For example, bacteria may be used to make the proteins found in spider's silk. Or cows may be used to produce human proteins. In some cases, this practice could produce a protein that is needed by a person who has a genetic disease. However, some scientists worry about the dangers of creating genetically engineered organisms.

Figure 5 *This genetically engineered tobacco plant contains firefly genes.*

Genetic Identification

Your DNA is unique, so it can be used like a fingerprint to identify you. *DNA fingerprinting* identifies the unique patterns in an individual's DNA. DNA samples are now used as evidence in crimes, as shown in **Figure 6.** Similarities between people's DNA can reveal other information, too. For example, DNA can be used to identify family relations or hereditary diseases.

Identical twins have truly identical DNA. Scientists are now able to create something like a twin, called a clone. A *clone* is a new organism that has an exact copy of another organism's genes. Clones of several types of organisms, including some mammals, have been developed by scientists. However, the possibility of cloning humans is still being debated among both scientists and politicians.

Reading Check What is a clone?

Figure 6 *This scientist is gathering dead skin cells from a crime scene. DNA from the cells could be used as evidence of a criminal's identity.*

CONNECTION TO Social Studies

Genetic Property Could you sell your DNA code? Using current laws and technology, someone could sell genetic information like authors sell books. It is also possible to file a patent to establish ownership of the information used to make a product. Thus, a patent can be filed for a unique sequence of DNA or for new genetic engineering technology. Conduct research to find an existing patent on a genetic sequence or genetic engineering technology.

Summary

- A gene is a set of instructions for assembling a protein. DNA is the molecular carrier of these genetic instructions.

- Every organism has DNA in its cells. Humans have about 2 m of DNA in each cell.

- Within a gene, each group of three bases codes for one amino acid. A sequence of amino acids is linked to make a protein.

- Proteins are fundamental to the function of cells and the expression of traits.

- Proteins are assembled within the cytoplasm through a multi-step process that is assisted by several forms of RNA.

- Genes can become mutated when the order of the bases is changed. Three main types of mutations are possible: insertion, deletion, and substitution.

- Genetic knowledge has many practical uses. Some applications of genetic knowledge are controversial.

Using Key Terms

1. Use each of the following terms in the same sentence: *ribosome* and *RNA*.

2. In your own words, write a definition for the term *mutation*.

Understanding Key Ideas

3. Explain the relationship between genes and proteins.

4. List three possible types of mutations.

5. Which type of mutation causes sickle cell anemia?
   - **a.** substitution
   - **b.** insertion
   - **c.** deletion
   - **d.** mutagen

Math Skills

6. A set of 23 chromosomes in a human cell contains 3.2 billion pairs of DNA bases in sequence. On average, about how many pairs of bases are in each chromosome?

Critical Thinking

7. **Applying Concepts** In which cell type might a mutation be passed from generation to generation? Explain.

8. **Making Comparisons** How is genetic engineering different from natural reproduction?

Interpreting Graphics

The illustration below shows a sequence of bases on one strand of a DNA molecule. Use the illustration below to answer the questions that follow.

9. How many amino acids are coded for by the sequence on one side (A) of this DNA strand?

10. What is the order of bases on the complementary side of the strand (B), from left to right?

11. If a G were inserted as the first base on the top side (A), what would the order of bases be on the complementary side (B)?

Developed and maintained by the National Science Teachers Association

For a variety of links related to this chapter, go to www.scilinks.org

Topic: Genetic Engineering
SciLinks code: HSM0654

Model-Making Lab

OBJECTIVES

Construct a model of a DNA strand.

Model the process of DNA replication.

MATERIALS

- bag, large paper
- paper, colored (4 colors)
- paper, white
- scissors

SAFETY

Base-Pair Basics

You have learned that DNA is shaped something like a twisted ladder. The side rails of the ladder are made of sugar parts and phosphate parts. The two side rails are connected to each other by parts called *bases*. The bases join in pairs to form the rungs of the ladder. Within DNA, each base can pair with only one other base. Each of these pairs is called a *base pair*. When DNA replicates, enzymes separate the base pairs, which breaks the rungs of the ladder in half. Then, each half of the DNA ladder can be used as a template for building a new half. In this activity, you will construct a paper model of DNA and use it to model the replication process.

Procedure

1. Trace the models of nucleotides below onto white paper. Label the pieces "A" (**a**denine), "T" (**t**hymine), "C" (**c**ytosine), and "G" (**g**uanine). Draw the pieces again on colored paper. Use a different color for each type of base. Draw the pieces as large as you want, and draw as many of the white pieces and as many of the colored pieces as time will allow.

2. Carefully cut out all of the pieces.

3. Put all of the colored pieces in the classroom into a large paper bag. Spread all of the white pieces in the classroom onto a large table.

4. Remove nine colored pieces from the bag. Arrange the colored pieces in any order in a straight column so that the letters *A, T, C,* and *G* are right side up. Be sure to fit the sugar notches to the phosphate tabs. Draw this arrangement.

5. Find the white bases that correctly pair with the nine colored bases. Remember the base-pairing rules, and pair the bases according to those rules.

6. Pair the pieces by fitting tabs to notches. The letters on the white pieces should be upside down. You now have a model of a double-stranded piece of DNA. The strand contains nine pairs of complementary nucleotides. Draw your model.

Nucleotides

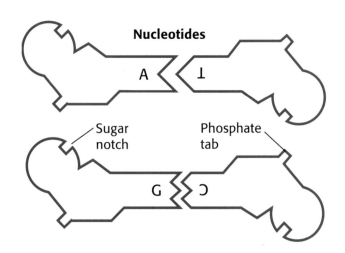

Sugar notch

Phosphate tab

Analyze the Results

1 **Identifying Patterns** Now, separate the two halves of your DNA strand along the middle of the base pair rungs of the ladder. Keep the side rails together by keeping the sugar notches fitted to the phosphate tabs. Draw this arrangement.

2 **Recognizing Patterns** Look at the drawing made in the previous step. Along each strand in the drawing, write the letters of the bases that complement the bases in that strand.

3 **Examining Data** Find all of the bases that you need to complete replication. Find white pieces to pair with the bases on the left, and find colored pieces to pair with the bases on the right. Be sure that the tabs and notches fit and the sides are straight. You have now replicated your model of DNA. Are the two models identical? Draw your results.

Draw Conclusions

4 **Interpreting Information** State the correct base-pairing rules. How do these rules make DNA replication possible?

5 **Evaluating Models** What happens when you attempt to pair thymine with guanine? Do they fit together? Are the sides straight? Do all of the tabs and notches fit? Explain.

Applying Your Data

Construct a 3-D model of a DNA molecule that shows DNA's twisted-ladder structure. Use your imagination and creativity to select materials. You may want to use licorice, gum balls, and toothpicks or pipe cleaners and paper clips.

1. Display your model in your classroom.
2. Take a vote to decide which models are the most accurate and the most creative.

Chapter Review

USING KEY TERMS

1 Use the following terms in the same sentence: *mutation* and *mutagen*.

The statements below are false. For each statement, replace the underlined term to make a true statement.

2 The information in DNA is coded in the order of <u>amino acids</u> along one side of the DNA molecule.

3 The "factory" that assembles proteins based on the DNA code is called a <u>gene</u>.

UNDERSTANDING KEY IDEAS

Multiple Choice

4 James Watson and Francis Crick
  a. took X-ray pictures of DNA.
  b. discovered that genes are in chromosomes.
  c. bred pea plants to study heredity.
  d. made models to figure out DNA's shape.

5 In a DNA molecule, which of the following bases pair together?
  a. adenine and cytosine
  b. thymine and adenine
  c. thymine and guanine
  d. cytosine and thymine

6 A gene can be all of the following EXCEPT
  a. a set of instructions for a trait.
  b. a complete chromosome.
  c. instructions for making a protein.
  d. a portion of a strand of DNA.

7 Which of the following statements about DNA is NOT true?
  a. DNA is found in all organisms.
  b. DNA is made up of five subunits.
  c. DNA has a structure like a twisted ladder.
  d. Mistakes can be made when DNA is copied.

8 Within the cell, where are proteins assembled?
  a. the cytoplasm
  b. the nucleus
  c. the amino acids
  d. the chromosomes

9 Changes in the type or order of the bases in DNA are called
  a. nucleotides.
  b. mutations.
  c. RNA.
  d. genes.

Short Answer

10 What would be the complementary strand of DNA for the following sequence of bases?

C T T A G G C T T A C C A

11 If the DNA sequence TGAGCCATGA is changed to TGAGCACATGA, what kind of mutation has occurred?

12 Explain how the DNA in genes relates to the traits of an organism.

13 Why is DNA frequently found associated with proteins inside of cells?

14 What is the difference between DNA and RNA?

CRITICAL THINKING

15 Concept Mapping Use the following terms to create a concept map: *bases, adenine, thymine, nucleotides, guanine, DNA,* and *cytosine.*

16 Analyzing Processes Draw and label a picture that explains how DNA is copied.

17 Analyzing Processes Draw and label a picture that explains how proteins are made.

18 Applying Concepts The following DNA sequence codes for how many amino acids?

T C A G C C A C C T A T G G A

19 Making Inferences Why does the government make laws about the use of chemicals that are known to be mutagens?

INTERPRETING GRAPHICS

The illustration below shows the process of replication of a DNA strand. Use this illustration to answer the questions that follow.

20 Which strands are part of the original molecule?

   a. A and B
   b. A and C
   c. A and D
   d. None of the above

21 Which strands are new?

   a. A and B
   b. B and C
   c. C and D
   d. None of the above

22 Which strands are complementary?

   a. A and C
   b. B and C
   c. All of the strands
   d. None of the strands

Standardized Test Preparation

EOG Prep

Read each of the passages below. Then, answer the questions that follow each passage.

Passage 1 The tension in the courtroom was so thick that you could cut it with a knife. The prosecuting attorney presented this evidence: "DNA analysis indicates that blood found on the defendant's shoes matches the blood of the victim. The odds of this match happening by chance are 1 in 20 million." The jury members were stunned by these figures. Can there be any doubt that the defendant is guilty?

DNA is increasingly used as evidence in court cases. Traditional fingerprinting has been used for more than 100 years, and it has been an extremely important identification tool. Recently, DNA fingerprinting, also called *DNA profiling*, has started to replace traditional techniques. DNA profiling has been used to clear thousands of wrongly accused or convicted individuals. However, there is some controversy over whether DNA evidence should be used to prove a suspect's guilt.

1. What does the first sentence in this passage describe?

  A the air pollution in a particular place

  B the feeling that a person might experience during an event

  C the motion of an object

  D the reason that a person was probably guilty of a crime

2. Which of the following best describes the main idea of the second paragraph of this passage?

  F A defendant was proven guilty by DNA analysis.

  G Court battles involving DNA fingerprinting are very exciting.

  H The technique of DNA profiling is increasingly used in court cases.

  I The technique of DNA profiling is controversial.

Passage 2 Most of the <u>biochemicals</u> found in living things are proteins. In fact, other than water, proteins are the most abundant molecules in your cells. Proteins have many functions, including regulating chemical activities, transporting and storing materials, and providing structural support.

Every protein is composed of small "building blocks" called *amino acids*. Amino acids are molecules that are composed of carbon, hydrogen, oxygen, and nitrogen atoms. Some amino acids also include sulfur atoms. Amino acids chemically bond to form proteins of many shapes and sizes.

The function of a protein depends on the shape of the bonded amino acids. If even a single amino acid is missing or out of place, the protein may not function correctly or may not function. Foods such as meat, fish, cheese, and beans contain proteins, which are broken down into amino acids as the foods are digested. Your body can then use these amino acids to make new proteins.

1. In the passage, what does *biochemical* mean?

  A a chemical found in nonliving things

  B a chemical found in living things

  C a pair of chemicals

  D a protein

2. According to the passage, which of the following statements is true?

  F Amino acids contain carbon dioxide.

  G Amino acids contain proteins.

  H Proteins are made of living things.

  I Proteins are made of amino acids.

INTERPRETING GRAPHICS

The diagram below shows an original sequence of DNA and three possible mutations. Use the diagram to answer the questions that follow.

Original sequence

Mutation A

Mutation B

Mutation C

1. In which mutation was an original base pair replaced?

   A Mutation A

   B Mutation B

   C Mutation C

   D There is not enough information to determine the answer.

2. In which mutation was a new base pair added?

   F Mutation A

   G Mutation B

   H Mutation C

   I There is not enough information to determine the answer.

3. In which mutation was an original base pair removed?

   A Mutation A

   B Mutation B

   C Mutation C

   D There is not enough information to determine the answer.

MATH

Read each question below, and choose the best answer.

1. Mary was making a design on top of her desk with marbles. She put 3 marbles in the first row, 7 marbles in the second row, 15 marbles in the third row, and 31 marbles in the fourth row. If Mary continues this pattern, how many marbles will she put in the seventh row?

   A 46

   B 63

   C 127

   D 255

2. Bobby walked 3 1/2 km on Saturday, 2 1/3 km on Sunday, and 1 km on Monday. How many kilometers did Bobby walk on those 3 days?

   F 5 1/6

   G 5 5/6

   H 6 1/6

   I 6 5/6

3. Marie bought a new aquarium for her goldfish. The aquarium is 60 cm long, 20 cm wide, and 30 cm high. Which equation could be used to find the volume of water needed to fill the aquarium to 25 cm deep?

   A $V = 30 \times 60 \times 20$

   B $V = 25 \times 60 \times 20$

   C $V = 30 \times 60 \times 20 - 5$

   D $V = 30 \times 60 \times 25$

4. How is the product of $6 \times 6 \times 6 \times 4 \times 4 \times 4$ expressed in scientific notation?

   F $6^4 \times 3^6$

   G $6^3 \times 4^3$

   H $3^6 \times 3^4$

   I 24^6

Science in Action

Scientific Debate

Supersquash or Frankenfruit?

Some food that you buy may have been developed in a new way. Food producers may use genetic engineering to make food crops easier to grow or sell, more nutritious, or resistant to pests and disease. More than half of the packaged foods sold in the United States are likely to contain ingredients from genetically modified organisms.

The U.S. government has stated that research shows that these foods are safe. But some scientists are concerned that genes introduced into crop plants could cause new environmental or health problems. For example, people who are allergic to peanuts might also be allergic to tomato plants that contain peanut genes.

Math ACTIVITY

Write a survey about genetically altered foods. Ask your teacher to approve your questions. Ask at least 15 people to answer your survey. Create graphs to summarize your results.

Science Fiction

"Moby James" by Patricia A. McKillip

Rob Trask and his family live on a space station. Rob thinks that his real brother was sent back to Earth. The person who claims to be his brother, James, is really either some sort of mutated plant or a mutant pair of dirty sweat socks.

Now, Rob has another problem—his class is reading Herman Melville's novel *Moby Dick*. As he reads the novel, Rob becomes convinced that his brother is a great white mutant whale—Moby James. To see how Rob solves his problems, read "Moby James" in the *Holt Anthology of Science Fiction*.

Language Arts ACTIVITY

WRITING SKILL Read "Moby James" by Patricia A. McKillip. Then, write your own short science-fiction story about a mutant organism. Be sure to incorporate some science into your science fiction.

People in Science

Lydia Villa-Komaroff

Genetic Researcher When Lydia Villa-Komaroff was young, science represented "a kind of refuge" for her. She grew up in a very large family that lived in a very small house. "I always wanted to find things out. I was one of those kids who took things apart."

In college, Villa-Komaroff became very interested in the process of embryonic development—how a simple egg grows into a complex animal. This interest led her to study genes and the way that genes code for proteins. For example, insulin is a protein that is normally produced by the human body. Often, people who suffer from diabetes lack the insulin gene, so their bodies can't make insulin. These people may need to inject insulin into their blood as a drug treatment.

Before the research by Villa-Komaroff's team was done, insulin was difficult to produce. Villa-Komaroff's team isolated the human gene that codes for insulin. Then, the scientists inserted the normal human insulin gene into the DNA of bacteria. This inserted gene caused the bacteria to produce insulin. This technique was a new and more efficient way to produce insulin. Now, most of the insulin used for diabetes treatment is made in this way. Many genetic researchers dream of making breakthroughs like the one that Villa-Komaroff made in her work with insulin.

Social Studies ACTIVITY

WRITING SKILL Do some research about several women, such as Marie Curie, Barbara McClintock, or Maxine Frank Singer, who have done important scientific research. Write a short biography about one of these women.

To learn more about these Science in Action topics, visit go.hrw.com and type in the keyword **HL5DNAF.**

Current Science

Check out Current Science® articles related to this chapter by visiting go.hrw.com. Just type in the keyword **HL5CS06.**

UNIT 5

TIMELINE

Motion, Forces, and Work

It's hard to imagine a world where nothing ever moves or where there are no machines. In this unit, you will learn about the relationship between force and motion and explore the scientific meaning of *work.* You will learn how to describe the motion of objects, how forces affect motion, how fluids exert force, and how machines make work easier. This timeline shows some events and discoveries that have occurred as scientists have advanced their understanding of the motion of objects here on Earth and in space, of work, and of machines.

Around 250 BCE

Archimedes, a Greek mathematician, develops the principle that bears his name. The principle relates the buoyant force on an object in a fluid to the amount of fluid displaced by the object.

1764

In London, Wolfgang Amadeus Mozart composes his first symphony—at the age of 8.

1846

After determining that the orbit of Uranus is different from what is predicted from the law of universal gravitation, scientists discover Neptune whose gravitational force is causing Uranus's unusual orbit.

1947

While flying a Bell X-1 rocket-powered airplane, American pilot Chuck Yeager becomes the first human to travel faster than the speed of sound.

PHILOSOPHIÆ
NATURALIS
PRINCIPIA
MATHEMATICA.
Autore JS. NEWTON, Trin. Coll. Cantab. Soc. Mathefeos
Profeffore Lucafiano, & Societatis Regalis Sodali.

Around 240 BCE

Chinese astronomers are the first to record a sighting of Halley's Comet.

1519

Portuguese explorer Ferdinand Magellan begins the first voyage around the world.

1687

Sir Isaac Newton, a British mathematician and scientist, publishes *Principia*, a book describing his laws of motion and the law of universal gravitation.

1905

While employed as a patent clerk, German physicist Albert Einstein publishes his special theory of relativity. The theory states that the speed of light is constant no matter what the reference frame is.

1921

Bessie Coleman becomes the first African American woman licensed to fly an airplane.

1971

American astronaut Alan Shepard takes a break from gathering lunar data to play golf on the moon during the *Apollo 14* mission.

1990

The *Magellan* spacecraft begins orbiting Venus for a four-year mission to map the planet. By using the sun's gravitational forces, it propels itself to Venus without burning much fuel.

2003

NASA launches *Spirit* and *Opportunity*, two Mars Exploration Rovers, to study Mars.

Matter in Motion

About the PHOTO↗

Speed skaters are fast. In fact, some skaters can skate at a rate of 12 m/s! That's equal to a speed of 27 mi/h. To reach such a speed, skaters must exert large forces. They must also use friction to turn corners on the slippery surface of the ice.

PRE-READING ACTIVITY

FOLDNOTES **Four-Corner Fold**
Before you read the chapter, create the FoldNote entitled "Four-Corner Fold" described in the **Study Skills** section of the Appendix. Label the flaps of the four-corner fold with "Motion," "Forces," "Friction," and "Gravity." Write what you know about each topic under the appropriate flap. As you read the chapter, add other information that you learn.

START-UP ACTIVITY

The Domino Derby

Speed is the distance traveled by an object in a certain amount of time. In this activity, you will observe one factor that affects the speed of falling dominoes.

Procedure

1. Set up **25 dominoes** in a straight line. Try to keep equal spacing between the dominoes.

2. Use a **meterstick** to measure the total length of your row of dominoes, and record the length.

3. Use a **stopwatch** to time how long it takes for the dominoes to fall. Record this measurement.

4. Predict what would happen to that amount of time if you changed the distance between the dominoes. Write your predictions.

5. Repeat steps 2 and 3 several times using distances between the dominoes that are smaller and larger than the distance used in your first setup. Use the same number of dominoes in each trial.

Analysis

1. Calculate the average speed for each trial by dividing the total distance (the length of the domino row) by the time the dominoes take to fall.

2. How did the spacing between dominoes affect the average speed? Is this result what you expected? If not, explain.

Measuring Motion

Look around you—you are likely to see something in motion. Your teacher may be walking across the room, or perhaps your friend is writing with a pencil.

Even if you don't see anything moving, motion is still occurring all around you. Air particles are moving, the Earth is circling the sun, and blood is traveling through your blood vessels!

Observing Motion by Using a Reference Point

You might think that the motion of an object is easy to detect—you just watch the object. But you are actually watching the object in relation to another object that appears to stay in place. The object that appears to stay in place is a *reference point.* When an object changes position over time relative to a reference point, the object is in **motion.** You can describe the direction of the object's motion with a reference direction, such as north, south, east, west, up, or down.

✓ **Reading Check** What is a reference point? (*See the Appendix for answers to Reading Checks.*)

Common Reference Points

The Earth's surface is a common reference point for determining motion, as shown in **Figure 1.** Nonmoving objects, such as trees and buildings, are also useful reference points.

A moving object can also be used as a reference point. For example, if you were on the hot-air balloon shown in **Figure 1,** you could watch a bird fly by and see that the bird was changing position in relation to your moving balloon.

Figure 1 *During the interval between the times that these pictures were taken, the hot-air balloon changed position relative to a reference point—the mountain.*

Speed Depends on Distance and Time

Speed is the distance traveled by an object divided by the time taken to travel that distance. Look again at **Figure 1.** Suppose the time interval between the pictures was 10 s and that the balloon traveled 50 m in that time. The speed of the balloon is (50 m)/(10 s), or 5 m/s.

The SI unit for speed is meters per second (m/s). Kilometers per hour (km/h), feet per second (ft/s), and miles per hour (mi/h) are other units commonly used to express speed.

Determining Average Speed

Most of the time, objects do not travel at a constant speed. For example, you probably do not walk at a constant speed from one class to the next. So, it is very useful to calculate *average speed* using the following equation:

$$average\ speed = \frac{total\ distance}{total\ time}$$

Recognizing Speed on a Graph

Suppose a person drives from one city to another. The blue line in the graph in **Figure 2** shows the total distance traveled during a 4 h period. Notice that the distance traveled during each hour is different. The distance varies because the speed is not constant. The driver may change speed because of weather, traffic, or varying speed limits. The average speed for the entire trip can be calculated as follows:

$$average\ speed = \frac{360\ km}{4\ h} = 90\ km/h$$

The red line on the graph shows how far the driver must travel each hour to reach the same city if he or she moved at a constant speed. The slope of this line is the average speed.

motion an object's change in position relative to a reference point

speed the distance traveled divided by the time interval during which the motion occurred

What's Your Speed?

Measure a distance of 5 m or a distance of 25 ft inside or outside. Ask an adult at home to use a stopwatch or a watch with a second hand to time you as you travel the distance you measured. Then, find your average speed. Find the average speed of other members of your family in the same way.

A Graph Showing Speed

Actual —— Average ——

Distance (km): 0, 100, 200, 300, 400
Time (h): 1, 2, 3, 4

Figure 2 *Speed can be shown on a graph of distance versus time.*

Calculating Average Speed An athlete swims a distance from one end of a 50 m pool to the other end in a time of 25 s. What is the athlete's average speed?

Step 1: Write the equation for average speed.

$$average\ speed = \frac{total\ distance}{total\ time}$$

Step 2: Replace the total distance and total time with the values given, and solve.

$$average\ speed = \frac{50\ m}{25\ s} = 2\ m/s$$

Now It's Your Turn

1. Kira jogs to a store 72 m away in a time of 36 s. What is Kira's average speed?
2. If you travel 7.5 km and walk for 1.5 h, what is your average speed?
3. An airplane traveling from San Francisco to Chicago travels 1,260 km in 3.5 h. What is the airplane's average speed?

Velocity: Direction Matters

Imagine that two birds leave the same tree at the same time. They both fly at 10 km/h for 5 min, 12 km/h for 8 min, and 5 km/h for 10 min. Why don't they end up at the same place?

Have you figured out the answer? The birds went in different directions. Their speeds were the same, but they had different velocities. **Velocity** (vuh LAHS uh tee) is the speed of an object in a particular direction.

Be careful not to confuse the terms *speed* and *velocity*. They do not have the same meaning. Velocity must include a reference direction. If you say that an airplane's velocity is 600 km/h, you would not be correct. But you could say the plane's velocity is 600 km/h south. **Figure 3** shows an example of the difference between speed and velocity.

Changing Velocity

You can think of velocity as the rate of change of an object's position. An object's velocity is constant only if its speed and direction don't change. Therefore, constant velocity is always motion along a straight line. An object's velocity changes if either its speed or direction changes. For example, as a bus traveling at 15 m/s south speeds up to 20 m/s south, its velocity changes. If the bus continues to travel at the same speed but changes direction to travel east, its velocity changes again. And if the bus slows down at the same time that it swerves north to avoid a cat, the velocity of the bus changes, too.

Reading Check What are the two ways that velocity can change?

Figure 3 *The speeds of these cars may be similar, but the velocities of the cars differ because the cars are going in different directions.*

460 Chapter 17 Matter in Motion

Figure 4 **Finding Resultant Velocity**

15 m/s east

1 m/s east

When you combine two velocities that are **in the same direction,** add them together to find the resultant velocity.

Person's resultant velocity
15 m/s east + 1 m/s east = 16 m/s east

1 m/s west

15 m/s east

When you combine two velocities that are **in opposite directions,** subtract the smaller velocity from the larger velocity to find the resultant velocity. The resultant velocity is in the direction of the larger velocity.

Person's resultant velocity
15 m/s east − 1 m/s west = 14 m/s east

Combining Velocities

Imagine that you are riding in a bus that is traveling east at 15 m/s. You and the other passengers are also traveling at a velocity of 15 m/s east. But suppose you stand up and walk down the bus's aisle while the bus is moving. Are you still moving at the same velocity as the bus? No! **Figure 4** shows how you can combine velocities to find the *resultant velocity*.

Acceleration

Although the word *accelerate* is commonly used to mean "speed up," the word means something else in science. **Acceleration** (ak SEL uhr AY shuhn) is the rate at which velocity changes. Velocity changes if speed changes, if direction changes, or if both change. So, an object accelerates if its speed, its direction, or both change.

An increase in velocity is commonly called *positive acceleration*. A decrease in velocity is commonly called *negative acceleration,* or *deceleration*. Keep in mind that acceleration is not only how much velocity changes but also how fast velocity changes. The faster the velocity changes, the greater the acceleration is.

velocity the speed of an object in a particular direction

acceleration the rate at which velocity changes over time; an object accelerates if its speed, direction, or both change

1 m/s   2 m/s   3 m/s   4 m/s   5 m/s

South

Figure 5 *This cyclist is accelerating at 1 m/s² south.*

Calculating Average Acceleration

You can find average acceleration by using the equation:

$$\text{average acceleration} = \frac{\text{final velocity} - \text{starting velocity}}{\text{time it takes to change velocity}}$$

Velocity is expressed in meters per second (m/s), and time is expressed in seconds (s). So acceleration is expressed in meters per second per second, or (m/s)/s, which equals m/s². For example, look at **Figure 5.** Every second, the cyclist's southward velocity increases by 1 m/s. His average acceleration can be calculated as follows:

$$\text{average acceleration} = \frac{5 \text{ m/s} - 1 \text{ m/s}}{4 \text{ s}} = 1 \text{ m/s}^2 \text{ south}$$

✓ **Reading Check** What are the units of acceleration?

Recognizing Acceleration on a Graph

Suppose that you are riding a roller coaster. The roller-coaster car moves up a hill until it stops at the top. Then, you are off! The graph in **Figure 6** shows your acceleration for the next 10 s. During the first 8 s, you move down the hill. You can tell from the graph that your acceleration is positive for the first 8 s because your velocity increases as time passes. During the last 2 s, your car starts climbing the next hill. Your acceleration is negative because your velocity decreases as time passes.

Calculating Acceleration

Use the equation for average acceleration to do the following problem.

A plane passes over point A at a velocity of 240 m/s north. Forty seconds later, it passes over point B at a velocity of 260 m/s north. What is the plane's average acceleration?

Figure 6 *Acceleration can be shown on a graph of velocity versus time.*

A Graph Showing Acceleration

Circular Motion: Continuous Acceleration

You may be surprised to know that even when you are completely still, you are experiencing acceleration. You may not seem to be changing speed or direction, but you are! You are traveling in a circle as the Earth rotates. An object traveling in a circular motion is always changing its direction. Therefore, its velocity is always changing, so it is accelerating. The acceleration that occurs in circular motion is known as *centripetal acceleration* (sen TRIP uht uhl ak SEL uhr AY shuhn). Centripetal acceleration occurs on a Ferris wheel at an amusement park or as the moon orbits Earth. Another example of centripetal acceleration is shown in **Figure 7.**

Figure 7 *The blades of these windmills are constantly changing direction. Thus, centripetal acceleration is occurring.*

SECTION Review

Summary

- An object is in motion if it changes position over time in relation to a reference point.
- Speed is the distance traveled by an object divided by the time the object takes to travel that distance.
- Velocity is speed in a given direction.
- Acceleration is the rate at which velocity changes.
- An object can accelerate by changing speed, direction, or both.
- Speed can be represented on a graph of distance versus time.
- Acceleration can be represented by graphing velocity versus time.

Using Key Terms

1. In your own words, write definitions for each of the following terms: *motion* and *acceleration*.

2. Use each of the following terms in a separate sentence: *speed* and *velocity*.

Understanding Key Ideas

3. Which of the following is NOT an example of acceleration?
   a. a person jogging at 3 m/s along a winding path
   b. a car stopping at a stop sign
   c. a cheetah running 27 m/s east
   d. a plane taking off

4. Which of the following would be a good reference point to describe the motion of a dog?
   a. the ground
   b. another dog running
   c. a tree
   d. All of the above

5. Explain the difference between speed and velocity.

6. What two things must you know to determine speed?

7. How are velocity and acceleration related?

Math Skills

8. Find the average speed of a person who swims 105 m in 70 s.

9. What is the average acceleration of a subway train that speeds up from 9.6 m/s to 12 m/s in 0.8 s on a straight section of track?

Critical Thinking

10. **Applying Concepts** Why is it more helpful to know a tornado's velocity rather than its speed?

11. **Evaluating Data** A wolf is chasing a rabbit. Graph the wolf's motion using the following data: 15 m/s at 0 s, 10 m/s at 1 s, 5 m/s at 2 s, 2.5 m/s at 3 s, 1 m/s at 4 s, and 0 m/s at 5 s. What does the graph tell you?

SCILINKS.

NSTA
Developed and maintained by the
National Science Teachers Association

For a variety of links related to this chapter, go to www.scilinks.org

Topic: Measuring Motion
SciLinks code: HSM0927

What Is a Force?

You have probably heard the word force *in everyday conversation. People say things such as "That storm had a lot of force" or "Our football team is a force to be reckoned with." But what, exactly, is a force?*

In science, a **force** is simply a push or a pull. All forces have both size and direction. A force can change the acceleration of an object. This acceleration can be a change in the speed or direction of the object. In fact, any time you see a change in an object's motion, you can be sure that the change in motion was created by a force. Scientists express force using a unit called the **newton** (N).

Forces Acting on Objects

All forces act on objects. For any push to occur, something has to receive the push. You can't push nothing! The same is true for any pull. When doing schoolwork, you use your fingers to pull open books or to push the buttons on a computer keyboard. In these examples, your fingers are exerting forces on the books and the keys. So, the forces act on the books and keys. Another example of a force acting on an object is shown in **Figure 1.**

However, just because a force acts on an object doesn't mean that motion will occur. For example, you are probably sitting on a chair. But the force you are exerting on the chair does not cause the chair to move. The chair doesn't move because the floor is also exerting a force on the chair.

Figure 1 *The bulldozer is exerting a force on the pile of soil. But the pile of soil also exerts a force by just sitting on the ground!*

Unseen Sources and Receivers of Forces

It is not always easy to tell what is exerting a force or what is receiving a force, as shown in **Figure 2.** You cannot see what exerts the force that pulls magnets to refrigerators. And you cannot see that the air around you is held near Earth's surface by a force called *gravity.*

Determining Net Force

Usually, more than one force is acting on an object. The **net force** is the combination all of the forces acting on an object. So, how do you determine the net force? The answer depends on the directions of the forces.

Forces in the Same Direction

Suppose the music teacher asks you and a friend to move a piano. You pull on one end and your friend pushes on the other end, as shown in **Figure 3.** The forces you and your friend exert on the piano act in the same direction. The two forces are added to determine the net force because the forces act in the same direction. In this case, the net force is 45 N. This net force is large enough to move the piano—if it is on wheels, that is!

✓ Reading Check How do you determine the net force on an object if all forces act in the same direction? (*See the Appendix for answers to Reading Checks.*)

Figure 2 *Something that you cannot see exerts a force that makes this cat's fur stand up.*

force a push or a pull exerted on an object in order to change the motion of the object; force has size and direction

newton the SI unit for force (symbol, N)

net force the combination of all of the forces acting on an object

25 N

Net force
25 N + 20 N = 45 N
to the right

20 N

Figure 3 *When forces act in the same direction, you add the forces to determine the net force. The net force will be in the same direction as the individual forces.*

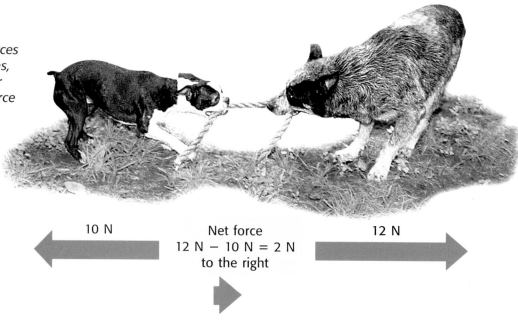

Figure 4 *When two forces act in opposite directions, you subtract the smaller force from the larger force to determine the net force. The net force will be in the same direction as the larger force.*

10 N

Net force
12 N − 10 N = 2 N
to the right

12 N

Forces in Different Directions

Look at the two dogs playing tug of war in **Figure 4.** Each dog is exerting a force on the rope. But the forces are in opposite directions. Which dog will win the tug of war?

Because the forces are in opposite directions, the net force on the rope is found by subtracting the smaller force from the larger one. In this case, the net force is 2 N in the direction of the dog on the right. Give that dog a dog biscuit!

✔ Reading Check What is the net force on an object when you combine a force of 7 N north with a force of 5 N south?

Balanced and Unbalanced Forces

If you know the net force on an object, you can determine the effect of the net force on the object's motion. Why? The net force tells you whether the forces on the object are balanced or unbalanced.

Balanced Forces

When the forces on an object produce a net force of 0 N, the forces are *balanced.* Balanced forces will not cause a change in the motion of a moving object. And balanced forces do not cause a nonmoving object to start moving.

Many objects around you have only balanced forces acting on them. For example, a light hanging from the ceiling does not move because the force of gravity pulling down on the light is balanced by the force of the cord pulling upward. A bird's nest in a tree and a hat resting on your head are also examples of objects that have only balanced forces acting on them. **Figure 5** shows another example of balanced forces.

Figure 5 *Because all the forces on this house of cards are balanced, none of the cards move.*

Unbalanced Forces

When the net force on an object is not 0 N, the forces on the object are *unbalanced*. Unbalanced forces produce a change in motion, such as a change in speed or a change in direction. Unbalanced forces are necessary to cause a nonmoving object to start moving.

Unbalanced forces are also necessary to change the motion of moving objects. For example, consider the soccer game shown in **Figure 6.** The soccer ball is already moving when it is passed from one player to another. When the ball reaches another player, that player exerts an unbalanced force—a kick—on the ball. After the kick, the ball moves in a new direction and has a new speed.

An object can continue to move when the unbalanced forces are removed. For example, when it is kicked, a soccer ball receives an unbalanced force. The ball continues to roll on the ground long after the force of the kick has ended.

Balanced and Unbalanced Forces in Action

Balanced and unbalanced forces and the interactions between them are important in all parts of your life. Balanced and unbalanced forces help you enjoy your free time, play sports, travel, and move your body.

Forces in Recreation

How do you spend your free time? Perhaps you play board games, read, or ride a skateboard. Forces are important in all these recreational activities. Your game piece stays on a game board because all of the forces on it are balanced. But you exert unbalanced forces to lift and roll the dice. Balanced forces keep your book open so that you can read it. But unbalanced forces are needed to turn the pages. Balanced and unbalanced forces are also important for the skateboarder in **Figure 7.**

Figure 6 *The soccer ball moves because the players exert an unbalanced force on the ball each time they kick it.*

Figure 7 *A skateboarder stays on his skateboard when the forces on him are balanced. But unbalanced forces let him have fun going down a ramp.*

Figure 8 *All the forces on this skater are balanced as she glides across the ice. But an unbalanced force was needed for her to start moving.*

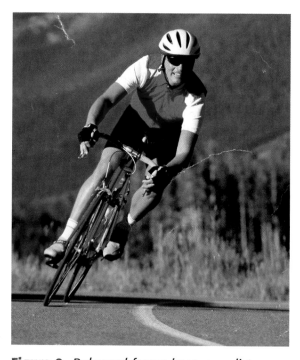

Figure 9 *Balanced forces keep a cyclist on his bicycle, but unbalanced forces are needed for him to turn corners or accelerate.*

Forces in Sports

Athletes use balanced and unbalanced forces all the time—even if they don't realize it. The figure skater in **Figure 8** probably doesn't know that balanced forces are helping her look graceful on the ice.

Now, think about what has to happen for a football placekicker to kick a field goal. First, the center exerts an unbalanced force on the football to snap the ball to the holder. Next, the holder makes sure that all the forces on ball are balanced as he or she holds the ball steady for the kicker. The kicker then exerts an unbalanced force on the ball to send it sailing through the goal posts.

A swimmer also uses balanced and unbalanced forces. The upward and downward forces on a swimmer have to be balanced so that the swimmer will stay afloat. If they weren't balanced, the swimmer would sink! To move forward, a swimmer pushes on the water with his or her arms and legs. These pushes create unbalanced forces that move the swimmer forward.

Forces in Transportation

The purpose of transportation is to move. And you already know that unbalanced forces are needed to start motion. The engines in cars, buses, and trains exert forces that turn their wheels to move forward or backward. Propellers on motorboats exert forces on the water to move the boat, and wind exerts forces on a sail to move a sailboat forward.

But balanced forces are also important in transportation. For example, the cyclist in **Figure 9** doesn't fall off his bicycle because the forces on him are balanced. Also, airplanes stay at their cruising altitude only when the downward force of gravity is balanced with an upward force called *lift*. Lift is created as an airplane moves through the air. The shape of an airplane's wings helps create lift, so a pilot can change the amount of lift by moving the flaps on the wings. If the pilot of the plane wants to land the plane, he or she has to decrease lift so that the force of gravity is greater than the lift. When this happens, gravity and lift are no longer balanced and the plane starts moving downward.

✓ Reading Check What two forces must be balanced so that a plane can fly at a certain altitude?

Forces in the Human Body

Nod your head. Now, hold it still. You've just experienced unbalanced and balanced forces on your body. To move any part of your body, your muscles have to exert unbalanced forces. For example, your muscles have to exert a force on your arm if you want to raise your hand in class. To hold any part of your body still, the forces on it have to be balanced, as shown in **Figure 10.** But unbalanced forces are always acting in your body even when you are completely still. For example, your blood flows through your body because the muscles of the heart exert unbalanced forces to keep the heart beating.

Figure 10 *To keep her hand up, this girl's muscles have to continue exerting a force to balance the force of gravity.*

SECTION Review

Summary

- A force is a push or a pull. Forces have size and direction and are expressed in newtons.

- Force is always exerted by one object on another object.

- Net force is determined by combining forces. Forces in the same direction are added. Forces in opposite directions are subtracted.

- Balanced forces produce no change in motion. Unbalanced forces produce a change in motion.

- Interactions of balanced and unbalanced forces are useful in recreation, sports, transportation, and the human body.

Using Key Terms

1. In your own words, write a definition for each of the following terms: *force* and *net force.*

Understanding Key Ideas

2. Which of the following may happen when an object receives unbalanced forces?

    a. The object changes direction.

    b. The object changes speed.

    c. The object starts to move.

    d. All of the above

3. Explain the difference between balanced and unbalanced forces.

4. Give an example of an unbalanced force causing a change in motion.

5. Give an example of an object that has balanced forces acting on it.

6. Explain the meaning of the phrase "Forces act on objects."

Math Skills

7. A boy pulls a wagon with a force of 6 N east as another boy pushes it with a force of 4 N east. What is the net force?

Critical Thinking

8. **Making Inferences** When finding net force, why must you know the directions of the forces acting on an object?

9. **Applying Concepts** List three forces that you exert when riding a bicycle.

10. **Analyzing Processes** Think about an activity that you do in your free time. Analyze the interactions of balanced and unbalanced forces needed to do that activity.

11. **Applying Concepts** How does the interaction of balanced and unbalanced forces help you get from your home to school?

SCiLINKS®

NSTA
Developed and maintained by the
National Science Teachers Association

For a variety of links related to this chapter, go to www.scilinks.org

Topic: Forces
SciLinks code: HSM0604

Friction: A Force That Opposes Motion

While playing ball, your friend throws the ball out of your reach. Rather than running for the ball, you walk after it. You know that the ball will stop. But do you know why?

You know that the ball is slowing down. An unbalanced force is needed to change the speed of a moving object. So, what force is stopping the ball? The force is called friction. **Friction** is a force that opposes motion between two surfaces that are in contact. Friction retards motion, which means that it can cause a moving object to slow down and eventually stop.

The Source of Friction

Friction occurs because the surface of any object is rough. Even surfaces that feel smooth are covered with microscopic hills and valleys. When two surfaces are in contact, the hills and valleys of one surface stick to the hills and valleys of the other surface, as shown in **Figure 1.** This contact causes friction.

The amount of friction between two surfaces depends on many factors. Two factors include the force pushing the surfaces together and the roughness of the surfaces.

The Effect of Force on Friction

The amount of friction depends on the force pushing the surfaces together. If this force increases, the hills and valleys of the surfaces can come into closer contact. The close contact increases the friction between the surfaces. Objects that weigh less exert less downward force than objects that weigh more do, as shown in **Figure 2.** But changing how much of the surfaces come in contact does not change the amount of friction.

READING WARM-UP

Objectives

- Explain why friction occurs.
- List the two types of friction, and give examples of each type.
- Explain how friction can be both harmful and helpful.

Terms to Learn

friction

READING STRATEGY

Brainstorming The key idea of this section is friction. Brainstorm words and phrases related to friction.

friction a force that opposes motion between two surfaces that are in contact

Figure 1 *When the hills and valleys of one surface stick to the hills and valleys of another surface, friction is created.*

Figure 2   Force and Friction

ⓐ There is more friction between the book with more weight and the table than there is between the book with less weight and the table. A harder push is needed to move the heavier book.

ⓑ Turning a book on its edge does not change the amount of friction between the table and the book.

Force acting on the book   Force of friction   Force acting on the book   Force of friction   Force acting on the book   Force of friction

The Effect of Rougher Surfaces on Friction

Rough surfaces have more microscopic hills and valleys than smooth surfaces do. So, the rougher the surface is, the greater the friction is. For example, a ball rolling on the ground slows down because of the friction between the ball and the ground. A large amount of friction is produced because the ground has a rough surface. But imagine that you were playing ice hockey. If the puck passed out of your reach, it would slide across the ice for a long while before stopping. The reason the puck would continue to slide is that the ice is a smooth surface that has very little friction.

✔ **Reading Check**   Why is friction greater between surfaces that are rough? (*See the Appendix for answers to Reading Checks.*)

The Friction 500

1. Make a short ramp out of **a piece of cardboard** and **one or two books** on a table.
2. Put a **toy car** at the top of the ramp, and let go of the car. If necessary, adjust the ramp height so that your car does not roll off the table.
3. Put the car at the top of the ramp again, and let go of the car. Record the distance the car travels after leaving the ramp.
4. Repeat step 3 two more times, and calculate the average for your results.
5. Change the surface of the table by covering the table with **sandpaper.** Repeat steps 3 and 4.
6. Change the surface of the table one more time by covering the table with **cloth.** Repeat steps 3 and 4 again.
7. Which surface had the most friction? Why? What do you predict would happen if the car were heavier?

Section 3   Friction: A Force That Opposes Motion   **471**

Types of Friction

There are two types of friction. The friction you observe when sliding books across a tabletop is called *kinetic friction*. The other type of friction is *static friction*. You observe static friction when you push on a piece of furniture and it does not move.

Kinetic Friction

The word *kinetic* means "moving." So, kinetic friction is friction between moving surfaces. The amount of kinetic friction between two surfaces depends in part on how the surfaces move. Surfaces can slide past each other. Or a surface can roll over another surface. Usually, the force of sliding kinetic friction is greater than the force of rolling kinetic friction. Thus, it is usually easier to move objects on wheels than to slide the objects along the floor, as shown in **Figure 3.**

Kinetic friction is very useful in everyday life. You use sliding kinetic friction when you apply the brakes on a bicycle and when you write with a pencil or a piece of chalk. You also use sliding kinetic friction when you scratch a part of your body that is itchy!

Rolling kinetic friction is an important part of almost all means of transportation. Anything that has wheels—bicycles, in-line skates, cars, trains, and planes—uses rolling kinetic friction.

Figure 3 **Comparing Kinetic Friction**

ⓐ Moving a heavy piece of furniture in your room can be hard work because **the force of sliding kinetic friction is large.**

ⓑ Moving a heavy piece of furniture is easier if you put it on wheels. **The force of rolling kinetic friction is smaller** and easier to overcome.

Figure 4 Static Friction

Block / **Table**

a There is no friction between the block and the table when no force is applied to the block.

Force applied / **Static friction**

b If a small force (purple arrow) is exerted on the block, the block does not move. The force of static friction (green arrow) balances the force applied.

Force applied / **Kinetic friction**

c When the force exerted on the block is greater than the force of static friction, the block starts moving. When the block starts moving, all static friction is gone, and only kinetic friction (green arrow) opposes the force applied.

Static Friction

When a force is applied to an object but does not cause the object to move, *static friction* occurs. The word *static* means "not moving." The object does not move because the force of static friction balances the force applied. Static friction can be overcome by applying a large enough force. Static friction disappears as soon as an object starts moving, and then kinetic friction immediately occurs. Look at **Figure 4** to understand under what conditions static friction affects an object.

Reading Check What does the word *static* mean?

Friction: Harmful and Helpful

Think about how friction affects a car. Without friction, the tires could not push against the ground to move the car forward, and the brakes could not stop the car. Without friction, a car is useless. However, friction can also cause problems in a car. Friction between moving engine parts increases their temperature and causes the parts to wear down. A liquid coolant is added to the engine to keep the engine from overheating. And engine parts need to be changed as they wear out.

Friction is both harmful and helpful to you and the world around you. Friction can cause holes in your socks and in the knees of your jeans. Friction by wind and water can cause erosion of the topsoil that nourishes plants. On the other hand, friction between your pencil and your paper is necessary to allow the pencil to leave a mark. Without friction, you would just slip and fall when you tried to walk. Because friction can be both harmful and helpful, it is sometimes necessary to decrease or increase friction.

INTERNET ACTIVITY

For another activity related to this chapter, go to **go.hrw.com** and type in the keyword **HP5MOTW**.

CONNECTION TO Social Studies

WRITING SKILL **Invention of the Wheel** Archeologists have found evidence that the first vehicles with wheels were used in ancient Mesopotamia sometime between 3500 and 3000 BCE. Before wheels were invented, people used planks or sleds to carry loads. In your **science journal,** write a paragraph about how your life would be different if wheels did not exist.

Quick Lab

Reducing Friction

1. Stack **two or three heavy books** on a table. Use one finger to push the books across the table.

2. Place **five round pens or pencils** under the books, and push the books again.

3. Compare the force used in step 1 with the force used in step 2. Explain.

4. Open a **jar** with your hands, and close it again.

5. Spread a small amount of **liquid soap** on your hands.

6. Try to open the jar again. Was the jar easier or harder to open with the soap? Explain your observations.

7. In which situation was friction helpful? In which situation was friction harmful?

Some Ways to Reduce Friction

One way to reduce friction is to use lubricants (LOO bri kuhnts). *Lubricants* are substances that are applied to surfaces to reduce the friction between the surfaces. Some examples of common lubricants are motor oil, wax, and grease. Lubricants are usually liquids, but they can be solids or gases. An example of a gas lubricant is the air that comes out of the tiny holes of an air-hockey table. **Figure 5** shows one use of a lubricant.

Friction can also be reduced by switching from sliding kinetic friction to rolling kinetic friction. Ball bearings placed between the wheels and axles of in-line skates and bicycles make it easier for the wheels to turn by reducing friction.

Another way to reduce friction is to make surfaces that rub against each other smoother. For example, rough wood on a park bench is painful to slide across because there is a large amount of friction between your leg and the bench. Rubbing the bench with sandpaper makes the bench smoother and more comfortable to sit on. The reason the bench is more comfortable is that the friction between your leg and the bench is reduced.

Reading Check List three common lubricants.

Figure 5 *When you work on a bicycle, watch out for the chain! You might get dirty from the grease or oil that keeps the chain moving freely. Without this lubricant, friction between the sections of the chain would quickly wear the chain out.*

Some Ways to Increase Friction

One way to increase friction is to make surfaces rougher. For example, sand scattered on icy roads keeps cars from skidding. Baseball players sometimes wear textured batting gloves to increase the friction between their hands and the bat so that the bat does not fly out of their hands.

Another way to increase friction is to increase the force pushing the surfaces together. For example, if you are sanding a piece of wood, you can sand the wood faster by pressing harder on the sandpaper. Pressing harder increases the force pushing the sandpaper and wood together. So, the friction between the sandpaper and wood increases. **Figure 6** shows another example of friction increased by pushing on an object.

Figure 6 *No one likes cleaning dirty pans. To get this chore done quickly, press down with the scrubber to increase friction.*

SECTION Review

Summary

- Friction is a force that opposes motion.
- Friction is caused by hills and valleys on the surfaces of two objects touching each other.
- The amount of friction depends on factors such as the roughness of the surfaces and the force pushing the surfaces together.
- Two kinds of friction are kinetic friction and static friction.
- Friction can be helpful or harmful.

Using Key Terms

1. In your own words, write a definition for the term *friction*.

Understanding Key Ideas

2. Why is it easy to slip when there is water on the floor?
   a. The water is a lubricant and reduces the friction between your feet and the floor.
   b. The friction between your feet and the floor changes from kinetic to static friction.
   c. The water increases the friction between your feet and the floor.
   d. The friction between your feet and the floor changes from sliding kinetic friction to rolling kinetic friction.

3. Explain why friction occurs.

4. How does the roughness of surfaces that are touching affect the friction between the surfaces?

5. Describe how the amount of force pushing two surfaces together affects friction.

6. Name two ways in which friction can be increased.

7. List the two types of friction, and give an example of each.

Interpreting Graphics

8. Why do you think the sponge shown below has a layer of plastic bristles attached to it?

Critical Thinking

9. **Applying Concepts** Name two ways that friction is harmful and two ways that friction is helpful to you when riding a bicycle.

10. **Making Inferences** Describe a situation in which static friction is useful.

Developed and maintained by the National Science Teachers Association

For a variety of links related to this chapter, go to www.scilinks.org

Topic: Force and Friction
SciLinks code: HSM0601

Gravity: A Force of Attraction

Have you ever seen a video of astronauts on the moon? They bounce around like beach balls even though they wear big, bulky spacesuits. Why is leaping on the moon easier than leaping on Earth?

The answer is gravity. **Gravity** is a force of attraction between objects that is due to their masses. The force of gravity can change the motion of an object by changing its speed, direction, or both. In this section, you will learn about gravity and its effects on objects, such as the astronaut in **Figure 1.**

The Effects of Gravity on Matter

All matter has mass. Gravity is a result of mass. Therefore, all matter is affected by gravity. That is, all objects experience an attraction toward all other objects. This gravitational force pulls objects toward each other. Right now, because of gravity, you are being pulled toward this book, your pencil, and every other object around you.

These objects are also being pulled toward you and toward each other because of gravity. So why don't you see the effects of this attraction? In other words, why don't you notice objects moving toward each other? The reason is that the mass of most objects is too small to cause a force large enough to move objects toward each other. However, you are familiar with one object that is massive enough to cause a noticeable attraction—the Earth.

READING WARM-UP

Objectives

● Describe gravity and its effect on matter.

● Explain the law of universal gravitation.

● Explain how an object's center of mass is used to determine gravitational force.

● Describe the difference between mass and weight.

Terms to Learn

gravity
weight
mass

READING STRATEGY

Paired Summarizing Read this section silently. In pairs, take turns summarizing the material. Stop to discuss ideas that seem confusing.

gravity a force of attraction between objects that is due to their masses

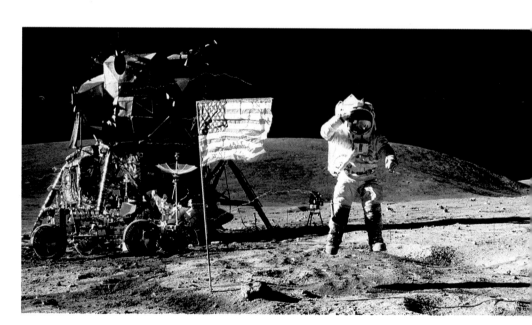

Figure 1 *Because the moon has less gravity than the Earth does, walking on the moon's surface was a very bouncy experience for the Apollo astronauts.*

The Size of Earth's Gravitational Force

Compared with all objects around you, Earth has a huge mass. Therefore, Earth's gravitational force is very large. You must apply forces to overcome Earth's gravitational force any time you lift objects or even parts of your body.

Earth's gravitational force pulls everything toward the center of Earth. Because of this force, the books, tables, and chairs in the room stay in place, and dropped objects fall to Earth rather than moving together or toward you.

Reading Check Why must you exert a force to pick up an object? (*See the Appendix for answers to Reading Checks.*)

Newton and the Study of Gravity

For thousands of years, people asked two very puzzling questions: Why do objects fall toward Earth, and what keeps the planets moving in the sky? The two questions were treated separately until 1665 when a British scientist named Sir Isaac Newton realized that they were two parts of the same question.

The Core of an Idea

The legend is that Newton made the connection between the two questions when he watched a falling apple, as shown in **Figure 2.** He knew that unbalanced forces are needed to change the motion of objects. He concluded that an unbalanced force on the apple made the apple fall. And he reasoned that an unbalanced force on the moon kept the moon moving circularly around Earth. He proposed that these two forces are actually the same force—a force of attraction called *gravity*.

Figure 2 *Sir Isaac Newton realized that the same unbalanced force affected the motions of the apple and the moon.*

The Birth of a Law

Newton summarized his ideas about gravity in a law now known as the *law of universal gravitation.* This law describes the relationships between gravitational force, mass, and distance. The law is called *universal* because it applies to all objects in the universe.

The Law of Universal Gravitation

The law of universal gravitation is the following: All objects in the universe attract each other through gravitational force. The size of the force depends on the masses of the objects and the distance between the objects. Understanding the law is easier if you consider it in two parts.

Part 1: Gravitational Force Increases as Mass Increases

Imagine an elephant and a cat. Because an elephant has a larger mass than a cat does, the amount of gravity between an elephant and Earth is greater than the amount of gravity between a cat and Earth. So, a cat is much easier to pick up than an elephant! There is also gravity between the cat and the elephant, but that force is very small because the cat's mass and the elephant's mass are so much smaller than Earth's mass. **Figure 3** shows the relationship between mass and gravitational force.

This part of the law of universal gravitation also explains why the astronauts on the moon bounce when they walk. The moon has less mass than Earth does. Therefore, the moon's gravitational force is less than Earth's. The astronauts bounced around on the moon because they were not being pulled down with as much force as they would have been on Earth.

✓ **Reading Check** How does mass affect gravitational force?

Figure 3 **How Mass Affects Gravitational Force**

The gravitational force between objects increases as the masses of the objects increase. The arrows indicate the gravitational force between two objects. The length of the arrows indicates the strength of the force.

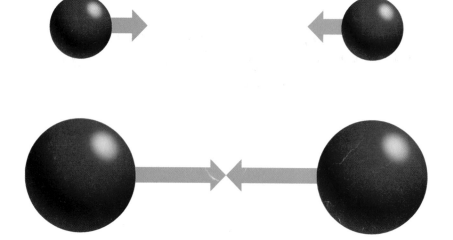

ⓐ Gravitational force is small between objects that have small masses.

ⓑ Gravitational force is large when the mass of one or both objects is large.

Part 2: Gravitational Force Decreases as Distance Increases

The gravitational force between you and Earth is large. Whenever you jump up, you are pulled back down by Earth's gravitational force. On the other hand, the sun is more than 300,000 times more massive than Earth. So why doesn't the sun's gravitational force affect you more than Earth's does? The reason is that the sun is so far away.

You are about 150 million kilometers (93 million miles) away from the sun. At this distance, the gravitational force between you and the sun is very small. If there were some way you could stand on the sun, you would find it impossible to move. The gravitational force acting on you would be so great that you could not move any part of your body!

Although the sun's gravitational force on your body is very small, the force is very large on Earth and the other planets, as shown in **Figure 4.** The gravity between the sun and the planets is large because the objects have large masses. If the sun's gravitational force did not have such an effect on the planets, the planets would not stay in orbit around the sun. **Figure 5** will help you understand the relationship between gravitational force and distance.

Figure 4 *Venus and Earth have approximately the same mass. But because Venus is closer to the sun, the gravitational force between Venus and the sun is greater than the gravitational force between Earth and the sun.*

Figure 5   How Distance Affects Gravitational Force

The gravitational force between objects decreases as the distance between the objects increases. The length of the arrows indicates the strength of the gravitational force between two objects.

ⓐ Gravitational force is strong when the distance between two objects is small.

ⓑ If the distance between two objects increases, the gravitational force pulling them together decreases rapidly.

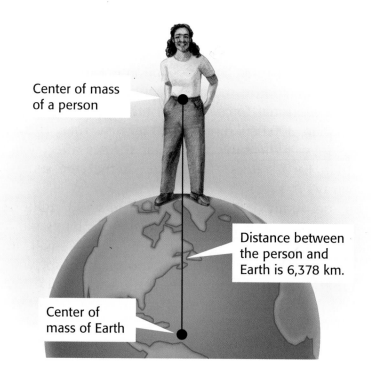

Figure 6 *The distance between a person standing on the ground and Earth is not 0 m! When finding distance to determine gravitational force, you always measure from the center of mass of each object.*

Center of mass of a person

Distance between the person and Earth is 6,378 km.

Center of mass of Earth

Gravitational Force and Center of Mass

You know that gravitational force depends on the distance between objects. But, how do you find the distance between objects? For example, if you need to know the distance between you and your friend, where would you measure? Would you measure from your nose to your friend's nose or from your foot to your friend's foot? When finding the distance between objects to determine gravitational force, scientists always measure from the center of mass of each object. The *center of mass* is the point at which all the mass of an object can be considered to be concentrated. **Figure 6** shows how the distance between a person and Earth is measured by using centers of mass.

Finding the Center of Mass

Finding the center of mass for regularly shaped objects, such as spheres and cubes, is easy. The center of mass is in the center of such objects. But finding the center of mass of an irregular object or an object that does not have a uniform density can be more difficult. However, one simple way to find the center of mass of an object is to spin the object. The point around which the object spins is its center of mass.

Scientists usually measure the motion of an object by the motion of its center of mass. Look at **Figure 7.** The hammer is spinning around its center of mass as it moves through the air. The line drawn on the photo shows how the center of mass moves. So, if you wanted to measure how far the hammer moved, you would measure from one end of the red line to the other end.

Figure 7 *Objects always spin around their center of mass. The motion of an object is usually described as the motion of its center of mass.*

Weight as a Measure of Gravitational Force

Gravity is a force of attraction between objects. **Weight** is a measure of the gravitational force on an object. When you see or hear the word *weight,* it usually refers to Earth's gravitational force on an object. But weight can also be a measure of the gravitational force exerted on objects by the moon or other planets.

The Differences Between Weight and Mass

Weight is related to mass, but they are not the same. Weight changes when gravitational force changes. **Mass** is the amount of matter in an object. An object's mass does not change. Imagine that an object is moved to a place that has a greater gravitational force—such as the planet Jupiter. The object's weight will increase, but its mass will remain the same. **Figure 8** shows the weight and mass of an astronaut on Earth and on the moon. The moon's gravitational force is about one-sixth of Earth's gravitational force.

Gravitational force is about the same everywhere on Earth. So, the weight of any object is about the same everywhere. Because mass and weight are constant on Earth, the terms *weight* and *mass* are often used to mean the same thing. This can be confusing. Be sure you understand the difference!

Reading Check How is gravitational force related to the weight of an object?

CONNECTION TO Language Arts

WRITING SKILL **Gravity Story**
Suppose you had a device that could increase or decrease the gravitational force of Earth. In your **science journal,** write a short story describing what you might do with the device, what you would expect to see, and what effect the device would have on the weight of objects.

weight a measure of the gravitational force exerted on an object; its value can change with the location of the object in the universe

mass a measure of the amount of matter in an object

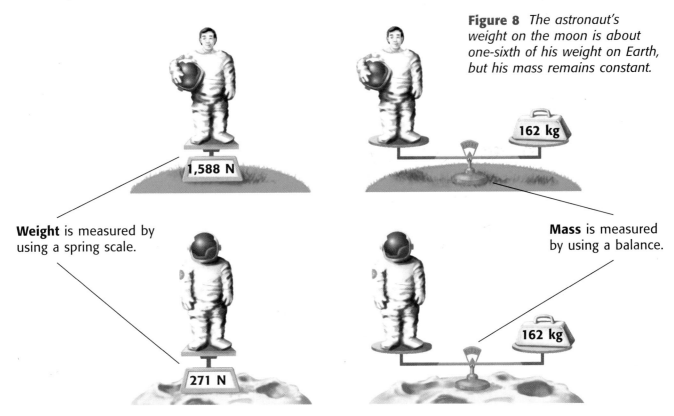

Figure 8 *The astronaut's weight on the moon is about one-sixth of his weight on Earth, but his mass remains constant.*

1,588 N

162 kg

Weight is measured by using a spring scale.

Mass is measured by using a balance.

271 N

162 kg

Figure 9 *A small apple weighs 1 N. The newton is the SI unit of weight.*

Units of Weight and Mass

You have learned that the SI unit of force is a newton (N). Gravity is a force, and weight is a measure of gravity. So, weight is also measured in newtons. The SI unit of mass is the kilogram (kg). Mass is often measured in grams (g) and milligrams (mg) as well. On Earth, a 100 g object, such as the apple shown in **Figure 9,** weighs about 1 N.

When you use a bathroom scale, you are measuring the gravitational force between your body and Earth. So, you are measuring your weight, which should be given in newtons. However, many bathroom scales have units of pounds and kilograms instead of newtons. Thus, people sometimes mistakenly think that the kilogram (like the pound) is a unit of weight.

✓ **Reading Check** What is the SI unit for force? What is the SI unit for mass?

The Influences of Weight on Shape

Gravitational force influences the shapes of living things. On land, large animals must have strong skeletons to support their mass against the force of gravity. For example, you would never see an elephant that has legs as thin as a person's legs! And the trunks of trees support the mass of the tree. For organisms that live in water, however, the downward force of gravity is balanced by the upward force of the water. For many of these creatures, strong skeletons are unnecessary. Jellyfish, such as the ones shown in **Figure 10,** have no skeleton. So, jellyfish drift gracefully through the water, but they collapse if they wash up on the beach.

Figure 10 *Jellyfish look like flying saucers when gravity is balanced by the upward force of water but are only lumps when washed up on the beach.*

Summary

- Gravity is a force of attraction between objects that is due to their masses.
- The law of universal gravitation states that all objects in the universe attract each other through gravitational force.
- Gravitational force increases as mass increases.

- Gravitational force decreases as distance increases.
- The distance between objects is measured between the centers of mass.
- Mass is the amount of matter in an object. Weight is a measure of the gravitational force on an object.

Using Key Terms

1. In your own words, write a definition for the term *gravity*.

2. Use each of the following terms in a separate sentence: *mass* and *weight*.

Understanding Key Ideas

3. If Earth's mass doubled without changing its size, your weight would

    a. increase because gravitational force increases.

    b. decrease because gravitational force increases.

    c. increase because gravitational force decreases.

    d. not change because you are still on Earth.

4. What is the law of universal gravitation?

5. How does the mass of an object relate to the gravitational force that the object exerts on other objects?

6. How does the distance between objects affect the gravitational force between them?

7. Why are mass and weight often confused?

8. How is an object's center of mass used to determine gravitational force?

Critical Thinking

9. **Applying Concepts** Your friend thinks that there is no gravity in space. How could you explain to your friend that there must be gravity in space?

10. **Making Comparisons** Explain why it is your weight and not your mass that would change if you landed on Mars.

Interpreting Graphics

A teacher placed four sets of objects around the classroom. A student measured the mass of each object and the distance between the two objects in each set. The data the student collected are shown in the table below. Use the table below to answer the questions that follow.

Data Collected			
Set	Mass A (g)	Mass B (g)	Distance (cm)
1	100	50	40
2	100	100	20
3	50	50	40
4	100	50	20

11. For which set of objects is the gravitational force between the two objects the greatest? Explain your answer.

12. Compare sets 1 and 4. For which set is the gravitational force smaller? Explain your answer.

For a variety of links related to this chapter, go to www.scilinks.org

Topic: Matter and Gravity
SciLinks code: HSM0922

Skills Practice Lab

Detecting Acceleration

Have you ever noticed that you can "feel" acceleration? In a car or in an elevator, you may notice changes in speed or direction—even with your eyes closed! You are able to sense these changes because of tiny hair cells in your ears. These cells detect the movement of fluid in your inner ear. The fluid accelerates when you do, and the hair cells send a message about the acceleration to your brain. This message allows you to sense the acceleration. In this activity, you will build a device that detects acceleration. This device is called an *accelerometer* (ak SEL uhr AHM uht uhr).

Procedure

1. Cut a piece of string that reaches three-quarters of the way into the container.

2. Use a pushpin to attach one end of the string to the cork or plastic-foam ball.

3. Use modeling clay to attach the other end of the string to the center of the inside of the container lid. The cork or ball should hang no farther than three-quarters of the way into the container.

4. Fill the container with water.

5. Put the lid tightly on the container. The string and cork or ball should be inside the container.

6. Turn the container upside down. The cork should float about three-quarters of the way up inside the container, as shown at right. You are now ready to detect acceleration by using your accelerometer and completing the following steps.

7. Put the accelerometer on a tabletop. The container lid should touch the tabletop. Notice that the cork floats straight up in the water.

8. Now, gently push the accelerometer across the table at a constant speed. Notice that the cork quickly moves in the direction you are pushing and then swings backward. If you did not see this motion, repeat this step until you are sure you can see the first movement of the cork.

9 After you are familiar with how to use your accelerometer, try the following changes in motion. For each change, record your observations of the cork's first motion.

   a. As you move the accelerometer across the table, gradually increase its speed.

   b. As you move the accelerometer across the table, gradually decrease its speed.

   c. While moving the accelerometer across the table, change the direction in which you are pushing.

   d. Make any other changes in motion you can think of. You should make only one change to the motion for each trial.

Analyze the Results

1 **Analyzing Results** When you move the bottle at a constant speed, why does the cork quickly swing backward after it moves in the direction of acceleration?

2 **Explaining Events** The cork moves forward (in the direction you were moving the bottle) when you speed up but moves backward when you slow down. Explain why the cork moves this way. (Hint: Think about the direction of acceleration.)

Draw Conclusions

3 **Making Predictions** Imagine you are standing on a corner and watching a car that is waiting at a stoplight. A passenger inside the car is holding some helium balloons. Based on what you observed with your accelerometer, what do you think will happen to the balloons when the car begins moving?

Applying Your Data

If you move the bottle in a circle at a constant speed, what do you predict the cork will do? Try it, and check your answer.

485

Chapter Review

USING KEY TERMS

Complete each of the following sentences by choosing the correct term from the word bank.

mass   gravity
friction   weight
speed   velocity
net force   newton

1 ___ opposes motion between surfaces that are touching.

2 The ___ is the unit of force.

3 ___ is determined by combining forces.

4 Acceleration is the rate at which ___ changes.

5 ___ is a measure of the gravitational force on an object.

UNDERSTANDING KEY IDEAS

Multiple Choice

6 If a student rides her bicycle on a straight road and does not speed up or slow down, she is traveling with a

  a. constant acceleration.

  b. constant velocity.

  c. positive acceleration.

  d. negative acceleration.

7 A force

  a. is expressed in newtons.

  b. can cause an object to speed up, slow down, or change direction.

  c. is a push or a pull.

  d. All of the above

8 If you are in a spacecraft that has been launched into space, your weight would

  a. increase because gravitational force is increasing.

  b. increase because gravitational force is decreasing.

  c. decrease because gravitational force is decreasing.

  d. decrease because gravitational force is increasing.

9 The gravitational force between 1 kg of lead and Earth is ___ the gravitational force between 1 kg of marshmallows and Earth.

  a. greater than   **c.** the same as

  b. less than   **d.** None of the above

Short Answer

10 Describe the relationship between motion and a reference point.

11 How is it possible to be accelerating but traveling at a constant speed?

12 What is the center of mass of an object? How can you find it?

13 Explain the difference between mass and weight.

Math Skills

14 A kangaroo hops 60 m to the east in 5 s. Use this information to answer the following questions.

   a. What is the kangaroo's average speed?

   b. What is the kangaroo's average velocity?

   c. The kangaroo stops at a lake for a drink of water and then starts hopping again to the south. Each second, the kangaroo's velocity increases 2.5 m/s. What is the kangaroo's acceleration after 5 s?

CRITICAL THINKING

15 Concept Mapping Use the following terms to create a concept map: *speed, velocity, acceleration, force, direction,* and *motion.*

16 Applying Concepts Your family is moving, and you are asked to help move some boxes. One box is so heavy that you must push it across the room rather than lift it. What are some ways you could reduce friction to make moving the box easier?

17 Analyzing Ideas Considering the scientific meaning of the word *acceleration,* how could using the term *accelerator* when talking about a car's gas pedal lead to confusion?

18 Identifying Relationships Explain why it is important for airplane pilots to know wind velocity and not just wind speed during a flight.

INTERPRETING GRAPHICS

Use the figures below to answer the questions that follow.

19 Is the graph below showing positive acceleration or negative acceleration? How can you tell?

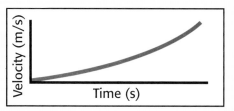

20 You know how to combine two forces that act in one or two directions. The same method can be used to combine several forces acting in several directions. Look at the diagrams, and calculate the net force in each diagram. Predict the direction each object will move.

READING

Read each of the passages below. Then, answer the questions that follow each passage.

Passage 1 If you look closely at the surface of a golf ball, you'll see dozens of tiny dimples. When air flows past these dimples, the air is stirred up and stays near the surface of the ball. By keeping air moving near the surface of the ball, the dimples help the golf ball move faster and farther through the air. Jeff DiTullio, a teacher at MIT in Cambridge, Massachusetts, decided to apply this principle to a baseball bat. When DiTullio tested his dimpled bat in a <u>wind tunnel</u>, he found that the bat could be swung 3% to 5% faster than a bat without dimples. That increase may not seem like much, but the dimpled bat could add about 5 m of distance to a fly ball!

1. Who is Jeff DiTullio?
  A the inventor of the dimpled golf ball
  B a teacher at Cambridge University
  C the inventor of the dimpled bat
  D a professional baseball player

2. Which of the following ideas is NOT stated in the passage?
  F Dimples make DiTullio's bat move faster.
  G MIT is in Cambridge, Massachusetts.
  H Air that is stirred up near the surface of DiTullio's bat makes it easier to swing the bat faster.
  I DiTullio will make a lot of money from his invention.

3. In the passage, what does *wind tunnel* mean?
  A a place to practice batting
  B a place to test the speed of objects in the air
  C a baseball stadium
  D a passageway that is shielded from the wind

Passage 2 The Golden Gate Bridge in San Francisco, California, is one of the most famous <u>landmarks</u> in the world. Approximately 9 million people from around the world visit the bridge each year.

The Golden Gate Bridge is a suspension bridge. A suspension bridge is one in which the roadway is hung, or suspended, from huge cables that extend from one end of the bridge to the other. The main cables on the Golden Gate Bridge are 2.33 km long. Many forces act on the main cables. For example, smaller cables pull down on the main cables to connect the roadway to the main cables. And two towers that are 227 m tall push up on the main cables. The forces on the main cable must be balanced, or the bridge will collapse.

1. In this passage, what does *landmarks* mean?
  A large areas of land
  B well-known places
  C street signs
  D places where people meet

2. Which of the following statements is a fact from the passage?
  F The roadway of the Golden Gate Bridge is suspended from huge cables.
  G The towers of the Golden Gate Bridge are 2.33 km tall.
  H The main cables connect the roadway to the towers.
  I The forces on the cables are not balanced.

3. According to the passage, why do people from around the world visit the Golden Gate Bridge?
  A It is the longest bridge in the world.
  B It is a suspension bridge.
  C It is the only bridge that is painted orange.
  D It is a famous landmark.

The graph below shows the data collected by a student as she watched a squirrel running on the ground. Use the graph below to answer the questions that follow.

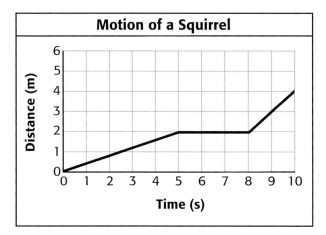

Motion of a Squirrel

1. Which of the following best describes the motion of the squirrel between 5 s and 8 s?

   A The squirrel's speed increased.

   B The squirrel's speed decreased.

   C The squirrel's speed did not change.

   D The squirrel moved backward.

2. Which of the following statements about the motion of the squirrel is true?

   F The squirrel moved with the greatest speed between 0 s and 5 s.

   G The squirrel moved with the greatest speed between 8 s and 10 s.

   H The squirrel moved with a constant speed between 0 s and 8 s.

   I The squirrel moved with a constant speed between 5 s and 10 s.

3. What is the average speed of the squirrel between 8 s and 10 s?

   A 0.4 m/s

   B 1 m/s

   C 2 m/s

   D 4 m/s

Read each question below, and choose the best answer.

1. The distance between Cedar Rapids, Iowa, and Sioux Falls, South Dakota, is about 660 km. How long will it take a car traveling with an average speed of 95 km/h to drive from Cedar Rapids to Sioux Falls?

   A less than 1 h

   B about 3 h

   C about 7 h

   D about 10 h

2. Martha counted the number of people in each group that walked into her school's cafeteria. In the first 10 groups, she counted the following numbers of people: 6, 4, 9, 6, 4, 10, 9, 5, 9, and 8. What is the mode of this set of data?

   F 6

   G 7

   H 9

   I 10

3. Which of the following terms describes the angle marked in the triangle below.

   42°

   A acute

   B obtuse

   C right

   D None of the above

4. Donnell collected money for a charity fundraiser. After one hour, he counted the money and found that he had raised $10.00 in bills and $3.74 in coins. Which of the following represents the number of coins he collected?

   F 4 pennies, 9 nickels, 18 dimes, and 6 quarters

   G 9 pennies, 7 nickels, 18 dimes, and 6 quarters

   H 6 pennies, 7 nickels, 15 dimes, and 8 quarters

   I 9 pennies, 8 nickels, 12 dimes, and 3 quarters

Standardized Test Preparation

Science in Action

Science, Technology, and Society

GPS Watch System

Some athletes are concerned about knowing their speed during training. To calculate speed, they need to know distance and time. Finding time by using a watch is easy to do. But determining distance is more difficult. However, a GPS watch system is now available to help with this problem. *GPS* stands for *global positioning system*. A GPS unit, which is worn on an athlete's upper arm, monitors the athlete's position by using signals from satellites. As the athlete moves, the GPS unit calculates the distance traveled. The GPS unit sends a signal to the watch, which keeps the athlete's time, and the watch displays the athlete's speed.

Math ACTiViTY

Suppose an athlete wishes to finish a 5 K race in under 25 min. The distance of a 5 K is 5 km. (Remember that 1 km = 1,000 m.) If the athlete runs the race at a constant speed of 3.4 m/s, will she meet her goal?

Weird Science

The Segway™ Human Transporter

In November 2002, a new people-moving machine was introduced, and people have been fascinated by the odd-looking device ever since. The device is called the *Segway Human Transporter*. The Segway is a two-wheeled device that is powered by a rechargeable battery. To move forward, the rider simply leans forward. Sensors detect this motion and send signals to the on-board computer. The computer, in turn, tells the motor to start going. To slow down, the rider leans backward, and to stop, the rider stands straight up. The Segway has a top speed of 20 km/h (about 12.5 mi/h) and can travel up to 28 km (about 17.4 mi) on a single battery charge.

Language Arts ACTiViTY

WRITING SKILL The inventor of the Segway thinks that the machine will make a good alternative to walking and bicycle riding. Write a one-page essay explaining whether you think using a Segway is better or worse than riding a bicycle.

People in Science

Victor Petrenko

Snowboard and Ski Brakes Have you ever wished for emergency brakes on your snowboard or skis? Thanks to Victor Petrenko and the Ice Research Lab of Dartmouth College, snowboards and skis that have braking systems may soon be available.

Not many people know more about the properties of ice and ice-related technologies than Victor Petrenko does. He has spent most of his career researching the electrical and mechanical properties of ice. Through his research, Petrenko learned that ice can hold an electric charge. He used this property to design a braking system for snowboards. The system is a form of electric friction control.

The power source for the brakes is a battery. The battery is connected to a network of wires embedded on the bottom surface of a snowboard. When the battery is activated, the bottom of the snowboard gains a negative charge. This negative charge creates a positive charge on the surface of the snow. Because opposite charges attract, the snowboard and the snow are pulled together. The force that pulls the surfaces together increases friction, and the snowboard slows down.

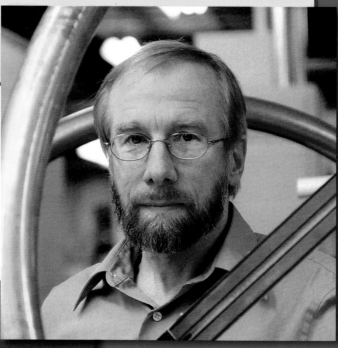

Social Studies ACTIVITY

Research the history of skiing. Make a poster that includes a timeline of significant dates in the history of skiing. Illustrate your poster with photos or drawings.

go.hrw.com

To learn more about these Science in Action topics, visit go.hrw.com and type in the keyword **HP5MOTF**.

Current Science

Check out Current Science® articles related to this chapter by visiting go.hrw.com. Just type in the keyword **HP5CS05**.

Forces and Motion

About the PHOTO

To train for space flight, astronauts fly in a modified KC-135 cargo airplane. The airplane first flies upward at a steep angle. Then, it flies downward at a 45° angle, which causes the feeling of reduced gravity inside. Under these conditions, the astronauts in the plane can float and can practice carrying out tasks that they will need to perform when they are in orbit. Because the floating makes people queasy, this KC-135 is nicknamed the "Vomit Comet."

PRE-READING ACTIVITY

**Graphic
Organizer**

Spider Map Before you read the chapter, create the graphic organizer entitled "Spider Map" described in the **Study Skills** section of the Appendix. Label the circle "Motion." Create a leg for each law of motion, a leg for gravity, and a leg for momentum. As you read the chapter, fill in the map with details about how motion is related to the laws of motion, gravity, and momentum.

Falling Water

Gravity is one of the most important forces in your life. In this activity, you will observe the effect of gravity on a falling object.

Procedure

1. Place a **wide plastic tub** on the floor. Punch a small hole in the side of a **paper cup,** near the bottom.

2. Hold your finger over the hole, and fill the cup with **water.** Keep your finger over the hole, and hold the cup waist-high above the tub.

3. Uncover the hole. Record your observations as Trial 1.

4. Predict what will happen to the water if you drop the cup at the same time you uncover the hole.

5. Cover the hole, and refill the cup with water.

6. Uncover the hole, and drop the cup at the same time. Record your observations as Trial 2.

7. Clean up any spilled water with **paper towels.**

Analysis

1. What differences did you observe in the behavior of the water during the two trials?

2. In Trial 2, how fast did the cup fall compared with how fast the water fell?

3. How did the results of Trial 2 compare with your prediction?

Gravity and Motion

Suppose you dropped a baseball and a marble at the same time from the top of a tall building. Which do you think would land on the ground first?

In ancient Greece around 400 BCE, a philosopher named Aristotle (AR is TAWT uhl) thought that the rate at which an object falls depended on the object's mass. If you asked Aristotle whether the baseball or the marble would land first, he would have said the baseball. But Aristotle never tried dropping objects with different masses to test his idea about falling objects.

Gravity and Falling Objects

In the late 1500s, a young Italian scientist named Galileo Galilei (GAL uh LAY oh GAL uh LAY) questioned Aristotle's idea about falling objects. Galileo argued that the mass of an object does not affect the time the object takes to fall to the ground. According to one story, Galileo proved his argument by dropping two cannonballs of different masses from the top of the Leaning Tower of Pisa in Italy. The people watching from the ground below were amazed to see the two cannonballs land at the same time. Whether or not this story is true, Galileo's work changed people's understanding of gravity and falling objects.

READING WARM-UP

Objectives

● Explain the effect of gravity and air resistance on falling objects.

● Explain why objects in orbit are in free fall and appear to be weightless.

● Describe how projectile motion is affected by gravity.

Terms to Learn

terminal velocity
free fall
projectile motion

READING STRATEGY

Reading Organizer As you read this section, create an outline of the section. Use the headings from the section in your outline.

Gravity and Acceleration

Objects fall to the ground at the same rate because the acceleration due to gravity is the same for all objects. Why is this true? Acceleration depends on both force and mass. A heavier object experiences a greater gravitational force than a lighter object does. But a heavier object is also harder to accelerate because it has more mass. The extra mass of the heavy object exactly balances the additional gravitational force. **Figure 1** shows objects that have different masses falling with the same acceleration.

Figure 1 *This stop-action photo shows that a table-tennis ball and a golf ball fall at the same rate even though they have different masses.*

Acceleration Due to Gravity

Acceleration is the rate at which velocity changes over time. So, the acceleration of an object is the object's change in velocity divided by the amount of time during which the change occurs. All objects accelerate toward Earth at a rate of 9.8 meters per second per second. This rate is written as 9.8 m/s/s, or 9.8 m/s^2. So, for every second that an object falls, the object's downward velocity increases by 9.8 m/s, as shown in **Figure 2.**

☑ **Reading Check** What is the acceleration due to gravity? (*See the Appendix for answers to Reading Checks.*)

Velocity of Falling Objects

You can calculate the change in velocity (Δv) of a falling object by using the following equation:

$$\Delta v = g \times t$$

In this equation, g is the acceleration due to gravity on Earth (9.8 m/s^2), and t is the time the object takes to fall (in seconds). The change in velocity is the difference between the final velocity and the starting velocity. If the object starts at rest, this equation yields the velocity of the object after a certain time period.

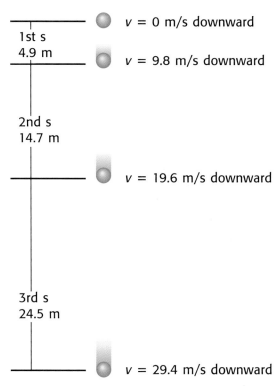

Figure 2 *A falling object accelerates at a constant rate. The object falls faster and farther each second than it did the second before.*

MATH FOCUS

Calculating the Velocity of Falling Objects A stone at rest is dropped from a cliff, and the stone hits the ground after a time of 3 s. What is the stone's velocity when it hits the ground?

Step 1: Write the equation for change in velocity.

$$\Delta v = g \times t$$

Step 2: Replace g with its value and t with the time given in the problem, and solve.

$$\Delta v = 9.8 \, \frac{\text{m/s}}{s} \times 3 \, s$$
$$= 29.4 \text{ m/s}$$

To rearrange the equation to find time, divide by the acceleration due to gravity:

$$t = \frac{\Delta v}{g}$$

Now It's Your Turn

1. A penny at rest is dropped from the top of a tall stairwell. What is the penny's velocity after it has fallen for 2 s?
2. The same penny hits the ground in 4.5 s. What is the penny's velocity as it hits the ground?
3. A marble at rest is dropped from a tall building. The marble hits the ground with a velocity of 98 m/s. How long was the marble in the air?
4. An acorn at rest falls from an oak tree. The acorn hits the ground with a velocity of 14.7 m/s. How long did it take the acorn to land?

Figure 3 **Effect of Air Resistance on a Falling Object**

a The **force of gravity** is pulling down on the apple. If gravity were the only force acting on the apple, the apple would accelerate at a rate of 9.8 m/s^2.

b The **force of air resistance** is pushing up on the apple. This force is subtracted from the force of gravity to yield the net force.

c The **net force** on the apple is equal to the force of air resistance subtracted from the force of gravity. Because the net force is not 0 N, the apple accelerates downward. But the apple does not accelerate as fast as it would without air resistance.

Air Resistance and Falling Objects

Try dropping two sheets of paper—one crumpled in a tight ball and the other kept flat. What happened? Does this simple experiment seem to contradict what you just learned about falling objects? The flat paper falls more slowly than the crumpled paper because of *air resistance*. Air resistance is the force that opposes the motion of objects through air.

The amount of air resistance acting on an object depends on the size, shape, and speed of the object. Air resistance affects the flat sheet of paper more than the crumpled one. The larger surface area of the flat sheet causes the flat sheet to fall slower than the crumpled one. **Figure 3** shows the effect of air resistance on the downward acceleration of a falling object.

Reading Check Will air resistance have more effect on the acceleration of a falling leaf or the acceleration of a falling acorn?

Acceleration Stops at the Terminal Velocity

As the speed of a falling object increases, air resistance increases. The upward force of air resistance continues to increase until it is equal to the downward force of gravity. At this point, the net force is 0 N and the object stops accelerating. The object then falls at a constant velocity called the **terminal velocity.**

Terminal velocity can be a good thing. Every year, cars, buildings, and vegetation are severely damaged in hailstorms. The terminal velocity of hailstones is between 5 and 40 m/s, depending on their size. If there were no air resistance, hailstones would hit the Earth at velocities near 350 m/s! **Figure 4** shows another situation in which terminal velocity is helpful.

Figure 4 *The parachute increases the air resistance of this sky diver and slows him to a safe terminal velocity.*

terminal velocity the constant velocity of a falling object when the force of air resistance is equal in magnitude and opposite in direction to the force of gravity

Free Fall Occurs When There Is No Air Resistance

Sky divers are often described as being in free fall before they open their parachutes. However, that is an incorrect description, because air resistance is always acting on the sky diver.

An object is in **free fall** only if gravity is pulling it down and no other forces are acting on it. Because air resistance is a force, free fall can occur only where there is no air. Two places that have no air are in space and in a vacuum. A vacuum is a place in which there is no matter. **Figure 5** shows objects falling in a vacuum. Because there is no air resistance in a vacuum, the two objects are in free fall.

Orbiting Objects Are in Free Fall

Look at the astronaut in **Figure 6.** Why is the astronaut floating inside the space shuttle? You may be tempted to say that she is weightless in space. However, it is impossible for any object to be weightless anywhere in the universe.

Weight is a measure of gravitational force. The size of the force depends on the masses of objects and the distances between them. Suppose you traveled in space far away from all the stars and planets. The gravitational force acting on you would be very small because the distance between you and other objects would be very large. But you and all the other objects in the universe would still have mass. Therefore, gravity would attract you to other objects—even if just slightly—so you would still have weight.

Astronauts float in orbiting spacecrafts because of free fall. To better understand why astronauts float, you need to know what *orbiting* means.

Figure 5 *Air resistance usually causes a feather to fall more slowly than an apple falls. But in a vacuum, a feather and an apple fall with the same acceleration because both are in free fall.*

free fall the motion of a body when only the force of gravity is acting on the body

Figure 6 *Astronauts appear to be weightless while they are floating inside the space shuttle— but they are not weightless!*

Figure 7 **How an Orbit Is Formed**

> **a** The space shuttle moves forward at a constant speed. If there were no gravity, the space shuttle would follow the path of the dotted line.

> **b** The space shuttle is in free fall because gravity pulls it toward Earth. The space shuttle would move straight down if it were not traveling forward.

> **c** The path of the space shuttle follows the curve of Earth's surface. Following this path is known as *orbiting*.

Two Motions Combine to Cause Orbiting

An object is orbiting when it is traveling around another object in space. When a spacecraft orbits Earth, it is moving forward. But the spacecraft is also in free fall toward Earth. **Figure 7** shows how these two motions combine to cause orbiting.

As you can see in **Figure 7,** the space shuttle is always falling while it is in orbit. So why don't astronauts hit their heads on the ceiling of the falling shuttle? Because they are also in free fall—they are always falling, too. Because astronauts are in free fall, they float.

Orbiting and Centripetal Force

Besides spacecrafts and satellites, many other objects in the universe are in orbit. The moon orbits the Earth. Earth and the other planets orbit the sun. In addition, many stars orbit large masses in the center of galaxies. Many of these objects are traveling in a circular or nearly circular path. Any object in circular motion is constantly changing direction. Because an unbalanced force is necessary to change the motion of any object, there must be an unbalanced force working on any object in circular motion.

The unbalanced force that causes objects to move in a circular path is called a *centripetal force* (sen TRIP uht uhl FOHRS). Gravity provides the centripetal force that keeps objects in orbit. The word *centripetal* means "toward the center." As you can see in **Figure 8,** the centripetal force on the moon points toward the center of the moon's circular orbit.

Reading Check What does the word *centripetal* mean?

Path of moon

Centripetal force on the moon

Figure 8 *The moon stays in orbit around Earth because Earth's gravitational force provides a centripetal force on the moon.*

Projectile Motion and Gravity

The motion of a hopping grasshopper is an example of projectile motion (proh JEK tuhl MOH shuhn). **Projectile motion** is the curved path an object follows when it is thrown or propelled near the surface of the Earth. Projectile motion has two components—horizontal motion and vertical motion. The two components are independent, so they have no effect on each other. When the two motions are combined, they form a curved path, as shown in **Figure 9.** Some examples of projectile motion include the following:

- a frog leaping
- water sprayed by a sprinkler
- a swimmer diving into water
- balls being juggled
- an arrow shot by an archer

projectile motion the curved path that an object follows when thrown, launched, or otherwise projected near the surface of Earth

Horizontal Motion

When you throw a ball, your hand exerts a force on the ball that makes the ball move forward. This force gives the ball its horizontal motion, which is motion parallel to the ground.

After you release the ball, no horizontal forces are acting on the ball (if you ignore air resistance). Even gravity does not affect the horizontal component of projectile motion. So, there are no forces to change the ball's horizontal motion. Thus, the horizontal velocity of the ball is constant after the ball leaves your hand, as shown in **Figure 9.**

Figure 9   Projectile Motion

a After the ball leaves the pitcher's hand, the ball's horizontal velocity is constant.

b The ball's vertical velocity increases because gravity causes it to accelerate downward.

c The two motions combine to form a curved path.

INTERNET ACTIVITY

For another activity related to this chapter, go to **go.hrw.com** and type in the keyword **HP5FORW**.

Figure 10 Projectile Motion and Acceleration Due to Gravity

The yellow ball was given a horizontal push off the ledge and follows projectile motion.

The red ball was dropped without a horizontal push.

The balls have the same acceleration due to gravity. The horizontal motion of the yellow ball does not affect its vertical motion.

Vertical Motion

Gravity pulls everything on Earth downward toward the center of Earth. A ball in your hand is prevented from falling by your hand. After you throw the ball, gravity pulls it downward and gives the ball vertical motion. Vertical motion is motion that is perpendicular to the ground. Gravity pulls objects in projectile motion down at an acceleration of 9.8 m/s^2 (if air resistance is ignored). This rate is the same for all falling objects. **Figure 10** shows that the downward acceleration of a thrown object and a falling object are the same.

Because objects in projectile motion accelerate downward, you always have to aim above a target if you want to hit it with a thrown or propelled object. That's why when you aim an arrow directly at a bull's-eye, your arrow strikes the bottom of the target rather than the middle of the target.

Reading Check What gives an object in projectile motion its vertical motion?

Penny Projectile Motion

1. Position a **flat ruler** and **two pennies** on a **desk or table** as shown below.

2. Hold the ruler by the end that is on the desk. Move the ruler quickly in the direction shown so that the ruler knocks the penny off the table and so that the other penny also drops. Repeat this step several times.

3. Which penny travels with projectile motion? In what order do the pennies hit the ground? Record and explain your answers.

SECTION Review

Summary

- Gravity causes all objects to accelerate toward Earth at a rate of 9.8 m/s^2.
- Air resistance slows the acceleration of falling objects. An object falls at its terminal velocity when the upward force of air resistance equals the downward force of gravity.
- An object is in free fall if gravity is the only force acting on it.
- Objects in orbit appear to be weightless because they are in free fall.

- A centripetal force is needed to keep objects in circular motion. Gravity acts as a centripetal force to keep objects in orbit.
- Projectile motion is the curved path an object follows when thrown or propelled near the surface of Earth.
- Projectile motion has two components—horizontal motion and vertical motion. Gravity affects only the vertical motion of projectile motion.

Using Key Terms

1. Use each of the following terms in a separate sentence: *terminal velocity* and *free fall*.

Understanding Key Ideas

2. Which of the following is in projectile motion?
   a. a feather falling in a vacuum
   b. a cat leaping on a toy
   c. a car driving up a hill
   d. a book laying on a desk

3. How does air resistance affect the acceleration of falling objects?

4. How does gravity affect the two components of projectile motion?

5. How is the acceleration of falling objects affected by gravity?

6. Why is the acceleration due to gravity the same for all objects?

Math Skills

7. A rock at rest falls off a tall cliff and hits the valley below after 3.5 s. What is the rock's velocity as it hits the ground?

Critical Thinking

8. **Applying Concepts** Think about a sport that uses a ball. Identify four examples from that sport in which an object is in projectile motion.

9. **Making Inferences** The moon has no atmosphere. Predict what would happen if an astronaut on the moon dropped a hammer and a feather at the same time from the same height.

Interpreting Graphics

10. Whenever Jon delivers a newspaper to the Zapanta house, the newspaper lands in the bushes, as shown below. What should Jon do to make sure the newspaper lands on the porch?

Newton's Laws of Motion

Imagine that you are playing baseball. The pitch comes in, and—crack—you hit the ball hard! But instead of flying off the bat, the ball just drops to the ground. Is that normal?

You would probably say no. You know that force and motion are related. When you exert a force on a baseball by hitting it with a bat, the baseball should move. In 1686, Sir Isaac Newton explained this relationship between force and the motion of an object with his three laws of motion.

Newton's First Law of Motion

> *An object at rest remains at rest, and an object in motion remains in motion at constant speed and in a straight line unless acted on by an unbalanced force.*

Newton's first law of motion describes the motion of an object that has a net force of 0 N acting on it. This law may seem complicated when you first read it. But, it is easy to understand when you consider its two parts separately.

Part 1: Objects at Rest

An object that is not moving is said to be at rest. A chair on the floor and a golf ball balanced on a tee are examples of objects at rest. Newton's first law says that objects at rest will stay at rest unless they are acted on by an unbalanced force. For example, objects will not start moving until a push or a pull is exerted on them. So, a chair won't slide across the room unless you push the chair. And, a golf ball won't move off the tee unless the ball is struck by a golf club, as shown in **Figure 1.**

Figure 1 *A golf ball will remain at rest on a tee until it is acted on by the unbalanced force of a moving club.*

Unbalanced force

Object at rest

Object in motion

Part 2: Objects in Motion

The second part of Newton's first law is about objects moving with a certain velocity. Such objects will continue to move forever with the same velocity unless an unbalanced force acts on them.

Think about driving a bumper car at an amusement park. Your ride is pleasant as long as you are driving in an open space. But the name of the game is bumper cars! Sooner or later you are likely to run into another car, as shown in **Figure 2.** Your bumper car stops when it hits another car. But, you continue to move forward until the force from your seat belt stops you.

Friction and Newton's First Law

An object in motion will stay in motion forever unless it is acted on by an unbalanced force. So, you should be able to give your desk a push and send it sliding across the floor. If you push your desk, the desk quickly stops. Why?

There must be an unbalanced force that acts on the desk to stop its motion. That unbalanced force is friction. The friction between the desk and the floor works against the motion of the desk. Because of friction, observing the effects of Newton's first law is often difficult. For example, friction will cause a rolling ball to slow down and stop. Friction will also make a car slow down if the driver lets up on the gas pedal. Because of friction, the motion of objects changes.

✓ **Reading Check** When you ride a bus, why do you fall forward when the bus stops moving? (*See the Appendix for answers to Reading Checks.*)

b The collision changes your car's motion, not your motion. Your motion continues with the same velocity.

a An unbalanced force from another car acts on your car and changes your car's motion.

c Another unbalanced force, from your seat belt, changes your motion.

Figure 2 *Bumper cars let you have fun with Newton's first law.*

First Law Skateboard

1. Place an **empty soda can** on top of a **skateboard.**
2. Ask a friend to catch the skateboard after you push it. Now, give the skateboard a quick, firm push. What happened to the soda can?
3. Put the can on the skateboard again. Push the skateboard gently so that the skateboard moves quickly but so that the can does not fall.
4. Ask your friend to stop the skateboard after he or she allows it to travel a short distance. What happened to the can?
5. Explain how Newton's first law applies to what happened.

inertia the tendency of an object to resist being moved or, if the object is moving, to resist a change in speed or direction until an outside force acts on the object

First-Law Magic

1. On a **table or desk**, place a **large, empty plastic cup** on top of a **paper towel.**

2. Without touching the cup or tipping it over, remove the paper towel from under the cup. How did you accomplish this? Repeat this step.

3. Fill the cup half full with **water,** and place the cup on the paper towel.

4. Once again, remove the paper towel from under the cup. Was it easier or harder to do this time?

5. Explain your observations in terms of mass, inertia, and Newton's first law of motion.

Inertia and Newton's First Law

Newton's first law of motion is sometimes called the *law of inertia.* **Inertia** (in UHR shuh) is the tendency of all objects to resist any change in motion. Because of inertia, an object at rest will remain at rest until a force makes it move. Likewise, inertia is the reason a moving object stays in motion with the same velocity unless a force changes its speed or direction. For example, because of inertia, you slide toward the side of a car when the driver turns a corner. Inertia is also why it is impossible for a plane, car, or bicycle to stop immediately.

Mass and Inertia

Mass is a measure of inertia. An object that has a small mass has less inertia than an object that has a large mass. So, changing the motion of an object that has a small mass is easier than changing the motion of an object that has a large mass. For example, a softball has less mass and therefore less inertia than a bowling ball. Because the softball has a small amount of inertia, it is easy to pitch a softball and to change its motion by hitting it with a bat. Imagine how difficult it would be to play softball with a bowling ball! **Figure 3** further shows the relationship between mass and inertia.

Figure 3 *Inertia makes it harder to accelerate a car than to accelerate a bicycle. Inertia also makes it easier to stop a moving bicycle than a car moving at the same speed.*

Newton's Second Law of Motion

The acceleration of an object depends on the mass of the object and the amount of force applied.

Newton's second law describes the motion of an object when an unbalanced force acts on the object. As with Newton's first law, you should consider the second law in two parts.

Part 1: Acceleration Depends on Mass

Suppose you are pushing an empty cart. You have to exert only a small force on the cart to accelerate it. But, the same amount of force will not accelerate the full cart as much as the empty cart. Look at the first two photos in **Figure 4.** They show that the acceleration of an object decreases as its mass increases and that its acceleration increases as its mass decreases.

Part 2: Acceleration Depends on Force

Suppose you give the cart a hard push, as shown in the third photo in **Figure 4.** The cart will start moving faster than if you gave it only a soft push. So, an object's acceleration increases as the force on the object increases. On the other hand, an object's acceleration decreases as the force on the object decreases.

The acceleration of an object is always in the same direction as the force applied. The cart in **Figure 4** moved forward because the push was in the forward direction.

Reading Check What is the relationship between the force on an object and the object's acceleration?

CONNECTION TO Environmental Science

Car Sizes and Pollution

On average, newer cars pollute the air less than older cars do. One reason for this is that newer cars have less mass than older cars have. An object that has less mass requires less force to achieve the same acceleration as an object that has more mass. So, a small car can have a small engine and still have good acceleration. Because small engines use less fuel than large engines use, small engines create less pollution. Research three models of cars from the same year, and make a chart to compare the mass of the cars with the amount of fuel they use.

ACTIVITY

Figure 4 **Mass, Force, and Acceleration**

Acceleration

Acceleration

Acceleration

If the force applied to the carts is the same, the acceleration of the empty cart is greater than the acceleration of the loaded cart.

Acceleration will increase when a larger force is exerted.

Figure 5 Newton's Second Law and Acceleration Due to Gravity

$m = 0.102$ kg

$F = 1$ N

1 N = 1 kg•m/s²

$$a = \frac{1 \text{ kg•m/s}^2}{0.102 \text{ kg}} = 9.8 \text{ m/s}^2$$

$m = 1.02$ kg

$F = 10$ N

10 N = 10 kg•m/s²

$$a = \frac{10 \text{ kg•m/s}^2}{1.02 \text{ kg}} = 9.8 \text{ m/s}^2$$

The apple has less mass than the watermelon does. So, less force is needed to give the apple the same acceleration that the watermelon has.

Expressing Newton's Second Law Mathematically

The relationship of acceleration (*a*) to mass (*m*) and force (*F*) can be expressed mathematically with the following equation:

$$a = \frac{F}{m}, \text{ or } F = m \times a$$

Notice that the equation can be rearranged to find the force applied. Both forms of the equation can be used to solve problems.

Newton's second law explains why objects fall to Earth with the same acceleration. In **Figure 5,** you can see how the large force of gravity on the watermelon is offset by its large mass. Thus, you find that the accelerations of the watermelon and the apple are the same when you solve for acceleration.

Second-Law Problems What is the acceleration of a 3 kg mass if a force of 14.4 N is used to move the mass? (Note: 1 N is equal to 1 kg•m/s²)

Step 1: Write the equation for acceleration.

$$a = \frac{F}{m}$$

Step 2: Replace *F* and *m* with the values given in the problem, and solve.

$$a = \frac{14.4 \text{ kg•m/s}^2}{3 \text{ kg}} = 4.8 \text{ m/s}^2$$

Now It's Your Turn

1. What is the acceleration of a 7 kg mass if a force of 68.6 N is used to move it toward Earth?
2. What force is necessary to accelerate a 1,250 kg car at a rate of 40 m/s²?
3. Zookeepers carry a stretcher that holds a sleeping lion. The total mass of the lion and the stretcher is 175 kg. The lion's forward acceleration is 2 m/s². What is the force necessary to produce this acceleration?

Newton's Third Law of Motion

> *Whenever one object exerts a force on a second object, the second object exerts an equal and opposite force on the first.*

Newton's third law can be simply stated as follows: All forces act in pairs. If a force is exerted, another force occurs that is equal in size and opposite in direction. The law itself addresses only forces. But the way that force pairs interact affects the motion of objects.

How do forces act in pairs? Study **Figure 6** to learn how one force pair helps propel a swimmer through water. Action and reaction force pairs are present even when there is no motion. For example, you exert a force on a chair when you sit on it. Your weight pushing down on the chair is the action force. The reaction force is the force exerted by the chair that pushes up on your body. The force is equal to your weight.

✓ Reading Check How are the forces in each force pair related?

Force Pairs Do Not Act on the Same Object

A force is always exerted by one object on another object. This rule is true for all forces, including action and reaction forces. However, action and reaction forces in a pair do not act on the same object. If they did, the net force would always be 0 N and nothing would ever move! To understand how action and reaction forces act on objects, look at **Figure 6** again. The action force was exerted on the water by the swimmer's hands. But the reaction force was exerted on the swimmer's hands by the water. The forces did not act on the same object.

SCHOOL to HOME

Newton Ball

Play catch with an adult. As you play, discuss how Newton's laws of motion are involved in the game. After you finish your game, make a list in your **science journal** of what you discussed.

ACTIVITY

Figure 6 *The action force and reaction force are a pair. The two forces are equal in size but opposite in direction.*

The action force is the swimmer's hands pushing on the water.

The reaction force is the water pushing on the hands. The reaction force moves the swimmer forward.

Figure 7 Examples of Action and Reaction Force Pairs

The rabbit's legs exert a force on Earth. Earth exerts an equal force on the rabbit's legs and causes the rabbit to accelerate upward.

The space shuttle's thrusters push the exhaust gases downward as the gases push the shuttle upward with an equal force.

The bat exerts a force on the ball and sends the ball flying. The ball exerts an equal force on the bat, but the bat does not move backward because the batter is exerting another force on the bat.

All Forces Act in Pairs—Action and Reaction

Newton's third law says that all forces act in pairs. When a force is exerted, there is always a reaction force. A force never acts by itself. **Figure 7** shows some examples of action and reaction force pairs. In each example, the action force is shown in yellow and the reaction force is shown in red.

The Effect of a Reaction Can Be Difficult to See

Another example of a force pair is shown in **Figure 8.** Gravity is a force of attraction between objects that is due to their masses. If you drop a ball, gravity pulls the ball toward Earth. This force is the action force exerted by Earth on the ball. But gravity also pulls Earth toward the ball. The force is the reaction force exerted by the ball on Earth.

It's easy to see the effect of the action force—the ball falls to Earth. Why don't you notice the effect of the reaction force—Earth being pulled upward? To find the answer to this question, think about Newton's second law. It states that the acceleration of an object depends on the force applied to it and on the mass of the object. The force on Earth is equal to the force on the ball. But the mass of Earth is much larger than the mass of the ball. Thus, the acceleration of Earth is much smaller than the acceleration of the ball. The acceleration of the Earth is so small that you can't see or feel the acceleration. So, it is difficult to observe the effect of Newton's third law on falling objects.

Action force

Reaction force

Figure 8 *The force of gravity between Earth and a falling object is a force pair.*

Reading Check Why do objects fall toward Earth?

SECTION Review

Summary

- Newton's first law of motion states that the motion of an object will not change if no unbalanced forces act on it.
- Objects at rest will not move unless acted upon by an unbalanced force.
- Objects in motion will continue to move at a constant speed and in a straight line unless acted upon by an unbalanced force.
- Inertia is the tendency of matter to resist a change in motion. Mass is a measure of inertia.

- Newton's second law of motion states that the acceleration of an object depends on its mass and on the force exerted on it.
- Newton's second law is represented by the following equation: $F = m \times a$.
- Newton's third law of motion states that whenever one object exerts a force on a second object, the second object exerts an equal and opposite force on the first object.

Using Key Terms

1. In your own words, write a definition for the term *inertia*.

Understanding Key Ideas

2. Which of the following will increase the acceleration of an object that is pushed by a force?
   a. decreasing the mass of the object
   b. increasing the mass of the object
   c. increasing the force pushing the object
   d. Both (a) and (c)

3. Give three examples of force pairs that occur when you do your homework.

4. What does Newton's first law of motion say about objects at rest and objects in motion?

5. Use Newton's second law to describe the relationship between force, mass, and acceleration.

Math Skills

6. What force is necessary to accelerate a 70 kg object at a rate of 4.2 m/s^2?

Critical Thinking

7. **Applying Concepts** When a truck pulls a trailer, the trailer and truck accelerate forward even though the action and reaction forces are the same size but are in opposite directions. Why don't these forces balance each other?

8. **Making Inferences** Use Newton's first law of motion to explain why airbags in cars are important during head-on collisions.

Interpreting Graphics

9. Imagine you accidentally bumped your hand against a table, as shown in the photo below. Your hand hurts after it happens. Use Newton's third law of motion to explain what caused your hand to hurt.

SCiLINKS® NSTA

Developed and maintained by the National Science Teachers Association

For a variety of links related to this chapter, go to www.scilinks.org

Topic: Newton's Laws of Motion
SciLinks code: HSM1028

Momentum

Imagine a compact car and a large truck traveling with the same velocity. The drivers of both vehicles put on the brakes at the same time. Which vehicle will stop first?

You would probably say that the compact car will stop first. You know that smaller objects are easier to stop than larger objects. But why? The answer is momentum (moh MEN tuhm).

Momentum, Mass, and Velocity

The **momentum** of an object depends on the object's mass and velocity. The more momentum an object has, the harder it is to stop the object or change its direction. In the example above, the truck has more mass and more momentum than the car has. So, a larger force is needed to stop the truck. Similarly, a fast-moving car has a greater velocity and thus more momentum than a slow-moving car of the same mass. So, a fast-moving car is harder to stop than a slow-moving car. **Figure 1** shows another example of an object that has momentum.

Calculating Momentum

Momentum (*p*) can be calculated with the equation below:

$$p = m \times v$$

In this equation, *m* is the mass of an object in kilograms and *v* is the object's velocity in meters per second. The units of momentum are kilograms multiplied by meters per second, or kg•m/s. Like velocity, momentum has a direction. Its direction is always the same as the direction of the object's velocity.

READING WARM-UP

Objectives
- Calculate the momentum of moving objects.
- Explain the law of conservation of momentum.

Terms to Learn
momentum

READING STRATEGY

Prediction Guide Before reading this section, write the title of each heading in this section. Next, under each heading, write what you think you will learn.

momentum a quantity defined as the product of the mass and velocity of an object

Figure 1 *The teen on the right has less mass than the teen on the left. But, the teen on the right can have a large momentum by moving quickly when she kicks.*

Momentum Calculations   What is the momentum of an ostrich with a mass of 120 kg that runs with a velocity of 16 m/s north?

Step 1: Write the equation for momentum.

$$p = m \times v$$

Step 2: Replace *m* and *v* with the values given in the problem, and solve.

$$p = 120 \text{ kg} \times 16 \text{ m/s north}$$
$$p = 19,200 \text{ kg} \cdot \text{m/s north}$$

Now It's Your Turn

1. What is the momentum of a 6 kg bowling ball that is moving at 10 m/s down the alley toward the pins?
2. An 85 kg man is jogging with a velocity of 2.6 m/s to the north. Nearby, a 65 kg person is skateboarding and is traveling with a velocity of 3 m/s north. Which person has greater momentum? Show your calculations.

The Law of Conservation of Momentum

When a moving object hits another object, some or all of the momentum of the first object is transferred to the object that is hit. If only some of the momentum is transferred, the rest of the momentum stays with the first object.

Imagine that a cue ball hits a billiard ball so that the billiard ball starts moving and the cue ball stops, as shown in **Figure 2.** The white cue ball had a certain amount of momentum before the collision. During the collision, all of the cue ball's momentum was transferred to the red billiard ball. After the collision, the billiard ball moved away with the same amount of momentum the cue ball had. This example shows the *law of conservation of momentum.* The law of conservation of momentum states that any time objects collide, the total amount of momentum stays the same. The law of conservation of momentum is true for any collision if no other forces act on the colliding objects. This law applies whether the objects stick together or bounce off each other after they collide.

Reading Check   What can happen to momentum when two objects collide? (*See the Appendix for answers to Reading Checks.*)

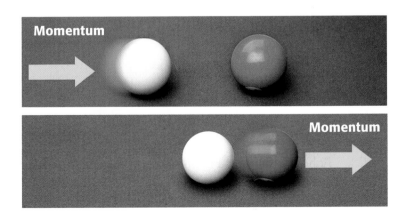

Figure 2 *The momentum before a collision is equal to the momentum after the collision.*

Objects Sticking Together

Sometimes, objects stick together after a collision. The football players shown in **Figure 3** are an example of such a collision. A dog leaping and catching a ball and a teen jumping on a skateboard are also examples. After two objects stick together, they move as one object. The mass of the combined objects is equal to the masses of the two objects added together. In a head-on collision, the combined objects move in the direction of the object that had the greater momentum before the collision. But together, the objects have a velocity that differs from the velocity of either object before the collision. The objects have a different velocity because momentum is conserved and depends on mass and velocity. So, when mass changes, the velocity must change, too.

Objects Bouncing Off Each Other

In some collisions, the objects bounce off each other. The bowling ball and bowling pins shown in **Figure 3** are examples of objects that bounce off each other after they collide. Billiard balls and bumper cars are other examples. During these types of collisions, momentum is usually transferred from one object to another object. The transfer of momentum causes the objects to move in different directions at different speeds. However, the total momentum of all the objects will remain the same before and after the collision.

Reading Check What are two ways that objects may interact after a collision?

CONNECTION TO
Language Arts

WRITING SKILL Momentum and Language

The word *momentum* is often used in everyday language. For example, a sports announcer may say that the momentum of a game has changed. Or you may read that an idea is gaining momentum. In your **science journal,** write a paragraph that explains how the everyday use of the word *momentum* differs from momentum in science.

Figure 3 Examples of Conservation of Momentum

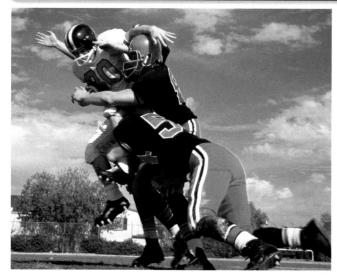

When football players tackle another player, they stick together. The velocity of each player changes after the collision because of conservation of momentum.

Although the bowling ball and bowling pins bounce off each other and move in different directions after a collision, momentum is neither gained nor lost.

Conservation of Momentum and Newton's Third Law

Conservation of momentum can be explained by Newton's third law of motion. In the example of the billiard ball, the cue ball hit the billiard ball with a certain amount of force. This force was the action force. The reaction force was the equal but opposite force exerted by the billiard ball on the cue ball. The action force made the billiard ball start moving, and the reaction force made the cue ball stop moving, as shown in **Figure 4.** Because the action and reaction forces are equal and opposite, momentum is neither gained nor lost.

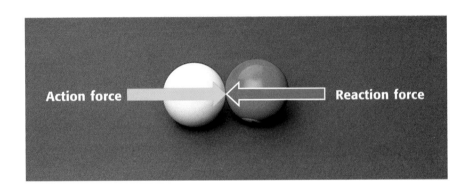

Figure 4 *The action force makes the billiard ball begin moving, and the reaction force stops the cue ball's motion.*

SECTION Review

Summary

- Momentum is a property of moving objects.

- Momentum is calculated by multiplying the mass of an object by the object's velocity.

- When two or more objects collide, momentum may be transferred, but the total amount of momentum does not change. This is the law of conservation of momentum.

Using Key Terms

1. Use the following term in a sentence: *momentum*.

Understanding Key Ideas

2. Which of the following has the smallest amount of momentum?
   a. a loaded truck driven at highway speeds
   b. a track athlete running a race
   c. a baby crawling on the floor
   d. a jet airplane being towed toward an airport

3. Explain the law of conservation of momentum.

4. How is Newton's third law of motion related to the law of conservation of momentum?

Math Skills

5. Calculate the momentum of a 2.5 kg puppy that is running with a velocity of 4.8 m/s south.

Critical Thinking

6. **Applying Concepts** A car and a train are traveling with the same velocity. Do the two objects have the same momentum? Explain your answer.

7. **Analyzing Ideas** When you catch a softball, your hand and glove move in the same direction that the ball is moving. Analyze the motion of your hand and glove in terms of momentum.

513

Skills Practice Lab

OBJECTIVES

Observe several effects of inertia.

Describe the motion of objects in terms of inertia.

MATERIALS

Station 1
- egg, hard-boiled
- egg, raw

Station 2
- card, index
- coin
- cup

Station 3
- mass, hanging, 1 kg
- meterstick
- scissors
- thread, spool

SAFETY

Inertia-Rama!

Inertia is a property of all matter, from small particles of dust to enormous planets and stars. In this lab, you will investigate the inertia of various shapes and kinds of matter. Keep in mind that each investigation requires you to either overcome or use the object's inertia.

Station 1: Magic Eggs

Procedure

1. There are two eggs at this station—one is hard-boiled (solid all the way through) and the other is raw (liquid inside). The masses of the two eggs are about the same. The eggs are not marked. You should not be able to tell them apart by their appearance. Without breaking them open, how can you tell which egg is raw and which egg is hard-boiled?

2. Before you do anything to either egg, make some predictions. Will there be any difference in the way the two eggs spin? Which egg will be the easier to stop?

3. First, spin one egg. Then, place your finger on it gently to make it stop spinning. Record your observations.

4. Repeat step 3 with the second egg.

5. Compare your predictions with your observations. (Repeat steps 3 and 4 if necessary.)

6. Which egg is hard-boiled and which one is raw? Explain.

Analyze the Results

1. **Explaining Events** Explain why the eggs behave differently when you spin them even though they should have the same inertia. (Hint: Think about what happens to the liquid inside the raw egg.)

Draw Conclusions

2. **Drawing Conclusions** Explain why the eggs react differently when you try to stop them.

Station 2: Coin in a Cup

Procedure

1. At this station, you will find a coin, an index card, and a cup. Place the card over the cup. Then, place the coin on the card over the center of the cup, as shown below.

2. Write down a method for getting the coin into the cup without touching the coin and without lifting the card.

3. Try your method. If it doesn't work, try again until you find a method that does work.

Analyze the Results

1. **Describing Events** Use Newton's first law of motion to explain why the coin falls into the cup if you remove the card quickly.

Draw Conclusions

2. **Defending Conclusions** Explain why pulling on the card slowly will not work even though the coin has inertia. (Hint: Friction is a force.)

Station 3: The Magic Thread

Procedure

1. At this station, you will find a spool of thread and a mass hanging from a strong string. Cut a piece of thread about 40 cm long. Tie the thread around the bottom of the mass, as shown at right.

2. Pull gently on the end of the thread. Observe what happens, and record your observations.

3. Stop the mass from moving. Now hold the end of the thread so that there is a lot of slack between your fingers and the mass.

4. Give the thread a quick, hard pull. You should observe a very different event. Record your observations. Throw away the thread.

Analyze the Results

1. **Analyzing Results** Use Newton's first law of motion to explain why the result of a gentle pull is different from the result of a hard pull.

Draw Conclusions

2. **Applying Conclusions** Both moving and non-moving objects have inertia. Explain why throwing a bowling ball and catching a thrown bowling ball are hard.

3. **Drawing Conclusions** Why is it harder to run with a backpack full of books than to run with an empty backpack?

Chapter Review

USING KEY TERMS

Complete each of the following sentences by choosing the correct term from the word bank.

free fall   projectile motion
inertia   terminal velocity
momentum

1 An object in motion has ___, so it tends to stay in motion.

2 An object is falling at its ___ if it falls at a constant velocity.

3 ___ is the path that a thrown object follows.

4 ___ is a property of moving objects that depends on mass and velocity.

5 ___ occurs only when air resistance does not affect the motion of a falling object.

UNDERSTANDING KEY IDEAS

Multiple Choice

6 When a soccer ball is kicked, the action and reaction forces do not cancel each other out because

 a. the forces are not equal in size.

 b. the forces act on different objects.

 c. the forces act at different times.

 d. All of the above

7 An object is in projectile motion if it

 a. is thrown with a horizontal push.

 b. is accelerated downward by gravity.

 c. does not accelerate horizontally.

 d. All of the above

8 Newton's first law of motion applies to

 a. moving objects.

 b. objects that are not moving.

 c. objects that are accelerating.

 d. Both (a) and (b)

9 To accelerate two objects at the same rate, the force used to push the object that has more mass should be

 a. smaller than the force used to push the object that has less mass.

 b. larger than the force used to push the object that has less mass.

 c. the same as the force used to push the object that has less mass.

 d. equal to the object's weight.

10 A golf ball and a bowling ball are moving at the same velocity. Which of the two has more momentum?

 a. The golf ball has more momentum because it has less mass.

 b. The bowling ball has more momentum because it has more mass.

 c. They have the same momentum because they have the same velocity.

 d. There is not enough information to determine the answer.

Short Answer

11 Give an example of an object that is in free fall.

12 Describe how gravity and air resistance are related to an object's terminal velocity.

13 Why can friction make observing Newton's first law of motion difficult?

Math Skills

14 A 12 kg rock falls from rest off a cliff and hits the ground in 1.5 s.

a. Without considering air resistance, what is the rock's velocity just before it hits the ground?

b. What is the rock's momentum just before it hits the ground?

CRITICAL THINKING

15 Concept Mapping Use the following terms to create a concept map: *gravity, free fall, terminal velocity, projectile motion,* and *air resistance.*

16 Identifying Relationships During a space shuttle launch, about 830,000 kg of fuel is burned in 8 min. The fuel provides the shuttle with a constant thrust, or forward force. How does Newton's second law of motion explain why the shuttle's acceleration increases as the fuel is burned?

17 Analyzing Processes When using a hammer to drive a nail into wood, you have to swing the hammer through the air with a certain velocity. Because the hammer has both mass and velocity, it has momentum. Describe what happens to the hammer's momentum after the hammer hits the nail.

18 Applying Concepts Suppose you are standing on a skateboard or on in-line skates and you toss a backpack full of heavy books toward your friend. What do you think will happen to you? Explain your answer in terms of Newton's third law of motion.

INTERPRETING GRAPHICS

19 The picture below shows a common desk toy. If you pull one ball up and release it, it hits the balls at the bottom and comes to a stop. In the same instant, the ball on the other side swings up and repeats the cycle. How does conservation of momentum explain how this toy works?

Standardized Test Preparation

READING

Read each of the passages below. Then, answer the questions that follow each passage.

Passage 1 How do astronauts prepare for trips in the space shuttle? One method is to use simulations on Earth that mimic the conditions in space. For example, underwater training lets astronauts experience reduced gravity. They can also ride on NASA's modified KC-135 airplane. NASA's KC-135 simulates how it feels to be in a space shuttle. How does this airplane work? It flies upward at a steep angle and then flies downward at a 45° angle. When the airplane flies downward, the effect of reduced gravity is produced. As the plane falls, the astronauts inside the plane can float like astronauts in the space shuttle do!

1. What is the purpose of this passage?

 A to explain how astronauts prepare for missions in space

 B to convince people to become astronauts

 C to show that space is similar to Earth

 D to describe what it feels like to float in space

2. What can you conclude about NASA's KC-135 from the passage?

 F NASA's KC-135 is just like other airplanes.

 G All astronauts train in NASA's KC-135.

 H NASA's KC-135 simulates the space shuttle by reducing the effects of gravity.

 I Being in NASA's KC-135 is not very much like being in the space shuttle.

3. Based on the passage, which of the following statements is a fact?

 A Astronauts always have to train underwater.

 B Flying in airplanes is similar to riding in the space shuttle.

 C People in NASA's KC-135 float at all times.

 D Astronauts use simulations to learn what reduced gravity is like.

Passage 2 There once was a game that could be played by as few as 5 or as many as 1,000 players. The game could be played on a small field for a few hours or on a huge tract of land for several days. The game was not just for fun—in fact, it was often used as a substitute for war. One of the few rules was that the players couldn't touch the ball with their hands—they had to use a special stick with webbing on one end. Would you believe that this game is the same as the game of lacrosse that is played today?

Lacrosse is a game that was originally played by Native Americans. They called the game *baggataway*, which means "little brother of war." Although lacrosse has changed and is now played all over the world, it still requires special, webbed sticks.

1. What is the purpose of this passage?

 A to explain the importance of rules in lacrosse

 B to explain why sticks are used in lacrosse

 C to describe the history of lacrosse

 D to describe the rules of lacrosse

2. Based on the passage, what does the word *substitute* mean?

 F something that occurs before war

 G something that is needed to play lacrosse

 H something that is of Native American origin

 I something that takes the place of something else

Read each question below, and choose the best answer.

1. Which of the following images shows an object with no momentum that is about to be set in motion by an unbalanced force?

A

B

C

D

2. During a laboratory experiment, liquid was collected in a graduated cylinder. What is the volume of the liquid?

F 30 mL
G 35 mL
H 40 mL
I 45 mL

Read each question below, and choose the best answer.

1. The table below shows the accelerations produced by different forces for a 5 kg mass. Assuming that the pattern continues, use this data to predict what acceleration would be produced by a 100 N force.

Force	Acceleration
25 N	5 m/s^2
50 N	10 m/s^2
75 N	15 m/s^2

A 10 m/s^2
B 20 m/s^2
C 30 m/s^2
D 100 m/s^2

2. The average radius of the moon is 1.74×10^6 m. What is another way to express the radius of the moon?

F 0.00000174 m
G 0.000174 m
H 174,000 m
I 1,740,000 m

3. The half price bookstore is selling 4 paperback books for a total of $5.75. What would the price of 20 paperback books be?

A $23.00
B $24.75
C $28.75
D $51.75

4. A 75 kg speed skater is moving with a velocity of 16 m/s east. What is the speed skater's momentum? (Momentum is calculated with the equation: *momentum = mass × velocity*.)

F 91 kg•m/s
G 91 kg•m/s east
H 1,200 kg•m/s east
I 1,200 kg•m/s^2 east

Standardized Test Preparation

Science in Action

Scientific Discoveries

The Millennium Bridge

You may have heard the children's song, "London Bridge is falling down . . .". London Bridge never fell. But some people who walked on the Millennium Bridge thought that it might fall instead! The Millennium Bridge is a pedestrian bridge in London, England. The bridge opened on June 10, 2000, and more than 80,000 people crossed it that day. Immediately, people noticed something wrong—the bridge was swaying! The bridge was closed after two days so that engineers could determine what was wrong. After much research, the engineers learned that the force of the footsteps of the people crossing the bridge caused the bridge to sway.

Language Arts ACTiViTY

WRITING SKILL Imagine that you were in London on June 10, 2000 and walked across the Millennium Bridge. Write a one-page story about what you think it was like on the bridge that day.

Science, Technology, and Society

Power Suit for Lifting Patients

Imagine visiting a hospital and seeing someone who looked half human and half robot. No, it isn't a scene from a science fiction movie—it is a new invention that may some day help nurses lift patients easily. The invention, called a power suit, is a metal framework that a nurse would wear on his or her back. The suit calculates how much force a nurse needs to lift a patient, and then the robotic joints on the suit help the nurse exert the right amount of force. The suit will also help nurses avoid injuring their backs.

Math ACTiViTY

The pound (symbol £) is the currency in England. The inventor of the suit thinks that it will be sold for £1200. How much will the suit cost in dollars if $1 is equal to £0.60?

Careers

Steve Okamoto

Roller Coaster Designer Roller coasters have fascinated Steve Okamoto ever since his first ride on one. "I remember going to Disneyland as a kid. My mother was always upset with me because I kept looking over the sides of the rides, trying to figure out how they worked," he says. To satisfy his curiosity, Okamoto became a mechanical engineer. Today he uses his scientific knowledge to design and build machines, systems, and buildings. But his specialty is roller coasters.

Roller coasters really do coast along the track. A motor pulls the cars up a high hill to start the ride. After that, the cars are powered by only gravity. Designing a successful roller coaster is not a simple task. Okamoto has to calculate the cars' speed and acceleration on each part of the track. He must also consider the safety of the ride and the strength of the structure that supports the track.

Social Studies ACTiViTY

Research the history of roller coasters to learn how roller coaster design has changed over time. Make a poster to summarize your research.

To learn more about these Science in Action topics, visit go.hrw.com and type in the keyword **HP5FORF**.

Current Science

Check out Current Science® articles related to this chapter by visiting go.hrw.com. Just type in the keyword **HP5CS06**.

19

Forces in Fluids

About the PHOTO

As you race downhill on your bicycle, the air around you pushes on your body and slows you down. "What a drag!" you say. Well, actually, it is a drag. When designing bicycle gear and clothing, manufacturers consider more than just looks and comfort. They also try to decrease drag, a fluid force that opposes motion. This photo shows cyclists riding their bikes in a wind tunnel in a study of how a fluid—air—affects their ride.

PRE-READING ACTIVITY

FOLD NOTES **Booklet** Before you read the chapter, create the FoldNote entitled "Booklet" described in the **Study Skills** section of the Appendix. Label each page of the booklet with a main idea from the chapter. As you read the chapter, write what you learn about each main idea on the appropriate page of the booklet.

START-UP ACTIVITY

Taking Flight

In this activity, you will build a model airplane to learn how wing size affects flight.

Procedure

1. Fold a **sheet of paper** in half lengthwise. Then, open it. Fold the top corners toward the center crease. Keep the corners folded down, and fold the entire sheet in half along the center crease.

2. With the plane on its side, fold the top front edge down so that it meets the bottom edge. Fold the top edge down again so that it meets the bottom edge. Turn the plane over, and repeat.

3. Raise the wings so that they are perpendicular to the body.

4. Point the plane slightly upward, and gently throw it. Repeat several times. Describe what you see.

5. Make the wings smaller by folding them one more time. Gently throw the plane. Repeat several times. Describe what you see.

6. Using the smaller wings, try to achieve the same flight path you saw when the wings were bigger.

Analysis

1. What happened to the plane's flight when you reduced the size of its wings? What did you have to do to achieve the same flight path as when the wings were bigger?

2. What gave your plane its forward motion?

Fluids and Pressure

What does a dolphin have in common with a sea gull? What does a dog have in common with a fly? What do you have in common with all these living things?

fluid a nonsolid state of matter in which the atoms or molecules are free to move past each other, as in a gas or liquid

pressure the amount of force exerted per unit area of a surface

pascal the SI unit of pressure (symbol, Pa)

atmospheric pressure the pressure caused by the weight of the atmosphere

One answer to these questions is that you and all these other living things spend a lifetime moving through fluids. A **fluid** is any material that can flow and that takes the shape of its container. Fluids include liquids and gases. Fluids can flow because the particles in fluids move easily past each other.

Fluids Exert Pressure

You probably have heard the terms *air pressure* and *water pressure.* Air and water are fluids. All fluids exert pressure. So, what is pressure? Think about this example. When you pump up a bicycle tire, you push air into the tire. And like all matter, air is made of tiny particles that are constantly moving.

Look at **Figure 1.** Inside the tire, the air particles collide with each other and with the walls of the tire. Together, these collisions create a force on the tire. The amount of force exerted on a given area is **pressure.**

Calculating Pressure

Pressure can be calculated by using the following equation:

$$pressure = \frac{force}{area}$$

The SI unit for pressure is the **pascal.** One pascal (1 Pa) is the force of one newton exerted over an area of one square meter (1 N/m^2).

Figure 1 *The force of the air particles hitting the inner surface of the tire creates pressure, which keeps the tire inflated.*

Pressure, Force, and Area What is the pressure exerted by a book that has an area of 0.2 m² and a weight of 10 N?

Step 1: Write the equation for pressure.

$$pressure = \frac{force}{area}$$

Step 2: Replace *force* and *area* with the values given, and solve. (Hint: Weight is a measure of gravitational force.)

$$pressure = \frac{10 \text{ N}}{0.2 \text{ m}^2} = 50 \text{ N/m}^2 = 50 \text{ Pa}$$

The equation for pressure can be rearranged to find force or area, as shown below.

$force = pressure \times area$ *(Rearrange by multiplying by area.)*

$area = \dfrac{force}{pressure}$ *(Rearrange by multiplying by area and then dividing by pressure.)*

Now It's Your Turn

1. Find the pressure exerted by a 3,000 N crate that has an area of 2 m².
2. Find the weight of a rock that has an area of 10 m² and that exerts a pressure of 250 Pa.

Pressure and Bubbles

When you blow a soap bubble, you blow in only one direction. So, why does the bubble get rounder instead of longer as you blow? The shape of the bubble partly depends on an important property of fluids: Fluids exert pressure evenly in all directions. The air you blow into the bubble exerts pressure evenly in all directions. So, the bubble expands in all directions to create a sphere.

Atmospheric Pressure

The *atmosphere* is the layer of nitrogen, oxygen, and other gases that surrounds Earth. Earth's atmosphere is held in place by gravity, which pulls the gases toward Earth. The pressure caused by the weight of the atmosphere is called **atmospheric pressure.**

Atmospheric pressure is exerted on everything on Earth, including you. At sea level, the atmosphere exerts a pressure of about 101,300 N on every square meter, or 101,300 Pa. So, there is a weight of about 10 N (about 2 lbs) on every square centimeter of your body. Why don't you feel this crushing pressure? Like the air inside a balloon, the fluids inside your body exert pressure. **Figure 2** can help you understand why you don't feel the pressure.

✓ Reading Check Name two gases in the atmosphere. (*See the Appendix for answers to Reading Checks.*)

Figure 2 *The air inside a balloon exerts pressure that keeps the balloon inflated against atmospheric pressure. Similarly, fluid inside your body exerts pressure that works against atmospheric pressure.*

Atmospheric pressure

Air pressure inside the balloon

Figure 3 Differences in Atmospheric Pressure

At 150,000 m above sea level, atmospheric pressure is almost 0 Pa. Humans cannot travel this high without protection. The space shuttle travels past this point on its way into orbit.

The atmospheric pressure at 12,000 m is about 20 kPa. Airplane cabins must be pressurized for passenger safety.

At the top of Mount Everest (8,847 m above sea level), atmospheric pressure is about a third of that at sea level.

Atmospheric pressure at La Paz, Bolivia (the world's highest capital city, at 4,000 m), is about 51 kPa.

At sea level (0 m), the full pressure of the atmosphere—101 kPa—is exerted on you.

Variation of Atmospheric Pressure

The atmosphere stretches about 150 km above Earth's surface. However, about 80% of the atmosphere's gases are found within 10 km of Earth's surface. At the top of the atmosphere, pressure is almost nonexistent. The pressure is close to 0 Pa because the gas particles are far apart and rarely collide. Mount Everest in south-central Asia is the highest point on Earth. At the top of Mount Everest, atmospheric pressure is about 33,000 Pa, or 33 kilopascals (33 kPa). (Remember that the prefix *kilo*- means 1,000. So, 1 kPa is equal to 1,000 Pa.) At sea level, atmospheric pressure is about 101 kPa.

Atmospheric Pressure and Depth

Take a look at **Figure 3.** Notice how atmospheric pressure changes as you travel through the atmosphere. The further down through the atmosphere you go, the greater the pressure is. In other words, the pressure increases as the atmosphere gets "deeper." An important point to remember about fluids is that pressure varies depending on depth. At lower levels of the atmosphere, there is more fluid above that is being pulled by Earth's gravitational force. So, there is more pressure at lower levels of the atmosphere.

Reading Check Describe how pressure changes with depth.

Pressure Changes and Your Body

So, what happens to your body when atmospheric pressure changes? If you travel to higher or lower points in the atmosphere, the fluids in your body have to adjust to maintain equal pressure. You may have experienced this adjustment if your ears have "popped" when you were in a plane taking off or in a car traveling down a steep mountain road. The "pop" happens because of pressure changes in pockets of air behind your eardrums.

Water Pressure

Water is a fluid. So, it exerts pressure like the atmosphere does. Water pressure also increases as depth increases, as shown in **Figure 4.** The deeper a diver goes in the water, the greater the pressure is. The pressure increases because more water above the diver is being pulled by Earth's gravitational force. In addition, the atmosphere presses down on the water, so the total pressure on the diver includes water pressure and atmospheric pressure.

Water Pressure and Depth

Like atmospheric pressure, water pressure depends on depth. Water pressure does not depend on the total amount of fluid present. A swimmer would feel the same pressure swimming at 3 m below the surface of a small pond and at 3 m below the surface of an ocean. Even though there is more water in the ocean than in the pond, the pressure on the swimmer in the pond would be the same as the pressure on the swimmer in the ocean.

Density Making a Difference

Water is about 1,000 times more dense than air. *Density* is the amount of matter in a given volume, or mass per unit volume. Because water is more dense than air, a certain volume of water has more mass—and weighs more—than the same volume of air. So, water exerts more pressure than air.

For example, if you climb a 10 m tree, the decrease in atmospheric pressure is too small to notice. But if you dive 10 m underwater, the pressure on you increases to 201 kPa, which is almost twice the atmospheric pressure at the surface!

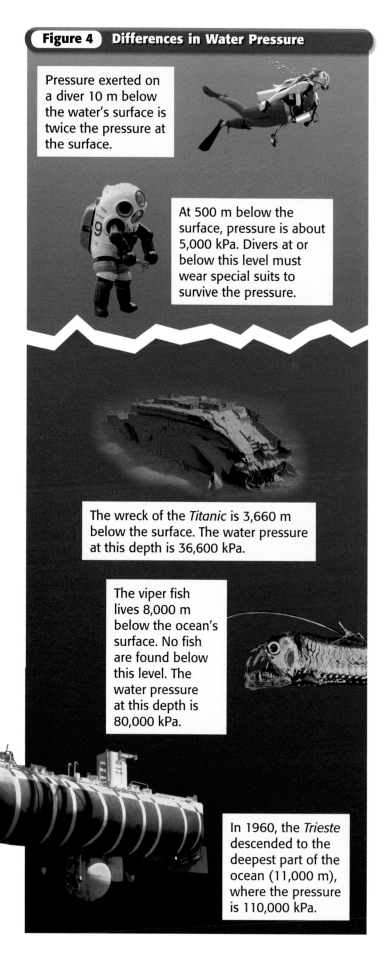

Figure 4 Differences in Water Pressure

Pressure exerted on a diver 10 m below the water's surface is twice the pressure at the surface.

At 500 m below the surface, pressure is about 5,000 kPa. Divers at or below this level must wear special suits to survive the pressure.

The wreck of the *Titanic* is 3,660 m below the surface. The water pressure at this depth is 36,600 kPa.

The viper fish lives 8,000 m below the ocean's surface. No fish are found below this level. The water pressure at this depth is 80,000 kPa.

In 1960, the *Trieste* descended to the deepest part of the ocean (11,000 m), where the pressure is 110,000 kPa.

Blown Away

1. Lay an **empty plastic soda bottle** on its side.

2. Wad a **small piece of paper** (about 4 × 4 cm) into a ball.

3. Place the paper ball just inside the bottle's opening.

4. Blow straight into the opening.

5. Record your observations.

6. Explain your results in terms of high and low fluid pressures.

Pressure Differences and Fluid Flow

When you drink through a straw, you remove some of the air in the straw. Because there is less air inside the straw, the pressure in the straw is reduced. But the atmospheric pressure on the surface of the liquid remains the same. Thus, there is a difference between the pressure inside the straw and the pressure outside the straw. The outside pressure forces the liquid up the straw and into your mouth. So, just by drinking through a straw, you can observe an important property of fluids: Fluids flow from areas of high pressure to areas of low pressure.

✔ **Reading Check** When drinking through a straw, how do you decrease the pressure inside the straw?

Pressure Differences and Breathing

Take a deep breath—fluid is flowing from high to low pressure! When you inhale, a muscle increases the space in your chest and gives your lungs room to expand. This expansion decreases the pressure in your lungs. The pressure in your lungs becomes lower than the air pressure outside your lungs. Air then flows into your lungs—from high to low pressure. This air carries oxygen that you need to live. **Figure 5** shows how exhaling also causes fluids to flow from high to low pressure. You can see a similar flow of fluid when you open a carbonated beverage or squeeze toothpaste onto your toothbrush.

Figure 5 **Exhaling, Pressure, and Fluid Flow**

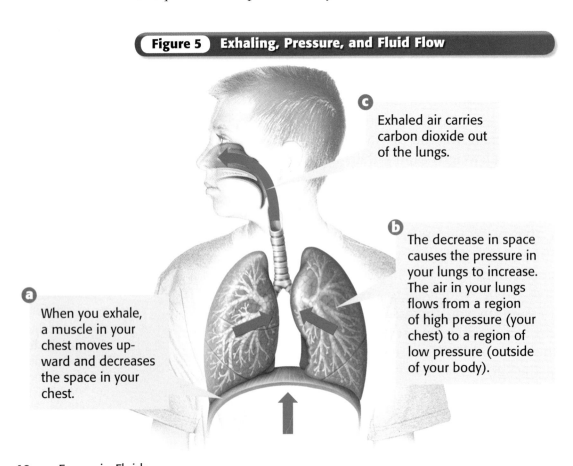

c Exhaled air carries carbon dioxide out of the lungs.

b The decrease in space causes the pressure in your lungs to increase. The air in your lungs flows from a region of high pressure (your chest) to a region of low pressure (outside of your body).

a When you exhale, a muscle in your chest moves upward and decreases the space in your chest.

Pressure Differences and Tornadoes

Look at the tornado in **Figure 6.** Some of the damaging winds caused by tornadoes are the result of pressure differences. The air pressure inside a tornado is very low. Because the air pressure outside of the tornado is higher than the pressure inside, air rushes into the tornado. The rushing air causes the tornado to be like a giant vacuum cleaner—objects are pushed into the tornado. The winds created are usually very strong and affect the area around the tornado. So, objects, such as trees and buildings, can be severely damaged by wind even if they are not in the direct path of a tornado.

Figure 6 *Tornadoes are like giant vacuum cleaners because of pressure differences.*

SECTION Review

Summary

- A fluid is any material that flows and takes the shape of its container.

- Pressure is force exerted on a given area.

- Moving particles of matter create pressure by colliding with one another and with the walls of their container.

- The pressure caused by the weight of the atmosphere is called *atmospheric pressure.*

- Fluid pressure increases as depth increases.

- As depth increases, water pressure increases faster than atmospheric pressure does because water is denser than air.

- Fluids flow from areas of high pressure to areas of low pressure.

Using Key Terms

1. In your own words, write a definition for each of the following terms: *fluid* and *atmospheric pressure.*

2. Use the following terms in the same sentence: *pressure* and *pascal.*

Understanding Key Ideas

3. Which of the following statements about fluids is true?

   a. Fluids rarely take the shape of their container.

   b. Fluids include liquids and gases.

   c. Fluids flow from low pressure to high pressure.

   d. Fluids exert the most pressure in the downward direction.

4. How do fluids exert pressure on a container?

5. Why are you not crushed by atmospheric pressure?

6. Explain why atmospheric pressure changes as depth changes.

7. Give three examples of fluids flowing from high pressure to low pressure in everyday life.

Math Skills

8. The water in a glass has a weight of 2.4 N. The bottom of the glass has an area of 0.012 m². What is the pressure exerted by the water on the bottom of the glass?

Critical Thinking

9. **Identifying Relationships** Mercury is a liquid that has a density of 13.5 g/mL. Water has a density of 1.0 g/mL. Equal volumes of mercury and water are in identical containers. Explain why the pressures exerted on the bottoms of the containers are different.

10. **Making Inferences** Why do airplanes need to be pressurized for passenger safety when flying high in the atmosphere?

529

Buoyant Force

Why does an ice cube float on water? Why doesn't it sink to the bottom of your glass?

Imagine that you use a straw to push an ice cube under water. Then, you release the cube. A force pushes the ice back to the water's surface. The force, called **buoyant force** (BOY uhnt FAWRS), is the upward force that fluids exert on all matter.

Buoyant Force and Fluid Pressure

Look at **Figure 1.** Water exerts fluid pressure on all sides of an object. The pressure exerted horizontally on one side of the object is equal to the pressure exerted on the opposite side. These equal pressures cancel one another. So, the only fluid pressures affecting the net force on the object are at the top and at the bottom. Pressure increases as depth increases. So, the pressure at the bottom of the object is greater than the pressure at the top. The water exerts a net upward force on the object. This upward force is buoyant force.

Determining Buoyant Force

Archimedes (AHR kuh MEE DEEZ), a Greek mathematician who lived in the third century BCE, discovered how to determine buoyant force. **Archimedes' principle** states that the buoyant force on an object in a fluid is an upward force equal to the weight of the fluid that the object takes the place of, or displaces. Suppose the object in **Figure 1** displaces 250 mL of water. The weight of that volume of displaced water is about 2.5 N. So, the buoyant force on the object is 2.5 N. Notice that only the weight of the displaced fluid determines the buoyant force on an object. The weight of the object does not affect buoyant force.

buoyant force the upward force that keeps an object immersed in or floating on a liquid

Archimedes' principle the principle that states that the buoyant force on an object in a fluid is an upward force equal to the weight of the volume of fluid that the object displaces

Figure 1 *There is more pressure at the bottom of an object because pressure increases with depth. This results in an upward buoyant force on the object.*

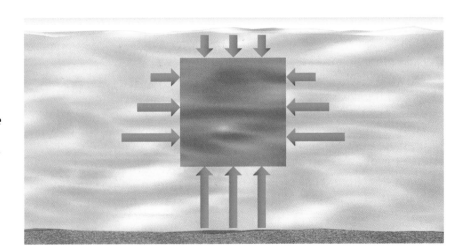

Weight Versus Buoyant Force

An object in a fluid will sink if its weight is greater than the buoyant force (the weight of the fluid it displaces). An object floats only when the buoyant force on the object is equal to the object's weight.

Sinking

The rock in **Figure 2** weighs 75 N. It displaces 5 L of water. Archimedes' principle says that the buoyant force is equal to the weight of the displaced water—about 50 N. The rock's weight is greater than the buoyant force. So, the rock sinks.

Floating

The fish in **Figure 2** weighs 12 N. It displaces a volume of water that weighs 12 N. Because the fish's weight is equal to the buoyant force, the fish floats in the water. In fact, the fish is suspended in the water as it floats. Now, look at the duck. The duck does not sink. So, the buoyant force on the duck must be equal to the duck's weight. But the duck isn't all the way underwater! Only the duck's feet, legs, and stomach have to be underwater to displace 9 N of water, which is equal to the duck's weight. So, the duck floats on the surface of the water.

Buoying Up

If the duck dove underwater, it would displace more than 9 N of water. So, the buoyant force on the duck would be greater than the duck's weight. When the buoyant force on an object is greater than the object's weight, the object is *buoyed up* (pushed up) in water. An object is buoyed up until the part of the object underwater displaces an amount of water that equals the object's entire weight. Thus, an ice cube pops to the surface when it is pushed to the bottom of a glass of water.

✓ **Reading Check** What causes an object to buoy up? (*See the Appendix for answers to Reading Checks.*)

Floating Fun

Fill a sink with water. Ask a parent to help you find five things that float in water and five things that sink in water. Discuss what the floating objects have in common and what the sinking objects have in common. In your **science journal,** list the objects, and summarize your discussion.

Figure 2 *Will an object sink or float? That depends on whether the buoyant force is less than or equal to the object's weight.*

Weight = 9 N
Buoyant force = 9 N
Duck floats on the surface.

Weight = 12 N
Buoyant force = 12 N
Fish floats and is suspended in the water.

Weight = 75 N
Buoyant force = 50 N
Rock sinks.

Floating, Sinking, and Density

Think again about the rock in the lake. The rock displaces 5 L of water. But volumes of solids are measured in cubic centimeters (cm^3). Because 1 mL is equal to 1 cm^3, the volume of the rock is 5,000 cm^3. But 5,000 cm^3 of rock weighs more than an equal volume of water. So, the rock sinks.

Because mass is proportional to weight, you can say that the rock has more mass per volume than water has. Mass per unit volume is density. The rock sinks because it is more dense than water is. The duck floats because it is less dense than water is. The density of the fish is equal to the density of the water.

More Dense Than Air

Why does an ice cube float on water but not in air? An ice cube floats on water because it is less dense than water. But most substances are *more* dense than air. So, there are few substances that float in air. The ice cube is more dense than air, so the ice cube doesn't float in air.

Less Dense Than Air

One substance that is less dense than air is helium, a gas. In fact, helium has one-seventh the density of air under normal conditions. A given volume of helium displaces an equal volume of air that is much heavier than itself. So, helium floats in air. Because helium floats in air, it is used in parade balloons, such as the one shown in **Figure 3.**

Reading Check Name a substance that is less dense than air.

Figure 3 *Helium in a balloon floats in air for the same reason an ice cube floats on water—helium is less dense than the surrounding fluid.*

Finding Density Find the density of a rock that has a mass of 10 g and a volume of 2 cm^3.

Step 1: Write the equation for density. Density is calculated by using this equation:

$$density = \frac{mass}{volume}$$

Step 2: Replace *mass* and *volume* with the values in the problem, and solve.

$$density = \frac{10 \text{ g}}{2 \text{ cm}^3} = 5 \text{ g/cm}^3$$

Now It's Your Turn

1. What is the density of a 20 cm^3 object that has a mass of 25 g?
2. A 546 g fish displaces 420 mL of water. What is the density of the fish? (Note: 1 mL = 1 cm^3)
3. A beaker holds 50 mL of a slimy green liquid. The mass of the liquid is 163 g. What is the density of the liquid?

Changing Overall Density

Steel is almost 8 times denser than water. And yet huge steel ships cruise the oceans with ease. But hold on! You just learned that substances that are more dense than water will sink in water. So, how does a steel ship float?

Changing Shape

The secret of how a ship floats is in the shape of the ship. What if a ship were just a big block of steel, as shown in **Figure 4**? If you put that block into water, the block would sink because it is more dense than water. So, ships are built with a hollow shape. The amount of steel in the ship is the same as in the block. But the hollow shape increases the volume of the ship. Remember that density is mass per unit volume. So, an increase in the ship's volume leads to a decrease in its density. Thus, ships made of steel float because their *overall density* is less than the density of water.

Most ships are built to displace more water than is necessary for the ship to float. Ships are made this way so that they won't sink when people and cargo are loaded on the ship.

CONNECTION TO Geology

Floating Rocks The rock that makes up Earth's continents is about 15% less dense than the molten (melted) mantle rock below it. Because of this difference in density, the continents are floating on the mantle. Research the structure of Earth, and make a poster that shows Earth's interior layers.

ACTIVITY

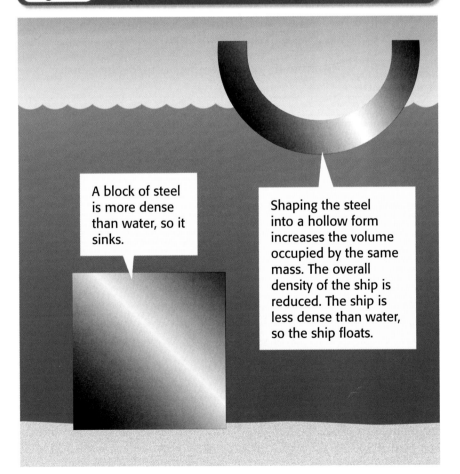

Figure 4 Shape and Overall Density

A block of steel is more dense than water, so it sinks.

Shaping the steel into a hollow form increases the volume occupied by the same mass. The overall density of the ship is reduced. The ship is less dense than water, so the ship floats.

INTERNET ACTIVITY

For another activity related to this chapter, go to **go.hrw.com** and type in the keyword **HP5FLUW**.

Quick Lab

Ship Shape

1. Roll a **piece of clay** into a ball the size of a golf ball, and drop it into a **container of water.** Record your observations.

2. With your hands, flatten the ball of clay until it is a bit thinner than your little finger, and press it into the shape of a bowl or canoe.

3. Place the clay boat gently in the water. How does the change of shape affect the buoyant force on the clay? How is that change related to the overall density of the clay boat? Record your answers.

Changing Mass

A submarine is a special kind of ship that can travel both on the surface of the water and underwater. Submarines have *ballast tanks* that can be opened to allow sea water to flow in. As water is added, the submarine's mass increases, but its volume stays the same. The submarine's overall density increases so that it can dive under the surface. Crew members control the amount of water taken in. In this way, they control how dense the submarine is and how deep it dives. Compressed air is used to blow the water out of the tanks so that the submarine can rise. Study **Figure 5** to learn how ballast tanks work.

✓ **Reading Check** How do crew members control the density of a submarine?

Figure 5 **Controlling Density Using Ballast Tanks**

When a submarine is floating on the ocean's surface, its ballast tanks are filled mostly with air.

Vent holes on the ballast tanks are opened to allow the submarine to dive. Air escapes as the tanks fill with water.

Vent holes are closed, and compressed air is pumped into the ballast tanks to force the water out, so the submarine rises.

Changing Volume

Like a submarine, some fish adjust their overall density to stay at a certain depth in the water. Most bony fishes have an organ called a *swim bladder,* shown in **Figure 6.** This swim bladder is filled with gases produced in a fish's blood. The inflated swim bladder increases the fish's volume and thereby decreases the fish's overall density, which keeps the fish from sinking in the water. The fish's nervous system controls the amount of gas in the bladder. Some fish, such as sharks, do not have a swim bladder. These fish must swim constantly to keep from sinking.

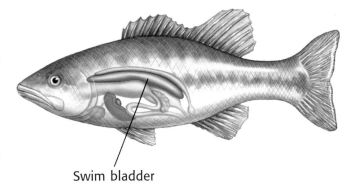

Swim bladder

Figure 6 *Most bony fishes have an organ called a* swim bladder *that allows them to adjust their overall density.*

SECTION Review

Summary

- All fluids exert an upward force called *buoyant force.*

- Buoyant force is caused by differences in fluid pressure.

- Archimedes' principle states that the buoyant force on an object is equal to the weight of the fluid displaced by the object.

- Any object that is more dense than the surrounding fluid will sink. An object that is less dense than the surrounding fluid will float.

- The overall density of an object can be changed by changing the object's shape, mass, or volume.

Using Key Terms

1. Use the following terms in the same sentence: *buoyant force* and *Archimedes' principle.*

Understanding Key Ideas

2. Which of the following changes increases the overall density of the object?

   a. A block of iron is formed into a hollow shape.

   b. A submarine fills its ballast tanks with water.

   c. A submarine fills its ballast tanks with air.

   d. A fish increases the amount of gas in its swim bladder.

3. Explain how differences in fluid pressure create buoyant force on an object.

4. How does an object's density determine whether the object will sink or float in water?

5. Name three methods that can be used to change the overall density of an object.

Math Skills

6. What is the density of an object that has a mass of 184 g and a volume of 50 cm^3?

Critical Thinking

7. **Applying Concepts** An object weighs 20 N. It displaces a volume of water that weighs 15 N.

   a. What is the buoyant force on the object?

   b. Will this object float or sink? Explain your answer.

8. **Predicting Consequences** Iron has a density of 7.9 g/cm^3. Mercury is a liquid that has a density of 13.5 g/cm^3. Will iron float or sink in mercury? Explain your answer.

9. **Evaluating Hypotheses** Imagine that your brother tells you that all heavy objects sink in water. Explain why you agree or disagree with his statement.

SCiLINKS®

NSTA

Developed and maintained by the National Science Teachers Association

For a variety of links related to this chapter, go to www.scilinks.org

Topic: Buoyant Force
SciLinks code: HSM0202

Fluids and Motion

Hold two sheets of paper so that the edges are hanging in front of your face about 4 cm apart. The flat faces of the paper should be parallel to each other. Now, blow as hard as you can between the two sheets of paper.

What's going on? You can't separate the sheets by blowing between them. In fact, the sheets move closer together the harder you blow. You may be surprised that the explanation for this unusual occurrence also includes how wings help birds and planes fly and how pitchers throw curve balls.

Fluid Speed and Pressure

The strange reaction of the paper is caused by a property of moving fluids. This property was first described in the 18th century by Daniel Bernoulli (ber NOO lee), a Swiss mathematician. **Bernoulli's principle** states that as the speed of a moving fluid increases, the fluid's pressure decreases. In the case of the paper, air speed between the two sheets increased when you blew air between them. Because air speed increased, the pressure between the sheets decreased. Thus, the higher pressure on the outside of the sheets pushed them together.

Science in a Sink

Bernoulli's principle is at work in **Figure 1.** A table-tennis ball is attached to a string and swung into a stream of water. Instead of being pushed out of the water, the ball is held in the water. Why? The water is moving faster than the air around it, so the water has a lower pressure than the surrounding air. The higher air pressure pushes the ball into the area of lower pressure—the water stream. Try this at home to see for yourself!

Bernoulli's principle the principle that states that the pressure in a fluid decreases as the fluid's velocity increases

Figure 1 *This ball is pushed by the higher pressure of the air into an area of reduced pressure—the water stream.*

Figure 2 **Wing Design and Lift**

ⓐ Airplane wings are made so that the air speed above the wing is greater than the air speed below the wing.

ⓑ According to Bernoulli's principle, a difference in air speed means a difference in pressure. The result is an upward force that contributes to lift.

ⓒ Another feature of wing design is that the shape of the wing forces the air downward. So, the air pushes the wing upward.

Factors That Affect Flight

A common commercial airplane in the skies today is the Boeing 737 jet. Even without passengers, the plane weighs 350,000 N. How can something so big and heavy get off the ground and fly? Wing shape plays a role in helping these big planes—as well as smaller planes and birds—achieve flight, as shown in **Figure 2.**

According to Bernoulli's principle, the fast-moving air above the wing exerts less pressure than the slow-moving air below the wing. The greater pressure below the wing exerts an upward force. This upward force, known as **lift,** pushes the wings (and the rest of the airplane or bird) upward against the downward pull of gravity.

lift an upward force on an object that moves in a fluid

✓Reading Check What is lift? (*See the Appendix for answers to Reading Checks.*)

Figure 3 **Increased Thrust Versus Increased Wing Size**

The engine of this jet creates a large amount of thrust, so the wings don't have to be very big.

This glider has no engine and therefore no thrust. So, its wings must be large in order to maximize the amount of lift achieved.

thrust the pushing or pulling force exerted by the engine of an aircraft or rocket

The First Flight The first successful flight of an engine-driven machine that was heavier than air happened in Kitty Hawk, North Carolina, in 1903. Orville Wright was the pilot. The plane flew only 37 m (about the length of a 737 jet) before landing, and the entire flight lasted only 12 s. Research another famous pilot in the history of flight. Make a poster that includes information about the pilot as well as pictures of the pilot and his or her airplane.

ACTIVITY

Thrust and Lift

The amount of lift created by a plane's wing is determined partly by the speed at which air travels around the wing. The speed of a plane is determined mostly by its thrust. **Thrust** is the forward force produced by the plane's engine. In general, a plane with a large amount of thrust moves faster than a plane that has less thrust does. This faster speed means air travels around the wing at a higher speed, which increases lift.

Wing Size, Speed, and Lift

The amount of lift also depends partly on the size of a plane's wings. Look at the jet plane in **Figure 3.** This plane can fly with a relatively small wing size because its engine gives a large amount of thrust. This thrust pushes the plane through the sky at great speeds. So, the jet creates a large amount of lift with small wings by moving quickly through the air. Smaller wings keep a plane's weight low, which also helps it move faster.

Compared with the jet, the glider in **Figure 3** has a large wing area. A glider is an engineless plane. It rides rising air currents to stay in flight. Without engines, gliders produce no thrust and move more slowly than many other kinds of planes. Thus, a glider must have large wings to create the lift it needs to stay in the air.

Bernoulli and Birds

Birds don't have engines, so birds must flap their wings to push themselves through the air. A small bird must flap its wings at a fast pace to stay in the air. But a hawk flaps its wings only occasionally because it has larger wings than the small bird has. A hawk uses its large wings to fly with very little effort. Fully extended, a hawk's wings allow the hawk to glide on wind currents and still have enough lift to stay in the air.

Figure 4 Bernoulli's Principle and the Screwball

ⓐ Air speed on the left side of the ball is decreased because air around the ball moves in the opposite direction of the airflow. So, there is a region of increased pressure on the left side of the ball.

Direction of spin

Direction of airflow

ⓒ Because air pressure on the left side is greater than air pressure on the right side, the ball is pushed toward the right in a curved path.

ⓑ Air speed on the right side of the ball is increased because air around the ball moves in the same direction as the airflow. So, there is a region of decreased pressure on the right side of the ball.

Bernoulli and Baseball

You don't have to look up at a bird or a plane flying through the sky to see Bernoulli's principle in your world. Any time fluids are moving, Bernoulli's principle is at work. **Figure 4** shows how a baseball pitcher can take advantage of Bernoulli's principle to throw a confusing screwball that is difficult for a batter to hit.

Drag and Motion in Fluids

Have you ever walked into a strong wind and noticed that the wind seemed to slow you down? It may have felt like the wind was pushing you backward. Fluids exert a force that opposes the motion of objects moving through the fluids. The force that opposes or restricts motion in a fluid is called **drag.**

In a strong wind, air "drags" on your body and makes it difficult for you to move forward. Drag also works against the forward motion of a plane or bird in flight. Drag is usually caused by an irregular flow of air. An irregular or unpredictable flow of fluids is known as *turbulence.*

drag a force parallel to the velocity of the flow; it opposes the direction of an aircraft and, in combination with thrust, determines the speed of the aircraft

✓ **Reading Check** What is turbulence?

Figure 5 *The pilot of this airplane can adjust these flaps to help increase lift when the airplane lands or takes off.*

Turbulence and Lift

Lift is often reduced when turbulence causes drag. Drag can be a serious problem for airplanes moving at high speeds. So, airplanes are equipped with ways to reduce turbulence as much as possible when in flight. For example, flaps like those shown in **Figure 5** can be used to change the shape or area of a wing. This change can reduce drag and increase lift. Similarly, birds can adjust their wing feathers in response to turbulence.

✓ **Reading Check** How do airplanes reduce turbulence?

Pascal's Principle

Imagine that the water-pumping station in your town increases the water pressure by 20 Pa. Will the water pressure be increased more at a store two blocks away or at a home 2 km away?

Believe it or not, the increase in water pressure will be the same at both locations. This equal change in water pressure is explained by Pascal's principle. **Pascal's principle** states that a change in pressure at any point in an enclosed fluid will be transmitted equally to all parts of that fluid. This principle was discovered by the 17th-century French scientist Blaise Pascal.

Pascal's principle the principle that states that a fluid in equilibrium contained in a vessel exerts a pressure of equal intensity in all directions

Pascal's Principle and Motion

Hydraulic (hie DRAW lik) devices use Pascal's principle to move or lift objects. Liquids are used in hydraulic devices because liquids cannot be easily compressed, or squeezed, into a smaller space. Cranes, forklifts, and bulldozers have hydraulic devices that help them lift heavy objects.

Hydraulic devices can multiply forces. Car brakes are a good example. In **Figure 6,** a driver's foot exerts pressure on a cylinder of liquid. This pressure is transmitted to all parts of the liquid-filled brake system. The liquid moves the brake pads. The pads press against the wheels, and friction stops the car. The force is multiplied because the pistons that push the brake pads are larger than the piston that is pushed by the brake pedal.

Figure 6 *Because of Pascal's principle, the touch of a foot can stop tons of moving metal.*

❶ When the driver pushes the brake pedal, a small piston exerts pressure on the fluid inside the brake system.

❷ The change in pressure is transmitted to the large pistons that push on the brake pads.

SECTION Review

Summary

● Bernoulli's principle states that fluid pressure decreases as the speed of the fluid increases.

● Wing shape allows airplanes to take advantage of Bernoulli's principle to achieve flight.

● Lift on an airplane is determined by wing size and thrust.

● Drag opposes motion through fluids.

● Pascal's principle states that a change in pressure in an enclosed fluid is transmitted equally to all parts of the fluid.

Using Key Terms

For each pair of terms, explain how the meanings of the terms differ.

1. *Bernoulli's principle* and *Pascal's principle*

2. *thrust* and *drag*

Understanding Key Ideas

3. The shape of an airplane's wing helps it gain
   a. drag.   c. thrust.
   b. lift.   d. turbulence.

4. What is the relationship between pressure and fluid speed?

5. What is Pascal's principle?

6. What force opposes motion through a fluid? How does this force affect lift?

7. How do thrust and lift help an airplane achieve flight?

Critical Thinking

8. **Applying Concepts** Air moving around a speeding race car can create lift. Upside-down wings, or spoilers, are mounted on the rear of race cars. Use Bernoulli's principle to explain how spoilers reduce the danger of accidents.

9. **Making Inferences** When you squeeze a balloon, where is the pressure inside the balloon increased the most? Explain.

Interpreting Graphics

10. Look at the image below. When the space through which a fluid flows becomes narrow, fluid speed increases. Using this information, explain how the two boats could collide.

SciLINKS®

NSTA
Developed and maintained by the
National Science Teachers Association

For a variety of links related to this chapter, go to www.scilinks.org

Topic: Bernoulli's Principle
SciLinks code: HSM0143

Skills Practice Lab

Fluids, Force, and Floating

Why do some objects sink in fluids but others float? In this lab, you'll get a sinking feeling as you determine that an object floats when its weight equals the buoyant force exerted by the surrounding fluid.

OBJECTIVES

Calculate the buoyant force on an object.

Compare the buoyant force on an object with its weight.

MATERIALS

- balance
- mass set
- pan, rectangular baking
- paper towels
- ruler, metric
- tub, plastic, large rectangular
- water

SAFETY

Procedure

1 Copy the table shown below.

Measurement	Trial 1	Trial 2
Length (l), cm		
Width (w), cm		
Initial height (h_1), cm		
Initial volume (V_1), cm^3 $V_1 = l \times w \times h_1$		
New height (h_2), cm		
New total volume (V_2), cm^3 $V_2 = l \times w \times h_2$	*DO NOT WRITE IN BOOK*	
Displaced volume (ΔV), cm^3 $\Delta V = V_2 - V_1$		
Mass of displaced water, g $m = \Delta V \times 1$ g/cm^3		
Weight of displaced water, N (buoyant force)		
Weight of pan and masses, N		

2 Fill the tub half full with water. Measure (in centimeters) the length, width, and initial height of the water. Record your measurements in the table.

3 Using the equation given in the table, determine the initial volume of water in the tub. Record your results in the table.

4 Place the pan in the water, and place masses in the pan, as shown on the next page. Keep adding masses until the pan sinks to about three-quarters of its height. Record the new height of the water in the table. Then, use this value to determine and record the new total volume of water plus the volume of water displaced by the pan.

5. Determine the volume of the water that was displaced by the pan and masses, and record this value in the table. The displaced volume is equal to the new total volume minus the initial volume.

6. Determine the mass of the displaced water by multiplying the displaced volume by its density (1 g/cm^3). Record the mass in the table.

7. Divide the mass by 100. The value you get is the weight of the displaced water in newtons (N). This is equal to the buoyant force. Record the weight of the displaced water in the table.

8. Remove the pan and masses, and determine their total mass (in grams) using the balance. Convert the mass to weight (N), as you did in step 7. Record the weight of the masses and pan in the table.

9. Place the empty pan back in the tub. Perform a second trial by repeating steps 4–8. This time, add masses until the pan is just about to sink.

Analyze the Results

1. **Identifying Patterns** Compare the buoyant force (the weight of the displaced water) with the weight of the pan and masses for both trials.

2. **Examining Data** How did the buoyant force differ between the two trials? Explain.

Draw Conclusions

3. **Drawing Conclusions** Based on your observations, what would happen if you were to add even more mass to the pan than you did in the second trial? Explain your answer in terms of the buoyant force.

4. **Making Predictions** What would happen if you put the masses in the water without the pan? What difference does the pan's shape make?

Chapter Review

USING KEY TERMS

In each of the following sentences, replace the incorrect term with the correct term from the word bank.

thrust   pressure
drag   lift
buoyant force   fluid
Pascal's principle
Bernoulli's principle

1 Lift increases with the depth of a fluid.

2 A plane's engines produce drag to push the plane forward.

3 A pascal can be a liquid or a gas.

4 A hydraulic device uses Archimedes' principle to lift or move objects.

5 Atmospheric pressure is the upward force exerted on objects by fluids.

UNDERSTANDING KEY IDEAS

Multiple Choice

6 The design of a wing
   a. causes the air above the wing to travel faster than the air below the wing.
   b. helps create lift.
   c. creates a low-pressure zone above the wing.
   d. All of the above

7 Fluid pressure is always directed
   a. up.   **c.** sideways.
   b. down.   **d.** in all directions.

8 An object surrounded by a fluid will displace a volume of fluid that is
   a. equal to its own volume.
   b. less than its own volume.
   c. greater than its own volume.
   d. denser than itself.

9 If an object weighing 50 N displaces a volume of water that weighs 10 N, what is the buoyant force on the object?
   a. 60 N   **c.** 40 N
   b. 50 N   **d.** 10 N

10 A helium-filled balloon will float in air because
   a. there is more air than helium.
   b. helium is less dense than air.
   c. helium is as dense as air.
   d. helium is more dense than air.

11 Materials that can flow to fit their containers include
   a. gases.
   b. liquids.
   c. both gases and liquids.
   d. gases, liquids, and solids.

Short Answer

12 Where is water pressure greater, at a depth of 1 m in a large lake or at a depth of 2 m in a small pond? Explain your answer.

13 Why are bubbles round?

14 Why are tornadoes like giant vacuum cleaners?

Math Skills

15 Calculate the area of a 1,500 N object that exerts a pressure of 500 Pa (500 N/m^2). Then, calculate the pressure exerted by the same object over twice that area.

CRITICAL THINKING

16 **Concept Mapping** Use the following terms to create a concept map: *fluid, pressure, depth, density,* and *buoyant force.*

17 **Forming Hypotheses** Gases can be easily compressed into smaller spaces. Why would this property of gases make gases less useful than liquids in hydraulic brakes?

18 **Making Comparisons** Will a ship loaded with beach balls float higher or lower in the water than an empty ship? Explain your reasoning.

19 **Applying Concepts** Inside all vacuum cleaners is a high-speed fan. Explain how this fan causes the vacuum cleaner to pick up dirt.

20 **Evaluating Hypotheses** A 600 N girl on stilts says to two 600 N boys sitting on the ground, "I am exerting over twice as much pressure as the two of you are exerting together!" Could this statement be true? Explain your reasoning.

INTERPRETING GRAPHICS

Use the diagram of an iceberg below to answer the questions that follow.

21 At what point (a, b, or c) is water pressure greatest on the iceberg?

22 How much of the iceberg has a weight equal to the buoyant force?

  a. all of it

  b. the section from a to b

  c. the section from b to c

  d. None of the above

23 How does the density of ice compare with the density of water?

24 Why do you think icebergs are dangerous to passing ships?

Standardized Test Preparation

READING

Read each of the passages below. Then, answer the questions that follow each passage.

Passage 1 The Mariana Trench is about 11 km deep—that's deep enough to swallow Mount Everest, the tallest mountain in the world. Fewer than a dozen undersea vessels have ever ventured this deep into the ocean. Why? Water exerts tremendous pressure at this depth. A revolutionary new undersea vessel, *Deep Flight*, has a hull made of an extremely strong ceramic material that can withstand such pressure. Although *Deep Flight* has not made it to the bottom of the Mariana Trench, some scientists think this type of undersea vessel will one day be used routinely to explore the ocean floor.

1. What is the meaning of the word *revolutionary* in this passage?
    A strange
    B overthrowing the government
    C radically different
    D disgusting

2. Based on the name of the undersea vessel described in this passage, what does the vessel look like?
    F a robot
    G a house
    H a car
    I an airplane

3. Based on the passage, which of the following statements is a fact?
    A Scientists hope to fly *Deep Flight* to the top of Mount Everest.
    B *Deep Flight* can withstand very high pressures.
    C Scientists cannot explore the ocean without using *Deep Flight*.
    D *Deep Flight* has gone to the bottom of the Mariana Trench a dozen times.

Passage 2 Buoyancy is an object's ability to float. An object will float if the water it displaces has a mass greater than the object's mass. It will sink if the water it displaces has a mass less than its own mass. But if an object displaces its own mass in water, it will neither float nor sink. Instead, it will remain suspended in the water because of what is called *neutral buoyancy*.

A goldfish has neutral buoyancy. A goldfish has a sac in its body called a *swim bladder*. Gases from blood vessels can diffuse into and out of the swim bladder. When the goldfish needs to rise in the water, for example, gases diffuse into the swim bladder and cause it to inflate. The swim bladder helps the goldfish maintain neutral buoyancy.

1. What is the purpose of this passage?
    A to explain how a goldfish maintains neutral buoyancy
    B to explain how to change the buoyancy of an object
    C to convince people to buy goldfish
    D to describe objects that float and sink

2. What is the meaning of the word *suspended* in this passage?
    F not allowed to attend school
    G stopped for a period of time
    H weighed down
    I supported from sinking

3. What is buoyancy?
    A a sac in a goldfish's body
    B the ability to float
    C the mass of an object
    D an inflated balloon

The graph below shows the water pressure measured by a scientist at different depths in the ocean. Use the graph below to answer the questions that follow.

Water Pressure Versus Depth

1. What is the pressure on the object when it is 100 m underwater?

   A 1.0 MPa

   B 1.1 MPa

   C 1.5 MPa

   D 2.0 MPa

2. Based on the data in the graph, which of the following is the best estimate of the pressure at 250 m below the surface of the ocean?

   F 1.7 MPa

   G 2.2 MPa

   H 2.6 MPa

   I 5.0 MPa

3. Which of the following statements best describes the relationship between the water pressure on an object and the depth of the object in the ocean?

   A Water pressure increases as the depth increases.

   B Water pressure decreases as the depth increases.

   C Water pressure does not change as the depth increases.

   D Water pressure has no predictable relationship to the depth.

Read each question below, and choose the best answer.

1. Anna-Marie has a coil of wire. She uses a balance to find that the wire has a mass of 17.8 g. She uses water displacement to find that the volume of the wire is 2.0 cm^3. Density is equal to mass divided by volume. What is the density of the wire?

   A 0.11 g/cm^3

   B 8.9 g/cm^3

   C 19.8 g/cm^3

   D 35.6 g/cm^3

2. Hussain rode his bike 30 km this weekend. What is this distance expressed in meters?

   F 0.3 m

   G 300 m

   H 30,000 m

   I 300,000 m

3. Olivia purchased 21 tubes of oil paint at $3.95 per tube, which includes tax. What was the total cost of the 21 tubes of paint?

   A $65.15

   B $82.95

   C $89.10

   D $93.50

4. Javi filled a container halfway full with water. The container measures 2 m wide, 3 m long, and 1 m high. How many cubic meters of water are in the container?

   F 2 m^3

   G 3 m^3

   H 5 m^3

   I 6 m^3

5. Pressure is equal to force divided by area. Jenny pushes a door with a force of 12 N. The area of her hand is 96 cm^2. What is the pressure exerted by Jenny's hand on the door?

   A 0.125 N/cm

   B 0.125 N/cm^2

   C 8 N/cm

   D 8 N/cm^2

Standardized Test Preparation

Science in Action

Science, Technology, and Society

Stayin' Aloft—The Story of the Frisbee®

In the late 1800s, a few fun-loving college students invented a game that involved tossing an empty tin pie plate. The pie plate was stamped with the name of a bakery: Frisbie's Pies. So, the game of Frisbie was created. Unfortunately, the metal pie plates tended to develop sharp edges that caused injuries. In 1947, plastic disks were made to replace the metal pie plates. These plastic disks were called Frisbees. How do Frisbees stay in the air? When you throw a Frisbee, you give it thrust. And as it moves through the air, lift is created because of Bernoulli's principle. But you don't have to think about the science behind Frisbees to have fun with them!

Math ACTIVITY

A Frisbee landed 10 m away from where it is thrown. The Frisbee was in the air for 2.5 s. What was the average speed of the Frisbee?

Science Fiction

"Wet Behind the Ears" by Jack C. Haldeman II

Willie Joe Thomas cheated to get a swimming scholarship. Now, he is faced with a major swim meet, and his coach told him that he has to swim or be kicked off the team. Willie Joe could lose his scholarship.

One day, Willie Joe's roommate, Frank, announces that he has developed a new "sliding compound." And Frank also said something about using the compound to make ships go faster. So, Willie Joe thought, if it works for ships, it might work for swimming.

See what happens when Willie Joe tries to save his scholarship by using Frank's compound at the swim meet. Read "Wet Behind the Ears," by Jack C. Haldeman II in the *Holt Anthology of Science Fiction*.

Language Arts ACTIVITY

Analyze the story structure of "Wet Behind the Ears." In your analysis, identify the introduction, the rising action, the climax, and the denouement. Summarize your analysis in a chart.

Alisha Bracken

Scuba Instructor Alisha Bracken first started scuba diving in her freshman year of college. Her first dives were in a saltwater hot spring near Salt Lake City, Utah. "It was awesome," Bracken says. "There were nurse sharks, angelfish, puffer fish and brine shrimp!" Bracken enjoyed her experience so much that she wanted to share it with other people. The best way to do that was to become an instructor and teach other people to dive.

Bracken says one of the biggest challenges of being a scuba instructor is teaching people to adapt and function in a foreign environment. She believes that learning to dive properly is important not only for the safety of the diver but also for the protection of the under-water environment. She relies on science principles to help teach people how to control their movements and protect the natural environment. "Buoyancy is the foundation of teaching people to dive comfortably," she explains. "Without it, we cannot float on the surface or stay off the bottom. Underwater life can be damaged if students do not learn and apply the concepts of buoyancy."

Social Studies ACTIVITY

Scuba divers and other underwater explorers sometimes investigate shipwrecks on the bottom of the ocean. Research the exploration of a specific shipwreck. Make a poster showing what artifacts were retrieved from the shipwreck and what was learned from the exploration.

To learn more about these Science in Action topics, visit go.hrw.com and type in the keyword HP5FLUF.

Current Science

Check out Current Science® articles related to this chapter by visiting go.hrw.com. Just type in the keyword HP5CS07.

20

Work and Machines

About the PHOTO

"One, two, stroke!" shouts the coach as the team races to the finish line. This paddling team is competing in Hong Kong's annual Dragon Boat Races. The Dragon Boat Festival is a 2,000-year-old Chinese tradition that commemorates Qu Yuan, a national hero. The paddlers that you see here are using the paddles to move the boat forward. Even though they are celebrating by racing their dragon boat, in scientific terms, this team is doing work.

PRE-READING ACTIVITY

FOLDNOTES **Booklet** Before you read the chapter, create the FoldNote entitled "Booklet" described in the **Study Skills** section of the Appendix. Label each page of the booklet with a main idea from the chapter. As you read the chapter, write what you learn about each main idea on the appropriate page of the booklet.

START-UP ACTIVITY

C'mon, Lever a Little!

In this activity, you will use a simple machine, a lever, to make your task a little easier.

Procedure

1. Stack **two books,** one on top of the other, on a **table.**

2. Slide your index finger underneath the edge of the bottom book. Using only the force of your finger, try to lift one side of the books 2 or 3 cm off the table. Is it hard to do so? Write your observations.

3. Slide the end of a **wooden ruler** underneath the edge of the bottom book. Then, slip a **large pencil eraser** or similar object under the ruler.

4. Again, using only your index finger, push down on the edge of the ruler and try to lift the books. Record your observations. **Caution:** Push down slowly to keep the ruler and eraser from flipping.

Analysis

1. Which was easier: lifting the books with your finger or lifting the books with the ruler? Explain your answer.

2. In what way did the direction of the force that your finger applied on the books differ from the direction of the force that your finger applied on the ruler?

Work and Power

Your science teacher has just given you tonight's homework assignment. You have to read an entire chapter by tomorrow! That sounds like a lot of work!

Actually, in the scientific sense, you won't be doing much work at all! How can that be? In science, **work** is done when a force causes an object to move in the direction of the force. In the example above, you may have to put a lot of mental effort into doing your homework, but you won't be using force to move anything. So, in the scientific sense, you will not be doing work—except the work to turn the pages of your book!

What Is Work?

The student in **Figure 1** is having a lot of fun, isn't she? But she is doing work, even though she is having fun. She is doing work because she is applying a force to the bowling ball and making the ball move through a distance. However, she is doing work on the ball only as long as she is touching it. The ball will keep moving away from her after she releases it. But she will no longer be doing work on the ball because she will no longer be applying a force to it.

Transfer of Energy

One way you can tell that the bowler in **Figure 1** has done work on the bowling ball is that the ball now has *kinetic energy*. This means that the ball is now moving. The bowler has transferred energy to the ball.

Differences Between Force and Work

Applying a force doesn't always result in work being done. Suppose that you help push a stalled car. You push and push, but the car doesn't budge. The pushing may have made you tired. But you haven't done any work on the car, because the car hasn't moved.

You do work on the car as soon as the car moves. Whenever you apply a force to an object and the object moves in the direction of the force, you have done work on the object.

✓ **Reading Check** Is work done every time a force is applied to an object? Explain. (*See the Appendix for answers to Reading Checks.*)

READING WARM-UP

Objectives

● Determine when work is being done on an object.

● Calculate the amount of work done on an object.

● Explain the difference between work and power.

Terms to Learn

work   power
joule   watt

READING STRATEGY

Reading Organizer As you read this section, make a table comparing work and power.

Figure 1
You might be surprised to find out that bowling is work!

Force and Motion in the Same Direction

Suppose you are in the airport and late for a flight. You have to run through the airport carrying a heavy suitcase. Because you are making the suitcase move, you are doing work on it, right? Wrong! For work to be done on an object, the object must move in the *same direction* as the force. You are applying a force to hold the suitcase up, but the suitcase is moving forward. So, no work is done on the suitcase. But work *is* done on the suitcase when you lift it off the ground.

Work is done on an object if two things happen: (1) the object moves as a force is applied and (2) the direction of the object's motion is the same as the direction of the force. The pictures and arrows in **Figure 2** will help you understand when work is being done on an object.

work the transfer of energy to an object by using a force that causes the object to move in the direction of the force

CONNECTION TO Biology

WRITING SKILL Work in the Human Body

You may not be doing any work on a suitcase if you are just holding it in your hands, but your body will still get tired from the effort because you are doing work on the muscles inside your body. Your muscles can contract thousands of times in just a few seconds while you try to keep the suitcase from falling. What other situations can you think of that might involve work being done somewhere inside your body? Describe these situations in your **science journal.**

Figure 2   Work or Not Work?

Example	Direction of force	Direction of motion	Doing work?
	→	→	Yes
	↑	→	No
	↑	↑	Yes
	↑	→	No

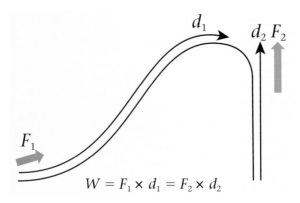

$$W = F_1 \times d_1 = F_2 \times d_2$$

Figure 3 *For each path, the same work is done to move the car to the top of the hill, although distance and force along the two paths differ.*

How Much Work?

Would you do more work on a car by pushing it up a long road to reach the top of a hill or by using a cable to raise the car up the side of a cliff to the top of the same hill? You would certainly need a different amount of force. Common use of the word *work* may make it seem that there would be a difference in the amount of work done in the two cases as well.

Same Work, Different Forces

You may be surprised to learn that the same amount of work is being done to push the car up a road as to raise it up the cliff. Look at **Figure 3**. A certain amount of energy is needed to move the car from the bottom to the top of the hill. Because the car ends up at the same place either way, the work done on the car is the same. However, pushing the car along the road up a hill seems easier than lifting it straight up. Why?

The reason is that work depends on distance as well as force. Consider a mountain climber who reaches the top of a mountain by climbing straight up a cliff, as in **Figure 4.** She must use enough force to overcome her entire weight. But the distance she travels up the cliff is shorter than the distance traveled by hikers who reach the top of the same mountain by walking up a slope. Either way, the same amount of work is done. But the hikers going up a slope don't need to use as much force as if they were going straight up the side of the cliff. This shows how you can use less force to do the same amount of work.

Figure 4 *Climbers going to the top of a mountain do the same amount of work whether they hike up a slope or go straight up a cliff.*

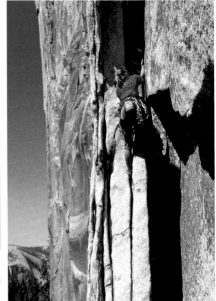

Calculating Work

The amount of work (*W*) done in moving an object, such as the barbell in **Figure 5,** can be calculated by multiplying the force (*F*) applied to the object by the distance (*d*) through which the force is applied, as shown in the following equation:

$$W = F \times d$$

Force is expressed in newtons, and the meter is the basic SI unit for length or distance. Therefore, the unit used to express work is the newton-meter (N × m), which is more simply called the **joule.** Because work is the transfer of energy to an object, the joule (J) is also the unit used to measure energy.

joule the unit used to express energy; equivalent to the amount of work done by a force of 1 N acting through a distance of 1 m in the direction of the force (symbol, J)

✔ **Reading Check** How is work calculated?

Figure 5 **Force Times Distance**

80 N

W = 80 N × 1 m = 80 J

The force needed to lift an object is equal to the gravitational force on the object—in other words, the object's weight.

160 N

W = 160 N × 1 m = 160 J

If you increase the weight, an increased force is needed to lift the object. This increases the amount of work done.

80 N

W = 80 N × 2 m = 160 J

Increasing the distance also increases the amount of work done.

Get to Work!

1. Use a **loop of string** to attach a **spring scale** to a **weight.**

2. Slowly pull the weight across a **table** by dragging the spring scale. Record the amount of force that you exerted on the weight.

3. Use a **metric ruler** to measure the distance that you pulled the weight.

4. Now, use the spring scale to slowly pull the weight up a **ramp.** Pull the weight the same distance that you pulled it across the table.

5. Calculate the work you did on the weight for both trials.

6. How were the amounts of work and force affected by the way you pulled the weight? What other ways of pulling the weight could you test?

Power: How Fast Work Is Done

power the rate at which work is done or energy is transformed

watt the unit used to express power; equivalent to joules per second (symbol, W)

Like the term *work,* the term *power* is used a lot in everyday language but has a very specific meaning in science. **Power** is the rate at which energy is transferred.

Calculating Power

To calculate power (*P*), you divide the amount of work done (*W*) by the time (*t*) it takes to do that work, as shown in the following equation:

$$P = \frac{W}{t}$$

The unit used to express power is joules per second (J/s), also called the **watt.** One watt (W) is equal to 1 J/s. So if you do 50 J of work in 5 s, your power is 10 J/s, or 10 W.

Power measures how fast work happens, or how quickly energy is transferred. When more work is done in a given amount of time, the power output is greater. Power output is also greater when the time it takes to do a certain amount of work is decreased, as shown in **Figure 6.**

Reading Check How is power calculated?

Figure 6 *No matter how fast you can sand by hand, an electric sander can do the same amount of work faster. Therefore, the electric sander has more power.*

MATH FOCUS

More Power to You A stage manager at a play raises the curtain by doing 5,976 J of work on the curtain in 12 s. What is the power output of the stage manager?

Step 1: Write the equation for power.

$$P = \frac{W}{t}$$

Step 2: Replace *W* and *t* with work and time.

$$P = \frac{5{,}976 \, \text{J}}{12 \, \text{s}} = 498 \, \text{W}$$

Now It's Your Turn
1. If it takes you 10 s to do 150 J of work on a box to move it up a ramp, what is your power output?
2. A light bulb is on for 12 s, and during that time it uses 1,200 J of electrical energy. What is the wattage (power) of the light bulb?

Increasing Power

It may take you longer to sand a wooden shelf by hand than by using an electric sander, but the amount of energy needed is the same either way. Only the power output is lower when you sand the shelf by hand (although your hand may get more tired). You could also dry your hair with a fan, but it would take a long time! A hair dryer is more powerful. It can give off energy more quickly than a fan does, so your hair dries faster.

Car engines are usually rated with a certain power output. The more powerful the engine is, the more quickly the engine can move a car. And for a given speed, a more powerful engine can move a heavier car than a less powerful engine can.

CONNECTION TO Language Arts

WRITING SKILL **Horsepower** The unit of power most commonly used to rate car engines is the *horsepower* (hp). Look up the word *horsepower* in a dictionary. How many watts is equal to 1 hp? Do you think all horses output exactly 1 hp? Why or why not? Write your answers in your **science journal.**

SECTION Review

Summary

- In scientific terms, *work* is done when a force causes an object to move in the direction of the force.
- Work is calculated as force times distance. The unit of work is the newton-meter, or joule.
- *Power* is a measure of how fast work is done.
- Power is calculated as work divided by time. The unit of power is the joule per second, or watt.

Using Key Terms

For each pair of terms, explain how the meanings of the terms differ.

1. *work* and *joule*

2. *power* and *watt*

Understanding Key Ideas

3. How is work calculated?
   a. force times distance
   b. force divided by distance
   c. power times distance
   d. power divided by distance

4. What is the difference between work and power?

Math Skills

5. Using a force of 10 N, you push a shopping cart 10 m. How much work did you do?

6. If you did 100 J of work in 5 s, what was your power output?

Critical Thinking

7. **Analyzing Processes** Work is done on a ball when a pitcher throws it. Is the pitcher still doing work on the ball as it flies through the air? Explain.

8. **Applying Concepts** You lift a chair that weighs 50 N to a height of 0.5 m and carry it 10 m across the room. How much work do you do on the chair?

Interpreting Graphics

9. What idea about work and force does the following diagram describe? Explain your answer.

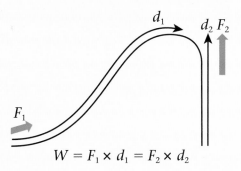

$$W = F_1 \times d_1 = F_2 \times d_2$$

For a variety of links related to this chapter, go to www.scilinks.org

Topic: Work and Power
SciLinks code: HSM1675

557

What Is a Machine?

You are in the car with your mom on the way to a party when suddenly—KABLOOM hisssss—a tire blows out. "Now I'm going to be late!" you think as your mom pulls over to the side of the road.

You watch as she opens the trunk and gets out a jack and a tire iron. Using the tire iron, she pries the hubcap off and begins to unscrew the lug nuts from the wheel. She then puts the jack under the car and turns the jack's handle several times until the flat tire no longer touches the ground. After exchanging the flat tire with the spare, she lowers the jack and puts the lug nuts and hubcap back on the wheel.

"Wow!" you think, "That wasn't as hard as I thought it would be." As your mom drops you off at the party, you think how lucky it was that she had the right equipment to change the tire.

Machines: Making Work Easier

Now, imagine changing a tire without the jack and the tire iron. Would it have been easy? No, you would have needed several people just to hold up the car! Sometimes, you need the help of machines to do work. A **machine** is a device that makes work easier by changing the size or direction of a force.

When you think of machines, you might think of things such as cars, big construction equipment, or even computers. But not all machines are complicated. In fact, you use many simple machines in your everyday life. **Figure 1** shows some examples of machines.

Figure 1 Some Everyday Machines

Wheelchair

Chopsticks

Scissors

Work In, Work Out

Suppose that you need to get the lid off a can of paint. What do you do? One way to pry the lid off is to use a common machine known as a *lever*. **Figure 2** shows a screwdriver being used as a lever. You place the tip of the screwdriver under the edge of the lid and then push down on the screwdriver's handle. The tip of the screwdriver lifts the lid as you push down. In other words, you do work on the screwdriver, and the screwdriver does work on the lid.

Work is done when a force is applied through a distance. Look again at **Figure 2.** The work that you do on a machine is called **work input.** You apply a force, called the *input force,* to the machine through a distance. The work done by the machine on an object is called **work output.** The machine applies a force, called the *output force,* through a distance.

How Machines Help

You might think that machines help you because they increase the amount of work done. But that's not true. If you multiplied the forces by the distances through which the forces are applied in **Figure 2** (remember that $W = F \times d$), you would find that the screwdriver does not do more work on the lid than you do on the screwdriver. Work output can never be greater than work input. Machines allow force to be applied over a greater distance, which means that less force will be needed for the same amount of work.

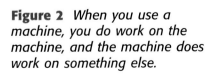 **Reading Check** How do machines make work easier? (*See the Appendix for answers to Reading Checks.*)

machine a device that helps do work by either overcoming a force or changing the direction of the applied force

work input the work done on a machine; the product of the input force and the distance through which the force is exerted

work output the work done by a machine; the product of the output force and the distance through which the force is exerted

Output force

Input force

Figure 2 *When you use a machine, you do work on the machine, and the machine does work on something else.*

Same Work, Different Force

Machines make work easier by changing the size or direction (or both) of the input force. When a screwdriver is used as a lever to open a paint can, both the size and direction of the input force change. Remember that using a machine does not change the amount of work you will do. As **Figure 3** shows, the same amount of work is done with or without the ramp. The ramp decreases the size of the input force needed to lift the box but increases the distance over which the force is exerted. So, the machine allows a smaller force to be applied over a longer distance.

The Force-Distance Trade-Off

When a machine changes the size of the force, the distance through which the force is exerted must also change. Force or distance can increase, but both cannot increase. When one increases, the other must decrease.

Figure 4 shows how machines change force and distance. Whenever a machine changes the size of a force, the machine also changes the distance through which the force is applied. **Figure 4** also shows that some machines change only the direction of the force, not the size of the force or the distance through which the force is exerted.

✔ **Reading Check** What are the two things that a machine can change about how work is done?

Figure 3 Input Force and Distance

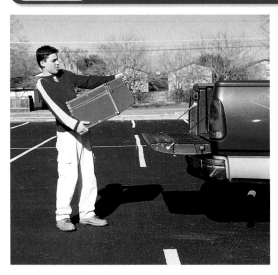

Lifting this box straight up requires an input force equal to the weight of the box.

$W = 450 \text{ N} \times 1 \text{ m} = 450 \text{ J}$

Using a ramp to lift the box requires an input force less than the weight of the box, but the input force must be exerted over a greater distance than if you didn't use a ramp.

$W = 150 \text{ N} \times 3 \text{ m} = 450 \text{ J}$

Figure 4 Machines Change the Size and/or Direction of a Force

Input force

Output force

A nutcracker *increases* the force but applies it over a *shorter* distance.

A hammer *decreases* the force, but applies it over a *greater* distance.

Output force

Input force

A simple pulley changes the *direction* of the input force, but the size of the output force is the same as the input force.

Input force

Output force

When a screw-driver is used as a lever, it *increases* the force and *decreases* the distance over which the force is applied.

Output force

Input force

Mechanical Advantage

Some machines make work easier than others do because they can increase force more than other machines can. A machine's **mechanical advantage** is the number of times the machine multiplies force. In other words, the mechanical advantage compares the input force with the output force.

mechanical advantage a number that tells how many times a machine multiplies force

Calculating Mechanical Advantage

You can find mechanical advantage by using the following equation:

$$mechanical\ advantage\ (MA) = \frac{output\ force}{input\ force}$$

For example, imagine that you had to push a 500 N weight up a ramp and only needed to push with 50 N of force the entire time. The mechanical advantage of the ramp would be calculated as follows:

$$MA = \frac{500\ N}{50\ N} = 10$$

A machine that has a mechanical advantage that is greater than 1 can help move or lift heavy objects because the output force is greater than the input force. A machine that has a mechanical advantage that is less than 1 will reduce the output force but can increase the distance an object moves. **Figure 4** shows an example of such a machine—a hammer.

Finding the Advantage

A grocer uses a handcart to lift a heavy stack of canned food. Suppose that he applies an input force of 40 N to the handcart. The cart applies an output force of 320 N to the stack of canned food. What is the mechanical advantage of the handcart?

Mechanical Efficiency

The work output of a machine can never be greater than the work input. In fact, the work output of a machine is always less than the work input. Why? Some of the work done by the machine is used to overcome the friction created by the use of the machine. But keep in mind that no work is lost. The work output plus the work done to overcome friction is equal to the work input.

The less work a machine has to do to overcome friction, the more efficient the machine is. **Mechanical efficiency** (muh KAN i kuhl e FISH uhn see) is a comparison of a machine's work output with the work input.

mechanical efficiency a quantity, usually expressed as a percentage, that measures the ratio of work output to work input; it can be calculated by dividing work output by work input

Calculating Efficiency

A machine's mechanical efficiency is calculated using the following equation:

$$\text{mechanical efficiency} = \frac{\text{work output}}{\text{work input}} \times 100$$

The 100 in this equation means that mechanical efficiency is expressed as a percentage. Mechanical efficiency tells you what percentage of the work input gets converted into work output.

Figure 5 shows a machine that is used to drill holes in metal. Some of the work input is used to overcome the friction between the metal and the drill. This energy cannot be used to do work on the steel block. Instead, it heats up the steel and the machine itself.

Reading Check How is mechanical efficiency calculated?

Useful Friction

Friction is always present when two objects touch or rub together, and friction usually slows down moving parts in a machine and heats them up. In some cases, parts in a machine are designed to increase friction. While at home, observe three situations in which friction is useful. Describe them in your **science journal**.

Figure 5 In this machine, some of the work input is converted into sound and heat energy.

Perfect Efficiency?

An *ideal machine* would be a machine that had 100% mechanical efficiency. An ideal machine's useful work output would equal the work done on the machine. Ideal machines are impossible to build, because every machine has moving parts. Moving parts always use some of the work input to overcome friction. But new technologies help increase efficiency so that more energy is available to do useful work. The train in **Figure 6** is floating on magnets, so there is almost no friction between the train and the tracks. Other machines use lubricants, such as oil or grease, to lower the friction between their moving parts, which makes the machines more efficient.

Figure 6 *There is very little friction between this magnetic levitation train and its tracks, so it is highly efficient.*

SECTION Review

Summary

- A machine makes work easier by changing the size or direction (or both) of a force.
- A machine can increase force or distance, but not both.
- Mechanical advantage tells how many times a machine multiplies force.
- Mechanical efficiency is a comparison of a machine's work output with work input.
- Machines are not 100% efficient because some of the work done is used to overcome friction.

Using Key Terms

For each pair of terms, explain how the meanings of the terms differ.

1. *work input* and *work output*

2. *mechanical advantage* and *mechanical efficiency*

Understanding Key Ideas

3. Which of the following is the correct way to calculate mechanical advantage?
   a. input force ÷ output force
   b. output force ÷ input force
   c. work input ÷ work output
   d. work output ÷ work input

4. Explain how using a ramp makes work easier.

5. Give a specific example of a machine, and describe how its mechanical efficiency might be calculated.

6. Why can't a machine be 100% efficient?

Math Skills

7. Suppose that you exert 60 N on a machine and the machine exerts 300 N on another object. What is the machine's mechanical advantage?

8. What is the mechanical efficiency of a machine whose work input is 100 J and work output is 30 J?

Critical Thinking

9. **Making Inferences** For a machine with a mechanical advantage of 3, how does the distance through which the output force is exerted differ from the distance through which the input force is exerted?

10. **Analyzing Processes** Describe the effect that friction has on a machine's mechanical efficiency. How do lubricants increase a machine's mechanical efficiency?

SCiLINKS.

NSTA
Developed and maintained by the
National Science Teachers Association

For a variety of links related to this chapter, go to www.scilinks.org

Topic: Mechanical Efficiency
SciLinks code: HSM0929

Types of Machines

Imagine that it's a hot summer day. You have a whole ice-cold watermelon in front of you. It would taste cool and delicious—if only you had a machine that could cut it!

The machine you need is a knife. But how is a knife a machine? A knife is actually a very sharp wedge, which is one of the six simple machines. The six simple machines are the lever, the inclined plane, the wedge, the screw, the pulley, and the wheel and axle. All machines are made from one or more of these simple machines.

Levers

Have you ever used the claw end of a hammer to remove a nail from a piece of wood? If so, you were using the hammer as a lever. A **lever** is a simple machine that has a bar that pivots at a fixed point, called a *fulcrum*. Levers are used to apply a force to a load. There are three classes of levers, which are based on the locations of the fulcrum, the load, and the input force.

First-Class Levers

With a first-class lever, the fulcrum is between the input force and the load, as shown in **Figure 1.** First-class levers always change the direction of the input force. And depending on the location of the fulcrum, first-class levers can be used to increase force or to increase distance.

Figure 1 **Examples of First-Class Levers**

When the fulcrum is closer to the load than to the input force, the lever has a **mechanical advantage of greater than 1.** The output force is increased because it is exerted over a shorter distance.

When the fulcrum is exactly in the middle, the lever has a **mechanical advantage of 1.** The output force is not increased because the input force's distance is not increased.

When the fulcrum is closer to the input force than to the load, the lever has a **mechanical advantage of less than 1.** Although the output force is less than the input force, distance increases.

Figure 2 Examples of Second-Class Levers

In a **second-class lever,** the output force, or load, is between the input force and the fulcrum.

Using a second-class lever results in a **mechanical advantage of greater than 1.** The closer the load is to the fulcrum, the more the force is increased and the greater the mechanical advantage is.

Second-Class Levers

The load of a second-class lever is between the fulcrum and the input force, as shown in **Figure 2.** Second-class levers do not change the direction of the input force. But they allow you to apply less force than the force exerted by the load. Because the output force is greater than the input force, you must exert the input force over a greater distance.

lever a simple machine that consists of a bar that pivots at a fixed point called a *fulcrum*

Third-Class Levers

The input force in a third-class lever is between the fulcrum and the load, as shown in **Figure 3.** Third-class levers do not change the direction of the input force. In addition, they do not increase the input force. Therefore, the output force is always less than the input force.

✔**Reading Check** How do the three types of levers differ from one another? (*See the Appendix for answers to Reading Checks.*)

Figure 3 Examples of Third-Class Levers

In a **third-class lever,** the input force is between the fulcrum and the load.

Using a third-class lever results in a **mechanical advantage of less than 1** because force is decreased. But third-class levers increase the distance through which the output force is exerted.

Pulleys

When you open window blinds by pulling on a cord, you're using a pulley. A **pulley** is a simple machine that has a grooved wheel that holds a rope or a cable. A load is attached to one end of the rope, and an input force is applied to the other end. Types of pulleys are shown in **Figure 4.**

pulley a simple machine that consists of a wheel over which a rope, chain, or wire passes

Fixed Pulleys

A fixed pulley is attached to something that does not move. By using a fixed pulley, you can pull down on the rope to lift the load up. The pulley changes the direction of the force. Elevators make use of fixed pulleys.

Movable Pulleys

Unlike fixed pulleys, movable pulleys are attached to the object being moved. A movable pulley does not change a force's direction. Movable pulleys do increase force, but they also increase the distance over which the input force must be exerted.

Block and Tackles

When a fixed pulley and a movable pulley are used together, the pulley system is called a *block and tackle*. The mechanical advantage of a block and tackle depends on the number of rope segments.

Figure 4 — Types of Pulleys

Fixed Pulley

Input force

Output force

A **fixed pulley** only spins. So the distance through which the input force and the output force are exerted—and thus the forces themselves—are the same. Therefore, a fixed pulley provides a mechanical advantage of 1.

Movable Pulley

Input force — Input force

Output force

A **movable pulley** moves up with the load as the load is lifted. The mechanical advantage of this movable pulley is 2.

Block and Tackle

Input force

Output force

The mechanical advantage of this **block and tackle** is 4 because there are four rope segments. It multiplies your input force by 4, but you have to pull the rope 4 m just to lift the load 1 m.

Figure 5 **How a Wheel and Axle Works**

Wheel

Input force

Axle

Output force

a When a small input force is applied to the wheel, the wheel rotates through a circular distance.

b As the wheel turns, so does the axle. But because the axle is smaller than the wheel, it rotates through a smaller distance, which makes the output force larger than the input force

Wheel and Axle

Did you know that a faucet is a machine? The faucet shown in **Figure 5** is an example of a **wheel and axle,** a simple machine consisting of two circular objects of different sizes. Doorknobs, wrenches, and steering wheels all use a wheel and axle. **Figure 5** shows how a wheel and axle works.

wheel and axle a simple machine consisting of two circular objects of different sizes; the wheel is the larger of the two circular objects

Mechanical Advantage of a Wheel and Axle

The mechanical advantage of a wheel and axle can be found by dividing the *radius* (the distance from the center to the edge) of the wheel by the radius of the axle, as shown in **Figure 6.** Turning the wheel results in a mechanical advantage of greater than 1 because the radius of the wheel is larger than the radius of the axle.

Reading Check How is the mechanical advantage of a wheel and axle calculated?

Radius of wheel **15 cm**

Radius of axle **3 cm**

$$MA = \frac{15 \text{ cm}}{3 \text{ cm}} = 5$$

Figure 6 *The mechanical advantage of a wheel and axle is the radius of the wheel divided by the radius of the axle.*

Figure 7 *The work you do on the piano to roll it up the ramp is the same as the work you would do to lift it straight up. An inclined plane simply allows you to apply a smaller force over a greater distance.*

$$MA = \frac{3 \text{ m}}{0.6 \text{ m}} = 5$$

Inclined Planes

Do you remember the story about how the Egyptians built the Great Pyramid? One of the machines they used was the **inclined plane.** An *inclined plane* is a simple machine that is a straight, slanted surface. A ramp is an inclined plane.

inclined plane a simple machine that is a straight, slanted surface, which facilitates the raising of loads; a ramp

Using an inclined plane to load a piano into a truck, as **Figure 7** shows, is easier than lifting the piano into the truck. Rolling the piano along an inclined plane requires a smaller input force than is needed to lift the piano into the truck. The same work is done on the piano, just over a longer distance.

Reading Check What is an inclined plane?

Mechanical Advantage of Inclined Planes

The greater the ratio of an inclined plane's length to its height is, the greater the mechanical advantage is. The mechanical advantage (*MA*) of an inclined plane can be calculated by dividing the *length* of the inclined plane by the *height* to which the load is lifted. The inclined plane in **Figure 7** has a mechanical advantage of 3 m/0.6 m = 5.

Mechanical Advantage of an Inclined Plane A heavy box is pushed up a ramp that has an incline of 4.8 m long and 1.2 m high. What is the mechanical advantage of the ramp?

Step 1: Write the equation for the mechanical advantage of an inclined plane.

$$MA = \frac{l}{h}$$

Step 2: Replace *l* and *h* with length and height.

$$MA = \frac{4.8 \text{ m}}{1.2 \text{ m}} = 4$$

Now It's Your Turn

1. A wheelchair ramp is 9 m long and 1.5 m high. What is the mechanical advantage of the ramp?
2. As a pyramid is built, a stone block is dragged up a ramp that is 120 m long and 20 m high. What is the mechanical advantage of the ramp?
3. If an inclined plane were 2 m long and 8 m high, what would be its mechanical advantage?

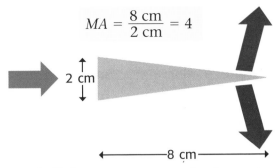

$$MA = \frac{8 \text{ cm}}{2 \text{ cm}} = 4$$

2 cm

← 8 cm →

Figure 8 *A knife is a common example of a wedge, a simple machine consisting of two inclined planes back to back.*

Wedges

Imagine trying to cut a melon in half with a spoon. It wouldn't be easy, would it? A knife is much more useful for cutting because it is a **wedge.** A *wedge* is a pair of inclined planes that move. A wedge applies an output force that is greater than your input force, but you apply the input force over a greater distance. For example, a knife is a common wedge that can easily cut into a melon and push apart its two halves, as shown in **Figure 8.** Other useful wedges include doorstops, plows, ax heads, and chisels.

Mechanical Advantage of Wedges

The longer and thinner the wedge is, the greater its mechanical advantage is. That's why axes and knives cut better when you sharpen them—you are making the wedge thinner. Therefore, less input force is required. The mechanical advantage of a wedge can be found by dividing the length of the wedge by its greatest thickness, as shown in **Figure 8.**

Screws

A **screw** is an inclined plane that is wrapped in a spiral around a cylinder, as you can see in **Figure 9.** When a screw is turned, a small force is applied over the long distance along the inclined plane of the screw. Meanwhile, the screw applies a large force through the short distance it is pushed. Screws are used most commonly as fasteners.

Mechanical Advantage of Screws

If you could unwind the inclined plane of a screw, you would see that the plane is very long and has a gentle slope. Recall that the longer an inclined plane is compared with its height, the greater its mechanical advantage. Similarly, the longer the spiral on a screw is and the closer together the threads are, the greater the screw's mechanical advantage is. A jar lid is a screw that has a large mechanical advantage.

wedge a simple machine that is made up of two inclined planes and that moves; often used for cutting

screw a simple machine that consists of an inclined plane wrapped around a cylinder

Figure 9 *If you could unwind a screw, you would see that it is actually a very long inclined plane.*

Compound Machines

You are surrounded by machines. You even have machines in your body! But most of the machines in your world are **compound machines,** machines that are made of two or more simple machines. You have already seen one example of a compound machine: a block and tackle. A block and tackle consists of two or more pulleys.

Figure 10 shows a common example of a compound machine. A can opener may seem simple, but it is actually three machines combined. It consists of a second-class lever, a wheel and axle, and a wedge. When you squeeze the handle, you are making use of a second-class lever. The blade of the can opener acts as a wedge as it cuts into the can's top. The knob that you turn to open the can is a wheel and axle.

Mechanical Efficiency of Compound Machines

The mechanical efficiency of most compound machines is low. The efficiency is low because compound machines have more moving parts than simple machines do, thus there is more friction to overcome. Compound machines, such as automobiles and airplanes, can involve many simple machines. It is very important to reduce friction as much as possible, because too much friction can damage the simple machines that make up the compound machine. Friction can be lowered by using lubrication and other techniques.

Reading Check What special disadvantage do compound machines have?

Wheel and axle

Wedge

Second class lever

Figure 10 *A can opener is a compound machine. The handle is a second-class lever, the knob is a wheel and axle, and a wedge is used to open the can.*

SECTION Review

Summary

- In a first-class lever, the fulcrum is between the force and the load. In a second-class lever, the load is between the force and the fulcrum. In a third-class lever, the force is between the fulcrum and the load.

- The mechanical advantage of an inclined plane is length divided by height. Wedges and screws are types of inclined planes.

- A wedge is a type of inclined plane. Its mechanical advantage is its length divided by its greatest thickness.

- The mechanical advantage of a wheel and axle is the radius of the wheel divided by the radius of the axle.

- Types of pulleys include fixed pulleys, movable pulleys, and block and tackles.

- Compound machines consist of two or more simple machines.

- Compound machines have low mechanical efficiencies because they have more moving parts and therefore more friction to overcome.

Using Key Terms

1. In your own words, write a definition for the term *lever*.

2. Use the following terms in the same sentence: *inclined plane, wedge,* and *screw.*

Understanding Key Ideas

3. Which class of lever always has a mechanical advantage of greater than 1?
   a. first-class
   b. second-class
   c. third-class
   d. None of the above

4. Give an example of each of the following simple machines: first-class lever, second-class lever, third-class lever, inclined plane, wedge, and screw.

Math Skills

5. A ramp is 0.5 m high and has a slope that is 4 m long. What is its mechanical advantage?

6. The radius of the wheel of a wheel and axle is 4 times the radius of the axle. What is the mechanical advantage of the wheel and axle?

Critical Thinking

7. **Applying Concepts** A third-class lever has a mechanical advantage of less than 1. Explain why it is useful for some tasks.

8. **Making Inferences** Which compound machine would you expect to have the lowest mechanical efficiency: a can opener or a pair of scissors? Explain your answer.

Interpreting Graphics

9. Indicate two simple machines being used in the picture below.

Skills Practice Lab

OBJECTIVES

Calculate the work and power used to climb a flight of stairs.

Compare your work and power with that of a 100 W light bulb.

MATERIALS

- flight of stairs
- ruler, metric
- stopwatch

A Powerful Workout

Does the amount of work that you do depend on how fast you do it? No! But the amount of time in which you do work does affect your power—the rate of work done. In this lab, you'll calculate your work and power for climbing a flight of stairs at different speeds. Then you'll compare your power with that of an ordinary household object—a 100 W light bulb.

Ask a Question

1 How does your power in climbing a flight of stairs compare with the power of a 100 W light bulb?

Form a Hypothesis

2 Write a hypothesis that answers the question in step 1. Explain your reasoning.

Data Collection Table				
Height of step (cm)	Number of steps	Height of stairs (m)	Time for slow walk (s)	Time for quick walk (s)
		DO NOT WRITE IN BOOK		

Test the Hypothesis

3 Copy the Data Collection Table onto a separate sheet of paper.

4 Use a metric ruler to measure the height of one stair step. Record the measurement in your Data Collection Table. Be sure to include units for all measurements.

5 Count the number of stairs, including the top step, and record this number in your Data Collection Table.

6 Calculate the height of the climb by multiplying the number of steps by the height of one step. Record your answer in meters. (You will need to convert your answer from centimeters to meters.)

7 Use a stopwatch to measure how many seconds it takes you to walk slowly up a flight of stairs. Record your measurement in your Data Collection Table.

8 Now measure how many seconds it takes you to walk quickly up a flight of stairs. Be careful not to overexert yourself. This is not a race to see who can get the fastest time!

Analyze the Results

1 **Constructing Tables** Copy the Calculations Table below onto a separate sheet of paper.

Calculations Table			
Weight (N)	Work (J)	Power for slow walk (W)	Power for quick walk (W)
		DO NOT WRITE IN BOOK	

2 **Examining Data** Determine your weight in newtons, and record it in your Calculations Table. Your weight in newtons is your weight in pounds (lb) multiplied by 4.45 N/lb.

3 **Examining Data** Calculate and record your work done in climbing the stairs by using the following equation:

$$work = force \times distance$$

(Hint: If you are having trouble determining the force exerted, remember that force is measured in newtons.)

4 **Examining Data** Calculate and record your power output by using the following equation:

$$power = \frac{work}{time}$$

The unit for power is the watt (1 watt = 1 joule/second).

Draw Conclusions

5 **Evaluating Methods** In step 3 of "Analyze the Results," you were asked to calculate your work done in climbing the stairs. Why weren't you asked to calculate your work for each trial (slow walk and quick walk)?

6 **Drawing Conclusions** Look at your hypothesis. Was your hypothesis correct? Now that you have measured your power, write a statement that describes how your power compares with that of a 100 W light bulb.

7 **Applying Conclusions** The work done to move one electron in a light bulb is very small. Write down two reasons why the power used is large. (Hint: How many electrons are in the filament of a light bulb? How did you use more power in trial 2?)

Communicating Your Data

Your teacher will provide a class data table on the board. Add your average power to the table. Then calculate the average power from the class data. How many students would it take to create power equal to the power of a 100 W bulb?

Chapter Review

USING KEY TERMS

For each pair of terms, explain how the meanings of the terms differ.

1 *work* and *power*

2 *lever* and *inclined plane*

3 *wheel and axle* and *pulley*

UNDERSTANDING KEY IDEAS

Multiple Choice

4 Work is being done when

  a. you apply a force to an object.

  b. an object is moving after you applied a force to it.

  c. you exert a force that moves an object in the direction of the force.

  d. you do something that is difficult.

5 What is the unit for work?

  a. joule

  b. joule per second

  c. newton

  d. watt

6 Which of the following is a simple machine?

  a. a bicycle

  b. a jar lid

  c. a pair of scissors

  d. a can opener

7 A machine can increase

  a. distance by decreasing force.

  b. force by decreasing distance.

  c. neither distance nor force.

  d. Either (a) or (b)

8 What is power?

  a. the strength of someone or something

  b. the force that is used

  c. the work that is done

  d. the rate at which work is done

9 What is the unit for power?

  a. newton

  b. kilogram

  c. watt

  d. joule

Short Answer

10 Identify the two simple machines that make up a pair of scissors.

11 Explain why you do work on a bag of groceries when you pick it up but not when you carry it.

12 Why is the work output of a machine always less than the work input?

13 What does the mechanical advantage of a first-class lever depend upon? Describe how it can be changed.

Math Skills

14 You and a friend together apply a force of 1,000 N to a car, which makes the car roll 10 m in 1 min and 40 s.

  a. How much work did you and your friend do together?

  b. What was the power output?

15 A lever allows a 35 N load to be lifted with a force of 7 N. What is the mechanical advantage of the lever?

CRITICAL THINKING

16 Concept Mapping Use the following terms to create a concept map: *work, force, distance, machine,* and *mechanical advantage.*

17 Analyzing Ideas Explain why levers usually have a greater mechanical efficiency than other simple machines do.

18 Making Inferences The amount of work done on a machine is 300 J, and the machine does 50 J of work. What can you say about the amount of friction that the machine has while operating?

19 Applying Concepts The winding road shown below is a series of inclined planes. Describe how a winding road makes it easier for vehicles to travel up a hill.

20 Predicting Consequences Why wouldn't you want to reduce the friction involved in using a winding road?

21 Making Comparisons How does the way that a wedge's mechanical advantage is determined differ from the way that a screw's mechanical advantage is determined?

22 Identifying Relationships If the mechanical advantage of a certain machine is greater than 1, what does that tell you about the relationship between the input force and distance and output force and distance?

INTERPRETING GRAPHICS

For each of the images below, identify the class of lever used and calculate the mechanical advantage of the lever.

23

Output force 120 N

Input force 40 N

Fulcrum

24

Input force 20 N

Fulcrum

Output force 4 N

Standardized Test Preparation

EOG Prep

Read each of the passages below. Then, answer the questions that follow each passage.

Passage 1 The Great Pyramid, located in Giza, Egypt, covers an area the size of 7 city blocks and rises about 40 stories high. The Great Pyramid was built around 2600 BCE and took less than 30 years to complete. During this time, the Egyptians cut and moved more than 2 million stone blocks, most of which average 2,000 kg. The workers did not have cranes, bulldozers, or any other heavy-duty machines. What they did have were two simple machines—the inclined plane and the lever. Archeologists have found the remains of inclined planes, or ramps, made from mud, stone, and wood. The Egyptians pushed or pulled the blocks along ramps to raise the blocks to the proper height. Notches in many blocks indicate that huge levers were used as giant crowbars to lift and move the heavy blocks.

1. What is the main idea of the passage?
   A Archeologists have found the remains of inclined planes near the pyramids.
   B The Great Pyramid at Giza was built in less than 30 years.
   C The Egyptians cut and moved more than 2 million stone blocks.
   D The Egyptians used simple machines to build the Great Pyramid at Giza.

2. Which of the following is a fact stated in the passage?
   F The Great Pyramid was made using more than 2 million stone blocks.
   G Each of the stone blocks used to build the Great Pyramid was exactly 2,000 kg.
   H Ancient Egyptians used cranes to build the Great Pyramid.
   I The Great Pyramid at Giza has a mass of about 2 million kg.

Passage 2 While riding a bicycle, you have probably experienced vibrations when the wheels of the bicycle hit bumps in the road. The force of the vibrations travels up through the frame to the rider. Slight vibrations can cause discomfort. Large ones can cause you to lose control of the bike and crash. Early bicycle designs made no attempt to dampen the <u>shock</u> of vibrations. Later designs used air-filled rubber tires and softer seats with springs to absorb some of the vibrations. Today's bike designs provide a safer, more comfortable ride. Various new materials—titanium, for example—absorb shock better than traditional steel and aluminum do. More important, designers are putting a variety of shock absorbers—devices that absorb energy—into bike designs.

1. In the passage, what does the term *shock* mean?
   A a medical emergency that can be caused by blood loss
   B a dry material used in early bicycles
   C a feeling of being stunned and surprised
   D a jolt or impact

2. Which of the following is a fact stated in the passage?
   F You have experienced vibrations while bicycle riding.
   G Slight vibrations can cause severe discomfort.
   H Titanium absorbs shock better than aluminum does.
   I Today's bike designs provide a more fashionable ride.

Use the diagram below to answer the questions that follow.

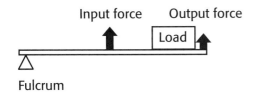

Input force   Output force
Load
Fulcrum

1. How does this lever make work easier?
   A by changing the direction of the force
   B by increasing both force and distance
   C by increasing force and decreasing distance
   D by decreasing force and increasing distance

2. What would the mechanical advantage of this lever be?
   F less than 1
   G 1
   H greater than 1
   I There is not enough information to determine the answer.

3. What type of lever is the lever in the diagram?
   A a first-class lever
   B a second-class lever
   C a third-class lever
   D There is not enough information to determine the answer.

4. Which of the following items is the same type of lever as the lever in the diagram?
   F a seesaw
   G a wheelbarrow
   H a bottle opener
   I an arm lifting a barbell

Read each question below, and choose the best answer.

1. For a special musical number during a school choir concert, 6 students stood in the first row, 10 students stood in the second row, and 14 students stood in the third row. If the pattern continued, how many students stood in the fifth row?
   A 18
   B 22
   C 26
   D 30

2. Michael baked some bread for his friends. He put 2½ cups of flour in each loaf. Altogether, he used 12½ cups of flour. How many loaves did he make?
   F 2 loaves
   G 4 loaves
   H 5 loaves
   I 15 loaves

3. A force of 15 N is exerted over a distance of 6 m. How much work was done? (Use the equation $W = F \times d$.)
   A 21 J
   B 21 N
   C 90 J
   D 90 N

4. If 350 J of work was done in 50 s, what was the power output? (Use the equation $P = W/t$.)
   F 7 W
   G 70 W
   H 1,750 W
   I 17,500 W

Standardized Test Preparation

Science in Action

Science, Technology, and Society

Kinetic Sculpture

The collection of tubes, tracks, balls, and blocks of wood shown in the photo is an audio-kinetic sculpture. A conveyor belt lifts the balls to a point high on the track, and the balls wind their way down as they are pulled by the force of gravity and pushed by various other forces. They twist through spirals, drop straight down tubes, and sometimes go up and around loops as if on a roller coaster. All this is made possible by the artist's applications of principles of kinetic energy, the energy of motion.

Math ACTIVITY

A conveyor belt on a kinetic sculpture lifts a ball to a point 0.8 m high. It exerts 0.05 N of force as it does so. How much work does the conveyor belt do on the ball?

Weird Science

Nanomachines

The technology of making things smaller and smaller keeps growing and growing. Powerful computers can now be held in the palm of your hand. But what can motors that are smaller than grains of pepper do? How can gnat-sized robots that can swim through the bloodstream be used? One possible field in which very small machines, *nanomachines,* can be used is in medicine.

Some scientists are looking into the possibility of creating cell-sized machines called *nanobots.* These tiny robots may have many uses in medicine if they can be injected into a person's bloodstream.

Language Arts ACTIVITY

WRITING SKILL Write a short story in which nanobots are used to save someone's life. Describe the machines the nanobots use in destroying deadly bacteria, clearing blood clots, or delivering medicine.

Mike Hensler

The Surf Chair Mike Hensler was a lifeguard at Daytona Beach, Florida, when he realized that it was next to impossible for someone in a wheelchair to come onto the beach. Although he had never invented a machine before, Hensler decided to build a wheelchair that could be driven across sand without getting stuck. He began spending many evenings in his driveway with a pile of lawn-chair parts, designing the chair by trial and error.

The result of Hensler's efforts looks very different from a conventional wheelchair. With huge rubber wheels and a thick frame of white PVC pipe, the Surf Chair not only moves easily over sandy terrain but also is weather resistant and easy to clean. The newest models of the Surf Chair come with optional attachments, such as a variety of umbrellas, detachable armrests and footrests, and even places to attach fishing rods.

Social Studies ACTIVITY

List some simple and compound machines that are used as access devices for people who are disabled. Research how these machines came to be in common use.

To learn more about these Science in Action topics, visit go.hrw.com and type in the keyword HP5WRKF.

Current Science

Check out Current Science® articles related to this chapter by visiting go.hrw.com. Just type in the keyword HP5CS08.

Contents

Skills Practice Lab

Go Fly a Bike!

Your friend Daniel just invented a bicycle that can fly! Trouble is, the bike can fly only when the wind speed is between 3 m/s and 10 m/s. If the wind is not blowing hard enough, the bike won't get enough lift to rise into the air, and if the wind is blowing too hard, the bike is difficult to control. Daniel needs to know if he can fly his bike today. Can you build a device that can estimate how fast the wind is blowing?

Ask a Question

1 How can I construct a device to measure wind speed?

Form a Hypothesis

2 Write a possible answer for the question above. Explain your reasoning.

Test the Hypothesis

3 Cut off the rolled edges of all five paper cups. They will then be lighter so that they can spin more easily.

4 Measure and place four equally spaced markings 1 cm below the rim of one of the paper cups.

5 Use the hole punch to punch a hole at each mark so that the cup has four equally spaced holes. Use the sharp pencil to carefully punch a hole in the center of the bottom of the cup.

6 Push a straw through two opposite holes in the side of the cup.

7 Repeat step 5 for the other two holes. The straws should form an X.

8 Measure 3 cm from the bottom of the remaining paper cups, and mark each spot with a dot.

9 At each dot, punch a hole in the paper cups with the hole punch.

10 Color the outside of one of the four cups.

MATERIALS

- clay, modeling
- cups, paper, small (5)
- hole punch
- marker, colored
- pencil, sharp, with an eraser
- ruler, metric
- scissors
- stapler, small
- straws, straight plastic (2)
- tape, masking
- thumbtack
- watch (or clock) that indicates seconds

SAFETY

11. Slide a cup on one of the straws by pushing the straw through the punched hole. Rotate the cup so that the bottom faces to the right.

12. Fold the end of the straw, and staple it to the inside of the cup directly across from the hole.

13. Repeat steps 11–12 for each of the remaining cups.

14. Push the tack through the intersection of the two straws.

15. Push the eraser end of a pencil through the bottom hole in the center cup. Push the tack as far as it will go into the end of the eraser.

16. Push the sharpened end of the pencil into some modeling clay to form a base. The device will then be able to stand up without being knocked over, as shown at right.

17. Blow into the cups so that they spin. Adjust the tack so that the cups can freely spin without wobbling or falling apart. Congratulations! You have just constructed an anemometer.

18. Find a suitable area outside to place the anemometer vertically on a surface away from objects that would obstruct the wind, such as buildings and trees.

19. Mark the surface at the base of the anemometer with masking tape. Label the tape "starting point."

20. Hold the colored cup over the starting point while your partner holds the watch.

21. Release the colored cup. At the same time, your partner should look at the watch or clock. As the cups spin, count the number of times the colored cup crosses the starting point in 10 s.

Analyze the Results

1. How many times did the colored cup cross the starting point in 10 s?

2. Divide your answer in step 21 by 10 to get the number of revolutions in 1 s.

3. Measure the diameter of your anemometer (the distance between the outside edges of two opposite cups) in centimeters. Multiply this number by 3.14 to get the circumference of the circle made by the cups of your anemometer.

4. Multiply your answer from step 3 by the number of revolutions per second (step 2). Divide that answer by 100 to get wind speed in meters per second.

5. Compare your results with those of your classmates. Did you get the same results? What could account for any slight differences in your results?

Draw Conclusions

6. Could Daniel fly his bicycle today? Why or why not?

Skills Practice Lab

Watching the Weather

Imagine that you own a private consulting firm that helps people plan for big occasions, such as weddings, parties, and celebrity events. One of your duties is making sure the weather doesn't put a damper on your clients' plans. In order to provide the best service possible, you have taken a crash course in reading weather maps. Will the celebrity golf match have to be delayed on account of rain? Will the wedding ceremony have to be moved inside so the blushing bride doesn't get soaked? It is your job to say yea or nay.

MATERIALS

- pencil

Procedure

1. Study the station model and legend shown on the next page. You will use the legend to interpret the weather map on the final page of this activity.

2. Weather data is represented on a weather map by a station model. A station model is a small circle that shows the location of the weather station along with a set of symbols and numbers around the circle that represent the data collected at the weather station. Study the table below.

Weather-Map Symbols					
Weather conditions		**Cloud cover**		**Wind speed (mph)**	
•• Light rain	○	No clouds	◎	Calm
•• Moderate rain	◐	One-tenth or less		3–8
•• Heavy rain	◔	Two- to three-tenths		9–14
, Drizzle	◕	Broken		15–20
** Light snow	◐	Nine-tenths		21–25
**,* Moderate snow	●	Overcast		32–37
⟁ Thunderstorm	⊗	Sky obscured		44–48
∿ Freezing rain		**Special Symbols**		55–60
∞ Haze	▲▲▲▲	Cold front		66–71
≡ Fog	●●●●	Warm front		
	H	High pressure		
	L	Low pressure		
	🌀	Hurricane		

Station Model

Wind speed is represented by whole and half tails.

A line indicates the direction the wind is coming from.

Air temperature

A symbol represents the current weather conditions. If there is no symbol, there is no precipitation.

Dew point temperature

Shading indicates the cloud coverage.

234

77
73

Atmospheric pressure in millibars (mbar). This number has been shortened on the station model. To read the number properly you must follow a few simple rules.

- If the first number is greater than 5, place a 9 in front of the number and a decimal point between the last two digits.

- If the first number is less than or equal to 5, place a 10 in front of the number and a decimal point between the last two digits.

Interpreting Station Models

The station model below is for Boston, Massachusetts. The current temperature in Boston is 42°F, and the dew point is 39°F. The barometric pressure is 1011.0 mbar. The sky is overcast, and there is moderate rainfall. The wind is coming from the southwest at 15–20 mph.

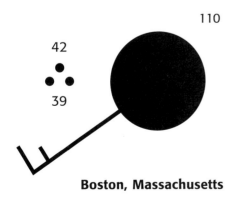

110

42

39

Boston, Massachusetts

Analyze the Results

1 Based on the weather for the entire United States, what time of year is it? Explain your answer.

2 Interpret the station model for Salem, Oregon. What is the temperature, dew point, cloud coverage, wind direction, wind speed, and atmospheric pressure? Is there any precipitation? If so, what kind?

3 What is happening to wind direction, temperature, and pressure as the cold front approaches? as it passes?

Draw Conclusions

4 Interpret the station model for Amarillo, Texas.

Skills Practice Lab

Let It Snow!

Although an inch of rain might be good for your garden, 7 cm or 8 cm could cause an unwelcome flood. But what about snow? How much snow is too much? A blizzard might drop 40 cm of snow overnight. Sure it's up to your knees, but how does this much snow compare with rain? This activity will help you find out.

Procedure

1. Pour 50 mL of shaved ice into your beaker. Do not pack the ice into the beaker. This ice will represent your snowfall.

2. Use the ruler to measure the height of the snow in the beaker.

3. Turn on the hot plate to a low setting. **Caution:** Wear heat-resistant gloves and goggles when working with the hot plate.

4. Place the beaker on the hot plate, and leave it there until all of the snow melts.

5. Pour the water into the graduated cylinder, and record the height and volume of the water.

6. Repeat steps 1–5 two more times.

Analysis

1. What was the difference in height before and after the snow melted in each of your three trials? What was the average difference?

2. Why did the volume change after the ice melted?

3. What was the ratio of snow height to water height?

4. Use the ratio you found in step 3 of the Analysis to calculate how much water 50 cm of this snow would produce. Use the following equation to help.

$$\frac{\text{measured height of snow}}{\text{measured height of water}} = \frac{50 \text{ cm of snow}}{? \text{ cm of water}}$$

5. Why is it important to know the water content of a snowfall?

- beaker, 100 mL
- gloves, heat-resistant
- graduated cylinder
- hot plate
- ice, shaved, 150 mL
- ruler, metric

SAFETY

Applying Your Data

Shaved ice isn't really snow. Research to find out how much water real snow would produce. Does every snowfall produce the same ratio of snow height to water depth?

Model-Making Lab

Gone with the Wind

Pilots at the Fly Away Airport need your help—fast! Last night, lightning destroyed the orange windsock. This windsock helped pilots measure which direction the wind was blowing. But now the windsock is gone with the wind, and an incoming airplane needs to land. The pilot must know which direction the wind is blowing and is counting on you to make a device that can measure wind direction.

MATERIALS

- card, index
- compass, drawing
- compass, magnetic
- pencil, sharpened
- plate, paper
- protractor
- rock, small
- ruler, metric
- scissors
- stapler
- straw, straight plastic
- thumbtack (or pushpin)

SAFETY

Ask a Question

1 How can I measure wind direction?

Form a Hypothesis

2 Write a possible answer to the question above.

Test the Hypothesis

3 Find the center of the plate by tracing around its edge with a drawing compass. The pointed end of the compass should poke a small hole in the center of the plate.

4 Use a ruler to draw a line across the center of the plate.

5 Use a protractor to help you draw a second line through the center of the plate. This new line should be at a 90° angle to the line you drew in step 4.

6 Moving clockwise, label each line "N," "E," "S," and "W."

7 Use a protractor to help you draw two more lines through the center of the plate. These lines should be at a 45° angle to the lines you drew in steps 4 and 5.

8 Moving clockwise from *N,* label these new lines "NE," "SE," "SW," and "NW." The plate now resembles the face of a magnetic compass. The plate will be the base of your wind-direction indicator. It will help you read the direction of the wind at a glance.

9 Measure and mark a 5 cm × 5 cm square on an index card, and cut out the square. Fold the square in half to form a triangle.

10 Staple an open edge of the triangle to the straw so that one point of the triangle touches the end of the straw.

11 Hold the pencil at a 90° angle to the straw. The eraser should touch the balance point of the straw. Push a thumbtack or pushpin through the straw and into the eraser. The straw should spin without falling off.

12 Find a suitable area outside to measure the wind direction. The area should be clear of trees and buildings.

13 Press the sharpened end of the pencil through the center hole of the plate and into the ground. The labels on your paper plate should be facing the sky, as shown on this page.

14 Use a compass to find magnetic north. Rotate the plate so that the *N* on the plate points north. Place a small rock on top of the plate so that the plate does not turn.

15 Watch the straw as it rotates. The triangle will point in the direction the wind is blowing.

Analyze the Results

1 From which direction is the wind coming?

2 In which direction is the wind blowing?

Draw Conclusions

3 Would this be an effective way for pilots to measure wind direction? Why or why not?

4 What improvements would you suggest to Fly Away Airport to measure wind direction more accurately?

Applying Your Data

Use this tool to measure and record wind direction for several days. What changes in wind direction occur as a front approaches? as a front passes?

Review magnetic declination in the chapter entitled "Maps as Models of the Earth." How might magnetic declination affect your design for a tool to measure wind direction?

Skills Practice Lab

Global Impact

For years, scientists have debated the topic of global warming. Is the temperature of the Earth actually getting warmer? In this activity, you will examine a table to determine if the data indicate any trends. Be sure to notice how much the trends seem to change as you analyze different sets of data.

Procedure

1. The table below shows average global temperatures recorded over the last 100 years.

2. Draw a graph. Label the horizontal axis "Time." Mark the grid in 5-year intervals. Label the vertical axis "Temperature (°C)," with values ranging from 13°C to 15°C.

3. Starting with 1900, use the numbers in red to plot the temperature in 20-year intervals. Connect the dots with straight lines.

4. Using a ruler, estimate the average slope for the temperatures. Draw a red line to represent the slope.

5. Using different colors, plot the temperatures at 10-year intervals and 5-year intervals on the same graph. Connect each set of dots, and draw the average slope for each set.

Analyze the Results

1. Examine your completed graph, and explain any trends you see in the graphed data. Was there an increase or a decrease in average temperature over the last 100 years?

2. What similarities and differences did you see between each set of graphed data?

Draw Conclusions

3. What conclusions can you draw from the data you graphed in this activity?

4. What would happen if your graph were plotted in 1-year intervals? Try it!

Average Global Temperatures											
Year	°C	Year	°C	Year	°C	Year	°C	Year	°C	Year	°C
1900	14.0	1917	13.6	1934	14.0	1951	14.0	1968	13.9	1985	14.1
1901	13.9	1918	13.6	1935	13.9	1952	14.0	1969	14.0	1986	14.2
1902	13.8	1919	13.8	1936	14.0	1953	14.1	1970	14.0	1987	14.3
1903	13.6	1920	13.8	1937	14.1	1954	13.9	1971	13.9	1988	14.4
1904	13.5	1921	13.9	1938	14.1	1955	13.9	1972	13.9	1989	14.2
1905	13.7	1922	13.9	1939	14.0	1956	13.8	1973	14.2	1990	14.5
1906	13.8	1923	13.8	1940	14.1	1957	14.1	1974	13.9	1991	14.4
1907	13.6	1924	13.8	1941	14.1	1958	14.1	1975	14.0	1992	14.1
1908	13.7	1925	13.8	1942	14.1	1959	14.0	1976	13.8	1993	14.2
1909	13.7	1926	14.1	1943	14.0	1960	14.0	1977	14.2	1994	14.3
1910	13.7	1927	14.0	1944	14.1	1961	14.1	1978	14.1	1995	14.5
1911	13.7	1928	14.0	1945	14.0	1962	14.0	1979	14.1	1996	14.4
1912	13.7	1929	13.8	1946	14.0	1963	14.0	1980	14.3	1997	14.4
1913	13.8	1930	13.9	1947	14.1	1964	13.7	1981	14.4	1998	14.5
1914	14.0	1931	14.0	1948	14.0	1965	13.8	1982	14.1	1999	14.5
1915	14.0	1932	14.0	1949	13.9	1966	13.9	1983	14.3	2000	14.5
1916	13.8	1933	13.9	1950	13.8	1967	14.0	1984	14.1	2001	14.5

Skills Practice Lab

For the Birds

You and a partner have a new business building birdhouses. But your first clients have told you that birds do not want to live in the birdhouses you have made. The clients want their money back unless you can solve the problem. You need to come up with a solution right away!

You remember reading an article about microclimates in a science magazine. Cities often heat up because the pavement and buildings absorb so much solar radiation. Maybe the houses are too warm! How can the houses be kept cooler?

You decide to investigate the roofs; after all, changing the roofs would be a lot easier than building new houses. In order to help your clients and the birds, you decide to test different roof colors and materials to see how these variables affect a roof's ability to absorb the sun's rays.

One partner will test the color, and the other partner will test the materials. You will then share your results and make a recommendation together.

MATERIALS

- cardboard (4 pieces)
- paint, black, white, and light blue tempera
- rubber, beige or tan
- thermometers, Celsius (4)
- watch (or clock)
- wood, beige or tan

SAFETY

Part A: Color Test

Ask a Question

1 What color would be the best choice for the roof of a birdhouse?

Form a Hypothesis

2 Write down the color you think will keep a birdhouse coolest.

Test the Hypothesis

3 Paint one piece of cardboard black, another piece white, and a third light blue.

4 After the paint has dried, take the three pieces of cardboard outside, and place a thermometer on each piece.

5 In an area where there is no shade, place each piece at the same height so that all three receive the same amount of sunlight. Leave the pieces in the sunlight for 15 min.

6 Leave a fourth thermometer outside in the shade to measure the temperature of the air.

7 Record the reading of the thermometer on each piece of cardboard. Also, record the outside temperature.

Analyze the Results

1 Did each of the three thermometers record the same temperature after 15 min? Explain.

2 Were the temperature readings on each of the three pieces of cardboard the same as the reading for the outside temperature? Explain.

Draw Conclusions

3 How do your observations compare with your hypothesis?

Part B: Material Test

Ask a Question

1 Which material would be the best choice for the roof of a birdhouse?

Form a Hypothesis

2 Write down the material you think will keep a birdhouse coolest.

Test the Hypothesis

3 Take the rubber, wood, and the fourth piece of cardboard outside, and place a thermometer on each.

4 In an area where there is no shade, place each material at the same height so that they all receive the same amount of sunlight. Leave the materials in the sunlight for 15 min.

5 Leave a fourth thermometer outside in the shade to measure the temperature of the air.

6 Record the temperature of each material. Also, record the outside temperature. After you and your partner have finished your investigations, take a few minutes to share your results.

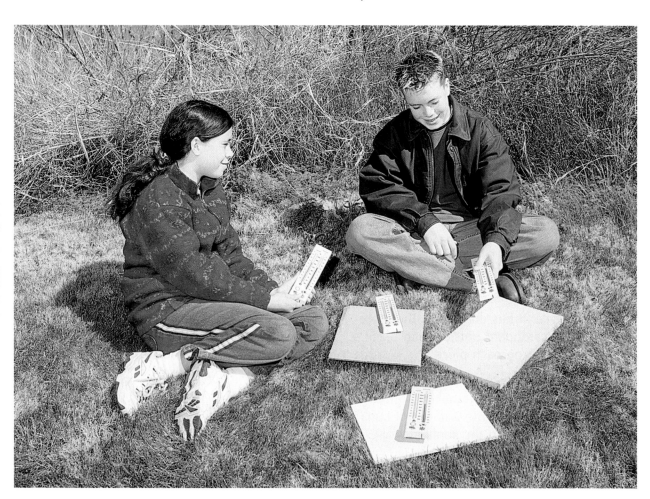

Analyze the Results

1 Did each of the thermometers on the three materials record the same temperature after 15 min? Explain.

2 Were the temperature readings on the rubber, wood, and cardboard the same as the reading for the outside temperature? Explain.

Draw Conclusions

3 How do your observations compare with your hypothesis?

4 Which material would you use to build the roofs for your birdhouses? Why?

5 Which color would you use to paint the new roofs? Why?

Applying Your Data

Make three different-colored samples for each of the three materials. When you measure the temperatures for each sample, how do the colors compare for each material? Is the same color best for all three materials? How do your results compare with what you concluded in steps 4 and 5 under Draw Conclusions of this activity? What's more important, color or material?

Inquiry Lab

Muscles at Work

Have you ever exercised outside on a cold fall day wearing only a thin warm-up suit or shorts? How did you stay warm? The answer is that your muscle cells contracted, and when contraction takes place, some energy is used to do work, and the rest is converted to thermal energy. This process helps your body maintain a constant temperature in cold conditions. In this activity, you will learn how the release of energy can cause a change in your body temperature.

Ask a Question

1 Write a question that you can test about how activity affects body temperature.

Form a Hypothesis

2 Form a group of four students. In your group, discuss several exercises that can produce a change in body temperature. Write a hypothesis that could answer the question you asked.

Test the Hypothesis

3 Develop an experimental procedure that includes the steps necessary to test your hypothesis. Be sure to get your teacher's approval before you begin.

4 Assign tasks to individuals in the group, such as note taking, data recording, and timing. What observations and data will you be recording? Design your data tables accordingly.

5 Perform your experiment as planned by your group. Be sure to record all observations in your data tables.

Analyze the Results

1 How did you determine if muscle contractions cause the release of thermal energy? Was your hypothesis supported by your data? Explain your results in a written report. Describe how you could improve your experimental method.

Applying Your Data

Why do humans shiver in the cold? Do all animals shiver? Find out why shivering is one of the first signs that your body is becoming too cold.

MATERIALS

- clock (or watch) with a second hand
- thermometer, small, hand held
- other materials as approved by your teacher

Model-Making Lab

Build a Lung

When you breathe, you actually pull air into your lungs because your diaphragm muscle causes your chest to expand. You can see this is true by placing your hands on your ribs and inhaling slowly. Did you feel your chest expand?

In this activity, you will build a model of a lung by using some common materials. You will see how the diaphragm muscle works to inflate your lungs. Refer to the diagrams at right as you construct your model.

MATERIALS

- bag, trash, small plastic
- balloon, small
- bottle, top half, 2 L
- clay, golf-ball-sized piece
- rubber bands (2)
- ruler, metric
- straw, plastic
- tape, transparent

Procedure

1. Attach the balloon to the end of the straw with a rubber band. Make a hole through the clay, and insert the other end of the straw through the hole. Be sure at least 8 cm of the straw extends beyond the clay. Squeeze the ball of clay gently to seal the clay around the straw.

2. Insert the balloon end of the straw into the neck of the bottle. Use the ball of clay to seal the straw and balloon into the bottle.

3. Turn the bottle gently on its side. Place the trash bag over the cut end of the bottle. Expand a rubber band around the bottom of the bottle to secure the bag. You may wish to reinforce the seal with tape. Before the plastic is completely sealed, gather the excess material of the bag into your hand, and press toward the inside of the bottle slightly. (You may need to tie a knot about halfway up from the bottom of the bag to take up excess material.) Use tape to finish sealing the bag to the bottle with the bag in this position. The excess air will be pushed out of the bottle.

Analyze the Results

1. What can you do with your model to make the "lung" inflate?

2. What do the balloon, the plastic wrap, and the straw represent in your model?

3. Using your model, demonstrate to the class how air enters the lung and how air exits the lung.

Applying Your Data

Do some research to find out what an "iron lung" is and why it was used in the past. Research and write a report about what is used today to help people who have difficulty breathing.

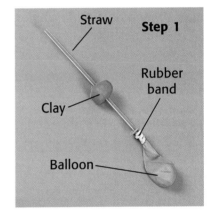

Step 1 — Straw, Rubber band, Clay, Balloon

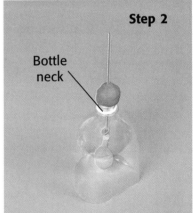

Step 2 — Bottle neck

Step 3

Skills Practice Lab

Enzymes in Action

You know how important enzymes are in the process of digestion. This lab will help you see enzymes at work. Hydrogen peroxide is continuously produced by your cells. If it is not quickly broken down, hydrogen peroxide will kill your cells. Luckily, your cells contain an enzyme that converts hydrogen peroxide into two nonpoisonous substances. This enzyme is also present in the cells of beef liver. In this lab, you will observe the action of this enzyme on hydrogen peroxide.

Procedure

1. Draw a data table similar to the one below. Be sure to leave enough space to write your observations.

Data Table

Size and condition of liver	Experimental liquid	Observations
1 cm cube beef liver	2 mL water	
1 cm cube beef liver	2 mL hydrogen peroxide	DO NOT WRITE IN BOOK
1 cm cube beef liver (mashed)	2 mL hydrogen peroxide	

MATERIALS

- beef liver, 1 cm cubes (3)
- gloves, protective
- graduated cylinder, 10 mL
- hydrogen peroxide, fresh (4 mL)
- mortar and pestle (or fork and watch glass)
- plate, small
- spatula
- test tube (3)
- test-tube rack
- tweezers
- water

SAFETY

2. Get three equal-sized pieces of beef liver from your teacher, and use your forceps to place them on your plate.

3. Pour 2 mL of water into a test tube labeled "Water and liver."

4. Using the tweezers, carefully place one piece of liver in the test tube. Record your observations in your data table.

5. Pour 2 mL of hydrogen peroxide into a second test tube labeled "Liver and hydrogen peroxide."
   Caution: Do not splash hydrogen peroxide on your skin. If you do get hydrogen peroxide on your skin, rinse the affected area with running water immediately, and tell your teacher.

6. Using the tweezers, carefully place one piece of liver in the test tube. Record your observations of the second test tube in your data table.

7. Pour another 2 mL of hydrogen peroxide into a third test tube labeled "Ground liver and hydrogen peroxide."

8. Using a mortar and pestle (or fork and watch glass), carefully grind the third piece of liver.

9. Using the spatula, scrape the ground liver into the third test tube. Record your observations of the third test tube in your data table.

Analyze the Results

1. What was the purpose of putting the first piece of liver in water? Why was this a necessary step?

2. Describe the difference you observed between the liver and the ground liver when each was placed in the hydrogen peroxide. How can you account for this difference?

Applying Your Data

Do plant cells contain enzymes that break down hydrogen peroxide? Try this experiment using potato cubes instead of liver to find out.

Skills Practice Lab

My, How You've Grown!

In humans, the process of development that takes place between fertilization and birth lasts about 266 days. In 4 weeks, the new individual grows from a single fertilized cell to an embryo whose heart is beating and pumping blood. All of the organ systems and body parts are completely formed by the end of the seventh month. During the last 2 months before birth, the baby grows, and its organ systems mature. At birth, the average mass of a baby is about 33,000 times as much as that of an embryo at 2 weeks of development! In this activity, you will discover just how fast a fetus grows.

MATERIALS

- paper, graph
- pencils, colored

Procedure

1. Using graph paper, make two graphs—one entitled "Length" and one entitled "Mass." On the length graph, use intervals of 25 mm on the y-axis. Extend the y-axis to 500 mm. On the mass graph, use intervals of 100 g on the y-axis. Extend this y-axis to 3,300 g. Use 2-week intervals for time on the x-axes for both graphs. Both x-axes should extend to 40 weeks.

2. Examine the data table at right. Plot the data in the table on your graphs. Use a colored pencil to draw the curved line that joins the points on each graph.

Increase of Mass and Length of Average Human Fetus		
Time (weeks)	Mass (g)	Length (mm)
2	0.1	1.5
3	0.3	2.3
4	0.5	5.0
5	0.6	10.0
6	0.8	15.0
8	1.0	30.0
13	15.0	90.0
17	115.0	140.0
21	300.0	250.0
26	950.0	320.0
30	1,500.0	400.0
35	2,300.0	450.0
40	3,300.0	500.0

Analyze the Results

1. Describe the change in mass of a developing fetus. How can you explain this change?

2. Describe the change in length of a developing fetus. How does the change in mass compare to the change in length?

Applying Your Data

Using the information in your graphs, estimate how tall a child would be at age 3 if he or she continued to grow at the same average rate that a fetus grows.

Model-Making Lab

Antibodies to the Rescue

Some cells of the immune system, called *B cells,* make antibodies that attack and kill invading viruses and microorganisms. These antibodies help make you immune to disease. Have you ever had chickenpox? If you have, your body has built up antibodies that can recognize that particular virus. Antibodies will attach themselves to the virus, tagging it for destruction. If you are exposed to the same disease again, the antibodies remember that virus. They will attack the virus even quicker and in greater number than they did the first time. This is the reason that you will probably never have chickenpox more than once.

In this activity, you will construct simple models of viruses and their antibodies. You will see how antibodies are specific for a particular virus.

MATERIALS

- craft materials, such as buttons, fabric scraps, pipe cleaners, and recycled materials
- paper, colored
- scissors
- tape (or glue)

Procedure

1 Draw the virus patterns shown on this page on a separate piece of paper, or design your own virus models from the craft supplies. Remember to design different receptors on each of your virus models.

2 Write a few sentences describing how your viruses are different.

3 Cut out the viruses, and attach them to a piece of colored paper with tape or glue.

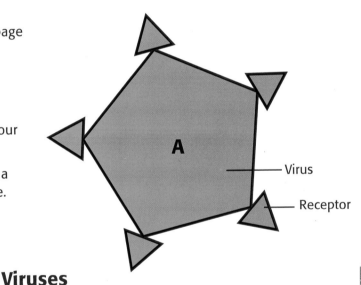

A — Virus

— Receptor

Viruses

Receptor

B — Virus

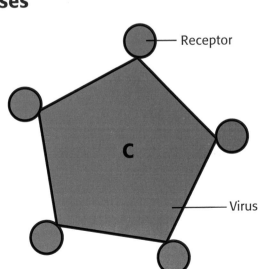

Receptor

C

Virus

4 Select the antibodies drawn below, or design your own antibodies that will exactly fit on the receptors on your virus models. Draw or create each antibody enough times to attach one to each receptor site on the virus.

Antibodies

5 Cut out the antibodies you have drawn. Arrange the antibodies so that they bind to the virus at the appropriate receptor. Attach them to the virus with tape or glue.

Analyze the Results

1 Explain how an antibody "recognizes" a particular virus.

2 After the attachment of antibodies to the receptors, what would be the next step in the immune response?

3 Many vaccines use weakened copies of the virus to protect the body. Use the model of a virus and its specific antibody to explain how vaccines work.

Draw Conclusions

4 Use your model of a virus to demonstrate to the class how a receptor might change or mutate so that a vaccine would no longer be effective.

Applying Your Data

Research in the library or on the Internet to find information about the discovery of the Salk vaccine for polio. Include information on how polio affects people today.

Research in the library or on the Internet to find information and write a report about filoviruses. What do they look like? What diseases do they cause? Why are they especially dangerous? Is there an effective vaccine against any filovirus? Explain.

Skills Practice Lab

To Diet or Not to Diet

There are six main classes of foods that we need in order to keep our bodies functioning properly: water, vitamins, minerals, carbohydrates, fats, and proteins. In this activity you will investigate the importance of a well-balanced diet in maintaining a healthy body. Then you will create a poster or picture that illustrates the importance of one of the three energy-producing nutrients—carbohydrates, fats, and proteins.

Procedure

1. Draw a table like the one below. Research in the library, on nutrition labels, in nutrition or diet books, or on the Internet to find the information you need to fill out the chart.

Nutrition Data Table			
	Fats	**Carbohydrates**	**Proteins**
Found in which foods			
Functions in the body		DO NOT WRITE IN BOOK	
Consequences of deficiency			

2. Choose one of the foods you have learned about in your research, and create a poster or picture that describes its importance in a well-balanced diet.

Analyze the Results

1. Based on what you have learned in this lab, how might you change your eating habits to have a well-balanced diet? Does the nutritional value of foods concern you? Why or why not? Write down your answers, and explain your reasoning.

Communicating Your Data

Write a paragraph explaining why water is a nutrient. Analyze a typical fast-food meal, and determine its overall nutritional value.

Skills Practice Lab

The Best-Bread Bakery Dilemma

The chief baker at the Best-Bread Bakery thinks that the yeast the bakery received may be dead. Yeast is a central ingredient in bread. Yeast is a living organism, a member of the kingdom Fungi, and it undergoes the same life processes as other living organisms. When yeast grows in the presence of oxygen and other nutrients, yeast produces carbon dioxide. The gas forms bubbles that cause bread dough to rise. Thousands of dollars may be lost if the yeast is dead.

The Best-Bread Bakery has requested that you test the yeast. The bakery has furnished samples of live yeast and some samples of the yeast in question.

Procedure

1. Make a data table similar to the one below. Leave plenty of room to write your observations.

2. Examine each yeast sample with a magnifying lens. You may want to sniff the samples to determine the presence of an odor. (Your teacher will demonstrate the appropriate way to detect odors in this lab.) Record your observations in the data table.

3. Label three test tubes or plastic cups "Live Yeast," "Sample A Yeast," and "Sample B Yeast."

4. Fill a beaker with 125 mL of water, and place the beaker on a hot plate. Use a thermometer to be sure the water does not get warmer than 32°C. Attach the thermometer to the side of the beaker with a clip so the thermometer doesn't touch the bottom of the beaker. Turn off the hot plate when the water temperature reaches 32°C.

MATERIALS

- beaker, 250 mL
- flour
- gloves, heat-resistant
- graduated cylinder
- hot plate
- magnifying lens
- scoopula (or small spoon)
- stirring sticks, wooden (3)
- sugar
- test-tube rack
- test tubes (3) (or clear plastic cups)
- thermometer, Celsius, with clip
- water, 125 mL
- yeast samples (live, A, and B)

SAFETY

Yeast sample	Observations	0 min	5 min	10 min	15 min	20 min	25 min	Dead or alive?
Live								
Sample A			DO NOT WRITE IN BOOK					
Sample B								

5. Add a small scoop (about 1/2 tsp) of each yeast sample to the correctly labeled container. Add a small scoop of sugar to each container.

6. Add 10 mL of the warm water to each container, and stir.

7. Add a small scoop of flour to each container, and stir again. The flour will help make the process more visible but is not necessary as food for the yeast.

8. Observe the samples carefully. Look for bubbles. Make observations at 5 min intervals. Write your observations in the data table.

9. In the last column of the data table, write "alive" or "dead" based on your observations during the experiment.

Analyze the Results

1. Describe any differences in the yeast samples before the experiment.

2. Describe the appearance of the yeast samples at the conclusion of the experiment.

3. Why was a sample of live yeast included in the experiment?

4. Why was sugar added to the samples?

5. Based on your observations, is either Sample A or Sample B alive?

Draw Conclusions

6. Write a letter to the Best-Bread Bakery stating your recommendation to use or not use the yeast samples. Give reasons for your recommendation.

Applying Your Data

Based on your observations of the nutrient requirements of yeast, design an experiment to determine the ideal combination of nutrients. Vary the amount of nutrients, or examine different energy sources.

Skills Practice Lab

Cells Alive!

You have probably used a microscope to look at single-celled organisms such as those shown below. They can be found in pond water. In the following exercise, you will look at *Protococcus*—algae that form a greenish stain on tree trunks, wooden fences, flowerpots, and buildings.

Euglena

Amoeba

Paramecium

Procedure

1. Locate some *Protococcus*. Scrape a small sample into a container. Bring the sample to the classroom, and make a wet mount of it as directed by your teacher. If you can't find *Protococcus* outdoors, look for algae on the glass in an aquarium. Such algae may not be *Protococcus,* but it will be a very good substitute.

2. Set the microscope on low power to examine the algae. On a separate sheet of paper, draw the cells that you see.

3. Switch to high power to examine a single cell. Draw the cell.

4. You will probably notice that each cell contains several chloroplasts. Label a chloroplast on your drawing. What is the function of the chloroplast?

5. Another structure that should be clearly visible in all the algae cells is the nucleus. Find the nucleus in one of your cells, and label it on your drawing. What is the function of the nucleus?

6. What does the cytoplasm look like? Describe any movement you see inside the cells.

Protococcus

Analyze the Results

1. Are *Protococcus* single-celled organisms or multicellular organisms?

2. How are *Protococcus* different from amoebas?

Skills Practice Lab

Stayin' Alive!

Every second of your life, your body's trillions of cells take in, use, and store energy. They repair themselves, reproduce, and get rid of waste. Together, these processes are called *metabolism.* Your cells use the food that you eat to provide the energy you need to stay alive.

Your Basal Metabolic Rate (BMR) is a measurement of the energy that your body needs to carry out all the basic life processes while you are at rest. These processes include breathing, keeping your heart beating, and keeping your body's temperature stable. Your BMR is influenced by your gender, your age, and many other things. Your BMR may be different from everyone else's, but it is normal for you. In this activity, you will find the amount of energy, measured in Calories, you need every day in order to stay alive.

MATERIALS
- bathroom scale
- tape measure

Procedure

1. Find your weight on a bathroom scale. If the scale measures in pounds, you must convert your weight in pounds to your mass in kilograms. To convert your weight in pounds (lb) to mass in kilograms (kg), multiply the number of pounds by 0.454.

   Example: If Carlos weighs 125 lb, his mass in kilograms is:

   $$\begin{array}{r} 125 \text{ lb} \\ \times\ 0.454 \\ \hline 56.75 \text{ kg} \end{array}$$

2. Use a tape measure to find your height. If the tape measures in inches, convert your height in inches to height in centimeters. To convert your height in inches (in.) to your height in centimeters (cm), multiply the number of inches by 2.54.

   If Carlos is 62 in. tall, his height in centimeters is:

   $$\begin{array}{r} 62 \text{ in.} \\ \times\ 2.54 \\ \hline 157.48 \text{ cm} \end{array}$$

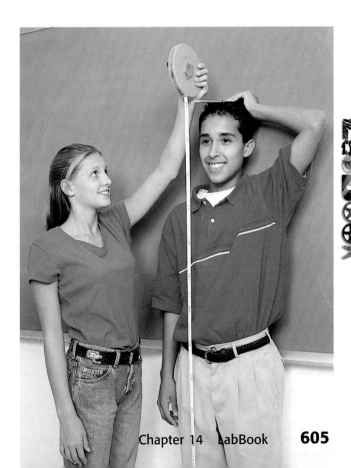

3 Now that you know your height and mass, use the appropriate formula below to get a close estimate of your BMR. Your answer will give you an estimate of the number of Calories your body needs each day just to stay alive.

Calculating Your BMR	
Females	**Males**
65 + (10 × your mass in kilograms)	66 + (13.5 × your mass in kilograms)
+ (1.8 × your height in centimeters)	+ (5 × your height in centimeters)
− (4.7 × your age in years)	− (6.8 × your age in years)

4 Your metabolism is also influenced by how active you are. Talking, walking, and playing games all take more energy than being at rest. To get an idea of how many Calories your body needs each day to stay healthy, select the lifestyle that best describes yours from the table at right. Then multiply your BMR by the activity factor.

Activity Factors	
Activity lifestyle	**Activity factor**
Moderately inactive (normal, everyday activities)	1.3
Moderately active (exercise 3 to 4 times a week)	1.4
Very active (exercise 4 to 6 times a week)	1.6
Extremely active (exercise 6 to 7 times a week)	1.8

Analyze the Results

1 In what way could you compare your whole body to a single cell? Explain.

2 Does an increase in activity increase your BMR? Does an increase in activity increase your need for Calories? Explain your answers.

Draw Conclusions

3 If you are moderately inactive, how many more Calories would you need if you began to exercise every day?

Applying Your Data

The best energy sources are those that supply the correct amount of Calories for your lifestyle and also provide the nutrients you need. Research in the library or on the Internet to find out which kinds of foods are the best energy sources for you. How does your list of best energy sources compare with your diet?

List everything you eat and drink in 1 day. Find out how many Calories are in each item, and find the total number of Calories you have consumed. How does this number of Calories compare with the number of Calories you need each day for all your activities?

Inquiry Lab

Tracing Traits

Have you ever wondered about the traits you inherited from your parents? Do you have a trait that neither of your parents has? In this project, you will develop a family tree, or pedigree, similar to the one shown in the diagram below. You will trace an inherited trait through a family to determine how it has passed from generation to generation.

Procedure

1. The diagram at right shows a family history. On a separate piece of paper, draw a similar diagram of the family you have chosen. Include as many family members as possible, such as grandparents, parents, children, and grandchildren. Use circles to represent females and squares to represent males. You may include other information, such as the family member's name, birth date, or picture.

2. Draw a table similar to the one on the next page. Survey each of the family members shown in your family tree. Ask them if they have hair on the middle segment of their fingers. Write each person's name in the appropriate square. Explain to each person that it is normal to have either trait. The presence of hair on the middle segment is the dominant form of this trait.

Pedigree

I Grandparents — Tom 1, Jane 2

II Parents — Fran 1, Harry 2, Mary 3, Bob 4

III Children — Luke 1, Mary 2, Dylan 3, Rosa 4

IV Grandchildren — Nathan 1, Alicia 2, Tara 3

Dominant trait	Recessive trait	Family members with the dominant trait	Family members with the recessive trait
Hair present on the middle segment of fingers (*H*)	Hair absent on the middle segment of fingers (*h*)	*DO NOT WRITE IN BOOK*	

③ Trace this trait throughout the family tree you diagrammed in step 1. Shade or color the symbols of the family members who demonstrate the dominant form of this trait.

Analyze the Results

① What percentage of the family members demonstrate the dominant form of the trait? Calculate this by counting the number of people who have the dominant trait and dividing this number by the total number of people you surveyed. Multiply your answer by 100. An example has been done at right.

Example: Calculating percentage

$$\frac{10 \text{ people with trait}}{20 \text{ people surveyed}} = \frac{1}{2}$$

$$\frac{1}{2} = 0.50 \times 100 = 50\%$$

② What percentage of the family members demonstrate the recessive form of the trait? Why doesn't every family member have the dominant form of the trait?

③ Choose one of the family members who demonstrates the recessive form of the chosen trait. What is this person's genotype? What are the possible genotypes for the parents of this individual? Does this person have any brothers or sisters? Do they show the dominant or recessive trait?

Draw Conclusions

④ Draw a Punnett square like the one at right. Use this to determine the genotypes of the parents of the person you chose in step 3. Write this person's genotype in the bottom right-hand corner of your Punnett square. **Hint:** There may be more than one possible genotype for the parents. Don't forget to consider the genotypes of the person's brothers and sisters.

Father

	?	?
Mother ?		
?		

Skills Practice Lab

Built for Speed

Imagine that you are an engineer at GoCarCo, a toy-vehicle company. GoCarCo is trying to beat the competition by building a new toy vehicle. Several new designs are being tested. Your boss has given you one of the new toy vehicles and instructed you to measure its speed as accurately as possible with the tools you have. Other engineers (your classmates) are testing the other designs. Your results could decide the fate of the company!

MATERIALS

- meterstick
- stopwatch
- tape, masking
- toy vehicle

SAFETY

Procedure

1. How will you accomplish your goal? Write a paragraph to describe your goal and your procedure for this experiment. Be sure that your procedure includes several trials.

2. Show your plan to your boss (teacher). Get his or her approval to carry out your procedure.

3. Perform your stated procedure. Record all data. Be sure to express all data in the correct units.

Analyze the Results

1. What was the average speed of your vehicle? How does your result compare with the results of the other engineers?

2. Compare your technique for determining the speed of your vehicle with the techniques of the other engineers. Which technique do you think is the most effective?

3. Was your toy vehicle the fastest? Explain why or why not.

Applying Your Data

Think of several conditions that could affect your vehicle's speed. Design an experiment to test your vehicle under one of those conditions. Write a paragraph to explain your procedure. Be sure to include an explanation of how that condition changes your vehicle's speed.

Skills Practice Lab

Relating Mass and Weight

Why do objects with more mass weigh more than objects with less mass? All objects have weight on Earth because their mass is affected by Earth's gravitational force. Because the mass of an object on Earth is constant, the relationship between the mass of an object and its weight is also constant. You will measure the mass and weight of several objects to verify the relationship between mass and weight on the surface of Earth.

Procedure

1. Copy the table below.

Mass and Weight Measurements		
Object	Mass (g)	Weight (N)

DO NOT WRITE IN BOOK

2. Using the metric balance, find the mass of five or six small classroom objects designated by your teacher. Record the masses.

3. Using the spring scale, find the weight of each object. Record the weights. (You may need to use the string to create a hook with which to hang some objects from the spring scale, as shown at right.)

Analyze the Results

1. Using your data, construct a graph of weight (y-axis) versus mass (x-axis). Draw a line that best fits all your data points.

2. Does the graph confirm the relationship between mass and weight on Earth? Explain your answer.

Skills Practice Lab

Science Friction

In this experiment, you will investigate three types of friction— static, sliding, and rolling—to determine which is the largest force and which is the smallest force.

MATERIALS

- rods, wood or metal (3–4)
- scissors
- spring scale (force meter)
- string
- textbook (covered)

SAFETY

Ask a Question

1 Which type of friction is the largest force—static, sliding, or rolling? Which is the smallest?

Form a Hypothesis

2 Write a statement or statements that answer the questions above. Explain your reasoning.

Test the Hypothesis

3 Cut a piece of string, and tie it in a loop that fits in the textbook, as shown on the next page. Hook the string to the spring scale.

4 Practice the next three steps several times before you collect data.

5 To measure the static friction between the book and the table, pull the spring scale very slowly. Record the largest force on the scale before the book starts to move.

6 After the book begins to move, you can determine the sliding friction. Record the force required to keep the book sliding at a slow, constant speed.

7 Place two or three rods under the book to act as rollers. Make sure the rollers are evenly spaced. Place another roller in front of the book so that the book will roll onto it. Pull the force meter slowly. Measure the force needed to keep the book rolling at a constant speed.

Analyze the Results

1 Which type of friction was the largest? Which was the smallest?

2 Do the results support your hypothesis? If not, how would you revise or retest your hypothesis?

Draw Conclusions

3 Compare your results with those of another group. Are there any differences? Working together, design a way to improve the experiment and resolve possible differences.

Skills Practice Lab

A Marshmallow Catapult

Catapults use projectile motion to launch objects. In this lab, you will build a simple catapult and determine the angle at which the catapult will launch an object the farthest.

Ask a Question

1 At what angle, from 10° to 90°, will a catapult launch a marshmallow the farthest?

Form a Hypothesis

2 Write a hypothesis that is a possible answer to your question.

Angle	Distance 1 (cm)	Distance 2 (cm)	Average distance	Data Collection
10°	DO NOT WRITE IN BOOK			

Test the Hypothesis

3 Copy the table above. In your table, add one row each for 20°, 30°, 40°, 50°, 60°, 70°, 80°, and 90° angles.

4 Using duct tape, attach the plastic spoon to the 1 cm side of the block. Use enough tape to attach the spoon securely.

5 Place one marshmallow in the center of the spoon, and tape it to the spoon. This marshmallow serves as a ledge to hold the marshmallow that will be launched.

6 Line up the bottom corner of the block with the bottom center of the protractor, as shown in the photograph. Start with the block at 10°.

7 Place a marshmallow in the spoon, on top of the taped marshmallow. Pull the spoon back lightly, and let go. Measure and record the distance from the catapult that the marshmallow lands. Repeat the measurement, and calculate an average.

8 Repeat step 7 for each angle up to 90°.

Analyze the Results

1 At what angle did the catapult launch the marshmallow the farthest? Explain any differences from your hypothesis.

Draw Conclusions

2 At what angle should you throw a ball or shoot an arrow so that it will fly the farthest? Why? Support your answer with your data.

Model-Making Lab

Blast Off!

You have been hired as a rocket scientist for NASA. Your job is to design a rocket that will have a controlled flight while carrying a payload. Keep in mind that Newton's laws will have a powerful influence on your rocket.

Procedure

1. When you begin your experiment, your teacher will tape one end of the fishing line to the ceiling.

2. Use a pencil to poke a small hole in each side of the cup near the top. Place a 15 cm piece of string through each hole, and tape down the ends inside.

3. Inflate the balloon, and use the twist tie to hold it closed.

4. Tape the free ends of the strings to the sides of the balloon near the bottom. The cup should hang below the balloon. Your model rocket should look like a hot-air balloon.

5. Thread the fishing line that is hanging from the ceiling through the straw. Tape the balloon securely to the straw. Tape the loose end of the fishing line to the floor.

6. Untie the twist tie while holding the end of the balloon closed. When you are ready, release the end of the balloon. Mark and record the maximum height of the rocket.

7. Repeat the procedure, adding a penny to the cup each time until your rocket cannot lift any more pennies.

Analyze the Results

1. In a paragraph, describe how all three of Newton's laws influenced the flight of your rocket.

Draw Conclusions

2. Draw a diagram of your rocket. Label the action and reaction forces.

Applying Your Data

Brainstorm ways to modify your rocket so that it will carry the most pennies to the maximum height. Select the best design. When your teacher has approved all the designs, build and launch your rocket. Which variable did you modify? How did this variable affect your rocket's flight?

MATERIALS

- balloon, long, thin
- cup, paper, small
- fishing line, 3 m
- meterstick
- pencil
- pennies
- straw, straight plastic
- string, 15 cm (2)
- tape, masking
- twist tie

SAFETY

Skills Practice Lab

Quite a Reaction

Catapults have been used for centuries to throw objects great distances. According to Newton's third law of motion (whenever one object exerts a force on a second object, the second object exerts an equal and opposite force on the first), when an object is launched, something must also happen to the catapult. In this activity, you will build a kind of catapult that will allow you to observe the effects of Newton's third law of motion and the law of conservation of momentum.

MATERIALS

- cardboard rectangles, 10 cm × 15 cm (3)
- glue
- marble
- meterstick
- pushpins (3)
- rubber band
- scissors
- straws, plastic (6)
- string

SAFETY

Procedure

1. Glue the cardboard rectangles together to make a stack of three.

2. Push two of the pushpins into the cardboard stack near the corners at one end, as shown below. These pushpins will be the anchors for the rubber band.

3. Make a small loop of string.

4. Put the rubber band through the loop of string, and then place the rubber band over the two pushpin anchors. The rubber band should be stretched between the two anchors with the string loop in the middle.

5. Pull the string loop toward the end of the cardboard stack opposite the end with the anchors, and fasten the loop in place with the third pushpin.

6. Place the six straws about 1 cm apart on a tabletop or on the floor. Then, carefully center the catapult on top of the straws.

7. Put the marble in the closed end of the V formed by the rubber band.

8. Use scissors to cut the string holding the rubber band, and observe what happens. (Be careful not to let the scissors touch the cardboard catapult when you cut the string.)

9 Reset the catapult with a new piece of string. Try launching the marble several times to be sure that you have observed everything that happens during a launch. Record all your observations.

Analyze the Results

1 Which has more mass, the marble or the catapult?

2 What happened to the catapult when the marble was launched?

3 How far did the marble fly before it landed?

4 Did the catapult move as far as the marble did?

Draw Conclusions

5 Explain why the catapult moved backward.

6 If the forces that made the marble and the catapult move apart are equal, why didn't the marble and the catapult move apart the same distance? (Hint: The fact that the marble can roll after it lands is not the answer.)

7 The momentum of an object depends on the mass and velocity of the object. What is the momentum of the marble before it is launched? What is the momentum of the catapult? Explain your answers.

8 Using the law of conservation of momentum, explain why the marble and the catapult move in opposite directions after the launch.

Applying Your Data

How would you modify the catapult if you wanted to keep it from moving backward as far as it did? (It still has to rest on the straws.) Using items that you can find in the classroom, design a catapult that will move backward less than the one originally designed.

Skills Practice Lab

Density Diver

Crew members of a submarine can control the submarine's density underwater by allowing water to flow into and out of special tanks. These changes in density affect the submarine's position in the water. In this lab, you'll control a "density diver" to learn for yourself how the density of an object affects its position in a fluid.

Ask a Question

1 How does the density of an object determine whether the object floats, sinks, or maintains its position in a fluid?

Form a Hypothesis

2 Write a possible answer to the question above.

Test the Hypothesis

3 Completely fill the 2 L plastic bottle with water.

4 Fill the diver (medicine dropper) approximately halfway with water, and place it in the bottle. The diver should float with only part of the rubber bulb above the surface of the water. If the diver floats too high, carefully remove it from the bottle, and add a small amount of water to the diver. Place the diver back in the bottle. If you add too much water and the diver sinks, empty out the bottle and diver, and go back to step 3.

5 Put the cap on the bottle tightly so that no water leaks out.

6 Apply various pressures to the bottle. Carefully watch the water level inside the diver as you squeeze and release the bottle. Record what happens.

7 Try to make the diver rise, sink, or stop at any level. Record your technique and your results.

Analyze the Results

1 How do the changes inside the diver affect its position in the surrounding fluid?

2 What relationship did you observe between the diver's density and the diver's position in the fluid?

Draw Conclusions

3 Explain how your density diver is like a submarine.

4 Explain how pressure on the bottle is related to the diver's density. Be sure to include Pascal's principle in your explanation.

MATERIALS

- bottle, plastic, with screw-on cap, 2 L
- dropper, medicine
- water

SAFETY

Skills Practice Lab

Inclined to Move

In this lab, you will examine a simple machine—an inclined plane. Your task is to compare the work done with and without the inclined plane and to analyze the effects of friction.

Ask a Question

1 Write a question that you can test regarding inclined planes.

Form a Hypothesis

2 Write a possible answer to the question you wrote.

Test the Hypothesis

3 Copy the table at right.

4 Tie a piece of string around a book. Attach the spring scale to the string. Use the spring scale to slowly lift the book to a height of 50 cm. Record the output force (the force needed to lift the book). The output force is constant throughout the lab.

5 Use the board and blocks to make a ramp 10 cm high at the highest point. Measure and record the ramp length.

6 Keeping the spring scale parallel to the ramp, as shown, slowly raise the book. Record the input force (the force needed to pull the book up the ramp).

7 Increase the height of the ramp by 10 cm. Repeat step 6. Repeat this step for each ramp height up to 50 cm.

Analyze the Results

1 The real work done includes the work done to overcome friction. Calculate the real work at each height by multiplying the ramp length (converted to meters) by the input force. Graph your results, plotting work (*y*-axis) versus height (*x*-axis).

Force Versus Height

Ramp height (cm)	Output force (N)	Ramp length (cm)	Input force (N)
10			
20			
30		DO NOT WRITE IN BOOK	
40			
50			

2 The ideal work is the work you would do if there were no friction. Calculate the ideal work at each height by multiplying the ramp height (cm) by the output force. Plot the data on your graph.

Draw Conclusions

3 Does it require more or less force and work to raise the book by using the ramp? Explain, using your calculations.

4 What is the relationship between the height of the inclined plane and the input force?

Skills Practice Lab

Wheeling and Dealing

A crank handle, such as that used in pencil sharpeners, ice-cream makers, and water wells, is one kind of wheel and axle. In this lab, you will use a crank handle to find out how a wheel and axle helps you do work. You will also determine what effect the length of the handle has on the operation of the machine.

Ask a Question

1 What effect does the length of a handle have on the operation of a crank?

Form a Hypothesis

2 Write a possible answer to the question above.

Test the Hypothesis

3 Copy Table 1.

4 Measure the radius (in meters) of the large dowel in the wheel-and-axle assembly. Record this in Table 1 as the axle radius, which remains constant throughout the lab. (Hint: Measure the diameter, and divide by 2.)

5 Using the spring scale, measure the weight of the large mass. Record this in Table 1 as the output force, which remains constant throughout the lab.

6 Use two C-clamps to secure the wheel-and-axle assembly to the table, as shown.

7 Measure the length (in meters) of handle 1. Record this length as a wheel radius in Table 1.

8 Insert the handle into the hole in the axle. Attach one end of the string to the large mass and the other end to the screw in the axle. The mass should hang down, and the handle should turn freely.

9 Turn the handle to lift the mass off the floor. Hold the spring scale upside down, and attach it to the end of the handle. Measure the force (in newtons) as the handle pulls up on the spring scale. Record this as the input force.

MATERIALS

- C-clamps (2)
- handles(4)
- mass, large
- meterstick
- spring scale
- string, 0.5 m
- wheel-and-axle assembly

SAFETY

Table 1 Data Collection

Handle	Axle radius (m)	Output force (N)	Wheel radius (m)	Input force (N)
1				
2				
3		*DO NOT WRITE IN BOOK*		
4				

10 Remove the spring scale, and lower the mass to the floor. Remove the handle.

11 Repeat steps 7 through 10 with the other three handles. Record all data in Table 1.

Analyze the Results

1 Copy Table 2.

Table 2 Calculations						
Handle	Axle distance (m)	Wheel distance (m)	Work input (J)	Work output (J)	Mechanical efficiency (%)	Mechanical advantage
1						
2						
3						
4						

DO NOT WRITE IN BOOK

2 Calculate the following for each handle, using the equations given. Record your answers in Table 2.

a. *Distance axle rotates =*
$2 \times \pi \times$ *axle radius*

Distance wheel rotates =
$2 \times \pi \times$ *wheel radius*

(Use 3.14 for the value of π.)

b. *Work input =*
input force × wheel distance

Work output =
output force × axle distance

c. *Mechanical efficiency =*
$\dfrac{work\ output}{work\ input} \times 100$

d. *Mechanical advantage =*
$\dfrac{wheel\ radius}{axle\ radius}$

Draw Conclusions

3 What happens to work output and work input as the handle length increases? Why?

4 What happens to mechanical efficiency as the handle length increases? Why?

5 What happens to mechanical advantage as the handle length increases? Why?

6 What will happen to mechanical advantage if the handle length is kept constant and the axle radius gets larger?

7 What factors were controlled in this experiment? What was the variable?

Inquiry Lab

Building Machines

You are surrounded by machines. Some are simple machines, such as ramps for wheelchair access to a building. Others are compound machines, such as elevators and escalators, that are made of two or more simple machines. In this lab, you will design and build several simple machines and a compound machine.

Ask a Question

1 How can simple machines be combined to make compound machines?

Form a Hypothesis

2 Write a possible answer to the question above.

Test the Hypothesis

3 Use the listed materials to build a model of each simple machine: inclined plane, lever, wheel and axle, pulley, screw, and wedge. Describe and draw each model.

4 Design a compound machine by using the materials listed. You may design a machine that already exists, or you may invent your own machine. Be creative!

5 After your teacher approves your design, build your compound machine.

Analyze the Results

1 List a possible use for each of your simple machines.

2 How many simple machines are in your compound machine? List them.

3 Compare your compound machine with those created by your classmates.

4 What is a possible use for your compound machine? Why did you design it as you did?

5 A compound machine is listed in the materials list. What is it?

Applying Your Data

Design a compound machine that has all the simple machines in it. Explain what the machine will do and how it will make work easier. With your teacher's approval, build your machine.

MATERIALS

- bottle caps
- cardboard
- clay, modeling
- craft sticks
- glue
- paper
- pencils
- rubber bands
- scissors
- shoe boxes
- stones
- straws
- string
- tape
- thread spools, empty
- other materials available in your classroom that are approved by your teacher

SAFETY

Contents

✓ *Reading Check* Answers

Chapter 1 Science in Our World

Section 1

Page 4: Science is the knowledge obtained by observing natural events and conditions in order to discover facts and formulate laws or principles that can be verified or tested.

Page 7: Society can influence technology development by identifying important problems that need technological solutions.

Page 9: A volcanologist studies volcanoes and their products, such as lava and gases.

Section 2

Page 10: a series of steps used by scientists to solve problems

Page 12: A hypothesis is testable if an experiment can be designed to test the hypothesis.

Page 14: only one

Page 16: because the scientist has learned something

Section 3

Page 19: a mathematical model

Page 20: to explain a broad range of observations, facts, and tested hypotheses, to predict what might happen, and to organize scientific thinking

Section 4

Page 22: stopwatch, graduated cylinder, meterstick, spring scale, balance, and thermometer

Page 25: the kilogram

Page 27: Safety symbols alert you to particular safety concerns or specific dangers in a lab.

Chapter 2 The Atmosphere

Section 1

Page 40: Water can be liquid (rain), solid (snow or ice), or gas (water vapor).

Page 42: The troposphere is the layer of turning or change. The stratosphere is the layer in which gases are layered and do not mix vertically. The mesosphere is the middle layer. The thermosphere is the layer in which temperatures are highest.

Page 44: The thermosphere does not feel hot because air molecules are spaced far apart and cannot collide to transfer much thermal energy.

Section 2

Page 47: Cold air is more dense than warm air, so cold air sinks and warm air rises. This produces convection currents.

Page 49: A greenhouse gas is a gas that absorbs thermal energy in the atmosphere.

Section 3

Page 51: Sinking air causes areas of high pressure because sinking air presses down on the air beneath it.

Page 52: the westerlies

Page 55: At night, the air along the mountain slopes cools. This cool air moves down the slopes into the valley and produces a mountain breeze.

Section 4

Page 56: Sample answer: smoke, dust and sea salt

Page 59: Answers may vary. Acid precipitation may decrease the soil nutrients that are available to plants.

Page 60: Powdered limestone is used to counteract the effects of acidic snowmelt from snow that accumulated during the winter.

Section 5

Page 62: Sample answer: coughing, headaches, and irritation to the eyes

Page 65: Sample answer: One way to reduce air pollution is to walk or bike to your destination instead of driving.

Chapter 3 Understanding Weather

Section 1

Page 76: The water cycle is the continuous movement of water from Earth's oceans and rivers into the atmosphere, into the ground, and back into the oceans and rivers.

Page 78: A psychrometer is used to measure relative humidity.

Page 79: The bulb of a wet-bulb thermometer is covered with moistened material. The bulb cools as water evaporates from the material. If the air is dry, more water will evaporate from the material, and the temperature recorded by the thermometer will be low. If the air is humid, less water will evaporate from the material, and the temperature recorded by the thermometer will be higher.

Page 81: Altostratus clouds form at middle altitudes.

Section 2

Page 85: A maritime tropical air mass causes hot and humid summer weather in the midwestern United States.

Page 87: An occluded front produces cool temperatures and large amounts of rain.

Page 89: An anticyclone can produce dry, clear weather.

Section 3

Page 91: A severe thunderstorm is a thunderstorm that produces high winds, hail, flash floods, or tornadoes.

Page 93: Hurricanes are also called *typhoons* or *cyclones.*

Page 94: Hurricanes get their energy from the condensation of water vapor.

Section 4

Page 98: Meteorologists use weather balloons to collect atmospheric data above Earth's surface.

Chapter 4   Climate

Section 1
Page 112:   Climate is the average weather condition in an area over a long period of time. Weather is the condition of the atmosphere at a particular time.

Page 114:   Locations near the equator have less seasonal variation because the tilt of the Earth does not change the amount of energy these locations receive from the sun.

Page 116:   The atmosphere becomes less dense and loses its ability to absorb and hold thermal energy, at higher elevations.

Page 117:   The Gulf Stream current carries warm water past Iceland, which heats the air and causes milder temperatures.

Page 118:   Each biome has a different climate and different plant and animals communities.

Section 2
Page 120:   You would find the tropical zone from 23.5° north latitude to 23.5° south latitude.

Page 123:   Answers may vary. Sample answer: rats, lizards, snakes, and scorpions.

Section 3
Page 124:   The temperate zone is located between the Tropics and the polar zone.

Page 126:   Temperate deserts are cold at night because low humidity and cloudless skies allow energy to escape.

Page 129:   Cities have higher temperatures than the surrounding rural areas because buildings and pavement absorb solar radiation instead of reflecting it.

Section 4
Page 131:   Changes in the Earth's orbit and the tilt of the Earth's axis are the two things that Milankovitch says cause ice ages.

Page 132:   Dust, ash, and smoke from volcanic eruptions block the sun's rays, which causes the Earth to cool.

Page 135:   The deserts would receive less rainfall, making it harder for plants and animals in the desert to survive.

Chapter 5   Body Organization and Structure

Section 1
Page 149:   Cells need nutrients moved into the cells and wastes moved out of the cells in order to maintain homeostasis.

Page 150:   A group of similar cells that work together form tissues.

Page 151:   The stomach works with other organs, such as the small and large intestines, to digest food.

Page 152:   Sample answer: The cardiovascular system includes the heart and blood vessels. These organs are also part of the circulatory system, which includes blood. Together, these systems deliver the materials cells need to survive.

Section 2
Page 155:   Sample answer: As people grow, most of the cartilage that they start out with is replaced with bone.

Page 156:   Sample answer: Joints are held together by ligaments. Cartilage cushions the area in a joint where bones meet.

Section 3
Page 159:   Sample answer: One muscle, the flexor, bends part of the body. Another muscle, the extensor, straightens part of the body.

Page 161:   Sample answer: Anabolic steroids can damage the heart, liver, and kidneys. They can also cause high blood pressure. Anabolic steroids can cause bones to stop growing.

Section 4
Page 163:   The dermis is the layer of skin that lies beneath the epidermis. It is composed of a protein called *collagen,* while the epidermis contains keratin.

Page 164:   Sample answer: A nail grows from living cells in the nail root at the base of the nail. As new cells form, the nail grows longer.

Chapter 6   Circulation and Respiration

Section 1
Page 176:   The four main parts of the cardiovascular system are the heart and the arteries, capillaries, and veins.

Page 178:   Arteries have thick, stretchy walls and carry blood away from the heart. Capillaries are tiny blood vessels that allow the exchange of oxygen, carbon dioxide, and nutrients between cells and blood. Veins are blood vessels that carry blood back to the heart.

Page 180:   Atherosclerosis is dangerous because it is the buildup of material inside an artery. When the artery becomes blocked, blood can't flow and can't reach the cells. In some cases, a person can have a heart attack from a blocked artery.

Section 2
Page 182:   plasma, red blood cells, white blood cells, and platelets

Page 183:   White blood cells identify and attack pathogens that may make you sick.

Page 184:   Systolic pressure is the pressure inside arteries when the ventricles contract. Diastolic pressure is the pressure inside the arteries when the ventricles are relaxed.

Page 185:   The red blood cells of a person who has type O blood have no A or B antigens. The A or B antibodies in another person's blood will not react to the type O cells. It is safe for anyone to receive type O blood.

Section 3
Page 186:   The lymphatic system is a secondary circulatory system in the body. The lymphatic system collects fluid and particles from between the cells and returns them to the cardiovascular system.

Page 188: The white pulp of the spleen is part of the lymphatic system. It helps fight infections by storing and producing lymphocytes. The red pulp of the spleen removes unwanted material, such as defective red blood cells, from the circulatory system.

Section 4
Page 191: Sample answer: In the lungs, each bronchiole branches to form thousands of alveoli. These small sacs allow for the exchange of oxygen and carbon dioxide. The alveoli provide a large amount of surface area, which allows gases to be exchanged efficiently.

Page 192: Cellular respiration is the process inside a cell in which oxygen is used to release energy stored in molecules of glucose. During the process, carbon dioxide (CO_2) and water are released.

Chapter 7   The Digestive and Urinary Systems
Section 1
Page 205 The digestive system works with the circulatory system to deliver the materials cells need to function. The digestive system breaks down food into a form that can be carried by the circulatory system.

Page 207 The stomach is a muscular, saclike organ with tiny glands that release enzymes and acids. This structure helps the stomach break down food mechanically and chemically.

Page 209 Bile breaks large fat droplets into very small droplets. This process allows more fat molecules to be exposed to digestive enzymes.

Page 210 Fiber keeps the stool soft and keeps material moving through the large intestine.

Section 2
Page 213 The function of kidneys is to filter blood. Nephrons are microscopic filters inside the kidneys that make this possible.

Page 214 Diuretics are chemicals that cause the kidneys to make more urine.

Chapter 8   Communication and Control
Section 1
Page 226: The CNS is the brain and the spinal cord. The PNS is all of the parts of the nervous system except the brain and the spinal cord.

Page 227: A neuron is a cell that has a cell body and a nucleus. A neuron also has dendrites that receive signals from other neurons and axons that send signals to other neurons.

Page 228: A nerve is a collection of nerve fibers, or axons, bundled together with blood vessels through which impulses travel between the central nervous system and other parts of the body.

Page 229: The PNS connects your CNS to the rest of your body, controls voluntary movements, and keeps your body's functions in balance.

Page 230: A voluntary action is an action over which you have conscious control. Voluntary activities include throwing a ball, playing a video game, talking to your friends, taking a bite of food, and raising your hand to answer a question in class. An involuntary action is an action that happens automatically. It is an action or process over which you have no conscious control.

Page 231: The medulla is important because it controls your heart rate, blood pressure, and ordinary breathing.

Page 232: When someone touches your skin, an impulse that travels along a sensory neuron to your spinal cord and then to your brain is created. The response travels back from your brain to your spinal cord and then along a motor neuron to a muscle.

Section 2
Page 234: Skin can detect pressure, temperature, pain, and vibration.

Page 235: Reflexes are important because they can protect you from injury.

Page 238: Neurons in the cochlea convert waves into electrical impulses that the brain interprets as sound.

Section 3
Page 241: Sample answer: The thyroid gland increases the rate at which the body uses energy. The thymus gland regulates the immune system, which helps your body fight disease.

Page 242: Insulin helps regulate the amount of glucose in the blood.

Chapter 9   Reproduction and Development
Section 1
Page 255: Sexual reproduction is reproduction in which the sex cells (egg and sperm) of two parents unite to form a new individual.

Page 256: External fertilization happens when the sex cells unite outside of the female's body. Internal fertilization happens when the sex cells unite inside the female's body.

Page 257: All mammals reproduce sexually and nurture their young with milk.

Section 2
Page 258: testes, epididymis, vas deferens, urethra, penis

Page 260: Twins happen about 30 times in every 1,000 births.

Section 3
Page 262: Fertilization happens when the nucleus of a sperm unites with the nucleus of an egg. Implantation happens after the fertilized egg travels down the fallopian tube to the uterus and embeds itself in the wall of the uterus.

Page 263: The placenta is important because it provides the embryo with oxygen and nutrients from the mother's blood. Wastes from the embryo also travel to the placenta, where they are carried to the mother so that she can excrete them.

Page 264: The embryo is now called a *fetus*. The fetus's face begins to look more human, and the fetus can swallow, grows rapidly (triples in size), and begins to make movements that the mother can feel.

Page 696: A person's reproductive system becomes mature.

Chapter 10   Body Defenses and Disease
Section 1
Page 281: Cooking kills dangerous bacteria or parasites living in meat, fish, and eggs.

Page 283: Frank's doctor did not prescribe antibiotics because Frank had a cold. Colds are caused by viruses. Antibiotics can't stop viruses.

Section 2
Page 285: Macrophages engulf, or eat, any microorganisms or viruses that enter your body.

Page 286: If a virus particle enters the body, it may pass into body cells and begin to replicate. Or it may be engulfed and broken up by macrophages.

Page 289: rheumatoid arthritis, diabetes, multiple sclerosis, and lupus

Page 290: HIV causes AIDS.

Chapter 11   Staying Healthy
Section 1
Page 303: An incomplete protein does not contain all of the essential amino acids.

Page 305: Sample answer: a peanut butter sandwich, a glass of milk, and fresh fruit and vegetable slices

Page 306: One serving of chicken noodle soup provides more than 10% of the daily recommended allowance of vitamin A and sodium.

Section 2
Page 309: Over-the-counter drugs can be bought without a prescription. Prescription drugs can be bought only with a prescription from a doctor or other medical professional.

Page 311: First-time use of cocaine can cause a heart attack or can cause a person to become addicted.

Page 312: Drug use is the proper use of a legal drug. Drug abuse is either the use of an illegal drug or the improper use of a legal drug.

Section 3
Page 315: Aerobic exercise strengthens the heart, lungs, and bones and reduces stress. Regular exercise also burns Calories and can give you more energy.

Page 317: Sample answers: Never hike or camp alone, dress for the weather, learn how to swim, wear a life jacket, and never drink unpurified water.

Page 319: CPR is a way to revive someone whose heart has stopped beating. CPR classes are available in many places in the community.

Chapter 12   It's Alive!! Or Is It?
Section 1
Page 333: Sample answer: They control their body temperature by moving from one environment to another. If they get too warm, they move to the shade. If they get too cool, they move out into the sunlight.

Page 334: making food, breaking down food, moving materials into and out of cells, and building cells

Section 2
Page 336: photosynthesis

Page 339: Simple carbohydrates are made of one sugar molecule. Complex carbohydrates are made of many sugar molecules linked together.

Page 340: Most fats are solid, and most oils are liquid.

Chapter 13   Cells: The Basic Units of Life
Section 1
Page 353: Sample answer: All organisms are made of one or more cells, the cell is the basic unit of all living things, and all cells come from existing cells.

Page 354: If a cell's volume gets too large, the cell's surface area will not be able to take in enough nutrients or get rid of wastes fast enough to keep the cell alive.

Page 355: Organelles are structures within a cell that perform specific functions for the cell.

Page 357: One difference between eubacteria and archaea is that bacterial ribosomes are different from archaebacterial ribosomes.

Page 358: The main difference between prokaryotes and eukaryotes is that eukaryotic cells have a nucleus and membrane-bound organelles and prokaryotic cells do not.

Section 2
Page 360: Plant, algae, and fungi cells have cell walls.

Page 361: A cell membrane encloses the cell and separates and protects the cell's contents from the cell's environment. The cell wall also controls the movement of materials into and out of the cell.

Page 362: The cytoskeleton is a web of proteins in the cytoplasm. It gives the cell support and structure.

Page 364: Most of a cell's ATP is made in the cell's mitochondria.

Page 366: Lysosomes destroy worn-out organelles, attack foreign invaders, and get rid of waste material from inside the cell.

Section 3
Page 368: Sample answer: larger size, longer life, and cell specialization

Page 369: An organ is a structure of two or more tissues working together to perform a specific function in the body.

Page 370: cell, tissue, organ, organ system

Chapter 14 The Cell in Action

Section 1

Page 383: Red blood cells would burst in pure water because water particles move from outside, where particles were dense, to inside the cell, where particles were less dense. This movement of water would cause red blood cells to fill up and burst.

Page 385: Exocytosis is the process by which a cell moves large particles to the outside of the cell.

Section 2

Page 387: Cellular respiration is a chemical process by which cells produce energy from food. Breathing supplies oxygen for cellular respiration and removes the carbon dioxide produced by cellular respiration.

Page 389: One kind of fermentation produces CO_2, and the other kind produces lactic acid.

Section 3

Page 391: No, the number of chromosomes is not always related to the complexity of organisms.

Page 392: During cytokinesis in plant cells, a cell plate is formed. During cytokinesis in animal cells, a cell plate does not form.

Chapter 15 Heredity

Section 1

Page 404: the passing of traits from parents to offspring

Page 407: During his second set of experiments, Mendel allowed the first-generation plants, which resulted from his first set of experiments, to self-pollinate.

Page 408: A ratio is a relationship between two different numbers that is often expressed as a fraction.

Section 2

Page 410: A gene contains the instructions for an inherited trait. The different versions of a gene are called *alleles*.

Page 412: Probability is the mathematical chance that something will happen.

Page 414: In incomplete dominance, one trait is not completely dominant over another.

Section 3

Page 417: 23 chromosomes

Page 418: During meiosis, one parent cell makes four new cells.

Chapter 16 Genes and DNA

Section 1

Page 435: Guanine and cytosine are always found in DNA in equal amounts, as are adenine and thymine.

Page 437: every time a cell divides

Section 2

Page 438: a string of nucleotides that give the cell information about how to make a specific trait

Page 441: They transfer amino acids to the ribosome.

Page 442: a physical or chemical agent that can cause a mutation in DNA

Page 443: Sickle cell disease is caused by a mutation in a single nucleotide of DNA, which then causes a different amino acid to be assembled in a protein used in blood cells.

Page 444: a near-identical copy of another organism, created with the original organism's genes

Chapter 17 Matter in Motion

Section 1

Page 458: A reference point is an object that appears to stay in place.

Page 460: Velocity can change by changing speed or changing direction.

Page 462: The unit for acceleration is meters per second per second (m/s^2).

Section 2

Page 465: If all of the forces act in the same direction, you must add the forces to determine the net force.

Page 466: 2 N north

Page 468: The force of gravity and the force of lift must be balanced for an airplane to stay at a certain altitude.

Section 3

Page 471: Friction is greater between rough surfaces because rough surfaces have more microscopic hills and valleys.

Page 473: *Static* means "not moving."

Page 474: Three common lubricants are oil, grease, and wax.

Section 4

Page 477: You must exert a force to overcome the gravitational force between the object and Earth.

Page 478: Gravitational force increases as mass increases.

Page 481: The weight of an object is a measure of the gravitational force on the object.

Page 482: The SI unit of force is the newton. The SI unit of mass is the kilogram.

Chapter 18 Forces and Motion

Section 1

Page 495: The acceleration due to gravity is 9.8 m/s^2.

Page 496: Air resistance will have more of an effect on the acceleration of a falling leaf.

Page 498: The word *centripetal* means "toward the center."

Page 500: Gravity gives vertical motion to an object in projectile motion.

Section 2

Page 503: When the bus is moving, both you and the bus are in motion. When the bus stops moving, no unbalanced force acts on your body, so your body continues to move forward.

Page 505: The acceleration of an object increases as the force exerted on the object increases.

Page 507: The forces in a force pair are equal in size and opposite in direction.

Page 508: Objects accelerate toward Earth because the force of gravity pulls them toward Earth.

Section 3

Page 511: When two objects collide, some or all of the momentum of each object can be transferred to the other object.

Page 512: After a collision, objects can stick together or can bounce off each other.

Chapter 19 Forces in Fluids

Section 1

Page 525: Two gases in the atmosphere are nitrogen and oxygen.

Page 526: Pressure increases as depth increases.

Page 528: You decrease pressure inside a straw by removing some of the air inside the straw.

Section 2

Page 531: An object is buoyed up if the buoyant force on the object is greater than the object's weight.

Page 532: Helium is less dense than air.

Page 534: Crew members control the density of a submarine by controlling the amount of water in the ballast tanks.

Section 3

Page 537: Lift is an upward force on an object that is moving in a fluid.

Page 539: An irregular or unpredictable flow of fluids is known as *turbulence.*

Page 540: Airplanes can reduce turbulence by changing the shape or area of the wings.

Chapter 20 Work and Machines

Section 1

Page 552: No, work is done on an object only if force causes the object to move in a direction that is parallel to the force.

Page 555: Work is calculated as force times distance.

Page 556: Power is calculated as work done (in joules) divided by the time (in seconds) in which the work was done.

Section 2

Page 559: Machines make work easier by allowing a decreased force to be applied over a greater distance.

Page 560: Machines can change the force or the distance through which force is applied.

Page 562: *mechanical efficiency = (work output − work input)* × 100

Section 3

Page 565: Each class of lever has a different set of mechanical advantage possibilities.

Page 567: the radius of the wheel divided by the radius of the axle

Page 568: a slanted surface that makes the raising of loads easier, such as a ramp

Page 570: They have more moving parts than simple machines do, so they tend to be less efficient than simple machines are.

Study Skills

FoldNote Instructions

Have you ever tried to study for a test or quiz but didn't know where to start? Or have you read a chapter and found that you can remember only a few ideas? Well, FoldNotes are a fun and exciting way to help you learn and remember the ideas you encounter as you learn science!

FoldNotes are tools that you can use to organize concepts. By focusing on a few main concepts, FoldNotes help you learn and remember how the concepts fit together. They can help you see the "big picture." Below you will find instructions for building 10 different FoldNotes.

Pyramid

1. Place a sheet of paper in front of you. Fold the lower left-hand corner of the paper diagonally to the opposite edge of the paper.

2. Cut off the tab of paper created by the fold (at the top).

3. Open the paper so that it is a square. Fold the lower right-hand corner of the paper diagonally to the opposite corner to form a triangle.

4. Open the paper. The creases of the two folds will have created an X.

5. Using scissors, cut along one of the creases. Start from any corner, and stop at the center point to create two flaps. Use tape or glue to attach one of the flaps on top of the other flap.

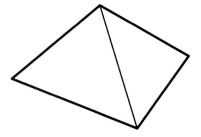

Double Door

1. Fold a sheet of paper in half from the top to the bottom. Then, unfold the paper.

2. Fold the top and bottom edges of the paper to the crease.

Booklet

1. Fold a sheet of paper in half from left to right. Then, unfold the paper.

2. Fold the sheet of paper in half again from the top to the bottom. Then, unfold the paper.

3. Refold the sheet of paper in half from left to right.

4. Fold the top and bottom edges to the center crease.

5. Completely unfold the paper.

6. Refold the paper from top to bottom.

7. Using scissors, cut a slit along the center crease of the sheet from the folded edge to the creases made in step 4. Do not cut the entire sheet in half.

8. Fold the sheet of paper in half from left to right. While holding the bottom and top edges of the paper, push the bottom and top edges together so that the center collapses at the center slit. Fold the four flaps to form a four-page book.

Layered Book

1. Lay one sheet of paper on top of another sheet. Slide the top sheet up so that 2 cm of the bottom sheet is showing.

2. Hold the two sheets together, fold down the top of the two sheets so that you see four 2 cm tabs along the bottom.

3. Using a stapler, staple the top of the FoldNote.

Key-Term Fold

1. Fold a sheet of lined notebook paper in half from left to right.

2. Using scissors, cut along every third line from the right edge of the paper to the center fold to make tabs.

Four-Corner Fold

1. Fold a sheet of paper in half from left to right. Then, unfold the paper.

2. Fold each side of the paper to the crease in the center of the paper.

3. Fold the paper in half from the top to the bottom. Then, unfold the paper.

4. Using scissors, cut the top flap creases made in step 3 to form four flaps.

Three-Panel Flip Chart

1. Fold a piece of paper in half from the top to the bottom.

2. Fold the paper in thirds from side to side. Then, unfold the paper so that you can see the three sections.

3. From the top of the paper, cut along each of the vertical fold lines to the fold in the middle of the paper. You will now have three flaps.

Appendix

Table Fold

1. Fold a piece of paper in half from the top to the bottom. Then, fold the paper in half again.

2. Fold the paper in thirds from side to side.

3. Unfold the paper completely. Carefully trace the fold lines by using a pen or pencil.

Two-Panel Flip Chart

1. Fold a piece of paper in half from the top to the bottom.

2. Fold the paper in half from side to side. Then, unfold the paper so that you can see the two sections.

3. From the top of the paper, cut along the vertical fold line to the fold in the middle of the paper. You will now have two flaps.

Tri-Fold

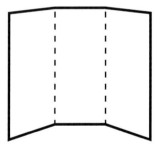

1. Fold a piece a paper in thirds from the top to the bottom.

2. Unfold the paper so that you can see the three sections. Then, turn the paper sideways so that the three sections form vertical columns.

3. Trace the fold lines by using a pen or pencil. Label the columns "Know," "Want," and "Learn."

Appendix

Graphic Organizer Instructions

 Have you ever wished that you could "draw out" the many concepts you learn in your science class? Sometimes, being able to *see* how concepts are related really helps you remember what you've learned. Graphic Organizers do just that! They give you a way to draw or map out concepts.

All you need to make a Graphic Organizer is a piece of paper and a pencil. Below you will find instructions for four different Graphic Organizers designed to help you organize the concepts you'll learn in this book.

Spider Map

1. Draw a diagram like the one shown. In the circle, write the main topic.

2. From the circle, draw legs to represent different categories of the main topic. You can have as many categories as you want.

3. From the category legs, draw horizontal lines. As you read the chapter, write details about each category on the horizontal lines.

Comparison Table

1. Draw a chart like the one shown. Your chart can have as many columns and rows as you want.

2. In the top row, write the topics that you want to compare.

3. In the left column, write characteristics of the topics that you want to compare. As you read the chapter, fill in the characteristics for each topic in the appropriate boxes.

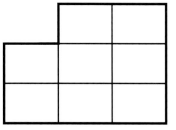

Appendix

Chain-of-Events-Chart

1. Draw a box. In the box, write the first step of a process or the first event of a timeline.

2. Under the box, draw another box, and use an arrow to connect the two boxes. In the second box, write the next step of the process or the next event in the timeline.

3. Continue adding boxes until the process or timeline is finished.

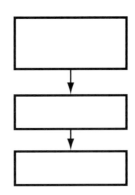

Concept Map

1. Draw a circle in the center of a piece of paper. Write the main idea of the chapter in the center of the circle.

2. From the circle, draw other circles. In those circles, write characteristics of the main idea. Draw arrows from the center circle to the circles that contain the characteristics.

3. From each circle that contains a characteristic, draw other circles. In those circles, write specific details about the characteristic. Draw arrows from each circle that contains a characteristic to the circles that contain specific details. You may draw as many circles as you want.

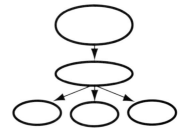

Appendix

SI Measurement

The International System of Units, or SI, is the standard system of measurement used by many scientists. Using the same standards of measurement makes it easier for scientists to communicate with one another.

SI works by combining prefixes and base units. Each base unit can be used with different prefixes to define smaller and larger quantities. The table below lists common SI prefixes.

SI Prefixes

Prefix	Symbol	Factor	Example
kilo-	k	1,000	kilogram, 1 kg = 1,000 g
hecto-	h	100	hectoliter, 1 hL = 100 L
deka-	da	10	dekameter, 1 dam = 10 m
		1	meter, liter, gram
deci-	d	0.1	decigram, 1 dg = 0.1 g
centi-	c	0.01	centimeter, 1 cm = 0.01 m
milli-	m	0.001	milliliter, 1 mL = 0.001 L
micro-	μ	0.000 001	micrometer, 1 μm = 0.000 001 m

SI Conversion Table

SI units	From SI to English	From English to SI
Length		
kilometer (km) = 1,000 m	1 km = 0.621 mi	1 mi = 1.609 km
meter (m) = 100 cm	1 m = 3.281 ft	1 ft = 0.305 m
centimeter (cm) = 0.01 m	1 cm = 0.394 in.	1 in. = 2.540 cm
millimeter (mm) = 0.001 m	1 mm = 0.039 in.	
micrometer (μm) = 0.000 001 m		
nanometer (nm) = 0.000 000 001 m		
Area		
square kilometer (km^2) = 100 hectares	1 km^2 = 0.386 mi^2	1 mi^2 = 2.590 km^2
hectare (ha) = 10,000 m^2	1 ha = 2.471 acres	1 acre = 0.405 ha
square meter (m^2) = 10,000 cm^2	1 m^2 = 10.764 ft^2	1 ft^2 = 0.093 m^2
square centimeter (cm^2) = 100 mm^2	1 cm^2 = 0.155 $in.^2$	1 $in.^2$ = 6.452 cm^2
Volume		
liter (L) = 1,000 mL = 1 dm^3	1 L = 1.057 fl qt	1 fl qt = 0.946 L
milliliter (mL) = 0.001 L = 1 cm^3	1 mL = 0.034 fl oz	1 fl oz = 29.574 mL
microliter (μL) = 0.000 001 L		
Mass		
kilogram (kg) = 1,000 g	1 kg = 2.205 lb	1 lb = 0.454 kg
gram (g) = 1,000 mg	1 g = 0.035 oz	1 oz = 28.350 g
milligram (mg) = 0.001 g		
microgram (μg) = 0.000 001 g		

Appendix

Temperature Scales

Temperature can be expressed by using three different scales: Fahrenheit, Celsius, and Kelvin. The SI unit for temperature is the kelvin (K).

Although 0 K is much colder than 0°C, a change of 1 K is equal to a change of 1°C.

Three Temperature Scales

	Fahrenheit	Celsius	Kelvin
Water boils	212°	100°	373
Body temperature	98.6°	37°	310
Room temperature	68°	20°	293
Water freezes	32°	0°	273

Temperature Conversions Table

To convert	Use this equation:	Example
Celsius to Fahrenheit °C → °F	$°F = \left(\frac{9}{5} \times °C\right) + 32$	Convert 45°C to °F. $°F = \left(\frac{9}{5} \times 45°C\right) + 32 = 113°F$
Fahrenheit to Celsius °F → °C	$°C = \frac{5}{9} \times (°F - 32)$	Convert 68°F to °C. $°C = \frac{5}{9} \times (68°F - 32) = 20°C$
Celsius to Kelvin °C → K	$K = °C + 273$	Convert 45°C to K. $K = 45°C + 273 = 318 K$
Kelvin to Celsius K → °C	$°C = K - 273$	Convert 32 K to °C. $°C = 32K - 273 = -241°C$

Measuring Skills

Using a Graduated Cylinder

When using a graduated cylinder to measure volume, keep the following procedures in mind:

1. Place the cylinder on a flat, level surface before measuring liquid.

2. Move your head so that your eye is level with the surface of the liquid.

3. Read the mark closest to the liquid level. On glass graduated cylinders, read the mark closest to the center of the curve in the liquid's surface.

Using a Meterstick or Metric Ruler

When using a meterstick or metric ruler to measure length, keep the following procedures in mind:

1. Place the ruler firmly against the object that you are measuring.

2. Align one edge of the object exactly with the 0 end of the ruler.

3. Look at the other edge of the object to see which of the marks on the ruler is closest to that edge. (Note: Each small slash between the centimeters represents a millimeter, which is one-tenth of a centimeter.)

Using a Triple-Beam Balance

When using a triple-beam balance to measure mass, keep the following procedures in mind:

1. Make sure the balance is on a level surface.

2. Place all of the countermasses at 0. Adjust the balancing knob until the pointer rests at 0.

3. Place the object you wish to measure on the pan. **Caution:** Do not place hot objects or chemicals directly on the balance pan.

4. Move the largest countermass along the beam to the right until it is at the last notch that does not tip the balance. Follow the same procedure with the next-largest countermass. Then, move the smallest countermass until the pointer rests at 0.

5. Add the readings from the three beams together to determine the mass of the object.

6. When determining the mass of crystals or powders, first find the mass of a piece of filter paper. Then, add the crystals or powder to the paper, and remeasure. The actual mass of the crystals or powder is the total mass minus the mass of the paper. When finding the mass of liquids, first find the mass of the empty container. Then, find the combined mass of the liquid and container. The mass of the liquid is the total mass minus the mass of the container.

Scientific Methods

The ways in which scientists answer questions and solve problems are called **scientific methods.** The same steps are often used by scientists as they look for answers. However, there is more than one way to use these steps. Scientists may use all of the steps or just some of the steps during an investigation. They may even repeat some of the steps. The goal of using scientific methods is to come up with reliable answers and solutions.

Six Steps of Scientific Methods

 Ask a Question

Good questions come from careful **observations.** You make observations by using your senses to gather information. Sometimes, you may use instruments, such as microscopes and telescopes, to extend the range of your senses. As you observe the natural world, you will discover that you have many more questions than answers. These questions drive investigations.

Questions beginning with *what, why, how,* and *when* are important in focusing an investigation. Here is an example of a question that could lead to an investigation.

Question: How does acid rain affect plant growth?

 Form a Hypothesis

After you ask a question, you need to form a **hypothesis.** A hypothesis is a clear statement of what you expect the answer to your question to be. Your hypothesis will represent your best "educated guess" based on what you have observed and what you already know. A good hypothesis is testable. Otherwise, the investigation can go no further. Here is a hypothesis based on the question, "How does acid rain affect plant growth?"

Hypothesis: Acid rain slows plant growth.

The hypothesis can lead to predictions. A prediction is what you think the outcome of your experiment or data collection will be. Predictions are usually stated in an if-then format. Here is a sample prediction for the hypothesis that acid rain slows plant growth.

Prediction: If a plant is watered with only acid rain (which has a pH of 4), then the plant will grow at half its normal rate.

 Test the Hypothesis

After you have formed a hypothesis and made a prediction, your hypothesis should be tested. One way to test a hypothesis is with a controlled experiment. A **controlled experiment** tests only one factor at a time. In an experiment to test the effect of acid rain on plant growth, the **control group** would be watered with normal rain water. The **experimental group** would be watered with acid rain. All of the plants should receive the same amount of sunlight and water each day. The air temperature should be the same for all groups. However, the acidity of the water will be a variable. In fact, any factor that is different from one group to another is a **variable.** If your hypothesis is correct, then the acidity of the water and plant growth are *dependant variables.* The amount a plant grows is dependent on the acidity of the water. However, the amount of water each plant receives and the amount of sunlight each plant receives are *independent variables.* Either of these factors could change without affecting the other factor.

Sometimes, the nature of an investigation makes a controlled experiment impossible. For example, the Earth's core is surrounded by thousands of meters of rock. Under such circumstances, a hypothesis may be tested by making detailed observations.

 Analyze the Results

After you have completed your experiments, made your observations, and collected your data, you must analyze all the information you have gathered. Tables and graphs are often used in this step to organize the data.

5 Draw Conclusions

After analyzing your data, you can determine if your results support your hypothesis. If your hypothesis is supported, you (or others) might want to repeat the observations or experiments to verify your results. If your hypothesis is not supported by the data, you may have to check your procedure for errors. You may even have to reject your hypothesis and make a new one. If you cannot draw a conclusion from your results, you may have to try the investigation again or carry out further observations or experiments.

6 Communicate Results

After any scientific investigation, you should report your results. By preparing a written or oral report, you let others know what you have learned. They may repeat your investigation to see if they get the same results. Your report may even lead to another question and then to another investigation.

Scientific Methods in Action

Scientific methods contain loops in which several steps may be repeated over and over again. In some cases, certain steps are unnecessary. Thus, there is not a "straight line" of steps. For example, sometimes scientists find that testing one hypothesis raises new questions and new hypotheses to be tested. And sometimes, testing the hypothesis leads directly to a conclusion. Furthermore, the steps in scientific methods are not always used in the same order. Follow the steps in the diagram, and see how many different directions scientific methods can take you.

Using the Microscope

Parts of the Compound Light Microscope

- The **ocular lens** magnifies the image 10×.
- The **low-power objective** magnifies the image 10×.
- The **high-power objective** magnifies the image either 40× or 43×.
- The **revolving nosepiece** holds the objectives and can be turned to change from one magnification to the other.
- The **body tube** maintains the correct distance between the ocular lens and objectives.
- The **coarse-adjustment knob** moves the body tube up and down to allow focusing of the image.
- The **fine-adjustment knob** moves the body tube slightly to bring the image into sharper focus. It is usually located in the center of the coarse-adjustment knob.
- The **stage** supports a slide.
- **Stage clips** hold the slide in place for viewing.
- The **diaphragm** controls the amount of light coming through the stage.
- The light source provides a **light** for viewing the slide.
- The **arm** supports the body tube.
- The **base** supports the microscope.

Ocular lens

Body tube

Revolving nosepiece

Objective

Stage clip

Stage

Diaphragm

Light

Coarse-adjustment knob

Arm

Base

Appendix

Proper Use of the Compound Light Microscope

1. Use both hands to carry the microscope to your lab table. Place one hand beneath the base, and use the other hand to hold the arm of the microscope. Hold the microscope close to your body while carrying it to your lab table.

2. Place the microscope on the lab table at least 5 cm from the edge of the table.

3. Check to see what type of light source is used by your microscope. If the microscope has a lamp, plug it in and make sure that the cord is out of the way. If the microscope has a mirror, adjust the mirror to reflect light through the hole in the stage. **Caution:** If your microscope has a mirror, do not use direct sunlight as a light source. Direct sunlight can damage your eyes.

4. Always begin work with the low-power objective in line with the body tube. Adjust the revolving nosepiece.

5. Place a prepared slide over the hole in the stage. Secure the slide with the stage clips.

6. Look through the ocular lens. Move the diaphragm to adjust the amount of light coming through the stage.

7. Look at the stage from eye level. Slowly turn the coarse adjustment to lower the objective until the objective almost touches the slide. Do not allow the objective to touch the slide.

8. Look through the ocular lens. Turn the coarse adjustment to raise the low-power objective until the image is in focus. Always focus by raising the objective away from the slide. Never focus the objective downward. Use the fine adjustment to sharpen the focus. Keep both eyes open while viewing a slide.

9. Make sure that the image is exactly in the center of your field of vision. Then, switch to the high-power objective. Focus the image by using only the fine adjustment. Never use the coarse adjustment at high power.

10. When you are finished using the microscope, remove the slide. Clean the ocular lens and objectives with lens paper. Return the microscope to its storage area. Remember to use both hands when carrying the microscope.

Making a Wet Mount

1. Use lens paper to clean a glass slide and a coverslip.

2. Place the specimen that you wish to observe in the center of the slide.

3. Using a medicine dropper, place one drop of water on the specimen.

4. Hold the coverslip at the edge of the water and at a 45° angle to the slide. Make sure that the water runs along the edge of the coverslip.

5. Lower the coverslip slowly to avoid trapping air bubbles.

6. Water might evaporate from the slide as you work. Add more water to keep the specimen fresh. Place the tip of the medicine dropper next to the edge of the coverslip. Add a drop of water. (You can also use this method to add stain or solutions to a wet mount.) Remove excess water from the slide by using the corner of a paper towel as a blotter. Do not lift the coverslip to add or remove water.

Periodic Table of the Elements

Each square on the table includes an element's name, chemical symbol, atomic number, and atomic mass.

The color of the chemical symbol indicates the physical state at room temperature. Carbon is a solid.

6	Atomic number
C	Chemical symbol
Carbon	Element name
12.0	Atomic mass

The background color indicates the type of element. Carbon is a nonmetal.

Background
- Metals
- Metalloids
- Nonmetals

Chemical symbol
- Solid
- Liquid
- Gas

Period 1
| 1 |
| **H** |
| Hydrogen |
| 1.0 |

	Group 1	Group 2		Group 3	Group 4	Group 5	Group 6	Group 7	Group 8	Group 9
Period 2	3 **Li** Lithium 6.9	4 **Be** Beryllium 9.0								
Period 3	11 **Na** Sodium 23.0	12 **Mg** Magnesium 24.3								
Period 4	19 **K** Potassium 39.1	20 **Ca** Calcium 40.1		21 **Sc** Scandium 45.0	22 **Ti** Titanium 47.9	23 **V** Vanadium 50.9	24 **Cr** Chromium 52.0	25 **Mn** Manganese 54.9	26 **Fe** Iron 55.8	27 **Co** Cobalt 58.9
Period 5	37 **Rb** Rubidium 85.5	38 **Sr** Strontium 87.6		39 **Y** Yttrium 88.9	40 **Zr** Zirconium 91.2	41 **Nb** Niobium 92.9	42 **Mo** Molybdenum 95.9	43 **Tc** Technetium (98)	44 **Ru** Ruthenium 101.1	45 **Rh** Rhodium 102.9
Period 6	55 **Cs** Cesium 132.9	56 **Ba** Barium 137.3		57 **La** Lanthanum 138.9	72 **Hf** Hafnium 178.5	73 **Ta** Tantalum 180.9	74 **W** Tungsten 183.8	75 **Re** Rhenium 186.2	76 **Os** Osmium 190.2	77 **Ir** Iridium 192.2
Period 7	87 **Fr** Francium (223)	88 **Ra** Radium (226)		89 **Ac** Actinium (227)	104 **Rf** Rutherfordium (261)	105 **Db** Dubnium (262)	106 **Sg** Seaborgium (263)	107 **Bh** Bohrium (264)	108 **Hs** Hassium (265)†	109 **Mt** Meitnerium (268)†

A row of elements is called a *period*.

A column of elements is called a *group* or *family*.

Values in parentheses are of the most stable isotope of the element.

† Estimated from currently available IUPAC data.

These elements are placed below the table to allow the table to be narrower.

Lanthanides
| 58 **Ce** Cerium 140.1 | 59 **Pr** Praseodymium 140.9 | 60 **Nd** Neodymium 144.2 | 61 **Pm** Promethium (145) | 62 **Sm** Samarium 150.4 |

Actinides
| 90 **Th** Thorium 232.0 | 91 **Pa** Protactinium 231.0 | 92 **U** Uranium 238.0 | 93 **Np** Neptunium (237) | 94 **Pu** Plutonium (244) |

Topic: **Periodic Table**
Go To: **go.hrw.com**
Keyword: **HN0 PERIODIC**
Visit the HRW Web site for
updates on the periodic table.

Group 18

| | | | | | | 2
He
Helium
4.0 |

| | | | Group 13 | Group 14 | Group 15 | Group 16 | Group 17 | |

This zigzag line reminds you where the metals, nonmetals, and metalloids are.

| | | | 5
B
Boron
10.8 | 6
C
Carbon
12.0 | 7
N
Nitrogen
14.0 | 8
O
Oxygen
16.0 | 9
F
Fluorine
19.0 | 10
Ne
Neon
20.2 |
| | | | 13
Al
Aluminum
27.0 | 14
Si
Silicon
28.1 | 15
P
Phosphorus
31.0 | 16
S
Sulfur
32.1 | 17
Cl
Chlorine
35.5 | 18
Ar
Argon
39.9 |

Group 10	Group 11	Group 12						
28 **Ni** Nickel 58.7	29 **Cu** Copper 63.5	30 **Zn** Zinc 65.4	31 **Ga** Gallium 69.7	32 **Ge** Germanium 72.6	33 **As** Arsenic 74.9	34 **Se** Selenium 79.0	35 **Br** Bromine 79.9	36 **Kr** Krypton 83.8
46 **Pd** Palladium 106.4	47 **Ag** Silver 107.9	48 **Cd** Cadmium 112.4	49 **In** Indium 114.8	50 **Sn** Tin 118.7	51 **Sb** Antimony 121.8	52 **Te** Tellurium 127.6	53 **I** Iodine 126.9	54 **Xe** Xenon 131.3
78 **Pt** Platinum 195.1	79 **Au** Gold 197.0	80 **Hg** Mercury 200.6	81 **Tl** Thallium 204.4	82 **Pb** Lead 207.2	83 **Bi** Bismuth 209.0	84 **Po** Polonium (209)	85 **At** Astatine (210)	86 **Rn** Radon (222)
110 **Ds** Darmstadtium (269)†	111 **Uuu** Unununium (272)†	112 **Uub** Ununbium (277)†		114 **Uuq** Ununquadium (285)†				

The names and three-letter symbols of elements are temporary. They are based on the atomic numbers of the elements. Official names and symbols will be approved by an international committee of scientists.

63 **Eu** Europium 152.0	64 **Gd** Gadolinium 157.2	65 **Tb** Terbium 158.9	66 **Dy** Dysprosium 162.5	67 **Ho** Holmium 164.9	68 **Er** Erbium 167.3	69 **Tm** Thulium 168.9	70 **Yb** Ytterbium 173.0	71 **Lu** Lutetium 175.0
95 **Am** Americium (243)	96 **Cm** Curium (247)	97 **Bk** Berkelium (247)	98 **Cf** Californium (251)	99 **Es** Einsteinium (252)	100 **Fm** Fermium (257)	101 **Md** Mendelevium (258)	102 **No** Nobelium (259)	103 **Lr** Lawrencium (262)

Appendix

Making Charts and Graphs

Pie Charts

A pie chart shows how each group of data relates to all of the data. Each part of the circle forming the chart represents a category of the data. The entire circle represents all of the data. For example, a biologist studying a hardwood forest in Wisconsin found that there were five different types of trees. The data table at right summarizes the biologist's findings.

Wisconsin Hardwood Trees	
Type of tree	Number found
Oak	600
Maple	750
Beech	300
Birch	1,200
Hickory	150
Total	3,000

How to Make a Pie Chart

1 To make a pie chart of these data, first find the percentage of each type of tree. Divide the number of trees of each type by the total number of trees, and multiply by 100.

$$\frac{600 \text{ oak}}{3{,}000 \text{ trees}} \times 100 = 20\%$$

$$\frac{750 \text{ maple}}{3{,}000 \text{ trees}} \times 100 = 25\%$$

$$\frac{300 \text{ beech}}{3{,}000 \text{ trees}} \times 100 = 10\%$$

$$\frac{1{,}200 \text{ birch}}{3{,}000 \text{ trees}} \times 100 = 40\%$$

$$\frac{150 \text{ hickory}}{3{,}000 \text{ trees}} \times 100 = 5\%$$

2 Now, determine the size of the wedges that make up the pie chart. Multiply each percentage by 360°. Remember that a circle contains 360°.

$20\% \times 360° = 72°$ $25\% \times 360° = 90°$
$10\% \times 360° = 36°$ $40\% \times 360° = 144°$
$5\% \times 360° = 18°$

3 Check that the sum of the percentages is 100 and the sum of the degrees is 360.

$20\% + 25\% + 10\% + 40\% + 5\% = 100\%$
$72° + 90° + 36° + 144° + 18° = 360°$

4 Use a compass to draw a circle and mark the center of the circle.

5 Then, use a protractor to draw angles of 72°, 90°, 36°, 144°, and 18° in the circle.

6 Finally, label each part of the chart, and choose an appropriate title.

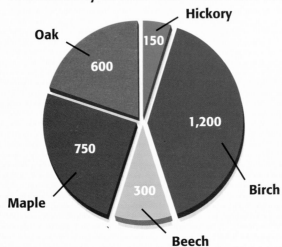

A Community of Wisconsin Hardwood Trees

Hickory 150 • Oak 600 • Maple 750 • Beech 300 • Birch 1,200

Line Graphs

Line graphs are most often used to demonstrate continuous change. For example, Mr. Smith's students analyzed the population records for their hometown, Appleton, between 1900 and 2000. Examine the data at right.

Because the year and the population change, they are the *variables*. The population is determined by, or dependent on, the year. Therefore, the population is called the **dependent variable,** and the year is called the **independent variable.** Each set of data is called a **data pair.** To prepare a line graph, you must first organize data pairs into a table like the one at right.

Population of Appleton, 1900–2000	
Year	Population
1900	1,800
1920	2,500
1940	3,200
1960	3,900
1980	4,600
2000	5,300

How to Make a Line Graph

1 Place the independent variable along the horizontal (*x*) axis. Place the dependent variable along the vertical (*y*) axis.

2 Label the *x*-axis "Year" and the *y*-axis "Population." Look at your largest and smallest values for the population. For the *y*-axis, determine a scale that will provide enough space to show these values. You must use the same scale for the entire length of the axis. Next, find an appropriate scale for the *x*-axis.

3 Choose reasonable starting points for each axis.

4 Plot the data pairs as accurately as possible.

5 Choose a title that accurately represents the data.

How to Determine Slope

Slope is the ratio of the change in the *y*-value to the change in the *x*-value, or "rise over run."

1 Choose two points on the line graph. For example, the population of Appleton in 2000 was 5,300 people. Therefore, you can define point *a* as (2000, 5,300). In 1900, the population was 1,800 people. You can define point *b* as (1900, 1,800).

2 Find the change in the *y*-value.
(*y* at point *a*) − (*y* at point *b*) =
5,300 people − 1,800 people =
3,500 people

3 Find the change in the *x*-value.
(*x* at point *a*) − (*x* at point *b*) =
2000 − 1900 = 100 years

4 Calculate the slope of the graph by dividing the change in *y* by the change in *x*.

$$slope = \frac{change\ in\ y}{change\ in\ x}$$

$$slope = \frac{3,500\ people}{100\ years}$$

$$slope = 35\ people\ per\ year$$

In this example, the population in Appleton increased by a fixed amount each year. The graph of these data is a straight line. Therefore, the relationship is **linear.** When the graph of a set of data is not a straight line, the relationship is **nonlinear.**

Appendix

Using Algebra to Determine Slope

The equation in step 4 may also be arranged to be

$$y = kx$$

where y represents the change in the y-value, k represents the slope, and x represents the change in the x-value.

$$slope = \frac{change\ in\ y}{change\ in\ x}$$

$$k = \frac{y}{x}$$

$$k \times x = \frac{y \times x}{x}$$

$$kx = y$$

Bar Graphs

Bar graphs are used to demonstrate change that is not continuous. These graphs can be used to indicate trends when the data cover a long period of time. A meteorologist gathered the precipitation data shown here for Hartford, Connecticut, for April 1–15, 1996, and used a bar graph to represent the data.

Precipitation in Hartford, Connecticut April 1–15, 1996			
Date	Precipitation (cm)	Date	Precipitation (cm)
April 1	0.5	April 9	0.25
April 2	1.25	April 10	0.0
April 3	0.0	April 11	1.0
April 4	0.0	April 12	0.0
April 5	0.0	April 13	0.25
April 6	0.0	April 14	0.0
April 7	0.0	April 15	6.50
April 8	1.75		

How to Make a Bar Graph

1 Use an appropriate scale and a reasonable starting point for each axis.

2 Label the axes, and plot the data.

3 Choose a title that accurately represents the data.

Math Refresher

Science requires an understanding of many math concepts. The following pages will help you review some important math skills.

Averages

An **average,** or **mean,** simplifies a set of numbers into a single number that *approximates* the value of the set.

Example: Find the average of the following set of numbers: 5, 4, 7, and 8.

Step 1: Find the sum.
$$5 + 4 + 7 + 8 = 24$$

Step 2: Divide the sum by the number of numbers in your set. Because there are four numbers in this example, divide the sum by 4.
$$\frac{24}{4} = 6$$

The average, or mean, is **6.**

Ratios

A **ratio** is a comparison between numbers, and it is usually written as a fraction.

Example: Find the ratio of thermometers to students if you have 36 thermometers and 48 students in your class.

Step 1: Make the ratio.
$$\frac{36 \text{ thermometers}}{48 \text{ students}}$$

Step 2: Reduce the fraction to its simplest form.
$$\frac{36}{48} = \frac{36 \div 12}{48 \div 12} = \frac{3}{4}$$

The ratio of thermometers to students is **3 to 4,** or $\frac{3}{4}$. The ratio may also be written in the form 3:4.

Proportions

A **proportion** is an equation that states that two ratios are equal.
$$\frac{3}{1} = \frac{12}{4}$$

To solve a proportion, first multiply across the equal sign. This is called *cross-multiplication*. If you know three of the quantities in a proportion, you can use cross-multiplication to find the fourth.

Example: Imagine that you are making a scale model of the solar system for your science project. The diameter of Jupiter is 11.2 times the diameter of the Earth. If you are using a plastic-foam ball that has a diameter of 2 cm to represent the Earth, what must the diameter of the ball representing Jupiter be?
$$\frac{11.2}{1} = \frac{x}{2 \text{ cm}}$$

Step 1: Cross-multiply.
$$\frac{11.2}{1} \diagup\!\!\!\!\diagdown \frac{x}{2}$$
$$11.2 \times 2 = x \times 1$$

Step 2: Multiply.
$$22.4 = x \times 1$$

Step 3: Isolate the variable by dividing both sides by 1.
$$x = \frac{22.4}{1}$$
$$x = 22.4 \text{ cm}$$

You will need to use a ball that has a diameter of **22.4** cm to represent Jupiter.

Percentages

A **percentage** is a ratio of a given number to 100.

Example: What is 85% of 40?

Step 1: Rewrite the percentage by moving the decimal point two places to the left.

0.85

Step 2: Multiply the decimal by the number that you are calculating the percentage of.

0.85 × 40 = 34

85% of 40 is **34.**

Decimals

To **add** or **subtract decimals,** line up the digits vertically so that the decimal points line up. Then, add or subtract the columns from right to left. Carry or borrow numbers as necessary.

Example: Add the following numbers: 3.1415 and 2.96.

Step 1: Line up the digits vertically so that the decimal points line up.

$$\begin{array}{r} 3.1415 \\ + \ 2.96 \\ \hline \end{array}$$

Step 2: Add the columns from right to left, and carry when necessary.

$$\begin{array}{r} 1 \ 1 \\ 3.1415 \\ + \ 2.96 \\ \hline 6.1015 \end{array}$$

The sum is **6.1015.**

Fractions

Numbers tell you how many; **fractions** tell you *how much of a whole*.

Example: Your class has 24 plants. Your teacher instructs you to put 5 plants in a shady spot. What fraction of the plants in your class will you put in a shady spot?

Step 1: In the denominator, write the total number of parts in the whole.

$$\frac{?}{24}$$

Step 2: In the numerator, write the number of parts of the whole that are being considered.

$$\frac{5}{24}$$

So, $\frac{5}{24}$ of the plants will be in the shade.

Reducing Fractions

It is usually best to express a fraction in its simplest form. Expressing a fraction in its simplest form is called *reducing* a fraction.

Example: Reduce the fraction $\frac{30}{45}$ to its simplest form.

Step 1: Find the largest whole number that will divide evenly into both the numerator and denominator. This number is called the *greatest common factor* (GCF).

Factors of the numerator 30:
1, 2, 3, 5, 6, 10, **15,** 30

Factors of the denominator 45:
1, 3, 5, 9, **15,** 45

Step 2: Divide both the numerator and the denominator by the GCF, which in this case is 15.

$$\frac{30}{45} = \frac{30 \div 15}{45 \div 15} = \frac{2}{3}$$

Thus, $\frac{30}{45}$ reduced to its simplest form is $\frac{2}{3}$.

Adding and Subtracting Fractions

To **add** or **subtract fractions** that have the **same denominator,** simply add or subtract the numerators.

Examples:

$$\frac{3}{5} + \frac{1}{5} = ? \quad \text{and} \quad \frac{3}{4} - \frac{1}{4} = ?$$

Step 1: Add or subtract the numerators.

$$\frac{3}{5} + \frac{1}{5} = \frac{4}{} \quad \text{and} \quad \frac{3}{4} - \frac{1}{4} = \frac{2}{}$$

Step 2: Write the sum or difference over the denominator.

$$\frac{3}{5} + \frac{1}{5} = \frac{4}{5} \quad \text{and} \quad \frac{3}{4} - \frac{1}{4} = \frac{2}{4}$$

Step 3: If necessary, reduce the fraction to its simplest form.

$\mathbf{\frac{4}{5}}$ cannot be reduced, and $\frac{2}{4} = \mathbf{\frac{1}{2}}$.

To **add** or **subtract fractions** that have **different denominators,** first find the least common denominator (LCD).

Examples:

$$\frac{1}{2} + \frac{1}{6} = ? \quad \text{and} \quad \frac{3}{4} - \frac{2}{3} = ?$$

Step 1: Write the equivalent fractions that have a common denominator.

$$\frac{3}{6} + \frac{1}{6} = ? \quad \text{and} \quad \frac{9}{12} - \frac{8}{12} = ?$$

Step 2: Add or subtract the fractions.

$$\frac{3}{6} + \frac{1}{6} = \frac{4}{6} \quad \text{and} \quad \frac{9}{12} - \frac{8}{12} = \frac{1}{12}$$

Step 3: If necessary, reduce the fraction to its simplest form.

The fraction $\frac{4}{6} = \mathbf{\frac{2}{3}}$, and $\mathbf{\frac{1}{12}}$ cannot be reduced.

Multiplying Fractions

To **multiply fractions,** multiply the numerators and the denominators together, and then reduce the fraction to its simplest form.

Example:

$$\frac{5}{9} \times \frac{7}{10} = ?$$

Step 1: Multiply the numerators and denominators.

$$\frac{5}{9} \times \frac{7}{10} = \frac{5 \times 7}{9 \times 10} = \frac{35}{90}$$

Step 2: Reduce the fraction.

$$\frac{35}{90} = \frac{35 \div 5}{90 \div 5} = \mathbf{\frac{7}{18}}$$

Dividing Fractions

To **divide fractions,** first rewrite the divisor (the number you divide by) upside down. This number is called the *reciprocal* of the divisor. Then multiply and reduce if necessary.

Example:

$$\frac{5}{8} \div \frac{3}{2} = ?$$

Step 1: Rewrite the divisor as its reciprocal.

$$\frac{3}{2} \rightarrow \frac{2}{3}$$

Step 2: Multiply the fractions.

$$\frac{5}{8} \times \frac{2}{3} = \frac{5 \times 2}{8 \times 3} = \frac{10}{24}$$

Step 3: Reduce the fraction.

$$\frac{10}{24} = \frac{10 \div 2}{24 \div 2} = \mathbf{\frac{5}{12}}$$

Appendix

Scientific Notation

Scientific notation is a short way of representing very large and very small numbers without writing all of the place-holding zeros.

Example: Write 653,000,000 in scientific notation.

Step 1: Write the number without the place-holding zeros.

653

Step 2: Place the decimal point after the first digit.

6.53

Step 3: Find the exponent by counting the number of places that you moved the decimal point.

6.53000000

The decimal point was moved eight places to the left. Therefore, the exponent of 10 is positive 8. If you had moved the decimal point to the right, the exponent would be negative.

Step 4: Write the number in scientific notation.

$$6.53 \times 10^8$$

Area

Area is the number of square units needed to cover the surface of an object.

Formulas:

$area\ of\ a\ square = side \times side$
$area\ of\ a\ rectangle = length \times width$
$area\ of\ a\ triangle = \frac{1}{2} \times base \times height$

Examples: Find the areas.

Triangle
$area = \frac{1}{2} \times base \times height$
$area = \frac{1}{2} \times 3\ cm \times 4\ cm$
$area = \textbf{6 cm}^2$

Rectangle
$area = length \times width$
$area = 6\ cm \times 3\ cm$
$area = \textbf{18 cm}^2$

Square
$area = side \times side$
$area = 3\ cm \times 3\ cm$
$area = \textbf{9 cm}^2$

Volume

Volume is the amount of space that something occupies.

Formulas:

$volume\ of\ a\ cube =$
$side \times side \times side$

$volume\ of\ a\ prism =$
$area\ of\ base \times height$

Examples:

Find the volume of the solids.

Cube
$volume = side \times side \times side$
$volume = 4\ cm \times 4\ cm \times 4\ cm$
$volume = \textbf{64 cm}^3$

Prism
$volume = area\ of\ base \times height$
$volume = (area\ of\ triangle) \times height$
$volume = (\frac{1}{2} \times 3\ cm \times 4\ cm) \times 5\ cm$
$volume = 6\ cm^2 \times 5\ cm$
$volume = \textbf{30 cm}^3$

Physical Science Refresher

Atoms and Elements

Every object in the universe is made up of particles of some kind of matter. **Matter** is anything that takes up space and has mass. All matter is made up of elements. An **element** is a substance that cannot be separated into simpler components by ordinary chemical means. This is because each element consists of only one kind of atom. An **atom** is the smallest unit of an element that has all of the properties of that element.

Atomic Structure

Atoms are made up of small particles called subatomic particles. The three major types of subatomic particles are **electrons, protons,** and **neutrons.** Electrons have a negative electric charge, protons have a positive charge, and neutrons have no electric charge. The protons and neutrons are packed close to one another to form the **nucleus.** The protons give the nucleus a positive charge. Electrons are most likely to be found in regions around the nucleus called **electron clouds.** The negatively charged electrons are attracted to the positively charged nucleus. An atom may have several energy levels in which electrons are located.

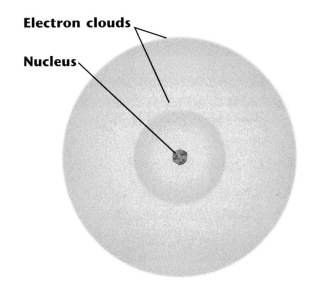

Electron clouds

Nucleus

Atomic Number

To help in the identification of elements, scientists have assigned an **atomic number** to each kind of atom. The atomic number is the number of protons in the atom. Atoms with the same number of protons are all the same kind of element. In an uncharged, or electrically neutral, atom there are an equal number of protons and electrons. Therefore, the atomic number equals the number of electrons in an uncharged atom. The number of neutrons, however, can vary for a given element. Atoms of the same element that have different numbers of neutrons are called **isotopes.**

Periodic Table of the Elements

In the periodic table, the elements are arranged from left to right in order of increasing atomic number. Each element in the table is in a separate box. An uncharged atom of each element has one more electron and one more proton than an uncharged atom of the element to its left. Each horizontal row of the table is called a **period.** Changes in chemical properties of elements across a period correspond to changes in the electron arrangements of their atoms. Each vertical column of the table, known as a **group,** lists elements with similar properties. The elements in a group have similar chemical properties because their atoms have the same number of electrons in their outer energy level. For example, the elements helium, neon, argon, krypton, xenon, and radon all have similar properties and are known as the noble gases.

Molecules and Compounds

When two or more elements are joined chemically, the resulting substance is called a **compound.** A compound is a new substance with properties different from those of the elements that compose it. For example, water, H_2O, is a compound formed when hydrogen (H) and oxygen (O) combine. The smallest complete unit of a compound that has the properties of that compound is called a **molecule.** A chemical formula indicates the elements in a compound. It also indicates the relative number of atoms of each element present. The chemical formula for water is H_2O, which indicates that each water molecule consists of two atoms of hydrogen and one atom of oxygen. The subscript number after the symbol for an element indicates how many atoms of that element are in a single molecule of the compound.

Acids, Bases, and pH

An ion is an atom or group of atoms that has an electric charge because it has lost or gained one or more electrons. When an acid, such as hydrochloric acid, HCl, is mixed with water, it separates into ions. An **acid** is a compound that produces hydrogen ions, H+, in water. The hydrogen ions then combine with a water molecule to form a hydronium ion, H_3O^+. A **base,** on the other hand, is a substance that produces hydroxide ions, OH^-, in water.

To determine whether a solution is acidic or basic, scientists use pH. The **pH** is a measure of the hydronium ion concentration in a solution. The pH scale ranges from 0 to 14. The middle point, pH = 7, is neutral, neither acidic nor basic. Acids have a pH less than 7; bases have a pH greater than 7. The lower the number is, the more acidic the solution. The higher the number is, the more basic the solution.

Chemical Equations

A chemical reaction occurs when a chemical change takes place. (In a chemical change, new substances with new properties are formed.) A chemical equation is a useful way of describing a chemical reaction by means of chemical formulas. The equation indicates what substances react and what the products are. For example, when carbon and oxygen combine, they can form carbon dioxide. The equation for the reaction is as follows: $C + O_2 \rightarrow CO_2$.

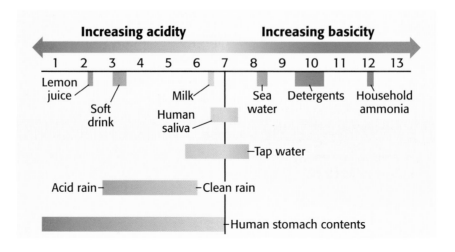

Physical Science Laws and Principles

Law of Conservation of Energy

The law of conservation of energy states that energy can be neither created nor destroyed.

The total amount of energy in a closed system is always the same. Energy can be changed from one form to another, but all of the different forms of energy in a system always add up to the same total amount of energy no matter how many energy conversions occur.

Law of Universal Gravitation

The law of universal gravitation states that all objects in the universe attract each other by a force called *gravity*. The size of the force depends on the masses of the objects and the distance between objects.

The first part of the law explains why a bowling ball is much harder to lift than a table-tennis ball. Because the bowling ball has a much larger mass than the table-tennis ball does, the amount of gravity between the Earth and the bowling ball is greater than the amount of gravity between the Earth and the table-tennis ball.

The second part of the law explains why a satellite can remain in orbit around the Earth. The satellite is carefully placed at a distance great enough to prevent the Earth's gravity from immediately pulling the satellite down but small enough to prevent the satellite from completely escaping the Earth's gravity and wandering off into space.

Newton's Laws of Motion

Newton's first law of motion states that an object at rest remains at rest and an object in motion remains in motion at constant speed and in a straight line unless acted on by an unbalanced force.

The first part of the law explains why a football will remain on a tee until it is kicked off or until a gust of wind blows it off.

The second part of the law explains why a bike rider will continue moving forward after the bike comes to an abrupt stop. Gravity and the friction of the sidewalk will eventually stop the rider.

Newton's second law of motion states that the acceleration of an object depends on the mass of the object and the amount of force applied.

The first part of the law explains why the acceleration of a 4 kg bowling ball will be greater than the acceleration of a 6 kg bowling ball if the same force is applied to both.

The second part of the law explains why the acceleration of a bowling ball will be larger if a larger force is applied to the bowling ball.

The relationship of acceleration (*a*) to mass (*m*) and force (*F*) can be expressed mathematically by the following equation:

$$acceleration = \frac{force}{mass}, \text{ or } a = \frac{F}{m}$$

This equation is often rearranged to the form

$$force = mass \times acceleration$$
$$or$$
$$F = m \times a$$

Newton's third law of motion states that whenever one object exerts a force on a second object, the second object exerts an equal and opposite force on the first.

This law explains that a runner is able to move forward because of the equal and opposite force that the ground exerts on the runner's foot after each step.

Law of Reflection

The law of reflection states that the angle of incidence is equal to the angle of reflection. This law explains why light reflects off a surface at the same angle that the light strikes the surface.

The beam of light traveling toward the mirror is called the *incident beam.*

The angle between the incident beam and the normal is called the *angle of incidence.*

A line perpendicular to the mirror's surface is called the *normal.*

The beam of light reflected off the mirror is called the *reflected beam.*

The angle between the reflected beam and the normal is called the *angle of reflection.*

Charles's Law

Charles's law states that for a fixed amount of gas at a constant pressure, the volume of the gas increases as the temperature of the gas increases. Likewise, the volume of the gas decreases as the temperature of the gas decreases.

If a basketball that was inflated indoors is left outside on a cold winter day, the air particles inside the ball will move more slowly. They will hit the sides of the basketball less often and with less force. The ball will get smaller as the volume of the air decreases.

Boyle's Law

Boyle's law states that for a fixed amount of gas at a constant temperature, the volume of a gas increases as the pressure of the gas decreases. Likewise, the volume of a gas decreases as its pressure increases.

If an inflated balloon is pulled down to the bottom of a swimming pool, the pressure of the water on the balloon increases. The pressure of the air particles inside the balloon must increase to match that of the water outside, so the volume of the air inside the balloon decreases.

Pascal's Principle

Pascal's principle states that a change in pressure at any point in an enclosed fluid will be transmitted equally to all parts of that fluid.

When a mechanic uses a hydraulic jack to raise an automobile off the ground, he or she increases the pressure on the fluid in the jack by pushing on the jack handle. The pressure is transmitted equally to all parts of the fluid-filled jacking system. As fluid presses the jack plate against the frame of the car, the car is lifed off the ground.

Archimedes' Principle

Archimedes' principle states that the buoyant force on an object in a fluid is equal to the weight of the volume of fluid that the object displaces.

A person floating in a swimming pool displaces 20 L of water. The weight of that volume of water is about 200 N. Therefore, the buoyant force on the person is 200 N.

Bernoulli's Principle

Bernoulli's principle states that as the speed of a moving fluid increases, the fluid's pressure decreases.

The lift on an airplane wing or on a Frisbee® can be explained in part by using Bernoulli's principle. Because of the shape of the Frisbee, the air moving over the top of the Frisbee must travel farther than the air below the Frisbee in the same amount of time. In other words, the air above the Frisbee is moving faster than the air below it. This faster-moving air above the Frisbee exerts less pressure than the slower-moving air below it does. The resulting increased pressure below exerts an upward force and pushes the Frisbee up.

Useful Equations

Average speed

$$average\ speed = \frac{total\ distance}{total\ time}$$

Example: A bicycle messenger traveled a distance of 136 km in 8 h. What was the messenger's average speed?

$$\frac{136\ km}{8\ h} = 17\ km/h$$

The messenger's average speed was **17 km/h.**

Average acceleration

$$\frac{average}{acceleration} = \frac{final\ velocity - starting\ velocity}{time\ it\ takes\ to\ change\ velocity}$$

Example: Calculate the average acceleration of an Olympic 100 m dash sprinter who reaches a velocity of 20 m/s south at the finish line. The race was in a straight line and lasted 10 s.

$$\frac{20\ m/s - 0\ m/s}{10s} = 2\ m/s/s$$

The sprinter's average acceleration is **2 m/s/s south.**

Net force

Forces in the Same Direction
When forces are in the same direction, add the forces together to determine the net force.

Example: Calculate the net force on a stalled car that is being pushed by two people. One person is pushing with a force of 13 N northwest, and the other person is pushing with a force of 8 N in the same direction.

$$13\ N + 8\ N = 21\ N$$

The net force is **21 N northwest.**

Forces in Opposite Directions
When forces are in opposite directions, subtract the smaller force from the larger force to determine the net force. The net force will be in the direction of the larger force.

Example: Calculate the net force on a rope that is being pulled on each end. One person is pulling on one end of the rope with a force of 12 N south. Another person is pulling on the opposite end of the rope with a force of 7 N north.

$$12\ N - 7\ N = 5\ N$$

The net force is **5 N south.**

Work

Work is done by exerting a force through a distance. Work has units of joules (J), which are equivalent to Newton-meters.

$$Work = F \times d$$

Example: Calculate the amount of work done by a man who lifts a 100 N toddler 1.5 m off the floor.

$Work = 100 \text{ N} \times 1.5 \text{ m} = 150 \text{ N}\bullet\text{m} = 150 \text{ J}$

The man did **150 J** of work.

Power

Power is the rate at which work is done. Power is measured in watts (W), which are equivalent to joules per second.

$$P = \frac{Work}{t}$$

Example: Calculate the power of a weightlifter who raises a 300 N barbell 2.1 m off the floor in 1.25 s.

$Work = 300 \text{ N} \times 2.1 \text{ m} = 630 \text{ N}\bullet\text{m} = 630 \text{ J}$

$P = \frac{630 \text{ J}}{1.25 \text{ s}} = \frac{504 \text{ J}}{\text{s}} = 504 \text{ W}$

The weightlifter has **504 W** of power.

Pressure

Pressure is the force exerted over a given area. The SI unit for pressure is the pascal (Pa).

$$pressure = \frac{force}{area}$$

Example: Calculate the pressure of the air in a soccer ball if the air exerts a force of 25,000 N over an area of 0.15 m².

$pressure = \frac{25,000 \text{ N}}{0.15 \text{ m}^2} = \frac{167,000 \text{ N}}{\text{m}^2} = 167,000 \text{ Pa}$

The pressure of the air inside the soccer ball is **167,000 Pa.**

Density

$$density = \frac{mass}{volume}$$

Example: Calculate the density of a sponge that has a mass of 10 g and a volume of 40 cm³.

$\frac{10 \text{ g}}{40 \text{ cm}^3} = \frac{0.25 \text{ g}}{\text{cm}^3}$

The density of the sponge is $\frac{0.25 \text{ g}}{\text{cm}^3}$.

Concentration

$$concentration = \frac{mass \ of \ solute}{volume \ of \ solvent}$$

Example: Calculate the concentration of a solution in which 10 g of sugar is dissolved in 125 mL of water.

$\frac{10 \text{ g of sugar}}{125 \text{ mL of water}} = \frac{0.08 \text{ g}}{\text{mL}}$

The concentration of this solution is $\frac{0.08 \text{ g}}{\text{mL}}$.

Glossary

A

acceleration (ak SEL uhr AY shuhn) the rate at which velocity changes over time; an object accelerates if its speed, direction, or both change (461)

acid precipitation rain, sleet, or snow that contains a high concentration of acids (59)

active transport the movement of substances across the cell membrane that requires the cell to use energy (384)

addiction a dependence on a substance, such as alcohol or drugs (308)

aerobic exercise physical exercise intended to increase the activity of the heart and lungs to promote the body's use of oxygen (315)

air mass a large body of air where temperature and moisture content are similar throughout (84)

air pollution the contamination of the atmosphere by the introduction of pollutants from human and natural sources (56)

air pressure the measure of the force with which air molecules push on a surface (41)

alcoholism a disorder in which a person repeatedly drinks alcoholic beverages in an amount that interferes with the person's health and activities (310)

allele (uh LEEL) one of the alternative forms of a gene that governs a characteristic, such as hair color (410)

allergy a reaction to a harmless or common substance by the body's immune system (289)

alveoli (al VEE uh LIE) any of the tiny air sacs of the lungs where oxygen and carbon dioxide are exchanged (191)

anemometer an instrument used to measure wind speed (99)

antibody a protein made by B cells that binds to a specific antigen (285)

anticyclone the rotation of air around a high-pressure center in the direction opposite to Earth's rotation (88)

Archimedes' principle (AHR kuh MEE DEEZ PRIN suh puhl) the principle that states that the buoyant force on an object in a fluid is an upward force equal to the weight of the volume of fluid that the object displaces (530)

area a measure of the size of a surface or a region (24)

artery a blood vessel that carries blood away from the heart to the body's organs (178)

asexual reproduction reproduction that does not involve the union of sex cells and in which a single parent produces offspring that are genetically identical to the parent (254, 334)

atmosphere a mixture of gases that surrounds a planet or moon (40)

atmospheric pressure the pressure caused by the weight of the atmosphere (525)

ATP **a**denosine **trip**hosphate, a molecule that acts as the main energy source for cell processes (340)

autoimmune disease a disease in which the immune system attacks the organism's own cells (289)

B

barometer an instrument that measures atmospheric pressure (99)

B cell a white blood cell that makes antibodies (285)

Bernoulli's principle (ber NOO leez PRIN suh puhl) the principle that states that the pressure in a fluid decreases as the fluid's velocity increases (536)

biome a large region characterized by a specific type of climate and certain types of plant and animal communities (118)

blood the fluid that carries gases, nutrients, and wastes through the body and that is made up of platelets, white blood cells, red blood cells, and plasma (182)

blood pressure the force that blood exerts on the walls of the arteries (184)

brain the mass of nerve tissue that is the main control center of the nervous system (230)

bronchus (BRAHNG kuhs) one of the two tubes that connect the lungs with the trachea (191)

buoyant force (BOY uhnt FAWRS) the upward force that keeps an object immersed in or floating on a liquid (530)

C

cancer a tumor in which the cells begin dividing at an uncontrolled rate and become invasive (290)

capillary a tiny blood vessel that allows an exchange between blood and cells in tissue (178)

carbohydrate a class of energy-giving nutrients that includes sugars, starches, and fiber; contains carbon, hydrogen, and oxygen (302, 339)

cardiovascular system a collection of organs that transport blood throughout the body (176)

cell in biology, the smallest unit that can perform all life processes; cells are covered by a membrane and contain DNA and cytoplasm (332, 352)

cell cycle the life cycle of a cell (390)

cell membrane a phospholipid layer that covers a cell's surface and acts as a barrier between the inside of a cell and the cell's environment (355)

cellular respiration the process by which cells use oxygen to produce energy from food (387)

cell wall a rigid structure that surrounds the cell membrane and provides support to the cell (360)

central nervous system the brain and the spinal cord; its main function is to control the flow of information in the body (226)

chromosome in a eukaryotic cell, one of the structures in the nucleus that are made up of DNA and protein; in a prokaryotic cell, the main ring of DNA (390)

climate the average weather conditions in an area over a long period of time (112)

cloud a collection of small water droplets or ice crystals suspended in the air, which forms when the air is cooled and condensation occurs (80)

cochlea (KAHK lee uh) a coiled tube that is found in the inner ear and that is essential to hearing (238)

compound machine a machine made of more than one simple machine (570)

condensation the change of state from a gas to a liquid (79)

consumer an organism that eats other organisms or organic matter (337)

controlled experiment an experiment that tests only one factor at a time by using a comparison of a control group with an experimental group (14)

convection the transfer of thermal energy by the circulation or movement of a liquid or gas (47)

Coriolis effect the apparent curving of the path of a moving object from an otherwise straight path due to the Earth's rotation (52)

cyclone an area in the atmosphere that has lower pressure than the surrounding areas and has winds that spiral toward the center (88)

cytokinesis the division of the cytoplasm of a cell (392)

D

decomposer an organism that gets energy by breaking down the remains of dead organisms or animal wastes and consuming or absorbing the nutrients (337)

density the ratio of the mass of a substance to the volume of a substance (26)

dermis the layer of skin below the epidermis (163)

diffusion (di FYOO zhuhn) the movement of particles from regions of higher density to regions of lower density (382)

digestive system the organs that break down food so that it can be used by the body (204)

DNA deoxyribonucleic acid, a molecule that is present in all living cells and that contains the information that determines the traits that a living thing inherits and needs to live (434)

dominant trait the trait observed in the first generation when parents that have different traits are bred (407)

drag a force parallel to the velocity of the flow; it opposes the direction of an aircraft and, in combination with thrust, determines the speed of the aircraft (539)

drug any substance that causes a change in a person's physical or psychological state (308)

E

egg a sex cell produced by a female (255)

elevation the height of an object above sea level (116)

embryo (EM bree OH) a developing human, from fertilization through the first 8 weeks of development (the 10th week of pregnancy) (262)

endocrine system a collection of glands and groups of cells that secrete hormones that regulate growth, development, and homeostasis; includes the pituitary, thyroid, parathyroid, and adrenal glands, the hypothalamus, the pineal body, and the gonads (240)

endocytosis (EN doh sie TOH sis) the process by which a cell membrane surrounds a particle and encloses the particle in a vesicle to bring the particle into the cell (384)

endoplasmic reticulum (EN doh PLAZ mik ri TIK yuh luhm) a system of membranes that is found in a cell's cytoplasm and that assists in the production, processing, and transport of proteins and in the production of lipids (363)

epidermis (EP uh DUHR mis) the surface layer of cells on a plant or animal (163)

esophagus (i SAHF uh guhs) a long, straight tube that connects the pharynx to the stomach (206)

eukaryote an organism made up of cells that have a nucleus enclosed by a membrane; eukaryotes include animals, plants, and fungi but not archaebacteria or eubacteria (358)

exocytosis (EK soh sie TOH sis) the process in which a cell releases a particle by enclosing the particle in a vesicle that then moves to the cell surface and fuses with the cell membrane (385)

external fertilization the union of sex cells outside the bodies of the parents (256)

F

fat an energy-storage nutrient that helps the body store some vitamins (303)

feedback mechanism a cycle of events in which information from one step controls or affects a previous step (235)

fermentation the breakdown of food without the use of oxygen (387)

fetus (FEET uhs) a developing human from seven or eight weeks after fertilization until birth (264)

fluid a nonsolid state of matter in which the atoms or molecules are free to move past each other, as in a gas or liquid (524)

force a push or a pull exerted on an object in order to change the motion of the object; force has size and direction (464)

free fall the motion of a body when only the force of gravity is acting on the body (497)

friction a force that opposes motion between two surfaces that are in contact (470)

front the boundary between air masses of different densities and usually different temperatures (86)

function the special, normal, or proper activity of an organ or part (371)

G

gallbladder a sac-shaped organ that stores bile produced by the liver (209)

gene one set of instructions for an inherited trait (410)

genotype the entire genetic makeup of an organism; also the combination of genes for one or more specific traits (411)

gland a group of cells that make special chemicals for the body (240)

global warming a gradual increase in average global temperature (49, 134)

Golgi complex (GOHL jee KAHM PLEKS) cell organelle that helps make and package materials to be transported out of the cell (365)

gravity a force of attraction between objects that is due to their masses (476)

greenhouse effect the warming of the surface and lower atmosphere of Earth that occurs when water vapor, carbon dioxide, and other gases absorb and reradiate thermal energy (48, 134)

H

heredity the passing of genetic traits from parent to offspring (334, 404)

homeostasis (HOH mee OH STAY sis) the maintenance of a constant internal state in a changing environment (148, 333)

homologous chromosomes (hoh MAHL uh guhs KROH muh SOHMZ) chromosomes that have the same sequence of genes and the same structure (391, 416)

hormone a substance that is made in one cell or tissue and that causes a change in another cell or tissue in a different part of the body (240)

humidity the amount of water vapor in the air (77)

hurricane a severe storm that develops over tropical oceans and whose strong winds of more than 120 km/h spiral in toward the intensely low-pressure storm center (93)

hygiene the science of health and ways to preserve health (314)

hypothesis (hie PAHTH uh sis) an explanation that is based on prior scientific research or observations and that can be tested (12)

I

ice age a long period of climate cooling during which ice sheets cover large areas of Earth's surface; also known as a *glacial period* (130)

immune system the cells and tissues that recognize and attack foreign substances in the body (285)

immunity the ability to resist an infectious disease (282)

inclined plane a simple machine that is a straight, slanted surface, which facilitates the raising of loads; a ramp (568)

inertia (in UHR shuh) the tendency of an object to resist being moved or, if the object is moving, to resist a change in speed or direction until an outside force acts on the object (504)

infectious disease a disease that is caused by a pathogen and that can be spread from one individual to another (280)

integumentary system (in TEG yoo MEN tuhr ee SIS tuhm) the organ system that forms a protective covering on the outside of the body (162, 234)

internal fertilization fertilization of an egg by sperm that occurs inside the body of a female (256)

J

jet stream a narrow belt of strong winds that blow in the upper troposphere (54)

joint a place where two or more bones meet (156)

joule the unit used to express energy; equivalent to the amount of work done by a force of 1 N acting through a distance of 1 m in the direction of the force (symbol, J) (555)

K

kidney one of the pair of organs that filter water and wastes from the blood and that excrete products as urine (213)

L

large intestine the wider and shorter portion of the intestine that removes water from mostly digested food and that turns the waste into semi-solid feces, or stool (210)

larynx (LAR ingks) the area of the throat that contains the vocal cords and produces vocal sounds (191)

latitude the distance north or south from the equator; expressed in degrees (113)

law a summary of many experimental results and observations; a law tells how things work (21)

lever a simple machine that consists of a bar that pivots at a fixed point called a *fulcrum* (564)

lift an upward force on an object that moves in a fluid (537)

lightning an electric discharge that takes place between two oppositely charged surfaces, such as between a cloud and the ground, between two clouds, or between two parts of the same cloud (91)

lipid a type of biochemical that does not dissolve in water; fats and steroids are lipids (340)

liver the largest organ in the body; it makes bile, stores and filters blood, and stores excess sugars as glycogen (209)

lymph the fluid that is collected by the lymphatic vessels and nodes (186)

lymphatic system (lim FAT ik SIS tuhm) a collection of organs whose primary function is to collect extracellular fluid and return it to the blood; the organs in this system include the lymph nodes and the lymphatic vessels (186)

lymph node an organ that filters lymph and that is found along the lymphatic vessels (187)

lysosome (LIE suh SOHM) a cell organelle that contains digestive enzymes (366)

M

machine a device that helps do work by either overcoming a force or changing the direction of the applied force (558)

macrophage (MAK roh FAYJ) an immune system cell that engulfs pathogens and other materials (285)

malnutrition a disorder of nutrition that results when a person does not consume enough of each of the nutrients that are needed by the human body (306)

mass a measure of the amount of matter in an object (25, 481)

mechanical advantage a number that tells how many times a machine multiplies force (561)

mechanical efficiency (muh KAN i kuhl e FISH uhn see) the ratio of output to input of energy or of power; it can be calculated by dividing work output by work input (562)

meiosis (mie OH sis) a process in cell division during which the number of chromosomes decreases to half the original number by two divisions of the nucleus, which results in the production of sex cells (gametes or spores) (417)

memory B cell a B cell that responds to an antigen more strongly when the body is reinfected with an antigen than it does during its first encounter with the antigen (288)

mesosphere the layer of the atmosphere between the stratosphere and the thermosphere and in which temperature decreases as altitude increases (43)

metabolism (muh TAB uh LIZ uhm) the sum of all chemical processes that occur in an organism (334)

meter the basic unit of length in the SI (symbol, m) (24)

microclimate the climate of a small area (128)

mineral a class of nutrients that are chemical elements that are needed for certain body processes (304)

mitochondrion (MIET oh KAHN dree uhn) in eukaryotic cells, the cell organelle that is surrounded by two membranes and that is the site of cellular respiration (364)

mitosis in eukaryotic cells, a process of cell division that forms two new nuclei, each of which has the same number of chromosomes (391)

model a pattern, plan, representation, or description designed to show the structure or workings of an object, system, or concept (18)

momentum (moh MEN tuhm) a quantity defined as the product of the mass and velocity of an object (510)

motion an object's change in position relative to a reference point (458)

muscular system the organ system whose primary function is movement and flexibility (158)

mutation a change in the nucleotide-base sequence of a gene or DNA molecule (442)

N

narcotic a drug that is derived from opium and that relieves pain and induces sleep; examples include heroine, morphine, and codeine (311)

nephron the unit in the kidney that filters blood (213)

nerve a collection of nerve fibers through which impulses travel between the central nervous system and other parts of the body (228)

net force the combination of all of the forces acting on an object (465)

neuron (NOO RAHN) a nerve cell that is specialized to receive and conduct electrical impulses (227)

newton the SI unit for force (symbol, N) (464)

nicotine (NIK uh TEEN) a toxic, addictive chemical that is found in tobacco and that is one of the major contributors to the harmful effects of smoking (310)

noninfectious disease a disease that cannot spread from one individual to another (280)

nucleic acid a molecule made up of subunits called *nucleotides* (341)

nucleotide in a nucleic-acid chain, a subunit that consists of a sugar, a phosphate, and a nitrogenous base (434)

nucleus in a eukaryotic cell, a membrane-bound organelle that contains the cell's DNA and that has a role in processes such as growth, metabolism, and reproduction (355)

nutrient a substance in food that provides energy or helps form body tissues and that is necessary for life and growth (302)

O

organ a collection of tissues that carry out a specialized function of the body (151, 369)

organelle one of the small bodies in a cell's cytoplasm that are specialized to perform a specific function (355)

organism a living thing; anything that can carry out life processes independently (370)

organ system a group of organs that work together to perform body functions (370)

osmosis (ahs MOH sis) the diffusion of water through a semipermeable membrane (383)

ovary in the female reproductive system of animals, an organ that produces eggs (259)

P

pancreas the organ that lies behind the stomach and that makes digestive enzymes and hormones that regulate sugar levels (208)

pascal the SI unit of pressure (symbol, Pa) (524)

Pascal's principle the principle that states that a fluid in equilibrium contained in a vessel exerts a pressure of equal intensity in all directions (540)

passive transport the movement of substances across a cell membrane without the use of energy by the cell (384)

pathogen a virus, microorganism, or other organism that causes disease (280)

pedigree a diagram that shows the occurrence of a genetic trait in several generations of a family (422)

penis the male organ that transfers sperm to a female and that carries urine out of the body (258)

peripheral nervous system (puh RIF uhr uhl NUHR vuhs SIS tuhm) all of the parts of the nervous system except for the brain and the spinal cord (226)

pharynx (FAR ingks) the passage from the mouth to the larynx and esophagus (191)

phenotype (FEE noh TIEP) an organism's appearance or other detectable characteristic (410)

phospholipid (FAHS foh LIP id) a lipid that contains phosphorus and that is a structural component in cell membranes (340)

photosynthesis (FOHT oh SIN thuh sis) the process by which plants, algae, and some bacteria use sunlight, carbon dioxide, and water to make food (386)

placenta (pluh SEN tuh) the partly fetal and partly maternal organ by which materials are exchanged between a fetus and the mother (263)

polar easterlies prevailing winds that blow from east to west between 60° and 90° latitude in both hemispheres (52)

polar zone the North or South Pole and the surrounding region (127)

power the rate at which work is done or energy is transformed (556)

precipitation any form of water that falls to the Earth's surface from the clouds (82)

pressure the amount of force exerted per unit area of a surface (524)

prevailing winds winds that blow mainly from one direction during a given period (115)

probability the likelihood that a possible future event will occur in any given instance of the event (412)

producer an organism that can make its own food by using energy from its surroundings (337)

projectile motion (proh JEK tuhl MOH shuhn) the curved path that an object follows when thrown, launched, or otherwise projected near the surface of Earth (499)

prokaryote (pro KAR ee OHT) an organism that consists of a single cell that does not have a nucleus (356)

protein a molecule that is made up of amino acids and that is needed to build and repair body structures and to regulate processes in the body (303, 338)

pulley a simple machine that consists of a wheel over which a rope, chain, or wire passes (566)

pulmonary circulation (PUL muh NER ee SUHR kyoo LAY shuhn) the flow of blood from the heart to the lungs and back to the heart through the pulmonary arteries, capillaries, and veins (179)

R

radiation the transfer of energy as electromagnetic waves (46)

recessive trait a trait that is apparent only when two recessive alleles for the same characteristic are inherited (407)

reflex an involuntary and almost immediate movement in response to a stimulus (235)

relative humidity the ratio of the amount of water vapor in the air to the maximum amount of water vapor the air can hold at a set temperature (77)

respiration in biology, the exchange of oxygen and carbon dioxide between living cells and their environment; includes breathing and cellular respiration (190)

respiratory system a collection of organs whose primary function is to take in oxygen and expel carbon dioxide; the organs of this system include the lungs, the throat, and the passageways that lead to the lungs (190)

retina the light-sensitive inner layer of the eye, which receives images formed by the lens and transmits them through the optic nerve to the brain (236)

ribosome a cell organelle composed of RNA and protein; the site of protein synthesis (363, 441)

RNA ribonucleic acid, a molecule that is present in all living cells and that plays a role in protein production (440)

S

science the knowledge obtained by observing natural events and conditions in order to discover facts and formulate laws or principles that can be verified or tested (4)

scientific methods a series of steps followed to solve problems (10)

screw a simple machine that consists of an inclined plane wrapped around a cylinder (569)

Glossary

sex chromosome one of the pair of chromosomes that determine the sex of an individual (421)

sexual reproduction reproduction in which the sex cells from two parents unite to produce offspring that share traits from both parents (255, 334)

skeletal system the organ system whose primary function is to support and protect the body and to allow the body to move (154)

small intestine the organ between the stomach and the large intestine where most of the breakdown of food happens and most of the nutrients from food are absorbed (208)

speed the distance traveled divided by the time interval during which the motion occurred (459)

sperm the male sex cell (255)

spleen the largest lymphatic organ in the body; serves as a blood reservoir, disintegrates old red blood cells, and produces lymphocytes and plasmids (188)

stimulus anything that causes a reaction or change in an organism or any part of an organism (333)

stomach the saclike, digestive organ between the esophagus and the small intestine that breaks down food by the action of muscles, enzymes, and acids (207)

stratosphere the layer of the atmosphere that is above the troposphere and in which temperature increases as altitude increases (43)

stress a physical or mental response to pressure (316)

structure the arrangement of parts in an organism (371)

surface current a horizontal movement of ocean water that is caused by wind and that occurs at or near the ocean's surface (117)

systemic circulation (sis TEM ik SUHR kyoo LAY shuhn) the flow of blood from the heart to all parts of the body and back to the heart (179)

T

T cell an immune system cell that coordinates the immune system and attacks many infected cells (285)

temperate zone the climate zone between the Tropics and the polar zone (124)

temperature a measure of how hot (or cold) something is; specifically, a measure of the average kinetic energy of the particles in an object (26)

terminal velocity the constant velocity of a falling object when the force of air resistance is equal in magnitude and opposite in direction to the force of gravity (496)

testes the primary male reproductive organs, which produce sperm cells and testosterone (singular, *testis*) (258)

theory an explanation that ties together many hypotheses and observations (20)

thermal conduction the transfer of as heat through a material (47)

thermometer an instrument that measures and indicates temperature (99)

thermosphere the uppermost layer of the atmosphere, in which temperature increases as altitude increases (44)

thrust the pushing or pulling force exerted by the engine of an aircraft or rocket (538)

thunder the sound caused by the rapid expansion of air along an electrical strike (91)

thunderstorm a usually brief, heavy storm that consists of rain, strong winds, lightning, and thunder (90)

thymus the main gland of the lymphatic system; it releases mature T lymphocytes (187)

tissue a group of similar cells that perform a common function (150, 369)

tonsils small, rounded masses of lymphatic tissue located in the pharynx and in the passage from the mouth to the pharynx (189)

tornado a destructive, rotating column of air that has very high wind speeds, is visible as a funnel-shaped cloud, and touches the ground (92)

trachea (TRAY kee uh) in insects, myriapods, and spiders, one of a network of air tubes; in vertebrates, the tube that connects the larynx to the lungs (191)

trade winds prevailing winds that blow from east to west from 30° latitude to the equator in both hemispheres (52)

tropical zone the region that surrounds the equator and that extends from about 23° north latitude to 23° south latitude (120)

troposphere the lowest layer of the atmosphere, in which temperature decreases at a constant rate as altitude increases (43)

Glossary

U

umbilical cord (uhm BIL i kuhl KAWRD) the structure that connects an embryo and then the fetus to the placenta and through which blood vessels pass (263)

urinary system the organs that make, store, and eliminate urine (212)

uterus in female mammals, the hollow, muscular organ in which a fertilized egg is embedded and in which the embryo and fetus develop (259)

V

vagina the female reproductive organ that connects the outside of the body to the uterus (259)

variable a factor that changes in an experiment in order to test a hypothesis (14)

vein in biology, a vessel that carries blood to the heart (178)

velocity (vuh LAHS uh tee) the speed of an object in a particular direction (460)

vesicle (VES i kuhl) a small cavity or sac that contains materials in a eukaryotic cell; forms when part of the cell membrane surrounds the materials to be taken into the cell or transported within the cell (365)

vitamin a class of nutrients that contain carbon and that are needed in small amounts to maintain health and allow growth (304)

volume a measure of the size of a body or region in three-dimensional space (25)

W

watt the unit used to express power; equivalent to joules per second (symbol, W) (556)

weather the short-term state of the atmosphere, including temperature, humidity, precipitation, wind, and visibility (76, 112)

wedge a simple machine that is made up of two inclined planes and that moves; often used for cutting (569)

weight a measure of the gravitational force exerted on an object; its value can change with the location of the object in the universe (481)

westerlies prevailing winds that blow from west to east between 30° and 60° latitude in both hemispheres (52)

wheel and axle a simple machine consisting of two circular objects of different sizes; the wheel is the larger of the two circular objects (567)

wind the movement of air caused by differences in air pressure (50)

work the transfer of energy to an object by using a force that causes the object to move in the direction of the force (552)

work input the work done on a machine; the product of the input force and the distance through which the force is exerted (559)

work output the work done by a machine; the product of the output force and the distance through which the force is exerted (559)

Spanish Glossary

A

acceleration/aceleración la tasa a la que la velocidad cambia con el tiempo; un objeto acelera si su rapidez cambia, si su dirección cambia, o si tanto su rapidez como su dirección cambian (461)

acid precipitation/precipitación ácida lluvia, aguanieve o nieve que contiene una alta concentración de ácidos (59)

active transport/transporte activo el movimiento de substancias a través de la membrana celular que requiere que la célula gaste energía (384)

addiction/adicción dependencia de substancia, tal como el alcohol u otra droga (308)

aerobic exercise/ejercicio aeróbico ejercicio físico cuyo objetivo es aumentar la actividad del corazón y los pulmones para hacer que el cuerpo use más oxígeno (315)

air mass/masa de aire un gran volumen de aire que tiene una temperatura y contenido de humedad similar en toda su extensión (84)

air pollution/contaminación del aire la contaminación de la atmósfera debido a la introducción de contaminantes provenientes de fuentes humanas y naturales (56)

air pressure/presión del aire la medida de la fuerza con la que las moléculas del aire empujan contra una superficie (41)

alcoholism/alcoholismo un trastorno en el cual una persona consume bebidas alcohólicas repetidamente en una cantidad tal que interfiere con su salud y sus actividades (310)

allele/alelo una de las formas alternativas de un gene que rige un carácter, como por ejemplo, el color del cabello (410)

allergy/alergia una reacción del sistema inmunológico del cuerpo a una substancia inofensiva o común (289)

alveoli/alveolo cualquiera de las diminutas bolsas de aire de los pulmones, en donde ocurre el intercambio de oxígeno y dióxido de carbono (191)

anemometer/anemómetro un instrumento que se usa para medir la rapidez del viento (99)

antibody/anticuerpo una proteína producida por las células B que se une a un antígeno específico (285)

anticyclone/anticiclón la rotación del aire alrededor de un centro de alta presión en dirección opuesta a la rotación de la Tierra (88)

Archimedes' principle/principio de Arquímedes el principio que establece que la fuerza flotante de un objeto que está en un fluido es una fuerza ascendente cuya magnitud es igual al peso del volumen del fluido que el objeto desplaza (530)

area/área una medida del tamaño de una superficie o región (24)

artery/arteria un vaso sanguíneo que transporta sangre del corazón a los órganos del cuerpo (178)

asexual reproduction/reproducción asexual reproducción que no involucra la unión de células sexuales, en la que un solo progenitor produce descendencia que es genéticamente igual al progenitor (254, 334)

atmosphere/atmósfera una mezcla de gases que rodea un planeta o una luna (40)

atmospheric pressure/presión atmosférica la presión producida por el peso de la atmósfera (525)

ATP/ATP adenosín trifosfato, una molécula orgánica que funciona como la fuente principal de energía para los procesos celulares (340)

autoimmune disease/enfermedad autoinmune una enfermedad en la que el sistema inmunológico ataca las células del propio organismo (289)

B

barometer/barómetro un instrumento que mide la presión atmosférica (99)

B cell/célula B un glóbulo blanco de la sangre que fabrica anticuerpos (285)

Bernoulli's principle/principio de Bernoulli el principio que establece que la presión de un fluido disminuye a medida que la velocidad del fluido aumenta (536)

biome/bioma una región extensa caracterizada por un tipo de clima específico y ciertos tipos de comunidades de plantas y animales (118)

blood/sangre el líquido que lleva gases, nutrientes y desechos por el cuerpo y que está formado por plaquetas, glóbulos blancos, glóbulos rojos y plasma (182)

blood pressure/presión sanguínea la fuerza que la sangre ejerce en las paredes de las arterias (184)

brain/encéfalo la masa de tejido nervioso que es el centro principal de control del sistema nervioso (230)

bronchus/bronquio uno de los dos tubos que conectan los pulmones con la tráquea (191)

buoyant force/fuerza boyante la fuerza ascendente que hace que un objeto se mantenga sumergido en un líquido o flotando en él (530)

C

cancer/cáncer un tumor en el cual las células comienzan a dividirse a una tasa incontrolable y se vuelven invasivas (290)

capillary/capilar diminuto vaso sanguíneo que permite el intercambio entre la sangre y las células de los tejidos (178)

carbohydrate/carbohidrato una clase de nutrientes que proporcionan energía; incluye los azúcares, los almidones y las fibras; contiene carbono, hidrógeno y oxígeno (302, 339)

cardiovascular system/aparato cardiovascular un conjunto de órganos que transportan la sangre a través del cuerpo (176)

cell/célula en biología, la unidad más pequeña que puede realizar todos los procesos vitales; las células están cubiertas por una membrana y tienen ADN y citoplasma (332, 352)

cell cycle/ciclo celular el ciclo de vida de una célula (390)

cell membrane/membrana celular una capa de fosfolípidos que cubre la superficie de la célula y funciona como una barrera entre el interior de la célula y el ambiente de la célula (355)

cellular respiration/respiración celular el proceso por medio del cual las células utilizan oxígeno para producir energía a partir de los alimentos (387)

cell wall/pared celular una estructura rígida que rodea la membrana celular y le brinda soporte a la célula (360)

central nervous system/sistema nervioso central el cerebro y la médula espinal; su principal función es controlar el flujo de información en el cuerpo (226)

chromosome/cromosoma en una célula eucariótica, una de las estructuras del núcleo que está hecha de ADN y proteína; en una célula procariótica, el anillo principal de ADN (390)

climate/clima las condiciones promedio del tiempo en un área durante un largo período de tiempo (112)

cloud/nube un conjunto de pequeñas gotitas de agua o cristales de hielo suspendidos en el aire, que se forma cuando el aire se enfría y ocurre condensación (80)

cochlea/cóclea un tubo enrollado que se encuentra en el oído interno y es esencial para poder oír (238)

compound machine/máquina compuesta una máquina hecha de más de una máquina simple (570)

condensation/condensación el cambio de estado de gas a líquido (79)

consumer/consumidor un organismo que se alimenta de otros organismos o de materia orgánica (337)

controlled experiment/experimento controlado un experimento que prueba sólo un factor a la vez, comparando un grupo de control con un grupo experimental (14)

convection/convección la transferencia de energía térmica mediante la circulación o el movimiento de un líquido o gas (47)

Coriolis effect/efecto de Coriolis la desviación aparente de la trayectoria recta que experimentan los objetos en movimiento debido a la rotación de la Tierra (52)

cyclone/ciclón un área de la atmósfera que tiene una presión menor que la de las áreas circundantes y que tiene vientos que giran en espiral hacia el centro (88)

cytokinesis/citoquinesis la división del citoplasma de una célula (392)

D

decomposer/descomponedor un organismo que, para obtener energía, desintegra los restos de organismos muertos o los desechos de animales y consume o absorbe los nutrientes (337)

density/densidad la relación entre la masa de una substancia y su volumen (26)

dermis/dermis la capa de piel que está debajo de la epidermis (163)

diffusion/difusión el movimiento de partículas de regiones de mayor densidad a regiones de menor densidad (382)

digestive system/aparato digestivo los órganos que descomponen la comida de modo que el cuerpo la pueda usar (204)

DNA/ADN ácido desoxirribonucleico, una molécula que está presente en todas las células vivas y que contiene la información que determina los caracteres que un ser vivo hereda y necesita para vivir (434)

dominant trait/carácter dominante el carácter que se observa en la primera generación cuando se cruzan progenitores que tienen caracteres diferentes (407)

drag/resistencia aerodinámica una fuerza paralela a la velocidad del flujo; se opone a la dirección de un avión y, en combinación con el empuje, determina la velocidad del avión (539)

drug/droga cualquier substancia que produce un cambio en el estado físico o psicológico de una persona (308)

E

egg/óvulo una célula sexual producida por una hembra (255)

elevation/elevación la altura de un objeto sobre el nivel del mar (116)

embryo/embrión un ser humano desde la fecundación hasta las primeras 8 semanas de desarrollo (décima semana del embarazo) (262)

endocrine system/sistema endocrino un conjunto de glándulas y grupos de células que secretan hormonas que regulan el crecimiento, el desarrollo y la homeostasis; incluye las glándulas pituitaria, tiroides, paratiroides y suprarrenal, el hipotálamo, el cuerpo pineal y las gónadas (240)

endocytosis/endocitosis el proceso por medio del cual la membrana celular rodea una partícula y la encierra en una vesícula para llevarla al interior de la célula (384)

endoplasmic reticulum/retículo endoplásmico un sistema de membranas que se encuentra en el citoplasma de la célula y que tiene una función en la producción, procesamiento y transporte de proteínas y en la producción de lípidos (363)

epidermis/epidermis la superficie externa de las células de una planta o animal (163)

esophagus/esófago un conducto largo y recto que conecta la faringe con el estómago (206)

eukaryote/eucariote un organismo cuyas células tienen un núcleo rodeado por una membrana; entre los eucariotes se encuentran los animales, las plantas y los hongos, pero no las arqueobacterias ni las eubacterias (358)

exocytosis/exocitosis el proceso por medio del cual una célula libera una partícula encerrándola en una vesícula que luego se traslada a la superficie de la célula y se fusiona con la membrana celular (385)

external fertilization/fecundación externa la unión de células sexuales fuera del cuerpo de los progenitores (256)

F

fat/grasa un nutriente que almacena energía y ayuda al cuerpo a almacenar algunas vitaminas (303)

feedback mechanism/mecanismo de retroalimentación un ciclo de sucesos en el que la información de una etapa controla o afecta a una etapa anterior (235)

fermentation/fermentación la descomposición de los alimentos sin utilizar oxígeno (387)

fetus/feto un ser humano en desarrollo de las semanas siete a ocho después de la fecundación hasta el nacimiento (264)

fluid/fluido un estado no sólido de la materia en el que los átomos o moléculas tienen libertad de movimiento, como en el caso de un gas o un líquido (524)

force/fuerza una acción de empuje o atracción que se ejerce sobre un objeto con el fin de cambiar su movimiento; la fuerza tiene magnitud y dirección (464)

free fall/caída libre el movimiento de un cuerpo cuando la única fuerza que actúa sobre él es la fuerza de gravedad (497)

friction/fricción una fuerza que se opone al movimiento entre dos superficies que están en contacto (470)

front/frente el límite entre masas de aire de diferentes desidades y, normalmente, diferentes temperaturas (86)

function/función la actividad especial, normal o adecuada de un órgano o parte (371)

G

gallbladder/vesícula biliar un órgano que tiene la forma de una bolsa y que almacena la bilis producida por el hígado (209)

gene/gene un conjunto de instrucciones para un carácter heredado (410)

genotype/genotipo la constitución genética completa de un organismo; *también* la combinación genes para uno o más caracteres específicos (411)

gland/glándula un grupo de células que elaboran ciertas substancias químicas para el cuerpo (240)

global warming/calentamiento global un aumento gradual de la temperatura global promedio (49, 134)

Golgi complex/aparato de Golgi un organelo celular que ayuda a hacer y a empacar los materiales que serán transportados al exterior de la célula (365)

gravity/gravedad una fuerza de atracción entre dos objetos debido a sus masas (476)

greenhouse effect/efecto de invernadero el calentamiento de la superficie y de la parte más baja de la atmósfera, el cual se produce cuando el vapor de agua, el dióxido de carbono y otros gases absorben y vuelven a irradiar la energía térmica (48, 134)

H

heredity/herencia la transmisión de caracteres genéticos de padres a hijos (334, 404)

homeostasis/homeostasis la capacidad de mantener un estado interno constante en un ambiente en cambio (148, 333)

homologous chromosomes/cromosomas homólogos cromosomas con la misma secuencia de genes y la misma estructura (391, 416)

hormone/hormona una substancia que es producida en una célula o tejido, la cual causa un cambio en otra célula o tejido ubicado en una parte diferente del cuerpo (240)

humidity/humedad la cantidad de vapor de agua que hay en el aire (77)

hurricane/huracán tormenta severa que se desarrolla sobre océanos tropicales, con vientos fuertes que soplan a más de 120 km/h y que se mueven en espiral hacia el centro de presión extremadamente baja de la tormenta (93)

hygiene/higiene la ciencia de la salud y las formas de preservar la salud (314)

hypothesis/hipótesis una explicación que se basa en observaciones o investigaciones científicas previas y que se puede probar (12)

I

ice age/edad de hielo un largo período de tiempo frío durante el cual grandes áreas de la superficie terrestre están cubiertas por capas de hielo; también conocido como período glacial (130)

immune system/sistema inmunológico las células y tejidos que reconocen y atacan substancias extrañas en el cuerpo (285)

immunity/inmunidad la capacidad de resistir una enfermedad infecciosa (282)

inclined plane/plano inclinado una máquina simple que es una superficie recta e inclinada, que facilita el levantamiento de cargas; una rampa (568)

inertia/inercia la tendencia de un objeto a no moverse o, si el objeto se está moviendo, la tendencia a resistir un cambio en su rapidez o dirección hasta que una fuerza externa actúe en el objeto (504)

infectious disease/enfermedad infecciosa una enfermedad que es causada por un patógeno y que puede transmitirse de un individuo a otro (280)

integumentary system/sistema integumentario el sistema de órganos que forma una cubierta de protección en la parte exterior del cuerpo (162, 234)

internal fertilization/fecundación interna fecundación de un óvulo por un espermatozoide, la cual ocurre dentro del cuerpo de la hembra (256)

J

jet stream/corriente en chorro un cinturón delgado de vientos fuertes que soplan en la parte superior de la troposfera (54)

joint/articulación un lugar donde se unen dos o más huesos (156)

joule/joule la unidad que se usa para expresar energía; equivale a la cantidad de trabajo realizada por una fuerza de 1 N que actúa a través de una distancia de 1 m en la dirección de la fuerza (símbolo: J) (555)

K

kidney/riñón uno de los dos órganos que filtran el agua y los desechos de la sangre y excretan productos en fomra de orina (213)

Spanish Glossary

668 Spanish Glossary

L

large intestine/intestino grueso la porción más ancha y más corta del intestino, que elimina el agua de los alimentos casi totalmente digeridos y convierte los desechos en heces semisólidas o excremento (210)

larynx/laringe el área de la garganta que contiene las cuerdas vocales y que produce sonidos vocales (191)

latitude/latitud la distancia hacia el norte o hacia el sur del ecuador; se expresa en grados (113)

law/ley un resumen de muchos resultados y observaciones experimentales; una ley dice cómo funcionan las cosas (21)

lever/palanca una máquina simple formada por una barra que gira en un punto fijo llamado *fulcro* (564)

lift/propulsión una fuerza hacia arriba en un objeto que se mueve en un fluido (537)

lightning/relámpago una descarga eléctrica que ocurre entre dos superficies que tienen carga opuesta, como por ejemplo, entre una nube y el suelo, entre dos nubes o entres dos partes de la misma nube (91)

lipid/lípido un tipo de substancia bioquímica que no se disuelve en agua; las grasas y los esteroides son lípidos (340)

liver/hígado el órgano más grande del cuerpo; produce bilis, almacena y filtra la sangre, y almacena el exceso de azúcares en forma de glucógeno (209)

lymph/linfa el fluido que es recolectado por los vasos y nodos linfáticos (186)

lymphatic system/sistema linfático un conjunto de órganos cuya función principal es recolectar el fluido extracelular y regresarlo a la sangre; los órganos de este sistema incluyen los nodos linfáticos y los vasos linfáticos (186)

lymph node/nodo linfático un órgano que filtra la linfa y que se encuentra a lo largo de los vasos linfáticos (187)

lysosome/lisosoma un organelo celular que contiene enzimas digestivas (366)

M

machine/máquina un aparato que ayuda a realizar un trabajo, ya sea venciendo una fuerza o cambiando la dirección de la fuerza aplicada (558)

macrophage/macrófago una célula del sistema inmunológico que envuelve a los patógenos y otros materiales (285)

malnutrition/desnutrición un trastorno de nutrición que resulta cuando una persona no consume una cantidad suficiente de cada nutriente que el cuerpo humano necesita (306)

mass/masa una medida de la cantidad de materia que tiene un objeto (25, 481)

mechanical advantage/ventaja mecánica un número que dice cuántas veces una máquina multiplica una fuerza (561)

mechanical efficiency/eficiencia mecánica la relación entre la entrada y la salida de energía o potencia; se calcula dividiendo la salida de trabajo por la entrada de trabajo (562)

meiosis/meiosis un proceso de división celular durante el cual el número de cromosomas disminuye a la mitad del número original por medio de dos divisiones del núcleo, lo cual resulta en la producción de células sexuales (gametos o esporas) (417)

memory B cell/célula B de memoria una célula B que responde con mayor eficacia a un antígeno cuando el cuerpo vuelve a infectarse con él que cuando lo encuentra por primera vez (288)

mesosphere/mesosfera la capa de la atmósfera que se encuentra entre la estratosfera y la termosfera, en la cual la temperatura disminuye al aumentar la altitud (43)

metabolism/metabolismo la suma de todos los procesos químicos que ocurren en un organismo (334)

meter/metro la unidad fundamental de longitud en el sistema internacional de unidades (símbolo: m) (24)

microclimate/microclima el clima de un área pequeña (128)

mineral/mineral una clase de nutrientes que son elementos químicos necesarios para ciertos procesos del cuerpo (304)

mitochondrion/mitocondria en las células eucarióticas, el organelo celular rodeado por dos membranas que es el lugar donde se lleva a cabo la respiración celular (364)

mitosis/mitosis en las células eucarióticas, un proceso de división celular que forma dos núcleos nuevos, cada uno de los cuales posee el mismo número de cromosomas (391)

model/modelo un diseño, plan, representación o descripción cuyo objetivo es mostrar la estructura o funcionamiento de un objeto, sistema o concepto (18)

momentum/momento una cantidad que se define como el producto de la masa de un objeto por su velocidad (510)

motion/movimiento el cambio en la posición de un objeto respecto a un punto de referencia (458)

muscular system/sistema muscular el sistema de órganos cuya función principal es permitir el movimiento y la flexibilidad (158)

mutation/mutación un cambio en la secuencia de la base de nucleótidos de un gene o de una molécula de ADN (442)

N

narcotic/narcótico una droga que proviene del opio, la cual alivia el dolor e induce el sueño; entre los ejemplos se encuentran la heroína, morfina y codeína (311)

nephron/nefrona la unidad del riñón que filtra la sangre (213)

nerve/nervio un conjunto de fibras nerviosas a través de las cuales se desplazan los impulsos entre el sistema nervioso central y otras partes del cuerpo (228)

net force/fuerza neta la combinación de todas las fuerzas que actúan sobre un objeto (465)

neuron/neurona una célula nerviosa que está especializada en recibir y transmitir impulsos eléctricos (227)

newton/newton la unidad de fuerza del sistema internacional de unidades (símbolo: N) (464)

nicotine/nicotina una substancia química tóxica y adictiva que se encuentra en el tabaco y que es una de las principales causas de los efectos dañinos de fumar (310)

noninfectious disease/enfermedad no infecciosa una enfermedad que no se contagia de una persona a otra (280)

nucleic acid/ácido nucleico una molécula formada por subunidades llamadas *nucleótidos* (341)

nucleotide/nucleótido en una cadena de ácidos nucleicos, una subunidad formada por un azúcar, un fosfato y una base nitrogenada (434)

nucleus/núcleo en una célula eucariótica, un organelo cubierto por una membrana, el cual contiene el ADN de la célula y participa en procesos tales como el crecimiento, metabolismo y reproducción (355)

nutrient/nutriente una substancia de los alimentos que proporciona energía o ayuda a formar tejidos corporales y que es necesaria para la vida y el crecimiento (302)

O

organ/órgano un conjunto de tejidos que desempeñan una función especializada en el cuerpo (151, 369)

organelle/organelo uno de los cuerpos pequeños del citoplasma de una célula que están especializados para llevar a cabo una función específica (355)

organism/organismo un ser vivo; cualquier cosa que pueda llevar a cabo procesos vitales independientemente (370)

organ system/aparato (o sistema) de órganos un grupo de órganos que trabajan en conjunto para desempeñar funciones corporales (370)

osmosis/ósmosis la difusión del agua a través de una membrana semipermeable (383)

ovary/ovario en el aparato reproductor femenino de los animales, un órgano que produce óvulos (259)

P

pancreas/páncreas el órgano que se encuentra detrás del estómago y que produce las enzimas digestivas y las hormonas que regulan los niveles de azúcar (208)

pascal/pascal la unidad de presión del sistema internacional de unidades (símbolo: Pa) (524)

Pascal's principle/principio de Pascal el principio que establece que un fluido en equilibro que esté contenido en un recipiente ejerce una presión de igual intensidad en todas las direcciones (540)

passive transport/transporte pasivo el movimiento de substancias a través de una membrana celular sin que la célula tenga que usar energía (384)

pathogen/patógeno un virus, microorganismo u otra substancia que causa enfermedades (280)

pedigree/pedigrí un diagrama que muestra la incidencia de un carácter genético en varias generaciones de una familia (422)

Spanish Glossary

penis/pene el órgano masculino que transfiere espermatozoides a una hembra y que lleva la orina hacia el exterior del cuerpo (258)

peripheral nervous system/sistema nervioso periférico todas las partes del sistema nervioso, excepto el encéfalo y la médula espinal (226)

pharynx/faringe en los gusanos planos, el tubo muscular que va de la boca a la cavidad gastrovascular; en los animales que tienen tracto digestivo, el conducto que va de la boca a la laringe y al esófago (191)

phenotype/fenotipo la apariencia de un organismo u otra característica perceptible (410)

phospholipid/fosfolípido un lípido que contiene fósforo y que es un componente estructural de la membrana celular (340)

photosynthesis/fotosíntesis el proceso por medio del cual las plantas, las algas y algunas bacterias utilizan la luz solar, el dióxido de carbono y el agua para producir alimento (386)

placenta/placenta el órgano parcialmente fetal y parcialmente materno por medio del cual se intercambian materiales entre el feto y la madre (263)

polar easterlies/vientos polares del este vientos preponderantes que soplan de este a oeste entre los 60° y los 90° de latitud en ambos hemisferios (52)

polar zone/zona polar el Polo Norte y el Polo Sur y la región circundante (127)

power/potencia la tasa a la que se realiza un trabajo o a la que se transforma la energía (556)

precipitation/precipitación cualquier forma de agua que cae de las nubes a la superficie de la Tierra (82)

pressure/presión la cantidad de fuerza ejercida en una superficie por unidad de área (524)

prevailing winds/vientos prevalecientes vientos que soplan principalmente de una dirección durante un período de tiempo determinado (115)

probability/probabilidad la probabilidad de que ocurra un posible suceso futuro en cualquier caso dado del suceso (412)

producer/productor un organismo que puede elaborar sus propios alimentos utilizando la energía de su entorno (337)

projectile motion/movimiento proyectil la trayectoria curva que sigue un objeto cuando es aventado, lanzado o proyectado de cualquier otra manera cerca de la superficie de la Tierra (499)

prokaryote/procariote un organismo que está formado por una sola célula y que no tiene núcleo (356)

protein/proteína una molécula formada por aminoácidos que es necesaria para construir y reparar estructuras corporales y para regular procesos del cuerpo (303, 338)

pulley/polea una máquina simple formada por una rueda sobre la cual pasa una cuerda, cadena o cable (566)

pulmonary circulation/circulación pulmonar el flujo de sangre del corazón a los pulmones y de vuelta al corazón a través de las arterias, los capilares y las venas pulmonares (179)

R

radiation/radiación la transferencia de energía en forma de ondas electromagnéticas (46)

recessive trait/carácter recesivo un carácter que se hace aparente sólo cuando se heredan dos alelos recesivos de la misma característica (407)

reflex/reflejo un movimiento involuntario y prácticamente inmediato en respuesta a un estímulo (235)

relative humidity/humedad relativa la proporción de la cantidad de vapor de agua que hay en el aire respecto a la cantidad máxima de vapor de agua que el aire puede contener a una temperatura dada (77)

respiration/respiración en biología, el intercambio de oxígeno y dióxido de carbono entre células vivas y su ambiente; incluye la respiración y la respiración celular (190)

respiratory system/aparato respiratorio un conjunto de órganos cuya función principal es tomar oxígeno y expulsar dióxido de carbono; los órganos de este aparato incluyen a los pulmones, la garganta y las vías que llevan a los pulmones (190)

retina/retina la capa interna del ojo, sensible a la luz, que recibe imágenes formadas por el lente ocular y las transmite al cerebro por medio del nervio óptico (236)

ribosome/ribosoma un organelo celular compuesto de ARN y proteína; el sitio donde ocurre la síntesis de proteínas (363, 441)

RNA/ARN ácido ribonucleico, una molécula que está presente en todas las células vivas y que juega un papel en la producción de proteínas (440)

science/ciencia el conocimiento que se obtiene por medio de la observación natural de acontecimientos y condiciones con el fin de descubrir hechos y formular leyes o principios que puedan ser verificados o probados (4)

scientific methods/métodos científicos una serie de pasos que se siguen para solucionar problemas (10)

screw/tornillo una máquina simple formada por un plano inclinado enrollado a un cilindro (569)

sex chromosome/cromosoma sexual uno de los dos cromosomas que determinan el sexo de un individuo (421)

sexual reproduction/reproducción sexual reproducción en la que se unen las células sexuales de los dos progenitores para producir descendencia que comparte caracteres de ambos progenitores (255, 334)

skeletal system/sistema esquelético el sistema de órganos cuya función principal es sostener y proteger el cuerpo y permitir que se mueva (154)

small intestine/intestino delgado el órgano que se encuentra entre el estómago y el intestino grueso en el cual se produce la mayor parte de la descomposición de los alimentos y se absorben la mayoría de los nutrientes (208)

speed/rapidez la distancia que un objeto se desplaza dividida entre el intervalo de tiempo durante el cual ocurrió el movimiento (459)

sperm/espermatozoide la célula sexual masculina (255)

spleen/bazo el órgano linfático más grande del cuerpo; funciona como depósito para la sangre, desintegra los glóbulos rojos viejos y produce linfocitos y plásmidos (188)

stimulus/estímulo cualquier cosa que causa una reacción o cambio en un organismo o cualquier parte de un organismo (333)

stomach/estómago el órgano digestivo con forma de bolsa ubicado entre el esófago y el intestino delgado, que descompone los alimentos por la acción de músculos, enzimas y ácidos (207)

stratosphere/estratosfera la capa de la atmósfera que se encuentra encima de la troposfera y en la que la temperatura aumenta al aumentar la altitud (43)

stress/estrés una respuesta física o mental a la presión (316)

structure/estructura el orden y distribución de las partes de un organismo (371)

surface current/corriente superficial un movimiento horizontal del agua del océano que es producido por el viento y que ocurre en la superficie del océano o cerca de ella (117)

systemic circulation/circulación sistémica el flujo de sangre del corazón a todas las partes del cuerpo y de vuelta al corazón (179)

T cell/célula T una célula del sistema inmunológico que coordina el sistema inmunológico y ataca a muchas células infectadas (285)

temperate zone/zona templada la zona climática ubicada entre los trópicos y la zona polar (124)

temperature/temperatura una medida de qué tan caliente (o frío) está algo; específicamente, una medida de la energía cinética promedio de las partículas de un objeto (26)

terminal velocity/velocidad terminal la velocidad constante de un objeto en caída cuando la fuerza de resistencia del aire es igual en magnitud y opuesta en dirección a la fuerza de gravedad (496)

testes/testículos los principales órganos reproductores masculinos, los cuales producen espermatozoides y testosterona (258)

theory/teoría una explicación que relaciona muchas hipótesis y observaciones (20)

thermal conduction/conducción térmica la transferencia de energía en forma de calor a través de un material (47)

thermometer/termómetro un instrumento que mide e indica la temperatura (99)

thermosphere/termosfera la capa más alta de la atmósfera, en la cual la temperatura aumenta a medida que la altitud aumenta (44)

thrust/empuje la fuerza de empuje o arrastre ejercida por el motor de un avión o cohete (538)

thunder/trueno el sonido producido por la expansión rápida del aire a lo largo de una descarga eléctrica (91)

thunderstorm/tormenta eléctrica una tormenta fuerte y normalmente breve que consiste en lluvia, vientos fuertes, relámpagos y truenos (90)

thymus/timo la glándula principal del sistema linfático; libera linfocitos T maduros (187)

tissue/tejido un grupo de células similares que llevan a cabo una función común (150, 369)

tonsils/amígdalas masas pequeñas y redondas de tejido linfático, ubicadas en la faringe y en el paso de la boca a la faringe (189)

tornado/tornado una columna destructiva de aire en rotación cuyos vientos se mueven a velocidades muy altas; se ve como una nube con forma de embudo y toca el suelo (92)

trachea/tráquea en los insectos, miriápodos y arañas, uno de los conductos de una red de conductos de aire; en los vertebrados, el conducto que une la laringe con los pulmones (191)

trade winds/vientos alisios vientos prevalecientes que soplan de este a oeste desde los 30° de latitud hacia el ecuador en ambos hemisferios (52)

tropical zone/zona tropical la región que rodea el ecuador y se extiende desde aproximadamente 23° de latitud norte hasta 23° de latitud sur (120)

troposphere/troposfera la capa inferior de la atmósfera, en la que la temperatura disminuye a una tasa constante a medida que la altitud aumenta (43)

U

umbilical cord/cordón umbilical la estructura que une al embrión y después al feto con la placenta, a través de la cual pasan vasos sanguíneos (263)

urinary system/sistema urinario los órganos que producen, almacenan y eliminan la orina (212)

uterus/útero en los mamíferos hembras, el órgano hueco y muscular en el que se incrusta el óvulo fecundado y en el que se desarrollan el embrión y el feto (259)

V

vagina/vagina el órgano reproductivo femenino que conecta la parte exterior del cuerpo con el útero (259)

variable/variable un factor que se modifica en un experimento con el fin de probar una hipótesis (14)

vein/vena en biología, un vaso que lleva sangre al corazón (178)

velocity/velocidad la rapidez de un objeto en una dirección dada (460)

vesicle/vesícula una cavidad o bolsa pequeña que contiene materiales en una célula eucariótica; se forma cuando parte de la membrana celular rodea los materiales que van a ser llevados al interior la célula o transportados dentro de ella (365)

vitamin/vitamina una clase de nutrientes que contiene carbono y que es necesaria en pequeñas cantidades para mantener la salud y permitir el crecimiento (304)

volume/volumen una medida del tamaño de un cuerpo o región en un espacio de tres dimensiones (25)

W

watt/watt (o vatio) la unidad que se usa para expresar potencia; es equivalente a un joule por segundo (símbolo: W) (556)

weather/tiempo el estado de la atmósfera a corto plazo que incluye la temperatura, la humedad, la precipitación, el viento y la visibilidad (76, 112)

wedge/cuña una máquina simple que está formada por dos planos inclinados y que se mueve; normalmente se usa para cortar (569)

weight/peso una medida de la fuerza gravitacional ejercida sobre un objeto; su valor puede cambiar en función de la ubicación del objeto en el universo (481)

westerlies/vientos del oeste vientos preponderantes que soplan de oeste a este entre 30° y 60° de latitud en ambos hemisferios (52)

wheel and axle/eje y rueda una máquina simple que está formada por dos objetos circulares de diferente tamaño; la rueda es el mayor de los dos objetos circulares (567)

wind/viento el movimiento de aire producido por diferencias en la presión barométrica (50)

work/trabajo la transferencia de energía a un objeto mediante una fuerza que hace que el objeto se mueva en la dirección de la fuerza (552)

work input/trabajo de entrada el trabajo realizado en una máquina; el producto de la fuerza de entrada por la distancia a través de la que se ejerce la fuerza (559)

work output/trabajo producido el trabajo realizado por una máquina; el producto de la fuerza de salida por la distancia a través de la que se ejerce la fuerza (559)

Index

Index

Index

Index

Index

Index

Index

Index

Acknowledgments
continued from page ii

Academic Reviewers
continued

Simonetta Frittelli, Ph.D.
Associate Professor
Department of Physics
Duquesne University
Pittsburgh, Pennsylvania

William Grisham, Ph.D.
Lecturer
Psychology Department
University of California,
Los Angeles
Los Angeles, California

David Haig, Ph.D.
Professor of Biology
Organismic and
Evolutionary Biology
Harvard University
Cambridge, Massachusetts

David S. Hall, Ph.D.
*Assistant Professor
of Physics*
Department of Physics
Amherst College
Amherst, Massachusetts

Deborah Hanley, Ph.D.
Meteorologist
State of Florida
Department of Agriculture
and Consumer Services
Division of Forestry
Tallahassee, Florida

William H. Ingham, Ph.D.
Professor of Physics
James Madison University
Harrisonburg, Virginia

**Ping H. Johnson, M.D.,
Ph.D., CHES**
*Assistant Professor of
Health Education*
Department of Health,
Physical Education
and Sport Science
Kennesaw State University
Kennesaw, Georgia

Linda Jones
Program Manager
Texas Department
of Public Health
Austin, Texas

David Lamp, Ph.D.
*Associate Professor
of Physics*
Physics Department
Texas Tech University
Lubbock, Texas

Joel S. Leventhal, Ph.D.
Emeritus Scientist
United States Geological
Survey (USGS)
Lakewood, Colorado

Mark Mattson, Ph.D.
Assistant Professor
Physics Department
James Madison University
Harrisonburg, Virginia

Nancy L. McQueen, Ph.D.
Professor of Microbiology
Department of Biological
Sciences
California State University,
Los Angeles
Los Angeles, California

**Madeline Micceri
Mignone, Ph.D.**
Assistant Professor
Natural Science
Dominican College
Orangeburg, New York

Eva Oberdoerster, Ph.D.
Lecturer
Department of Biology
Southern Methodist
University
Dallas, Texas

Dork Sahagian, Ph.D.
Research Professor
Department of Earth
Sciences
Institute for the Study of
Earth, Oceans, and Space
University of New
Hampshire
Durham, New Hampshire

Laurie Santos, Ph.D.
Assistant Professor
Department of Psychology
Yale University
New Haven, Connecticut

Patrick K. Schoff, Ph.D.
Research Associate
Natural Resources Research
Institute
University of Minnesota—
Duluth
Duluth, Minnesota

**H. Michael Sommermann,
Ph.D.**
Professor of Physics
Physics Department
Westmont College
Santa Barbara, California

Daniel Z. Sui, Ph.D.
Professor
Department of Geography
Texas A&M University
College Station, Texas

Dwight L. Whitaker, Ph.D.
Assistant Professor of Physics
Department of Physics
Williams College
Williamstown,
Massachusetts

Lab Testing

Barry L. Bishop
*Science Teacher and
Department Chair*
San Rafael Junior High
Ferron, Utah

Yvonne Brannum
*Science Teacher and
Department Chair*
Hine Junior High School
Washington, D.C.

Daniel Bugenhagen
*Science Teacher and
Department Chair*
Yutan Junior–Senior High
Yutan, Nebraska

Gladys Cherniak
Science Teacher
St. Paul's Episcopal School
Mobile, Alabama

James Chin
Science Teacher
Frank A. Day Middle School
Newtonville, Massachusetts

Randy Christian
Science Teacher
Stovall Junior High School
Houston, Texas

Vicky Farland
*Science Teacher and
Department Chair*
Centennial Middle School
Yuma, Arizona

Susan Gorman
Science Teacher
North Ridge Middle School
North Richmond Hills,
Texas

C. John Graves
Science Teacher
Monforton Middle School
Bozeman, Montana

Janel Guse
*Science Teacher and
Department Chair*
West Central Middle School
Hartford, South Dakota

Norman Holcomb
Science Teacher
Marion Local Schools
Maria Stein, Ohio

Kerry A. Johnson
Science Teacher
Isbell Middle School
Santa Paula, California

M. R. Penny Kisiah
*Science Teacher and
Department Chair*
Fairview Middle School
Tallahassee, Florida

Kathy LaRoe
Science Teacher
East Valley Middle School
East Helena, Montana

Edith C. McAlanis
*Science Teacher and
Department Chair*
Socorro Middle School
El Paso, Texas

Jan Nelson
Science Teacher
East Valley Middle School
East Helena, Montana

Terry J. Rakes
Science Teacher
Elmwood Junior High
Rogers, Arkansas

Elizabeth Rustad
Science Teacher
Higley School District
Gilbert, Arizona

Debra A. Sampson
Science Teacher
Booker T. Washington
Middle School
Elgin, Texas

David M. Sparks
Science Teacher
Redwater Junior High
School
Redwater, Texas

Larry Tackett
*Science Teacher and
Department Chair*
Andrew Jackson Middle
School
Cross Lanes, West Virginia

Ivora Washington
*Science Teacher and
Department Chair*
Hyattsville Middle School
Washington, D.C.

Elsie N. Waynes
*Science Teacher and
Department Chair*
R. H. Terrell Junior High
School
Washington, D.C.

Christopher Wood
Science Teacher
Western Rockingham
Middle School
Madison, North Carolina

Sharon L. Woolf
Science Teacher
Langston Hughes Middle
School
Reston, Virginia

Walter Woolbaugh
Science Teacher
Manhattan School System
Manhattan, Montana

Gordon Zibelman
Science Teacher
Drexel Hill Middle School
Drexel Hill, Pennsylvania

Teacher Reviewers

Laura Buchanan
*Science Teacher and
Department Chairperson*
Corkran Middle School
Glen Burnie, Maryland

Sarah Carver
Science Teacher
Jackson Creek Middle
School
Bloomington, Indiana

Robin K. Clanton
Science Department Head
Berrien Middle School
Nashville, Georgia

Karen Dietrich, S.S.J., Ph.D.
*Principal and Biology
Instructor*
Mount Saint Joseph
Academy
Flourtown, Pennsylvania

Meredith Hanson
Science Teacher
Westside Middle School
Rocky Face, Georgia

Denise Hulette
Teacher
Conway Middle School
Orlando, Florida

Debra S. Kogelman, MAed.
Science Teacher
University of Chicago
Laboratory Schools
Chicago, Illinois

Deborah L. Kronsteiner
Teacher
Science Department
Spring Grove Area Middle
School
Spring Grove, Pennsylvania

Jennifer L. Lamkie
Science Teacher
Thomas Jefferson Middle
School
Edison, New Jersey

Augie Maldonado
Science Teacher
Grisham Middle School
Round Rock, Texas

Bill Martin
Science Teacher
Southeast Middle School
Kernersville, North
Carolina

Maureen Martin
Science Teacher
Jackson Creek Middle
School
Bloomington, Indiana

Alyson Mike
Science Teacher
East Valley Middle School
East Helena, Montana

Jean Pletchette
Health Educator
Winterset Community
Schools
Winterset, Iowa

Susan H. Robinson
Science Teacher
Oglethorpe County Middle
School
Lexington, Georgia

Elizabeth Rustad
Science Teacher
Higley School District
Gilbert, Arizona

Helen Schiller
Instructional Coach
Greenville County Schools
Greenville, South Carolina

Mark Schnably
Science Instructor
Thomas Jefferson Middle
School
Winston-Salem, North
Carolina

Stephanie Snowden
Science Teacher
Canyon Vista Middle
School
Round Rock, Texas

Martha Tedrow
Science Teacher
Thomas Jefferson
Middle School
Winston-Salem,
North Carolina

Martha B. Trisler
Science Teacher
Rising Starr Middle School
Fayetteville, Georgia

Sherrye Valenti
Curriculum Leader
Science Department
Wildwood Middle School,
Wildwood, Missouri

Florence Vaughan
Science Teacher
University of Chicago
Laboratory Schools
Chicago, Illinois

Angie Williams
Teacher
Riversprings Middle School
Crawfordville, Florida

Roberta Young
Science Teacher
Gunn Junior High School
Arlington, Texas

Answer Checking

Hatim Belyamani
Austin, Texas

John A. Benner
Austin, Texas

Catherine Podeszwa
Duluth, Minnesota

Staff Credits

Editorial

Leigh Ann García,
Executive Editor
Kelly Rizk,
Senior Editor
David Westerberg,
Senior Editor
Laura Zapanta,
Senior Editor

Editorial Development Team

Karin Akre
Monica Brown
Jen Driscoll
Shari Husain
Michael Mazza
Karl Pallmeyer
Laura Prescott
Bill Rader
Jim Ratcliffe
Dennis Rathnaw
Betsy Roll
Kenneth Shepardson

Copyeditors

Dawn Marie Spinozza,
Copyediting Manager
Simon Key
Jane A. Kirschman
Kira J. Watkins

Editorial Support Staff

Debbie Starr,
Managing Editor
Kristina Bigelow
Suzanne Krejci
Shannon Oehler

Online Products

Bob Tucek,
Executive Editor
Wesley M. Bain

Design

Book Design

Kay Selke,
Director of Book Design
Lisa Woods,
Page Designer
Holly Whittaker, *Project Administrator*

Media Design

Richard Metzger,
Design Director
Chris Smith,
Developmental Designer

Image Acquisitions

Curtis Riker, *Director*
Jeannie Taylor,
Photo Research Manager
Diana Goetting,
Senior Photo Researcher
Elaine Tate,
Art Buyer Supervisor
Angela Boehm,
Senior Art Buyer

Publishing Services

Carol Martin, *Director*

Graphic Services

Bruce Bond, *Director*
Jeff Bowers, *Graphic Services Manager*

Katrina Gnader,
Graphics Specialist
Cathy Murphy, *Senior Graphics Specialist*
Nanda Patel,
Graphics Specialist
JoAnn Stringer, *Senior Graphics Specialist II*

Technology Services

Laura Likon, *Director*
Juan Baquera, *Technology Services Manager*
Lana Kaupp,
Senior Technology Services Analyst
Margaret Sanchez, *Senior Technology Services Analyst*
Sara Buller, *Technology Services Analyst*
Patty Zepeda, *Technology Services Analyst*
Jeff Robinson, *Ancillary Design Manager*

New Media

Armin Gutzmer, *Director*
Melanie Baccus,
New Media Coordinator
Lydia Doty,
Senior Project Manager
Cathy Kuhles, *Technical Assistant*
Marsh Flournoy, *Quality Assurance Analyst*
Tara F. Ross, *Senior Project Manager*

Design New Media

Ed Blake, *Director*
Kimberly Cammerata, *Design Manager*
Michael Rinella,
Senior Designer

Production

Eddie Dawson,
Production Manager
Sherry Sprague,
Project Manager
Suzanne Brooks, *Production Coordinator*

Teacher Edition

Alicia Sullivan
David Hernandez
April Litz

Manufacturing and Inventory

Jevara Jackson
Ivania Quant Lee
Wilonda Ieans

Ancillary Development and Production

General Learning Communications,
Northbrook, Illinois

Credits

Abbreviations used: (t) top, (c) center, (b) bottom, (l) left, (r) right, (bkgd) background

PHOTOGRAPHY

Front Cover (tl) Mike Powell/Getty images; (bl) Daryl Benson/Masterfile; (r) Andrew Syred/Getty Images; (DNA strand) David Mack/Science Photo Library

Skills Practice Lab Teens Sam Dudgeon/HRW

Connection to Astrology Corbis Images; **Connection to Biology** David M. Phillips/Visuals Unlimited; **Connection to Chemistry** Digital Image copyright © 2005 PhotoDisc; **Connection to Environment** Digital Image copyright © 2005 PhotoDisc; **Connection to Geology** Letraset Phototone; **Connection to Language Arts** Digital Image copyright © 2005 PhotoDisc; **Connection to Meteorology** Digital Image copyright © 2005 PhotoDisc; **Connection to Oceanography** © ICONOTEC; **Connection to Physics** Digital Image copyright © 2005 PhotoDisc

Table of Contents iii (t), Peter Van Steen/HRW; iii (b), Uniphoto; iv (t), Chip Simmons/Discover Channel; iv (b), Wolfgang Bayer; vi (t), Ned M. Seidler/National Geographic Society Image Collection; vi (b), Sam Dudgeon/HRW; vii (tl), James Beveridge/Visuals Unlimited; vii (tr), © Gail Shumway/Getty Images/FPG International; viii (t), © G. Randall/Getty Images/FPG International; viii (b), CNRI/Science Photo Library/Photo Researchers; viii-ix (t), © Stan Osolinski/Getty Images/FPG International; ix (c), SuperStock; ix (b), Digital Image copyright © 2005 PhotoDisc; x (t), Breck P. Kent/Animals Animals/Earth Scenes; x (b), Ron Kimball; xi (t), © Jeffrey L. Rotman/CORBIS; xi (c), © Kevin Schafer/CORBIS; xi (b), Kenneth Fink/Bruce Coleman, Inc.; xii (t), Sylvain Cordier/Photo Researchers; xiii (t), Kim Heacox/DRK Photo; xiii (bl), © Jeff Hunter/Getty Images/The Image Bank; xiv (tl), © Sindre Ellingsen/Alamy Photos; xiv (b), Sam Dudgeon/HRW; xiv-xv (tc), © Nih/Science Source/Photo Researchers, Inc.; xvi (t), Sam Dudgeon/HRW; xvi (b), Photo Lennart Nilsson/Albert Bonniers Forlag AB, A Child Is Born, Dell Publishing Company; xvii (b), © Rob Van Petten/Getty Images/The Image Bank; xviii-xxxiii (all), HRW

Chapter One 2-3 Craig Line/AP/Wide World Photos; 4 Peter Van Steen/HRW Photo; 5 (t) Peter Van Steen/HRW Photo; 5 (b) Sam Dudgeon/HRW Photo; 6 (b) Peter Van Steen/HRW Photo; 6 (t) Hank Morgan/Photo Researchers, Inc.; 7 Dale Miquelle/National Geographic Society Image Collection; 8 (b) John Langford/HRW Photo; 8 (t) NC: Science VU/PNNL/Visuals Unlimited; 9 Jeremy Bishop/Science Photo Library/Photo Researchers, Inc.; 11 (t) Peter Van Steen/HRW Photo; 12 Peter Van Steen/HRW Photo; 14 John Mitchell/Photo Researchers; 16 Sam Dudgeon/HRW Photo; 17 (t) John Mitchell/Photo Researchers; 18 (l) © Fujifotos/The Image Works; 18 (r) © Fujifotos/The Image Works; 20 Art by Christopher Sloan/Photograph by Mark Thiessen both National Geographic_Image Collection/© National Geographic Image Collection; 24 David Austen/Publishers Network, Inc.; 25 (l) Peter Van Steen/HRW Photo; 25(r) Peter Van Steen/HRW Photo; 26 (tl) Tony Freeman/PhotoEdit; 26 (tr) Victoria Smith/HRW; 26 (bl) Corbis Images; 34 (l), Craig Fugii/©1988 The Seattle Times; 35 (r), Bettman/CORBIS; 35 (bl), Layne Kennedy/CORBIS

Unit One 36 (t), Ronald Sheridan/Ancient Art & Architecture Collection; 36 (c), The Huntington Library, Art Collections, and Botanical Gardens, San Marino, California/SuperStock; 37 (tl), NASA; 37 (tr), Sam Dudgeon/HRW; 37 (cr), SuperStock; 37 (bc), Lawrence Livermore Laboratory/Photo Researchers, Inc.; 37, S.Feval/Le Matin/Corbis Sygma

Chapter Two 38-39, Robert Holmes/CORBIS; 41, Peter Van Steen/HRW; 43 (t), SuperStock; 43 (b), NASA; 44, Image Copyright ©2005 PhotoDisc, Inc.; 45, Patrick J. Endres/Alaskaphotographics.com; 50, Terry Renna/AP/Wide World Photos; 51 (b), Moredun Animal Health Ltd./Science Photo Library/Photo Researchers, Inc.; 54 (t), NASA/Science Photo Library/Photo Researchers, Inc.; 56 (c), Argus Fotoarchiv/Peter Arnold, Inc.; 56 (r), David Weintraub/Photo Researchers, Inc.; 56 (l), Digital Image copyright © 2005 PhotoDisc/Getty Images; 57 CORBIS; 59, Simon Fraser/SPL/Photo Researchers, Inc.; 60 David R. Frazier Photolibrary; 62 (t), Goddard Space Flight Center Scientific Visualization Studio/NASA; 62 ©UNEP/Peter Arnold, Inc.; 64, (b) AP Wide World/Joe Giblin; 64, (t) Tampa Electric; 65 Francis Dean/The Image Works; 66-67, Sam Dudgeon/HRW; 69 (t), Goddard Space Flight Center Scientific Visualization Studio/NASA; 72 (b), James McInnis/Los Alamos National Laboratories; 72 (t), Jonathan Blair/CORBIS; 73 (r), Fred Hirschmann; 73 (bl), Fred Hirschmann

Chapter Three 74-75, Tim Chapman/Miami Herald/NewsCom; 78, Sam Dudgeon/HRW; 79, Victoria Smith/HRW; 80 (tc), NOAA; 80 (tr), Joyce Photographics/Photo Researchers, Inc.; 80 (tl), Corbis Images; 82, Gene E. Moore; 82 (tl), Gerben Oppermans/Getty Images/Stone; 83 (c), Corbis Images; 83 (t), Victoria Smith/HRW; 85, Image Copyright ©2005 PhotoDisc, Inc.; 85 (t), Reuters/Gary Wiepert/NewsCom; 88, NASA; 90, William H. Edwards/Getty Images/The Image Bank; 91 (br), Jean-Loup Charmet/Science Photo Library/Photo Researchers, Inc.; 92 (all), Howard B. Bluestein/Photo Researchers, Inc.; 93 (t), Red Huber/Orlando Sentinel/SYGMA/CORBIS; 93 (b), NASA; 94 (tl), NASA/Science Photo Library/Photo Researchers, Inc.; 95, Dave Martin/AP/Wide World Photos; 96 (b), Joe Raedle/NewsCom; 97 (t), Will Chandler/Anderson Independent-Mail/AP/Wide World Photos; 97 (t), Jean-Loup Charmet/Science Photo Library/Photo Researchers, Inc.; 98 (c), NASA/Science Photo Library/Photo Researchers, Inc.; 98, Graham Neden/Ecoscene/CORBIS; 99, Sam Dudgeon/HRW; 99 (t), G.R. Roberts Photo Library; 99 (t), Guido Alberto Rossi/Getty Images/The Image Bank; 100, National Weather Service/NOAA; 104, Sam Dudgeon/HRW; 105 (tl), Corbis Images; 108 (tr), Lightscapes Photography, Inc./CORBIS; 105 (b), Joyce Photographics/Photo Researchers, Inc.; 109 (t), Michael Lyon; 109 (bl), Corbis Images

Chapter Four 110-111, Steve Bloom Images; 112 (bkgd), Tom Van Sant, Geosphere Project/Planetary Visions/Science Photo Library/Photo Researchers, Inc.; 112 (tl), G.R. Roberts Photo Library; 112 (tr), Index Stock; 112 (c), Yva Momatiuk & John Eastcott; 112 (bl), Gary Retherford/Photo Researchers, Inc.; 112 (br), SuperStock; 113 (t), CALLER-TIMES/AP/Wide World Photos; 113 (b), Chase Jarvis/CORBIS; 114 (t) Duomo/CORBIS; 115 Will & Deni McIntyre/CORBIS; 116 (bl), Larry Ulrich Photography; 116 (br), Paul Wakefield/Getty Images/Stone; 119, Index Stock; 120 ©Harold & Esther Edgerton Foundation, 2003, Courtesy of Palm Press, Inc.; 121 (tl), Carlos Navajas/Getty Images/The Image Bank; 121 (tr), Michael Fogden/Bruce Coleman, Inc.; 122,(l) Kevin Schafer/CORBIS, (r) Peter Johnson/CORBIS; 123, Larry Ulrich Photography; 124 (br), Tom Van Sant/Geosphere Project, Santa Monica/Science Photo Library/Photo Researchers, Inc.; 125 (b), Tom Bean/Getty Images/Stone; 125 (t), CORBIS Images/HRW; 126 (b), Steven Simpson/Getty Images/FPG International; 126 (t), Fred Hirschmann; 127 (b), Harry Walker/Alaska Stock; 127 (tr), Tom Van Sant/Geosphere Project, Santa Monica/Science Photo Library/Photo Researchers, Inc.; 128, SuperStock; 132 (br), Roger Werth/Woodfin Camp & Associates; 133, D. Van Ravenswaay/Photo Researchers, Inc.; 138, Gunter Ziesler/Peter Arnold, Inc.; 139, SuperStock; 142, Roger Ressmeyer/CORBIS; 142 (b), Terry Brandt/Grant Heilman Photography, Inc.; 143 (t), Courtesy of The University of Michigan

Unit Two 144 (t), Geoffrey Clifford/Woodfin Camp; 144 (c), J & L Weber/Peter Arnold; 144 (b), AP/Wide World Photos; 145 (cl), Brown Brothers; 145 (cr), SuperStock; 145 (tl), Gamma-Liaison/Getty News Images; 145 (bl), Enrico Ferorelli; 145 (tr), Sheila Terry/Science Photo Library/Photo Researchers, Inc.; 145 (br), © CORBIS

Chapter Five 146-147 AFP/CORBIS; 148 © Kevin Schafer/Getty Images/Stone; 149 Bob Daemmrich/Stock Boston; 150-151 © David Madison/Getty Images/Stone; 152 SamDudgeon/HRW; 157 Scott Camazine/Photo Researchers, Inc.; 158 (bkgd), © Bob Torrez/Getty Images/Stone; 158 (bl-inset), Dr. E.R. Degginger; 158 (r-inset), Manfred Kage/Peter Arnold, Inc. ; 158 (tl-inset), © G.W. Willis/Biological Photo Service; 160 (r), Sam Dudgeon/HRW; 160 (l), Chris Hamilton; 162 Sam Dudgeon/HRW; 164 (bkgd), Peter Van Steen/HRW; 164 (l), Dr. Robert Becker/Custom Medical Stock Photo; 164 (r), Peter Van Steen/HRW; 169 (t), Sam Dudgeon/HRW; 169 (b), Peter Van Steen/HRW; 172 (l), © Dan McCoy/Rainbow; 172 (r), Reuters/David Gray/NewsCom; 173 (t), Photo courtesy of Dr. Zahra Beheshti; 173 (b), Creatas/PictureQuest

Chapter Six 174-175 © Nih/Science Source/Photo Researchers, Inc.; 178 (l), O. Meckes/Nicole Ottawa/Photo Researchers, Inc.; 178 (r), O. Meckes/Nicole Ottawa/Photo Researchers, Inc.; 610 © John Bavosi/Photo Researchers, Inc.; 182 Susumu Nishinaga/Science Photo Library/Photo Researchers, Inc.; 183 (b), Don Fawcett/Photo Researchers; 185 © Getty Images/The Image Bank; 188 © Collection CNRI/Phototake Inc./Alamy Photos; 193 (l), Matt Meadows/Peter Arnold, Inc.; 193 (r), Matt Meadows/Peter Arnold, Inc.; 194 (b), Sam Dudgeon/HRW; 200 (l), Richard T. Nowitz/Phototake; 200 (r), © Paul A. Souders/CORBIS; 201 Courtesy of the Boggy Creek Gang Camp

Chapter Seven 202-203 © ISM/Phototake; 211 (t), Victoria Smith/HRW; 214 Getty Images/The Image Bank; 215 Stephen J. Krasemann/DRK Photo; 216 (b), Sam Dudgeon/HRW; 222 (l), J.H. Robinson/Photo Researchers; 222 (r), REUTERS/David Gray/NewsCom; 223 (t), Peter Van Steen/HRW

Chapter Eight 224-225 Omikron/Photo Researchers, Inc.; 231 (t), Sam Dudgeon/HRW; 235 Sam Dudgeon/HRW; 242 (c), Sam Dudgeon/HRW; 243 Will & Deni McIntyre/Photo Researchers; 244 (r), Sam Dudgeon/HRW; 244 (l), Sam Dudgeon/HRW; 245 Sam Dudgeon/HRW; 247 (t), Sam Dudgeon/HRW; 250 (l), Victoria Smith/HRW; 250 (r), Mike Derer/AP/Wide World Photos; 251 (t), Photo courtesy of Dr. Bertha Madras; 251 (b), SPL/Photo Researchers, Inc.

Chapter Eighteen 492-493 (all), NASA; 493 (br), NASA; 494 (bl), Richard Megna/ Fundamental Photographs; 496 (cl), Toby Rankin/Masterfile; 497 (tr), James Sugar/ Black Star; 497 (bl), NASA; 499 (bl), Michelle Bridwell/Frontera Fotos; 499 (br), Image copyright © 2005 PhotoDisc, Inc.; 500 (tc), Richard Megna/Fundamental Photographs; 501 (tr), Toby Rankin/Masterfile; 502 (b), John Langford/HRW; 504 (br), Mavournea Hay/HRW; 504 (bc), Michelle Bridwell/Frontera Fotos; 505 (all), Victoria Smith/HRW; 506 (all), Image copyright © 2005 PhotoDisc, Inc.; 507 (b), David Madison; 508 (tc), Gerard Lacz/Animals Animals/Earth Scenes; 508 (tr), Sam Dudgeon/HRW; 508 (tr), Image copyright © 2005 PhotoDisc, Inc.; 508 (tl), NASA; 509 (br), Lance Schriner/HRW; 509 (tr), Victoria Smith/HRW; 511 (all), Michelle Bridwell/HRW; 512 (br), Zigy Kaluzny/Getty Images; 512 (bl), © SuperStock; 513 (cl), Michelle Bridwell/HRW; 514 (bl), Image ©2001 PhotoDisc, Inc.; 515 (all), Sam Dudgeon/HRW; 516 (tc), Gerard Lacz/Animals Animals/Earth Scenes; 517 (all), Sam Dudgeon/HRW; 520 (tl), AP Photo/Martyn Hayhow; 520 (tr), Junko Kimura/Getty Images/NewsCom; 521 (tr), Steve Okamoto; 521 (br), Lee Schwabe

Chapter Nineteen 522-523 (all), © Nicholas Pinturas/Getty Images; 526 (tl), © I.M. House/Getty Images; 526 (tcl), David R. Frazier Photolibrary; 526 (cl), Dieter and Mary Plage/Bruce Coleman, Inc.; 526 (bcl), Wolfgang Kaehler/CORBIS; 526 (bl), © Martin Barraud/Getty Images; 527 (tr), © SuperStock; 527 (tcr), Daniel A. Nord; 527 (cr), © Ken Marschall/Madison Press Books; 527 (bcr), Dr. Paul A. Zahl/Photo Researchers, Inc.; 527 (br), CORBIS/Bettman; 529 (tr), © Charles Doswell III/Getty Images; 532 (tl), Bruno P. Zehnder/Peter Arnold, Inc.; 536 (br), Richard Megna/ Fundamental Photographs/HRW Photo; 538 (tl), Larry L. Miller/Photo Researchers, Inc.; 538 (tr), Richard Neville/Check Six; 540 (tr), John Neubauer/PhotoEdit; 541 (br), Check Six; 543 (b), Sam Dudgeon/HRW; 544 (tr), © SuperStock; 548 (tc), © Victor Malafronte; 548 (tl), Sam Dudgeon/HRW; 549 (bl), Corbis Images; 549 (tr), Courtesy of Alisha Bracken

Chapter Twenty 550-551 (all), age fotostock/Photographer, Year; 552 (bl), John Langford/HRW; 553 (all), John Langford/HRW; 554 (all), © Galen Rowell/CORBIS; 555 (all), Sam Dudgeon/HRW; 556 (all), John Langford/HRW; 558 (cr), Scott Van Osdol/HRW; 558 (br), Robert Wolf/HRW; 558 (bc), Digital Image copyright © 2005 Artville; 559 (br), Sam Dudgeon/HRW; 560 (all), Scott Van Osdol/HRW; 561 (tr, cr), Sam Dudgeon/HRW; 561(tl), John Langford/HRW; 562 (br), CC Studio/Science Photo Library/Photo Researchers, Inc.; 563 (tr), © Reuters NewMedia Inc./CORBIS; 564 (all), Robert Wolf/HRW; 565 (tr), Robert Wolf/HRW; 565 (br), Scott Van Osdol/HRW; 565 (bc), Sam Dudgeon/HRW; 565 (tc), John Langford/HRW; 567 (t), Robert Wolf/ HRW; 568 (tr), Lisa Davis/HRW; 569 (tl, cr), Sam Dudgeon/HRW; 569 (br), Peter Van Steen/HRW ; 570 (b), Robert Wolf/HRW; 571 (tr), Robert Wolf/HRW; 571 (br), John Langford/HRW; 572 (bl), Stephanie Morris/HRW; 573 (br), Paul Dance/Getty Images; 574 (tl), John Langford/HRW; 575 (cl), Helmut Gritscher/Peter Arnold, Inc.; 575 (tr), Robert Wolf/HRW; 575(cr), John Langford/HRW; 575 (br), Stephanie Morris/HRW; 576 (tr), © Visuals Unlimited; 578 (tl), Wayne Sorce; 579 (cr), A.W. Stegmeyer/ Upstream; 579 (bl), Digital Image copyright © 2005 PhotoDisc

Lab Book 582, Sam Dudgeon/HRW; 585, Kuni Stringer/AP/Wide World Photos; 586, Victoria Smith/HRW; 587, Jay Malonson/AP/Wide World Photos; 589, 592, Sam Dudgeon/HRW; 593, Andy Christiansen/HRW; 594 Sam Dudgeon/HRW; 595 (t), Sam Dudgeon/HRW; 595 (c), Sam Dudgeon/HRW; 595 (b), Sam Dudgeon/HRW; 596 Sam Dudgeon/HRW; 597 Sam Dudgeon/HRW; 601 Peter Van Steen/HRW; 603 Sam Dudgeon/HRW; 604 (tl), Runk/Schoenberger/Grant Heilman; 604 (tc), Runk/ Schoenberger/Grant Heilman; 604 (tr), Michael Abbey/Photo Researchers, Inc.; 604 (tr), Sam Dudgeon/HRW; 604 (br), Runk/Schoenberger/Grant Heilman; 605 (b), Sam Dudgeon/HRW; 605 (c), Sam Dudgeon/HRW; 606 Sam Dudgeon/HRW; 609 (all), Sam Dudgeon/HRW; 610 (br), Sam Dudgeon/HRW; 612 (c), Sam Dudgeon/HRW; 617 (br), Sam Dudgeon/HRW; 618 (b), Sam Dudgeon/HRW; 619 (br), John Langford/ HRW; 612 (tr, cr), Robert Wolf; 621 (br), John Langford/HRW; 623 (l), Matt Meadows/Peter Arnold, Inc.; 623 (r), Matt Meadows/Peter Arnold, Inc.; 624 (b), Sam Dudgeon/HRW; 630 (br), Victoria Smith; 631 (br), Victoria Smith; 637 (tr), Peter Van Steen/HRW; 637 (br), Sam Dudgeon/HRW, 640 CENCO; 655 (tr), Sam Dudgeon/HRW